The Casebook of Doctor Sababa

Lawrence Winkler

שלם יהיה אז ,שלי אלוהים, אותי לרפא אתה אם
אותי לשרוף לא שלך הכעס אש את ייתן מי
טוב אם, של הם שלי התרופות
חלש או חזק אם, רע או
ו לא, אתה, שבוחר זה שאתה מכיוון
מטרתה כדי חצים להנחות ואינה מדריכים שלכם הידיעה
ריפוי שלי הכוח תסמוך
שלך התרופה של רק חלק ליטול עשוי

If you heal me, my God, then I shall be whole.
May the fire of your anger not burn me.
My medicines are of you, whether good
Or bad, whether strong or weak.
Because you are the one who chooses, you, not I, and
Your omniscience guides and does not guide your
arrow to its goal.
Not upon my power of healing I rely;
May I only partake of your medicine.'
    Yehudah HaLevi (1075 - 1141 AD), *The Sick Physician*

To my patients

Table of Contents

Acknowledgements

This book is of me, and my thirty years in practice as an Internal Medicine consultant on Vancouver Island. But it is not me, although it may have been who I wanted to become.

I continue to live (amazing as this phenomenon is all by itself) in eternal debt to the people who made me what I was, in the quest to become as good as I should have been. For those I have forgotten to pay proper homage to, minds I have been inspired by or borrowed from, I would ask your forgiveness.

These are the people I want to thank: The best of my old professors, dear colleagues and friends Gerald Winkler, Raymond Adams, David Bird, David Rush, John Heath, Jerry Simice, Don Hilton, Robin Molineaux, Randy Marback, John Whitelaw, Stuart Ross, Paul Mitenko, Geoff Spry, Larry Sterns, Kam Bandali, Peter King, Jessie Gordon, John 'Hawkeye' Rutka, Ron Wigle, Kevin Morrison, Bill Griswold, Eric Grantner, David Westwood, Bill Leslie, Sati Murty, Bill Cameron (both of them), Murray Welte, Mike Kenyon and Kevin Lai; Iwona Jozwiak for her brilliant painting of the plague doctor cover art, Ken Hamm for the use of *Fishing Grounds*, and Dean Whitfield for *Three Feet Off Gabriola*, all the other musicians and poets, Jenny Engwer for putting it all together, and my patient and loving wife, Robyn, through whose tender loving care I am still alive.

Disclaimer

This is a work of fiction. Any similarity to any person, dead or alive, is purely coincidental and unintended. I mean it.

Prologue

You will love Harbour City. Most visitors to the island drive right through, without taking time to explore its attractions. But you're not most visitors. You will get to spend some time.

Go head. Turn on your radio. That's BC Bud, 101.3 FM on your Home and Native Band. He will announce your special arrival.

And if you catch something more than a salmon, you could be referred to Doctor Sababa, an Internal Medicine consultant at Harbour City Regional, the Sage of the Salish Sea. He would amuse you with his wit and wisdom, and the spontaneous combustion and thrust they generate, often mixed in unequal proportions, as he dances with the devil in the pale moonlight. Before there was artificial intelligence, he was the real thing, working in the mysterious old ways of a masterless samurai. In the myriad motions of all celestial objects, he was a meteor.

With proper care, you might even survive your encounter. Welcome to the spring and summer of his Casebook. Welcome to Sababaland.

The Making of Doctor Sababa

At the beginning and the end, there was chaos. Between the beginning and the end, there was Sababa. Between Sababa and the end was order. Between Sababa and order was more chaos, in paper and protocol.

Eleazar Mordechai wasn't born Sababa. He became Sababa. His flight path began as ether, burst into flame, made landfall, and dissolved. *Wind. Fire. Earth. Water.* Sababa didn't study the Four Humours. Sababa was the Four Humours, a living perfect embodiment of the Diatessaron, the grace of the fourth voice, the honeyed treacle of gentian, Aristochlia rotunda, laurel berries, and myrrh.

"Someday, you might find a cure for cancer." His mother had once said. But Sababa was too preoccupied being a carrier of everything, to find a cure for anything.

The portly professor was not a religious man—he was a natural philosopher, a secular scientist. If you couldn't know for sure, Sababa reasoned, there was no point in going around guessing.

This might explain how the Good Doctor had become such a misanthrope. It was not that he didn't like individual people, it was that he didn't trust them in groups. Hospital politics, to Sababa, was anathema. Committees were cul-de-sacs down which brilliant ideas were lured and quietly strangled.

"There is no 'I' in team." The portly professor would say. "But there is in kiss my ass." In one of his more memorable meetings, a prominent Health Authority luminary had set up a question he thought would finally bell the cat.

"But surely, Doctor Sababa." He said. "You believe in collaboration?"

"Nope." He replied. "France. 1945. Shaved 'em... shot 'em."

To Sababa, human beings were inherently unable to overcome their alienation and suffering by joining together—all became inauthentic and destined to disintegrate. Neither the nation nor its neighbourhoods, neither colleagues nor their congregations, provided enough commonality to form a community. Committees were bogus because they attempted to paper and protocol over the fundamental human experience hiding the ultimate reality for those unable to see it. The best they could aspire to was distraction.

People were alone. Everyone died alone. Life was about confronting that reality and still struggling anyway. Being authentic, being a man, being a sanative samurai, was to understand the emptiness. Sababa had recognized fundamental truths about the human condition—death was the critical experience, and that most of the things we did before we died were meaningless. Sababa found meaning, and humbling heroism, in his fight against disease. Fleeting moments of joy came from the endeavour, but the stocky savant didn't want to be happy—he wanted to be right. The Good Doctor rejected relationships based on fakery, willing to be miserable if he could be true to himself.

Sababa found authenticity in Nature, and by facing his own death with dignity and courage. In rare down times, he climbed up the ridges above the lake with his dog and, in the right months of the year, with his Italian mushroom knife, seeking the simpler pleasures there were in foraging for anonymity.

He looked forward to his trips with Dasco Boet, his Intensivist colleague, and their mutual immersion in a struggle for shells and scales. Fish were what they were, and devoid of deliberation. The two Good Doctors were loyal ichthyophiles together, away from the civilizing influences and deadfall misconceptions that swam in their usual habitat. It was the men and the fish, although sometimes there may have been ribeyes and rare wines and Cuban cigars.

Sababa walked across Paris one day, on a sacred quest to find a special seafood seasoning for their fishing cabin. In the small shop, he met another customer, an attractive Parisian of Sababa's vintage. She asked him where he was going, where he would need such a *recherché* concoction. Sababa told her of Barkley Sound, and Chinook salmon and barn-door halibut, and oysters and Manila clams, and Dungeness crab and Spot prawns. When the owner finally located the rare condiment, Sababa paid him and turned to leave the premises.

"Monsieur?" She called.

"Oui?"

"Bonne pêche." She mewed, her spirit longing after him. *Good fishing.*

Sababa's formal education had been formidable. He left his hometown at the age of 16, for M.I.T. in Boston, where he double majored in aerospace engineering and biology. He was enamoured of the cosmos, the possibility of extraterrestrial life, the greatest mystery there was, in the theory of everything. After medical school and an internship in medicine, he took five years off to hitchhike around the world. This was a career path that should have crashlanded, but his program director remembered him when he called from Bangkok that many years later, and once more his ascendant signs were restored. After completing his residency, Sababa took his Internal Medicine American board exams at the Mayo Clinic. For three days in a row, he was the first to put down his pencil, a good hour before any of the other candidates in the room finished theirs. He began to wonder if they were writing the same test papers, but he took the highest mark with him when he left Rochester. To study for his Canadian fellowship examination, while his frazzled colleagues were drugging themselves to stay awake that much longer to learn that much more, Sababa took his young wife, Jane, to Rio, and lay in a hammock until the spirit moved him. *My Harrison's Miguel. The urge is strong today.*

After some postdoctoral work in various other geographies, Sababa and Jane landed in Harbour City, where he would dedicate the next thirty years of his existence to the care of his patients. There was some fun to be had.

Inside his Colombian leather briefcase, Sababa kept his black bound handwritten micrographic medical manual, a repository of divine revelation. Sababa called it his 'Sefer Refuot,' a play on *Asaph's Book of Remedies*, the most ancient Hebrew medical text from the 6th century and a work of mystery, so exalted as to have been recorded twice in the Babylonian Talmud. Everyone else who worked with the portly professor called it his little Black Book.

Inside, it was strangely divided into conditions affecting the classical humours originally proposed in the cosmogenic theory of a pre-Socratic philosopher from Agrigentum, a classical Greek city in Sicily. Empedocles proposed that all the structures in the world were made from four ultimate elements—Wind and Fire and Earth and Water—and that health and disease were a function of their balance, under the influence of the two forces of attraction and repulsion, Love and Strife.

Like its inspiration, Sababa's Black Book of Remedies ended with the Oath of Asaph.

'Take heed that ye kill not any man with the sap of a root; and ye shall not dispense a potion to a woman with child by adultery to cause her to miscarry; and ye shall not lust after beautiful women to commit adultery

13

with them; and ye shall not disclose secrets confided unto you; and ye shall take no bribes to cause injury and to kill; and ye shall not harden your hearts against the poor and the needy, but heal them...'

Asaph had enjoined his physicians to treat any patient, regardless of their means to pay a fee, something not mentioned by Hippocrates at all. While the Hippocratic oath was a contract between the student and his teacher, Asaph's was a covenant of the medical community. *Be ye pure and faithful and upright.* Although not always successful, Sababa worked hard to keep up his end of the bargain.

His referring colleagues were aware, and grateful, for the insight they had acquired in their interactions with the stocky savant, that their best option for solving a complicated medical problem, was to front-end load the expertise. Sababa was not a sub-specialist but a super-specialist, a phenomenal phenomenologist phenomenon.

And that was where you could find him, in the fertile fields of forever, making mythology, becoming legend.

At Work and Play in the House of God

The pager awoke in his pocket. In the Medical Advisory Committee meeting Sababa had been compelled to attend, the sensation came as a welcome reprieve. Not only did the vibration remind him of the location and continued presence of his genitals, but it also provided a convenient excuse to leave before any further attempt was made to remove them.

The new Chief of Staff, writhing in her last throes of building a fragile legacy, determined to nail them above her desk, for his sin of trying to protect his patients from the virtues of 'Managed Care.'

"Duty calls." He said. And there was nothing any of them could do. Sababa had not divulged his complicity in the summons timing, so elegantly prearranged with the hospital operators who would always protect him from the ubiquitous intramural forces of evil.

At the speed of systemic circulation and cerebral perfusion, Sababa cruised the hallways where the angels and demons lived. His hospital was a regional referral centre and, back in the Age of Samurai, had been the ultimate destination for families all over the island, who would exhale in relief, when informed that their loved ones would be transferred there. Doctor Sababa provided the most comfort, for his name was among the illustrious champions of survival their hopes could aspire to.

But malevolence had come to live at Harbour City Regional. The administrative epicentre was about to migrate south to the capital, and the local health region had been assimilated, if that was the proper term, into the control of an alien authority.

Here are twelve stories of one of the last lone gunmen. Read them in the sequence they are. Savour the struggle between the science and the suits and the snowflakes, and give thanks.

15

Spring—The Book of Wind

☷

'Behold, my friends, the spring is come;
the earth has gladly received the embraces of the sun,
and we shall soon see the results of their love!'
                                                    Sitting Bull

Spring came in like a halting tide, surging as warm white sunshine, receding into bitter gusting winds. Sleet turned to soft rain. Spirits rose into balmy air.

Sunlight dispersed clouds reflected on the lake. Sababa's shoreline exploded into cherry blossoms, irregular salmon pink clusters swirling in breeze-blinding bursts of pigment. Perfection in medieval Japan came off the austere branches of Buddhism, in the imperfect *wabi-sabi* impermanence of their own *sakura* blossoms. It couldn't be helped, there or here.

Harbour City deposited its Daylight Savings in an interest-bearing account of shorter nights and longer days. Morning danced on open-mouthed swallows soaring over lake shimmer, infiltrated pineal glands of awakening bears, and split everything else into prisms of life creation. Ivory snowdrops and crocuses broke free from buried bulbs. Erupting yellow daffodil blooms bowed fluted heads in homage to forsythia gold, iris cadmium, and dandelion sulfur. White returned with gifts of apple and plum and lilac. Dogwoods shed popcorn showers with pink peach petals, in a falling carpet of blush.

Rembrandt painted a venerable variegated tulip mania. Azaleas dazzled vermilion fireworks. Tiger Swallowtails beat the thickening air with paper wings, striped black and yellow.

Sababa planted juice and joy in his garden, savouring newly turned soil, pungent from the bacteria reactivated by the warm rains. Backyard bonfire woodsmoke was an intoxicant. In the forest, anise scents of oyster mushrooms on alder hosts mixed with acrid aromas of skunk cabbage swamp lanterns.

But it was green that defined the season. New light climbed tree trunks and nude branches and cracked open tight arboreal buds to reveal soft nascent leaves, unfurling. Matted grasses grew lush; curly-headed fern fiddlenecks unravelled. Moss on the ridgeline became a sea of emeralds.

Water striders skated the ponds; frogspawn hatched into tadpoles below them. Newborn spotted fawns gambolled on clumsy matchsticks. Turkey vultures soared high, sniffing for any who hadn't completed the journey.

A busy-happy symphony of eagles chirping, ravens clonking, ducks quacking, hummingbirds buzzing, and quail chattering accompanied the songbird dawn chorus.

Spring blew ephemeral lessons from Musashi's *The Book of Wind*, refining Sababa's vision and skill, sweeping the web of winter from his mind. Wisdom sailed with wind and time.

It was in such a season that Sababa could sit on his deck at dusk and think calm quiet thoughts, setting his mind free to wander the paths of ethereal lands. These were the days of light under the dark, and laughter beneath cloudy skies. You could consume such a day as a tonic. Live in the sunshine. Swim in the sea. Drink the wild air.

1. The Case of the Ultimate Artery

'In Harbour City, Vancouver's rusty town
No-hoper Angels they got the place locked down
Nobody can be certain if it ain't just that floatplane
that went down, down, down...'
Dean Whitfield, *Three Feet Off Gabriola*

The sunrise down Newcastle Channel scattered its first frail photons into a landscape of smoked glass, chasing grey mists off the green and blue conifer-coated sandstone archipelago. The sheer mercurial beauty of the place would smack you silly.

On the Harbour City side of the water, seagulls flew sorties through the rigging of the fishing boats, screaming at the new dawn.

The young pilot pushed his twin-engine silver floatplane from the dock, climbed the left ladder and left wing and fuselage, and dropped into his cockpit. His company's Beech 18 logo splashed onto the twin tail rudders. *Rainbow Air.*

The eight charter passengers were quiet with the weight of the early hour and the anticipation of becoming airborne. They were flying to new jobs in the small mainland logging community of Port Mellon in Howe Sound, and the withdrawal of tobacco and alcohol and sleep was a further impediment to casual conversation.

The pilot pumped the two central throttles back and forth for effect, set the flaps, flicked switches and fired up the two 450 HP Pratt and Whitney engines on each wing. Blue smoke blew out from under him and curved scimitars whirled into an *eliche perforante* resonant reverberation that rumbled rudely through the numbness. *RrrRRRrRRRRR...*

The aviator pushed on the glass of his flight instruments to read them more accurately through the vibration. He pushed harder on the two central throttles and the seaplane began to move forward, leaving a triangular turbulent wake of ripples on the Salish saltwater below.

The young flier knew that if you pulled the bow tie pasta stick of the Beechcraft back, the rocks and trees would get smaller. If you pushed the stick forward (or if you pulled the stick all the way back too fast), they would get bigger again. He pulled the control stick back gently, and five tons of metal and men and avgas and baggage and other cargo rose into where the wind lived. Had the passengers been more fortunate, they would soon be falling logs in Howe Sound, instead of just falling.

The last thing that went through the pilot's mind was the Strait of Georgia, as the Air Rainbow plane exploded in a fireball across the sky, into as many colours again, before the black smoke extinguished the sunrise.

> 'Once upon a time I was falling in love
> Now I'm only falling apart
> There's nothing I can do
> A total eclipse of the heart.'
> Bonny Tyler, *Total Eclipse of the Heart*

The floatplane had disintegrated only two blocks from him, but inside the sealed cabin of his own silver conveyance, Sam Kee was oblivious to everything but the eight speakers of his Audi's Bose Surround Sound system.

Good Morning Harbour City... This is CNDN Coast Salish radio, 101.3 FM on your Home and Native Band. I'm your host, BC Bud...

Sam's family had prospered from the time his great-grandfather, Mah Bing Kee, left Canton for *Gam Saan* Gold Mountain at the tender age of 14, to pan the California gold rush in 1861. Six years later, Bing found *shuāngxǐ* double happiness in his marriage to Wong Foon, the daughter of a wealthy San Francisco merchant. The couple and their four children moved north to Harbour City in 1890, where Bing farmed and logged, and built a new house. He began to capitalize new Chinese immigrants in establishing businesses as bakers and cooks and tailors and herbalists, receiving a half-share of any profits for his risk. Before long, Bing owned two laundries, a tailor shop, a restaurant, a hotel, a gambling house, several residential properties, and a small logging and sawmill operation. He had timber cut into slabs and sent by railway to his lumberyard in Cassidy, where dealers bought it wholesale.

In 1903, Bing Kee's luck began to turn to bat shit. He purchased the 159-acre Ganner Estate, south of Harbour City, which contained valuable forest and coal seams. Bing wanted to mine the coal, but the estate executors asked the government to revoke the coal rights. The court in Victoria ruled in Bing's favour. The executors then appealed to the Supreme Court in Ottawa, and again the ruling went to Bing. The executors finally appealed to the court in London, England. Bing's lawyer refused to defend him, and men in wigs rescinded his coal rights.

In the same year, over a bowl of Hong Kong mulligan at the Nam King Low Chop Suey House, Mah Bing Kee and Ching Chung Yung incorporated the Hop Sing Company, formed to buy Harbour City's original Chinatown and the thirty acres of farmland behind it. There was no time for 'foolishment.'

Five years later, they purchased the site of the second Chinatown. When the Chinese residents tried to tear down and move their buildings, Bing sought an injunction and had them arrested. Seventeen went on trial before a packed courtroom June 1, 1908, and were required to swear to the 'Chinese Oath' administered by the Chief Magistrate.

'To establish a yellow oath, I... the Attester, do swear... that I will give the evidence in court today to speak the truth, pertaining to the case. If I had any biased mind to invent lies or to utter falsehood, the high Heaven, the true God, will punish me, sink me in the river and drown me in the deep sea, forfeit my future generations and cast my soul into hell to suffer forever and ever.'

The provincial court ruled that the buildings belonged to the Chinese who had built them. Bing's next appeal to the Supreme Court of Canada was dismissed and the frame buildings were rebuilt with overhanging balconies and wooden sidewalks inside the large timber gates of the third Chinatown.

Bing had also endured the payment of a $500 head tax, and continuous simmering white resentment and endemic racism, but he was luckier than the 104 Chinese coal miners killed in underground explosions, and those who never got to Gold Mountain at all, in the humiliation of the Chinese Immigration Act, which halted all further admission to Canada. He had left a wealthy legacy to a large established family, and his great-grandson was making out just fine. Besides his ownership of two hotels, a pub, a liquor store, and a nightclub, Sam was an elected city council member, respected for his sagacity and sense of fair play.

First, the weather. Today's forecast: Showers followed by rain. Tomorrow's forecast: Rain followed by showers...

He wasn't double happy about this tempestuous time of year. It made him want to do to his girlfriend what March was doing to the cherry trees. And today was the day.

Just to remind you that Daylight Saving Time begins at 3:00 a.m. on March 11th... So, spring forward one hour, fall behind on your sleep and feel like crap all day long... Only a Wašicu fool would tell you that if you cut a foot off the top of a blanket and sew it to the bottom, you'll have a longer blanket...

Sam looked at his Rolex. He feathered the Audi's 6-speed manual transmission and 32 dual overhead cammed valves roared into a 280 horsepower choral accelerando. He took the corner of the iconic intersection of Dufferin Crescent at Dufferin Crescent in the last millisecond of yellow light. One of the other city staff had pasted a yellow 'C' sticker in the right-sided blind spot of his windshield, with the words 'Chinese Driver' underneath. Sam sported it as a badge of pride.

In nine more days, on March 20th, five days after they stabbed Julius Caesar two thousand years ago, is the first day of spring—the season of the eagle, tobacco, fire, mental health, birth, childhood, mineral, the sun, the dawn, growth, the east, and oriental yellow people...

Exactly in front of the entrance to Harbour City Regional Hospital, Sam felt his teeth go numb, like he was at the dentist, just before the thunder exploded in his chest, just before his airbag deployed. His disoriented Audi departed the lane and any hope of resurrection, crashed into a towering red and white utility pole, and knocked the breath out of the heliport windsock.

And remember, your first teacher is your own heart.

'Help is on the way
Help is on the way
Hold my hand, to help see, right there in front of me
Help is on the way.'
Rise Against, *Help Is On The Way*

The day before the two accidents found a young man wandering the halls of Harbour City Regional Hospital, blown off course by the same spring winds of the Salish Sea. He had entered a medical maze of waiting rooms and treatment pods, pathways and parking lots, atria and courtyard gardens, a labyrinthine leprosarium of brick and Douglas fir and concrete and glass.

Lost in his brooding imbroglio, he finally found Cheri Sundae, the ER ward clerk, sitting at the counter behind her polycarbonate protective window. On her flank, she faced a wide entrance with automatic sliding frosted glass doors, ambulances lined up outside, paramedics wheeling in patients on gurneys, and a carnival of Care Card numbers, wristbands, and pain.

"Can I help you?" She asked.

"I'm Jamie Dunne, the new medical resident." He said. "I'm looking for Doctor Sababa."

"He's on the Bridge of the Death Star." She said.

"Huh?"

"He's in the ICU." She said.

"Where's that?" He looked at the various corridors radiating out from her nuclear core.

Cheri pointed to a procession of yellow rectangles receding down a passageway to a far-off vanishing point.

"Follow the Yellow Brick Road." She said.

Jamie thanked her and set off in the designated direction.

Nowhere was the chronic underfunding of Harbour City Regional clearer than in the corridors. The air in the passage was stuffy, with undertones of bleach, and worse. The monotone linoleum floor was highly polished, to better illuminate the hallway that stretched beyond. The dove and magnolia and pale blue walls were scraped and scored deep by the hundreds of metal trolleys that had collided with them, the drywall showing through in white scars.

23

There were cheap insipid commercial prints on the walls, of scenes meant to be uplifting but even more dull and depressing for hanging in measured institutional intervals like death row inmates in an antechamber to the great beyond. Above him, the ceiling was a grid of perforated polystyrene tiles and naked fluorescent tubes, flickering abrasive in their own end-of-life death throes. Large spotless signs trimmed every double-door frame he passed under, indicating in bold capitalized lettering the areas of the hospital that lay ahead.

At the end of the Yellow Brick Road, Jamie entered a small vestibule, furnished with several retro vintage chairs, a coffee table on which sat a vase of withering gladiolas, and a wire rack of support group pamphlets. It could have been a cave if there had been more light. But all the radiance was straight ahead of him, soft and translucent, behind the frosted automatic door with a hand sanitizer dispenser and a red buzzer button on a brushed metal speaker protruding from its frame. A sign hung overhead. *ICU—Tranquility Base.*

Jamie pushed on the button.

"Yes?" Came the tinny answer from the metal speaker.

"It's Dr. Dunne." Jamie spoke his words slowly. "Doctor Sababa's new resident." The translucency slid sideways with ease. A warm draft hit his face, with a tincture of bleach, and worse. Inside was a bizarre absurd conundrum of simultaneous sensory deprivation and overload.

The glare was subtle and harsh. The world stopped at the windows, portholes that had devolved into vestigial lancets. No light could enter; no screams could leave. Any illumination of any form attempting to seek ingress into the unit was snuffed out by the sickness and suffering which contaminated the air and tinted the glass.

Time was hazy, measured in microseconds and eternities.

The ICU was quiet. Most sounds were dampened by sterile drapes and gauze, and curtains and consequence. Voices whispered. Until the shit happened, and the machines began dinging and buzzing and beeping in hair-raising Devil's Tritones, dissonant chords that would have been banned in any Renaissance church.

Pumps on IV poles beeped as they ran out of their fluid or medication. Cardiac and hemodynamic monitors alarmed when heart rates or pacemaker parameters or blood pressures dipped too low, climbed too high, registered abnormal rhythms or with other ECG changes. Ventilators screamed for more or less respiratory rate or pressure or dead space or oxygen or carbon dioxide, or during circuit leaks or patient suctioning. Other

24

sensors warned of abnormal temperature or movement artifact or electromagnetic interference or electrode disconnection or cuff distortion. Every ICU patient would generate over seven hundred distress signals per day, and nearly all of them would be an error. This resulted in a phenomenon called alarm fatigue, where nurses and clinicians ignored device warnings, assuming them to be false, device limits to inaudible, or even moved physiologic specifications into unsafe zones, to regain some peace.

They couldn't do the same with human noise—loud voices, confused voices, moaning voices, screaming voices, footfalls, cartwheel squeaks, and cell phone cacophony.

Jamie had noted the warning signs throughout the hospital corridors. *Scent-Free Zone. Fragrance-Free Space. We Share the Air.*

But he just laughed to himself. Jamie knew all the smells from his training. He could identify them easily, as they decayed as the square of the distance from his nose. He knew the mouse smell of liver failure, the ammonia of kidney failure dialysis, the fishy aroma of infected piss and the metallic tang of bloody leg bag urine. He could identify the guilty bacteria and the antibiotic used for any wound infection—oozing, necrotic, tunnelling, abscess, or pressure ulcer—the almondy grape juice of Pseudomonas, the rotten meat of Clostridium or other anaerobic gas gangrene, the fecal odour of E. coli, the decomposition stench of MRSA, the old sweat stink of S. epidermis, and the cat pee perfume of Ceftriaxone. He was *au fait* with the odours that came from ventilated patients, the trachs that reeked, the drooling beard with too much pustular sputum that no amount of oral care would ever fix. Gastrointestinal miasmas were some of the worst—vomit and gastric lavage contents, the burning leather and tar black stools of an upper GI bleed and the iron and death smell of bleeding further down the GI pipeline; the burst colostomy bag, the C. difficile megacolon and defecated infarcted dead bowel, the genital effluvia of retained tampons or the eye-watering rotten crotch candle of trichomonas and bacterial vaginosis.

Jamie knew the nuanced nose of skin gone wrong—fresh burns hot out of the mercy flight, the scent of chronic lustre-lost AIDS skin flaking into dust storms at the slightest touch in that rare ray of sunshine that straddled the bed, or the whiff of now translucent hair, matted by perspiration and molded by pillow. Brain damage imparted its own notes to the olfactory orchestra, the sweetish, sickly earthy smell of 'neuro funk.'

Any ICU nurse might receive any aromatic admission just before the end of her shift— an incontinent drunk homeless man with an extraterrestrial body odor and springtime swamp feet, or an elderly morbidly obese matron with so much diabetes and disease she would throw Lt. Col. Frank Slade's *Scent of a Woman* into total darkness—weeping edema and white gooey yeast cheese under pendulous breasts and abdominal aprons and other skin folds, all wrapped up in soiled clothing permeated with it all. Then there were the chemical and endemic bouquets that the hospital brought to the picnic—The sweet ketones of iodoform disinfectant, the artificial fragrances of soaps and cleansers, bitter antiseptics, old tube feeding formula, morning breakfast tray powdered eggs and bad cafeteria food, and the acrid burnt earthworm fetor of linen fresh from the overheated hospital laundry dryers. And finally, there were the overpowering combinations of peculiar and pungent and putrid and poisonous pongs of sweat and stool and sputum and serum that collided into an experience not that far from opening the lid of a two-week-old dumpster. For this, when no one was looking, the ICU nurses nebulized Febreze.

The positive atmosphere in the ICU was pressurized to prevent the invasion of any foreign fragrances or other influences. Jamie entered the unit through the air that was trying to escape. Ahead, on the Bridge of the Death Star, behind a polycarbonate window like the one protecting Cheri Sundae in the ER, sat a wizened elderly Chinese ward clerk with Coke bottle wire-rimmed glasses and an Empress Consort's demeanor. He read her nametag as he approached. *Betty Boop*.

"Hello. I'm Jamie Dunne, the new medical resident." He said. "I'm looking for Doctor Sababa."

"You already said that." Her voice was husky and Jamie could tell from the lines in her face and her nicotinic acerbity that she was counting down to her next cigarette.

"Take a number." She grinned. "He's putting in a Swan-Ganz catheter in the cubicle behind Curtain #3." Jamie surveyed his new kingdom. There were 12 cubicles that surrounded the Bridge, each with its own draping and nurse and avionics that were displays on the bank of monitors arrayed behind Betty Boop. The white noise of the ventilators softened the starkness. His eyes converged on the object of his search. *Cubicle 3*. Jamie strolled over and pulled back the curtain. Inside were several machines, two nurses, a patient buried under sterile drapes and, at the head of the bed, a stout man in a surgical cap and face mask and shield and booties, wearing cheerful pale blue scrubs still starched into wrinkles. He was calling out instructions and the nurses were calling back numbers. Jamie cleared his throat.

"Hey, Dude." He said. The calling out and back stopped dead.

"What happened?" Asked Mary, the first nurse.

"He called him Dude." Answered Charmeine, the second nurse.

"How did that work out?" Mary inquired.

"I don't plan on being here to find out." Charmeine glared over her face mask.

"Sorry, Doctor Sababa. I'm Jamie Dunne, your new resident from UBC."

"Ah, yes." Said the stocky savant. "The University of Bourbon and Cannabis. Your program director send you across the strait for some bracing sea air?

"Something like that."

"Spectacular mistake." Sababa said. "Is your CV a list of things you never want to do again?"

"Sorry if I gave any offense."

"Welcome to Thoracic Park, Jamie." He pointed to a cart outside the cubicle. "Gown up and put on a pair of gloves."

Jamie did this with efficiency, and entered the Sababa's sanctum.

"Those forceps." Sababa pointed. Jamie took the forceps.

"You know where the left supraspinatus muscle is?"

"Of course." Jamie was insulted at the interrogation of such a simple fact. Sababa turned away.

"Now scratch behind my left shoulder blade." Jamie scratched, and Sababa's pager went off in his right pocket. *Doctor Sababa, 2071. Doctor Sababa, 2071.*

"Betty, can you get that for me, please?" Sababa projected past the curtain. He grabbed a tenaculum off the tray and reached down to turn off his pager.

"I'm on it." She said. Her left hand gesticulated in the air for a few seconds, and then she replaced the handset.

"Dr. Capitaine in Emerg." She said. "He wants you to see a patient."

"Jamie?" Sababa looked at him.

"Yes, Doctor Sababa?"

"Go see the patient in Emerg. And Jamie?"

"Yes, Doctor Sababa?"

"If you ever call me Dude again, the next heart you see will be your own. We clear?"

"Yes, Doctor Sababa."

'Why, universal plodding poisons up
The nimble spirits in the arteries,
As motion and long-during action tires
The sinewy vigour of the traveller.'
William Shakespeare, *Love's Labour Lost*

Wide Emergency Room glass doors slid open and shut in symphonic saccades. The first contact any patient would have was with the triage nurse inside, a drum majorette diverting and disposing patients, like Mengele meeting the trains. It was all an elaborate contemporary ballet danced to divide and conquer the myriad chaotic presentations of disability and disease.

Less or more fortunate performers were directed to the capacious waiting room, a purgatory of anxiety and bandages and boredom—a knuckle-cracking, backward-glancing, magazine-flipping, watch-checking, phone-texting, iPod-scrolling, feet-tapping, hand-wringing, purse-fiddling, button-twirling, ring-twisting, eye-rubbing, nose-pinching, arm-stroking, floor-pacing sickscape of wheezing, whispering, whimpering and weeping, immobilized in wheelchairs and tortured plastic chairs slung with sweaters and jackets and resignation and metal arm rails digging into flesh.

The contaminated sterile amalgam reeked of air-borne pathogens, antiseptics, latex gloves, body odor, stale cigarette smoke, old urine, and fear. All attempts to alter the atmosphere with filtration or fresheners had rendered it more pathetic.

An acoustic arcade of periodic vending machine dispensation broke the monotony—coins clinking in and out, the thud of chocolate bars or sodas hitting the tray, the hiss of opening aluminum cans, the rustle of candy and chip wrappers.

Beyond the defensive perimeter of the ER ward clerk, sounds of the servants, the venerable, the blessed beatified, the canonized saints of medical science, came in the form of rustling paperwork, clicking pens, and mumbling mobile phones. Doctors and nurses, porters and phlebotomists, respiratory therapists and ECG technicians intermingled with itinerant janitorial staff.

Jamie approached her polycarbonate barrier for the second time that day.

"Cheri, I'm looking for a patient named Man Singh." He said.

28

"Bed 9." She pointed to the cubicle. "His entire family is living with him behind the curtain." Jamie pulled the chart from its slot and read the ER Referral note. *Doctor Sababa to see. Discussed.*

Jamie pulled back the drape. An elderly patriarch with a mesmerizing orange turban and long white beard lay half-conscious, surrounded by the standing horseshoe of a devoted family. The old man wore the 5 K's of his faith—*kashera* cotton breeches, a *kirpan* short dagger, a *kara* steel bangle on his dominant arm, the *kesh* uncut hair under his turban, and a small *kanga* comb to groom it twice a day. His progeny appeared less traditional in their appearance, although they likely carried more hidden signs of their devoutness. The oldest son's eyes caught Jamie's attention.

"*Sat Shri Akall.* Good morning." He began. "My father understands only Punjabi, so I will speak for him. All medical treatment to avert the threat to his life should be provided without question and without delay." Jamie looked at the near moribund man, and then the chart. Man Singh was a 79-year-old retired blueberry farmer. His gaze drifted up to the old man's chest. It was pulsating in time to the horizontal moving electric QRS complexes on the screen of the cardiac monitor above him. There was nothing good happening here.

Jamie asked the family for the medical history of their elder and probed for clues to his recent deterioration. After some initial resistance, they finally agreed to leave for a few minutes to allow the young resident to examine him. Jamie knew he was running the clock.

As he finished synthesizing the result of his history and physical and the available lab work and imaging data into an analysis he thought he could present to his own guru, Sababa bounced into Jamie's peripheral vision. He was a different animal outside the calm cubicles of the ICU—buoyant, fast, incisive, intuitive, and ruthlessly efficient. Internal Medicine specialists were at the top of their game. Favorable clinical outcomes depended on it. He watched the burly medical machine springboard into the department. A mop of curly black hair and the stethoscope around his collar recoiled off his resilient gait. He was neatly dressed but wore no tie. The old leather briefcase he had picked up in Colombia from his hitchhiking days contained examining tools, instruments, and an infamous hand-scribed Black Book. The prevailing folklore suggested that if you knew the contents of Sababa's Black Book of Remedies, you not only knew all there was to know about the secrets of medicine, you knew all there was to know about the secrets of life.

Sababa collided with Jamie's space at the same time an ER doc in green scrubs converged on both of them. He had been working the antibacterial hand dispenser like a gambling addict at a slot machine. His breath smelled of Code Brew coffee. Sababa made the introductions.

"Jamie, meet the one, the only, Dr. Myles Capitaine." Sababa said. "Single-handed sailor on the Sea of Tranquillity. How are you, Myles?"

"Living the dream." Said the Emergency doctor.

"The ER is blanketed by a wild majesty that beckons dreamers." Sababa said. "Jamie, know how to confuse an ER doc?" Jamie shrugged.

"Ask him what the second dose is."

"Listen Sababa, just a heads up." Said Myles. "The Singh family may be expecting some kind of miracle here, but whatever is going on with grandpa is not going to welcome one."

"Immature strategy is the cause of grief." Sababa replied.

"Who said that?" Asked Myles.

"Miyamoto Musashi." Sababa said. "And me." Myles didn't have the time to ask. Sababa turned his attention to the young resident.

"A consultant is sometimes sent in after the battle to bayonet the wounded, Jamie. He said. "Tell me a story."

Jamie began to recite what he had concluded were the salient details of the case, trying to include everything material to the ultimate clinical plan for Man Singh, and leaving out what he thought Sababa would consider unnecessary extraneous information. He related episodes of near fainting, worsening shortness of breath, weight gain, progressive swallowing difficulty, poor balance, and lower limb lightning pains and swelling, delusions, and gradual mental decline. His examination had found head bobbing, bounding pulses, sternal pulsation, and various complicated abnormal heart sounds and murmurs. Hemogram showed all the blood cell lines reduced in number. Electrocardiogram was abnormal in a dozen different ways. Chest x-ray showed something big and full of fluid and calcium behind the breastbone.

"You are looking at history here, Jamie." Sababa said. "It appears our man, Man Singh, was walking, when he was walking, in the illustrious company of such notables as Guy de Maupassant and Charles Baudelaire, Schubert and Schopenhauer, Édouard Manet and Toulouse-Lautrec, Tolstoy and Lenin, Hitler and Mugabe, and Al Capone and Idi Amin. Let's go see him."

30

At the bedside, Sababa pulled a small penlight from his bag, and swung it from eye to eye and back again. Man's pupils contracted when Sababa asked him to look at his own nose but failed to constrict in the brightness of applied light.

"Plot twist." Sababa said. "Like the doxy that gave Man her gift—accommodating but unreactive." Sababa raised one of the elderly man's legs and asked him to point to his big toe. Man was off by a mile. Jamie's brow furrowed.

"I don't understand."

"Internal Medicine is a Confucian discipline, Jamie. Numerological, in big strokes. First to know are the three steps to proper fact acquisition for meaningful clinical intervention: (1) What you got, you got. (2) What you don't got, you don't got, and (3) What you do with what you got and what you don't got depends on context."

"OK."

"So then, what have you got?" Jamie recounted his findings.

"An elderly man with a mass in his chest and some form of neurological decline." He said.

"And the light-near dissociation of his pupils? Sababa asked.

"Five possible causes." Jamie said. "Deafferented pupils, midbrain lesions, aberrant regeneration of the third nerve, tonic pupils, and... and..."

"And?"

"I forget." He said.

"Across from this valley of ashes is the office of our own faceless oculist guru, Dr. T.J. Eckleburg, who I will ask to see our sick Sikh, for his own erudition." Said Sababa. "Argyll-Robertson pupils. Prostitute pupils. And in combination with General Paresis of the Insane, Tabes Dorsalis, and a giant eroding thoracic aneurysm that has been like sighting a rare white spirit bear since the day that penicillin arrived (but obviously not to Man Singh), and what have you got? What is the name of the 'Revenge of the Americas,' the 'French disease,' the "Neapolitan disease,' the 'Great Pox,' Sir William Osler's 'Great Imitator,' the injected Tuskegee Institute pathogen for which Bill Clinton apologized too little too late, the 'that which cannot be spoken?'"

"Syphilis?" Jamie said. "But Man Singh is a Sikh."

"As was Mahant Narayan Das." Sababa offered.

"Who?"

"Some other time." He said.

"Man Singh's family is concerned." Jamie said. "His eldest son told me they want all medical treatment without question or delay. His ascending aortic diameter is greater than 5.5 cm. He should be a candidate for surgical resection."

"Confucius said there are three stages of life, Jamie: (1) Birth. (2) What the fuck is this? and (3) Death. We're still in the second stage. What's the most important question?"

"Dunno."

"The most important question is 'What's the question?'" Our Man's aneurysm is expanding according to Laplace's law. It may soon rupture through his sternum. The management choices might have been difficult, falling between Scylla and Charybdis, if he didn't have tertiary syphilitic dementia. But now it's easier. No one is going to use sharp objects on the tree bark that has replaced his main artery. So I ask again, what's the question?"

"What is the best way to treat this patient, in these circumstances?"

"Much to learn you still have, my young Padawan." Sababa said. "And what is the most important thing?"

"What we do with the most important question?"

"The most important thing is to keep the most important thing the most important thing." Sababa said. "In Man Singh's case, it will be palliation, and reassuring the family of our first obligation to the patient. *To cure sometimes, to relieve often, to comfort always.*

"How do you tell a religious East Indian family that their patriarch and benefactor is about to become a scene from *Alien* because he has syphilis?"

"One tells them." Said Sababa. "Not because they need to know that he was one of the fools who wrangled over *ganika* flesh, but because they also need to be tested."

"He's not infectious now."

"But he was." Sababa said. "I'll tell them, while you go and see the next patient."

"There's another one?" Jamie asked.

"I'm thinking your ability to thrive under pressure is what drove you into Internal Medicine." He said. "In this game, the reward for excellence is always more. You see that ER doc over there? His name is Trace Pangloss. He's going to be a fine administrator some day, but he doesn't know it yet. He wants us to see the young Japanese women behind Curtain #5. Go get 'em, tiger." Sababa went to call in the Singh family. He took the eldest son by his elbow and guided him, and began to speak of the recitation of Gurbani and sacred hymns, and serenity. No one could hear what he was humming in his head.

> 'There was a young man of Bombay,
> Who thought syphilis just went away,
> And felt that a chancre,
> Was merely a canker,

Acquired in lascivious play.

With symptoms increasing in number,
His aorta's in need of a plumber,
His heart is cavorting,
From previous consorting
And now he's acquired a gumma.

Consider his terrible plight,
His eyes won't react to the light,
His hands are apraxic
His gait is ataxic,
He's developing gun-barrel sight.

Though treated in every known way,
His spirochetes grow by the day,
He's developed paresis,
And converses with Jesus,
On his float in the Kalsa parade.'
JAMA, Jan 31 1942 (with apologies), *The Limerick of Syphilis*

"What you got?" Sababa asked, an hour later.

"Murasaki Shikibu." Jamie said. "27-year-old right-handed pianist and composer with a chief complaint of recurrent loss of consciousness with changes in posture, occurring over the previous month. History of some kind of stroke a year ago." Sababa looked at Trace's consult referral sheet. *Fall down, go boom.*

"What you don't got?" Sababa asked.

"Seizures, fever, joint pain, rash, other systemic symptoms." Jamie said. Sababa smiled.

"Exam?" He asked.

"Weird." Jamie said. "She has no pulses or discernible blood pressure in her neck and arms. Pulses and pressures in her legs are normal. Mild spastic weakness on her right side and an expressive aphasia, presumably from her previous stroke.

"Lab?"

"Blood work, chest X-ray, electrocardiogram all normal. CT brain shows an old stroke exactly where you would expect to find it."

"Context?"

"Young Asian woman in her reproductive years. Clearly not atherosclerosis or giant cell." Jamie said. "You likely don't want to bury this one." Sababa scowled.

"You said weird, Jamie." He said. "Disease usually falls into one of three categories of natural imbalance: (1) too much, (2) too

33

little, and (3) weird. In Mrs. Shikibu's situation, there is also a dimensional vector variant as a clue: (1) up, (2) down, and (3) sideways. Murasaki has no pulses in the upper half of her body. What if she had no pulses in the lower half instead?"

"I'd think of a coarctation narrowing in the arch of her aorta." He said. "But she has the opposite problem, something that's blocking off the more northern tributaries coming off her arch."

"You have a name?" Said Sababa.

"Pulseless disease?"

"Half points." Sababa pulled out his thick Black Book and flipped to an illuminated papyrus page. There were several tiny beautiful hand-sketched drawings of arteries, annotated with flow equations and miniature multicolored cursive hieroglyphs. Jamie let out a low whistle.

"It's like the *Egyptian Book of the Dead*."

"I'd like to rather think of it as the *Book of Emerging Forth into the Light*." Sababa said.

"The *Gospel According to Sababa*." Jamie asked.

"Something like that." At the top of the page was a heading. *Takayasu's Arteritis.*

"Book her a CT angiogram." He said. "It will show severe gross thickening of the aortic arch and proximal ascending aorta with near-complete obstruction of both carotid and subclavian arteries. She likely doesn't have any ocular involvement because she lives in British Columbia, or renal artery involvement because her blood pressure is normal. Add a sedimentation rate and HLA-Bw52 to her blood work, and start her on prednisone at a dose of 1 mg/kg. Today. She'll need other steroid-sparing immunosuppressive therapy soon, and she may still need new plumbing. And Jamie?"

"Yes?"

"Mikito Takayasu was the ophthalmologist who first described the condition in 1908." Sababa said. "He was a professor at Kanazawa University."

"And?"

"Kanazawa is on the north coast of Honshu in Ishikawa Prefecture." He said. "Same climate and amazing seafood as we have. It has the finest Japanese garden, and the best preserved Samurai house and old Geisha district in Japan."

"And?"

"When you visit, go see my old friend Kazuhiko Tsurumi at *Otomezushi*. He's only the third designated *taisho* sushi master chef in the country. Makes Jiro Ono look like a line cook. Order a nice bottle of *junmai daijingo*. You will see God."

"And when do I get to make this pilgrimage?" Jamie asked.

"A few years after you've seen these next consults on the wards."
Sababa handed him a piece of paper with two names. "The
morning is only half over."

'We view things not only from different sides, but with different eyes;
we have no wish to find them alike.'

Blaise Pascal

Dr. Ernie Hacker was an Internal Medicine colleague of Sababa,
but Jamie hadn't met him yet. Indeed, he would never meet him
because Dr. Hacker was elusive. Ernie was a Jackal of the
jugular, a Ponzi of patient care, a Madoff of medicine, and a
Rumpelstiltskin of responsibility. Of the three considered
attributes of a good doctor, availability, ability, and affability,
Ernie compensated for the absence of the first and the
mediocrity of the second, with an explosive expert effusiveness of
the third. He cultivated the patronage of wealthy widows and
verily did his office runneth over with hams and turkeys at
Christmas. The nurses called him Dr. Upan Atom, after his
encouraging bedside manner. The doctors called him 'The Big
Easy' because every day was a potential golf day. Ernie was a
master of dreams and schemes and putting greens, keeping his
eye on the ball, and his balls on the table. His consult notes were
fast and messy, and sparse. On one occasion, his only comment
was 'This guy is a crock.' The specialist that found the patient's
bowel tumour asked Ernie to see him again. 'This crock has
cancer.' He wrote. On the rare occasion that Dr. Hacker was
blessed with a resident of his own, he would preempt his case
review by writing in the bottom half of the consult page. *I agree
with the above.* One brave resident who came to see the patient
later had the temerity to write above Ernie's insightful
assessment. *I agree with the below.*
A legend made its own rounds that Ernie had jumped on a plane
to Quebec one fall on call day. In Montreal, he shouted across
Rue Saint-Paul, after finding another hospital associate, the
pulmonologist Dr. Edward Hyde, on the same street.
"I signed out to you." He said.

"I signed out to you." Said Dr. Hyde, most emphatically.

Jamie would never meet Dr. Hacker but he would, in his time at Harbour City Regional, meet many of his casualties, two of which were written on the piece of paper Sababa had just given him. He took the elevator up to the 5th floor, where the less acute medical problems lived. A lovely Filipino nurse named Sophia was the first to welcome him. Jamie knew that the Philippines produced some of the best nurses in the world. Every smiling Pinoy he met was rocking it—compassionate and caring, quick-learning mood-lifting hard workers, with unmatched inner strength and dedication.

"I'm Doctor Sababa's resident." He began.

"You are his aso shit?" She asked. Jamie nodded.

"As a mutter of puck, he is my payborit ductor." Sophia said.

Jamie showed her the names of the two patients. *Julius Noh... Paul Hewson.*

"Uktoowally, I cun help wheat dat." She said. "Ductor Hacker must be playing wack wack today. Eat snot pear. Palo me." They walked down the hall to a brightly lit double room.

"I will open delight." She said. Two young men looked up. One was digging into his morning meal. The other near the window had finished and had buried himself in the Harbour City Star.

"Dey are peeling pine today." Sophia said. "East-tart pursed with Meester Noh. Den Meester Hewson, upter he penis her brick-pus." Sophia left Jamie to conduct his interviews.

Exactly two hours later, Sababa stepped off the elevator on the fifth floor, to find Sophia smiling, and Jamie finishing his consult notes at the nursing station.

"What you got?" He asked.

"Both patients were referred to Dr. Hacker, but nobody remembered that today was a golf day." Jamie began. "First is Julius Noh, 47-year-old unmarried stamp dealer admitted for recurrent community-acquired pneumonia. He's had five previous hospitalizations for same, on a background of frequent bronchitis and sinus infections. Exam reveals a right nasal polyp, but the rest of his physical is weird. His heart sounds are on the wrong side of his body, and his liver taps out on the left. Blood work was normal but the QRS voltage on his ECG goes backward. Here's his chest x-ray." Jamie threw the film up on the viewer. Sababa took it down, turned it over, and replaced it on the illuminated screen.

"That's backward." Jamie said.

"Look at the anatomical side markers." Sababa said. It took a few seconds for the recognition software to kick in.

"His organs are on the wrong side of his body." Jamie said.

"He's a stereoisomer of normal organ position." Said Sababa. "He has his heart and abdominal organs on the opposite side from yours and mine, recurrent respiratory tract infections and probable sterility. You have a name?"

"Kartagener's Syndrome?"

"Head of the class." Sababa said. "Type of disorder?" Jamie pulled out his cell phone and held out his dominant hand, in supplication to the signal. Sababa snatched it away.

"Welcome to the end of the internet, Jamie." He said. "Kartagener's is a defect in the movement of the tiny hairs that move fluids in the direction they're supposed to go—in the sinuses, Eustachian tubes, middle ear, fallopian tubes, and in the forward flagellar motion of sperm. They also produce nitric oxide, but we'll save that for another day. What do you want to do with him?"

"Repeat his ECG with reversed leads, CT of his paranasal sinuses, and a High-resolution CT of his chest. Jamie said. "Change his antibiotic to something that will work, and an abdominal ultrasound to confirm the organ reversal."

"Get a sperm analysis." Sababa said. "And do a Saccharin test."

"A what?"

"Put a small particle of saccharin here in his nasal cavity." Sababa drew a diagram. "If he doesn't taste sweetness inside of twenty minutes, his mucociliary clearance is faulty. When you want to know how things work, Jamie, study them when they're coming apart. Who's the second of The Big Easy's admissions?"

"Paul Hewson." Jamie began. "58-year-old Catholic priest. I haven't figured out why he's here. His only complaint is failing vision but on exam he has these cloudy corneas that make him look like a fish. His blood work is noteworthy only for a lipid panel that shows low high-density lipoprotein and high triglycerides. Dr. Hacker admitted him because of concern about his kidney function but it's normal." The Good Doctor's forehead formed a fretwork of frown.

"When all else fails, Jamie, go to the bedside." They bounced down the hallway to the room of the two men. Sababa introduced himself to both, before pulling the curtain to speak to the patient whose eyes looked like those of a five day old boiled fish.

"You have a rare condition known as incomplete lecithin cholesterol acyltransferase or LCAT deficiency, also known as Fish-eye disease. The complete form of the defect is associated with anemia and kidney problems but you won't have either. The most you might need is corneal transplantation and an exercise stress test, which I can organize as an outpatient. You can go home."

The man looked relieved and gathered his things before anyone could change their mind. Sababa turned his attention to his young protégé.

"I assume you have a motorized means of linear transport." Jamie nodded.

"Go grab some lunch." He said. "I'll finish here later. Meet me at my clinic at one."

"For?"

"Some light afternoon doctoring." Sababa opened the door to the stairwell.

"How long is the clinic?" Jamie asked.

"All things entail rising and falling timing." He began descending the stairs. "Live your life by a compass, not a clock." His voice faded away. Jamie turned to find Sophia, smiling.

"Welcome to Sababaland."

⚕ ⚕ ⚕

'I try but nothing's ever gonna fill me up.
Why won't anything fill me up?
When you're born with a leak in your heart
It stays so dark...'

Joe Hedges, *Mitral Valve Prolapse*

Doctor Sababa's clinic was halfway across Harbour City, an eight-minute drive from the hospital. Jamie did it in ten. Sababa would do it in five, right behind him.

The young resident pulled into the parking lot next to a beautiful old white two-storey heritage building. The main floor entrance was adorned with a small brass plaque. *Harbour City Research Institute.* Jamie was aware that Sababa was a principal investigator in several Phase III clinical trials, including some from the Harvard TIMI and Canadian Vigour research groups. He climbed the stairs to another doorway, inlaid with stained glass, and marked by another sign. *Manzanita Medical.* Sababa had told him that other clinics were named for native trees, but his office was denominated after a local shrub that lived on the ridges behind the city because he loved its flowers.

He followed Jamie up the stairs and into a sunlit foyer. A redheaded middle-aged woman with cat-eyed frame glasses sat typing behind a counter and a big screen PowerMac G4, under a photo of a bowl of multicoloured cereal with a diagonal red line through it. *No fruit loops.*

"Hi, Mercy." Sababa said.

"It's buggered blood vessel week, Boss." She said.

"Mercy among the virtues is like the moon among the stars, dispensing a calm radiance that hallows the whole." He replied.

"What?" Jamie asked, in vain.

"Put your phone down and pull your pants up, Jamie." Sababa said. "We have work to do."

The first patient had been referred by a family physician, Dr. Tictac Tarmac, for a clinical suspicion of coronary artery disease. Yuri Heilongjiang was a 78-year-old retired ferry worker from Damansky Island on the Amur River, the waterway that formed the border between China and the old Soviet Union. When a territorial conflict broke out in 1969, the Soviets imprisoned Yuri as a Chinese spy. When they released him twenty years later, the Chinese arrested him as a Soviet spy. When he was finally freed, twenty years after that, Yuri lit out for Canada. He worked for BC Ferries until his retirement, which he spent running up the mountains around Harbour City. Sababa had Jamie take a history, and then they examined Yuri together. Jamie went on to see the next referral in the apprentice examining room while Sababa supervised the retired ferry worker's graded exercise test. Manzanita Medical was wired for sound. Yuri Heilongjiang ran the machine into the ground to the accompaniment of the complete Red Army choral rendition of Max Kyuss's *Amur Waves*. What it wasn't wired for was something that Sababa would only discover after many years. He had purchased the defibrillator for his stress room on eBay from a medical supply house in Las Vegas. He hadn't realized why it was so cheap until his friend and Harbour City Regional biomedical engineer, Murray 'Leatherman' MacGyver, tested it one day.

"You'll need a new battery." He said.

"Why?" Sababa asked.

"It didn't come with one."

"Oh." Sababa said.

"You know why they call us biomedical engineers, right?" Leatherman asked.

"No."

"Because 'fucking miracle worker' isn't an official job title."

With the assurance that he could handle any clinical situation restored, Sababa went ahead with Yuri's stress test. Twelve minutes and as many metabolic equivalents later, Sababa shut him down out of boredom. The note to Dr. Tarmac was brief. *That which does not kill us makes us stronger. You'll need another diagnosis.* When he had finished his assessment, Jamie presented Edie Sitwell, a 24-year-old dental hygienist, referred by her GP, Dr. Nicholas Rivera, for assessment of pain in her neck and arms.

"What you got?" Sababa observed a fidgety young woman, cracking and popping her joints, bouncing her legs, and readjusting her posture in attempts to get comfortable.

"She says she is in constant pain." Jamie said. "Her arms look blue."

"They are blue." Sababa bent his thumb back toward his wrist. "Can you do that, Edie?" Edie bent her thumb far behind her wrist. She pulled the skin of her neck out until she looked like a frilled lizard.

"Whenever I eat or brush my teeth, I have to push on my lower jaw to put it back in because it slips out." Sababa performed a series of specific manoeuvres with Edie's arms and rounded shoulders.

"Her arms are blue from shoulder girdle laxity and hypermobility, which cause costoclavicular compression of the bicuspid valves within the internal jugular, external jugular and subclavian veins, and the thoracic outlet syndrome you're looking at." Sababa said. "Edie, this explains your symptoms of numbness and tingling, headache, ear swooshing and ringing, visual floaters, fainting, nausea, and pain in your jaw, shoulders, chest, back, groin, and tailbone." Edvard Munch could have painted Edie's facial expression. Sababa turned his attention back to Jamie.

"You have a name?" He asked. Jamie had the same expression.

"Ehlers-Danlos Syndrome." Sababa said. "What you don't got?" Nothing persisted in coming out of his mouth.

"The eyes are open, the mouth moves, but Mr. Brain has long since departed, hasn't he?" Sababa smiled. "There are disease continua and *formes frustes* of too much, too little and weird, Jamie.

Some conditions occur in greater frequency with thehyperelasticity/hypermobility syndromes—smooth muscle hyperreactivity (in the form of migraine, Raynaud's, vasomotor rhinitis, Prinzmetal's angina, asthma, biliary dyskinesia, and irritable bowel syndrome), mitral valve prolapse, hyperthyroidism, and Marfan's. You won't find this online or in any standard medical reference." Sababa flicked to a page in his Black Book.

"Edie will need a bilateral brachial plexus MRI, MRA/MRV with saline waterbags placed alongside her neck to enhance signal-to-noise ratio. Book an echo, tertiary genetics, physiatry and orthopedic consults, occupational and physiotherapy referrals, and a time in outpatients for me to perform a skin biopsy. Please formulate your letter for Dr. Rivera to read like a consultant dictated it. And then, Jamie."

"Uh huh."

"Go interview the last patient while I see the next one."

When he had finally finished explaining everything to Edie Sitwell, booked the necessary further investigations and referrals, and dictated his assessment to her family physician, Jamie walked by Mercy to retrieve the final patient of the afternoon. Above the fast feline fingers typing transcription and beneath her cat-eyed frame glasses, she was grinning like the Cheshire rest of her.

"Last year UBC nominated Doctor Sababa an educational influential physician." She said.

"And?"

"He's still not happy about it."

"Like a wasp nest at a piñata party." Jamie said. "Is he this abrupt with everyone?"

"I don't get the impression you're special." She said.

Jamie found Linda Blare in the waiting room, reading her most recent copy of *Clean Eating* magazine. She was weaponized with several file folders of articles she had compiled for this occasion and showed no small displeasure at being interviewed by a resident, which could only delay her own planned interrogation.

"Are you a vegan?" She asked. "Because you should be."

Sababa, meanwhile, had called in Rod Duterte, a patient from the practice of his own GP, Dr. James Ruben Andrews. He read the referral letter, twice. *Please see this 31-year-old drywaller with leg pain during exercise and at rest. I've been telling him for years that he needs to quit smoking. Perhaps he'll pay attention to what you have to say.*

Sababa listened to the tradesman's story. He asked him how much he smoked.

"Two packs a day." Rod said. He asked him how much cannabis.

"How do you know?"

"It is my business to know what other people don't know." He said. "How much?" It was a lot. Sababa asked the drywaller to sit up on his Cabernet-coloured examining table. He found no pulses in Rod's purple hands and feet and tiny areas of dead tissue. The rest of his skin was thin and shiny. A part of his scrotum was the same colour as the table. The Good Doctor retrieved Jamie, from his case in the next room, to expound.

"Mr. Duterte here has a progressive problem with clotting and inflammation of the small and medium blood vessels of his hands and feet and happy bits." He said. "Like King George VI of Britain. According to Olin's 2000 article in the New England Journal, Mr. Duterte meets criteria for the diagnosis of Buerger's disease. You know what that is, Rod?" Rod shook his head.

"Jamie?" Jamie shook his head in the other direction.

"It was first reported by an Austrian named Felix von Winiwarter, in 1879, but it wasn't until 1908 that Leo Buerger at Mount Sinai Hospital in New York provided a more accurate description. He called it 'presenile spontaneous gangrene.' Do you know what else we call it?" Rod shook his head. Sababa looked at his apprentice.

"Thromboangiitis obliterans." Jamie said.

"The obliterans part should get your attention, Rod." Sababa continued. "If you quit smoking today, you'll have a 94% chance of avoiding major amputation. If you don't stop smoking today, you will have more than a 50% likelihood of losing your legs and more fun body parts. That thing playing near your joystick is called migratory superficial thrombophlebitis. We usually only use big words when rewards and punishments enter the high stakes poker room. Capice?" Rod nodded.

"You're going to have some more blood work, and an echocardiogram and arteriography to exclude other causes." He said. "Stop smoking today. Everything. Don't come back here chewing smokeless tobacco." He wrote a prescription.

"Take these pills. I've indicated what they're for and how they work. I'll refer you on for physical therapy, to an anesthetist friend of mine for consideration of an epidural, a vascular surgeon to see if you're a candidate for either bypass or amputation, and, depending on your motivation, a neurosurgeon about lumbar sympathectomy. If I find a good hyperbaric oxygen facility in the neighbourhood, I'll let you know. And Rod?"

Rod nodded.

"The King had lung cancer and died in his bed of a heart attack." He said. "So far as I know they never had to cut off his penis. Tell Mercy to book you a return appointment in a month. Make me proud." Rod left the room. Sababa's letter to Dr. James Ruben Andrews was succinct. *He's paying attention.*

"What you got?" Sababa asked. Jamie rolled his eyes.

"Let's go see her." He said. In the residents' examining room, Jamie made the introductions.

"Ms. Blare is a 43-year-old animal rights advocate and health food shop owner, a vegan, referred by her GP, Dr. Poldy Bloom,

42

for problems of anemia and a low platelet count. Examination reveals an enlarged spleen, and subcutaneous xanthomas of her Achilles and hand extensor tendons."

"What's that?" She asked.

"Irregular yellow nodules, caused by fat deposition." Sababa answered.

"That's impossible." She said. "My body is a temple." She handed him a photocopied quote out of one of her manila folders.

"This is from Dr Caldwell Esselstyn's famous book *Forks Over Knives*." She said. *Some people think plant-based diet, whole foods diet is extreme. Half a million people a year will have their chests opened up and a vein taken from their leg and sewn onto their coronary artery. Some people would call that extreme.*

"Ah, yes, the Reverend Dr Caldwell Blakeman Esselstyn Jr." Sababa said. "Olympic rowing champion and, after young interns, Bill Clinton's favorite diet. But in your case, there appears to be one small problem."

"What's that?" She asked.

"I added serum plant sterol concentrations to Dr. Bloom's blood work." He said. "They came back 25 times normal."

"What does that mean?" She asked.

"It means you have a rare genetic disorder of increased absorption and decreased excretion of sterols from plant sources." He said. "It's called Sitosterolemia. We can fix it with a combination of a cholesterol absorption inhibitor called ezetimibe, and a bile acid-binding resin called cholestyramine."

"Drugs?" She sputtered. "You want to give me artificial chemicals?"

"No, I want to give you real chemicals." Sababa said.

"Isn't there a more natural way of treating this?" She said. "Something more holistic, like diet?"

"It's your diet that's killing you, Linda." Sababa said. "You need to back off the vegetable oils, olives, and avocados. Pick up a quarter pounder on your way home. If God didn't intend for us to eat animals, then why did he make them out of meat?"

"What if I refuse to take your poisons?" She was foaming.

"Untreated, you win a premature death from atherosclerotic coronary heart disease." Sababa said. He handed her a prescription, some online website references and a checklist with the *Graded Exercise Test* box ticked off. "Give this to Mercy on your way out. I'll explain more when I see you next." He turned to Jamie.

"That could be one reason why people who work in health food shops always look so unhealthy." He said. "We're on call tonight."

"I have a squash game."

"What?"

"I have a squash game."

"What?"

"I have a squash game."

"If you're on call every other night you're missing half the action." Sababa said.

"I'll risk it." Jamie thanked him for the too much fun he had already drowned in.

'When you sow blood you reap blood
That's what the Good Book says
Between The Hatfields and McCoys
The Tug River's running red.'
David Adkins, *Blood Feud*

Sababa arranged for Jamie to find him the next morning and drove back to Harbour City Regional alone. So far he had received only a single referral request from the ER while he was finishing up his clinic dictation, but that would change.

Dr. Gung Ho met him inside the sliding doors. He and Sababa went way back before the *Stout Men* days of the Himalayas, on the same trip that Gung's face fell forward into his bowl of peanuts in the Long Bar at Raffles Hotel, after a few sips of a Singapore Sling.

"It's an enzyme called alcohol dehydrogenase, Gung." Sababa had mused. "You don't have any."

This evening, Gung was his usual clear-headed self, explaining the reason he wanted Sababa to see the man in Bed #4.

"Behind that curtain is Randy McCoy, a 40-year-old cattle rancher with two-months of belly pain and blurred right vision." Gung began. "On exam, his pressure is through the roof at 220/120 mmHg, despite being on three drugs to control it. His right eye visual acuity is reduced, and normal on the left. I dilated him up and found a tangerine-coloured mass over the right optic nerve head, fed by snaky-looking vessels. I thought of you."

"How kind." Sababa said. "Optic head hemangioma and secondary hypertension. Sometimes you have to go to the bedside." He left Gung and slid open the curtain.

"Howdy." He said on a hunch.

"Howdy." He got back.

"Mr. McCoy?"

"Call me Randy." He said.

"OK." Sababa pulled the Black Book of Remedies from his Colombian leather briefcase. "Where's your family from, Randy."

"Kentucky."

"Tug Fork?" Sababa asked.

"How do you know?"

"It is my business to know what other people don't know." He said. "Your great great great great great great grandfather, William, was born in Ireland in 1750. In 1878, his great-grandson, Randolph, began a fight with a West Virginian, Floyd Hatfield, over a set of notches on the ear of a hog, claiming they were his marks. The feud that followed resulted in a New Year's Massacre, the Battle of the Grapevine Creek, a series of trials, and the deaths of two dozen people in both families, including a hanging at Pikeville. The feud between the Hatfields and the McCoys is an iconic Appalachian cautionary tale of the perils of family honor, justice, and revenge."

"Sumnabitch." Randy said. "And how is that relevant to my current problem?" Sababa asked if he could look in his eye before he answered.

"Can't fault a man for looking you in the eye." Randy said. Sababa pulled his ophthalmoscope from his Colombian leather bag, held open his patient's right upper eyelid, and dove in.

"Question is 'What's the question.'" Sababa leaned in on the scope. "Question is 'What made the McCoys so dang nab ornery.' Turns out, there's an uncommon condition which causes high blood pressure, racing hearts, severe headaches, and too much adrenaline and other 'fight or flight' stress hormones. It can make a man short-tempered."

"You got a name?" Randy asked. Sababa asked him to look into the light.

"Von Hippel-Lindau disease." He said. "Also known as familial cerebelloretinal angiomatosis. Mutation in a suppressor gene on the short arm of chromosome 3. Tumours in the eyes, ears, pancreas, kidney, brain, and spine. Roughly three-quarters of your ancestry had something called a pheochromocytoma, a growth in a part of the adrenal gland."

"My wife says I have a wicked temper." Randy said.

45

"We might fix that." Sababa put his scope away. "I'll admit you to the hospital for a few days, do some tests, get your blood pressure off the ceiling, that sort of thing. Your family will need screening."

"Who'll look after my cattle?"

"Who'd look after your cattle if you got hit by a truck?" Sababa asked.

"We'd have to find a way."

"Find a way, Randy." Sababa said. "You just got hit by a truck." The men shook hands. Sababa changed the song on his ER computer, as he wrote the admission orders.

> 'Let's go to Luckenbach, Texas
> With Waylon and Willie and the boys
> This successful life we're livin'
> Got us feuding like the Hatfields and McCoys...'
> Waylon Jennings, *Luckenbach, Texas*

Dr. Cliffy Carlton had referred the second patient of the evening. Cliffy and Sababa also went way back before the *Stout Men* days of the Himalayas, on the same trip that Cliffy nearly got them all killed by calling an armed Chinese soldier 'a small man with no soul.' In one of his rare moments of diplomacy, Sababa managed to talk the enraged guard out of shooting his company of adventurers, and into raising the frontier gate blocking their way.

"Britney Pratt." Cliffy began. "38-year-old known methhead, glamping along the Millstone River, who presents with confusion, fever, and low blood pressure. The ambulance crew that found her said she had vomited.

I found her disheveled, blue and agitated, with a temperature of 40.3°C, a pulse rate of 136 beats per minute, and blood pressure of 60/48. No skin lesions or track marks and no signs of trauma. Rest of her exam was unremarkable. I intubated her with vecuronium and sux, ran in two litres of intravenous saline, started her on dopamine, and then had to add Levophed. She may have three kinds of shock. The peaked T waves on her electrocardiogram were compatible with her high potassium, so I started IV calcium chloride, insulin/D50W, and bicarbonate. Cultures are in the lab. Urine drug test was positive for amphetamines. Duh.

Lactate and white cell count and serum muscle and liver enzymes are all in the sky, but that's your problem."

Sababa knew the other name for Levophed. *Leave 'em dead.* He looked across the ER at Britney Pratt, intubated, sedated, and paralyzed. Bright red blood began to flow out of her nasogastric

46

tube. He looked at the sheets under her. They were turning the same colour. He went over and placed his hand on her abdomen. It was as rigid as the will of fate.

"Who's the slasher tonight?" He asked.

"Dr. Doughnut." Cliffie said. There were three general surgeons at Harbour City Regional, one cerebral, one visceral and one somatic, each not as good as the next. The top gun of the group was Dr. Julius Martino, fast, good with his hands, smooth operator, and as sharp as his scalpels (except for a slight predisposition to use healing steel where Sababa's erudite medical management might have provided the same outcome. *A chance to cut is a chance to cure.*). Dr. John Falstaff was the second best surgeon—just as smart, more cautious, but an English epicurean oenophile with a jubilant brain, a British Bacchus, the wittiest and the weightiest of his department. He was bright, he was round, his footing not quite sound. And finally, there was Dr. Buddy Benway, golf partner of Ernie 'The Big Easy' Hacker, captain and crew of his own ship, sometimes wrong but never in doubt, a double-edged scalpel who preferred the unhurried financial rewards of endoscopy to the more rigorous demands of cut and paste. It pleased Sababa to hear Falstaff's voice.

"One for you, John." He said, relating the story of his Amphetamine Annie in as few words as possible.

"Do you have any imaging?" Falstaff asked.

"Only a useless flat plate x-ray." Sababa said. "No time for anything more, and besides, her kidneys would never handle an IV contrast load. You'll find lots of dead small and large bowel. Gangrene. Your own dinner will be much later."

Falstaff arrived faster than he would at his own chosen pace, usually like that of a ceremonial Indian elephant. He was babbling of green fields.

"You know the difference between God and a surgeon, Cliffie?" Sababa asked.

"Nope."

"God doesn't think he's a surgeon." Falstaff shook his head and placed a hand on Britney's abdomen. Three minutes later, she was on her way to the operating room.

"I'll make a post-op bed in the Death Star." Sababa said. "She'll still need high cutoff filter continuous veno-venous hemodialysis for what the muscle breakdown is doing to her kidneys, further rehydration, ventilation and blood pressure support, and the right bug juice."

"I can order the antibiotics." Falstaff said.

"John, a surgeon with an antibiotic is like a fish with a bicycle." He replied. "So listen to the whispering wind. It sounds like a big storm rolling in." Dr. Doughnut left the department for the OR, and Sababa changed the music on his ER computer, as he wrote out his consultation.

'It's gonna rock you like a hurricane, It's gonna rock you 'til you lose sleep
It's gonna rock you 'til you're out of a job, It's gonna rock you 'til you're out on the street
It's gonna rock you 'til you're down on your knees, It's gonna have you begging pretty please
It's gonna rock you like a hurricane... Methamphetamine.'
Old Crow Medicine Show, Methamphetamine

'It is difficult to understand the universe if you only study one planet.'
Miyamoto Musashi

On some call nights, Sababa might get home for dinner or, if he was especially lucky, sleep in his own bed for a few hours. Tonight was not one of those nights. His wife Jane might always have something ready, but Sababa also knew which hospital refrigerators held all the army surplus egg salad or minced chicken sandwiches, for when the hypoglycemia got militant.

Sababa lived up at the lake. On his rare days off, he would work in his vineyard or garden, or take his dog, Shiva, up the mountain to look for edible mushrooms in the fall, or swim across the lake in the summer. He and Jane had been inseparable for over thirty years. Their back acreage was always teeming with Columbian white-tailed deer, bald eagles, osprey, raccoons, herons, kingfishers, or an occasional black bear.

At one American Heart Association meeting in Chicago, several years before, a group of hotshot Windy City cardiologists invited Sababa to join them at a posh restaurant. In a private dining room at Gene and Georgetti's, they asked Sababa about his hospital's amenities. Sababa told them. There was a prolonged silence.

"Doctor Sababa." One specialist finally responded. "You can't run with the big dogs if'n you pee like a puppy." Another asked him why on earth he was working 'in the boondocks' when he could live in a big smoke penthouse on the North Shore and fish in Wisconsin for two weeks a year. Sababa knew that cardiologists were like Dungeness crabs in a bucket, each one

48

trying to crawl over the ones on top. He told them of the rich mélange of fascinating cases he got to manage all by his little lonesome, about the ocean and the air and the rainforest, and the wine he made from his own grapes. In most matters of the heart, Sababa would get to the heart of the matter. He was the only one who finished dessert.

Sababa had seventeen phone calls, and ten more consultations overnight. He had flown in on two wheels for three of them.

Working on the last of his referrals and reserves at sunrise, Sababa asked one of the ER nurses, Michaela, to help with a procedure.

"You ever get used to this?" She asked.

"Used to what?"

"Getting by on three hours sleep a night." She said.

"Michaela, three hours of sleep is a Caribbean cruise."

'A committee should consist of three men, two of whom are absent.'
Herbert Beerbohm Tree

Sababa got home for long enough to grab a shower and a coffee. On the five-kilometer drive to the hospital, there were sometimes occasional cars in front of him. He tried hard not to run them off the road.

His first appointment of the same next day was a monthly Department of Medicine meeting. Mandatory assemblies always seemed to be scheduled after he had had a night from hell. Sababa hated meetings at the best of times but he liked his colleagues. He found most of them trying to grab a quick java in the main lobby at Code Brew.

It is inhumane to force people who have a genuine medical need for coffee to wait in line behind people who view it as some kind of recreational activity, but there they were, the movers and shakers of Internal Medicine, queued up like a tour group at the Sistine Chapel. Sababa waved to Dr. Marquis Shu Ying, the electrodiagnostic expert, a strong-willed, focused and successful sweet soul, the first person to help out anyone in need. He did stand up paddle Tai Chi every morning to center himself. Shu ordered a piccolo latte. Behind him was Dr. Ernie 'The Big Easy' Hacker, the smooth champion of charm, golfing his way through life, and around the world. He had a flat white. Next was Dr. Dasco Boet, Sababa's purist old school straight-shooting bold fishing buddy. Straight black, the blacker the better. Following him was Dr. Ed Hyde, an anal-retentive OCD health nut and control freak, who would consume enough caffeine to get the coffee jolt without the jitters. What's black and never works? Decaf (you racist bastard). Finally, there was Dr. Sid Shalimar, an optimistic, fun-loving, sociable, loyal groovy hipster who wasn't afraid to spend money on luxury. The cappuccino was his poison.

"And for you?" Asked the barista.

"Espresso doppio doppio." Sababa said. She looked confused.

"Two times two is four." He added. "It's four shots of espresso." She looked horrified.

All the men walked together down a side hallway, to the Administration Board Room. For Sababa, it was always a journey to the Forbidden Zone. Already waiting inside a large secluded but expansive space on the main floor of Harbour City Regional was the patriarch of the department, Dr. Peter Zaias, a big bear of a man, Chief Defender of the Faith, seer of the Sacred Scrolls. He never drank coffee. Sababa remembered when Zaias had offered him employment, at a barbeque on the back of his sailboat, one brilliant summer day.

"You ever thought about joining us full-time?"

"You have an opening?" Sababa asked.

"Can you dance with the devil in the pale moonlight?"

"Yeah." He said. "I can dance..."

Sababa called the capacious space the Oracle of Oversight, and he meant it both ways.

The light green-yellow padded walls were fuzzy from the static electricity, lined with picture frames of previous hospital administrators and their lives of black and white mediocre supervision, their plaques awarded for nebulosity, and the occasional spider web. The walls and the white stippled acoustic tile ceiling had been constructed to absorb the screams of the defeated. It was bored out with pot lights and grooved in a railway yard of track lighting, controlled by a far wall bank of controls and switches and potentiometers to focus photons and heat.

A long teak conference table, halfway between a boat and a racetrack, polished with oil and buffed with a soft towel, filled the centre, racing the waist-high wooden wall sideboard cabinet next to it down the length of the room. The only two items on the table were an open box of tissues, and a multifunction business class conference digital phone console. Dr. Zaias picked up a handset and dialed zero.

50

"Lana, can you announce the beginning of the Department of Medicine meeting?" The hospital switchboard operator's Big Voice broadcast the assembly overhead.

At the far end, a wall mounted HDTV screen hung next to a melamine whiteboard on an easel with a tray of desiccated multicoloured felt markers. Whoever had written this message on the whiteboard would have had to have picked the lock to the Board Room.

> Are you lonely?
> Hate to make decisions?
> Rather talk about it than do it?
> Then why not hold a meeting?
> You can: Get to see other people
> > Sleep in peace
> > Offload decisions
> > Learn to write volumes of meaningless notes
> > Feel important
> > Impress (or bore) your colleagues
> And all in work time!
> Meetings... The Practical Alternative to Work

But if the visual was of opulent government largesse, the sniff test produced powerful earthy union odours of dust and must and rotting corpses. The fabric seats of the Mayline chairs that held both fat and lean arses sported new crumbs and old spills. Particulate debris lurked under the table on the claret pile carpet.

All these urbane appurtenances in this palace of administration enveloped these clinical courtiers with a semblance of security. But it was an antechamber to Hell, a black hole for light. For any young physician with any delusions of constructive change, no matter how aware and despite his plan in place, here was the morgue of ambition.

The final department member strolled into the midst of his peers after they had all taken their seats. Dr. Wayward Woods was always late. He was missing an internal clock, and made no effort to look at the strange contraption on his wrist. The only reason for time was so that everything didn't happen all at once. The one thing he made time for was his children. Wayward had eight of them. He once told Sababa how much he loved his wife. Sababa gave him Groucho. *I love my cigar but I take it out of my mouth once in a while.* Wayward was a good caring internist, but he treated every patient encounter like it was the last chopper out of Saigon. On the rare occasion when Sababa looked after his patients, the nurses called it 'deforestation.' Wayward arrived

51

with a Double Double, purchased from his secret hiding place at Tim Hortons.

Dr. Zaias called the council to order and requested approval of the previous meeting's minutes. A cacophony of grunts echoed around the table. They dealt with the more mundane aspects of their otherwise exciting existences, leaving a paper trail of 'ayes' and 'nays' and tabled motions until the next time. Halfway through the proceedings, they were joined by the man in the thousand dollar suit, held together with impeccable cuffs and collars, silk ties and linen handkerchiefs, and silver cuff-links in his Cardin shirt. In his manicured fingers, he held a matched pen or pencil of platinum, poised to doodle on monogrammed paper holding the timeless, the ageless, reports. Malcolm Canmore was the Chief Hospital Administrator of Harbour City Regional, the CHA, the CEO, the COO, the COG, the CAD, the CON, the CUR, the grand omnipotent stomper of supermen. In a universe that used chaos as fuel, Malcolm represented order. Every day, he cleaned his navel with a cotton bud soaked in witch hazel.

Sababa remembered his grandfather's definition of a civil servant. *A civil servant should be dressed in clean second-hand clothes, make half as much money as a contributing taxpayer, and be polite to one and all.* Times had changed.

"Something wicked this way comes." Sababa muttered under his breath. He and Malcolm were natural foes, and the Good Doctor preferred it that way.

"I subscribe to the atomic theory of bureaucracy." He would say. "Don't trust them. They make up everything. Also, the human body has eleven organ systems, all doing different things at the same time. To keep us alive, they need one voice, a leader, a master. And at the base of our brains, that job belongs to the pituitary gland. It works hard, sensing needs before they arise, communicating with all other glands, telling them when to produce the vital hormones we need to function. It keeps everything running in perfect order. It has the toughest job in the room. The problem is, Malcolm thinks he's a pituitary, but he's just a self-licking ice cream cone. Bureaucrats know the sorrows of being powerless even when in power. They know that we know that they don't know... anything."

Malcolm disliked men like Sababa because, whereas men made the rules for Malcolm, Sababa knew that only Mother Nature made the rules for him, and Sababa was scornful of the ones made for and by Malcolm.

"You're wasting your time with a small hospital like this, Sababa." He once told the stocky savant. "Why don't you try wasting your time with a larger hospital?"

"Coal face, Malcolm." Sababa replied. "I battle the Angel of Death a hundred hours a week. I can do that anywhere, but I like the variety show here. What do you do?"

Malcolm had a special agenda item he wanted to add at the last minute, in the way he always did.

"We have some dignitaries from the Ministry of Health and the Central Vancouver Island Health Region who would like to bring us up to speed on their new initiatives, New Directions, Closer to Home, the replacement of the paradigms of Disease with Wellness and Patients with Clients, and other innovations."

"Don't let them in." Sababa smiled. "These managers are like Harbour City seagulls. They arrive squawking around our heads, eat everything, shit all over the place, and then leave us with the mess to clean up. And they're never around in the middle of the night when the wolves come out." Dr. Zaias overruled his motion to block the door.

A gaggle of suits and pantsuits entered and filled the remaining Mayline chairs around the table. Their spokesperson spoke. He presented bizarre theories about collective causes of individual disease, and the cost of having overqualified doctors treating their clients. He provided a ministerial solution, comprised of a fifteen-year plan to better define their vision statement, placing signs in all hospital elevators, the appointment of Program Managers and Team Leaders, the continuous quality improvement intensive monitoring of managed care models, and access and utilization rationing through physician review committees. There were military terms in play. *Mission statement. Strategic initiative. Action Plan. Task force. Front line. Leading edge. Launched. Bullet points.*

"Our new Minister of Health, Corky Macfail, calls it 'The Great Leap Forward.'"

"Confusion now hath made his masterpiece." Sababa had trouble holding back. "We're not running a seance here. Even Stalin had only 5-year plans. If you want to maximize efficiency and minimize cost, the simplest solution is a seventeen-cent bullet at the front door. Bureaucrats incapable of solving problems can only rearrange them. They have perfected the art of looking for trouble, finding it everywhere, diagnosing it incorrectly and applying the wrong remedies. You're attempting to convince us that we're going to be able to get sick cheaply, and that is correct. Getting sick has always been cheap, often free. It's getting well that costs the money. When the price of an item is fixed above market value, there is a surplus of that item, like the tulip mania that infected the Dutch Golden Age of the 17th Century. When the price of an item is fixed below market value, that item disappears. This is a basic law of economics. The price of health care is fixed below market value, and we're all going to die. Charlie Mayo, you may have heard of him, founder of the clinic that bears his name, said it all more than a hundred years ago. *The government has dabbled in medical affairs at enormous expense for what has been accomplished.*

Now, I need a pacemaker program. I've been asking for one for years now. I can get a pacemaker for your cat faster than I can get one for your grandmother. But this morning I'm putting you on notice. I have a tin can, a broom closet, and a slasher who's trained up and ready to roll. The next 'client' that walks through these doors in complete heart block will pass Go and collect a device implanted by our dream team. Questions?" There were no questions. Malcolm glared.

Sababa's pager went off in his pocket. He called the number. It was Jamie, on the Bridge of the Death Star. He was excited.

Dr. Zaias thanked everyone and adjourned the meeting before any bloodshed could occur.

'This heart   attack I've gotta get
away I'm not   coming back
I'm 'bout to flatline so call me when you can some other time...'
Faker, *This Heart Attack*

On his way to the ICU, Sababa left the Board Room with Marquis Shu Ying. Shu was a crackerjack internist, but he maintained a robust fascination for Chinese metaphysics in medicine. He would delight Sababa with explanations of how the forces of *yin-yang* duality were complementary, interconnected, and interdependent in the natural world, and gave rise to each other as they interrelated in medical diagnosis and treatment.

"Yin is the cosmic influence of dark, slow, soft, yielding, diffuse, cold, wet, and passive, associated with water, earth, the moon, femininity, and nighttime. Yang, in contrast, is illuminated, fast, hard, solid, focused, hot, dry, and active, associated with fire, sky, the sun, masculinity, and daytime." Shu had told him. "Together they constitute a oneness in the Tao, a whole greater than the sum of the assembled parts. Confucianism may have a moral dimension but the Tao does not. There is no good and bad. Shadow cannot exist without light. The bigger the front, the bigger the back. Illness is the doorway to health. Tragedy turns to comedy. Disasters turn out to be blessings. A stone dropped in a calm pool of water will raise waves and lower troughs between them. Grain that reaches its full height in summer produces seeds and dies back in winter in an endless cycle. Every advance of an ocean wave is complemented by a retreat, and every rise transforms into a fall." Sababa wasn't having it.

"My medical world can be categorized into too much, too little, and weird. Your *yin-yang* duality doesn't cover weird." He said.

"True." Shu said. "But the Five Elements theory can help." He explained how the four diagnostic methods of inspection, auscultation and olfaction, inquiring, and palpation could be used to determine how the five elements of wood, fire, earth, metal, and water, in the four possible relationships of mutual generation, mutual subjugation, extreme subjugation, and counter subjugation, were acting on the five Yin organs of heart, liver, spleen, lung and kidney and the six Yang organs of gallbladder, stomach, small intestine, large intestine, and bladder." Sababa's eyes rolled behind his upper eyelids.

"This patient you're going to see in the unit." Shu continued. "According to the Five Elements, his element is fire, his emotional activity joy, his environmental factor heat, his generation spleen, his subjugation lung, his five senses taste, his taste bitter, his yang organ small intestine."

"You're not helping me here, Shu." The sweet soul smiled.

"His time of the day is 11 a.m. to 3 p.m., his colour is red, his yin organ is his heart, his five tissues his blood vessels, his direction is south, and his sound..."

"Is?"

"Laughing." Shu veered off towards the Electrodiagnostic lab.

But nobody was laughing on the Bridge of the Death Star. Sababa's first clue came from Betty Boop, who seemed to be in even more nicotine withdrawal than usual. Two of the critical care nurses, Mary and Charmeine, pointed to cubicle six, behind which he could hear Angie trying to take orders from Jamie. He frowned at the patient's ECG monitor tracing and pulled back the curtain.

"Your resident here just ordered IV morphine for a patient whose pressure is 80 systolic." Angie said. "I thought I'd check with you before I go to prison."

"He's having chest pain." Jamie said. "And his ST segments are rising again."

"Why is his pressure low?" Sababa indicated for Angie to open up a hanging IV bag of saline. "Tell me a story, Jamie. A short story." Perspiration broke on the young man's forehead.

"Sam Kee, 46-year-old local businessman, and city councillor, extracted from his vehicle by the Jaws of Life in front of the hospital. Lost consciousness immediately before or as the result of crashing into a heliport utility pole outside. Assessed by Dr. Capitaine in the ER who found no evidence of trauma, but did find this on his electrocardiogram, for which Myles gave him a clot-buster." Jamie showed Sababa the ECG. Sam Kee's blood pressure had risen 20 mmHg, the ST segments had normalized, and his pain had gone.

"Ah, yes. Cholesterol." Sababa said. "The patient man's suicide attempt. What do you see on this first cardiogram?" Jamie pointed to the evidence of an extensive heart attack.

"We call them tombstones." He said, referring to the shape of the elevated segments.

"We have them in the Third World, too." Sababa said. "Any clues on the culprit artery?" Jamie shook his head.

"You see how the tombstones run all across the ECG?" Sababa asked. "And how they get bigger as they move towards the high lateral part of the heart?" Jamie nodded.

"So we usually all have a Papa Artery called the left anterior descending, affectionately referred to as 'the artery of sudden death' or 'the widowmaker.' We all have a Mama Artery called the right coronary, and we all have a Baby artery called the circumflex, which supplies blood and oxygen and nutrients to the high lateral part of the heart. So what you got?" Jamie shook his head.

"The culprit artery can't just be the circumflex, because his entire heart is affected." He said. "Unless he has a monster dominant Papa Artery that supplies everything."

"Or?" Sababa asked. Jamie shook his head.

"What if Sam Kee had already slowly clotted off his Papa and Mama arteries and his Baby Artery had become an orphan, having been or become dominant through the development of a collateral circulation? And then today was not his day?" They both saw the tombstones rise again on the bedside monitor. Sam's heart rate rose to 100 bpm and his pressure dropped to where it had been before the thought shower. His face became contorted from the pain.

"Angie, please give Mr. Kee a milligram of IV propranolol." Sababa said.

"But his pressure is low." Jamie remonstrated.

"When do the coronary arteries fill, Jamie?"

56

"When the heart relaxes." He said. Angie fired in the propranolol.

"And what is a major determinant of the time the heart is relaxing?"

"Heart rate." Jamie said. Sam's tombstones and heart rate came down, his pressure came up, and his pain once again disappeared.

"Should we give him another dose of clot-buster?" Jamie asked.

"Well, I might agree with you, but then we'd both be wrong." Sababa said. "It doesn't appear to have done the trick the first time. Someday, every heart attack that comes in the door will automatically go for an urgent angiogram but for now, in the vast reaches of the known universe, the interventional cardiologists in Victoria will only accept in transfer those that have 'failed' thrombolysis. What do you think, Jamie? Has Mr. Kee failed?" They all watched Sam's tombstones rise again on the bedside monitor. Sam's pressure dropped and his face deformed, but this time his heart rate did not go up.

"Square root of negative shit squared." Sababa said.

"Huh."

"Shit just got real." He said. "Angie, put 10 milligrams of nifedipine under Mr. Kee's tongue."

"But his pressure is low and his heart rate is normal." Jamie scratched his head.

"Between the desire and the spasm, between the potency and the existence, between the essence and the descent, falls the shadow." Sababa said.

"T.S. Eliot." Angie said as she popped the pill under Sam's tongue.

"One of my favorite antisemitic poets." Sababa said. "Let's make it a true daily double, Jamie." Sam's tombstones returned to baseline, his pressure came up, his pain disappeared, and his heart rate did not change.

"Looks like spasm to me." Sababa said. "Betty, can you get me the cath jockey on call in Victoria?"

"I'm on it." She said. Her left hand gesticulated in the air for a few seconds, and then she spoke into the phone.

"Now." She said. "It's Doctor Sababa in Harbour City." A few minutes later Sababa was multitasking, speaking to a cardiologist in the southern capital of the Middle Kingdom, and giving orders to Angie for alternating doses of propranolol and nifedipine, as Sam Kee's ultimate artery tried to repeatedly shuffle him off this mortal coil. Sababa was using the words 'medevac' or 'dustoff' in every second sentence.

"Call in the Big Bird, Betty." He hung up his handset and watched Betty Boop pick hers up again.

"Now." She said. After four more medicated squeeze sessions of rising and falling tombstones, everyone heard the blade slapping pulsations approaching outside the wire. *Dubdubdubdub whumpawhumpa whupwhup wuppawuppa whopwhop batabata tocotoco flacflac chakkchackk chakachak akk-chk thiththith sssssssss...*

Five minutes later, two blue air ambulance jumpsuits rolled a shortbox stretcher into the unit. It was piled high with advanced life support instruments and equipment—oral and nasal airways, bag-valve masks, portable suction, combitubes, King laryngeal tubes, laryngeal mask airways, endotracheal tubes and laryngoscopes with blades and handles, stylets and lubricant, Magill forceps, bougies, tourniquets, cleaning agents, IV catheters, fluid bags, and tubing, meds for rapid sequence intubation, and an automated external defibrillator. Sababa greeted them.

"Well, lookee what the bling boys brought to the picnic." He said.

"What you got?" Asked the big bling boy with the beard. Sababa's smiled widened.

"Mr. Sam Kee, 46-year-old male with an acute global myocardial infarction, who failed thrombolytic therapy because his only coronary circulation is a trickle from a circumflex artery that keeps trying to go into spasm and finish the story. Cath lab staff is assembled and waiting in Victoria. We'll send Braveheart here off with two box tops, a syringe full of propranolol, and a bucket of sublingual nifedipine. Give him a milligram of propranolol when his heart rate gets above 90, and a nifedipine under his tongue if his ST segments are up and he's still having chest pain. Kick the tires and light the fires, boys. Adios."

"We can't do that." Said the bearded bling boy.

"Huh?" Sababa said. "How come?"

"We're not authorized." He said. "Only you can do that." The blue streak that Sababa swore made the color of their jumpsuits blush, but he knew he had no choice.

"OK." He said. "Here's my pager, Jamie. Go see all the referrals. Don't make me look bad. Betty, please call Mercy and tell her I might be late but not to cancel the office. Let's go, gentlemen."

"I'm not sure I want this." Jamie said.

"Any man's death diminishes me because I am involved in mankind." Sababa said. "And therefore never send to know for whom the beeper beeps; it beeps for thee."

58

Sam Kee left Harbour City Regional even faster than he had arrived, ahead of the small tornado the pilot had blasted on the ground below him. Twenty minutes later, they touched down on the helipad at Victoria Hospital. Sababa had given Sam one more course of his double cocktail en route. *Dubdubdubdub whumpawhumpa whupwhup wuppawuppa whopwhop batabata tocotoco flacflac chakkchackk chakachak akk-chk thiththith sssssssss...*

"OK, Doc." Big beard said. "We'll take it from here. You can go now." The paramedics began to roll Sam toward the hospital entrance.

"Hang on." Sababa said. "I have a clinic beginning at one. You got me here. You get me back."

"Can't Doc." The helmeted pilot in dark glasses shouted from the cockpit. "We have to pick up the Minister of Health." Sababa remembered his last encounter with Corky Macfail. She had used an air ambulance to take her up to Mount Washington to go cross-country skiing. Sababa nearly collected her around a downhill corner on a steep backcountry trail. If he had recognized her in time, she might have been particles, instead of waves.

"Let me talk to your dispatcher." He said. It took two minutes before they were airborne again. *Sssssssss thiththith akk-chk chakachak chakkchackk flacflac tocotoco batabata whopwhop wuppawuppa whupwhup whumpawhump dubdubdubdub...*

"We still have to stop at the airfield to refuel." The pilot had to shout above the rotor noise.

"Hell of a life isn't it?" Sababa asked.

"What?" Yelled the pilot.

"It's a hell of a life." The pilot shook his head and pointed to his ear.

"I said, 'How would you ever know if I slept with your wife?'" The pilot gave Sababa a thumbs up.

In five minutes more, he was landing at the aerodrome to refuel. Ten minutes after that, they were lifting off again. Sababa looked out through his polycarbonate protective window, across the expanse of tarmac. On the edge, flanked by a retinue of subordinate sycophants, stood Corky Macfail, fuming so hard that, if the whirlybird had been any closer, it would have burst into flames. Sababa smiled a Sababa smile at her and wiggled his fingers. *His time of the day is 11 a.m. to 3 p.m., his colour is red, his yin organ is his heart, his five tissues his blood vessels, his direction is south, and his sound..."*

"Is?"

"Laughing."

Helicopters actually cannot fly. Their passengers are so contrary the earth repels them.

'This is why Why we fight Why we lie awake
This is why This is why we fight
When we die We will die with our arms unbound
And this is why This is why we fight.'
The Decembrists, *This Why We Fight*

The casual reader must resist the temptation to think of Sababa only as he appeared. His mind was a big thing with small holes through which his passions seeped. He could be rude to inertial forces that placed themselves in the way of his need for speed. He made enemies, sometimes deliberately, rather than seeking a corrupt compromise. For his friends, no explanation was ever necessary; for his enemies, none would ever have sufficed; they may have indulged his idiosyncrasies, but they would never excuse his genius.

Sababa forgave almost every slight committed against him after a good night's sleep (although sometimes that took several weeks). He loved his wife Jane, his dog Shiva, and the patients under his care, about in that order. He kept his circle small and was loyal to the end. He lived like he would die tomorrow and studied like he would live forever, embracing the continual acquisition of knowledge for its own sake. He made a point of having no prejudices, and of following where the facts led. He aspired to teach better ways.

Sababa was the embodiment of Marquis Shu Ying's *yin-yang* duality of complementary, connected, and interdependent characteristics in the natural world—the bad, the good, the bad in the good, and the good in the bad—especially in how they gave rise to each other, interrelated in medical diagnosis and treatment. To heal others, he had to be incurably himself.

He knew what mattered most was how well you walked through the fire. *Can you dance with the devil in the pale moonlight?*

There is never any real ending. It's just the place where you stop the story. But laughter is not at all a bad beginning for a casebook, and it is far the best ending for a case.

Man Singh passed away peacefully without the *Alien* theatrics, surrounded by his family, who still loved him despite his earlier weakness of the flesh. None of them tested positive for syphilis. Murasaki Shikibu stabilized on her new drugs but had to undergo reconstructive surgery of her aortic arch. She has quit the piano but is still composing and has dedicated a sonata to Sababa.

Julius Noh is still suffering from recurrent chest and sinus infections, but his physicians have a plan in place to catch and treat them early. His stamp collection is worth millions. Paul Hewson had successful corneal transplants and moved to another parish for some undisclosed reason.

Edie Sitwell has managed to avoid surgery unless you count the successful delivery of a baby girl. She quit her job as a dental hygienist and collects disability insurance premiums, but still has to put her jaw back into place after eating and brushing her teeth. Rod Duterte wasn't paying attention after all and died of a heart attack four months after Sababa told him to quit smoking. Linda Blare is taking Sababa's poisons and still plans to live forever.

The CT scan and surgeon found both of Randy McCoy's adrenal tumours. His blood pressure is now normal and his wife loves him again. Britney Pratt recovered but left the hospital against medical advice. She returned dead on admission three days later.

It takes a strong heart to drive on clogged arteries. Sam Kee has recovered from his ordeal, still an entrepreneur but no longer a city councillor. The cath jockey found a 99% narrowing in the only functioning artery he still had, his circumflex. He ballooned and stented the Baby, but Sam still had to undergo coronary bypass to get back behind the wheel of his Audi. His wife and girlfriend are grateful. Sababa's discharge summary was as prescient as Marquis Shu Ying's prediction. *He continued to have pain and was transferred to Victoria for evasive assessment.*

And the man in the thousand-dollar suit? Juan Leyblanca, the on-call pathologist, slammed the door in Malcolm Canmore's face when the administrator showed up for a photo-op at the coroner's confidential forensic proceedings for the victims of the Rainbow Air crash.

"Not today, Pendejo." He said. "We don't need no stinkin' badges."

2. The Case of the Broken Heart

'Works at the jewelry store
Down in the harbor
Where the ferries come to shore
She never really knew how good it would feel
To finally find herself in a place so warm and real.'
                                    Kenny Chesney, *Boston*

In the springtime, the winds blow over Mount Benson and along the Salish Sea into the heart of Harbour City. Some days the rain falls gently, its winter iciness gone. But today was a different day. Heaven's door was knocking back, determined to wash away all the sins of the earth.

Steady silver sheets and heavy curtains and walls and waves of water poured from tumbling dark clouds slung low. Streams swelled over new waterfalls. Tumultuous torrents fell on the intemperate rainforest and West Coast luxury homes and mean downtown streets the same. Great heavy raindrops pelted down with intense anxiety, in fear of falling short in the space between the sky and the earth. At their destination, they beaded on and trickled down and bounced from every hard surface, splattering and pooling into puddles of mercury across the pavement. Everything was some shade of black and white, grey smudges of light like Monet would have painted it.

The sound of the storm drowned out every other noise. Car tires hissed on glistening roads, windscreen wipers swooshed, storm drains gurgled, and the sidewalks of Commercial Street crackled like an old radio coming to life. The deluge drove horizontal, blowing umbrellas inside out.

Rain thundered and hammered and battered and lashed the blurred windows of the Scotiabank in a relentless drumming of fingernails, or a hail of bullets.

The only thing that could spoil a spring shower was people. People were always the limiters of happiness except for the few that were as good as spring itself. Victoria Huckell looked up from her cash drawers and paperwork as a steady cold draught from the opening storefront door washed through her. Except for the big-nosed mask, he had dressed for the weather. He left a trail of water on the clean floor from his hooded American military camouflage poncho raincoat, as he advanced on her teller window. She recognized the mask as a comical *Basler Fasnacht larva* from a Swiss carnival she had attended, on a previous holiday with her German boyfriend. The man began singing as he approached. The words were garbled. She noticed a clothes peg in his grimace, from out of which two wires disappeared down the neck of his poncho.

> 'Ist das nicht ein Schnitzelbank? Ja das ist ein Schnitzelbank.
> Oh du schöne Schnitzelbank, oh du schöne Schnitzelbank.'

He pulled a shotgun and a large hockey duffle bag out from under his poncho.

> 'Ist das nicht ein kreuz und quer? Ja das ist ein kreuz und quer.
> Ist das nicht ein Schiessgewehr? Ja das ist ein Schiessgewehr.
> Schiessgewehr, kreuz und quer, hin und her, kurz und lang,

Oh du schöne Schnitzelbank, oh du schöne Schnitzelbank.'

She knew the song. *Is that not a shooting gun? Yes, that is a shooting gun. Shooting gun, crooked and straight, here and there, short and long...* The man handed her a damp note, and then the duffel bag, through the polycarbonate window. He smelled like bleach.

Act normal. Place all the cash drawer money in the bag, then the cash from the teller stations on either side of you. No alarms, dye packs, no funny money, no one will get hurt. I am armed with explosives that will be triggered by the dead man's switch detonator in my teeth, if anything stupid happens.

He opened his poncho enough for her to see a vest of TATP plastic bottles wired in parallel to a battery. Victoria emptied her cash drawers and those immediately adjacent, into the duffel bag. She pushed it back over her window and stood back. He grabbed the handles, turned on his heels, and left. The cold draught from the reopening door allowed her to exhale, and break into tears. The wind threw the rain harder against the blurred windows.

The camouflage poncho floated back up Commercial Street, to a pickup truck parked outside Bastion Jewellers. Cathy Bates watched from behind a display case, as he fiddled for the keys inside his raincoat. The truck's lights flashed once, and he pulled open the driver side door. From the corner of her peripheral vision on her left, Cathy could make out an RCMP Ford Interceptor cruising toward the half-ton. The officer inside was speaking into her vest radio. The police car stopped and Veronica Marsden was out in the downpour behind her engine, pointing a Smith and Wesson pistol. People put so much effort into starting a relationship and so little effort into ending one. Cathy heard the policewoman shout instructions, but then she couldn't hear at all.

In one last heartbeat, the blast had blown out most of the shop windows on Commercial Street. People were crying and screaming, Canadian banknotes and colourful confetti floated in the air, and debris lay shattered and strewn everywhere.

Acrid smoke covered the downtown. Everything smelled of burnt flesh and hair for a week. The bandit's head, mask intact, had been severed at the moment of detonation and found in a state of perfect preservation several metres from the torso's shredded remains. Part of his leg with the boot and foot was hanging on a streetlight a block away. The rest of him had dissolved in the rain.

Veronica organized the cleanup and the police investigation. She questioned Victoria Huckell and Cathy Bates, and a hundred others, but no one knew anything more than their own experience.

"You have a name?" Her Superintendent asked, at the end of the detective work.

"Oliver D. Place." She offered.

'Heartbreaker, your time has come
Can't take your evil way
Go away heartbreaker...'
Led Zeppelin, *Heartbreaker*

An hour earlier and one block further up, at the top of Commercial Street, Linley Valley was unaware of what would soon happen downstream. In the heart of Harbour City's business district, Linley had an opulent office in a heritage building that dominated the triangular-shaped lot at the pointed junction of three streets.

The Great National Land Building was a hundred years old, rising in 1914 as the Frontier Building, a new icon of corporate dominance, strength, and stability, after suppression of the Island coal miners' attempts to form a union during the turbulent Great Strike of the preceding two years. *I require you to walk out in single file to the courthouse and anyone attempting to run away will be bayoneted or shot.* But none of the building's commercial tenants knew anything about that now.

The Neo-classical architecture of the three-story flat-roofed flatiron-shaped exterior was stylish and imposing—a prominent prowed parapet curved over a facade of pilasters, keystones, elaborate cornices, transoms, and four massive fluted columns, all clad in brick and stone and terra cotta.

Every great story begins with a snake. Two large bas-reliefs of Greek *caduceus* insignias hovered in the centre line, near the roof and above the front doors. The emblem of two snakes entwined around a winged staff was not a medical symbol, contrary to its adoption and misuse by the U.S. Army Medical Corps in 1902 (the proper symbol of medicine is the Rod of Aesculapius, which is a coarse stick entwined by a single serpent).

In Greek mythology, the caduceus herald staff was a stave carried by the messengers of the gods of the high road and the

66

market place, Hermes and Mercury, silver-tongued patrons of commerce and the fat purse. It was a representation of trade, eloquence, negotiation, prudence, fertility, luck, wisdom, protection of the travelling salesman, cheating, thievery, lying, and the passage into the underworld. The only possible relationship to medicine might have been its association with the alchemical 'Universal Solvent,' Azoth, and its allusion by Homer as 'possessing the ability to charm the eyes of men,' which could also describe the business of our Harbour City oculist, T.J. Eckleburg. Otherwise, conflating the two was like misusing the logo of the National Rifle Association for the Audubon Society.

The survival of its safety deposit boxes in a fire that destroyed the ten buildings around it in 1930 reinforced the eternal solid durability of the Great National Land Building, both physical and metaphorical. Its bricks and stone had halted the spread of the blaze.

Oblivious to these nuances of architecture and history, just inside a tempest of water and not fire, the middle-aged realtor stood smoking a cigarette at the apex of the triangular entrance, and his career. Linley Valley was a decorated agent at Harbour City Realty. In his short 58 years on the planet, he had earned his company's Hall of Fame and Lifetime Achievement awards, a REIC Emeritus and Community Services award, VIREB Realtors Care award, and dozen other medals and decorations and rewards that hung on the walls of his office, among framed quotations of his lifelong impersonal trainer, Donald Trump. *First and foremost, I'm a real estate person. And that's what I love the most... Real estate is a contact sport... It's tangible, it's solid, it's beautiful. It's artistic, from my standpoint, and I just love real estate...*

An oversized painting of Trump hung behind his Eames executive chair and a well-thumbed signed copy of *The Art of the Deal* lay inert on his desk. Linley worshipped Donald Trump. His colleagues and customers knew the agent for his witty repartee and insights into the trade. *The best investment on earth is earth... Buy land, they're not making it anymore... Don't wait to buy real estate. Buy real estate and wait... Every sale has five basic obstacles: no need, no money, no hurry, no desire, no trust.*

Back inside the Great National main entrance, Linley strutted through the echoes and ozone of the grand circular hall, on an Italian white marble floor, along maple wainscoting and wall murals, under a matrix of glazed frozen pendulous lights, to his executive office. It was spacious and filled with light, with an oak floor and a Roman brick fireplace.

And yet, for all his success, Linley Valley was a troubled man. His children wouldn't talk to him since his wife had left him a month earlier. He had stopped eating properly, had taken up smoking again after quitting ten years earlier and began draining a bottle of Canadian rye every night. Linley only drank Crown Royal XR, because he could afford it. To sleep, he accompanied his firewater with a double dose of Xanax from his doctor, who was unaware he was burning through his prescription that fast.

In his workaday world, the minimum daily requirement of information and connectivity had grown stupid, to feed an existence increasingly devoid of meaning. His life was as shallow as the Great National front facade. Serpents gathered around him.

Linley was becoming more anxious and restless by the day. He was always tired and his muscles ached. His colleagues noticed that he was tremulous and sweaty, more detached, plagued with irritable mood swings, and even occasional hostility.

Two days earlier, Linley had decided it was time to stop the pills cold turkey. He didn't tell anyone. He needed another cigarette.

Outside, at the apex of his career again, Linley fired up a Sobranie Black Russian and pulled. The lung burn lifted him back into focus. He smiled at his white Alfa Romeo Mito parked on the curb. The *biscione* serpent in the heraldic ornament on the front grill swallowed the Moor in its mouth and then slithered through the triangular black hole. A toothache began deep in his chest and spread to his back and down both arms. He sat on the wet stone steps outside the portico, offering no resistance to the downpour to soaking through him.

A Dodge Viper braked at the triple intersection. Linley could hear his radio.

Knock Knock... Who's there... Dishes... Dishes who... Dishes BC Bud, your Harbour City morning host, for CNDN Coast Salish radio, 101.3 FM on your Home and Native Band... What was British Columbia called before the white man? Ours... Then we had a real estate problem...

The young driver got out and knelt beside him, asked him what was wrong, and called 911 on his cell at the same time. Linley's head lolled from side to side. He grabbed at his chest.

The viper on the Dodge hood smiled and slid into one of the front bumper air dams. Linley looked up at the caduceus above the main entrance. The snakes had unraveled and were gliding down two of the giant columns toward him. BC Bud continued to narrate.

When a man moves away from Nature his heart becomes hard.

An Emergency Paramedic ambulance pulled up in front of the gathering crowd. Linley noticed the six-pointed 'star of life' logo on the side. The coiled serpent on the Rod of Asclepius in the middle stuttered into a skid down the face of the vehicle and under the running board. All the pressures of the world rained down on Linley Valley, mixed with the salt of his tears. Two paramedics cracked open a wheeled gurney, and the realtor was in the air a few seconds later. Before his conveyance entered the back of the ambulance, Linley's peripheral vision registered a phantom in a hooded camouflage poncho wearing a strange mask, heading down Commercial Street. After all the other twisted apparitions that he had already seen, Linley didn't give the man another glance, or a second thought. They would both go their separate ways. One would go many ways.

It may be true that stress can cause a broken heart, but don't blame me for today, white boy. I didn't make it rain.

'I don't break the rules. I merely test their elasticity.'
Bill Veeck

The morning before the Scotiabank robbery and Linley Valley's unfortunate journey of the serpents, Jamie Dunne had paged his mentor from the Harbour City Regional Emergency Room.
"What you got?" Sababa was on the Bridge of the Death Star.
"Meisie van der Merwe." He said. "35-year-old travel agent with right-sided heart failure. She can do that skin-pulling thing that Edie Sitwell demonstrated for us."
"She has something different going on, Jamie." Sababa said. "I'll be down in a few minutes." It was less than a few minutes later when the black-curled medusan medico jounced into the ER.
"This one of your specials, Gung?" Dr. Ho nodded, and introduced Sababa to a virtual copy of himself, dressed in green scrubs.
"This is my little brother, Westwood." He said. "For some reason, he wants to be an internist. I've tried to warn him." The young man was acting like he wanted an autograph.
"Send Westwood my way when he has more body hair." Sababa turned his attention to Jamie, who took him to the bedside of Meisie van der Merwe and made introductions.
"Goeie more, jong vrou." Said Sababa.

"Goeie more, Dokter. Howzit? My frriends call me Stretch." She pulled the skin of her neck out until she looked like a frilled lizard.

"She presents with a two-month history of chest and leg pain on exertion, and a one month story of swollen legs." Jamie began. Exam shows an elevated jugular venous pressure, loud P2, right ventricular S3, pulsation in her solar plexus, an enlarged liver and well, see for yourself." Sababa examined her heart, and then pushed his right index finger into an ankle. It left a dimple.

"You were going to tell me about these raised yellow papules and the diagonal grooves in the skin on her chin." Sababa said.

"My neck looks like eh plucked chicken ehs well." Stretch told them of her embarrassment.

"Did you look in her eyes, Jamie?" Sababa pulled his ophthalmoscope from his leather bag, held open his patient's right upper eyelid, and dove in. Jamie folded.

"Oh yes." He said. "Separation and mineralization of the elastic fibers of the Bruch membrane from the pigmented layer of the retina, resulting in *peau d'orange*, and angioid streaks radiating out from the optic nerve. She'll need to see our oculist, T.J. Eckleburg.

"What else you got?"

"ECG shows trifascicular block and enlargement of both atria." Jamie handed him the tracing. "Chest x-ray shows an enlarged heart." He threw the film up on the bedside viewer.

"What else you got?" Jamie looked puzzled.

"Where is she from?

"Seth Ehfrikeh." Meisie offered.

"Right heart failure and angioid streaks of the retina." Sababa continued. "What if Stretch were of South African Indian or Mediterranean origin?"

"β Thalassemia?" Jamie offered.

"Ja." Sababa said. "Lekker. But she's not of South Asian or Mediterranean origin, is she Sangoma? So, you got a name?" Jamie winced.

"Eina." Meisie felt sorry for him. "Agchh, shame."

"Autosomal recessive mutation in the ABCC6 gene on the short arm of chromosome 16, which codes for the MRP6 ATP-binding cassette transporter protein, causing mineralization and fragmentation of the mid laminar elastin-containing fibers of the dermis, Bruch's membrane and midsized arteries, and the inability of vitamin K metabolites to reach peripheral tissues. *Elastodysplasia calcificans.*" Sababa said. "Rigall first called it Grönblad-Strandberg syndrome in 1881."

"Izzit?" Stretch yawned and crossed her eyes.

"You have a condition called Pseudoxanthoma Elasticum, Meisie." Sababa said. "It's what we call a founder effect, inherited from your Afrikaner ancestors."

"What does it do?" She asked.

"It can affect the skin, eyes, blood vessels, and ticker." He said. "Causes the heart's interior to lose blood supply, causing a restriction of the normal recoil mechanism."

"So it's brauken." She said. "Skrik vir niks."

"What?" Jamie asked.

"She's not afraid of anything." Sababa said. "Good, We'll make a plan. Just now."

"Jamie, consults to Genetics and T.J. Eckleburg." He said. "Inpatient echo and CTA of her coronary and limb arteries, outpatient exercise stress test and Holter and skin biopsy. Start her on the anti-failure regimen we discussed." He turned to Stretch.

"Meisie, you won't be able to take any aspirin or nonsteroidal anti-inflammatories." Sababa handed Jamie a piece of paper with two names on it.

"But wait. There's more."

"What's this?" He asked.

"Ward referrals." Sababa said. "He who studies medicine without books sails an uncharted sea, but he who studies medicine without patients does not go to sea at all. We should totally go for coffee, but I have a few other things to attend to. Call me when you're done, sailor." And then he was gone.

"That muti oke is ubuntu, neh?" Stretch was stuck in her founder effect.

"Sorry?" Jamie was trying to concentrate.

"I couldn't help but notice how your shoelaces untied when he spoke to you." She said.

"Noka etlatswa ke dinokana." *A river is filled by its streams.*

'Critics have been amusing themselves for a long time by auscultating fiction for signs of heart failure.'

Storm Jameson

The telemetered Step Down Unit on the first floor of Harbour City Regional was indeed a step down from the intensity of the

Intensive Care Unit, a few steps down the hall. But although the sudden cardiac and respiratory arrests and other emergencies that occurred here were no less exciting, the attempted interventions, for various reasons, were often fated to be neither as fast, nor as effective. *Fast, cheap, and good... pick two words to live by. If it's fast and cheap it won't be good. If it's cheap and good it won't be fast. If it's fast and good it won't be cheap.*

Outside its doors, boxes of rubber gloves in assorted sizes sat on an aluminum trolley, next to a laundry bin for scrubs and linens, and a garbage bin for disposable masks and shoe covers and bouffant caps. The Health Authority had spent $130,000 to teach staff how to wash their hands. A battery of wall-mounted sanitizers and infection control notices flanked the entrance. Jamie bypassed the display and entered unscathed.

Inside, the walls were just cream, and the floor just gray. There was no decoration at all, save the limp sun-bleached curtains that separated and encircled the beds. They may have once been a revitalizing colour of green that could have awakened memories of springtime and hope, but that had all faded away in the passage of time. The frosted windows were frozen in their frames. Monitors hung behind the pillows of every bay, above the clinical chrome clutter of medical gas outlets and aspirators that penetrated the walls, and the aneroid gauges and dials and meters and valves, and rubber and plastic tubing, that measured and regulated their flow. It was here, Sababa had observed, was where you could suck and blow at the same time. The hissibilation of this activity, and that of the infusion alarms, alerts and prompts, and automatic blood pressure devices, reverberated off the chrome and were then swallowed in the somberness. Jamie knew that patient prognosis was an inverse function of the number of CADD pumps on the IV poles surrounding the bed. The contract for every gas and liquid and solid had gone to the lowest bidder. Each patient was on a diet and each amenity was on a budget.

No flowers or scents, or other forms of natural beauty were allowed entry to aid in the healing process. In their efforts not to offend or inspire, the bureaucrats had succeeded in sinking the spirit.

The charge nurse, Serafina, was hovering over her applesauce and medication administration record MAR chart, dispensing the ten o'clock drugs. A nursing school mantra of dispensation echoed in her head. *Right dose, right route, right patient... three checks...*

Jamie timed his introduction and handed her the names that Sababa had provided him. *Fred Hundertwasser... Mingtao Wang.* She pulled two charts from the racks.

72

"Mr. Hundertwasser is doing better this morning." She said. "Mr. Wang is the same." Jamie sat down at the nursing station to peruse the records. The plastic binder covers were the colour of blood. There was a post-it note on the front of Hundertwasser's chart. *Do Not Resuscitate order... clarification, please.* He found a referral letter from Dr. Tictac Tarmac, deep inside Mingtao Wang's casebook. *Increasing shortness of breath. Does not want to die.*

Jamie went to see both men and, when he had finished his assessments, paged Sababa to the unit. He arrived with a raised eyebrow.

"What's the matter?' Asked the portly professor.

"At my age, Bobby Orr was already retired." Jamie said.

"At your age, Mozart was already dead."

"How long does it take before this gets better?" Jamie tilted his head like a Labrador.

"You're here now, Jamie. When you're somewhere you ought to be there, because it's not about how long you stay in a place. It's about what you do while you're there. And is that place any better for you having been there when you leave? Am I answering your question?" Jamie nodded.

"So, tell me what you got?"

"First patient is Fred Hundertwasser." He began. "83-year-old owner of the Wandering Salamander Guest House downtown. Patient of Dr. Hyde, but he's off today running a marathon."

"Why are we seeing him?" Sababa asked.

"Dunno." Jamie said. "His GP wanted us involved for some reason. I'm getting the impression you get to see a lot of Dr. Hyde's patients when there's an opening for another opinion." Sababa shrugged.

"For the patient, a second opinion can be the difference between life and death. For the doctor, it can mean picking a fight with everyone who was there before you."

"Anyway, Dr. Hyde admitted him yesterday for investigation of multiple lung nodules. Longstanding history of hypertension treated to target. Unremarkable exam. This is from a week ago." Jamie threw up a chest x-ray on the nursing station viewer.

"OK."

"There's just one problem." Jamie said.

"What's that?"

"This one is from this morning." He said. The nodules were gone.

"Hmmm." Sababa asked. "What happened overnight?"

"Nothing." Jamie hesitated. "As far as I know."

"Serafina, what happened to Mr. Hundertwasser in the middle of the night?"

"We had to call Dr. Hacker." She said. "He was on call. Mr. Hundertwasser developed sudden shortness of breath and we received an order for a diuretic IV. It seemed to work."

"Did Dr. Hacker come in to see him?" Sababa asked. Her face told him the answer. He flipped to the nursing notes. 0425. *Lasix 40 mg given IV, with excellent response.*

"You might want to read this part of the chart every once in a while." Sababa said. "The medicolegal atmosphere loses some of its oxygen."

"So, is this too much, too little, or weird?" Jamie asked.

"Nope, this is just true or false."

"Huh?"

"Either Fred had multiple nodules in his lungs or he didn't." Sababa said. "Whatever they had been disappeared along with his shortness of breath after a single nocturnal dose of loop diuretic. That should give you a name." Jamie had that Labrador look.

"Pulmonary pseudotumour, phantom effusions in the lung lining from diastolic heart failure." Sababa said. "CHF drug regimen and home."

"But Dr. Hyde has him booked for a bronchoscopy tomorrow morning." Jamie protested.

"Cancel it." Sababa said, sliding the sagging curtain around its rail.

"Good news, Mr. Hundertwasser." Sababa was ebullient. "You're too sexy for this party, and we'll make you hale and hearty. Honourable discharge time."

"Right." Said Fred, packing his things. Sababa turned back to Jamie.

"And?" Jamie handed him the second chart, flipped open to Dr. Tarmac's referral request. Sababa smiled.

"Mr. Mingtao Wang." He began. "59-year-old owner of the Hip Sing Tong Chinese restaurant. Admitted last night in florid heart failure. Only history is surgery for colon cancer five years ago before he emigrated."

"From where?" Sababa asked.

"China." Jamie said. But this was too imprecise. Sababa slid back the faded curtain. He introduced himself in Mandarin, to the appreciation of the focus of his attention.

"Nǐ zài nǎ lǐ?" Sababa continued. *Where are you from.*

"Qí qí hā ěr shì." He said. "Zài hēi lóng jiāng shěng." *Qiqihar, in Heilongjiang province.*

74

"Nǐ zì jǐ zhòng shū cài ma?" Sababa asked him if he grew his own vegetables. Mr. Wang related his skill as a market gardener, and how he raised his own livestock. Sababa asked him if his animals ever had white flesh. Mingtao nodded. He asked him if he had been sick with a viral illness before he came to Canada.

"Kē sà qí B bìng dú." He said. *Coxsackie B virus*. Sababa blew on his fingers.

"What?" Jamie was agitated. "What?"

"Middle-aged man from Northeastern China comes to the Island after a Coxsackie B infection. He leases local farmland, and raises his own crops and livestock which he notes have 'white muscle disease.' Our soil is deficient in selenium and, because of his previous bowel surgery, Wang's absorption is likely reduced to some extent anyway. And now, he presents in heart failure. You have a name?"

"No, I don't have a name." Jamie said. "Sometimes, you don't play fair."

"Welcome to the game, Jamie." He said. "Mother Nature doesn't play fair, and she has the only poker table in town where you get to play with other people's chips."

"So what is it?" Jamie asked.

"Mingtao Wang has a mitochondrial cardiomyopathy called Keshan's Disease." Sababa said. "It's named after the county he's from in China, where the disease was first noted. It's a weird, and a too little—a weird effect of too little dietary selenium causing mutation in an infecting virus, and the direct effect of too little selenium on the heart as well."

"Can we fix it?" He asked.

"You bet." Sababa said. "First, get us a serum selenium and selenoprotein P determination, echo, nuclear ventriculogram, and these." Sababa wrote down a list. "His ECG is abnormal. Get another one." He wrote some more.

"Then begin this anti-failure drug regimen, and start him on vitamin E and selenium supplements."

"How much selenium?" Jamie asked. Sababa turned to Mr. Wang.

"Xìng shēng huó huó yuè ma?" He asked. Mingtao blushed like Gung Ho at a Singapore Sling convention.

"He appears to be sexually active." Sababa said. "Let's make it 100 micrograms a day."

"Will you explain all this to him?"

"Oh no, Jamie." Sababa said. "Mr. Wang speaks perfect English. I just needed the practice. You enlighten him and write these two gentlemen up. By the time you finish here and grab a bite to eat, our clinic at the office should be starting."

Dr. Das Boet waved to them, on his way into the unit, as Sababa was leaving.

"You one of Sababa's sharks?" He asked.

"Shark?" Jamie puzzled.

"Don't stop moving." Boet said. "Or you'll die."

'There is only a finger's difference between a wise man and a fool.'
Diogenes

Two hours later, Jamie watched a white hatchback streak into the Manzanita Medical parking lot from the safe vantage point of a large second-storey window. Previous encounters with Newton's Laws of Motion had disfigured the vehicle that came to a sudden halt in the only reserved clinic parking space. Sababa's Honda Civic was an automobile of provenance. It was as dimpled and dented as a Caribbean steel drum.

Some of its markings were from its frequent collision with local fauna. Despite Jane's disapproval, Sababa would sometimes serve portions of his nighthawk road kill, masterfully prepared, to unsuspecting dinner guests. Others were from the acute obligations of his employment, jumping curbs in a life or death race to *dance with the devil in the pale moonlight*, or nudging the illegally parked from his on-call bay in front of the Emergency Department. The interior of his hatchback had fared no better, used as it was to transport sword ferns or edible mushrooms or other native flora back to the rejuvenating garden of his lakeside domain. The original Civic carpet colour had transmuted into a breathing lifeform of its own.

But Sababa's aerobatic airframe of stealth was predominantly known for the reckless speed of its pilot. One group of new millennial mothers, running to keep up with their jogging strollers, accosted him one day as he made the turn into his driveway, during a rare brief lunch break.

"What is this teaching our children, when you drive like that?" Asked the one with the twins.

"Natural selection." Sababa said.

He took the stairs two at a time to the front door of his clinic.

"It's broken heart week, Boss." Mercy was typing behind the sunlit counter. Jamie came out of the residents' room.

"Mercy rides to the door of my heart upon the black horse of affliction." Sababa smiled.

"What?"

"Every sadonecrobestiophile is just beating a dead horse."

"Huh?" Sababa handed him the chart on the top of the pile.

"Later, Jamie." He said. "Now is the time to heal the country by ridding ourselves of the unwell. You get the first patient." Jamie looked at the name and called her into his space. *Victoria Huckell.*

Sababa invited the woman with the next appointment into his office. He had looked after Cathy Bates for two years now, ever since the chemotherapy for her breast cancer had poisoned her heart. She had asked him why the doxorubicin had murdered her pump. He could have told her about how quinones cause redox reactions that generate superoxides and other reactive oxygen species, which creates lipid peroxidation in biomolecules, signalling the cell into the apoptotic transduction pathway, specifically because of phosphatidylserine, flipping them from the cytosolic to the extracellular side of the plasma membrane. He could have told her of the 50% mortality she faced. But he didn't.

Instead, he suggested she drink green tea (for its Epigallocatechin-3-gallate polyphenol content) and take his poisons, special β-blockers, and some other drugs. In the intervening two years that she drank her tea and took Sababa's pills, the pumping action of Cathy's heart had risen from 11% of normal, to normal. She was back to work at Bastion Jewellers, and her husband had taken Sababa fly fishing for steelhead. It was a win-win.

Cathy had arrived with a new problem, but he would fix that. He gave her a requisition for some investigations and asked her to make a return appointment with Mercy for a month's time. Sababa loved fishing for steelhead.

When Jamie was ready, he presented Victoria Huckell's case to Sababa. He handed him the referral letter from her family doctor, James Ruben Andrews. *32-year-old bank teller with unexplained heart failure. She wants to know why, and so do I.*

Jamie told Victoria's story and demonstrated the findings of his physical examination. He finished with a review of her investigations.

"You got a name?" Sababa asked. Jamie shook his head.

"From one thing, know ten thousand things." He said. "Look at Victoria again. Narrow face with a broad nasal base and small chin, low-lying eyelid margins, and joint hyperextensibility" Sababa asked her to bend her fingers back. They bent way back. He took his Queen Square reflex hammer and tapped her large tendons. They barely flinched.

"And hypotonia." He said. The antique instrument consisted of a stout ring of *caoutchouc* India rubber encircling a bell metal spherical centre from which protruded an eight-inch tapering whalebone shaft. It was an antique. Jamie noted that it was inscribed with the name of the inventor, and the date of its creation. *Henry Vernon, 1858.* Sababa replaced it beside another later version fashioned from a ring pessary around a solid brass wheel on a bamboo cane. He noticed Jamie's curiosity.

"Made by a Miss Wintle, a head nurse at the National Hospital for Nervous Diseases, in Queen Square, London. They called her 'Sister Electrical,' but that doesn't address the most important thing now, Jamie. What's the most important thing?"

"What we do with the most important question?"

"The most important thing is to keep the most important thing the most important thing." Sababa said. He turned to his patient.

"Victoria, you have an inherited condition which causes heart congestion and malformation of the ovaries, which can cause infertility. We call that part hypergonadotropic hypogonadism, but it doesn't matter. What matters is that we can treat both problems."

"You have a name?" She asked. Sababa smiled.

"Malouf Syndrome." He said. "Named after Joe Malouf, the cardiologist at the American University of Beirut who first described it." Jamie ordered investigations and provided Victoria with a prescription. Mercy made a follow-up appointment for six weeks later.

After reviewing several more patients, Doctors Sababa and Dunne saw the last one together. Pinky Floyd was a referral from Dr. Poldy Bloom, the Hibernian emergency physician who shared Sababa's tent on the first night of their Stout Men Himalayan adventure. Poldy had only lasted that one sleep before descending a kilometer down to an airstrip to take him home. In Nepal, they had referred to him as 'Small Man.' *Small man must go in front seat.* He was bigger than that but he had slowed down and transitioned to family practice. His consultation request described Pinky as *a 26-year-old Pamela Anderson Plaza busker with a loud heart murmur and ECG abnormalitiees. I told her that your cooking poisoned us in Nepal.*

78

Sababa asked Jamie to examine her cardiac system. Jamie had Pinky properly draped and went through the inspection-palpation-percussion-auscultation routine of her chest. He listened longest with the diaphragm at the pulmonic position, then wrapped his stethoscope back around his collar, and beamed.

"What you got?" Sababa asked.

"Splitting of the first heart sound. Fixed splitting of the second heart sound, and brief diamond-shaped murmurs in both contraction and relaxation."

"You got a name?"

"Atrial septal defect."

"Well done, Earthling." Sababa was pleased. "And the ECG?"

Jamie studied the tracing.

"Sinus brady, right superior axis, first degree AV and right bundle branch blocks."

"You got a name?"

"I just gave you a name." Jamie said.

"Context, Jamie. Context."

"I don't get it." He said.

"I know." Sababa turned to the young patient.

"What instrument do you play when you're busking, Pinky?"

"Ukelele." She said.

"How come?" Sababa asked.

"What else could I play with these?" Her thumbs looked like fingers, there were only four digits on her left hand, and her left arm was shorter than her right. Jamie swore under his breath.

"Holt-Oram Syndrome, Jamie." Sababa said. "Also known as Heart-Hand Syndrome. Usually from a spontaneous mutation in the TBX5 gene. Someday, after four more years of Internal Medicine training, you will find yourself in a random hospital in a random city with a random examiner. If he or she asks you to examine the cardiac system and you don't start with the patient's hands, you will find yourself in a random hospital in a random city with a random examiner a year later."

"I think I'm doing well." Jamie had taken offense.

"Only one person in this room has two thumbs and cares more about you than Pinky Floyd. I'll leave you to dictate a concise consultation letter to Dr. Bloom, order the tests you think Pinky needs, and explain to her what she has, to her satisfaction. Also, if you're interested, I am on call tonight, and you are more than welcome to join me. The darkest nights produce the brightest stars."

"OK." He said. Sababa handed him his pager and twiddled an air cigar on his way out the door.

"Hello, I must be going."

Before he left the clinic, Jamie paused for too long at Mercy's counter. She unplugged her earphones.

"Doctor Sababa also rides the black horse of affliction." She said. "He is trying to help you be your best, Jamie. You should take what he says with a grain of salt."

"I'm trying?"

"Also, sometimes, it goes even farther with a litre of lime juice and a forty pounder of tequila."

'How can you mend a broken heart?
How can you stop the rain from falling down
How can you stop the sun from shining
What makes the world go round'
Bee Gees, *How Can You Mend a Broken Heart*

The Good Doctor was finishing the last of the Spanish stew that Jane had lovingly prepared when his landline burst into Blue Oyster Cult. *Then the door was open and the wind appeared, the candles blew then disappeared...* Sababa had programmed his ringtones to announce the identity of certain callers. *The curtains flew then he appeared, saying don't be afraid...* This one was from Harbour City Regional. *Come on baby, don't fear the reaper...*

The cowbell was insistent.

Sababa didn't own a mobile phone. He reasoned that if it was an emergency, the hospital switchboard operator would call him on his pager; if it wasn't an emergency, the universe should leave him alone; and there was never any other good news coming through a cell phone. But there was no good news coming through his landline either. Jamie had his pager, and he was agitated on the other end of it.

"You need to come in." He said. Now."

Sababa took one last bite of rabbit and kissed Jane on the way out the door. She heard the Honda scream in protest, as it barreled through the downpour and out of their long driveway. The Doppler shift matched that of the manual transmission down the Mount Benson hillside.

As he braked for the red light at the Quarterway School on Bowen Road, an RCMP Ford Interceptor cruised up beside him. Sababa took a quick look at the female police officer at the wheel and waved his stethoscope through the windshields.

Veronica Marsden held up her handcuffs, with the same motion. Sababa slinked through the light change until he was sure she wasn't following him.

In the acute room of the ER, Jamie and Trace Pangloss were doing all they could, but it wasn't enough. Whatever they were doing was beading tiny droplets of perspiration on both their foreheads. Two busy nurses were in fully committed mode.

"What you got?" Sababa asked.

"William Paxton." Jamie began. "57-year-old manager of the Port Theatre and a history of mechanical aortic valve replacement two years ago because of an infection. Presents today with sudden chest pain and shortness of breath. Initial exam showed a low blood pressure, bounding pulses, abnormal prosthetic heart sounds with a big diastolic decrescendo murmur everywhere, creps in the lung bases, and cool bluish legs.

"He was in cardiogenic shock and heart failure." Trace said. "We gave him some IV Lasix and started him on Levophed. His pressure is back up to normal." Sababa looked at the infusion rate. It was atmospheric.

"ECG shows a normal heart rate and signs of lack of blood flow across his heart." Trace threw a chest x-ray up on the viewer. "Enlarged heart with lung congestion." Sababa looked at the patient. No one was happy.

"Dina, mix up nitroglycerine and dobutamine infusions." Sababa said. "Tack them onto the Levo at 5 and 10 mg/kg/minute respectively."

"You're going to reduce afterload in a patient with an acutely leaking aortic valve?" Jamie asked.

"No, I'm going to increase his heart rate, decrease the time his heart is in the relaxation phase, and thereby decrease regurgitant volume, left ventricular relaxation and pulmonary artery pressures, and improve the heart's output." Sababa said. "If my old friend Arthur Kantrowitz was still alive, I could ask him to bring me one of his intra-aortic balloon pumps, but I can't, cause he's dead. Michaela, have Cheri Sundae patch me through to the chest cracker on call in Victoria and get me the Big Bird. Have the lab come back and draw a set of blood cultures." He rolled a portable ultrasound machine to William Paxton's bedside and showed him the problem.

"Bill, it appears you have a mechanical aortic valve that's trying to escape." He said. "We're going to get you a new one." Paxton raised one eyebrow.

"I tell ya, if it ain't one thing, it's somethin' else."

A few minutes later, Sababa had spoken to the cardiothoracic surgeon, who accepted the patient in transfer and would alert the OR staff in Victoria. Paxton's heart rate had increased but he was breathing easier. Then the music arrived. *Dubdubdubdub whumpawhumpa whupwhup wuppawuppa whopwhop batabata tocotoco flacflac chakkchackk chakachak akk-chk thiththith ssssssssss...*

"I love the nightlife." Said Sababa.

Once William Paxton was airborne, Jamie told him of two more referrals. One he had already seen. He handed Sababa the chart.

"That's my contribution to your evening festivities." Dr. Capitaine stood on the other side of the desk, writing some discharge orders.

"How are you, Myles?" Sababa asked.

"Living the dream."

"Trust in dreams, for in them is hidden the gate to eternity." Sababa asked Jamie what he had.

"Hank Gathers," Jamie started. "62-year-old maintenance man at the Dorchester Hotel. Presents with a week-long story of recurrent temporary loss of consciousness and an electrical conduction problem."

"Go on." Sababa said.

"A couple of weeks worth of breathlessness with exertion on a longstanding background of high blood pressure. On exam, there is III/VI murmur during heart contraction. His ECG shows a slow heart rate with first degree AV and bifascular block." Sababa looked at Hank's monitor. Some atrial discharges were not followed by ventricular ones.

"And that?" He asked. Jamie's eyes opened.

"Wasn't there before."

"Let's go see him." He said. Jamie made the introductions. Sababa took Hank's pulse and then asked his protégé to do the same.

"Bisferiens." Jamie said. "Double pulse. Compatible with my diagnosis of aortic valve narrowing."

"What else causes it?"

"Normal hearts in a hyperdynamic state, patent ductus arteriosus, arteriovenous fistulas, and hypertrophic obstructive cardiomyopathy, but..."

"But what?" Sababa unwrapped his Littman Master Cardiology black and brass stethoscope from around his neck. "But did you get him to Valsalva and squat while listening to his heart?" He asked Hank to get out of bed, bear down while standing, and then to squat. He asked Jamie to listen to Hank's chest during the dynamic manoeuvres.

"The murmur gets louder with Valsalva and lessens with squatting."

82

"So does he have a narrowed aortic valve?"

"No." Jamie said. "He has HOCM."

"And why did he lose consciousness?"

"Because of his HOCM." Jamie said.

"I suppose it's possible that Hank's hypertrophic cardiomyopathy may have worsened in the last 62 years." Sababa pointed to the monitor. "But his development of Mobitz II second degree atrioventricular block hasn't helped."

"The likelihood of that being responsible for his symptoms is next to nothing." Jamie said.

"Last time I checked, next to nothing is higher than nothing." Sababa said. "It happens to 6% of HOCM patients, or in Mr. Gather's case, 100%." Hank's monitor demonstrated a run of unconnected atrial and ventricular discharges, before firing off a fusillade of atrial discharges only. He lost consciousness, and then revived when his electrical conduction improved spontaneously. Sababa called to his nurse.

"Regina, Dr. Dunne will need to put in a temporary pacemaker here."

"I will?"

"I assume you've done this before." Sababa said.

"I've seen it done." Regina moved the implantation cart to the bedside.

"See one, do one, teach one, Jamie." Sababa said. "Not do one, teach one, kill one. Let's remember that. Gown and glove." The Good Doctor explained the situation to Hank, proceeded to help Jamie guide a balloon-tipped temporary ventricular pacemaker through an internal jugular central line, attach it to a generator, and adjust the output settings.

"Until I get my pacemaker program, Mr. Gather will have to be transferred to Victoria for his permanent device." Sababa said. "But he would have to be transferred anyway, even if we could implant at Harbour City Regional. Know why?"

"Because he'll need a dual chamber automatic implantable cardioverter-defibrillator for his HOCM?" Sababa patted his shoulder.

"And we can give him β-blockers." He said. "Well done. You know what the Brockenbrough-Braunwald-Morrow sign is?" Jamie shook his head.

"Some other time. Let's go see the next patient together."

Trace Pangloss approached them on an angled trajectory, as they went for the patient's emergency record.

"Pfeffer Bach Reiter." He said. "42-year-old Commercial Street second-hand bookstore owner. Saw his GP yesterday for a six-days of fever, chills, red eyes, vomiting and diarrhea, left knee pain, and frequent and urgent urination. Presents today with shortness of breath and chest pain. History of hypertension and recurrent inflammation of the ocular white coating of his eyes, four times in the last eight years. No previous story of sexually transmitted disease. No family history of weird. Exam shows low-grade fever but otherwise normal vital signs, conjunctivitis, soft S1, single S2, LV S3, and short diastolic murmur, pericardial rub, congested lungs, and a warm and tender left knee. Normal complete blood count and ECG, but high sedimentation rate at 56 mm/hr. Chest x-ray shows pulmonary venous congestion. He's all yours."

"Hmmm... Can't see, can't pee, can't climb a tree." Sababa said.

"Sorry?" Trace looked puzzled.

"What causes the classic triad of conjunctivitis, nongonococcal urethritis, and asymmetric oligoarthritis?" Sababa asked. "This man's namesake."

"Reiter's syndrome." Trace offered.

"We don't call it that anymore."

"Why not?" Jamie asked.

"Because the son of a bitch was a Nazi." Sababa said. "Hans Conrad Julius Reiter conducted forced medical experiments on Buchenwald concentration camp prisoners. He was prosecuted in Nuremberg as a war criminal. Reiter was just one of many fascist fuckwits who had medical conditions and terminology named for them."

"Like who?" Jamie and Trace asked simultaneously.

"Like Hans Asperger of Asperger syndrome, who colluded with the child 'euthanasia' program." He said. "Like Max Clara of the Clara cell, who based his work on a tissue sample taken from an executed 'prisoner'; like Hans Eppinger of Cauchois–Eppinger–Frugoni syndrome, who conducted cruel experiments on gypsy prisoners at Dachau to test the potability of seawater; like Julius Hallervorden of Hallervorden–Spatz disease, who was present at the killing of more than 60 children in the Brandenburg Psychiatric Institution, and removed material from the brains of 697 euthanasia victims for his investigations; like Franz Seitelberger of Seitelberger disease, who worked on the brains of 3 children from the killing institute of Landesanstalt Görden in Brandenburg; like Hugo Spatz of Hallervorden–Spatz disease and Georg Stiefler of the Spatz–Stiefler reaction and, who directed the murders there, and experimented on hundreds of brains from the mentally ill of all ages; like Hans Joachim Scherer of Van Bogaert–Scherer–Epstein syndrome, who analyzed brains from over 300 Polish and German children

84

executed in the nearby Loben Psychiatric Clinic for Youth at the Neurology Institute in Breslau, Silesia; and like Friedrich Wegener of Wegener's granulomatosis, whose investigations exploited the genocide machinery in Lodz."

"What's different now?" Trace asked.

"We don't name diseases after Nazis." Sababa said. "Although we have named them after their victims."

"So what do we call Reiter's syndrome now?" Jamie asked.

"We call it reactive arthritis." Sababa said.

"What's it reacting against?" Trace asked.

"Chlamydia, shigella, salmonella, campylobacter, ureaplasma, or yersinia." He said. "Take your pick of triggers. Let's go see him." Trace Pangloss pulled back the curtain of Bed #6. A frail-looking middle-aged man with white hair and blue eyes and glasses looked uncomfortable and unamused. Sababa pointed to the soles of his feet, covered in small hard nodules.

"Psoriasis?" Jamie asked.

"Keratoderma blennorrhagicum." Sababa said. "That clinches the diagnosis." He asked Pfeffer if he could listen to his heart. The bookseller shrugged. Sababa frowned through his exam, and then called to the nurse, taking vital signs in the next bed over.

"Dina, I'll need a dobutamine and nitro cocktail for this patient as well." He leaned over to catch the ward clerk's attention.

"Cheri, can you get me the chest cracker again, and call dispatch for Big Bird to make another run?" Cheri Sundae reactivated her phone headset and began dialing. Sababa turned to the subject of his attention.

"Pfeffer, it appears you have the same disease that Christopher Columbus may have had." Herr Reiter looked perturbed.

"I've never seen it happen in this condition so quickly before, but you've developed a considerable leak in your aortic valve." He said. "You may have to have it replaced, and I'm having you assessed in Victoria."

"What is the cause?" Pfeffer asked.

"We don't know for sure." Sababa said. "But it has something to do with a gene component called HLA-B27 and the production of an excess signaling cytokine protein called TNFα."

"Must be such a pleasure to live in your head." Pfeffer pointed to his ear.

"It's not my planet, Pfeffer." Sababa said. "I just work here." He turned to his colleagues.

"Gentlemen, permit me to make a few notes for Herr Reiter's upcoming journey to the dark side of our moon. I will need mood music to accompany my labour." He wrote out his consultation, accompanied by the *Horst-Wessel-Lied* from the nearest computer.

> 'Die Strasse frei den braunen Batallionen
> Die Strasse frei dem Sturmabteilungsmann
> Es schau'n auf's Hackenkreuz voll Hoffung schon Millionen
> Der Tag für Freiheit und für Brot bricht an.'

The street free for the brown battalions, the street free for the Storm Troopers. Millions, full of hope, look up at the swastika; The day breaks for freedom and for bread.

"I'll leave the rest for you to finish, Jamie." He pulled the pager out of the young man's pocket. "But I'll take the rest of the night. Get switchboard to call me tomorrow after you've seen your first patient." Sababa bounced out of the automatic sliding frosted glass doors.

"I still trying to decide if working with this guy is a blessing or a curse." Jamie said. Trace shook his head.

"It's just a matter of time before they add the word 'syndrome' after his name."

Back on the road home in the downpour, Sababa glimpsed a blue and red flash in his rearview mirror. He braked hard and slowed into the first available pullout. *Speaking of Nazis...*

The female officer cruised to a halt behind him and turned on the interior light of her Ford Interceptor. She began to write a ticket of her own. It may forever remain a mystery whether Veronica Marsden had it in for Doctor Sababa. She was definitely not in a happy place. Her daddy was an RCMP deputy commissioner in Vancouver, but despite her request for assignment to a unit in the big smoke, she learned much later that her father had helped exile her to the bright lights of Harbour City, for 'further professional development.' For that she would never forgive him and someone would have to pay.

Sababa watched the waterproof yellow jacket-clad traffic policewoman exit the vehicle and make her way to his driver-side door. As he rolled down his window, Veronica shone a full-beam flashlight into his eyes.

"I've been waiting for you." She smiled.

"Yeah, well, I got here as fast as I could."

mend this broken

'And how can you man?

How can a loser ever win?
Please help me mend my broken heart
And let me live again'
    Bee Gees, *How Can You Mend a Broken Heart*

The new day brought more cascades and torrents falling through the gunmetal gloom onto the wet washed streets.

Specializing in the aggressive speed that forces a choice between compliance and casualty, the ambulance driver screeched his tires through a blurred gauntlet of downtown morning traffic, parting it like a hot knife through butter. The siren echoed and wailed and reverberated in rising and falling glissandos, and sequential staccato jagged bursts of urgent chirping. Stroboscopic flashing lights illuminated Linley Valley's blanketed body inside the vehicle. Everything behind the interior polycarbonate wall shields rattled. Linley could see the paramedic's mouth move, but his words bounced off and dissolved into the downpour outside. The smells of gasoline and cleaning chemicals and crisp sheets mixed with the earthy geosmin of the rain. His tongue tasted like roasted beets. In his terror, Linley had been incontinent.

As the ambulance slowed to a stop in front of the neon yellow stripes and automatic sliding frosted glass doors of the Harbour City Regional ER entrance, the cloudbank fractured for one electric moment, letting out a flood of glistening white light, falling onto the Japanese cherry blossoms, as if God himself was breaking through.

It was fine to respect the gods and Buddhas, as long as you didn't depend on them, but Linley Valley needed a miracle to rescue him from his delirium and make his pain and breathlessness go away.

The emergency nurses instilled confidence and made him comfortable with morphine. Dr. Cliffy Carlton quickly determined, based on his story and exam and ECG, that he was having a heart attack and ran a clot buster into his veins. It didn't make any difference to his symptoms or his electrocardiogram. The next physician up the food chain was an Internal Medicine resident named Dr. Jamie Dunne, who admitted him to the ICU. A porter and his assigned critical care nurse, Charmeine, wheeled his gurney under the sign on the transom. *Tranquility Base.* A warm draft hit his face, with a tincture of bleach, and worse.

Linley not only wasn't feeling the tranquillity, he was still seeing the snakes. They slithered for no clear purpose—not to eat, not for love, but perhaps towards him for the heat.

Dr. Dunne was already in the unit, on and then off the phone.

"He's on his way in." Jamie announced and gave some orders to Charmeine. Linley was multitasking, trying to sell her a condo and pushing the snakes away at the same time.

"For someone who's short of breath, you sure do talk a lot." She said. "You may have arrived by ambulance, but you'll be staying in the van. The *Ativan*, Doctor Sababa's special snake oil." She tried to put a milligram tablet under his tongue but he wouldn't stop talking long enough. She fired a double dose into a vein, followed by 100 milligrams of thiamine.

"Anxiety does not empty tomorrow of its sorrows, but only empties today of its strength." She said.

"If you don't own a home, buy one. If you own a home, buy another one." He was blabbering. "If you own two homes, buy a third. And, lend your relatives the money to buy a home." Linley heard the whoosh of the translucent door, sliding sideways with ease. He watched a stout man close the space between them at a clip. His black curls bounced with each stride. He threw a Colombian leather briefcase over the elevated centre of the room. It careened over a wall of telemetry monitors and came to rest upright beside a computer. The man approached Linley's bedside, Black Book in hand.

"This is Doctor Sababa." Charmeine said. "He is never bothered by stress, but he is a carrier. Relax, he appears to be in a good mood."

"Are all your needs being met?" Sababa asked.

"I'm a real estate guy." Linley said. "He is not a full man who does not own a piece of land. To me, I love real estate because you can feel it."

"Where do you feel it?" Sababa asked.

"Here." He put his fist on his chest. Sababa took his wrist.

"Location. Location. Location."

"Real estate is a contact sport." He said. "If you think hiring a professional is expensive, wait until you hire an amateur." Sababa smiled a Sababa smile.

"Charmeine, you know why people take an instant dislike to real estate agents?" She shook her head.

"To save time. Only one thing worse than a realtor, but at least that can be lanced, drained and surgically dressed. What you got?" Jamie came over with the lab results and a series of ECG tracings taken since Linley's arrival at Harbour City Regional.

88

"His markers are only slightly up." The resident said. "But his electrocardiogram shows an anterior wall heart attack and QT segment prolongation."

"You don't say." Sababa turned his attention to Betty Boop."

"Betty, can you patch me through to whichever shadow puppet is on for ultrasound today?" He said. "I need a portable echo."

"They don't do portable echos." She said. Her left hand gesticulated in the air as she held the handset high.

"They do today."

"Dr. Mako Brisk on line one." She said. Sababa picked up line one. The banter captivated an attentive audience of nurses and respiratory technicians. A few minutes later, they heard the whoosh of the translucent door, sliding sideways with ease. An ultrasound technician guided a large mobile Zamboni through a torment of high fives.

"Bed #4." Betty Boop pointed toward Linley's cubicle. A few minutes later, Dr. Mako Brisk entered, scowling at Doctor Sababa.

"Jamie, you know the name of a radiologist's favorite plant?" Sababa asked. Jamie shook his head.

"The hedge." He said, deepening the lines on Brisk's face. The technician had already set up the study windows for Linley's ultrasound. Sababa and Brisk, and Jamie and Charmeine hovered beside the screen. As he adjusted his probe, a pulsating shape hove into view.

"Whoah." Mako said. Sababa let out a low whistle.

"Nippon no tako no wana o mita koto ga arimasu ka, Jamie?"

"Huh?"

"Have you ever seen a Japanese octopus trap?" Sababa asked.

"No."

"It looks like that." He pointed to the bulging, ballooned-out motionless tip of the lower chamber and hard pumping base. "Like the ceramic fishing pots they use to capture octopus. That's why we call it Takotsubo Syndrome. Or Broken Heart Syndrome. Or Stress Cardiomyopathy. First described by Dr. Sato in Japan in 1991. The worst cases cause shock, heart failure, rhythm disturbances, wall clots or rupture. It's a masquerader. Think of the Japanese proverb." *Beware the octopus's eighth leg.*

"Is it caused by stress?" Charmeine asked.

"Emotional or physical." He said. "Sometimes none. Sometimes even extreme joy."

"You mean I might die of happiness?" Linley said.

"If you want a happy ending, that depends, of course, on where you stop your story. It's not stress that kills us, but our reaction to it. This can recur, usually from the same trigger." Sababa said. "So if happiness caused this... welcome to the end of the thought process."

"I'm a realtor, Doc." Linley was becoming agitated again. "I need closure." Charmeine slipped another Ativan under his tongue. Mako Brisk and his ultrasound technician took their leave and drove the Zamboni from the Death Star.

"I still need to transfer you to Victoria for an angiogram, Linley." Sababa said.

"Can't you do that stuff here?"

"I am a simple village internist." Sababa said. "They don't let me play with their toys. We will, however, start you on medication, aspirin, and ACE inhibitors. β-blockers don't work. When you come back, we will talk about the snakes, and you will need to see my favorite psychiatrist, Dr. Robert La Capuche. If you survive, and there's every reason to think you will, you should return to normal within two months. Time mends a broken heart. You'll be back to high ball cocktails and low ball offers in no time."

"Crown Royal XR?" He asked.

"The snake that cannot shed its skin perishes." Sababa said. "I'd switch to Domaine Renegade Pinot Noir."

"Who makes that?" He asked.

"I do." The stocky savant left the bedside to compose his consultation and orders and arrange ambulance transfer for Linley's angiography. He navigated to the five thousand tunes stored on the hard drive of his Death Star computer and played the most appropriate accompaniments to his activities. It could have been *Heartbreaker* or *Stairway to Heaven*, but that would have gone over like a Led Zeppelin. For every snake, there is a ladder; for every ladder, a snake.

'I show you doubt, to prove that faith exists.'
Robert Browning

The casual reader must resist the temptation to think of Sababa as impervious to doubt. His immersion in any case often waded into mangroves where he couldn't always see the bottom. But if uncertainty occasionally plagued him, he never let his disaffection show. *I'm not stressed... beyond the stress induced by you telling me how stressed I am.*

He handled the stress of being wrong better than anyone. He knew that introspection caused most of the trouble in the world and that those who were the most awake did the most harm. He learned from his mistakes and could repeat every one of them exactly. He recognized that it was in the nature of medicine that he was going to screw up, even kill someone. But he could handle that reality. *If it works, I was right. If he dies, it was something else... You want to make things right? Nothing's ever right.*

But the stress he didn't handle well was the insecurity of getting older in an ever-younger world, of becoming obsolete and irrelevant, of losing his intellectual and moral authority, and the attention and affection of his patients it provided. He could see his own future reflected in their eyes. When a lion is old he becomes a plaything of jackals. The Shadow was that dark cloud of doubt that followed even the best of them into battle. Sababa had to pretend the Shadow wasn't there, hoping that if he saved more lives, mastered more difficult techniques, and ran faster and farther, it would get tired and give up the chase. But you can't outrun your Shadow. Most of the insecurity it generated was because of fear. And most of the fear was, in its purest essence, a fear of death.

In the music that is our lives, you can't rewind love, or fast-forward heartbreak.

No one can repair all the damaged desire chilled and drowned in the spring rains.

Stretch van der Merwe responded well to Sababa's medications and T.J. Eckleburg's ocular biologicals. She now spends more time travelling Around the World than working there.

Fred Hundertwasser still runs the Wandering Salamander Guest House. He sees his family doctor every three months for medication renewals. Mingtao Wang's heart function is now normal. He sold the Hip Sing Tong Restaurant to spend more time in his garden and augments his soil with bags of selenium supplements.

Victoria Huckell still works as a teller at the Commercial Street Scotiabank but watches the front door more. Cathy Bates's heart function is now normal. She fills in part-time at Bastion

Jewellers. Her husband still takes Sababa steelhead fishing on remote island rivers. Pinky Floyd is fine, and her ukelele playing draws big crowds and lucrative tips in Pamela Anderson Square. William Paxton's mechanical valve was found infected with Staph aureus, so they gave him a new one. He retired as the manager of the Port Theatre, but still helps from the wings. Hank Gathers received a brand new pacemaker-defibrillator. He boasts of his new stamina as the head of maintenance at the Dorchester Hotel. Pfeffer Bach Reiter got his first valve replacement, from an anonymous involuntary pig donor. He still has recurring attacks of reactive arthritis, and his bookstore sales are down from recurring attacks by Amazon. His grandfather, Hans Conrad Julius Reiter, who died on his country estate in 1969, at the ripe old age of 88, is still dead.

Linley Valley's heart function returned to normal, as Sababa predicted. The crack in his heart, like the fractured cloudbank that illuminated the cherry blossoms, let in the light. He quit smoking and drinking and reunited with his wife and family. Last year, he was invested as a proud member in his company's Circle of Legend, having generated more than $10 million of gross commissions in ten years of service. He still fondly remembers Sababa's jibes. *Q. What can you do with a gun with only two bullets, in a room with a lawyer, a used car salesman, and a real estate agent? A. Shoot the realtor twice to make sure.*

They never found out the identity of the masked bank robber. His molecules never made it back to a class reunion, and his DNA never appeared on any Interpol computer or genealogy website.

Oh, and Sababa's affair with the disgruntled road traffic warrior? Veronica Marsden continued to hound Sababa at every turn. On one occasion, he suggested she adopt a feral cat to take the edge off whatever was bothering her. But you can't pin your heart to a wild thing. It gets very expensive, very frequently, very fast.

3. The Case of the Cornelian Dilemma

'The world has room to make a bear feel free.'
Robert Frost, *The Bear*

Springtime is the land awakening. The coho winds were back upon us—bleak easterlies sweeping in like a morning yawn after a night of sour wine, blasting our marrow for signs of life.

Savage squalls swept up the streets, howled around the houses and rattled along the rooftops, menacing hearth flames that struggled against the darkness, and scattering their feeble curls of chimney smoke into invisibility. They roared through the wild dark groves and great bare trees along the seashore of Harbour City, riding harmonic woodwind valkyries of ephemeral air falling in love with itself. Branches bowed and bent downward in a hypnotic dance of creaking chaos, arms swaying like a stadium swarm. All flying creatures were grounded.

He shuffled down the steps that led to the water at the end of Stephenson Point Road, turning back along the beach toward the Pacific Biological Station. Previous brawls had scarred his head and neck. All his brothers were dead, but he was smart enough to have survived. The trail of the scent she had left, outside her comfort zone, he followed in a hurried frenzy.

The sea was a tumult of giant waves, roaring and crashing and pounding the shore, moaning from the depths of itself, mourning memories of lost men long tossed overboard. Wild gusts of cold sea spray lashed the coastline. The harshness bit bitter and salty into his bones. Ashen clouds scuttled across the sky,

He was a being of Heaven and Earth, of thunder and lightning, of rain and wind, of the galaxies. His eyes glowed luminous in the reflected dawn light.

His sense of smell was seven times greater than any hound, able to detect her scent over twelve hours after she had passed this way. He could smell a dead deer carcass three miles away and go a hundred days without eating, defecating, or urinating, converting his urea back into muscle mass. If you put him next to a wild coyote, he would ignore it; if you put him next to a dog, he would kill it with a single blow.

He was an excellent swimmer and capable of running bursts at fifty kilometres an hour. Fifty metres away, he could still get to you in three heartbeats. He had lost forty per cent of his weight over the winter but was still a 400-pound giant, an agile and powerful and unpredictable and indestructible bloodhound, with claws and teeth and night vision goggles. He shook off his torpor and put his hips and shoulders into his pursuit, his pace never slackening.

Brad Eggleston sat in the cab of his truck, a blue Dodge RAM 2500 equipped with a bull bar and motorized winch in the front, a rack of floodlights and sirens across the top, and a caged flatbed in the back. The logos painted on both doors were simple enough. *Conservation Officer Service*. He sipped his Tim Hortons Double Double through the flip-backed spout cover below the maple leaf embossed on the lid.

He had lost sight of the bear at the Stephenson Point steps but figured that the animal might walk along the beach toward the Biological Station, and waited for him there. Wisdom sails with wind and time.

Brad had parked his truck around the back, under the flapping cotton of the Fisheries and Oceans flag, hanging on to the flagpole above him. He watched the bear lumber from one side to another up the bank and onto the front lawn of the Pacific Biological Station. His eyeshine held no fear.

Upwind from the bear, Brad opened the driver side door of his truck and climbed down from the cab. He moved much slower than he used to. His legs wobbled and he got dizzy if he stood up too fast or chased after something.

Powerful gusts crackled his Gore-Tex rain jacket like a silken sail. The badge on the shoulders of his uniform spoke to his mission. *Integrity... Service... Protection.* But oaths are but words and words are but wind, and this was an ill one. It flowed between his buttonholes, chilling his skin beneath, swirling his hair around his head, salting his eyelashes, and hitting his face like it intended to go right through it. It caught the brim of his caph and swept it away. Tornados of cold air coiled around his legs. The draft blew him backwards, raced around Mount Benson and returned for another go. Brad drank in the wild air before it was all gone.

His eyes squinted into two more looking back. The big black bruin stood straight up on two hind legs, nose in the air, head nodding in agitation, then came back to the ground broadside.

Brad averted a direct gaze and pulled his 12-gauge pump action shotgun from its sleeve. He put two shells into the breech. The first shot would have to count. Both head and heart began with the same three letters, but Brad knew you had to read all the way to the end, and neither shot was a good idea. The bear's brain was a small target. A narrow miss might cause a broken jaw, lost eye, or another sort of unpleasant, slow death. The heart was also a small target and is often covered by the upper leg. A discharge too far forward was a non-fatal brisket shot; too low and he'd hit muscle or break a leg. Too far back is a gut-shot animal. The only practical way to kill this bear was to shoot high and take out the lungs.

Brad raised his weapon smooth and slow, concentrating on ensuring his body and clothing didn't touch or rub against the exterior of his vehicle. He rested the gun barrel in his left arm on the hood of his truck, and in his mind traced the back of the bear's left front leg up to about one-third of the way into the chest, behind the shoulder. He wondered how the boar couldn't hear his own heart thumping. His mouth filled with cotton, his knees and hands trembled, and his palms glistened with rain where the sweat should have been. He fought back other calls of nature.

The conservation officer froze in a punishing pose, not blinking, keeping his mouth closed, breathing small and shallow, taking his time, waiting. The bear extended his near foreleg, and Brad saw the perfect angle. He braced his left arm so as not to fall, took in a deep breath, let it out, held it, and squeezed. *BRUSUSUHHHHHH!*

The bear became the dust in the wind knocked out of him, lost on it, gone with it. He plunged forward in the direction he was facing, through everything in his path, panicked and reckless and noisy, roaring and growling, twenty metres towards the doors of the Biological Station, before falling on his side less than ten seconds later. It seemed like forever. The scent trail had become a blood trail, and the groans became weaker against the wind.

Brad came around his truck and behind the animal to put the second shell into its neck. *SJIKK SJIKK. BRUSUSUHHHHHH!* He waited more, and then, turning on his headlamp to illuminate the bear's face, he leaned out and touched an exposed eye with the end of a stick. No one blinked.

Brad felt drained, limbs heavy and shaking. It took him ten minutes to make it back to his truck, and longer to compose himself and write his report.

Nuisance black bear boar, following a scent trail of a female in estrus, showing signs of being habituated and reluctant to leave the area, was euthanized at Pacific Biological Station at 0700 hours. Suspect a second competing male may still be at large.

96

He looked through his windshield at the Harbour City skyline, waking from its slumber. The first Vancouver ferry of the morning was entering Departure Bay. It would be one of those spring days when the sun shone hot and the wind blew cold, when it was summer in the light and winter in the shade.

'One often hears of writers that rise and swell with their subject, though it may seem but an ordinary one. How, then, with me, writing of this Leviathan?'

Herman Melville, *Moby-Dick; or, The Whale*

Rick Erscurve parked his Tucson SUV in the space designated for him at the Pacific Biological station. He hesitated at the blood trail that splattered towards the doors of his employment. It wasn't as if he didn't see a lot of it inside the building, but this wasn't a colour he recognized. What he was familiar with was whale blood.

Rick had cut his scientific teeth on modeling the bell-shaped relationship between female fish spawning stock and the number of young recruits that survive to maturity or are captured by the fishery. It was a lousy model, and its application to Canada's enormous fisheries stocks of Atlantic cod, anchovy, and salmon had managed them into near-extinction. Rick made a successful lateral career move into studying whales and was now the director of the station's Cetacean Research Program.

His primary interest lay in how humpback whales handled oxygen, deep in their ocean abode. The first focus of his research had been on the 'Bohr effect,' and how much oxygen was bound to an animal's hemoglobin, as an inverse relation to the amount of acid and carbon dioxide in its blood. This was thought to be dependent on the size of the animal, but Rick had determined that humpbacks had a strong Bohr effect, approaching that of a guinea pig. As an adaptation to deep long dives, its unique physiology allowed for almost all hemoglobin-bound oxygen to dissociate and supply the whale's body underwater. He also discovered that a humpback muscle protein, myoglobin, because of the way its structure was folded, was even better at holding oxygen than hemoglobin, and was productively used to prolong its repose in the briny depths of its existence.

Rick knew that peripheral oxygen extraction was only one part of peripheral oxygen delivery and had explored the physiology of

97

humpback hearts to complete the equation. He entered his lab, where his postdoc, Dick Squamish, and a technician, were disassembling 200 kilograms of cardiac tissue. The whale's heart was the size of a small car and weighed about as much as three human adults. The lab radio was tuned to a local station.

Hi how are ya Hi how are ya Hi how are ya... Good Morning Indian country, CNDN Coast Salish radio, 101.3 FM on your Home and Native Band... This is BC Bud, bringing you Waŝícus and Twinkies all the stuff you missed in history class...
"What are we doing today?" He asked.
"Working on the conduction system." Dick said. The humpback team had already determined some static and dynamic factors of whale blood volume and flow. They knew the average humpie had 850 litres of blood in its circulation, 190 times that of an average human. They knew that an average humpie had a heart rate of 6 beats per minute, 12 times less than that of an average human. They knew, therefore, that the cardiac output of the humpie was a staggering 270 L/min, pumped by a heart with a relatively enlarged and thickened right ventricle, an adaptation to the hemodynamic changes and collapse of the thorax associated with apneic diving.

The beauty of the trees, the softness of the air, the fragrance of the grass, speaks to me.

"And what little treasures have you discovered over the weekend?" Rick asked.
"Well, we know from single-lead ECG recordings in the water that the electrical conduction between the top and bottom of the humpie heart, and down through the ventricles is fast for an animal of this size." Dick said.

The summit of the mountain, the thunder of the sky, the rhythm of the sea, speaks to me.

"And?"
"We've found out the reason for this adaptation." Dr. Squamish pointed to the dense His-Purkinje network in the ventricular wall.

The strength of the fire, the taste of salmon, the trail of the sun, and the life that never goes away, they speak to me.

"What?" Rick asked.

98

"Since the humpback heart is so much bigger, the electrical signals that make it contract must travel faster to reach the entire muscle in time." Dick said. "It may be that this type of conduction is more accurate so that whales might be less prone to arrhythmias than we are."

"Anything else?" Rick asked.

"Yeah." Squamish said. There was no evidence of atherosclerosis or calcification in any arteries."

"A cetacean is as old as his arteries." Rick said. "Like us." But although the humpback heart in front of them was the same age as the biologist, Rick's arteries were a lot older than the whale's.

"Have you ever seen a rainbow heart from a humpback's blowhole?" Squamish asked.

Rick had seen such rainbows blown, and would now witness his own foolish heart pick the worst time to attack him, in this charades endgame at the apex of his career.

The pressure in his chest breached like a baleen bull in spring mating season and landed on him as if harpooned. The agony radiated down his arms and distorted his face in a terrified grimace and his breathing into pathetic gasps. Extravagant sweat drenched his shirt. Dick Squamish dialed 911 and jabbered into his cell phone. There came sirens.

And my heart soars.

> 'Heartbreaker, you've got the best of me
> But I just keep on coming back incessantly.'
> Mariah Carey, *Heartbreaker*

Dr. Trace Pangloss was the oracle of the ER, the greatest philosopher in the province, and thus in the best of all worlds. *It has been proved that things cannot be otherwise than they are; for, everything being made for a certain end, the end for which everything is made is necessarily the best end...*

The day before Brad Eggleston shot his bear and Rick Erscurve had his heart attack, Trace Pangloss paged Jamie Dunne from the emergency department.

"There is no effect without a cause." He said. "I need you and your Mahatma to find the cause of my patient's bouts of high blood pressure. Jamie walked down to the department.

"Mr. Sam McGee." Trace began. "33-year-old Stephenson Lookout B&B owner with a three-year history of recurrent spasms of severe hypertension. He presents today with a blood pressure of 220/140 mmHg, associated with a two-hour history of dizziness, weakness, throbbing headache, visual blurring, facial flushing, nausea, sweating, chest pain, rapid palpitations, and frequent urination. These episodes occur several weeks apart and persist for up to twelve hours, resolving with or without treatment. Between attacks, his blood pressure is normal. He can't function."

"Sam has a pheochromocytoma." Jamie said. "Adrenal tumour."

"That's what the last eight consultants said." Trace handed Jamie the chart. "There's just one problem."

"What's that?"

"Nobody can find one." Trace said. "Repeated random assays of serum and urinary catecholamines, plasma renin activity, CT scan of his kidneys, renal angiography, MRI of his brain and abdomen, and urinary 5-hydroxyindoleacetic acid determination were all normal. They even did an FDP PET scan and an MIBG scan, looking for the tumour outside where it would normally live, neither of which were any help. He's had every test in the book, to no avail."

"I'll bet my spiritual mentor will think of a few more." Jamie said.

"He was one of the eight consultants." Trace smiled his best of all worlds smile.

"Oh." Jamie went to see Sam. He pulled back the curtain around the man's bed.

"How do you feel now, Mr. McGee?" He asked

"Exhausted." Sam said. "I'll be sapped for days." Jamie began a careful review of the details of the B&B owner's case, performed an examination, and formulated his analysis and plan. Then he called Sababa.

"You've seen him before." Jamie said.

"What? Did he make a follow-up appointment?" Asked the stocky savant. Jamie found the order in the chart.

"Did he?" Jamie asked the patient.

"Doesn't appear so."

"Then it doesn't count." Sababa said. "I'll be there." Jamie presented his findings a few minutes later.

"No alcohol or illicit drugs, no herbal remedies, no nonsteroidal anti-inflammatory or pressor medication, no sleep apnea, no familial history, no abnormal physical findings or investigations, no nothing." Jamie said. Sababa suggested they go to the bedside.

"I remember you." Said Sam McGee.

"Likewise." Sababa offered.

"You weren't much help."

"You didn't come back like you were supposed to." Sababa said.

"My part in your story ends in the chapter you cut me out of."

"I don't believe in allopathic medicine." He said. "I'm having all my mercury fillings pulled." Sababa scowled.

"What's wrong?" Sam asked.

"I'm not responsible for what my face does when you talk." He said. "Stupidity is not a crime. You're free to go."

"But what about my problem?" Sam was agitated.

"Your Google search doesn't trump our expertise, Sam. Your habitual reappearance in the epicentre of something you declare no belief in does not coexist with your insistence on having nothing done." Sababa said. "You're stuck on the bank of a river and you won't swim, you won't take the boat, and you won't fly on the wings of an eagle. So you won't be getting this fixed."

"But even you don't know what's wrong." Said Sam. Sababa placed a blood pressure cuff back on Sam's arm, and asked him to bear down as he repeated the measurement.

"I didn't." Sababa said. "But I do now."

"What is it then?"

"Sam, what's bothering you?" Sababa leaned on the bed railing.

"What do you mean?" Sam asked his own question.

"What are you most afraid of?" Sababa asked.

"Last night I had a bear in my garbage bins."

"That's not it." Sababa said. "How's the B&B business?" Sam's combat face withered.

"Not great." He said. "What with increasing overhead, Airbnb cutting in on the dance floor, the bank's threatening to foreclose, bureaucratic interference... one bad TripAdvisor review and I'm sunk. I'm dying by degrees and you guys can't even tell me what's going on."

"You have a condition we call pseudo-pheochromocytoma, Sam." Sababa said.

"How did you know that?" Jamie asked first.

"Hmmm. Episodes of sudden high blood pressure without any evidence of biochemical excess." Sababa said. "In the presence of subliminal emotional distress, and a higher systolic blood pressure response to Valsalva manoeuvre."

"Can you fix it?" Sam asked.

"You'll need α-1 and β-blockers." Sababa said. "And a referral to our homeboy headshrinker, Dr. Robert La Capuche, to help with your anxiety. Don't mind the sign on his office door. 'Psycho the rapist' should have been one word." He discharged McGee only after he promised to call Mercy for a follow-up appointment, then handed Jamie a piece of paper with a name. *Stephen Dedalus.*

"Telemetry unit, first floor, Grasshopper." He said. "Call me when you're done."

As he sat down to write out his consultation, Sababa selected a tune from his music library on a secret drive hidden deep inside the hospital computer network.

> 'Oh it takes a worried man, to sing a worried song
> Takes a worried man, to sing a worried song
> Well it takes a worried man to sing a worried song
> I'm worried now, won't be worried long.'

'Blessed are the pacemakers, for they shall be called...'
Matthew 5: 9

An hour later, Doctor Sababa rolled through the frosted doors of the Harbour City Regional first floor telemetry unit.

"Morning, Serafina." He said. "Where's my boy?"

"Bed #6, Doc." She said. "He's wound fairly tight." Sababa pulled back the curtain to find Jamie listening to the chest of a tanned bearded fit-looking middle-aged man.

"What you got?" He asked. Jamie unplugged the stethoscope from his ears.

"Mr. Stephen Dedalus, 63-year-old Harbour City Parks and Recreation works supervisor admitted by Dr. Rivera last night for increasingly frequent loss of consciousness."

"What do you do?" Stephen asked.

"I solve problems you didn't know you had in ways you can't understand." He said. "What happened?"

"I fainted yesterday afternoon while working with my crew on the Planta Park trail near the Pacific Biological Station." Stephen said.

"He didn't get any warning it would happen." Jamie added.

"Ever faint when you're shaving?' Sababa asked.

102

"That's why I grew the beard." Said the supervisor. "My wife said I had a seizure once afterwards." Sababa turned to Jamie. "And?"

"And his physical exam is normal. No drop in his blood pressure on standing. Bloodwork, ECG and echo all unremarkable. But late last night, his telemetry showed a four-second pause followed by a slow heart rate." Sababa leaned his head out of the curtain.

"Serafina, run a strip for me, please." The nurse tapped the touch-sensitive screen and a paper strip began to slither from the printer, recording Stephen's electrical heart complexes in real time. Sababa asked him to extend his head, and then gently massaged a small area of his neck.

The ECG tracing became a flat line, the monitor alarms screamed in pain, Stephen lost consciousness, and Serafina contacted Lana to call a Code Blue over the Big Voice. Mary and Angie flew in the door from the Death Star, followed by Dr. Marquis Shu Ying and his resident. Serafina had already rolled the crash cart next to Stephen's bed. The fluorescent hum above them crackled in fury. Stephen's heart rhythm returned as fast as it had departed. His blood pressure rose to the occasion.

"What happened here?" Shu asked.

"He had a positive controlled carotid sinus massage test." Sababa explained.

"Controlled usually implies patient consent and collegial advanced warning." He said.

"More fun this way, Shu."

"What happened?" Stephen had regained his power of speech.

"You have carotid sinus syndrome." Sababa said. "It's a hypersensitivity of the small organ responsible for regulating your blood pressure. It lives in the bulb of your carotid artery. You blacked out when I pushed on it."

"Can you fix it?" Stephen asked.

"You bet." Sababa said. He picked up a handset. At the exact time Sababa dialed the number, before their metamorphosis into 'team leaders," only three nursing administrators worked at Harbour City Regional—the Director of Medical Nursing, the Director of Surgical Nursing, and the Grand Galactic Governess of Nightingales. Sababa referred to them as the Clipboards and Pearls Brigade. Edith Mortley was the Medical Nursing Director and wore a string of natural pearls, uncultured. Sababa once asked her why she wanted to become a nursing administrator.

"Every little girl wants a pony until they have to clean up after it." She said.

Daisy Daws was the Director of Surgical Nursing. She wore a string of imitation pearls. Road hard and put away wet, she was the total embodiment of everything a surgeon needed and feared. But Sababa wasn't calling these divas. He was calling Big Nurse, the Grand Galactic Governess of Nightingales. Mildred Ratschet wore a string of natural pearls, cultured.

"What do you want?" Came the greeting.

"You. Me. And a rainy afternoon."

"I've said it once, and I'll say it again. I never repeat myself." She said. "What do you want?"

"I have this patient..." He began.

"And?"

"He needs a pacemaker, Mildred"

"Send him to Victoria." She said.

"I can get a one faster on eBay." Sababa said. "I want to implant here. I have a tin can, a broom closet, and a slasher who's trained up and ready to roll."

"Over my dead body."

"I knew you'd understand." He said.

"You know the rules, Sababa." She said. "First, we need a program proposal. Then we need approval, then we need start-up and maintenance funding. Then, and only then, do you get your pacemaker and not a moment before."

"Deja Moo." He said.

"What?"

"It's the feeling that I've heard this bullshit before. You know I'm not good with following rules and needing approval."

"No."

"OK, my mistake. Here I called you, and you gave me the impression that you cared, which is so wrong." Sababa said. "Can you at least get this rolling?"

"I'll put it on my fucket list." She hung up.

"How was that?" Shu asked.

There are three kinds of pearls, but there are also three kinds of olives." Sababa said.

"Which are?'

"Green, black... and stuffed." Sababa told Jamie to get some lunch and meet him at his afternoon clinic. Before leaving, he brought Stephen back into his own picture and arranged the transfer.

On his way out of the unit, Jamie confided in Serafina.

"Not sure I'm cut out for this. I'm sleep-deprived and crazy all the time. Every day is a series of massive crises that screws up my ability to decide what's normal. And yet patients ask me how they're doing. Hell, I don't even know how I'm doing. And I get little support from Doctor Swami." Serafina nodded.

"Sababa is a trainee's worst nightmare, Jamie. He's smarter than you, he never sleeps, he digests the inside of every medical journal like it's his last meal, and he devours lesser mortals. Just when you think you know what you're doing, he shows that you don't. You will go to sleep at night cursing his relatives and wake up every morning seeking his approval. And because he considers what you do too important to need it, you'll never see it happen."

'Licorice is the liver of candy.'

Michael O'Donoghue

"It's fall down go boom week, Boss." She said. Sababa and Jamie entered before the clinic was due to begin.

"I'm at the Mercy of whatever character comes into her head." Said the stocky savant.

Jamie looked puzzled. Sababa handed him the first chart.

"Go see this patient." He said.

"Go see this patient?"

"Or repeat everything I say as a question." Jamie looked at the name. *Aurora Leigh*. He called her into the residents' examining room.

Sababa picked up the next manila folder. *Jerome Van Conn*. He looked at Mercy. She didn't take her eyes off her transcription.

"Urgent from Dr. James Ruben Andrews." She said. Sababa shrugged and called the patient into his office. He spent a few minutes pouring over the referral letter and the thick sheaf of accompanying documentation.

"What do you do, Mr. Van Conn?" He asked.

"I work for DFO as a south coast regional salmon officer."

"How's business?" Sababa closed the folder.

"Buoyant." He said.

"Your GP thinks you have a tumour of your adrenal gland." Sababa said. "Why would he think that?"

"My high blood pressure isn't controlled." Jerome said. "My legs swell and my muscles are weak. He says that I'm retaining salt water, and I have too little potassium and too much baking soda in my blood."

105

"Ten per cent of hypertension is caused by an overproduction of a hormone called aldosterone. About a third of these people have a tumour of the adrenal gland." Sababa said, "Many suffer from fatigue, poor vision, confusion, headaches, muscular aches and spasm and weakness, low back and flank pain, trembling, tingling sensations, numbness, and excessive urination, all caused by the potassium deficiency and high blood pressure from the excess hormone. This can lead to strokes, heart attacks, kidney failure, and abnormal heart rhythms."

"Can't you fix this by taking out the tumour?" Van Conn asked.

"We could if that were the problem." Sababa said. " But your imaging studies don't show one, and your aldosterone levels are actually low."

"So what is my problem?" He asked.

"Your problem is the duty-free shop in Schipol Airport."

"How do you know that I go back to Holland every year?" Van Conn asked.

"It is my business to know what other people don't know." He said. "I can smell it."

"What do you mean?" He asked.

"What are you chewing, Jerome?" Sababa wrote notes.

"Dubbel Zout." He said, pulling a small canister from his pocket. "I order it online." He opened the lid.

"Would you like one?" Inside the tin container was an array of small black diamond-shaped lozenges.

"Salmiak." Sababa said. "Inedible pieces of rubber filled with toilet cleaning crystals."

"They're lekker." Van Conn insisted. "I eat them all the time. Good for your health."

"No." Sababa said. "They're not."

"What do you mean?"

"That astringent tongue-numbing mouth-stinging doubled salted licorice you're so fond of is ten per cent ammonium chloride." Sababa began. "The licorice root part contains glycyrrhizinic acid and enoxolone, which not only inhibit the breakdown of another adrenal hormone called cortisol but cause it to inappropriately stimulate mineralocorticoid receptors, by interfering with the enzyme, 11-beta-hydroxysteroid dehydrogenase. *Or have we eaten on the insane root that takes reason prisoner?*"

"I have no idea what you said." Jerome stared at the black pastilles in the tin.

"The licorice you eat so much of mimics the action of a hormone that helps regulate salt and water balance in your body." Sababa said. "You don't have a tumour causing Primary

Aldosteronism, Jerome, you have a habit causing Pseudoaldosteronism."

Van Conn shook his head.

"But wait. There's more."

"What more?" Jerome asked.

"The *sal ammoniac* part, the ammonium chloride, was made by medieval apothecaries as an expectorant.

"A what?"

"Cough medicine." Sababa said. "You used to take snus, didn't you?"

"I used to buy it from the same duty free shop in Amsterdam." Jerome admitted.

"And then you began to buy oral tobacco laced with salmiak, because you developed a cough, and you found it went away with a pinch between the lips and the gums."

"It did go away." Jerome said.

"But it scared you so much that, after more than thirty years of cigarette smoking and a downshift to chewing tobacco in a half measure attempt to quit the evil weed, you finally managed a switch to Dubbel Zout licorice."

"You know that?" Jerome was not comfortable.

"But your cough has come back, hasn't it?" Sababa asked.

Van Conn nodded.

"Your blood pressure will likely go back to normal." Sababa threw a film up on his office viewer. "But it appears the radiologist may have missed a small abnormality on your chest x-ray."

"Small?"

"Small." Sababa said. "But possibly significant. The most important thing is to keep the most important thing the most important thing. It appears that your GP was half right, Jerome. You do have a tumour, but not where he thought it would be. We'll need to spend more time together."

After Van Conn had left his office to see Mercy, Jamie arrived to discuss his patient.

"Aurora Leigh." He began. "22-year-old hairdresser at the Blue Heron Salon referred by Dr. Poldy Bloom for a ruptured spleen."

"I don't do ruptured spleens." Sababa said. "What's the question?"

"Why did her spleen rupture?" Jamie asked.

"So what you got?"

"She fell four feet off an unloading ski chairlift at Mount Washington a month before they had to take out her ruptured spleen. She was medically cleared at the time of the fall."

"They missed it the first time."

"They did." Jamie said. "She began having fainting episodes, dizziness on sitting up, and persistent lower abdominal pain before they clued in and ordered an abdominal CT scan."

"So tell me again why she's here." Sababa said.

"She's still fainting. Four or five times a day."

"Was she fainting before she ruptured her spleen?" Sababa stood up from his chair.

"No."

"Exam?"

"Normal, except for her splenectomy scar."

"Lab?"

"Normal blood work, ECG, Holter, echo." Jamie said. "She refused to use an event recorder."

"Let's go see her." Sababa said.

"Are you sure you had no history of fainting before your accident, Aurora?" Sababa asked after Jamie had made the introductions.

"Positive." She said.

"And when do you faint now?"

"Anytime." She said. "Day or night."

"But never at work, standing all day cutting hair?"

"Nope." She said.

"Do you get any warning?" Sababa asked. "Lightheadedness, nausea, sweating, ringing in your ears, chest pain, fuzzy thoughts, speech stuttering, weakness, or visual disturbances?"

Aurora fell off her chair onto the floor, unconscious. Her breathing seemed labored and her eyelids began to flutter. Jamie went to protect her airway but Sababa grabbed his arm.

"Wait." He said. "The moment I squeeze her left wrist, she'll recover." Sababa squeezed her left wrist. Aurora opened her eyes.

"Hello, Sleeping Beauty." He said, helping her back onto her chair.

"A few more questions, if I may." Sababa said. Aurora nodded.

"Are you in a relationship?" She glared and then shook her head.

"When did the last one end?" He asked.

"On our last skiing trip." She said.

"The one when you fell off the chairlift?" Aurora nodded. Sababa paused for a moment.

"Aurora, it appears you have a rare but treatable form of what we call pseudosyncope." He said. "It's not dangerous, and the treatment is simple." Aurora wrote the name.

108

"What's the treatment?" She asked. Sababa produced a saltshaker from his pocket.

"Salt?" She asked. "That's it?"

"That's it." He said. "It should begin working immediately and by two weeks from now, you shouldn't need it at all. I'll write Dr. Bloom a letter, and explain all this to him. You can go now."

After Aurora left, Jamie asked Sababa why he didn't accept her story.

"Never ask why patients lie, Fledgling, just assume they do." He said. "Everybody lies. Truth begins in lies."

"But she injured herself falling off the chairlift." He said. "Whatever is causing her loss of consciousness has to be physical. I would have said vasovagal syncope, from a mixture of abnormal cardioinhibitory and vasodepressor responses."

"Always good to know the pathophysiology and the causes of syncope—autonomic, orthostatic, cardiovascular or metabolic, or reflex, of which vasovagal is a subset." Sababa said. "But she had no history before her accident, her fall occurred on the same trip as the breakup with her partner, she doesn't faint standing all day cutting hair, she refused to use an event recorder, and there are no warning symptoms or identifiable triggers."

"Shouldn't we at least do a tilt table test?" Jamie asked.

"No more tests." Sababa said. "No one flutters their eyelids like that when they're unconscious."

"Won't she figure it out from the name you gave her?"

"That was the idea." Sababa said. "Far enough removed in time and space to be gentle, and close enough to be informative."

They saw the last clinic patient together, a referral from Dr. Tictac Tarmac. *Louisa Musgrove, 28-year-old Departure Bay school teacher with a two-month history of fatigue, chest and abdominal pain, problem swallowing, and fainting episodes.*

"How can we help you, Louisa?" Sababa asked.

"I have three problems." She said.

"What's the fourth?" He asked.

"I'm not sure you can make me better." She said. "I've seen a gastroenterologist, an endocrinologist, an immunologist, a neurologist, and a cardiologist, and none of them have helped me so far." Sababa turned to his apprentice.

"What's the question, Jamie?"

"The cause of her fainting episodes." He said.

"Of all the professions, physicians are the most proficient at not listening." Sababa said. "You heard what you thought she meant, rather than what she said. The question was whether we could make her better. Always remember—speak to listen, not listen to speak." But Louisa had three problems.

"What's the first issue, Louisa?" Sababa asked.

"Whenever I stand up, my heart races and I get dizzy and blurry vision and short of breath." She said. "My legs get heavy and I want to vomit. Sometimes I faint."

"And the second?" He asked.

"I get hives." She said. "Ever since the virus."

"You had a viral infection?"

"That's what Dr. Tarmac called it." Louisa rolled up her sleeves to show them a rash of round welts.

"When did that start?"

"About seven months ago now." She said.

"What's the third problem?" He asked.

"My joints hurt." She said. "And I have back pain." Sababa handed her a gown and pointed to the dressing room.

"Please." He said. "Down to your panties."

On physical examination, Louisa's heart rate jumped to 120 beats a minute in the first 10 minutes of a standing upright test, but her blood pressure didn't fall at all. Sababa bent his thumb back toward his wrist.

"Can you do that, Louisa?" The teacher bent her thumb far behind her wrist. All her joints showed excess mobility.

"Do you know Edie Sitwell, Louisa?" He asked.

"She's my cousin." Jamie let out a low whistle.

"What's going on?" She asked.

"You have three problems, Louisa." Sababa said. "But they're related. The first is something we call POTS, postural orthostatic tachycardia syndrome. The viral illness you had may have disrupted that part of your nervous system that controls certain functions. It's only had a name for it since two doctors at the Mayo clinic decided on one in 1993." Mercy interrupted to give Sababa a note. He wrote another and handed it to Jamie.

"The name for your rash is MCAS, or mast cell activation syndrome, and the third problem is Ehlers-Danlos syndrome Type III, an inherited connective tissue condition of joint laxity and chronic back pain. The combination is what we refer to as a trifecta, like predicting the first three horse race finishers or other grand events in their correct order."

"Some grand events." She said.

"Over 60% of POTS patients return to normal within five years. In the meantime, and for those that don't recover completely, there is treatment, to which over 90% respond." Sababa said. "Your rash should also resolve, and there are specific therapies for certain aspects of your Ehlers-Danlos syndrome. Jamie will fill you in on the details, organize more investigations, and dictate a note to Dr. Tarmac. I'm afraid I've been paged to the hospital emergency department, but tell Mercy I'll see you in follow-up in four weeks. Good luck. Jamie, meet me in the ER when you're finished here."

"I have a hockey game."

"What?"

"I have a hockey game."

"What?"

"I have a hockey game."

"What position?"

"Goalie."

"As you will be." Sababa said. "On call."

"But..."

"Eat. Sleep. Internal Medicine." Sababa twiddled an air cigar on his way out the door.

"I hear he's a legend." Louisa said. Jamie shook his head.

"He's not dead yet."

'He was just blinded by the light
Cut loose like a deuce, another runner in the night...'
Bruce Springstein, *Blinded by the Light*

Dr. Cliffy Carlton met Doctor Sababa bouncing through the automatic sliding frosted glass doors of the Harbour City Regional emergency room. It would be an understatement to acknowledge that, among the other more refined members, and many of the frequent patrons of his department, Cliffy enjoyed a somewhat more refreshing reputation. *Here's a prescription to get the hell out of my ER and go see your Family Doctor about this crap.* He loved the unconventional acronym. *GPO: Good for Parts Only... TSTL: Too Stupid to Live... PRATFO: Patient Reassured And Told to Fuck Off... GOMER: Get out of my emergency room... AMFYOYO: Adios... You're On Your Own.*

"You want me to see Brad Eggleston?" Sababa said.

"53-year-old conservation officer who presents with JAR syndrome." Cliffy handed him the chart.

"JAR syndrome?" An eyebrow ascended at an angle under Sababa's curls.

"Just Ain't Right." He said. "But you'll figure it out.'

"Indeed." Sababa said.

Cliffy pulled back the curtain of Bed #5. A sinewy middle-aged man in a blue uniform reclined uneasily. He had run out of fun.

"Brad, this is Doctor Sababa. He's too brilliant for introductions." Cliffy waved. "Gotta go. People to meet, preconceptions to maim and kill." Eggleston studied Sababa with not quite the same intensity that Sababa studied Eggleston.

"Tell me about it, Brad."

"Nothing much to tell." His voice was hoarse. "I've slowed down so much it scares me. Tired all the time. My legs are wobbly and I can't stand up or exert myself without getting dizzy. My pulse doesn't go up when it needs to, I don't sweat anymore, but I have to pee all the time. Dry mouth. Not good habits when you're chasing bears and cougars all day."

"Constipated?" Brad nodded.

"Morning erections?"

"Gone." Brad said. "All gone. My wife says I snore, and she keeps elbowing me to breathe."

"What brought you in tonight?" Sababa asked.

"I fainted." He said. "While loading a rifle." There was a melancholic pause.

"Have you seen a neurologist?" Sababa asked.

"Local guy named Oliver Lax." He said. "Diagnose. Adios."

"What was his diagnosis?"

"He missed that part." Brad shook his head.

"Did he do any tests?"

"Blood work." He said. "CT and MRI of my brain."

Sababa asked the officer if he could examine him.

"It would be a first." He said.

Brad's blood pressure dropped into his boots on standing. His muscles were stiff to move and his writing was small and spidery.

"I'll be back." Sababa said. He logged on to a nearby computer, pulled up Brad's head scans, and returned to his bedside.

"Nothing is certain." Sababa straightened his elbows on the bedrail. "Nothing is ever what it seems to be, but everything is exactly what it is."

"You have a name?" Asked the officer.

"Nothing is certain." He said.

"What have I got?"

"Something called Multiple System Atrophy." Sababa wrote it down for him. *MSA-P.*

"Doesn't sound good."

"Not good." Sababa said. "We used to call it Shy-Drager syndrome, but that doesn't matter. It's a rare degenerative disorder of the autonomic nervous system, the part of you that

112

regulates certain body functions. It's a kind of synucleinopathy, caused by an abnormal accumulation of α-synuclein protein, resulting in scarring of certain cells in the brain. It may be a viral protein called a prion. Wipes out your adrenalin and your nervous system response to it."

"Is it treatable?" He asked.

"Treatable." Sababa said. "Not curable. I'll start you on some medication to raise your blood pressure. You'll need to drink more water, add salt to your food, wear compression stockings while you're up, and tilt the head of your bed up ten degrees when you're not. No alcohol."

"I'd rather die."

"Careful what you wish for." Sababa said. "I'll arrange a swallowing assessment, refer you to a neurologist in Vancouver who has a special interest in this stuff, and prepare consults with a physiatrist, and physio and occupational and speech therapists."

"But I have to work."

"Wrap it up." Sababa said. "I'll write you a note. That's what disability insurance is for."

"How long have I got?"

"Nothing is certain." Sababa said.

"How long have I got?"

"Average lifespan after symptom onset is eight years." Sababa said. "But 20 per cent survive past twelve years, and there's mesenchymal stem cell therapy on the horizon."

"Not in this place." Brad said.

"Not in this place." Sababa agreed.

Jamie had arrived in the department. He was wearing a Vancouver Canucks jersey, and a frown.

"Each day as I go through the hospitals surrounded by younger men, they give me of their dreams and I give them of my experience, and I get the better of the exchange." Sababa said.

"Who said that?" Jamie asked.

"Dr. Will Mayo. You may have heard of him. Ran a medical lemonade stand down in Minnesota. Bet he never had a resident who dreamt he was a Vancouver Canuck."

"I can still make the game."

"Sorry." Sababa said. "The lifestyle you ordered is currently out of stock." As Jamie took off his jersey, Dr. Gung Ho approached the two men with a chart.

"Where do you hide a hundred-dollar bill from an emergency doc?" Jamie shrugged.

"In the past medical history." He said. "What you got, Gung?"

"Sherry Rogers." Gung handed Sababa a chart. "34-year-old single mother of five presenting today with a sudden onset of flank pain."

"Which side?" Jamie asked.

"Both sides." Gung said.

Sababa handed the chart off to Jamie.

"You deal with Dr. Ho's pain therapy session." He said. "I have some urgent business to attend to elsewhere."

"As opposed to emergent business here?" Jamie asked.

"Medicine is a science of uncertainty and an art of probability." Sababa said. "I'll be back before you're finished. Where we go depends on what we know, and what we know depends on where we go. You stay here."

"And you?"

"I have to see a man about a dog." He said.

Jamie was more than ready to present his case by the time Sababa returned to the ER.

"How's your dog?" Jamie asked.

"Worms." Sababa said. "What you got?"

"As Dr. Ho first introduced her." Jamie began. "34-year-old single mother of five children with a sudden onset of flank pain."

"How many fathers?" Sababa said.

"Why is that even relevant?" Jamie asked.

"Father to progeny ratio." He said. "It does tell us something. Though I have no idea what. Go on."

"No previous medical history." Jamie continued. "Exam demonstrated her blood pressure in the sky at 194/129 mmHg and lower abdominal tenderness, and abnormal whooshing sounds on both sides. Blood work showed only an elevated white blood cell count and reduced kidney function. Urine was abnormal, full of red and white blood cells. Abdominal CT scan revealed several wedge-shaped areas of dead kidney tissue, as well as multiple short dissections and beading of the supply arteries. Echocardiogram didn't show any clot or growths on the heart valves."

"You got a name?"

"Fibromuscular dysplasia." Jamie said. "Must be."

"When you have eliminated the impossible, whatever remains, however improbable, must be the truth. Let's go see her."

"Are you in a lot of pain, Sherry?" Sababa asked.

"Ms. Rogers please."

"Are you in a lot of pain, Ms. Rogers?" Sababa corrected himself.

"Yes, but I don't want anything artificial for it." She said.

"How about morphine?" Sababa said. "That's natural."

114

"I have these." She said, pulling a receptacle from her purse. *Strauss Heartdrops. We cure heart disease (since 1980). We solve cholesterol problems for life.*

Sababa tried to explain the genetic problem responsible for her presentation, but Sherry Rogers was resistant to any explanation of her condition that wasn't constructed in terms she considered correct.

"Why come to me?" Sababa said. "I'm only a humble superspecialist. You should see a homeopathic health-care provider."

"There aren't any alternative holistic emergency choices yet, for those of us who are more discriminating about our wellness options." She said.

"Alternative medicine is an alternative universe, so let me explain your radical recourses." Sababa said. "We can image the rest of your arteries to see if you have these abnormalities in other vascular beds, bring your blood pressure under control with medications that block certain pathways in your own unique renin-aldosterone-angiotensin system, add in some low dose acetylsalicylic acid bark from a willow tree, make sure you don't have any related conditions, surgically fix parts of your circulation if we need to, and screen your five kids for the disease."

"Or what?" She asked.

"Or else we remove all the warning labels, let the problem sort itself out, and allow Mother Nature to empty the gene pool and kill all the stupid people." He said. "Which door would you like?"

"I'll take door number one." She said. "Until I find better choices." Sababa nodded.

"One last thing, Ms. Snowflake." Sherry glared.

"You'll need to quit those cigarettes I can smell on your breath." He said. "They're no longer considered fashionable in either of the worlds we live in."

Sababa was about to ask Jamie to finish the casework on Ms. Rogers, but he perceived his resident's agitation.

"I can just make it." Jamie put his jersey back on.

"Go enjoy, my golden goalie." He said. "I'll take the rest of the night, but you're on intake first thing tomorrow morning."

"Done deal." Jamie said.

"Dunne deal." Sababa sat down to write out his consultation, and selected an old Huey Smith tune from his music library, on a secret drive hidden deep inside the hospital computer network.

'My heart just a-jumpin' up and down in vain

115

Shivers up and down my spine it's true
My face started sweatin' and it's all because of you
I get a high blood pressure 'cause I'm your man.'

He was finishing his orders when Michaela delivered him a hand-written note.

"Guy in Bed #9 is a physician." She said. "Dr. Jeremy Bentham. His wife is with him. He had an appointment to see you tomorrow but insists it couldn't wait." Sababa read the note. It was from Dr. Manfred Mann, a cardiologist in Victoria.

Dear Up Island Doc,
The ultrasound I performed in my echo lab on this family doctor this afternoon demonstrated that he has WHO Group 1 Idiopathic Pulmonary Hypertension. Please modify your clinical record accordingly. I've advised him that you will need to refer him to a cardiologist in Vancouver with a special interest in this condition.

Dr. Manfred Mann

Sababa pulled back the curtain of Bed #9.

"Hello, Jeremy. Daphne." He said. "To what do we owe this honour?"

"I fainted, Sab." He said. "I took my first dose of calcium channel blocker and fainted."

"He's been a bundle of nerves since his echo this afternoon." Daphne said. "Dr. Mann told Jeremy that he has a fatal disease."

"We all have a fatal disease." Sababa said. "What did he say?"

"He asked me if I was short of breath, tired, or had palpitations, fainting episodes, chest pain or leg swelling. I told him no."

"Jeremy uses his elliptical trainer for 30 minutes every day." Daphne added.

"I know this condition." Jeremy said. "It's a death sentence. No one knows what causes it and there's no known cure."

"But there is treatment." Sababa said.

"Oh sure." Jeremy's legs trembled on the bed. "If I want to have a continuous infusion of some medication until I can get a lung transplant."

"Hang on, Jeremy." Sababa said. "You're way ahead of yourself. And me."

"That would be a first." He said. Sababa unwrapped his Littman Master Cardiology black and brass stethoscope from around his neck.

"Let me into your heart." He grinned. Jeremy pulled open his gown. Sababa listened.

116

"I don't believe it." He said, placing his scope back where he found it.

"But it was there on the echo." Jeremy said.

"Sensitivity and specificity of 88% and 56%, respectively." Sababa said. "It isn't the gold standard. You have no symptoms, no reduction in your exercise tolerance, and a normal cardiac exam. I don't believe it."

"What's the gold standard?" Daphne asked.

"Right heart catheterization." Sababa said.

"Let's do it." Jeremy said.

"We will." Sababa said. "I'll have to bring you in as an outpatient."

"Let's do it tonight." Jeremy said. Sababa was going to say no, but he made the mistake of looking at Daphne, before picking up a handset. He found Marquis Shu Ying on the other end of it.

"Shu, can you spare a nurse for a few minutes? He asked.

"What for?" Shu inquired.

"I want to do a right heart cath here in the ER." He said.

"We don't do heart caths in the ER, Doctor Sababa." It was Michaela. She had overheard the conversation.

"A little impatience will spoil great plans." Shu said.

"He who asks is a fool for five minutes." Sababa said. "But he who does not ask remains a fool forever."

"Half an hour." Shu said. "Not a minute more. I'll send Mary down with a Swan-Ganz catheter."

"Doctor Sababa." It was Michaela. "You are not going to do this procedure in this emergency room.

"Tell me I can't." He said. "I will. Watch me." Michaela went for the phone.

Two things happened within the next five minutes. Mary came down from the Death Star with the tools Sababa ordered, and Michaela managed to find the Nursing Administrator on call. It was Big Nurse, the Grand Galactic Governess of Nightingales. She was less than amused by the news.

"Mildred Ratschet on line two, Doctor Sababa." Michaela shouted.

"Tell her I'm gowned and gloved." Sababa said.

"But you're not."

"Tell her anyway." Sababa gowned and gloved.

"She says now." Michaela bellowed. Sababa had fired a central port into Jeremy Bentham's right jugular vein and was threading in a balloon catheter while Mary activated and began to calibrate the monitor module.

"Tell her I'll call her back in five." Michaela stuttered on the phone.

"She says to make sure you do." Sababa read the numbers to Mary, as she wrote them down.

"Pulmonary artery pressure 17 mm Hg." Sababa said. "We're done here." He removed the catheter and central line. Mary positioned a dressing.

"Nursing supervisor on line one for you, Doctor Sababa." Cheri Sundae handed him the handset. There came a cacophony of agitated chirping.

"Hi, Mildred." Sababa said. "Can I call you back? I'm driving."

"You don't own a cell phone." She said.

"Oh, yeah." He said.

"Now listen carefully." She said. "That little stunt you pulled tonight, you will never, ever do that again. Do you understand?"

"I'll put it on my fucket list."

"Never, ever again." She was furious.

"There's no need to repeat yourself, Mildred." Sababa said. "I ignored you just fine the first time." A loud click from the other side of the galaxy followed. Sababa went back to speak to Jeremy and Daphne.

"You're fine." He said. "Your pulmonary pressures are normal."

"And Dr. Mann's echo?" Jeremy asked.

"He was blinded by the light." Sababa dictated his letter before he left the department.

Dear Down Island Doc,

The right heart cath I performed in my ER tonight demonstrated that this highly respected Family Physician has normal cardiac pressures. Please modify your clinical record accordingly. I've advised him that sometimes you need to kiss a few frogs before you get a prince.

Doctor Eleazar Sababa

'Forget about your worries and your strife...'
Terry Gilkyson, *The Bare Necessities*

It was after 3:00 a.m. when the low beams of Sababa's dimpled and dented Honda Civic swept around the last corner onto Westwood Lake Road, in the predawn rush to catch a few minutes of sleep, before it started all over again. It was on these last efforts to escape the serious illness of others of his species that the stocky savant gained his roadkill recipes. But sometimes you eat the alligator; sometimes the alligator eats you.

About 15,000 black bears lived on Vancouver Island. The five-hundred-pound boar that stood the width of the road was the biggest he had ever seen. Both mammals were in their own latent states of torpor, and no one was going anywhere fast. Sababa approached, stopped, and turned off his ignition. He looked out at the bear. He looked down at his dashboard. His better judgement decided to wait it out.

Sababa awoke to the blue and red flashing lights in his rearview mirror. Another kind of man-eater had turned on the interior light of her Ford Interceptor. She finished writing her ticket, exited her vehicle, and approached his driver-side door. As he rolled down his window, Veronica Marsden shone a full-beam flashlight into his eyes.

"What are you doing here, parked in the middle of the road?" She asked.

"Waiting for the bear." He said.

"What bear?" She asked. Sababa looked out his windshield. There was no bear.

"Blow into this tube." She said. Sababa blew.

"Lucky this time, Soy boy." She said.

Sababa thanked her for the ticket. In our deepest moments, we say the most inadequate things.

'And if you tell my heart
My achy breaky heart
He might blow up and kill this man.'
Billy Lee Cyrus, *Achy Breaky Heart*

Sababa's pager had a full-blown seizure on his way to the hospital the next morning. He took the corner of the iconic intersection of Dufferin Crescent at Dufferin Crescent on two wheels. A minute later he was flying through the wide automatic sliding frosted glass doors of the Harbour City Regional ER. His Colombian leather briefcase did a barrel roll through the air before coming to rest beside the computer on the consultants' desk. Cheri Sundae pointed towards the acute room.

"Other side, Doctor Sababa." He walked in on Drs. Jamie Dunne and Myles Capitaine by the bedside of a breathless middle-aged man in obvious discomfort. Two ER nurses stood beside them, awaiting instructions.

"How are you, Myles?"

"Living the dream."

"Myles, you gotta have a dream." Sababa said. "If you don't have a dream, how you gonna make a dream come true?" Everyone seemed glad to see him.

"What's going on?" He said.

"Rick Erscurve." Jamie said. "54-year-old marine researcher at the Pacific Biological Station who arrives with a forty-minute history of central chest pain radiating down both arms." No one was happy. One glance at the monitor gave it away.

"He's in complete heart block." Sababa rolled up his sleeves.

"Because of this." Jamie handed him an ECG. There were tombstones everywhere. The bottom of his heart was no longer talking to the top. "Anterior myocardial infarction with electrical conduction system failure. Whatever happened to the Golden Hour?" Myles and Jamie took Sababa aside.

"You've seen this movie before, Sab." Myles said. "It's not long before we'll have no electrical activation at all. What do we do first, put in a temporary pacemaker, or give him a clotbuster and hope for the best?"

"Hmmm... C'est un dilemme cornélien." Sababa said. "Classique."

"What?" Jamie and Myles asked together.

"You know who Pierre Corneille was?" Sababa translated. Both men shook their heads.

"One of the three great seventeenth-century French dramatists, along with Molière and Racine. Wrote a tragicomedy play called *Le Cid*, denounced for breaching morality and Aristotle's classic dramatic unities of time, place and action."

"And?"

"In the play, the protagonist, Rodrigue, is torn between two desires: the love of Chimène, or avenging his family, who had been wronged by Chimène's father." He said. "Rodrigue can either seek revenge and lose the love of his beloved, or renounce revenge and lose his honour, thus embodying the Cornelian Dilemma."

"What the hell does that have to do with Rick Erscurve?" Myles asked.

120

"Rick's heart is obliging us to choose between two courses of action, either of which can lead to a detrimental outcome." He said. "Putting in a pacemaker will restore his electrical conduction for a period of time, but may still be inadequate if his heart attack progresses, and will preclude us from giving him a clot buster because of the increased risk of bleeding from our first intervention. If we give him the clot buster and it doesn't result in the restoration of his electrical conduction, we'll still have to put in a pacemaker, with the same increased risk of bleeding we would have had in the first option. Your choice, Gentlemen. Love or honour."

"Jeezuz." Jamie said. "It's a choice between two evils, the horns of a dilemma, between the devil and the deep blue sea, between a rock and a hard place, from the frying pan into the fire."

"Incidit in scyllam cupiens vitare charybdim." Sababa had switched to Latin. *He runs into Scylla, wishing to avoid Charybdis.*

"Have I got a heart condition?" Rick asked.

"Something like that." Sababa said. "The main artery that supplies the front part of your heart decided to close shop without consulting any of your other organs. The lack of blood flow is affecting the electrical system."

"The His-Purkinje network in the ventricular wall?" Rick asked.

"Yeah, that one." Myles said.

"What are you going to do?" Rick winced in pain.

"We will give you a recombinant fibrin-specific plasminogen activator, something to dissolve the clot." Sababa said. "It's called Tenecteplase."

"Dina, fire up the TNK protocol." He said. "Regina, please get an external pacer and attach it to Mr. Erscurve's chest." The ER nurses bolted into action. Two minutes later, the top and bottom of Rick Erscurve's heart were speaking to each other again. A minute after that and the tombstones on the monitor dissolved into the electrical baseline of his ECG tracing. Rick's face resumed its normal colour.

"So fuck Death and all his little friends." Sababa picked up a handset.

"Cheri, get me the cath jockey on call in Victoria and an ACLS ambulance ground crew please." He said. "Rick, you're going on a road trip."

An hour later, Jamie and Sababa arrived on the floor one medical ward. It was nursing student day in the clinical teaching unit and the Vancouver Island University instructors were there in full revolutionary relish and regalia. Long gone were the days of nursing caps and uniforms. The young novitiates were now attired and perforated in pronouncements of personal preference, with transdermal metal and subdermal ink, and hair all colours of the rainbow. They sported badges supplied by the nursing union. *We can't stop caring.*

"If you can't stop something, it's an addiction, a runaway train, or both." Sababa said. "You know the difference between a VIU Nursing instructor and a bullet?" Jamie shook his head.

"A bullet can draw blood." He said. "A bullet moves fast." He was rolling. "A bullet only kills once. You can fire a bullet. Amber alert."

Amber was Sababa's least favorite nursing instructor, not because she wasn't a good nurse and role model because she wasn't, but because she was always trying to show how her little flock could embarrass or catch out or lord it over the physicians at Harbour City Regional. She called it team empowerment. Sababa called it a fascist distraction. She was hovering above the two physicians, with a student in tow.

"Ahem." Amber began her gambit. Her face was a brown paper bag, crinkled after all the candy was gone. Her eyes were small and mean.

"Why do nurses wear colors and doctors wear white, Jamie?" The resident shrugged his shrug.

"Because doctors are pure and good." Sababa said.

"This is Dreamcatcher." Amber's arm tried to encircle an ample amalgam of acne and attitude, pierced in metal and traced in tattoos, and chewing gum. "She has a question." Sababa smiled.

"All the ward's a stage." Sababa said. "What can we possibly help you with, Dreamcatcher?" He may have meant it in many ways.

"Well, I'm like taking care of our client, Mr. Phillips, today." She said. Sababa's face tinted towards crimson. "And like I know that he came in with chest pain."

"Yes." Sababa said. "That's correct."

"Well, I see you're like sending him home today on Nexium." She continued.

"Yes." He said. "He has gastroesophageal reflux, and the medication is a proton pump inhibitor that will reduce the production of hydrochloric acid in his stomach."

"Well, I've been like reading about this chemical." Dreamcatcher closed in for the kill. "And it says that it can like cause chest pain." Sababa smashed his forehead on his hands. There was the smell of ozone.

"Well, Dreamcatcher." He said. "The rare side effect of a therapy does not prevent its use to treat a disease, even if the presenting symptom is the same as the rare side effect. It's an illusory correlation called *Post hoc ergo propter hoc*, a logical fallacy, an assumptive error of causation. If the rooster crows immediately before sunrise, it doesn't immediately follow that the rooster caused the sun to rise." Dreamcatcher was as dumbfounded as Amber was apoplectic.

"Two more little tidbits." He said. "There are only two professions with clients, the legal one and the oldest one, and I'm assuming you are not a member of either. Clients have a choice. Our patients, in their captivity to our ministrations, do not."

"That's only one tidbit." Amber fumed. "What's the other?"

"Sometimes young sloths grab their own arms, thinking they're tree branches."

'If ands and buts were candy and nuts,
Then every day would be Christmas.'
Don Meredith

We can forgive the casual reader for assuming that the results of Sababa's deliberations were always optimal and unconditional. True, he knew all the 'ands and buts' of a case. It was the 'ifs' that threatened to trip him up:

If you theorize before the facts, you will make mistakes. If a condition you didn't know a patient had disappeared, did you miss it? If you don't try, can you still fail? If what you're doing is working, keep doing it. If what you're doing is not working, stop doing it. If you don't know what you're doing, do nothing. If you are looking for a safe space, this isn't it.

If you carry your specialty training too far, uneducated cults slip in. If you fix your eyes on details and neglect important things, your spirit will become bewildered, and victory will escape you. If you are first, you are first. If you are second, you are nothing. If you can keep your head when all about you are losing theirs and blaming it on you...

If you ever lose Jane, the next thing you will lose will be your soul. No ifs, ands, or buts.

The good physician treats the disease. The great physician treats the patient who has the disease.

Sam McGee had no more emergency episodes of sky-high blood pressure after he changed his Stephenson Lookout B&B to the Bear Bottom Backpackers and Coffeehouse.

Stephen Dedalus experienced no further fainting episodes after his pacemaker procedure and still runs Parks and Recreation work crews throughout Harbour City's green spaces.

Aurora Leigh and her new boyfriend terrorize the slopes of Mount Washington without her worrying about falling from the ski lifts. Jerome Van Conn is receiving chemotherapy for his lung cancer. His blood pressure is normal, but he misses his Dutch double licorice drops.

Louisa Musgrove's POTS problem and hives have resolved, but she still has back and joint pain after a long day teaching school. Brad Eggleston passed away in his sleep.

Sherry Rogers quit smoking the day she met Doctor Sababa. Her complaint to the College of Physicians and Surgeons about his bedside manner resulted in an admonition that, in the future, he must not refer to his patients as 'snowflakes.' Her kidney function returned to normal, but her high blood pressure still required treatment. She is looking forward to having another baby, just as soon as she can get off Sababa's evil poisons. Dr. Jeremy Bentham is back on his treadmill in the office and back on his elliptical at home.

Rick Erscure had a successful angioplasty. He received the Order of Canada for his research on humpback cardiovascular physiology.

And the other male black bear that Brad Eggleston wondered about, the one Sababa stopped his dimpled and dented Honda for in the middle of the night? He woke Sababa's dog, Shiva, now cured of her worm infestation, at five o'clock one morning. The stocky savant opened his French doors to find the cause of the barking, and the biggest boar he had ever seen. Jane called out from behind him.

"What is it, a bear?" She was grumpy from having her sleep interrupted.

"Yep." Sababa said.

"What are you going to do about it?" She asked.

"Call animal control, I guess." He dialed a number and woke the voice that answered it.

"Conservation Officer Bradshaw." Said the voice. "What's the problem?"

"There's a bear in my backyard." Sababa looked at the number he had dialed. It began with 1-800. "Wait a minute. Where are you?"

"Victoria." Bradshaw said.

"Fat lot of good you'll do me down there." Sababa said. "What am I supposed to do?"

"Tell it to go away." The officer hung up.

"What did he say?" Jane asked.

"He said I should tell it to go away." Sababa said.

"So what are you going to do?" Sababa went out on his deck.

"Go away." He said. The 500-pound bear jumped the fence and shuffled off down the boardwalk towards the parking lot at the public beach. The first group of early morning joggers would meet it halfway. The rendezvous would squander the longevity they had gained by the exercise. *Can you dance with the devil in the pale moonlight?*

Sababa fell back to sleep, smiling.

4. The Case of the Parthian Shot

'Life is not measured by the number of breaths we take,
but by the moments that take our breath away.'

Anon

The locals called it the Pineapple Express, the heavy warm spring rains that roll in from the Hawaiian Islands. Its coastal collision with the Great Bear Rainforest smelled of salt spray and mountain lions and untamed wilderness. The earth was heavy with snowmelt and water from the sky.

She drove through a grey shroud of muted mist and dark diffusion, able to see only as far as her headlights. It was like her marriage, a torch that gleamed through the gloom without dispelling it. But she had made the whole trip that way in the silence. The fog was a cage without a key.

It had been after midnight when Bernadine Soulier began her journey from Nanoose back to Honeymoon Bay in the Cowichan. She had visited an old school friend, Elizabeth Barnes, for some comfort talk. Her husband was an avid golfer and raconteur, and Bernadine was feeling like Tiger Wood's first wife. The incision under her right breast still nagged like a toothache.

Tragedy is not black and white. Most consequential choices involve shades of gray, suspended in murky bewilderment. The haze made everything larger and more grotesque than it was. There were foghorns.

The mist morphed back into a downpour as she crossed into Lantzville. Bernadine drove along Rumming Road, into her own ghost story. She had no way of knowing that the flooding had already closed the main highway. Creeks had turned into rushing rivers; roads had turned into lakes. It even played on her radio. *Hard rain gonna fall.*

In her rearview mirror, Bernadine saw the road wash out behind her. She floored her accelerator trying to outrun it, but the disappearing edge caught up to her too fast. The mudslide that washed away what had been Rumming Road flipped her backwards and upside-down, twenty-five metres into the new hole it had made in the planet's surface. The windshield and windows exploded outwards as her vehicle crash-landed hard on its roof. Tumbling rocks and plummeting waterfalls pummeled and smashed its vulnerable belly. The wreck continued to slide, headlights illuminating its course, gliding toward the ocean, slowed only by the water and dirt still pouring through the windows.

Bernadine lay upside down, dazed inside her still-fastened seatbelt. She felt the impact of every boulder that bombarded and battered her undercarriage, each impact slipping her caged terror further toward the waves far below. Through the roar of the deluge, she could make out the sound of approaching sirens. Minutes later, there were kaleidoscopic strobes and flashlight beams shining in the mud and water swirling around her vehicle. Dr. Nicholas Rivera, manager of Harbour City Search and Rescue, dropped off a rope ladder beside her. Dodging the rocks falling around him, he helped Bernadine wriggle out of the driver side window and hooked her to a harness. He watched the rope system haul her up to the ambulance crew waiting at the top, as her car slid off out of the crevasse, down the mudslide and into the sea.

'Yet who would have thought the old man
to have had so much blood in him?'
William Shakespeare, *Macbeth V.1. 44-45*

The head office of Hub Geotechnical Incorporated was up the street from the Great National Land Building. Harewood Mines, its chief engineer, had a view of the harbour from his office. The thirty years he had worked for the company had seen explosive growth in the need for his abilities. New earthquake regulations in an unprecedented construction boom, the resurgence in mining, and a professorial appointment in a nascent department at Vancouver Island University had kept Harewood more than occupied. Gazing out his window at the fishing boats in the harbour fog, he turned on his Bose radio and felt the warmth inside.

Awaken the canoes, powwows and pale faces... This is BC Bud, for CNDN Coast Salish radio, 101.3 FM on your Home and Native Band... You might be from Harbour City if you know all the seasons: Almost Winter, Winter, Still Raining, Road Construction, and Raining Again...

Harewood's inside got warmer as he downloaded his geotech analysis for the new RV development planned for up at the lake. There had been some opposition from some neighbourhood residents, but that's what the high-priced lawyers were for.

You might be from Harbour City if you do not understand humidity without precipitation, you know what 'light-mist rain' means, you think that people who use umbrellas are either tourists or wimps, and you never go camping without waterproof matches and a poncho...

He had calculated the thickness of the asphalt and the resultant hydrocarbon runoff from the twelve-acre parking lot into the lake. There was no way to prevent that, but he could play with the topography so the drainage would occur too fast to measure. Mallory Weiss, the paving contractor, should have provided his quote two days ago. Harewood made a note to remind him.

You might be from Harbour City if you think if it has no snow, it is not a real mountain, and if you notice it's 'out' when it's a pretty day and you can actually see it...

The warmth inside rose higher into his chest and began to poke at the edges of his awareness of it.

You might be from Harbour City if you carry jumper cables in your car and your wife knows how to use them...

Harewood had bought the acreage four months ago through Harbour City Realty. Linley Valley was a silent partner and had manoeuvred the asking price into roadkill range. It was too bad about his heart attack. They had made a fortune from the timber alone.

You might be from Harbour City if you can wear Gore-tex as business casual...

The warmth inside Harewood Mine's chest roared into fever, cut off his breathing, and stabbed at his ribs. His heart tried to pound itself out of his chest. From out of his open mouth a plume of bright red blood streaked across the vastness of his white wool carpet.

You might be from Harbour City if you buy new sunglasses every year because you can't find the old ones after such a long time...

He heard the radio humming to itself. Its tiny lights swam in circles. It was the last thing he remembered.

'Well, won't you lend your lungs to me?
          Mine are collapsing
          Plant my feet and bitterly breathe
          Up the time that's passing.
          Breath I'll take and breath I'll give...'
          Steve Earle, *Lungs*

The day before the mudslides and the collapse of Harewood Mines, Sababa awoke to his pager, in a fog of his own, from a dream not altogether mood and not quite weather, uncertain of its destination. It was still early, but it was Jamie.
"What you got?" He asked.
"Dr. Capitaine wants us to see a man that Dr. Benway just scoped." Jamie said.
"Why doesn't he get Buddy to come back and reassess his patient?"
"He tried." Jamie was trying to be tactful. "Dr. Benway told Myles to get you to see him."
"He must have an endoscopy clinic." Sababa said. "Rather spend the morning looking up some friends."

"He does." Jamie said.

"It's difficult to describe these slashers sometimes." Sababa mused. "Are they little boys unaccustomed to being told 'no,' or is it the 'god-complex' part? Hard to choose, they're both so good... I'll be there in twenty."

A short time later, Sababa met Jamie and Myles in the ER.

"How are you, Myles?" He asked.

"Living the dream."

"Harbour City Regional is a magical poetic place full of promise, excitement, and surprises, where all your dreams can come true." He said. "What did Buddy Benway say?"

"The surgeon is the captain of the ship." Dr. Capitaine chortled. "Although this morning he would rather be a Rear Admiral."

"Where do you hide a hundred-dollar bill from a general surgeon?" Myles and Jamie shrugged.

"In the patient's room." He said. "Tell me the story."

"Mallory Weiss in Bed #6." Jamie began. "52-year-old paving contractor who developed continuous violent hiccups two days ago, followed by an upset stomach and blood-stained vomiting last night. No prior history of anything, although he thinks he may have had a slight problem swallowing for a couple of weeks prior. Nothing on initial exam. I consulted Dr. Benway, and he performed an upper GI endoscopy around six a.m."

"Did he find anything? Bleeding? Did he take any biopsies?" Sababa asked.

"None of the above." Myles said. "But he blew in a lot of air."

"Ah, insufflation." Sababa said. "Last resort and benediction of the blind endoscopist. And then?"

"After the procedure, a few minutes ago, Mr. Weiss complained of shortness of breath and neck pain." Myles threw a chest x-ray up on the nearest viewer. "And then we got this."

Sababa caught the attention of a favorite nurse.

"Dina, can you help us set up for a chest tube in Bed #6?" He said. "#24 French, left side. We'll be there when you're ready."

"Large pneumothorax on the left." Jamie said. "And all these tiny air bubbles in the soft tissues of the chest and mediastinum."

"And thickening of the gastric fundus and junction, with air tracking posterior to the crus of the diaphragm." Sababa said. "Buddy must have perforated his esophagus. And here I thought the only weapon with which a patient could immediately retaliate upon an incompetent surgeon was hemorrhage. Let's go see him and fix this fustercluck."

Myles made the introductions. Sababa explained the problem and the need for a chest tube to Mallory Weiss, while Jamie

130

pressed on the skin of the man's neck and chest. There was a popping sound, like bubble wrap.

"Subcutaneous emphysema." Sababa said. "I know it's addictive, but you can stop now, Jamie." Dina had finished setting up the tray and the underwater seal to which Sababa would attach the chest tube. The stocky savant selected a Sade tune from his music library, on a secret drive hidden deep inside the hospital computer network. *No need to ask, he's a smooth operator... smooth operator, smooth operator...*

The men gowned and gloved and, after painting the space between two of Mallory's left ribs with an iodinated disinfectant solution, Sababa placed a series of sterile drapes around the field he would insert the tube through.

"What do you call the surgical drape separating the patient from the surgeon, Mallory?"

"Dunno." He said.

"The blood-brain barrier." Sababa froze the skin between the two ribs with 2% Xylocaine, and infiltrated the local anesthetic deeper, into the pleural lining on the inside of the chest wall.

"So why did this happen?" Mallory asked. Sababa used a scalpel blade to make an incision wide enough, and then expanded the opening with his finger to allow the insertion of the chest tube.

"It's called Boerhaave Syndrome." Sababa said. "Named after the Dutchman that first described it in 1724. In your case, accidental barotrauma from Dr. Benway's procedure may have caused it. But your original problem likely started as a small tear at the junction of your stomach and esophagus from the retching."

"And why did I have that?" Mallory asked. Sababa unsheathed the chest tube from its scabbard, slipped it into the space between the chest wall and the collapsed lung, and attached it to the underwater seal drain.

"Well, that's the real question, isn't it?" He said. "To answer it, I need to scope you again."

"No way." Mallory said. " There is no chance of my ever going through that again."

"Well, that presents a problem." Sababa said. "Because we need to know. Unfortunately, Dr. Benway didn't take any biopsies of your esophagus in his enthusiasm to take part in its perforation."

"Don't you have any other way of finding out?"

"We have a white blood cell count that shows a small increase in some pink staining leukocytes called eosinophils." Sababa said. "That may be a clue, but it ain't the whole enchilada. We need tissue from your food pipe."

"I'm not having another scope." Mallory was adamant.

"Hmmm... I may have another way." Sababa reached deep into his Colombian leather briefcase and pulled out a tiny robot still sealed in its original packaging. "But it's not legal."

"What is it?" Mallory asked.

"Meet Piehole Pete." He said. "It's a MASCE, a magnet-actuated soft capsule endoscope, a camera that can take biopsies on the voyage through your gut. Supposed to work like a hot damn."

"Supposed to?"

"I haven't tried it yet." Sababa admitted.

"How does it operate?" Mallory asked.

"It has this delivery chamber that releases hundreds of tiny untethered thermosensitive self-folding Micro-Grippers which take small biopsies and retrieves them with a wet adhesive patch on the bottom of the MASCE. They look like sharp miniature ninja *shuriken* star-shaped discs."

"Does it retrieve all the little ninja stars all the time?" Mallory asked.

"It's supposed to."

"Supposed to?"

"I told you." Sababa said. "I haven't tried it yet."

"Doesn't it need approval from the Medical Advisory Committee?" Michaela had been eavesdropping.

"Too small for that, Michaela." Sababa said. "Nobody would ever know unless somebody told them, although we do have a meeting tonight."

"Let's do it." Mallory said.

"We shouldn't until your lung reinflates and the hole in your esophagus heals over." Sababa put the drone back in his Colombian leather briefcase, beside his Black Book of Remedies. "Tell you what. Let's admit you to Dr. Benway's ward, organize more blood work, a gastrograffin swallow, CT scan of your chest and when no one's looking you can try out Piehole Pete in a few days' time." Mallory Weiss nodded his approval.

"God willin' and the creek don't rise." Sababa said. Cheri Sundae waved at him from behind her polycarbonate window.

"It's Dr. Troy in the OR." She said. "He says he needs you to see a patient there." Sababa looked at Jamie.

"I'm on it." He said.

'This life is filled with hurt

Dr. Christian 'Pretty Boy' Troy was the only plastic surgeon at Harbour City Regional. His main source of patient referrals derived from his looking younger than his age, although his appearance (and behaviour) hovered somewhere between Doogie Howser and Ted Bundy.

"Is he a good doctor?" One of Sababa's patients once asked.

"It's too early to tell." He said. Pretty Boy's specialty was gender-reaffirming surgery, something he called the 'Mommy Makeover,' breast implants combined with a tummy tuck and liposuction. It was during one of these that Sababa got the call. Jamie paged him from Operating Room #3.

"Bernadine Soulier." He said. "44-year-old homemaker admitted for one of Dr. Troy's plastic transmogrifications. He made an incision under her right breast, and she won't stop bleeding from it."

"What does her coagulation profile look like?" Sababa asked.

"Her PT is normal." Jamie said. "But her PTT is prolonged. No one noticed."

"What's her blood group?"

"Type O." Jamie said.

"She likely has Von Willebrand disease, Jamie." He said. "Type 1 or some subtype of Type 2. Not Type 3 nor Pseudo nor Hemophilia A. Give her 600 IU of Humate P, not purified monoclonal or recombinant factor VIII concentrates because they don't contain enough vWF, and sponge some topical rhThrombin to the wound before they apply a pressure dressing. I'll be up shortly."

"Dr. Troy wants to know if he can continue with his surgery."

"Tell him all bleeding stops, eventually." Sababa said. "That should shut it down for today." Several minutes later, a gowned and garbed Doctor Sababa bounded into OR #3.

"Where do you hide a hundred-dollar bill from a plastic surgeon?" Jamie shrugged.

"You can't hide a hundred-dollar bill from a plastic surgeon." Sababa said. "You do remember that women also bleed, don't you Christian?"

"You sure I can't continue, Sababa?" Pretty Boy said.

"Not unless she's a Doberman Pinscher, if you want to keep your license intact and the bottom feeding away." He said. "You just cut into a human with an abnormal coagulation profile. Last

133

time I checked, it was still illegal to perform an autopsy on a living person."

"What's going on here, Sababa?" Pretty Boy was sweating behind his mask.

"It may be Von Willebrand disease, but nothing is certain. After the dust settles on her wound and her hemostasis returns to whatever is normal for her, she'll need a proper history and physical exam, repeat complete blood count, PT and PTT, thrombin time, fibrinogen level, a vWF antigen assay, a glycoprotein Ib binding assay, ristocetin cofactor activity, and Factor VIII levels. She may also need as many as a dozen other studies. Then, and only then, once we've figured out the name of this thing, will we know what to give her preoperatively, so you can continue your little magic show."

The sound of clapping arrived from the head of the bed. It was coming from the anesthetist, Dr. Banjo Paterson.

"I see you're still adhering to the ABCs of your trade, Banjo." Sababa said. "Airway, breakfast, crossword, donut, expedia.com." Banjo grinned and blew the icing sugar off his fingers.

'My brain says I'm receiving pain
A lack of oxygen from my life support
My iron lung.'
Radiohead, My Iron Lung

Sababa's pager went off in Jamie's pocket. It was Floor 5.

"Hillo? Hostess?"

"It's Dr. Dunne." Jamie said.

"Doctor Sababa's aso shit?"

"Yes, Sophia." Jamie said. "Do you have a problem?"

"Marta Lillard." Sophia answered. "She was udmeetted by Doctor Clippy Carlton lust ebening."

"And?"

"Chicken-nut bread." Sophia said.

"What?" Jamie didn't understand.

"Chicken-nut bread." Sophia repeated herself.

Sababa asked Jamie what the problem was.

"Chicken-nut bread?" Jamie said.

"She cannot breathe." Sababa said. "Let's go." They took the stairs two at a time.

134

"Ah, Sophia, one of the four prides of the Philippines." Sababa said.

"What are the other three?" Jamie asked. Sababa opened his hand towards Sophia.

"Pride fish. Pride chicken. Pride rice." She beamed. "Palo me queeklee." She handed Jamie the patient's chart.

Inside the second last room was a young woman propping herself up on extended arms, both hands white-knuckled on the bed rails. Her breathing came in short gasps, and there was a radial spray of bright red blood spattering her linen.

"Pipty Shades ob Grey." Observed the head nurse. "Marta, dees ees Doctor Sababa, choo-tore to Ductor Dunne here. He is a UBC medicule grad-waite.

"Page respiratory, Sophia." Sababa examined the patient while Jamie retook her vital signs. "Call for a portable chest film and ECG stat. Let's get her on some oxygen by nasal cannula at 3L/minute." He continued to refine his orders as he better determined the situation, and the data rolled in. Sophia conveyed them to her RNs.

"More peen, pibe meeleegrums anak... one bucks tee-shoes... fresh bed shits... electric pun... Ees eet carjack, Doctor Sababa?" She asked.

"No, Sophia." Sababa looked at the portable chest x-ray his resident held up against the window. "It's pulmonary. What did Cliffy write in the chart, Jamie?"

"27-year-old Landlubber Pub waitress with relapsing episodes of fever spikes accompanied by general fatigue, treated with oral antibiotics by her family doctor with poor clinical response. Nonsmoker with no exposure to illicit drugs, environmental or occupational allergens, toxic fumes, chemicals, or dust."

"She deedn't cutch da plew?" Sophia asked.

"No flu Sophia." Sababa said. "Cliffy's exam?"

"Normal except for mild end-inspiratory crackles in the bottom of both lungs."

"They're not mild today." Sababa said. "Labs?"

"Iron deficiency anemia." Jamie said. "Chest x-ray showed infiltrates in both lung bases. Pulmonary function test last week showed reduced diffusing capacity. High-resolution CT scan at the same time showed areas of alveolar hemorrhage. She has an appointment to see our respirologist, Dr. Hyde, for a bronchoscopy."

"Not dut mun-yak." Sophia blurted. Martha Lillard's breathlessness was improving all by itself, enough to pose questions. Her oxygen saturation had returned to normal.

"What is this?" She asked Jamie. He looked at Sababa.

"Nothing is certain." Sababa said. "But you have the triad of coughing up blood, diffuse lung infiltrates on your chest imaging studies, and iron deficiency anemia. With your other blood work being normal, and if Dr. Hyde's investigations are confirmative, you may have a condition we call Idiopathic Pulmonary Hemosiderosis."

"What causes it?" Martha asked.

"That's what idiopathic means." Sababa said. "We don't know. We also used to refer to it as 'Iron Lung.'"

"Can you fix it?"

"We do have treatment." He said. "But I'd like to see the other investigations performed before we start them." Sophia was on a new high.

"I um berry huppy." She said. "What a the prince prom bee-pore und up-ter. She hus her boys buck. She weel rice a-bub as a sir bye bore. Ay-bree-buddy weel let you slip now, Marta. I weel watts her berry care-pullee, Doctor Sababa."

"Let's get to the office, Jamie." Sababa said. "We have a busy clinic this afternoon."

"No offense, but..." Jamie said.

"You started that sentence with no offense." Sababa said. "That doesn't mean you can end it with whatever you want."

"Are you penis, Ductor Dunne?" Sophia asked.

"Sometimes he's a penis, Sophia." Sababa said. "Sometimes."

'A watermelon that ⚕ ⚕ ⚕ breaks open by itself tastes better than one cut with a knife.'

Hualing Nieh Engle

Under the *No Fruit Loops* sign above her counter, Mercy was typing furiously.

"It's clotting and bleeding week, Boss." She said between flying finger flurries.

"The depths of misery are never below the depths of Mercy." Sababa said. Jamie had given up trying.

"Here's the one you need to respond to first." She said, pushing a letter across the divide. It was already opened, but that was what Mercy did.

Dear Sir or Madam,
Job Application: Medical Office Assistant
Upon scrutinizing your add for the position above, I am compelled to send you my resume as an application for the same.

136

I am a recent graduate with a Bachelor of Arts degree accompanying an interesting combination of a double major in Psychology and Business Management. I have a total of more than 18 months working in office, administration and customer service. I am confident that I possess both the business savvy and human relations skills for the position. I also believe that my services could not go to a better organization or towards a better cause.

It is my personal testament that I thrive in challenging and versatile environments and am an apt pupil of any milieu. This is exemplified by my ability to conquer new horizons and explore new roles, cultures, countries and organizations from a very young age. In essence, I will bring unique integrity and diversity to any work culture. Hence, I invite you to peruse my resume for details. Reference list and a copy of reference letter is available on request.

Please contact me at your convenience for an opportunity to assess each other at a more personal level. A favorable and early response on your part would greatly be appreciated.

Sincerely yours,

Dominica Perkins

"I guess you're fired, Mercy." Sababa said. "She can start tomorrow." He felt the burn through his back as he and Jamie retreated to his office. He turned around only long enough to tell her he hadn't advertised for a new medical office assistant.

"I never placed an advertisement. She made it up." He said, turning his attention back to his protégé.

"You take the first patient, Jamie. I need to catch up on some paperwork. Come and get me when you're penis."

Sababa made a priority out of reviewing the vast number of referrals that arrived on Mercy's desk every day. Most could wait a few weeks if they had to. *Diagnosis: multimedical... If you cannot see this chap within a week, I am going to rip out all your vines and run off with your wife... I've arranged for him to start detrimentally decreasing doses of Warfarin...* He should have seen a few in the ER, yesterday. *Help... TSH < 0.1 Free T4 86.6 Anything worth treating?... Stay on white sheets... pneumonia getting worse...*

Some could wait forever. *I pretended to run a battery of tests and they came back positive for hypochondria... Would you kindly see this 56-year-old male who is awaiting rehab? He is in denial. He works for the Central Vancouver Island Health Authority and has been using the company credit card for alcohol purchases. Would you consider him for a stress test?... Wife cancelled appointment as this would cost them half a tank of gas... Sab, You told me Mr. Sanderson died last week, so I cancelled his appointment. He is here now. Thanks.*

Jamie appeared in his doorway.

"What you got?" Sababa asked.

"Henri Mygold." He began. "37-year-old Canadian Tire auto parts specialist referred in by Dr. Ho for a one-day history of sudden chest pain. No cardiovascular risk factors, and normal ECG, echo, and chest x-ray. Exam shows a swollen, red, lumpy, tender cord over the front of his chest wall. Come, I'll show you." Jamie introduced Sababa to Henri Mygold, still without his shirt again from his examination.

"1939." Sababa said.

"1939?" Jamie asked.

"1939." Sababa rolled the rubber ribbon with his fingers. "The year a Parisian surgeon gave his name to the condition. Mondor's disease."

"What is it?" Henri asked.

"It's thrombophlebitis, a blood clot of the superficial veins of the anterior chest wall." Sababa said. "You're a lucky man, Mr. Mygold."

"How so?"

"Sometimes it involves the dorsal vein of the penis." He said.

"What's the treatment?" Henri asked.

"Warm compresses, ibuprofen, and 4 weeks of waiting for it to go away." Henri shook Sababa's hand far too much as he left. Mercy stuck her head into the residents' room.

"Sab, there's a man out here who thinks he's invisible."

"Tell him I can't see him." He said. "Jamie, there's one more patient, an urgent referral from Drs. Benway and Rivera, in the waiting room. Let me know when you're finished. I'll be in my office reviewing some lab reports."

Sputum culture: normal genital flora?!... Holter Diary Activity: sex, Symptoms: great!... C Spine Partial Exam: Incomplete views were obtained as the patient died prior to completion of the exam. No gross abnormalities were seen... Steven Smith: Normal obstetrical ultrasound...

"Ready, Effendi." Jamie said.

"What have you got?"

"Herbert Hancock." Jamie said. "56-year-old Fireman First Responder referred by Dr. Nicholas Rivera for longstanding black and bright red blood per rectum and iron deficiency anemia. Dr. Buddy Benway scoped him last week and found a watermelon stomach."

"A what?" Herbert asked.

"It's also called GAVE." Sababa said. "Gastric antral vascular ectasia." When Dr. Benway retroflexed his endoscope he saw streaky long red dilated blood vessels that look like the skin markings of a watermelon."

"What causes it?" Herbert asked.

"No one knows." Sababa said. "Although it is associated with Vitamin B12 deficiency, connective tissue diseases, liver and kidney problems."

"Can you make it go away?"

"To some extent." Sababa said. "Dr. Benway ablated some of the vessels with electrocautery, but there are other surgical procedures if it becomes more of a nuisance. You'll need to take iron and a proton pump inhibitor, and we'll need to do more blood work. Make an appointment with Mercy for me to see you in eight weeks."

"Dr. Benway says I'll need him to rescope me every six months." Herbert said. Sababa pulled Piehole Pete out of his Colombian leather bag.

"Buddy has to continue to make the payments on his brand new jet black Jaguar, but we can make it less likely for him to get flecks of your vital organs all over the upholstery."

'There's too many people
Making too many problems
And not much love to go round
Can't you see
This is a land of confusion.'
Genesis, *Land of Confusion*

Sababa already had two consults waiting for him in the Harbour City Regional ER when he left his office, but he had to send Jamie ahead to see them first. Once a month, there occurred a collision (or a collusion, depending on the character and mood of the participants) between the medical staff and the health authority bureaucrats. They held the Medical Advisory Committee meeting in the Boardroom, that same Oracle of Oversight, that identical morgue of ambition, in which Dr. Zaias chaired his Department of Medicine meetings. The only differences were that the light green-yellow padded walls were fuzzier from the static electricity, the white stippled acoustic tile ceiling worked harder to absorb the screams of the defeated, and the Mayline chairs fabric seats running the length of the long teak conference table held fatter asses, and more of them. The particulate debris lurking under the table on the claret pile carpet became even more agitated.

139

New graffiti marred the melamine whiteboard on an easel at the far end of the room.

$$x = \frac{Power}{(Knowledge + Accountability)}$$

where $x_{ideal} = 1$,
$x_{bureaucrat} = $ Infinity, and
$x_{physician} = 0$

Jamie had written it out correctly. It was Sababa's Equation of Medical-Bureaucratic Inequity. The ideal ratio of power to knowledge and accountability for any therapeutic intervention was unity, just enough control, balanced off by an appropriate amount of knowledge and accountability; but the bureaucratic ratio was infinite, not so much because they enjoyed limitless authority (although they did) but more because, as Sababa was always quick to remind them, they had no knowledge and no accountability. The physician ratio was zero, not so much because they had maximal expertise and responsibility (although they did), but because they had little systemic authority.

The committee was made up of medical staff departmental representatives—Jules Martino from Surgery, Juan Leyblanca from Pathology, Mako Brisk from Radiology, Trace Pangloss from Emergency, Banjo Paterson from Anesthesia, and Eleazar Sababa from Internal Medicine; and courtiers from the Palace of Administration, and all their urbane appurtenances—Malcolm Canmore, the Chief Hospital Administrator of the silk ties, linen handkerchiefs, silver cuff-links, manicured fingernails, and platinum pens, Foster Concord, the 'innovative' CEO of the Central Vancouver Island Health Region, Big Nurse Mildred Ratschet, the Grand Galactic Governess of Nightingales, sporting her string of cultured natural pearls, and a gaggle of other suits and pantsuits. They would collaborate to achieve the magnetic goals that drew their obscene destinies together, always ready and willing to judge and bludgeon the independent outsider.

But the committee chairperson, the most prepotent master of control, was a diminutive general practitioner named Dr. Petronilla de Meath, a Napoleanna bone apart, a harpy hag of a harridan henpecking harassment.

"Who's the chairperson?" Asked a visiting dignitary.

"Our new Chief of Staff." Sababa said. "She's a doctor."

"Oh? Which kind?"

"Witch."

140

"Which which?"

"Which what?"

"Which doctor?"

"Right." Sababa said. He and Petronilla were natural foes, and the Good Doctor preferred it that way. His euphemism for her enchantment with 'Managed Care' was to refer to it as 'Damaged Care.' Petronilla accused the Internists of being 'dysfunctional,' despite Sababa's claim to have put the fun back into it. "Something wicked this way comes." He muttered under his breath.

Petronilla picked up a handset from the multifunction business class conference digital phone console and dialled zero.

"Lana, can you announce the beginning of the Medical Advisory meeting?" The hospital switchboard operator's Big Voice broadcast the assembly overhead.

Petronilla called the council to order and requested approval of the previous meeting's minutes. A cacophony of grunts echoed around the room.

"I've tabled the old business." She said. "So we can hear a progress report from Foster Concord, the 'innovative' CEO of the CVIHR. Foster, please proceed." The innovator rose to the occasion and called for the first slide.

"Thank you for that excellent introduction, Petronilla." He said. "Let me begin by thanking all of you for your patience in the last six months since the new Regional Board's inception, while we were working hard to formulate our Vision and Mission Statements." The first slide was a quote from the new authority's internal newsletter.

CEO Health Matters: The Need for a New Approach

Foster Concord, our Chief Executive Officer, has reiterated the need for innovative thinking and process proposals that include a variety of stakeholders and are open to different ideas. We need to encourage other such initiatives to continue to come up with new and innovative ways of responding to challenges in health care.

"We finally have our Vision and Mission Statements, and now we're working on steps to formulate a 15-year Action plan, which should be a value-added best-in-class game changer." He said in an interview last week.

"Next slide, please." Foster was on a roll. "This is from the Vancouver Island University Executive Bulletin yesterday."

Health board builds partnerships... The regional health board met with new partners Saturday, including school districts and area colleges, in their fight against child poverty. One of Central Vancouver Island Health Regions's goals is advocacy through strategic partnerships. In the first step toward that, it met with representatives from other involved groups to discuss advocacy strategies.

"Next slide." He said. "I'm pleased to be able to present the interim results of our first large sponsored research project."

A Knowledge Management Approach to Making Sense of Regional Health Indicators and Related Information Systems...
This is a progress report on a project funded by the Canadian Population Health Initiative to use a knowledge management approach to make sense of selected population health indicators. Our research question is 'Can KM be used to enhance the development and implementation of policies and programs for regional health indicators and related information systems?' The scope of this project covers those health indicators and information systems (IS) identified by two stakeholders (BC's Provincial Health Officer, Central Vancouver Island Health Region) as pertinent to ensuring the health of the local populations within the region. The main goals of this project are to (a) produce a set of policy, evidence and experience knowledge on selected regional health indicators and related IS; (b) use the knowledge produced to make sense of existing regional health indicator policies and programs; (c) refine this knowledge to enhance regional health indicator policies and programs. Our major project tasks are to (a) confirm stakeholders, selected health indicators and related IS; (b) initiate knowledge production on policy, evidence, and experience; (c) engage stakeholders in knowledge use; (d) foster knowledge refinement; (e) formalize results and recommendations. This project has major policy implications in terms of how the Canadian health system should address the ongoing production, use and refinement of its population health policy, evidence and experience as intellectual assets in the field setting. This project can provide much-needed insights and lessons on effective transfer and utilization of population health knowledge.

"Last slide, please." Foster's laser pointer jiggled to an executive organizational blueprint of Health Region administrative directors and officials. Every branch forked many times. Foster jiggled the ruby pinpoint through the bottom half of the complex diagram.

"At this point in the flowchart, we don't know what these people do." He admitted. "But we know they are thinking innovatively, and we would like to have a consensus statement to make sure we're all on the same page." It was too much for Sababa.

"Just what size piece of paper are you people on? A consensus statement allows us to say collectively what no one believes

142

individually." He said. "I'd be happy to give you some innovative thinking if you provide me the guidelines?"

"Foster, this is Doctor Sababa." Petronilla scowled. "Still spreading peace and love wherever you go, I see."

"Was I talking to you?" Sababa asked. "I've seen bush monkey shit fights more organized than this outfit."

"We all know Doctor Sababa." Admitted the CEO. Petronilla called for order, thanked Foster Concord, and then called for the other two items of new business.

Trace Pangloss presented a provisional plan for the establishment of a roving band of nurses, sent to patients' houses to administer a dose of powerful diuretic, making it unnecessary for those in sudden heart failure to clog up the emergency room.

"And how would you determine the cause of each of the cases of heart failure you propose to manage all the same way?" Sababa asked.

"Does it matter?" Trace asked.

"There are hundreds of reasons for a heart to fail, and you can't treat them all the same." Sababa said. "Apparently, rock bottom has a basement. Sometimes, Trace, you're as about as useful as a white crayon."

"Perhaps you should present a more formal proposal, Dr. Pangloss." Petronilla said. "And Doctor Sababa, I believe you have the last item of new business." Sababa pulled a robot from his Colombian leather briefcase.

"This is Piehole Pete." He said. "It has a camera and a chamber of microgrippers that can biopsy tissue on the way through the gut. Consider it an adjunct to endoscopy. It works a lot better for a lot less money than most of the people in this room."

"I'm sure the Department of Surgery would have something to say about any drone that threatens to displace the endoscopic expertise of our specialists." Jules Martino gave Sababa one of his rare looks of disapproval.

"Same for you, Doctor Sababa." Petronilla said. "A more detailed and properly prepared proposal will be necessary."

The stocky savant's pager went off in his pocket.

"Did your beeper go off, or are you ditching the conversation?" Petronilla asked

"Why can't both be true?" Sababa called the number. It was Jamie, in the ER, and he could hardly contain his excitement.

As he arrived in the emergency department, Sababa selected a tune from his music library on a secret drive hidden deep inside the hospital computer network. *'Now you're under control, and now you do what they told ya... I won't do what you tell me!... I won't do what you tell me!'*

"Why are you playing Rage Against the Machine?" Jamie asked.

"Because I want to." He said. "What you got?"

"Hillary Flintston." Jamie began. "30-year-old female MLA presenting with a sudden thunderclap headache and neck pain, and forward bulging of both eyes, associated with vomiting. She had been fasting to lose weight and was taking an oral contraceptive.

On examination she had a low-grade fever, pulse was fast and regular, and blood pressure normal. She was pale, and both eyeballs protruded forward and down. She had a left-sided third nerve palsy. Both optic discs were swollen. Blood work revealed an elevated white cell count of 15,000, and a positive D-dimer indicative of endogenous fibrinolysis. CT brain scan showed a cord sign and an empty delta sign. MRI confirmed the findings."

"You have a name?" Sababa asked.

"Cerebral vein thrombosis." He said. "Clot involving her transverse and sigmoid and cavernous sinuses."

"Let's go see her." Sababa said. Jamie made the introductions.

"What happened, Hillary?" Asked the portly professor.

"My head exploded." She said. "And then my eyes fell down."

"You have an unusual condition." Sababa said. "First described by a French physician named Ribes in 1825. There are blood clots in some veins in your brain. They're causing your symptoms and increasing the pressure inside your head. They have likely occurred because of the combination of your oral contraceptive therapy and your dehydration, but we will look for other possible contributing causes. We need to rehydrate you and begin blood thinners immediately."

"And if you don't?" She asked.

"Even with the anticoagulants, acute phase mortality is still 5.6% and 9.4% in total." He said. "It's far higher without it, and sometimes these clots fly off into your lungs. Not good."

"OK." She said.

"We must also watch your neurovital signs as we may have to decrease the pressure in your brain with a simple surgical

144

procedure. We'll start you on an anticonvulsant to prevent any seizures. And we'll need more blood tests when the situation stabilizes." He turned to Jamie.

"Factor V Leiden, prothrombin gene mutation, protein C and protein S, antithrombin III, Factor XIII, homocysteine, serum viscosity, blood cultures... you know the rest." The resident nodded.

"Put in a referral for Oliver Lax to see her. I'll take the rest of the night." Jamie handed him the pager with no small pleasure. Dr. Gung Ho approached Sababa, not five minutes after Jamie had left the department.

"Don't like this one, Sab." He said. "Amato Lusitano, 69-year-old retired coast guard officer. His platelet count is low."

"How low?" Sababa asked.

"Two thousand."

"I'm at the point in my life where I need a stronger word than 'fuck.'" He said. "Where is he?"

"Bed 2."

"I'm on it." Sababa pulled back the curtain to find a portly old Portuguese man and his slender spouse. They both smiled at his arrival.

"Dr. Ho said you were the best." Amato said.

"The only problem with that theory is it's based on the assumption that the universe is a just place." Sababa said. "There's something serious going on here, Mr. Lusitano."

"What is it?" He asked.

"Your platelet count is low at 2,000 per microlitre of blood."

"What should it be?" Asked his wife.

"Around 150,000 is a good number."

"What's causing it to be so low?" She asked.

"I'm working on it right now." Sababa asked Amato some quick questions. The retired coast guard officer showed him the mass of blood inside his mouth and the thousands of tiny red specks all over his lower extremities.

"I'll be back." Sababa said. He ran down to the hematology lab and asked the tech to place the peripheral smear of Amato's blood on a microscope stage. After peering through the eyepieces for less than a minute, he ran back to the ER to deliver stat orders.

"Regina, please give Mr. Lusitano in Bed #2 a gram of IV Solumedrol. Now." Sababa said. "Cheri Sundae, get me the blood bank please." He watched as Regina ran in the steroid.

"Line 3 for the blood bank, Doctor Sababa." Cheri said. He picked up line 3.

"Blood bank." Said the voice.

"How much IVIg do you have in stock?" Sababa asked.

"None." The voice said. "That's a new therapy and we don't have approval yet. They have some at St. Paul's in Vancouver."

"Thanks." He hung up. "Cheri, please patch me through to the blood bank at St. Paul's." A few minutes later, Sababa had spoken to both the St. Paul's blood bank and the on-call hematologist at the Vancouver hospital.

"Do you know how much this stuff costs?" He asked.

"Do you know how much I need it?" Sababa countered. The hematologist agreed to a transfer of six units of IV immunoglobulin to Harbour City Regional as soon as possible. Big Bird was in the air to fetch it a few minutes later. Sababa breathed a sigh and returned to the Lusitano bedside.

"Amato, here's the problem." He said. "One of your blood marrow products is low. Platelets are the small cell fragments responsible for the initial steps in shutting down any bleeding in your body. Yours are low because your own immune system is destroying them in your bloodstream because it thinks they're a foreign menace. It's called Idiopathic Thrombocytopenic Purpura—'idiopathic', from the Latin meaning we're idiots because we can't figure out what's causing it, 'thrombocytopenic' meaning low platelets, and 'purpura' meaning a rash of purple spots on the skin caused by internal bleeding from small blood vessels."

"How do you know this?" He asked.

"Because you have the characteristic rash, your spleen is not enlarged, you don't have any secondary causes of immune-mediated platelet destruction, and some platelets in your peripheral smear are larger than normal." He said. "We could wait for the results of antiplatelet antibody determinations or do a bone marrow biopsy to be sure, but these tests take time. Treatment's quicker."

"That's why Regina gave me the steroid?"

"Correct." Sababa said. "But for the raging activity of platelet destruction going on in your bloodstream, it's not enough. There's a new form of therapy I'm having flown over from Vancouver tonight. Works like a hot damn."

"Well, then." He said. "Hot damn!" Sababa admitted Amato to the ICU and called the nurses there to appraise them of the situation, and the need for alacrity when the immune globulin arrived from Vancouver.

"Don't let him do anything but breathe until we get that IVIg into him." He said. Everything was set for victory.

A half hour later, Sababa was playing what he called the Tranquility Base Trifecta, three different heart attacks in three

146

different beds, all receiving clot busting therapies. He had an anterior myocardial infarction in Bed #9, an inferior MI in Bed #8, and a high lateral heart attack in Bed #7. And so far, he was winning. His one-armed banditry was paying out.

In the background of his chaos, he heard rotors. *Dubdubdubdub whumpawhumpa whupwhup wuppawuppa whopwhop batabata tocotoco flacflac chakkchackk chakachak akk-chk thiththith sssssssss...* An ACLS ambulance attendant ran a styrofoam container past the ER towards the ICU. But nothing is never simple. Ten minutes later, Cheri Sundae held up a handset.

"ICU, line 1." She said.

"I'm busy." Sababa said. "Tell them to give the IVIg and take a message."

"They say they need to talk to you." Cheri said. Sababa picked up line 1. It was Charmeine.

"This better not be about what I think it is." He said.

"We can't give this blood product, Sab." She said.

"Why not?" He asked.

"We're not authorized." Charmeine was upset. "Hell, we haven't even been inserviced. If you want it given, you'll have to do it yourself."

"Charmeine, I'm up to my ass in gators here." He said. "It's real simple. You mix it with distilled water and hang the bag. And if you don't, this pleasant little retired Portuguese coast guard officer will bleed into his head. In this universe effect follows cause. I've complained about it but..." He hung up.

Three minutes later, Cheri Sundae held up the handset again.

"Nursing supervisor on call, Doctor Sababa." She said. "Edith Mortley, line 2."

"Wonderful." He thought. "Clipboards and Pearls Brigade. Natural and uncultured."

"What is it, Edith?" Sababa's fuse was getting short.

"If you want that stuff from St. Paul's administered, you must give it yourself." She said. "I will not have my nurses put in medicolegal jeopardy."

"You want to play jeopardy, Edith?" He said. "Well, let's make it a true daily double. Mr. Amato Lusitano has a platelet count of two thousand, and will definitely have an intracerebral hemorrhage quicksmart unless he gets this St. Paul's 'stuff.' And right this minute I'm managing three acute MIs here in Lotus Land."

"No." She said.

"It looks like my watch has stopped. It appears that never has arrived." Sababa said. "You know what's worse than useless? Useless and oblivious. Look, I take risks, sometimes patients die.

147

But not taking risks causes more patients to die, so my biggest problem is I'm cursed with the ability to do the math. Please allow these nurses to administer the IVIg."

"Over my dead body." She said.

"OK. Yours and his." Edith's intransigence crushed Sababa's spirit and Amato's hope. "What's the opposite of 'thank you'? I'm sure it also ends in 'you.' I'll get there as soon as I can." *Can you dance with the devil in the pale moonlight?* History is made at night. Character is what you are in the dark. Character is fate. Two minutes later, Cheri Sundae again held up her handset.

"ICU on line 1, Doctor Sababa." She said. It was Charmeine.

"Mr. Lusitano appears to have had a stroke." She said. "His family is at the bedside." People don't get what they deserve. They just get what they get. Sababa swore a blue streak all the way to the Death Star. He spent as long as he could afford to spend with Amato's family, apologizing for what hadn't happened the way he planned it. Saltwater ran down his cheeks. Charmeine held up her handset.

"Sab, it's Edith Mortley." She said.

"I heard about what happened, Doctor Sababa." She said. "But I had no choice."

"If nobody takes responsibility, Edith, then nothing is anybody's fault." He said. "Messianic slogans lead to the disablement of serious analysis, then to the denial of error or failure, and then to systemic cover-up and abuse. You not only get to watch it happen, but you also get to take part. When the cock crows three times..." He hung up.

If the battle chooses us, and not the other way around, that's when the sacrifice can be more than we can bear. Later in the wee hours, Sababa was finishing his admission notes, when Dr. Buddy Benway walked by, on the way out to his brand new jet black Jaguar.

"Hey, Buddy." He said. "Mine's the white one."

'You wound, like Parthians, while you fly,
And kill with a retreating eye.'
Samuel Butler, *An Heroical Epistle of Hudibras to His Lady*

The tiny lights still swam in circles, although there were so many more of them. The hum of the radio had reawakened as dissonant chords of dinging and buzzing and beeping. Harewood Mines looked up into the eyes of an Angel. She called through the partition that separated them from something bigger.

"In here, Sab." Angie said. The curtain parted to a spectre of black curly hair and burning eyes, followed by another of more humble proportions.

"Tell me again why you paged me stat, Jamie." said the big one.

"Harwood Mines." Jamie said. "52-year-old geotechnical engineer brought in twenty minutes ago from the ER, admitted under Dr. Hyde."

"Where's Dr. Hyde?" Sababa said.

"Hyding?" Jamie offered. "I don't think Dr. Pangloss wanted to refer him that way, but he was on call at the time."

"A sunset is only the backside of a sunrise." Sababa said. "Even snakes are afraid of other snakes. What you got?"

"His staff heard him fall in his office, and opened the door to find him unconscious, and his white carpet sprayed in bright red blood." Jamie said. "It had come from his mouth. They called 911, and an ambulance crew found him with a fast pulse and breathing rate and low blood pressure. They ran in a litre of saline on the way in."

"And?"

"And his pressure is still low, 80/40, his breathing is still fast, his oxygen saturation is in his boots, and his blood gas shows a respiratory acidosis." Jamie said.

"We sometimes have a name for patients with low blood pressure and inadequate peripheral oxygen delivery." Sababa said.

"Shock?"

"Welcome to the dark side, Jamie, where all the fun shit happens." Sababa said. "And what kinds of shock do you know about?"

"Cardiogenic, obstructive, and redistributive." Jamie said.

"Redistributive?" Sababa asked.

"Subdivided into septic, anaphylactic, endocrine and toxic, and neurogenic causes."

"Every generation of doctors regards itself as having reached the pinnacle of understanding." Sababa said. "But here on the Death Star, we prefer resuscitation to fluffing around. So have you any other clues about which one of these little shock categories our Mr. Mines may be in the throes of before we put in lines?"

"Well, his exam and chest x-ray are normal, but his ECG has abnormalities and his troponin is up." Jamie said. "And there's that." A run of ventricular tachycardia tickled its way across the monitor. "I'd say cardiogenic."

Sababa had been examining Harewood during the conversation. "Would you now?" Sababa asked. "You don't think his blue lips and fingers, his sky-high jugular neck veins, his parasternal heave and thumping loud pulmonic heart sound are of any significance?"

"His breath sounds are normal." Jamie said.

"$DO_2I = CI*SaO_2*10Hgb*1.34$." Sababa said. "Equation of perfusion. He's ventilating the square root of fuck all. His ECG shows a rapid heart rate, an S1Q3T3 pattern, inverted T waves in leads V1-V4, ST elevation in aVR, and a complete right bundle branch block, and his chest x-ray shows a prominent hilum and oligemia, and low-density lung fields."

"But no Westermark sign or Hampton's hump." Jamie lost the only expression on his face.

"Jamie, three rules of medical analysis: (1) what you got you got, (2) what you don't got, you don't got, and (3) context is everything."

"So you think it's a clot causing obstructive shock?" Jamie asked.

"Harewood Mines has a massive pulmonary embolism, likely a saddle blocking both of his main pulmonary arteries." He said.

"But according to his Wells and Geneva probability scores..."

"His D-dimer is high." Sababa said.

"Excuse me, Doctor Sababa." Angie interjected. "But if you would consider postponing your trenchant exercise in medical scholarship, we could continue with our little resuscitation here. I have a systolic pressure of 60 mmHg of mercury, and Elvis appears to have left the building."

"Sorry, Angie." Sababa said. "There is nothing more stimulating than a case where everything goes against you. Give Mr. Mines 100 mg of recombinant tissue plasminogen activator over the next ninety minutes."

"Thank Christ." She said. As he sat down to write out his consultation, Sababa selected a tune from his music library on a secret drive hidden deep inside the hospital computer network.

'Every breath you take
Every move you make
Every bond you break
Every step you take
I'll be watching you.'
The Police, *Every Breath You Take*

"You'll give him a clot buster without getting a spiral CT scan first?" Jamie asked.

"There are two kinds of people, Jamie." Sababa said. "Those that can extrapolate from incomplete data."

"And?"

"Who am I, Hercule Fucking Poirot?" Sababa asked. "The world is divided into people who think they're right. You know who the Parthians were, Jamie?" The young man shook his head.

"The Parthian Empire was a major Iranian political and cultural power in ancient Persia from 247 BC to 224 AD, on the Silk Road trade route between the Roman Empire in the Mediterranean and the Han Empire of China. Have you ever heard of the Battle of Carrhae?" Jamie shook his head again.

"It occurred in 53 BC, near the ancient Mesopotamian town of Harran. The Parthian general Surena obliterated the superior Roman invasion force commanded by Marcus Licinius Crassus. It was one of the most crushing defeats in Roman history. You know why?" Again Jamie nodded no.

"Crassus's army was comprised of seven Roman legions and auxiliaries and outnumbered Surena's army mounted on horseback by four to one. A baggage train of a thousand camels provided the Parthian horse archers with a constant supply of arrows. During real or feigned retreat, they turned their bodies back in full gallop to shoot at the pursuing enemy. The cavalry manoeuvre required superb equestrian skills since the rider's composite bow required both hands. Also, because the stirrup didn't exist yet, the rider relied on pressure from his legs to guide his horse. The tactic that became famous as the 'Parthian shot,' devastated the Roman army. In chess, we call it *zugzwang*, a situation in which the obligation to move can cause a serious, often decisive, disadvantage."

"What has that got to do with Harewood Mines?" Jamie asked.

'Every single day
Every word you say
Every game you play
Every night you stay
I'll be watching you'
The Police, *Every Breath You Take*

"Think about what happened here." Sababa pulled an object from his open Colombian leather briefcase and held out a large bronze coin in the palm of his hand.

"What's that?" Jamie saw the coin detail through the green patina of time. He could make out a single cornucopia tied with ribbons on one side and vine leaves and grapes on the other. He couldn't understand the inscription. *ΒΑΣΙΛΕΟΣ ΑΝΤΙΓΟΝΟΥ.*

"It's in Paleo Hebrew." Sababa said. "It says Mattathias Antigonus."

"Who's he?"

"He was the High Priest of the Council, the last king of the Hasmonean-Maccabean Dynasty. After the Battle of Carrhae, Parthian forces captured the whole of the Levant from the Romans. They set their ally, Antigonus II Mattathias, on the throne of Judea, sending Herod fleeing to his fort at Masada, and then to Rome."

"And?"

"And Judean independence didn't last but three years." Sababa said. "Mark Anthony counterattacked Parthia, reinvaded Judea, laid siege to Jerusalem, and designated Herod the new vassal King. Herod handed Antigonus Mattathias over to the Romans for execution. Josephus and Plutarch said they beheaded him. Roman historian Cassius Dio said they crucified him. It doesn't matter. This is all there is left. Except for one other thing. An ancient proverb validates Parthian protection of their Judean minority. *When you see a Parthian charger chained to a tombstone in the Land of Israel, the hour of the Messiah will be near.*

"And?"

"The world's most populous religion still thinks it happened that way." Sababa said. "My namesake, Eleazar, son of Eliud, in the Gospel of Matthew, is listed in the genealogy of Jesus as the great-grandfather of Joseph, husband of Mary."

"He wasn't likely the only Eleazar in those times."

"True." Replied the portly professor. "It was not an uncommon name—Eleazar, the nephew of Moses and companion in the Exodus, Eleazar, keeper of the Ark of the Covenant, Eleazar, a warrior of King David, Eleazar, in charge of the sacred vessels brought back to Jerusalem after the Babylonian Exile, Eleazar, the slayer of a battle elephant in I Maccabees, Eleazar, a scribe martyred under Antiochus IV Epiphanes, or Eleazar, an Essene who cured a possessed person in the presence of the Roman Emperor Vespasian."

"Which one did your mother name you after?" Jamie asked.

"None of those men." Sababa said. "She named me after Eleazar ben Simon, the leader of the resistance against the armies of Cestius Gallus, Vespasian, and Titus Flavius before the Romans destroyed the Second Temple. He was never given a formal office because of his temperament and his political party."

"Which was?"

"He was a Zealot." Sababa said.

> 'Oh can't you see
> You belong to me
> My poor heart aches
> With every step you take.'
> The Police, *Every Breath You Take*

"Pressures coming up." Angie said, "He's regaining consciousness."

"Thank ya. Thank ya very much." Sababa blew on his fingertips. "When you hear hoofbeats, you first think of horses, not zebras. The best riders are still Parthians."

"Oxygen saturation and pressure now normal."

> 'Every move you make
> Every vow you break
> Every smile you fake
> Every claim you stake
> I'll be watching you.'
> The Police, *Every Breath You Take*

Sababa caught Buddy Benway out of the corner of his eye, entering the Death Star.

"I presume you have room in the unit for one of my post-op patients, Sab." He asked.

"What's the problem?"

"I need to remove his right lung." He said, firing up a chest x-ray on the nearest viewer. "He has a wee bit of bronchiectasis."

"He only has one lung, Buddy." Sababa said.

"Oh, well then." Benway said. "Never mind."

The morning slid into the usual busy barrage of infirmity and illness that Harbour City Regional inflicted on its specialists. Jamie admitted Elizabeth Barnes, a middle-aged lady from Nanoose Bay to the unit. She was also in severe respiratory distress. Sababa called for a stat portable chest x-ray and had written something novel in the 'Reason for Examination' line on the requisition. *Because I said so.*

The receiving radiologist, Mako Brisk, wasted no time in reaching the frosted sliding doors of the Death Star, to land on Sababa for his breach of protocol. He was spuming.

"Jamie, where do you hide a hundred-dollar bill from a radiologist?" Jamie shrugged.

"On top of the patient." Sababa said. "Mako, we need to have a repository of our patient's x-rays here in the ICU. It takes too much time for us to have to run down to your department every time we want to see and compare film images. Someday, someone is going to pay the ultimate price for this idiocy."

"Over my dead body." Mako said.

"Why does every bureaucrat and department head in this place volunteer their lives to prevent improvements in patient care?" Sababa asked. "We can act like these walls mean nothing. But then we'd hurt our noses."

'Oh, a storm is threat'ning
My very life today
If I don't get some shelter
I'm gonna fade away...
It's just a shot away
It's just a shot away...'
      Rolling Stones, *Gimme Shelter*

'For this is the day you know too little
against the day when you will know too much...'
      John Stone, *Gaudeamus Igitur*

Forgive the casual reader for assuming that Sababa's Three States of Natural Imbalance (too much, too little, and weird) applied to only molecules and organ function. But his system covered many more circumstances. How to reconcile the German quantifier scope ambiguity of 'alles ist zuviel, nichts zu wenig?' *Everything is too much, nothing is too little.* And how is it possible to be both too much and not enough at the same time? The Good Doctor Sababa was a good and bad example.

He questioned too much. He read too much. He thought too much. He researched too much. He knew too much. He did too much. He felt too much. He was too curious, too smart, too intense, too intuitive, too analytical, too creative, too idealistic, too obsessive, too sensitive, too empathetic, too emotional, too self-absorbed, too compassionate, too introspective... too weird.

But he still felt he knew too little, achieved too little, appreciated too little, had too little time to spend with too few friends, laughed too little, made too little music... missed too much in his search for more.

He had a rainforest mind that could appreciate the paradox of having more and not enough at the same time, which is weird. Absurdity is the ecstasy of intellectualism.

Profusion is poison. Paucity is paralysis. Peculiar is perversion. Too much ends in smoke. Too little ends in a vacuum. Weird never ends. Too much mystery is merely an annoyance. Too much adventure is exhausting. And a little terror goes a long way. The Swedes have a word, *lagom*, which means 'not too much, not too little, just right.' Sababa knew it but had never used it in a sentence.

"It's a strange world." He would say. "Let's keep it that way."

Not everyone has to or gets to make a Parthian shot, hitting their target from behind while riding into oblivion. Every day in an ocean fog of bleeding and clotting, internists make decisions that can go one of two ways, either vitally good or fatally bad. The problem is that the great decisions and the bad ones look exactly the same when they're being made.

Mallory Weiss swallowed Sababa's secret robot two days into his hospital admission on Buddy Benway's ward. After an equally clandestine retrieval, Piehole Pete's microgrippers had collected enough photos and tissue samples of Mallory's food pipe lining to provide a diagnosis of eosinophilic esophagitis, and a stern phone call from the pathologist Dr. Juan Leyblanca, who had figured out exactly how Sababa had got his biopsies.

"¿Do ju have permission to use jor machine?" He asked.

"You always have permission to use yours?" Sababa said. "It's easier to get forgiveness."

"I call ju." He hung up.

Mallory's malady responded well to a proton-pump inhibitor, and four puffs of a steroid inhaler swallowed three times a day for six weeks. He saw an allergist, who is still eliminating his way through Mallory's favorite food groups, to find the one that may have caused his problem. Mallory profited from the paving contract that now runs the hydrocarbons off the trailer park, up at Sababa's lake.

Bernadine Soulier went to Victoria to have her 'Mommy Makeover.' Her plastic surgeon wasn't as pretty as Christian Troy, but he at least had a hematologist premedicate her before surgery, so she wouldn't bleed in any abnormal way. Unfortunately, her husband's golf handicap did not notice her transformation, as futile and foreseen as the false fruits of unrequited love can sometimes be.

Dr. Hyde performed his bronchoscopy on Martha Lillard, which confirmed Sababa's diagnosis of idiopathic pulmonary hemosiderosis. After a course of corticosteroids, she is off treatment, free of relapses, and still pouring pints at the Landlubber Pub. Henri Mygold has also recovered from his Mondor's disease and is planning his retirement party from Canadian Tire.

Dr. Buddy Benway kicked up such a fuss about Sababa's plan to use Piehole Pete to monitor Herbert Hancock's watermelon stomach disease activity, that any plan to introduce the robot as even an adjunct to the lucrative lonely business of endoscopy was shelved far into the future. Herbert gets his routine hosing from Buddy, and follow-up with a rheumatologist in Vancouver, for the connective tissue disease that Sababa found was causing it.

Hillary Flintston died the day following her admission, even before Dr. Lax could see her. Dr. Leyblanca found blood clots in her lungs and a large bleed in her brain at autopsy. It was the second fatal case of pulmonary emboli he had dissected out that day, but because of the demise of Elizabeth Barnes, the ICU got their own x-ray repository; and, because of the unfortunate death of Amato Lusitano, the blood bank got its own supply of IVIg. Tragedy is a strong acid that dissolves away all but golden truth.

The day after Harewood Mines received a dose of clot buster, a spiral CT scan of his chest showed his saddle embolism had dissolved away. Sababa found the cause of his clotting predisposition, an unusual condition known as primary antiphospholipid antibody syndrome. He now treats Harewood with rat poison warfarin and willow bark aspirin. Mines prospered from his trailer park project and, when he's not listening to his Bose radio in his white-carpeted office, woos young South American girls on his ever more frequent Latin America holidays.

Oh, and Buddy Benway's brand new Jaguar? Some strapping saboteur ran an ancient Parthian bronze coin down the jet black paint job late one night. The closed-circuit camera behind the

On-call Physician Parking Bay missed the face of the burly barbarian as he receded into the darkness. But it caught him firing a small object into an open Colombian leather briefcase behind him, on the back seat of a dimpled and dented white Honda Civic.

5. The Case of the Syncopated Rhythm

'Rhythm is the life of space of time danced through.'
Cecil Taylor

The back alley behind the Grizzly B'ar was called Beat Street, and not because of the dance music. More stroboscopic scintillation than any other policed area in Harbour City floodlit the dead of any night.

A saloon is a place that sells madness by the bottle. Inside this one, the miasmic stench of stale smoke and sour suds and steroidal and spermatic swaggering, the booming tempo of what passed for musical accompaniment, and the hockey games on the big screens no one was watching, animated the insanity.

No one was watching what was about to happen under the suspended fluorescent illumination in the middle of the tavern. The Kirkwood brothers owned the Grizzly B'ar pool table. Damian and Jason had dorsal fins, chomped through the bait of every challenger, and usually left the pub with enough pocket money to sleep through their days.

Eddie Felson hadn't meant to provoke the two men when he picked up the cue ball from the table, during one of Damian's shots. It was likely that he expected the Kirkwoods to take the gesture in the more lighthearted spirit in which he thought he was making it. Seriousness is the only refuge of the shallow. Eddie hadn't expected Damian to jump the table to get to him, smashing him so hard that he fell across the playing surface he had removed the ball from, into blows now raining down from Damian's brother, Jason.

But no one expected the bouncer, Siddartha Sauve, to join in the brawl, and if they did, they didn't expect him to enter the arguement on the side of the Kirkwoods, against a man now lying splayed and unconscious across the surface of the pool table. It was just one punch, but what had been Eddie Felson's humorous intentions now seeped a crimson coast into the green felt under him. Sauve and other bouncers carried him outside the bar and propped him up against a nearby telephone pole in the early morning rain. Someone called an ambulance.

'Listen to  the rhythm of the falling rain
Telling me just what a fool I've been
I wish that it would go and let me cry in vain
And let me be alone again.'
The Cascades, *Rhythm of the Rain*

159

In the same rain a few hours later, Jasmine Place noticed a thin pool of diluted crimson under the telephone pole across the alleyway, as she opened the doors to her ballet studio. It wasn't anything she hadn't seen there before. Mr. Rogers had done a poor job of preparing her for the people in her neighborhood.

Jasmine switched on the bank of hanging lights that illuminated the main stage and mirrors and shiny hardwood floors of Harbour Dancentre. Along the entire length of a far wall ran a different kind of grisly barre. She turned on the radio before the end of Michael Jackson.

Just bead it, bead it, bead it... Roc your mocs and Cowichan socks. This is BC Bud, for CNDN Coast Salish radio, 101.3 FM on your Home and Native Band...

Jasmine had opened Harbour Dancentre two years earlier, in partnership with two other ballet teachers, Karen Kaine, and Jane Sababa. They all delighted in the pure joy of motion and were passionate about bringing that enthusiasm to their students. But their unbeatable reputations as dance instructors had rewarded their egos a great deal more than their balance sheets.

Jasmine changed into her practice clothes and pointes. A mélange of wafting aromas had assembled the dressing room—moisture and sweat—of underarms and feet, of socks and tights, of spandex and nylon, of canvas and leather, musty costumes and new costumes and the steamers used to take out creases from the dresses; the stale scents of young dancers' cotton candy perfume and hairspray and Harpix and styling gel mixed with deodorant and old wooden pancake makeup, candles, stuffy air, the strong notes of Tiger Balm and Deep Heat and Arnica Gel, rosin, old 'Skittles' candy, and that acetone accessory of clear nail polish, for runs in their tights, ends of their pointe shoelaces, ballet shoe elastic bands, and their nails.

Due to the recent loss in our community, out of respect of the family, Sobriety Group tonight is cancelled.

Soon there would be the excited screaming and laughter of Jasmine's young students, anticipating their use of the *barre*, and then their centre work. Some balanced like they were born to it, others wobbled like jelly on a plate. Scarlet cheeks returned breathless to the changing room, to rip apart a bowl of sweet oranges.

160

As they grew into ballet, students would graduate from spaghetti straps to long-sleeve leotards, to provide more support during *changements*. Jasmine had forbidden them from wearing leg warmers because she knew they were bending their knees during their *arabesques*. Their first tutus were more exciting than their first kiss and just as awkward.

They would remember their first time they were *en pointe*. On top of the world, they could stay up there forever, and then how it felt immediately after. Hell was that moment after they took off their shoes to find feet covered in blisters. Art was pain. Goodbye to peep toe shoes forever. Their brand new pointe shoes were beautiful, but they would break their feet and their wallets with the same wild abandon—at a hundred dollars a pair times at least twelve new pairs a year. They were all undanceable until they suffered the same pain, of bending and beating, and then microwaves. And Heaven? Heaven was that moment when they graduated from lambswool to gel pads.

What's the difference between John Wayne and Jack Daniels? Jack Daniels is still killing Indians... Alcohol—helping white people to dance for centuries.

Jasmine's students would learn about studio rivalries and dance moms and elite examiners and the catty cruelty of competition. The losers committed social suicide in full sole shoes and footed tights under their leotards, with a pink wrap skirt, or in garbage bag shorts.

The ones that made it through their exams and festivals to rehearsals for more serious performances would absorb the molecules of their new Sansha split soles and convertible Capezios. Their closets began to resemble leather graveyards.

They would begin to savour the heat of the lights, the linoleum warming up beneath them, and the ancient dust of old theatres, and dancers now long dead.

Always together, never apart. ABC, 1, 2, 3, baby, plié, grand plié. No matter how much they practiced, most of their arches and turnouts and adagios and postures were never good enough. In the chasm between triumph and despair, most would fall away, like booster rockets on an interplanetary probe. And the few star seekers left at the end of this combustion and carnage would continue to compete in a world of mood and eating disorders, up through innumerable performances of Nutcracker and Giselle and Sleeping Beauty, into the countless chaîné turns of Coppelia. Then came live accompaniment in every class, and more polished teachers yelling at pianists about when to begin an eight count exactly.

161

And finally, after years of sublime sacrifice, the primas that made it to opening night centre stage would smell powder and floral wreaths and roses and expensive perfume—Hermes Kelly Caleche, Bottega Veneta, Acqua di Parma, Magnolia Nobile Special Edition, Roxana Illuminated Perfume Gracing the Dawn, Lorenzo Villoresi Teint de Neige, Guerlain Vol de Nuit or L'Heure Bleue, Chanel N°22 or Bois des Iles.

But most of all, they would smell the scent of passion, and it was beautiful.

May the moon keep you centered...

Jasmine began with her usual stretching exercises, with far less flexibility than she once enjoyed. The chain of her St. Vitus necklace, patron saint of dancers, swung in wide arcs around her neck as she increased the amplitude of her movements.

She began to sway and spin, and whirl and twirl, glissade and assemblé, and pirouette and trip the light fantastic, first for technique, then for Terpsichore, the classical muse of dance, and finally for herself, and the sheer exhilaration of being.

May the sun keep you dancing...

She reached for the sign over the stage above her. 'You must have chaos within you to give birth to a dancing star.' It was Nietzsche. But also from Nietzsche, was Jasmine's fate to be wrecked against infinity in the chaos that erupted in her chest. Be still my heart. She staggered to an open window. Outside, the cherry blossoms blew sideways, through all the air she struggled to devour.

And the stars shed light on your dreams.

'Quit playin' games with my heart
Before you tear us apart...'
Backstreet Boys, *Quit Playing Games With My Heart*

The day before the episodes at the Grizzly B'ar and grisly barre, Dr. Trace Pangloss stat-paged Doctor Sababa to the ER resuscitation room. Dr. Jamie Dunne got there only moments before his mentor to find a young man in obvious distress. His monitor showed his heart racing along at a speed that would have killed a lesser mortal.

"Brian Hugh Warner." Trace began. "26-year old lead singer in a local rock band, just brought in. Longstanding history of episodic dizziness, shortness of breath and palpitations with several bouts of recent fainting with exercise."

"He must be going 180 beats a minute." Jamie said. Trace handed him the ECG.

"Oh yeah." He said. "Michaela, give him 5 mg of verapamil IV. Now." Michaela drew up the drug.

"Stop!" Said the doorway. "Put that down."

"But Sab, he's booming along like a bat out of hell." Trace said. "We need to block down his AV node."

"No, you don't." Sababa said. "As my old samurai rōnin, the Saint of the Sword Miyamoto Musashi used to say: 'Concerning speed, we say that something is fast or slow depending on whether it misses the rhythm of things.' You need to block down his accessory pathway."

"What accessory pathway?"

"Michaela, give Mr. Warner 100 mg of IV procainamide." Micheala drew up and gave the drug. His rhythm snapped into normal. There were tiny delta waves among the others on the monitor.

"That one." Sababa said. "He was in atrial flutter and threatening to conduct 1:1 down his Bundle of Kent."

"What would have happened if I had given him the verapamil?" Trace asked.

"He would have gone into ventricular fibrillation and arrested. To hell in a handbasket." Sababa asked Micheala to call for another ECG. "Although all arrhythmias straighten themselves out in the end."

"What is this, Doc?" Brian asked.

"You have an extra electrical pathway connecting the top and bottom parts of your heart, Brian." Sababa said. "Every once in a while it wants to be the boss."

"You have a name?" He asked.

"Wolff-Parkinson-White syndrome, type A." Sababa said. "Meat Loaf has it."

"Can you fix it?" He asked.

"You'll be going from here to a buddy of mine in Victoria." Sababa asked Cheri Sundae to get Dr. Gerry Genial on the phone. "He faints at the sight of blood, but he's a cracker-jack in the EP Lab. He'll destroy your accessory pathway with radiofrequency catheter ablation."

Dr. Capitaine broke into the gathering from the other side of the ER.

"How are you, Miles?" Sababa asked.

"Living the dream."

"Dream no small dreams for they have no power to move the hearts of men." He said. "What you got?" Myles handed him an ECG.

"Hmmm." Sababa handed it off to Jamie. "I assume you've already fixed this rhythm or you wouldn't have drifted in here so casually."

"Electricity sorted it." Myles nodded.

"Hmmm." Jamie said.

"What?" Sababa asked.

"Wide complex tachycardia with a left bundle branch block morphology." He said.

"And an inferior axis." Sababa said. "RV outflow tract ventricular tachycardia."

"Here's the second ECG after we fixed it." Myles handed them the tracing.

"Hmmm... QRS complex prolongation in leads V1-V3, Epsilon waves, and incomplete RBBB." Sababa said. "Seriously? Where is this patient from?"

"20-year-old guy visiting his uncle here in Harbour City. He's from Greece." Myles said.

"Let's go see him." Sababa led the entourage to the other side. Myles opened the curtain on a woolly haired young man with an unusual yellow thickening of his palms.

"Πως σε λένε?" Sababa asked. *What is your name.*

"Αλέξανδρος αστέρι." Said the boy. *Alexander Asteras.*

"Από που είσαι, Αλέξανδρος?" Sababa asked. *Where are you from, Alex.*

"Νάξος." He said. *Naxos.*

"Λοιπόν, ο Αλέξανδρος, ο Εύρικα." Sababa opened his hands. *Well then, Alexander, eureka.*

"I'm here visiting my Uncle Peter." Alex said. "What do I tell him is going on?"

164

"There's a rare recessive condition that affects people from your Aegean island, Alex." Sababa turned to his colleagues. "It causes abnormal, incomplete development and fibro-fatty failure of the right ventricle, and rhythm disturbances from the same part of the heart. It's from a two base-pair deletion in the Pk2157del2TG gene encoding the desmosomal cell adhesion protein 17q21plakoglobin."

"You have a name?" Jamie asked.

"Naxos disease." Sababa said.

"Is there a treatment?" Alex asked.

"You have travel medical insurance from Greece?" Sababa asked.

"Full coverage." Alex said.

"We'll need to implant an automatic cardioverter defibrillator in Victoria, Alex." Sababa said. "I'll make the arrangements today with Dr. Genial. You may also need medication to control the rhythm disturbances and the weakened wall of your heart."

"Do I have to?" Alex asked.

"Or you can do everything in moderation and wait for your genes to kill you." Sababa said. "Fight like you're the third monkey trying to get onto the Ark." There was a pause.

"Ευχαριστώ Γιατρέ." Alex said. *Thank you, Doctor.*

"Είστε ευπρόσδεκτοι, Άλεξ." Sababa said. *You're welcome, Alex.*

He took Jamie and Myles aside after speaking with his patient.

"He may need a heart transplant, and he may still die a sudden cardiac death. Let me tell you another little story. Once, when I was doing a locum in my old home town, one of the family docs on call in emergency asked me to see a lady who had driven 100 kilometers to the hospital.

"She says she's in ventricular tachycardia." He said.

"What did the ECG show?" I asked.

"I haven't done one yet." He answered.

"Why not?" I asked.

"I told her that if she was in ventricular tachycardia, she'd be dead."

"What happened?" Myles asked.

"We did the ECG." Sababa said. "She was in ventricular tachycardia. As you get the rhythm, you discern how to win."

"Miyamoto Musashi?" Jamie asked.

"The same." Sababa said. "Wrote the Book of Five Rings." *Go Rin No Sho*. His life's lessons on the essential elements of Wind, Fire, Earth, Water, and The Void. You should read it, but it studies best in the original.

"Just how many languages do you speak, Sab?" Myles asked.

165

"English to colleagues, French to Michelin star chefs, Newspeak to bureaucrats, Japanese to my Akita dog, a smattering of enough of several others to get by, and I'm fluent in sarcasm and profanity." A throat cleared itself beside them. Michaela held a handset to her sternum.

"It's Shekina on Floor 6, Doctor Sababa. She says you need to come now."

The sixth floor of Harbour City Regional shared the odd surgical specialties of orthopedics and urology. The head of orthopedics, Dr. Piggy Muldoon, was a knuckle dragger and avid sailor—an overbearing stern brigand of bulkheaded booms, rolling bilge, and rigged gaffs and messes. The head of the urology stream team was Dr. Harry 'Doc' Martin who, like his calling, was usually pissed. Martin's heavy drinking was a legend. On one occasion, he passed out on the floor at a party. When a guest pointed him out to his wife, she hadn't seemed concerned. *Let Docky sleep. He has to operate in the morning.*

Doc Martin had operated on a volunteer the day before Sababa and Jamie made it up to the low oxygen levels of the sixth floor. Shakina was waiting for them at the top of the stairs.

"What you got?" Sababa asked.

"Larry Bird." Shakina said. "73-year-old Robbins Parking attendant, a patient of Doc Martin, one-day post-op transurethral prostate resection for benign enlargement."

"We don't do that kind of plumbing." Said the stocky savant.

"He's in a weird fast rhythm, and his blood pressure is low." She handed him an ECG. Sababa noted the imaginative reason given for its requisition. *Failure to cope.*

"How low?" Sababa asked.

"So low we can barely feel a pulse."

"So 70 mmHg systolic." He said. "Where is he?"

166

"Room 609."

"Bring the crash cart." He said.

"You know why they call it a crash cart, Shekina?" She shook her head backwards as she ran down the hallway. "Because they haven't yet invented a crash tractor for me to drive around the hallways."

The two men hurried into Larry Bird's room to find a thin old man, semiconscious. There was no IV. Sababa pulled a #14 cannula from his Colombian leather bag and fired it into a vein on Larry's thumb that no one else could see, attached it to a litre of saline he retrieved from the same divine repository and hung it high on an IV pole. Shekina rolled in the crash cart. Jamie attached three ECG electrodes to Larry's chest and to the monitor leads of the defibrillator.

"Unchain my heart. Give me a rhythm I can dance to." Sababa said. "Yep, that's one."

"He's in atrial fibrillation with a rapid ventricular response." Jamie added.

"Yes, he is. What's his pressure now, Jamie?" The resident pumped up the sphygmomanometer bulb and let the mercury fall.

"Just audible at 70 mmHg." He said. Sababa placed two large electrolyte pads on Larry Bird's chest and pulled the paddles from the defibrillator. He fired up the capacitor to deliver 200 joules. *Whirhrrhhrrrhhhrrrr....*

"Go big or go home." Sababa looked up into the eyes of Daisy Daws, the Director of Surgical Nursing. She was carrying a clipboard and wearing a string of imitation pearls. Road hard and put away wet, Daisy went through life holding onto the sides. She may have been the total embodiment of everything a surgeon needed and feared, but she had no appreciation for the finer nuances of Internal Medicine and its practitioners.

"And just what do you think you're going to do here, Doctor Sababa?" She was in a foul mood.

"Healing touch." Sababa said.

"Over my dead body." Daisy's back went rigid. "You will transfer this patient to the ER and perform your little magic trick there, with proper anesthesia management under controlled conditions."

"These are teachable moments, Jamie." Sababa said. "How do you tell a urologist from an anesthesiologist?" Jamie shrugged.

"When they're in the OR, the urologist has his hand on someone else's wiener. And a bureaucrat is someone who, when he or she sees light at the end of the tunnel, orders more tunnel." He looked up at Daisy Daws.

"What is that hole in your face that all those noises are coming out of, Daisy?" He asked. "The problem with your threat is that it will be Mr. Bird's body that will be dead if you transfer him. Playing it safe will always end in disaster. Clear! Fire in the hole." The next sound sailed all the way to the nursing station. *Craaaaccckkkkk!!!*

It woke Larry Bird, who was now holding his chest.

"Jesus Fucking Christ." He said. Jamie looked at the monitor through the smoke. Larry was back in a normal rhythm. He took his pressure. It was now also normal. He looked at Sababa, smiling as Sababa smiled.

"Who's your daddy?" Sababa blew on his fingers. "Sometimes it is better to light a flamethrower than to curse the darkness."

"It smells kind of like a BBQ in here." Shekina offered. Daisy Daws stormed out to file a complaint and her nails.

"Attention! Code Blue. Floor One." It was Big Voice. "Code Blue. Floor One." Sababa turned to Jamie again.

"I'll get this." He said. "You stay here and finish up. And don't forget to make sure that Mr. Bird hasn't had a blood clot to his lungs." Jamie watched an unkempt mop of curly black hair recoil out the door, down the hallway, and into the stairwell.

Once his feet hit the linoleum of the first floor, his eyes converged on a crushing crowded commotion draining through the frosted doors into the telemetry unit. The assembled multitude of nurses and ECG and respiratory technicians parted a path for Sababa to enter through. Gathered around a bed in a far corner were three nurses and Dr. Trace Pangloss, pulling a long monitor strip through his fingers.

"What happened here?" Sababa asked.

"You're too late, Sab." Trace said. "He fixed himself."

"Tell me about it." Sababa said.

"Barry Keliher." It was Sarafina. "59-year-old government liquor store worker admitted by Dr. Ernie Hacker yesterday afternoon. He was in atrial fibrillation."

"What rhythm is he in now?"

"He's back in normal sinus rhythm." She said.

"So why did you call the code?"

"Because of this." She handed him a rhythm strip. It was two minutes long. Sababa's hands streamed through it. The entire record was nothing but a flat line.

"What meds did Dr. Hacker order for him last night?"

She handed him the MAR. *Amiodarone 300mg po, Sotalol 80 mg po, Digoxin 0.25mg po, Procainamide 100mg po...*

"You gave him all this?" Sababa asked. Serafina nodded.

168

The following day Sababa would ask The Big Easy about the chemical cocktail he had ordered for Barry Keliher.

"It is the vice of a vulgar mind to be thrilled by bigness." Sababa said.

"It worked, didn't it?" Ernie was late for a round of golf. Trust nothing that can think for itself if you can't see where it keeps its brain."

"Hearts are wild creatures. That's why our ribs are cages."
Anon

"It's rhythm and blues week, Boss." Mercy was transcribing furiously under what had been Sababa's *No Fruit Loops* sign. She had replaced it with one of her own.

Uptown Internal Medicine
Valet Parking
Spacious Waiting Rooms
Complimentary WiFi
Perrier and Bottled Still Water
Designer Gowns
French Varietal Examining Tables
Warmed Gloves and Instruments
Boutique Gift Shop
Courier Concierge Consultations
'You've seen the rest, now try the best'

"The quality of Mercy is not strain'd." Sababa said to Jamie. "Take it down and put the Fruit Loops back up." He handed Jamie the second chart and called in his first patient, a young woman with a brand new baby.

Daisy Miller was on maternity leave for her first infant. Sababa had initially seen her as an inpatient referral from an obstetrician, Dr. Olaf Octagon, calling from the telemetry ward.

"Hey, Olaf." Sababa said. "What are the four most common OB-GYN surgical procedures?"

"What?" Said the weed puller.

"C-section, hysterectomy, transection of left ureter, and transection of right ureter." Sababa said. "I could never figure out why you guys leave the room when your patients get undressed." Humour was not Olaf's strong suit.

"Daisy Miller." Olaf said. "23-year-old Canada Post letter carrier, $P_0G_1A_0$, in her 17th week of pregnancy, admitted with complaints of rapid heart action and shortness of breath, which had progressed over the previous month. No history of any cardiac disease. Her ECG showed a supraventricular tachycardia with a heart rate of 152 beats per minute."

"What kind?" Sababa had asked.

"Dunno. I just pop babies." He said. "The ER doc thought it was abnormal enough to give her adenosine, and when that failed, he tried to cardiovert her."

"How did that work out?"

"Nothing changed." Olaf said.

"She was in sinus rhythm." Sababa said. "Just fast."

"He passed her off to one of your colleagues, who admitted her to telemetry, and gave her sequential IV esmolol and oral metoprolol, followed by verapamil and then digoxin."

"And?"

"All that got her heart rate down to 120 beats a minute, but she couldn't get out of bed without fainting." Olaf continued. "Serial inpatient echo showed progressively failing pump function of her heart and a worsening leak of her mitral valve. Your buddy had to give her a diuretic to keep her out of heart failure."

"If we can rule out all the other causes of a fast rate but normal rhythm, she has what's called inappropriate sinus tachycardia. Sometimes we ablate plus or minus pace these patients, but we have to avoid x-rays and risky procedures because of the pregnancy. There's only one option if we don't want her heart to beat itself to death."

Twenty weeks later, Daisy Miller was sitting in Manzanita Medical, bouncing her new son on a knee. Sababa had applied to Ottawa for the urgent release of a controlled drug called ivabradine. No matter how fast light travels, darkness got there first and was waiting for it. They denied permission on the first day of the application. But a desk is a dangerous place from which to view the world. Sababa called the bureaucrat responsible for the refusal the minute the doors opened three time zones ahead.

"You can't have it." Said the apparatchik. "You have requested it for an off-label purpose. The answer is still no."

Throwing acid is wrong... in some people's eyes. Sababa asked him to spell his name for the national media outlets he would call after he hung up. FedEx delivered the drug the next morning. If you're going to kick authority in the teeth, you might as well use two feet.

Sababa informed Daisy of the risks and with her consent and trust, started her on 5mg of ivabradine twice a day. Her pulse dropped to 90 beats a minute the first day, and the fetal heart rate never changed. Daisy delivered a normal baby boy, her pump and mitral valve function returned to normal, and here she sat, breastfeeding in Sababa's office.

"You know his name?" She asked. Sababa shook his head.

"Eleazar." She said. All three blushed together. Jamie poked his nose in the door.

"I'll be there in a minute." Sababa said. "Let me finish this little basking exercise first."

A few minutes later, Sababa knocked on the residents' room door. Jamie opened it as wide as his eyes.

"What you got?" Sababa asked.

"Torsade Depointes." He said. "32-year-old chef at Café de la Paix referred by Dr. Rivera for a problem of recurrent fainting spells." Sababa studied the man.

"Have you any oriental relatives?" He asked.

"My motheer is Chinese." He said. "Thees is embarrassing for me." Torsade said. "I fall on the keetchen floor more and more."

"They occur more often when he's tired after working too hard, after a heavy meal or sleeping, or he has a fever." Jamie added.

"Or drinks too much alcohol?" Sababa asked. The chef nodded.

"Nothing else in the history, family history, or on physical exam." Jamie handed the portly professor some tracings. "But his ECG and the Holter study Mercy did is interesting."

"What about the ECG?" Sababa asked.

"First degree AV block, right bundle branch block with coved ST elevation in leads V1-V3 with over 0.2 mV J-point elevation and descending ST segments." Jamie offered.

"And?"

"I see nothing more." He said. "I thought I was doing good."

"You were doing well." Sababa said. "Except for the prolonged QT interval."

"Oh."

"And Mercy's Holter?"

"It shows occasional polymorphous VT."

"Yes, it does." Sababa agreed. "God's little Ctrl-Alt-Delete. You have a name?"

"Type 1 Brugada Syndrome." Jamie said.

"Close." Sababa said.

"What ees eet?" Torsade was not getting any of this.

"Once upon a time." Sababa said. "In 1992, two brothers in Spain named Pedro and Josep described an abnormal condition of how the electrical energy of the heart either discharges or recharges. It allows some waves to pass others in a phenomenon known as wavebreak. They named the disorder. It's called Brugada Syndrome. You have what we call an overlap syndrome, Brugada and long QT syndrome, in your case caused by a mutation in a gene, SCN5A, which reduces the peak sodium current while simultaneously leaving a persistent current leak. Vive la différence. The Holter monitor showed that sometimes you faint because of a rhythm disturbance, and sometimes because you just faint. It's complicated, but everything is vague to a degree you do not realize until you've tried to make it precise."

"So what do we do now?" Torsade asked.

"Dr. Dunne will refer to you Dr. Gerry Genial in Victoria for an implantable machine that should prevent you from coming to harm. You'll like him. He wears cowboy boots to work. We should get your immediate family tested for the condition. You may need medication, but you definitely must not take certain other drugs. Dr. Dunne will give you a list. No cocaine; no alcohol, at least for now."

"But wine makes me feel alive." Torsade protested.

"Me too, Torsade." Sababa said. But no matter how many ways there may be of being alive, there are vastly more ways of being dead. No alcohol. We must now stop this interview as I have come to the end of my personality." Mercy interrupted the conclusion.

"Jane on line 1, Boss." Sababa picked up the phone and grunted through a brief conversation.

"Two things, Jamie." He said.

"Yassa, Massa."

"My wife has invited you to join us for dinner tomorrow night." Sababa said. "I'll see what I can pick up on the way home later."

"And the second thing?" Jamie asked.

"We're on call tonight."

"But..."

"There are no shortcuts to excellence, Jamie." Sababa said. "Many people never use their initiative because no one told them to."

"But I'm tired." He said.

"Life is a long process of getting tired." He said. "If you're not tired, you're not doing it right. You can sleep when you die."

'Oh yeah, I wanna feel your power
Shock me, make me feel better.'
Kiss, *Shock Me*

Dr. Cliffy Carlton was not in a playful mood that evening. All his patients were 'trainwreck' serial complications or confused 'purse positive' little old ladies lying on their stretchers and clutching their handbags.

"You couldn't afford your asthma inhaler, but those cigarettes hanging out of your pocket were free?" He'd ask. "Did you think that big 'H' on the building meant Hilton?" Cliffy introduced Sababa and Jamie to their first referral of the evening.

"Welcome to our little shit-stained, drug-soaked, degenerate, morose, despondent, permadrizzle freak show, Gentlemen." He said. "Recipe for today: One cup cluster. Two cups fuck."

"What you got, Cliffy?" Sababa asked.

"Mathew Damon." He said. "69-year-old Harbour City Casino croupier who went to see the new acupuncturist in town."

"OK."

"He has an automatic implantable cardioverter defibrillator." Cliffy said. "Implanted."

"So?"

"She hooked up his acupuncture needles to DC current." There was a pause.

"How many discharges?" Sababa asked.

"He bounced off the table seven times before she decided to call the game on account of rain." Cliffy said. "Lucky bed number 7."

"Jeezuz." Jamie said.

"Hang up a shingle, condemn the narrowness and greed of Western medicine, and you'll make a damn fine living." Sababa added. They all went to see him.

The senior casino employee behind the lucky curtain seemed uncomfortable.

"Playing the low voltage lottery with your device tonight, Matt?" Sababa asked. "Death is usually like the rumble of distant thunder at a picnic. In your case, it brought lightning."

"I didn't know she was going to attach the needles to a battery." He said.

"The rest of your life is already a gamble at terrible odds." Sababa said. "If you were a bet, I wouldn't take it."

"I'll never do that again." Matt said. "Do you think my defibrillator is OK?"

"I'm bringing in one of the techs to answer that question." Sababa said. "But the answer is likely in the affirmative. You should be able to go home after she interrogates your device."

"Are you going to tell my acupuncture therapist?" He asked.

"Right now." Sababa left to make a phone call. Jamie could hear parts of the conversation. *Been living on the edge, baby doll... This isn't a pop quiz anymore. It's an intervention... You don't ever take a fence down until you know the reason it was put up...If you ever...* It went something like that.

After Sababa had spoken with his EP technician, Dr. Gung Ho approached the medicine man and his mentor.

"Careful Jamie, an ER doc's favorite hallucinogen is exhaustion." Sababa said.

"Cara Cicatriz." Gung handed the portly professor a chart. "Young woman presenting today with a two-week history of increasing fatigue and shortness of breath."

Sababa saw Dr. Peter Zaias waving at him from the hospital corridor entrance. He handed the chart off to Jamie.

"You get started." He said. "I have some urgent business to attend to elsewhere."

"As opposed to emergent business here?" Jamie asked.

"The teacher is as a needle, the disciple is as thread. You must practice constantly." He said. "I'll be with Dr. Zaias at the end of the known universe." Sababa left the fluorescent hum of the ER for the hospital hallway and the company of Zaias. Two mineshaft shadows faded from Gung and Jamie's view.

"Residents are like puppies, Sab." Zaias said. "Eager and enthusiastic. You can teach them without crushing their spirit."

"He'll be fine, Peter." Sababa said. "Did you bring the weapons of mass deconstruction?" Zaias handed him one of two Robinson screwdrivers he had secured for the occasion. They marched in silence, arriving at the main internal lifts of Harbour City Regional. Zaias pressed all the elevator buttons. The excitement pressed all of Sababa's. Both men entered the lifts in sequence as their doors opened. They disabled each one long enough to unscrew the new signs that had been posted inside earlier that day.

Mission Statement
The Central Vancouver Island Health Region is committed to the total quality management of timely, seamless, innovative care for all our

174

consumers, facilitated by a multidisciplinary collaboration of providers, promoted with restructured preventative paradigms of diverse, progressive client empowerment.
Check out our new website: www.defalcation.ca.
'Healthy Stakeholders in Healthy Communities.'

As the two men were collecting all the new signs under their arms, an older man entered an elevator. He pushed a button and flew backwards across the space. *Whummmph!* He got up in obvious pain, only to be flung at the rear wall of the lift for a second time. *Whummmph!* There was no obvious assailant. He lay on the floor, afraid to get up.

"Damned implantable defibrillators." Sababa said. "Why do you think these elevators would be out to get me?"

He called Marquis Shu Ying and his reinforcements on the Bridge of the Death Star from the nearest handset.

"Richard Cheney, Shu." He said. "76-year-old retired firearms expert playing handball with his defibrillator all over the elevator walls. A hundred no's are less agonizing than one insincere yes."

"Better to light a candle than to curse the darkness." Came the reply.

After Marquis Shu Ying and his Tranquility Base jumpers picked up their new patient, Sababa and Dr. Zaias walked through the valley of the shadow to their cars.

"What will you do with yours, Peter?"

"Compost bins in my garden shed." He said. "You?"

"Tasting tables for my wine cellar." Sababa admitted. "And what better material for what better causes?"

Jamie was more than ready to present his case by the time Sababa returned to the ER.

"What you got?" Sababa asked.

"As Dr. Ho presented." He said. "Cara Cicatriz, a 33-year-old London Drugs cosmetician with increasing breathlessness and fatigue. No significant past medical history, but physical examination tonight shows areas of skin discoloration on her back, neck, and face. She has thickening of the skin on her fingertips, red hands, spider blood vessels on her chest wall, bulging neck veins, Velcro crackles on listening to her lungs, normal heart sounds, and swelling of her legs."

"Blood tests?" Sababa asked.

"Elevated brain natriuretic peptide level suggesting heart failure, and lots of positive autoimmune tests from a recent visit to her family doctor—antinuclear, antithyroid and anti-Scl70 antibodies. CPK from skeletal muscle is up. Her c-ANCA is

175

positive. Here's her ECG." Sababa noted the low voltage and right and left anterior bundle branch blocks. "She had an echo yesterday, Sab." Jamie continued. "It showed four-chamber enlargement with severe loss of pump function to both sides of her circulation. There's a big clot in her left ventricle."

"We need to go see her." Sababa said.

"Bed #4." Jamie pointed the way and made introductions behind the curtain.

"This is Doctor Sababa, Cara." He said. "For every expert we have, he's the equal and opposite expert." Sababa scowled.

"How long have you had these scars on your skin, Cara?" He asked.

"They've been breaking out in clusters for the past two years." She said. Sababa pulled an ophthalmoscope from his Colombian leather bag.

"May I look at your fingernails through this instrument?" He asked. The cosmetician held out her hands. Sababa unwrapped his Littman Master Cardiology black and brass stethoscope from around his neck.

"May I listen to your chest?" Cara leaned back and looked away. "What's going on?" She asked when he finished.

"It appears you have a condition affecting both your skin and your internal organs." Sababa began. "In your case, it appears to have caused some inflammation of your heart muscle."

"How much inflammation?" She asked.

"A lot." Sababa said. "The positive c-ANCA blood test and the amount of skeletal muscle involvement are rather accurate predictors of disease activity."

"You have a name?"

"Autoimmune myocarditis." He said. "From a disorder we call scleroderma."

"It's a skin problem?"

"You could describe it like that."

"That figures. I'm a cosmetician." She said. "Can you fix it?"

"Most likely." Sababa said. "I'm sending you down to a cardiologist friend of mine in Victoria tonight. Sometimes you need to get out of town. Get a new perspective. But you can't always see that you need a new perspective because you, well, need a new perspective to see that. It's complicated. His name is Wineburger, two of my favorite comestibles."

"What will he do that you can't?" Cara asked.

"He has better toys than I do." Sababa said. "He can arrange for a cardiac magnetic resonance study, skin and heart biopsies, and the other tertiary referrals you will need, and heart failure and immunosuppressive therapy, if you need it."

176

"But I have to work." She said. "I don't have time for this."

"OK Cara, let's leave it a couple of months. Maybe you'll be feeling better by then." Sababa said. "Oh wait, which way does time go? Even though it is not a rigid construct, yours still goes forward. The time for this has come today. Do I make the phone call?"

Cara nodded.

From his secret drive hidden deep inside the hospital computer network, Sababa selected some mood music to build the suspense.

It's astounding... Time is fleeting... Madness takes its toll... But listen closely... Not for very much longer... I've got to keep control... Let's do the Time Warp again... Let's do the Time Warp again...

Richard O'Brien, Time Warp

'Get taps on your toes and get gone
Get rhythm when you get the blues.'
Johnny Cash, *Get Rhythm*

"It's not a clue." Sababa said. He had found Jamie staring at Jasmine's St.Vitus necklace.

"He's the patron saint of dancers." She said. "Like me." The only thing Jamie knew about St. Vitus' dance was that it was a complication of rheumatic fever, which affected the heart. Whatever was affecting Jamie's made it dance.

"You want to tell me what she's doing in my ICU or are you just going to stare into her eyes?" Sababa knew his adherents believed St. Vitus protected against lightning strikes. "Concentrate, Grasshopper. I'm already having one of those days. The voices in my head are fighting, my imaginary friend is running with scissors, and one of my personalities has wandered off."

"Jasmine Place, 27-year-old dance teacher admitted this morning by Dr. Pangloss." He began. "In atrial fibrillation."

"To the ICU?" Sababa asked.

"It took Trace three tries to convert her into normal sinus rhythm." He said. "And her pressure's all over the place."

"What do you do?" It was from Jasmine.

"I'm a phenomenologist." Sababa said. "I find out what's wrong with people, and I fix it if I can."

177

"Don't all doctors do that?" She asked.

"Yeah, but they can't dance like I can." Jasmine smiled.

"She's had a cough and shortness of breath for a year." Jamie continued.

"My breathing gets better when I lie down. I get these chest pains and joint pains and fevers and dizziness." Jasmine added. "And I'm losing weight. It's affecting my dance and my exercise tolerance."

"Exam?" Sababa asked.

"Well, that's it then." Jamie said.

"What's what when?"

"She has a murmur across her mitral valve."

"So?"

"There's this other sound I can't figure out." Jamie said. Sababa unwrapped his Littman Master Cardiology black and brass stethoscope from around his neck. He asked Jasmine to move in various positions and hold and release her breath. Dr. Dasco Boet passed through the unit and came over to extend his morning greetings.

"What are you trying to hear?" He asked.

"Tumour." Sababa said.

"They're usually quiet because they don't have vocal cords." He said.

"Listen to this, Das." Boet unwrapped his own scope from his shoulders. He placed his instrument's diaphragm on Jasmine's chest from where Sababa had removed his. Everyone watched his eyes grow large.

"There's a tumour plop." He said.

"Now listen to the other side." Sababa said. Dasco listened to the other side.

"There are two tumour plops." He said. "Left and right." The conversation had become unnerving for Jasmine.

"What's going on?" She asked. "What's a tumour plop?"

"All in good time, Jasmine." Sababa said. "Betty, get me the shadow puppet on call, please."

"I'm on it." She said. Her left hand gesticulated in the air for a few seconds. "Dr. Brisk, line 1." Sababa picked up the nearest handset.

"No." Said the radiologist.

"You don't even know what I'm asking for."

"No." He repeated.

"Mako, I need a portable transesophageal echo in the unit." Sababa said.

"I'll send down the transthoracic machine." He said.

178

"Not good enough." Sababa said. "I'm sitting on two independent wrecking ball atrial myxomas here and I need to find out now before they throw a clot or block off this girl's circulation."

"We'll be down." He said.

"Thanks, Mako. I'm sorry for the mean awful accurate things I've said about you."

"And I'm sorry." Dasco Boet said behind him. "I have a clinic."

"No worries, Dasco." Sababa said. "We understand."

"No, you don't." Boet said. "I said 'I'm sorry I have a clinic,' not 'I'm sorry. I have a clinic.' But I'll be late for it because I'm not going anywhere. I wouldn't miss this for the world."

While they waited for Mako Brisk and his technician to bring down the portable TEE machine, Jamie challenged the two older internists' findings.

"She most likely has only one problem." He said. "Occam's razor. The simplest explanation is always the best."

"And you think one is simpler than two?" Dasco asked.

"I'm pretty sure it is, yeah." Jamie said.

"The diagnostic parsimony of 13th century Occam's razor." Boet continued. "The simplest explanation is usually that somebody screwed up."

"It's a matter of taste more than of truth." Sababa said "Let me introduce you to Hickam's dictum. In 1946, John Hickam was a house staff member at Grady Memorial Hospital in Atlanta. 'A patient can have as many diseases as they damn well please.'"

"At no stage in the analytic process should you exclude a particular diagnosis because it does not fit Occam's razor." Dasco agreed. "In fact, it is statistically more likely that a patient has several common conditions rather than having a single, rarer disease. Read Walter Chatton's 'anti-razor' principle, which advises 'no less than is necessary.' He used to argue with William Ockham's 'no more than is necessary' long before you were born; the two men were, in fact, not that different. The first expressed negatively what the second expressed in positive terms, and together they made manifest the irreducible tension between simplicity and complexity, in our investigation of reality."

"Reality is always wrong." Jamie said. "If I could get a firm grip on reality, I'd choke it."

"Well, get a grip on it now, Jamie, because here it comes." Sababa said. They heard the whoosh of the translucent door sliding sideways with ease. An ultrasound technician guided a large mobile Zamboni into the Death Star.

179

"Bed #6." Betty Boop pointed toward Jasmine's cubicle. A few minutes later, Dr. Mako Brisk entered, scowling at Doctor Sababa.

"How does a radiologist have sex, Jamie?" Said the stocky savant. Jamie shrugged.

"They don't." He said. "They just enjoy looking at the pictures." He and his technician had Jasmine swallow the ultrasound probe. Sababa and Boet and Brisk, and Jamie and Jasmine's nurse, Mary, hovered around the screen. As Mako adjusted the probe, three pulsating shapes hove into view.

"Whoah." He said. Everyone else let out a low whistle.

"Large 6.6 x 3.1 cm left atrial mass attached to the interatrial septum moving in and out of the left ventricular inflow." Mako adjusted the probe. "And another smaller separate mass, here in the right atrium." Sababa shouted through the curtain.

"Betty, get me the chest cracker on call in Victoria please."

"I'm on it." She said. A few minutes later, Sababa told Jasmine he was transferring her to Victoria.

"What will happen?" She asked.

"You have two benign tumours in the top part of your heart, Jasmine." Sababa said. "The down-island heart surgeon will remove them. And then you'll be fine."

"What are they called?" She asked.

"Myxomas." He said.

"That's a catchy name." She looked at Jamie. "You could slow dance to that."

"Life is about rhythm." Jamie opened her window shade to a view of cherry blossoms. "We vibrate, our hearts pump blood. We are rhythm machines."

"Never lose control of your feet." She was speaking to Jamie.

Dasco Boet rolled his eyes into the back of his head until he could see his brain. Sababa began writing his transfer notes. Ugly music emerged from the computer beside him.

> 'You can dance
> You can jive
> Having the time of your life
> Ooh, see that girl
> Watch that scene
> Digging the dancing queen'
> ABBA, *Dancing Queen*

180

"I hope you like rabbit, Jamie." Jane said.

"Love it." Jamie said.

"Sab brought it home last night." She said. "I've made a hunter's stew."

"Good thing he didn't hit a bear." Jamie mused aloud.

"It could happen." Sababa poured three glasses of young Italian red. The dinner conversation revolved around Jamie's career plans.

"Whom the gods wish to destroy they first call promising." Sababa said. "Never pick a career based on a single 3 a.m. orgasm."

"Did you always want to go into medicine, Jamie?" Jane asked.

"I think so." He said. "I'll never forget when I became a doctor. A switch flipped. I wasn't playing dress-up anymore. I owned the white coat and it owned me. At that moment... it changed me, but nothing like this residency has changed me."

"How so?" Jane passed Jamie more early salad greens from their garden.

"My survival depends on my denial." He said. "Of how badly I want to succeed, that I'm scared, that I'm tired, that I'm in denial even. After a while, the lies become the truth, and the truth becomes unrecognizable."

"But surely you're enduring these hardships for a greater end?" She asked.

"My chances depend on what else I'm prepared to abandon to achieve that success—sleep, natural light, decent food, time, friends, love, self-esteem, a normal life. This residency is the ultimate sensory deprivation trip. There are days that make the burnt offerings worthwhile. There are days where everything feels like ritual slaughter. There are sacrifices that I can't even figure out why I'm making. And all for that one moment when I can call myself an internist."

"Destiny has no pager, Jamie" Sababa said. "Destiny always leans trench-coated out of an alley with a whisper that you can't even hear because you're rushing to something you think is more important and different from your destiny. If you want to do something, you do it. You don't save it for a sound bite."

181

"Where did you find your destiny?" Jamie asked. Sababa looked across the table.

"In the Cairo airport." He said. "At 3 a.m." Jane blushed.

"So why did you want to come to Harbour City Regional for your elective?" She asked.

"They say you should walk a mile in someone else's shoes." Jamie said. "I thought I'd try to walk in Doctor Sababa's. The eyes can mislead, the smile can lie, but the shoes always tell the truth."

"And now?"

"Big shoes." He said.

"And when you finish here?" Jane asked.

"Well, the sacrifice continues." He said. "I have other rotations, and all the while I have to find study time to pass my board exams."

"You know, Jamie, you don't study to pass the test." Sababa said. "You study to prepare for the day when you are the only thing between a patient and the grave. If you do that with the right stuff, you'll pass the exams with no difficulty. And when you finish your training, you will follow your bliss and do your work with love and not for financial reward. But I'm sure you already know all this."

After dessert, Jamie thanked Jane and excused himself to follow Sababa into his study. The portly professor poured him a vintage port and opened the lid of a box on his desk.

"The most futile and disastrous day is well spent when revived through the blue fragrant smoke of a Havana cigar." He said. Jamie partook of the generosity. Both men were soon blowing rings for their own reasons.

"I need to talk to you about today in the Death Star, Jamie." Sababa said.

"I can't show interest in someone?" He asked.

"You can, and I can remind you of your responsibility not to confuse and conflate your conduct."

"OK." He said. "You're right."

"Everyone carries all kinds of conflicting loyalties." Sababa said. "But you can't ever mix professional priority with pleasure, even in your own mind. Ever."

"I know." He said. "How's everything otherwise?"

"Good." It was the best he could do to reassure his protégé. "Just remember that when everything is going against you, airplanes take off into the wind."

Later that night, after Jamie had left, Jane turned to her husband.

"I'm worried about that young man." She said. "He uses the word 'sacrifice' far too much."

'Time is a valuable thing
Watch it fly by as the pendulum swings
Watch it count down to the end of the day
The clock ticks life away.'
Linkin Park, *In the End*

We can excuse the casual reader for not living in real time. Life is so much more intense when one can indulge in worrying about the future and feeling guilty about the past.

Sababa's interest in the past extended only so far as helping him find solutions to problems in the here and now. Those who forget that were doomed to repeat it. But does history repeat itself, the first time as tragedy, the second time as farce? Nope, too grand. History burps, and we taste again the raw onion it swallowed centuries ago. As a snake sheds its skin, so must we shed our past over and over.

"What's the point of the present?" One might ask. "You're born, you walk about and then you die. Waste of time, except that time is all you have for a time." Time after time. Time and tide wait for no man. In time, most things work to one's advantage when one pursues them with an open heart.

And the future? It wasn't necessary to imagine Sababa's world ending in fire or ice. There were two other possibilities. One was paperwork, and there was no way that would ever happen. The other was nostalgia. Nostalgia. How long had that been around?

"Why should I care about posterity?" Sababa might ask. "What has posterity ever done for me?" Sometimes he wondered about trying to slow the unrelenting persecutory movement of time with rebellious and deliberate linear motion through space, on a blockhead Harley, on a sailboat, or hiking the mountains behind his homestead forever. He had already hitchhiked around the world for five years as a young man, running from or searching for, it was sometimes difficult to be sure which.

But in the end, there was no end. There was only the future, and that would begin tomorrow, for the foreseeable future. He was doing what he loved to do and so he let the good times roll. *Showtime.*

Time flies. Time heals all wounds. Time to let go. Time is the direction and distance covered by the inscription in the pasha's celebrated ancient signet ring, for every occasion, comic or tragic. *This too shall pass.*

Dr. Gerry Genial ablated Brian Hugh Warner's extra conduction tract in the Victoria EP lab. Brian sent Sababa two tickets to his next concert. He gave them to Mercy, who went with her daughter.

Thanks to his extensive Greek travel medical insurance, Alexander Asteras got a cardioverter-defibrillator implanted in Athens. Sababa still thinks his Uncle Peter makes the best roast lamb in Harbour City.

Larry Bird's episode of atrial fibrillation after his prostate surgery turned out just one of those things. As grateful as he was for Sababa's quick intervention to save him, he never forgot the delivery of 200 watts/sec of electrical energy across his chest while he was still half awake. The reason he returned to work as a Robbins Parking attendant was to hide in wait for a dimpled and dented white Honda Civic, and exact retribution with stiff shocks of his own. Between his efforts and those of Veronica Marsden, Sababa began to wonder why his air space seemed to have become so hostile.

Barry Keliher ended up in stable permanent atrial fibrillation. He tries hard to find the wines that Sababa orders from the provincial liquor store, but like most endeavors the government pursues, all he usually receives are cases of too little too late.

Daisy Miller has retired from Canada Post for a job as a stay-at-home mom to her son Eleazar and is planning another pregnancy, as soon as her husband forgets about the last one.

Torsade Depointes also got his defibrillator and returned to his work as a chef at Café de la Paix. He did not heed Sababa's advice about wine and cocaine and reappeared in the Harbour

City Regional ER one night in a full-blown 'electrical storm' that even Dr. Capitaine's isoproterenol infusion couldn't calm.

Mathew Damon gave up acupuncture forever; his therapist still doesn't understand what happened to him on her table.

After Cara Cicatriz's biopsy in Victoria confirmed the diagnosis of scleroderma heart disease, Sababa resumed her treatment in Harbour City. An echo one year later showed complete recovery of cardiac function. There was no progression of her skin and lung involvement. New interest and study of pharmacology resulted in a lateral employment move from the makeup to the pharmacy department of London Drugs.

Eddie Felson died from a brain hemorrhage in hospital the afternoon after he picked up the Grizzly B'ar cue ball. Damian Kirkwood received a two-year conditional sentence after pleading guilty to manslaughter. His brother Jason pleaded guilty to assault causing bodily harm and received an eight-month conditional sentence. Siddartha Sauve, because of his 'specialized position as a trained bouncer,' got twelve months in jail, for his part in the fatal attack. They ordered him to give a sample of his DNA and prohibited any possession of firearms for ten years. He now runs an organic farm in the interior of British Columbia.

Jasmine Place had successful surgery to remove her two cardiac tumours. Her Victoria chest cracker replaced the wall between the two upper chambers with a patch from the membrane that lines the outside of the heart. The inside of her heart reached out to Jamie on her return home, but Jamie didn't reach back. She is otherwise symptom-free and still teaching ballet at her studio.

The signs in the Harbour City Regional elevators are still doing useful work in Dr. Zaias's greenhouse and Doctor Sababa's wine cellar. No one ever replaced them.

6. The Case of the Lush Vegetation

'Livin' on the edge, You can't help yourself from fallin''
Livin' on the edge, You can't help yourself at all...'
Arrowsmith, *Livin' on the Edge*

Errington is a small village of three thousand souls, in the Arrowsmith foothills on the east coast of Vancouver Island, northwest of Harbour City. Founded after WWI, British officers settled in, hoping to become chicken ranchers. Local attractions include spectacular cataracts and swimming holes and spawning salmon of Englishman River Falls, the free-spirited rooftop goats of Coombs Old Country market, the North Island Wildlife Recovery Centre, and the last great stand of first growth Cathedral Grove rainforest. *A growing shrine more holy than God, more patient than time...*

Bobby 'Bigmouth' Bass lived alone in the Doug Fir Estates trailer park off Sugarbowl Road. According to one of his rare female guests, the 47-year-old loner worked as a deliveryman for the Shanghai Garden restaurant in Parksville. Originally from Ontario, Bigmouth had lived in his trailer for three years. Because of his pit bull and the rumors he was a drug dealer who owed a lot of money, his neighbours gave him and his trailer a wide berth. They heard frequent loud disturbances coming from his single-wide. Someone threw Bigmouth out of a party in another camper when he had arrived with a broken nose after a drunken brawl.

"We'd wave to him." Said the couple in the mobile home next door. "But that's all."

Ever since the Harbour City detachment of the Combined Forces Special Enforcement Unit seized the local Hells Angels clubhouse under the Civil Forfeiture Act, other criminal mobs had begun to 'assert their dominance and control over the gang landscape' in the region. That kind of healthy competition was bad news for public safety.

Paul Gary Claymore of 'no fixed address' had a red scorpion tattooed on his chest. No one could have known of his whereabouts the night he paid his visit to the Doug Fir Estates trailer park. He had stolen a car in Parksville earlier that day and loaded the back seat and trunk with the forbidden fruits of other labours, including a loaded .40-calibre handgun. Later that night, Paul cut the fuel line on a marked fire truck at the Coombs-Hilliers Fire Department and siphoned off the gas. An hour later, Bigmouth Bass's neighbours heard an 'upset man.' After Bobby's visitor left, they found blood all over his door and called the police.

Paul Gary Claymore drove out towards Coombs, flush with a hundred thousand dollars' worth of cocaine, methamphetamine, and cash. He stopped at the Midway gas station to celebrate with ice cream. Back behind the wheel of his stolen vehicle he licked around the rim to prevent the double-wide cone from dripping on his pants, turned the key, and threw the automobile into gear. It was at that precise moment that the E-Comm officer who had tracked his GPS movements and monitored the bait car interior with audio and video surveillance, disabled Paul's engine with the click of a mouse button. Try as he might, his machine refused to start. As Paul licked at his ice cream, he looked up into the full-beam flashlight and precisely pointed sidearm of Veronica Marsden.

"Rocky Road?" She asked.

'Some dream of India, where their cousins are stars
But they don't like the crowds, so they stay where they are...'
John Gorka, *Winter Cows*

Down the road from the Midway gas station, Gulch Galloway climbed into his denim coveralls at 4:30 a.m. that morning and made a pot of cowboy coffee even before his eyes could focus. There were no weekends for a dairy farmer, no five-day cows. He splashed a dollop of cream from the previous afternoon's milking into a steaming cup of joe, wobbled into the aging Wellingtons two sizes too big for him, and set off out the door into the slip of farmyard muck towards the stanchion barn, through the rays of the new day struggling to light the dawn, and the manure-infused dew-laden Errington air.

His first stop was to check the cattle in the hospital pen, to make sure they were getting better, with the medicine the vet had prescribed for their ruminal acidosis and feedlot bloat. Gulch would milk these sacred cows separate from the rest of the herd. He flicked on the radio after turning on the lights in the main milking shed.

Open your knees and feel the breeze, because BC Bud is back in the trees... This is your host with the most, the bear in your beauty parlour, Fifty Shades of Eh infected with love, for CNDN Coast Salish radio, 101.3 FM on your Home and Native Band...

Gulch moved all the stock to a holding pen and remade their beds with clean and dry comfortable straw and cedar shavings. *The cow is of the bovine ilk; one end is moo, the other milk.* For the next two hours, his new Tie-Stall AMS mobile automated milking system would travel the centre aisle of the barn, approaching his cows from behind to milk them in their stalls. The robotic arm unit, with the aid of a laser teat position sensor, assumed the tasks of automatic teat cleaning, teat-cup application and removal, milking, and last teat spraying.

The Errington dairy farmer remained patient and kind, so his livestock remained calm to maximize their output. Gulch knew that to lose his temper was to lose his usefulness. Moo may represent an idea, but only the cow knows. The bovine is not a reasoning being, but it is the foster mother of humanity. Gulch's farm was a home for mothers. Milk was their gift. Any flow lessened by rough treatment would injure him and the source.

Diamonds are nice and so are pearls, but nothing compares to Coast Salish girls... Bead me like one of your French girls, Snag Eyes, and I'll bang you like a drum... You're the pow in my wow, the sweet to my grass, the choke to my cherry, the star to my quilt...

After the early morning collection, Gulch would clean the parlour and flip on the wash cycle to clean the AMS. Hygiene was critical. Next, he fed the calves milk, the young stock grain and hay, and his milking cows a healthy blend of ingredients to promote lactation. Only then would Gulch Galloway get to have his own breakfast, when most of his neighbours were just waking up. If he did one thing late, he would be late in all his work.

During the rest of the day, depending on the season, Gulch tended his other crops, made hay and silage for his cows, repaired trucks, tractors, and other equipment and outbuildings, and ran errands and attended meetings with veterinarians, vendors, buyers, and government bureaucrats. Dairy farming was simple if your plow was a pencil a thousand miles from udder terror. These alien grass eaters weren't even able to convert what they ate into useful protein. They suspected anyone who made an honest living with his hands and considered independent men like Gulch Galloway 'farmed and dangerous.' They accused Gulch's cows of being the biggest cause of greenhouse gases in the atmosphere but were always trying to milk his dead ones for more. Gulch told them they should go after the 135,000-head Almarai dairy megafactories in Saudi Arabia and they might have, but for the petroleum involved in the equation. Gulch knew that his was a profession of hope, the most useful, the most dignified, and the noblest employment of man.

What is life? It is the flash of a firefly in the night. It is the breath of a buffalo in the wintertime. It is the little shadow that runs across the grass and loses itself in the sunset.

At 4:30 in the afternoon, twelve hours after his first coffee of the day, the second round of milking, and the chores associated with it, started all over again. Seven days a week, 365 days a year, forever, regardless of social responsibilities or personal health.

Gulch Galloway had crossed the threshold of his 45th birthday. His joints creaked and his bones ached. But it was the rash and the fevers that were killing him. The first had started two weeks before as itchy red splotches on his ankles that had now spread to his arms and torso and when he looked in his bathroom mirror, his back. The fevers started a week ago. They came every day, with teeth-chattering chills, soaking his sheets with sour-smelling sweat every night.

When you were born, you cried and the world rejoiced... Live your life so that when you die the world cries and you rejoice.

190

After his second round of chores, it was time for dinner. Gulch checked all the animals one more time before going to bed. Tomorrow would be better. Tomorrow he was going into town to see the hotshot specialist that Dr. Rivera had referred him to. Tomorrow couldn't come soon enough for Gulch Galloway. He fell asleep immediately.

'Un-break my heart
My heart
Don't leave me in all this pain...'
Toni Braxton, *Un-Break My Heart*

"What do you want?"
"Espresso doppio doppio." He said.
"What's that?" Asked the barista.
"It's a double shot of a double espresso." He said. "Two times two is four."
"OK." She said. "How do you take it?"
"Black." He said. "Like my soul."
Sababa had been to Ethiopia, where coffee was born in the ninth century, from white blooms cresting out of evergreen plants, getting goat herders high, spinning them like dervishes. It had made its way along a giant plume from Africa to Europe to cafés, where famous people in berets and scarfs stirred sugar and curled lemon rind, and left crumbs and suitcase bombs beneath small tables.

The day before the events in Errington, Sababa had arrived in front of a glass case of muffins and croissants and sausage rolls, to the smell of old milk and sadness, and jets of black coffee taking off like they were backed up on an airport runway. From the transdermal metal and subdermal ink and perfect pouring hand of the barista, he looked down into his cup, at a face shimmering on the surface like a dark star, in a serum of steam rising. *Hello darkness, my old friend, I've come to talk with you again... within the sound of sirens...*

He was moody because he was on call that day and he hadn't slept well the previous night, because the ER docs preferred calling him than risk the merciless opprobrium and questionable clinical judgement of Dr. Ed Hyde when he was on call. *Well, obviously we're not going to have an intelligent conversation, so I'll just examine you.*

Sababa had made it home in time to grab a quick shower before the pleasures of his own beck and call day would begin.

Perhaps he was moody because of the vehicle he discovered parked in his on-call bay at the front of the ER. Sababa drove up behind it, pushed it over the curb into where the ambulances pulled up to the emergency entrance and told security on his way through the wide automatic sliding frosted glass doors. A Robbins tow truck arrived in less time than Sababa had taken to bounce the rest of the way to the main lobby location of Code Brew.

Resuscitation fluid in hand, Sababa dropped a floor to the room where the monthly medical rounds were being held. The guest speaker for this educational hour of effort was the renowned Victoria cardiologist, Dr. Ricardo Wineburger, who waxed eloquent about cardiac imaging until half the attendees in the dim shadows were asleep. When the lights came back up, Dr. Wineburger asked if there were any questions.

Dr. Mako Brisk's right arm flew into the air. The lecturer knew of the shadow puppet from Sababa's reports of his difficulty procuring heart studies from the radiologists in Harbour City that the cardiologists in Victoria would have been more than happy to perform.

"Yes, Sir." Ricardo said.

"Dr. Brisk, Head of Radiology." Mako said. "We have some difficulty with one of our internists who feels he can requisition a cardiac ultrasound in any phase of the moon. When do you order an echocardiogram?"

"Whenever I want one." Dr. Wineburger said. Sababa high-fived Dr. Dasco Boet in the back of the room before the pager went off in his pocket. It was from the ER. He snuck out before the cardiologist could soften the message. He met Jamie and Dr. Capitaine standing beside the computer on the consultants' desk.

"How are you, Myles?" He asked.

"Living the dream."

"I dream of a better world where chickens can cross the road without having their motives questioned." Sababa said. "What you got?"

"Toni Brachstone." Myles began. "57-year-old Laughter Yoga teacher with type 2 diabetes mellitus and hypertension and a week-long history of shortness of breath and cough, and malaise and confusion, much worse in the last two days. She's not laughing anymore."

"Exam?" Sababa asked.

192

"Mild respiratory distress." Jamie said. "Breathing rate 18 a minute and pulse oximetry of 99% on two litres of oxygen. Pressure's a bit low, likely dehydration. Jugular veins are up, probably not significant. Heart sounds a little muffled, but it just could have been my stethoscope. Creps in both lower lobes."

"Labwork?"

"Anemia of chronic disease and mild elevation of white blood cells. ECG revealed sinus tachycardia and low voltage. Chest x-ray shows an enlarged cardiac silhouette and left lower lobe infiltrate. Urine was cloudy with bugs on microscopy."

"You have a name?" Sababa asked.

"Community-acquired pneumonia." Jamie said. "Pure and simple."

"Make everything as simple as possible, but not simpler." Sababa said. "It was a sign on Einstein's study wall at Princeton. Let's go see her."

At the bedside, Sababa took more time than Jamie expected to use the blood pressure cuff, examine her neck veins, and listen to her heart.

"What did you say about her pressure and jugular veins and heart sounds?"

"Pressure's a bit low, likely dehydration. Jugular veins are up, probably not significant. Heart sounds a little muffled, but it just could have been my stethoscope." Jamie said.

"You just gave me a perfect description of Beck's triad, and you didn't even recognize it." Sababa said. "All your clever reasons were wrong. Riddle me this. Did you find a contracted pulse pressure and a pulsus paradoxicus on exam, the electrical alternans on her ECG, and the water bottle appearance of her heart on the chest x-ray?"

"Nope."

"Well, I did." Sababa said. "We don't set our standards this high to watch our best and brightest hopes for the future fail to meet them." Jamie's expression was crestfallen.

"I've started her on empiric azithromycin and ceftriaxone." He said.

"That part was correct." Sababa said. "Cheri Sundae, please find me the shadow puppet on call for echo today." Less than a minute later, she raised her handset in a victory salute.

"Dr. Brisk on line 2, Doctor Sababa." She said.

"Mako, you either need you to bring the portable transthoracic echo machine down to the ER, or I can bring the patient to your department."

"What do you need this for?" Brisk was brusque.

"Cardiac tamponade." Sababa said. "I need to drain her pericardial sac."

"Oh." Mako said. "I guess we better do this in resusc. We'll be right down."

"Enjoy that little lecture this morning?" Sababa asked. Mako hung up. A few minutes later, an ultrasound technician guided a large mobile Zamboni through the whoosh of a translucent door, sliding sideways with ease.

Michaela and Regina had already set up for the pericardiocentesis. Sababa and Jamie, and Mako and his technician gowned and gloved, and the stocky savant prepped and painted and draped the area around Toni Brachstone's sternum. Sababa placed an alligator clip on his needle, grounded to an ECG machine to warn him of any heart muscle contact. He remembered a story his cousin Gerry had told him about trying to resuscitate a cardiac arrest patient in Boston before any such thing existed. Gerry had drained a similar effusion from around a dying patient's heart when the man flat-lined. The needle he was using had inadvertently pierced into heart muscle and generated a contraction every time Gerry flicked it with his index finger and thumb. The man began to regain consciousness with each more rapid flick of Gerry's digits until he was tweaking it at 70 beats a minute. The head nurse knew he had a broad grin under his mask and removed it with a single poignant question. *Now what, Hotshot?*

The ultrasound probe showed a lake around Toni's heart, and collapse of the right atrium and ventricle during relaxation. Sababa froze the skin and infiltrated lidocaine under the notch that joined her rib cage in the middle of her chest. With continuous negative pressure on the plunger of a 50 ml glass syringe, he began to aspirate the bloody fluid surrounding her pump. He removed 800 ccs and sent it to the lab for a dozen different cultures and other analytical tests. Toni's breathing eased and her cognition improved. Sababa left a cannula in place in case he had to repeat the procedure if the need arose. Michaela finished the dressing.

"From here it's just calculus." He pulled off his mask and gloves.

"What do you think she's got, Sab?" Myles asked.

"It's some kind of fastidious bug." He said. "Too quick to be TB, too slow to be anything common. We'll have to wait for the cultures."

"There are two consults on the telemetry ward, Jamie." Sababa said. "After this little picnic, they shouldn't be too challenging."

Toni Brachston burst out laughing.

194

'I'd unravel ev'ry riddle for any
Individdle
In trouble or in pain.'
Wizard of Oz, *If I Only Had a Brain*

"Dr. Hacker treated him for a heart attack last week." Poldy Bloom was about to look in on his patient after Jamie had finished working up his first referral in the telemetry ward. "Michael Verigin, 66-year-old Doukhobor Meats and Delicatessen owner who initially presented with a two-day history of chest discomfort and fever. The pain was behind the sternum and associated with palpitations and sweating. Exam was normal but his cardiac enzymes were elevated and his ECG showed a pattern consistent with an ST-elevation myocardial infarction affecting the bottom of his heart. The Big Easy saw him between rounds of golf, gave him a clot buster, and sent him to Victoria for angiography."

"Sounds reasonable." Jamie said. "He had a heart attack."

"No, he didn't." It was Sababa, who rolled through the frosted doors of the Harbour City Regional first floor telemetry unit.

"I'm rejecting your current diagnosis because it's wrong, and treating for wrong diagnoses can result in certain side effects." Sababa said. "Like death."

"But why?" Jamie asked.

"He had a fever." Sababa said.

"You can have a fever with an MI, can't you?"

"Feel free to exclude any symptom if it makes the job easier." Sababa said. "What did the heart cath and angio show, Poldy?" Dr. Bloom flipped to the imaging part of the chart.

"Normal." He said. "All normal." Sababa looked at Jamie.

"So he had a MINCA." He said. "You know. Myocardial infarction with normal coronary arteries. It can happen."

"Hmmm... You're sort of like a child genius, without being either a child or a genius." Sababa said. "As much as I'd like to take your word for it, I have no interest in taking your word for it."

"Anyway, Ernie's off on a golf day, so I'd appreciate your seeing him." Poldy said. "Although I'm not sure where we got this idea that you're better than everyone else?"

"Dunno." Sababa said. "Possibly all that pulling people back from the brink of death. Just a guess."

"I admitted him last night with more chest tightness, but now with shortness of breath, fatigue, low blood pressure, and high fever." Poldy said. "Labs showed high white blood cell count and mild elevation of hepatic bilirubin. He's back from an abdominal ultrasound." Sababa called the radiology department.

"Who's the shadow puppet on for ultrasound today?" He asked. It was Dr. Alan Statham. "Let me speak to him." A few minutes later, Sababa hung up the phone.

"Well?" Poldy and Jamie chimed in together.

"Gosh, it would be awful pleasing, to reason out the reason, for things I can't explain." Sababa said. "I'd unravel every riddle, for any individual, in trouble or in pain."

"What did it show?" Poldy asked.

"Liver abscess." He said. "Let's go see him."

"This is Doctor Sababa." Poldy made the introductions. "He's aggressive, nasty, and unstoppable. Just the man you want on your side when you're in trouble."

"Am I in trouble?" Michael asked.

"Not as much now." Sababa told him about the infection.

"Well, I guess that explains this catheter drain in my belly." He said. "But they told me I had a heart attack."

"It's the abscess." Sababa said. "Likely a bacterium called Klebsiella. Caused a noxious inflammation of your heart muscle, a toxic myocarditis that mimicked an acute MI. We'll also start you on some IV antibiotics, and they'll be some other tests." Dr. Bloom stayed with Michael to explain.

"Did you finish working up the other patient here?" Jamie handed Sababa Cliffy Carlton's ER referral note. It was short and approximately to the point. *Diagnosis: Multimedical. To see Doctor Sababa. Discussed.*

"So tell me a story." Said the stocky savant.

"Edmond Nocard." Jamie began. "43-year-old Errington Horse Trail Ride Guide two weeks status-post porcine Medtronic Freestyle biological prosthetic aortic valve replacement for an inherited narrowed and calcified two-cusped valve. It was found during an annual physical exam, required because he also works as a volunteer firefighter for the Coombs-Hilliers Fire Department. Dr. Carlton admitted him last night and started him on intravenous antibacterial drugs for a high fever, persistent two days after his GP had given him the first course of

196

oral antibiotics. Like Cliffy says: One cup cluster. Two cups fuck."

"Did he draw any blood cultures before he started the IV bug killers?" Sababa asked.

"Yep. Two sets." Jamie said. "Both with an antibiotic removal device."

"So we have a chance to ID the culprit." Sababa said. "Why did they give him a pig valve instead of a metal one?"

"He decided against a mechanical valve because his lifestyle was incompatible with lifelong blood thinners."

"Fair enough." Sababa said. "It's a durable enough device they chose, made without a frame and allowing movement more like a natural valve. What else do we know at this point?"

"Vital signs are now normal, sternal incision shows no signs of infection, and his cardiac and lung exam is otherwise normal." Jamie said. "I found a splinter hemorrhage under the fingernail of his right thumb."

"Good man." Sababa said.

"He's anemic and his C-reactive protein is in the stratosphere. ECG and chest x-ray are normal." Jamie brought up an image on a nearby computer screen. "Here's his transesophageal echo from this morning." He pointed out a string-like structure in the left ventricular outflow tract attached to the prosthetic valve.

"You have a name?" Sababa asked.

"Early onset prosthetic valve endocarditis."

"Care to hazard a guess at the culprit organism?" Sababa asked.

"Could be anything." Jamie said.

"I smell horse hoof dust."

"Meaning?"

"What are the great systemic imitators in medicine?" Sababa asked. "The great masqueraders."

"You mean like TB and syphilis and lupus and..."

"And various cancers and intravascular large B-cell lymphoma and fibromyalgia and psoriatic arthritis and sarcoid and multiple sclerosis and celiac disease and Addison's and pulmonary embolism and sleep disorders and Lyme and malaria and brucellosis." Sababa said. "And one more."

"I give up."

"Your hard drive appears to be out of free space." Sababa said.

"Nocardiosis."

"You think?" Jamie asked. "Normally when you hear hoofbeats its horses, not zebras."

"I don't make predictions. Never have and never will." Sababa said. "Nocardia farcinica, to be more precise. We'll treat it. Even

if the cultures come back negative if he gets better, I'm right; if
he dies, you're right."

"You taught me that if your patient gets better, it isn't proof that
your diagnosis was correct." Jamie said. "It's not even logical."

"Logic allows you to be wrong with authority." Sababa said.
"Instinct follows intuition. Change Cliffy's milquetoast
antimicrobials to IV imipenem and cotrimoxazole. We wait five
days for the culture results. I'll go see him. You write him up.
Grab a bite to eat and meet me in the office at one."

On his way out of the unit, Jamie once again confided in
Serafina.

"Sababa is that guy who follows you into a revolving door and
comes out first." The young man said. "He'll lift your all hopes
and aspirations, carry those dreams across the most radioactive
proving ground, and then feed them to his dog."

"Life is a complex texture of conflicting moralities." Serafina
said.

"I'll bet when he deletes a cell phone app, all his icons shake in
panic over who he'll cut next."

"He doesn't own a cell phone." She said.

"Jeezuz."

'Like a man in a
trance
     You know darn well that I don't stand a chance
     Unchain my heart let me go my way.'
     Joe Cocker, *Unchain my heart*

"It's infected heart week, Boss."

"Act justly. Love Mercy. Walk humbly." Sababa said. "Where's
Jamie?"

"Not here yet." She said.

"When he arrives, give him the next patient." Sababa took the
first chart off the top of the pile and called his first puzzle.

"Gulch Galloway." A thin man in denim overalls got up from his
waiting room chair. Sababa was already analyzing the visible
rash on his arms. "Come in, Sir." He pointed to a door.

Sababa's office was large and spacious. The light poured in from
the windows behind his desk. Sometimes he left the blinds open
if he thought he required an advantage. His bookshelves went to
the ceiling, filled as they were with rare and exotic medical texts
and antique instruments. He had catalogued his wooden file
cabinets with a unique system designed to categorize human

198

disease from subatomic particles and physical threats, up through molecules to viruses, bacteria, protozoa, fungi, worms, to venomous animals. He could put his finger on any article in any drawer within a few heartbeats. A bone-chilling wooden skeleton from a Guatemalan church in Chichicastenango smiled down on the proceedings. Sababa would point to it when the absence of patient compliance became evident. Beside his desk was a Shaolin monastery rubbing of Da Mo, the monk who brought Buddhism to China. There were two chairs on the other side of his desk, comfortable but not too comfortable. No third chair assured his control over any extraneous interrogation.

Gulch Galloway sat in one of the seats. Sababa read Dr. Rivera's referral. *Skin failure.*

"How can I help?" He began.

"I have this rash." Gulch said. "And these fevers."

"You're a dairy farmer?"

"How did you know?"

"It is my business to know what other people don't know." Sababa spent the next half hour collecting the recent and remote life history of Gulch Galloway. He took him into his examining room across the hall and spent another half hour looking and listening, and percussing and probing every organ. The rash was now everywhere, his ankles were swollen, and his rectal exam Hemoccult test turned blue, evidence for microscopic blood in his stool.

"You need to be in hospital." Sababa said, finally.

"I can't. I have cows." Gulch protested. "What's wrong?"

"You have an inflammation of your small blood vessels." Sababa said. "We call it vasculitis. Yours is from an infection. All the blood work that Dr. Rivera did yesterday hasn't come back, but we know that you have a high white blood cell count, two kinds of anemia, and an elevated sedimentation rate, which is a nonspecific marker for inflammation."

"I need to find someone to look after my herd." Gulch said. "Can I come in tomorrow?"

"I may call you to come in sooner, if I get notification of anything more significant going on, Gulch." Sababa said. "But definitely tomorrow. You come in through the emergency department. I'll let them know to expect you. How are your cows?"

"Most are good. I have a few with feedlot bloat." He looked up. Sababa hadn't liked the answer.

"Tomorrow. Be there. Give these requisitions to Mercy as you leave." Gulch shook Sababa's hand before Jamie appeared in his doorway.

199

"How kind of you to come."

"Sorry." Jamie said.

"I'm not a big fan of apologies." Sababa said. "As a doctor, 'sorry' is not a happy word. It usually means this will hurt, or you're dying and I can't help you."

"Sorry." He said again.

"OK. What you got?"

"Edward Derrick." Jamie said. "50-year-old North Island Wildlife Recovery Centre volunteer referred by Dr. Tarmac for a one-week history of progressive shortness of breath on exertion and at rest, made worse by lying down. He was well until a month before when he developed a brief flu-like illness with fever, malaise, night sweats, recurrent throbbing headaches, muscle and joint pain, loss of appetite, dry cough, nausea, and diarrhea."

"Past medical history?" Sababa asked.

"A year ago he had coronary artery bypass grafting and bioprosthetic aortic valve placement." Jamie said. "There is a five-year history of insulin-treated diabetes, and remote alcohol, marijuana, and cocaine use. He still smokes a pack of cigarettes a day. Used to work on a nearby dairy farm."

"Exam?"

"Shows a well-healed sternal scar from his earlier cardiac surgeries. He has a faint mitral murmur, creps to both mid-lungs, and minimal leg swelling. Labs are normal except for an elevated sed rate and some kidney dysfunction. Chest x-ray this morning shows lung congestion."

"Let's go see him." Sababa opened the door to the residents' examining room. Inside was a thin, tanned, middle-aged male with a face creased and craggy from years of smoking. He wasn't bald but had grown somewhat taller than his hair.

"You had something like the flu about a month ago, Ed?" Sababa began.

"Yeah." He said. "Horrible."

"What happened two to three weeks before that?" Sababa asked.

"What do you mean?"

"Anything unusual happen at the wildlife recovery centre?" Sababa's gaze narrowed to a focal point.

"Nothing I can think of..." Ed said. "Wait a minute, there was that problem with the Coombs rooftop goat."

"What problem?" Sababa asked.

"Damnedest thing I ever seen." Ed continued. "Market owner couldn't raise the vet so he brought one of his goats down to us. She aborted a kid and died in front of us. Nothing we could do."

200

"Right." Sababa said. "Ed, Dr. Dunne here will admit you to hospital today. Wait here." He and Jamie went back to Sab's office to discuss the case.

"You got a name?" Jamie asked.

"Q fever endocarditis." Sababa said. "On his prosthetic valve."

"How did you come up with that?"

"Goats are a host for the ticks that carry Coxiella burnetii, a proteobacterium known to cause spontaneous abortions in ruminants. The incubation timing is right. It only takes one bug to cause the disease, the lowest known ID50 of any bacterial agent, which is why the Americans developed and manufactured over five thousand gallons of the stuff as a biological weapon at Pine Bluff Arsenal in the 1960s."

"You want me to arrange admission?"

"Please." Sababa said. "Give him a diuretic. After they draw six sets of blood cultures, get a C. burnetii IgG assay and the other fastidious organism serologies you know about, and start him on an antibiotic regimen for culture-negative endocarditis—vancomycin, rifampin, and ciprofloxacin. Leave off the gentamicin because of his kidney dysfunction. I'll meet you in the ER after I finish here." His glance up at Jamie couldn't find his eyes.

"What's wrong?" Sababa asked. "You look like you're trying to shit a sea urchin."

"Uh, I have a... date... tonight." He said.

"Must be the reception." Sababa said. I didn't quite get that."

"I have a date tonight."

"I'm sorry. I was calculating the mass of the sun." Sababa said. "No hablo Inglés."

"I have a date."

"Did I ever tell you about the cool life-size bronze statue of a Burmese healing deity I found in Mandalay? The locals rubbed the spot that ailed them. Some places were still green with centuries of verdigris corrosion. They had polished others to a high shine. But there was this gaping hole where the crotch should have been. And I always thought carrying around a penis made everything so shiny and happy."

"Does that mean I can go?"

"Life is a short, meaningless journey filled with emptiness and pain, Jamie." He said. "Get all the patchouli you can."

'You're in my heart, you're in my soul
You'll be my breath should I grow old...'
Rod Stewart, *You're In My Heart*

Doctor Sababa walked past something that could have begun life as a hominid.

"What happened to you?" He asked.

"I was drinking with a friend." He said. "He got to the axe first."

"Life in the vast lane." Dr. Gung Ho crossed the ER in ten strides. "I keep asking for a Valium fountain in the waiting room, but the mandarins just ignore me."

"Maybe a phenobarb salt lick instead." Sababa said. "What you got?"

"Duck Jones." Dr. Gung Ho pulled Sababa into a cubicle. "19-year-old worker at the Qualicum Trading Post in Whiskey Creek."

"Native art and souvenirs." Duck said.

"Says he had a bad sore throat two weeks ago." Gung said. "And just in the last 24 hours can't walk properly."

"My muscles won't do what they're supposed to." Duck's face was trying to go in different directions. "Arms jerk all over the place. I can't write, I slur my words, and I've had this boomer headache."

"Pleased to make your acquaintance." Sababa extended his hand. Duck took it with a relapsing grip of alternate increases and decreases in tension.

"Milk sign." He said. "Open your mouth." The tongue inside flickered in random spontaneous contractions.

"Bag of worms." Sababa said. "Did you get any antibiotics for your sore throat?"

"Nope." Duck said. "Couldn't find time to get into town."

"You ever had this before?"

"I remember my mom saying I had something like this when I was six years old." Duck said. "Came with a rash like a snake."

"Erythema marginatum." Sababa said. "Well, you've got it again."

"Got what?" He asked.

"Sydenham's chorea." Sababa said. "Also called St. Vitus' dance, after the patron saint of dancers. Thomas Sydenham was the British doctor that first described it. He also gave us the dictum *Primum non nocere*. First, do no harm. As doctors, we're pledged to live by this oath. But harm happens and then guilt happens. And guilt travels nowhere on its own without its friends, doubt and insecurity. But I digress."

"I didn't get much of that." Duck admitted.

202

"Sababa's different." Gung said. "He sometimes suffers from paralysis by analysis."

"You've got rheumatic fever." Sababa said. "For the second time. It's caused by your immune system confusing certain parts of you with a Group A β-hemolytic streptococcus. Right now, it's confused the dopamine 2 receptor in your brain's corpus stratum with the molecular mimicry of the bacterial antigens. You're producing antibodies against your own brain."

"My boss always says I don't know myself anymore."

"Rheumatic fever licks at the joints, but bites at the heart." Sababa said.

"Meaning what?"

"Your movement disorder will get better, although sometimes it takes a while." Sababa said. "The real problem is what this type II immune reaction can do to your ticker."

"Like what?"

"About half the time it will attack the lining of your heart, your valves, or the heart muscle itself. We need to find out if you've developed rheumatic heart disease."

"How does that work?" Duck asked.

"I need to bring you into hospital for a few days." Sababa said. "We'll do some throat and blood cultures, other blood tests, CT scan your brain, echo your heart, and give you courses of short and long-term penicillin, perhaps as long as forty years. I'll also prescribe a course of corticosteroids and some medication for the movement disorder. Everyone should believe in something. I believe in Haldol."

"If you could lick my heart, it would poison you." Duck said.

"Wearing your heart on your sleeve isn't a good plan, Duck." Sababa said. "It's better on the inside where it's designed to function."

Cliffy Carlton's face poked through the curtains of Duck Jones's cubicle.

"My ER is filled to the brim with acute exacerbations of chronic nonsense." He said. "But I have this one guy you need to see."

Sababa came out from Duck's cubbyhole.

"Who's that?"

"Les Hart." Cliffy said. "27-year-old Coombs Old Country Market produce manager. Recently got back from South America and now complains of shortness of breath and dizziness. Only other problem is low thyroid, treated to target. Exam shows a slow pulse. Chest X-ray and most baseline bloods are normal but his cardiac markers and BNP are up and his ECG is abnormal."

"How abnormal?" Sababa asked.

"This abnormal." Cliffy handed him the tracing. It showed complete heart block, a right bundle branch block, elevation in some unrelated leads, and depression in others. "And then there's that." Sababa glanced over at the monitor. There were frequent runs of nonchalant slow sustained ventricular tachycardia flying across the screen.

"I'm all over it." Sababa pulled back the curtain.

"Mr. Hart?" The man nodded. "I'm Dr. Sababa. Dr. Carlton asked me to look in on you."

"What kind of doctor are you?"

"I'm an internist."

"An intern?"

"No, that's a doctor in training." Sababa said. "I solve complex problems. Everything except barbershop, bat shit and babies."

"I don't feel good at all."

"Where were you in South America?" Sababa asked.

"Peru, Ecuador, Argentina." He said. "Around."

"Do you remember any significant insect bites?"

"No." Sababa watched another run of VT ricochet across the monitor. He opened the curtain wide enough.

"Regina, can I have a slow load amiodarone here please?"

"Coming right up, Sab." She disappeared into the med room.

"What's that for?" Les asked.

"You're having some rhythm disturbances from the bottom part of your heart."

Sababa continued his exam. "We're not fond of them."

"What's wrong with me?"

"That's what I'm working on finding out, Les." Sababa said. "I need to send you to a friend of mine in Victoria. Tonight."

"Is it serious?" He asked.

"You're will need more investigations to be sure." Sababa said.

"Like what?"

"Like ultrasounds and angiograms and a biopsy of your heart muscle."

"You're kidding."

"If I was kidding, I'd have goats on my roof." Sababa said. "Dr. Richard Wineburg. That's who I'm phoning right now." Cliffy cornered the stocky savant after he made his call.

"If this guy's still here in the morning, I will bring a shovel and bury him in the parking lot."

"You won't need to do that, Cliffy." Sababa said. "He's trying to do that all by himself. There's an ACLS ambulance on its way."

"What do you think?"

"Giant cell myocarditis." Sababa said. "Median survival is only 6 months. Ninety percent are dead by the end of one year or have received a heart transplant. In this country, he'll be lucky to live long enough to get one."

"Will it work?"

"In a quarter of the allografts, the disease destroys the new heart." Sababa said. "He'll be back if he survives."

"We always assume the serious changes in our life happen slowly, over time." Cliffy said. "But it's not true, is it Sab? The big stuff happens in a heartbeat. Sometimes you don't even recognize that anything has changed."

"Dr. Will Mayo once said that life is a matter of chemistry." Sababa said. "But those reactions all follow the second law of thermodynamics. Stuff rarely comes together, but it always comes apart. Finally, only one thing is certain. No one is getting out of here alive."

Cheri Sundae waved at Sababa from across the ER.

"Microbiology on line 3, Doc." She shouted. Sababa picked up the nearest handset.

"Yes?"

"You have a patient named Gulch Galloway?" The lab tech asked.

"Yes."

"He's growing Strep bovis in his blood cultures." She said. "Six positive out of six sets."

Sababa made another phone call to a dairy farmer in Errington.

'It ⚕ ⚕ ⚕ was warm in the
night   I   was cold as a stone
           But I still haven't
found
What I'm looking for...
U2, *I Still Haven't Found What I'm Looking For*

As with most other planetary forms of corruption, progress moved faster inside the Death Star in the presence and with the provision of extra anomalous forms of payment. The hush money units of negotiable currency in the Harbour City Regional Hospital ICU came in two principal denominations— Purdy's chocolates and Mambo's pizza. It was the latter of this comestible capital that found its way onto Doctor Sababa's credit card late that night, when Virginia, one of the night staff, found its upper limit in the Good Doctor's wallet. It's not that Sababa hadn't offered to buy midnight pizzas for his Angels of

Mercy. He had. But Virginia's tenacious grip on the card had shown none, and her lavish order had required delivery by two drivers, much to the astonishment of the assembled intended beneficiaries and, a few weeks later, when the VISA bill arrived, of Jane Sababa.

"I hope you're hungry, Sab." Virginia said as she replaced the lifeless plastic remains back in his billfold.

Sababa hadn't made it home that night. There had been too much deadly and destructive carnage wrought by Mother Nature and her surgical colleagues. The best of them were also on call that night. Dr. Jules Martino and Sababa shared the patient with a record for the longest stay in the unit. Walt Gropius had been on a ventilator for four months. Every fortnight the suits would come down from their clouds and ask Sababa how much longer they would have to pay to maintain the elderly architect on life-support, and every two weeks Doctor Sababa would tell them they could unplug his star patient, if they were also willing to provide their reasons for their little euthanasia exercise to the national media.

Walt came in with pancreatitis, brought on by his irrepressible fondness for Northern Harvest Crown Royal rye whiskey. He hadn't had a drink now for four months, and his wife promised his doctors he never would again, provided they saved his miserable soul this time, so she could beat it to death when she got him home. His black and blue arms told the tale of his staying and his staying power.

Every other two weeks, Dr. Martino would whisk Walt off to the OR, for what he referred to as 'debridement,' a term which Sababa suspected was scalpel and staple gun code for 'gilding the lily,' although Walt continued to improve after each surgical furlough from the Death Star.

The anesthetist, Dr. Banjo Paterson, brought him back to his cubicle this time. Sababa welcomed him with a Mötley Crüe music library excerpt from a secret drive hidden deep inside the hospital computer network. *He's the one they call Dr. Feelgood, he's the one that makes ya feel all right...*

Sababa knew the data on music in the ICU—how brain blood flow dropped more listening to *Va pensioero* from Verdi's *Nabucco* compared to *Libiam nei lieti calici* from his *La Traviata*, or Bach's Cantata No. 169 *Gott soll allein mein Herze haben*.

He knew that *Beethoven's Ninth Symphony* made no difference at all, that Bach, Mozart, and Italian composers caused his critical care patients to get better faster, and that Heavy Metal tunes were not only ineffective but dangerous, and led to life-threatening arrhythmias. He didn't give a rat's ass.

"Anesthesia is so weird, Sab." Banjo said. "You go to sleep in one room, then wake up four hours later with some stranger in a different one, just like at university." Sababa knew the story of how Banjo once sedated a young boy and left him anesthetized while he went into town to go shopping, but now was not the time to reminisce. He read the gas passer's OR note. *Stable, but in multi-organ failure.* Banjo turned to the new patient in the next cubicle.

"Be nice to your nurse." He said. "She's the only heart your doctor has." And then to the stocky savant.

"Plug and play, my friend." He said. "à bientôt."

Gulch Galloway was in the next bed, already admitted through the ER at 4:00 a.m. Sababa had greeted him with an old bovine canard from Tommy Douglas.

"Canada is like an old cow, Gulch." He said. "The West feeds it. Ontario and Quebec milk it. And you can well imagine what it's doing in the Maritimes." Sababa told the dairy farmer about how he knew which bacteria was causing all the trouble.

"You had feedlot bloat and ruminant acidosis affecting a part of your herd." He said. "Certain lactic acid bacteria which ferment the carbohydrates in your cows' high starch and sugar diet did that, the same kind of Group D Streptococcus gallolyticus, S. bovis, that grew the vegetation on your heart valve."

"Vegetation?" Gulch had asked.

"That's what we call the growth of bacteria and infected blood products that attaches itself in the turbulence. Your heart valves don't have a blood supply of their own." *One who neglects or disregards the existence of earth, air, fire, water, and vegetation disregards his own existence that is entwined with them... Vegetation is the basic instrument the creator uses to set all of nature in motion...*

"There's one more little connection I need to tell you about." Sababa said.

"What's that?" Gulch asked.

"Your bug is S. bovis biotype I."

"What does that mean?" He asked.

"Sometimes we find this bacterium in association with tumours of the colon." Sababa said. "You have two kinds of anemia, and I found microscopic traces of blood on your rectal exam."

"I have bowel cancer as well?"

"I'm not sure." Sababa said. "But you'll need a colonoscopy before you get home."

"How long is all this going to take?" Gulch asked. "My herd is missing me."

"If your echo today shows that your vegetation is less than 5 mm in diameter, if you don't develop any complications, if the

207

minimum inhibitory concentration of the antibiotic is high enough, if your response is rapid and we clear your bloodstream infection immediately, and if we don't find a tumour on colonoscopy, you may get away with a two-week course of IV benzylpenicillin plus another bug killer."

"You think so?" He asked.

"No, I don't think so." Sababa said. "But it's possible. We'll talk again after your ultrasound."

"What if I refuse to do all this stuff?"

"Then you will die." Sababa said. "And we will miss you."

The day-shifters had arrived and turned on all the lights. For as long as it took the night nurses to give report, there were two Angels of Mercy seated in front of every cubicle. Betty Boop flew in like a banshee, swirling vortices of smoke off her trailing edges. Jamie, who had come to say goodbye, followed her.

"Don't you have one more day?" Sababa said.

"I have something important to attend to." He said. "I didn't think you'd mind."

"No, that's fine."

"I brought you something for all the help you've given me." Jamie handed Sababa a gift-wrapped box. Sababa removed a scalpel from his Colombian leather briefcase and made short work of the wrapping. Inside was an elaborate life-sized model of a human heart.

"It's a heart." Jamie said. "It comes apart so you can see inside. I thought you could use one." Sababa smiled. There was a card attached, inscribed with an excerpt from a Rush song. *And the men who hold high places... must be the ones who start... to mold a new reality... closer to the heart.*

"Thank you, Jamie." He said. "Help yourself to some pizza."

"It's cold."

"That's why God made microwaves." Sababa said. "Breakfast of Champions."

'There's a feeling I get when I look to the west
And my spirit is crying for leaving
In my thoughts I have seen rings of smoke through the trees
And the voices of those who stand looking...
Ooh, it makes me wonder...'
Led Zeppelin, *Stairway To Heaven*

The casual reader can be absolved of misunderstanding the meaning of life. Life was planned by a committee while the clever ones had popped outside for a smoke. They wasted their lives drawing the lines that Sababa decided he would live his life crossing. Boundaries didn't keep other people out; they fenced you in. Life was messy and something he found difficult to avoid. They had tried to make the lines way too dangerous to cross, but the view from the other side was so spectacular, he couldn't resist. It was a quality of life issue, larger than life. You bet your life. In learning how to save a life, he became the Jaws of Life. It set Sababa to ponder that ontological riddle: was life random or systematic? He opted for the systematic approach, algebraic, if you will—an eye for an eye, a tooth for a tooth.

Of the three choices he had in life: be good, get good or give up, he chose 'get good.' Life was everywhere. The earth was throbbing with it. It was music. The plants, the creatures, the ones he saw, the ones he didn't see, it was one, big, pulsating symphony. Beyond wine and women and song, beyond sex and drugs and rock 'n' roll, life was not a fairy tale. The great tragedy of life was that something always changed. The comforting vision of Newton's neat, orderly, predictable universe functioning like clockwork and a well-oiled machine was shot to pieces by relativity and quantum mechanics, and all the other trolls of 20th-century physics. The truth was a lizard, leaving its tail in your fingers and running away, knowing it would grow a new one in the twinkling.

Sababa considered the donning of his white coat the moment his life started; it would still fit him when it ended. We are all serving a life sentence in the dungeon of self.

There may have been life after death. It just didn't involve him. There was no next life. Though he would give up his life, he would never give up his honor. Drama was life with the dull bits cut out, and the drama was coming.

In medicine, it's called the Golden Hour. That magical window of time that often determines whether someone lives or dies. It takes only six minutes for a brain to die, but the rest of you can live without a brain if we get to you within an hour. Sababa gave

Jane an exact six-minute radial limit to Harbour City Regional Hospital when she went looking for their homestead property. It was as much time as he ever had to forgive himself if he needed to. For who knew what the next hour had in store for him?

Toni Brachstone's blood grew round granular colonies of Ureaplasma on A8 agar after 48 hours of incubation at 37°C in an atmosphere enriched with 7.5% CO2. The drain around her heart was removed on Day 4 and she was discharged laughing from hospital two weeks later. She still teaches laughter yoga in Harbour City.

The Doukhobor Meats and Delicatessen owner, Michael Verigin, had his liver abscess drained. This and his antibiotic treatment returned his toxic heart to normal and allowed him to return home to his four wives.

Five days after admission, Edmond Nocard's blood cultures turned positive with an organism later identified as N. farcinica, on the basis of its comparable growth on tryptic soy agar slopes at 45°C and 35°C, and acid production from rhamnose. His oral antibiotic therapy continued for six months. A repeat echo showed complete resolution of the thread-like vegetation on his pig valve. Edmond is back kicking up the Errington dust as a horse trail ride guide and volunteer firefighter. He still smokes a pack a day.

Ed Derrick's phase I immunoglobulin G against C. burnetii returned at a titre of 1:2048, consistent with Sababa's provisional diagnosis of Q fever endocarditis. He was started on oral antibiotics but he developed a posterior circulation stroke that required an emergency simultaneous replacement of his aortic valve and root. He made a miraculous complete recovery and now works with the eagles and other raptors at the North Island Wildlife Recovery Centre.

Duck Jones developed a severe obsessive-compulsive disorder after his initial treatment for rheumatic fever. It may not have been a totally unhappy circumstance. Duck quickly bought out his boss and now owns the Qualicum Trading Post in Whiskey Creek. His movement disorder resolved after only two months but his echo showed enough evidence for rheumatic carditis to require monthly injections of long-acting penicillin for the next forty years.

Les Hart was wheeled into an operating room, and then had a change of heart. He received a cardiac transplant and a brand new shiny defibrillator in Vancouver, but his giant cell myocarditis reinfiltrated his hopes and dreams and took less than a year longer to kill him. There is a small bronze statue to

210

commemorate his quiet heroism at the Coombs Old Country Market.

After five months on a ventilator in the Harbour City Regional ICU, Walt Gropius was extubated and went home two weeks later. He still holds the record for the longest stay in the Death Star. He sometimes looks longingly at the shelf of Northern Harvest rye whiskey in the government liquor store, but his wife is never far away, and Walt knows how distinctly preferable it would be to die peacefully in his sleep.

Gulch Galloway's echo showed a mobile 8 mm vegetation arising from the ventricular surface of the aortic valve. Dr. Jules Martino performed his screening colonoscopy, which found a resectable cancer in his sigmoid bowel. With Banjo Paterson officiating, Martino removed it the following day. Unfortunately, despite six weeks of IV antibiotics, Gulch's blood cultures remained persistently positive, and repeat echo showed a penetrating lesion with abscess formation. He is not happy with the plan to replace his aortic valve in Victoria, but he is delighted that the Avalus bioprosthesis he is scheduled to receive is from a cow.

Paul Gary Claymore was sentenced to thirteen years in prison for the murder of Bobby 'Bigmouth' Bass in the Doug Fir Estates trailer park. In commemoration, the Red Scorpions have adopted Rocky Road as their official gang ice cream flavour.

A week after the stories of all the lush vegetations, Mercy appeared in the doorway of Doctor Sababa's office.

"They found Jamie." She said.

"Generally, if you find someone you're not looking for, it's not a good thing."

"He took an overdose of fentanyl." She said.

Sababa picked up the heart model that Jamie had given him. He held it in his hands for a long time, time he could hardly afford.

Summer—The Book of Fire

'The finest steel has to go through the hottest fire.'
Richard Nixon

Summer came in on her time off, to ensure we still loved our swelter and suffering. First light separated into rainbows on the homestead's white walls. Sababa was gone by dawn and back after dusk, in enough sunlight to see but not enough to burn. Petals fell on garden paths.

Birds improvised soulful jazz until the air warmed so thick their song fell silent, breathing with open beaks high in the rough limbs of the two old growth fir trees on the lakeshore. Jane and the Good Doctor hovered drowsy on their cotton hammock hung between them in dappled shade, watching clouds float across the sky, listening to bumblebees, or the *Clack clack clack clack clack*... of chunky blue dragonflies on the water. It was a marvellous waste of time. Underneath, the ground was lumpy with projecting roots, twisted like snakes turned to stone, writhing upward one last time before descending deep into the earth to take cool draughts from the water far below.

There were fragrances of leaf and soil, wild rose perfume, and the floral honey of cottonwood snow.

They hiked up to the ridges for picnics of asiago and arugula and avocado sandwiches, and sparkling water splashed with tangy citrus. They ate strawberries and raspberries and blueberries from their garden, and blackberries picked on the climb, glossy purple clots of sanguine wine exchanged for sticky hands scratched by briar thorns. The arbutus trees had moulted like snakes with bad sunburn, exposing satin smooth trunks of yellow and silver ghost and pistachio. Cool to the touch, impossible not to touch. In the rain, they glistened like a fresh oil painting, trains of boxcar droplets running down the undulations. Sababa brought back Manzanita blooms for his clinic.

The heat grew unbearable as the summer intensified, trickling sweat, forcing open windows, switching on fans, turning wands of knee-high grasses golden. Sababa's work in his vineyard ended in a swim across the lake, or a beer, or both. Banana slugs buried themselves in protective mucus, under forest debris. Raccoons shrieked and herons squawked in the night. The biggest of fears was of a blazing forest inferno.

Sababa's high summer glowed with ephemeral lessons from Musashi's *The Book of Fire*, refining timing strategy on the high ground to gain advantage, treading down the sword. The Good Doctor was no stranger to conflagration. He was heir to the Israelite Exodus, conferred by a burning bush unconsumed by its own flaming fractals. He lived on the Ring of Fire. In his work, Sababa fought fire with fire all the time, cutting to repair, hurting to heal. Talent was flame; genius was fire.

The season would eventually subside as imperceptibly as grief, but not quite yet. Stars would rise until the rain would fall, bringing all the good things that summer could bring.

7. The Case of the Flushed Fisherman

'It's always ourselves we find in the sea.'
E. E. Cummings, *maggie and milly and molly and may*

It had been a wonderful vacation. Darryl and Madelaine Hope had driven their two daughters out from Alberta to visit Maddy's mother in Harbour City. Shirley MacMillan always looked forward to seeing her grandchildren Dawn and Carrie and played havoc with her son-in-law's head when it was time for them to leave.

"Why don't you move the family out to the Island, Darryl?" She'd save the question for the last pancake breakfast of the summer holiday. "You could go fishing and I could have my family living closer. I won't be here forever, you know." But Darryl never bit back. He knew how difficult it was for Maddy and her mother to be so far apart, but he still had a well-paying job back in the Alberta oil patch, and moving to B.C. wouldn't likely happen until the girls grew up. Dawn was fourteen but Carrie was only still eleven years old, and Darryl and Maddy were still in their early forties.

"Someday, Shirley." He would say. "You never know." There were hugs and tears when they left this year, more than before. For Shirley, it was like drowning on dry land. Dawn and Carrie piled into the back of the brown minivan. Darryl fired up the engine and waited for Maddy to finish saying goodbye to her mother. Everyone waved backwards as they drove away.

There was a two-sailing wait at the B.C. Ferry terminal in Departure Bay. Darryl knew it was a stiff price to pay for coming to Harbour City during the summer holidays, but it must have been worth it because everyone came. This year he was smart and paid for a reservation on the 9:00 a.m. Queen of Alberni. The pleasure in his own cleverness forced a grin as he pulled past all the vehicles without as much foresight or money.

"Lane 3." Said the ticket vendor in the booth. "You're the last." Darryl steered across the back of several painted white lines to take his place behind a red Thunderbird convertible with California license plates. The cavernous metal doors of the Queen of Alberni were already gaping, and the first lane of vehicles began to pour into the top decks of the ship. Every sort of conveyance, every colour of the rainbow, drove past Darryl— camper vans and sedans, sports cars and SUVs, trucks and trailers and the boats they carried. Dogs drooled out open windows. The smells of coffee and cinnamon and sea air and diesel intermingled over crossword puzzles and cell phones. The California convertible lurched ahead of him, and Darryl followed. One of the ferry workers directing traffic up ahead stopped waving and held out an outstretched arm.

Darryl knew it was OK. He had a reservation and the ticket vendor in the booth told him he was the last. No one told him how true that would be in so many ways.

They speak of slow motion, of life flashing before your eyes, whoever they are. But not that way at all today. The minivan rolling forward off what had been the loading ramp for the receding ferry produced an initial feeling of sinking nausea, but

216

the thirty-foot plunge off the upper car deck was all too quick and unspectacular.

Darryl fumbled to close the electric windows but the freezing salt water had already shorted their circuitry and was now silencing every Hope. He looked around his cockpit, to his wife and two daughters, gasping and holding their breaths, unbuckling their seat belts, moving their arms like they were climbing rocks but it was only the Strait of Georgia. The panic hammered their hearts against their ribs, like birds trapped in cages too small. They tried rolling over on their backs to float. Desperate hot waves washed over them. As the minivan sank, the increasing hydrostatic pressure set their lungs on fire.

They were all strong swimmers but their breathing reflexes were stronger, and they weren't swimming. Ice water rushed up their nostrils, streaming in cascades into the back of their throats. When the carbon dioxide concentrations in their bloodstream overwhelmed their breath-hold breakpoints and throat spasms, they began to swallow and then aspirate large volumes of swirling dark indigo, in exchange for strings of bubbles. The cold salt water rushed in like it owned them, enveloped them and triggered their diving reflexes, slowing their heart rates, constricting the blood flow to their extremities, shifting their blood volume to the inside of their chests, and leaving different concentrations of sodium and chloride ions in the left and right chambers of their hearts. But it also diffused into their blood, making it thicker, requiring more work from their hearts to circulate. They could taste the salt and seaweed and the diesel. Microscopic diatoms unique to this place passed through their lung membranes into capillaries, seeding their internal organs with tiny shells.

The feeble light from above had dimmed. Red and black splotches danced in their vision.

Their hair rose upwards like the kelp beds below them. The cabin was full of freezing seawater and vomit and partially digested pancakes.

They floated like the seaweed, heads back, mouths agape, empty eyes of glass open wide. The red blotches had long since disappeared, faded to black. Their minds had unravelled like a turning spiral of wool, slipping skyward through gaps in the universe, floating away. The chaotic sounds of the sea had drowned in a low hum, muted into silence, one with the darkness. No one heard the last sounds of stopping hearts.

One witness said the ferry appeared to move away slowly.

217

"Either the driver shouldn't have tried to drive on at the time, or the ferry moved early." He said. "It was a lack of communication, I guess."

'A ship is safe in harbor, but that's not what ships are built for.'
John A. Shedd

The day had broken bright and early above the rainforest, transfixing the coastal cumulus in naked mountain peaks. During any other season, the Harbour City skyline would have been a snow-covered postcard, but this was not that other time. This was summer.

Light shimmered cerulean dipped in silver. The wind from the west carried wisps of vapour and the minor melancholic strumming of a busker's ukelele over the harbourfront southeast of Departure Bay.

Water reflected and rippled against the hulls of the boats that rose and fell on their C Dock moorings—gillnetters and seiners, collectors and crab boats, herring punts and prawners, halibut longliners and draggers, each built in their own style. The smell of fish guts festered in the sun. Seagulls cried overhead, coming for whatever they could get.

Summer had ignited the chunky blue dragonflies and the weeds in the cracks of the path along the water's edge. A tiger swallowtail landed on the stem of a fluffy sphere of what had been a dandelion butter bloom only yesterday. The butterfly opened and shut its yellow and black wings like a miniature drone controlled by a remote servo.

The old man had come along the esplanade in no particular hurry. Jacob Berzelius was an American yachtie who believed he had cured himself of prostate cancer. Every summer for the past eleven years, Jake had sailed to Harbour City from Seattle. He envied the slower lives of the many friends he had made on the island. Gary Shadling, the bartender at the Dinghy Dock Pub, would often top up his pint glass of Blue Buck for free. Rhea Bolger, the line cook at Trawlers Fish and Chips, had hooked him good and proper with her generous portions of battered halibut. Quinten Massys, the owner of The Pirate Chandler, let him run a line of credit for any odd item he needed to keep his ship afloat. Jake had no way of knowing about Dawn Hope, who would soon drown inside a sinking van not far away. He reached down and picked a dandelion, from which a tiger swallowtail had launched a few seconds earlier. With a single deep breath, he puffed at a globe of delicate white parachutes, launching them in clusters into the warm air.

Jake wandered onto C Dock in a random walk, drawn to the fishing vessels and the men that worked them, those who had bet their whole lives on an endless war with the deep wild ocean, not just fair-weather hobbyists. He paused in front of an old traditional double-ended salmon troller and digested its name. *Relic.*

The man who stood on its deck lacked the bellies and multiple chins of other men his age. Every part of him was a rough lean, and a leather brown alchemy of sun and sea and weather. He looked like nothing could break him. Jake watched him pat the pockets of his jeans and then his shirt, with spade-like calloused hands. The man retrieved a tobacco tin, rolled a cigarette between his fingers, sealed it with a smooth, beefy red tongue, found fire, and curled smoke into the salty breeze. A sudden flood of briny tears welled up in the cracks of his lips. Then Jake noticed the painful-looking red sores all over his exposed brown skin.

"You all right?" He asked. The man tilted his head back and blew a whale spout of smoke.

"Yep."

"It's just that..." Jake said. Coal Tyee leaned out over the foredeck railing.

"You see this boat?" He said. "She was built in 1954 by the Sather Boat Works in New Westminster. My father bought her in Bristol condition, when she still smelled like wood and diesel and paint and not mildew and disuse, although the old fridge he hauled off, sealed with duct tape, was full of new mushrooms growing in a lake of ancient liquid rotten meat and eggs." Jake took another hard look at the fisherman. His eyes bore the same hue of the ocean but with none of its warmth or sparkle. The corners of his mouth had slumped into his posture. Every cry of the gulls cut at him, layering invisible wounds over his hide and dreams, both wrinkled beyond their years.

"Welcome to the dock side. Come aboard." Jake bowed his head as he did. Coal went into the wheelhouse and turned on his radio.

This is Silas Seaweed, standing in for BC Bud, who hit a snag on the weekend... Today is June 21, the first day of summer—the season of the

219

wolf, sweetgrass, earth, physical and spiritual health, adolescence, cedar, the moon, noon, the south, and red aboriginal people...

Coal removed a dollar bill, taped inside a cabinet door, and handed it to the American sailor. A short phrase was hand-scrawled in black ink. *This is why we're here.*

"My first." Coal said. "If I had one of those for every time I thought about it, I'd have as many as I do now. But there were never enough. It was only fish prices that kept my father from swinging from the rafters for as long as he didn't. He eventually died of his environment. I'm still grateful for the twenty years I spent with him as his deckhand, rebuilding a relationship that had crashed on the rocks when I was a teen. We found respect and understanding that few fathers and sons had ever seen, through hard work and fishing. He gave me the fire in my belly, my physical and mental endurance and ability to do the work, taught me about diesel engines and hydraulics and electronics and 12-Volt systems and dependability, how to shift gears in extreme weather without losing my nerve and to keep my head on a swivel. He led me into the Game Theory of putting each other's needs ahead of our own. With every sacrifice of sleep or convenience or time or effort, we would always take a bullet for the team. When you live in a cabin the size of most people's bathroom for months on end, you learn to get along, or you perish.

Just to remind you of the Canning workshop at the Coast Salish First Nation Big House kitchen tomorrow... Please bring your fish guts to the hole at the point of the Rez... Make sure you log onto our website, www.savethesalmon.net... and bring your fishing license... HaHa... Just kidding...

My old man was part native Nootka wizard. Every year, before we put to sea, he would make an image of a swimming fish and put it in the water in the direction from which the chinook would appear. Then he said a prayer louder than any of the other fisherman, to encourage the salmon to arrive faster.

Here's a hymn for our men on the high seas...

Silas Seaweed pushed a button, and Ken Hamm's voice and resonant dobro guitar pervaded the pilot house space.

Well, light comes early, it's early in the day, It's four o'clock and we're on our way,

220

Ah we're looking for smiley, but he can't be found, Bitter days, on the fishing grounds.

"We tried to sleep in shifts of four hours out of twenty-four. I mostly braced myself in my bunk staring at the ceiling less than a foot away from the back of my eyeballs, because we had anchored in ten feet of water in a fifty-kilometre Small Craft Advisory wind coming from the wrong direction, and the waves stacked up six feet high rolling in arcs on the back of a giant cobra.

I slept for an hour and then another, all the while thinking about that dollar taped to the inside of the cabinet and how the season still held that many days and how tired I was and how the engine has been sounding weird and leaking coolant and how old the bilge pumps were. And what my girlfriend might be doing while I wasn't there. If there ever was any such a thing as beauty sleep, we left our bunks uglier than when we got in.

When the alarm went off, I'd commando-crawl out of my bunk and, testing the limits of the human olfactory system, put on the same sweats I'd been marinating in for the last five days, slap on another coat of deodorant because I hadn't showered in a week, wolf down some food, collect a few more bruises and new curses from pinballing around the cabin, stomp into my Xtratuf boots, fire up the engine, and kick the anchor winch into gear.

I'd jam on my heavy rubber gloves, clip on my life jacket, and stagger out on a pitching deck into clammy rain gear that weighed a ton. The cold wind blew the rain sideways."

And we tacked off Hippa, in a dirty lump, And the pigs were bouncing, man, and you could see them jump, And a cold southeaster, right in your face, And a three day skunk on, that's some disgrace.

"We'd set the stored gear, reeling out six winch gurdies of wound stainless steel lines of hooks and spoon lures and line springs and cannonballs and giant vaned Styrofoam pig floats onto and behind the large suspended poles angled on their mounting points out from the port and starboard decks. Back in the cockpit, we needed to react in a split second to any problems, including those created by other boats in the area. When the time was right, we started rolling up the lines. The salmon came alongside flopping and jerking, hundreds of gills and bodies and tails twisted up in the lines. I had about a second apiece to gaff them off into the boat without losing any tackle.

Knee-deep in chinook, I'd take a step back to make room for more. *Relic* was pitching from 45 to 45, I was gasping for breath,

221

my forearms and hands burned like molten lead and the sharp lashes of jellyfish tentacles lacerated my face in pain, but there was never any choice but to keep hauling. Feet planted, hood up, face pointed at the deck as much as possible, I guided the smileys into our holds twelve feet away. My head covered in blood and scales and sea salt, and up to my ass in fish, with nowhere to collapse like I'd want to, the buoys on the end of the lines finally coming in over the rollers was the most beautiful sight in the world."

On the fishing grounds, on smiley's trail, Down around Hippa, in a rising gale,
On the fishing grounds, on smiley's trail, Lord we ain't quitting till we got fish for sale.

There were now two hours at most to stow the catch and reset the gear, and every minute counted. I stretched molten muscles, cracked stiff joints and bad jokes, and got to work. Dawn had crept into the steely gray sky. The wind and the rain may have died down. After the lines were out again, I could stop and make some hot food. Just another day at the office."

We fished it low, and we fished it deep, And a medium red now, that's our only keep,
I had a thirty pounder, with a real good fight, But when we gaffed him aboard, lord it was just a white.

"I've never had a savings account." Coal stared at the dollar bill. "My father always told me. *Save your money for fuel to get up to God's country.* "I guess he's there now."
"And you?" Jake asked. Coal collapsed back into his moaning chair.
"I've spent half my money on gambling, alcohol, and wild women." He said. "The other half I wasted. Look at my one true love here. Boats should be an antidote for technology but it's all projects on top of projects. Working on her for four months non-stop. I dropped a new bulkhead all the way down and tied it into the floors and hull, with an access panel ahead of the engine, rerouted the coolant lines, replaced the four-row crank pulley with a two-row and cut back the steel engine stringers. I raked out the cabin and coach-bolted right through the cleat, carlin, and shelf to pull it all up tight in one go. I refastened the staves with galvanized wood screws. Everything loose was rereefed and recaulked and resealed with Dolphinite and Duraglass. The pilothouse roof got new ply and glass and epoxy. The pilothouse

window frames are all rewooded and reframed. I installed a new outside helm to starboard of the wheelhouse door with a sixteen-inch Hamilton Marine bronze wheel connected to the Capilano hydraulic steering and a new servo-motor coupled autopilot. I unstepped the cracked and collapsing wooden mast and replaced it with old-growth aluminum. The new small cast-iron Neptune diesel stove I bought is ideal for *Relic*. I replaced the dry stack, replanked the flush foredeck, and built an aft deck railing out of black iron pipe, retapped the fittings to bury all the pipe threads, primed it with Rustoleum zinc, and then painted it rust-coloured, anyway. It's a work of art I call *Mortality and the Sea*, a study in the transient nature of life, entropy and the ocean through the inevitable failure of all human efforts to resist decay."

And we fished it low, and we fished it down, At twenty fathoms-lord, that was the fishy ground, But there's nothing but shrimp here, there's no damn birds, Tell me where was smiley, lord that's all I heard.

"Are you done?" Jake asked.
"Done? Hell no, I'm not done." Coal Tyee became agitated and aggressive. "I'm a shoestring mariner. Here on this fragment detached from the earth, this small planet of mine, I have no functioning ground tackle, no running lights, no place to sleep, no interior to speak of in fact, and I should tear out and rebuild the crumbling engine bed of my temperamental Detroit 3-53. But it's a lifetime of more work, and if I didn't do it right, I'd get annoyed every time I looked at it. The annoyance would fester and keep me up at night. I'd question my worth as a human, the choices I made that led me to compromise my ideals and what lessons I had learned about hard work and craftsmanship. I would lose the will to measure twice. Who cares how many cuts you have to make? It's all just time. And what is time when time stretches out across the grim landscape of failed dreams to the horizon of mortality?
It would always be the symbol of my failure as a man. One night, alone with my despair, I'd stare deep into a can of spar varnish and a vision of my father would form in its depths. He would speak to me, granting me absolution from the sin of the imperfect engine bed, and point towards my path of redemption. The next evening I'd stumble into an anonymous backyard bowshed to see a circle of men in faded jackets, lines of their addiction etched on their faces. Tilting a lukewarm coffee from the urn in the corner, I would sit and introduce myself. 'Hi, I'm Coal Tyee, and I'm a perfectionist.'"

No luck on the brass spoon, no luck on the chrome, We were thinking of the pleasures now, the pleasures of home, Cause there's nothing but coho here, too early to sell, We're just staring at the linespring, listening for the bell.

"And I'd like to build in some engine room soundproofing, a cockpit 'verandah' at the stern with a small doghouse over the hatch and two berths below. I need to put a cage around the old prop. It has a patina now, although some might call it rust. Someday I'll repaint this life of mine—green hull, off-white sheer band and house, and Bristol beige decks. But I can't. I have this stupid rash, mouth sores, my hair is falling out, I can't sleep, I have belly pains and continuous explosive diarrhea, I'm clumsy and can't think straight anymore, I wheeze and I can't catch my breath, I can't stand my body odour, the light bothers my skin and eyes, my legs swell up, and I flush like a schoolgirl with her panties down. " He broke down into more tears. Jake could see Coal Tyee's life now. There should have been years of fishing ahead of him but his *Relic* had sailed her last voyage. The ocean that had been his sanctuary only yesterday was now as remote as a far off land. He who has known its bitterness shall have its taste forever in his mouth.

And the damned old rock cod, twisting up our lines, Shaking these coho, man am I wasting my time,
Gonna go hand logging, build me up a raft, Take it all into Charlotte, and sell it quick for cash.

Jake's eyes found three books on a shelf. First was a dog-eared copy of Jack London's *Small Boat Sailing*, an ode to adventure, but with too much emphasis on the enjoyment of mishap. Beside it stood *Tranquility* by Billy Sparrow, set in the same Salish Sea. The last was no surprise, a Hemingway anthology. *Ask not for whom the salmon troller trolls. It trolls for thee.*
"Many men go fishing all their lives without knowing that it is not fish they are after." He said. Coal Tyee blushed crimson and scarlet and held his head before he fell onto the deck of his boat. *Sudden a thought came like a full-blown rose, flushing his brow.*
For far too long, the fisherman had been burning the candle at both ends, and the flames had met in the middle. Jake called for an ambulance from the wheelhouse radio.

'But never have I been a calm blue sea
I have always been a storm.'
Fleetwood Mac, *Storms*

The smell separating night from day forged the morning rush.
Fragrant as musk thy berry is, yet black as ink in sooth.
"Your usual, Doctor Sababa?" Said the transdermal metal and
subdermal ink.
"Quadruple espresso." He said. "Black as hell, strong as death,
sweet as love." Sababa ignored the other aromas of Code Brew,
the cloying muffins and marijuana, stale dishwater and old
garbage juice. He needed fresh ground hot scalding truth serum
to combat the powers of darkness and sorcerers' lies that he
sensed were to come.
The stocky savant turned to find two pairs of lost eyes.
"Excuse me." Said the lean one in the TipTop suit. "Can you
tell us where the Board Room is?"
"Bureaucrats." He mumbled to himself, but loud enough that
they heard it.
"We prefer to refer to ourselves as Health Care Managers." Said
the fat one in the Armani. "How did you know?"
"Well. You don't know where you are, you don't know where
you are going, and somehow it will be my fault." Sababa was
used to seagulls, but it was never a good sign, he thought, when
the crows showed up. He pointed them in the wrong direction,
as some other members of his department lined up behind him.
Dasco Boet ordered his straight black, Sid Shalimar a
cappuccino, Ernie 'The Big Easy' Hacker a flat white, Marquis
Shu Ying a piccolo latte, and Ed Hyde, a decaf.
"Big day today, Sab?" Peter Zaias, walked by the line of
assembled specialists on his way to chair the meeting. "You
should stick to water."
"True, Peter, there is no life without water." Sababa said.
"Because without water there is no coffee. And without coffee,
I'd kill you all."
Dr. Wayward Woods trailed behind the other department
members, clutching a Tim Hortons Double Double.
Malcolm Canmore sat at the head of the long teak conference
table, halfway between a boat and a racetrack, polished with oil
and buffed with a soft towel, filling the centre, racing the waist-

225

high wooden wall sideboard cabinet next to it down the length of the room. The only two items on the table were an open box of tissues and a multifunction business class conference digital phone console. Dr. Zaias picked up a handset and dialled zero.

"Lana, can you announce the beginning of the Department of Medicine meeting?" The hospital switchboard operator's Big Voice broadcast the assembly overhead.

At the far end, a wall-mounted HDTV screen hung next to a melamine whiteboard on an easel with a tray of desiccated multicoloured felt markers. Whoever had written this message on the whiteboard would have had to have picked the lock to the Board Room.

The Creation
In the Beginning was the plan
And then came the assumptions
And the Assumptions were without form
And the plan was completely without substance
And the Darkness was upon the faces of the workers
And they spake unto their Group Heads, saying:
'It is a crock of shit, and it stinketh.'
And the Group Heads went unto their Section Heads, and Sayeth:
'It is a pail of dung, and none may abide the odour thereof'
And the Section Heads went unto their Managers and sayeth unto them:
'It is a container of Excrement, and it is very strong,
such that none here may abide by it'
And the Manager went unto their Director, and sayeth unto him:
'It is a vessel of fertilizer, and none may abide its strength'
And the Directors went unto their Director-General, and sayeth:
'It contains that which aids plant growth, and it is very strong.'
And the Director-General went unto the Assistant Deputy Minister, and sayeth unto him:
'It promoteth growth, and it is very powerful'
And the Assistant Deputy Minister went unto the Deputy Minister, and sayeth unto him:
'This powerful new plan will actively promote the growth and efficiency of the Department, and this area in particular'
And the Deputy Minister looked upon the plan,
And saw that it was good
And the Plan became Policy.
Amen

Two suits, a fat Armani and a lean TipTop, walked into the Board Room.

"Sorry we're late." Said the fat Armani. "Someone misinformed us about the geography."

226

"And the history and science and mathematics and ethics." Sababa said. The administrators scowled.

"Gentlemen, permit me to introduce you to Doctor Sababa." Malcolm said.

"We've already had the pleasure." The fat one said.

"Here comes the pain." Sababa averted his gaze.

"As you are now well aware, the CVIHR is no more." Malcolm continued. "We have replaced it with a larger jurisdiction called the Vancouver Island Health Authority domiciled in Victoria. VIHA for short."

"Very Iffy Helicopter Access." Sababa mumbled.

"This is William Bligh, the CEO of VIHA." Malcolm gestured toward the fat Armani.

"And this is Dr. Milo Mindbender." Bligh said. "He's an emergency physician who had just recently ascended to the new VIHA position of Executive Vice President and Chief Medical Officer.

"Dr. Apoptosis." Sababa said.

"What's that?" Bligh asked.

"Programmed cell death." Sababa said. "Another useful idiot, gone over to the Dark Side." Milo glowered back at him.

"Dr. Mindbender would like to take this opportunity to present the details of our new VIHA contract for physicians and our new innovative rules and regulations." Bligh said. "Milo, if you please." the lean TipTop suit stood at the far end of the long Board Room table and handed out a single sheet of white paper to each of the internists, inscribed with only one line. *www.VIHA.ca/New Era/PhysicianConstraint/Contract/Rules*

"For far too long, certain members of our medical staff have subjected the Health Authority to arbitrary criticism." Mindbender gave Sababa a death stare. "They have shared their denunciations with local and provincial media outlets, often to the detriment of our administrative reputation, despite a long tradition of management excellence. Instead of working within the system to build bridges, some of our physicians prefer the fires they kindle when burning them. I am here today to inform you that the days of antagonism without accountability are over. There will be no more public displays of policy disagreement, no more attempts to herd stray cats. We will hammer down any nail that lifts its head above conformity. There will be no 'I' in team."

"By the pricking of my thumbs, something wicked this way comes." Sababa said. "I could eat a bowl of alphabet soup and shit a better arguement than that. Or what?"

"The new VIHA physician contract will allow you to function in your capacity as health authority employees, and direct how to

227

follow the practice guidelines for your specialty." Milo said. "The new rules and regulations will define your responsibilities and obligations, and the boundaries of acceptable behaviour."

"War is peace. Freedom is slavery. Ignorance is strength." Sababa said. "What about your responsibility to provide enough resources for us to do our jobs? Where is your accountability?"

"Not here." Bligh said. "Not with you."

"A tale told by an idiot, full of sound and fury, signifying nothing." Sababa leaned on his hands. "Besides this bombastic juggling, what else can you do?"

"We can rescind your medical privileges, Doctor Sababa." Milo Mindbender raised his voice. "We now have that power. And we will do just that, if anyone refuses to sign this contract, or violates any of the twenty-seven pages of new rules and regulations."

"Treat us good, we'll treat you better." Sababa said. "Treat us bad, we'll treat you worse."

"You're addicted to conflict." Bligh seethed.

"And pinot noir." He said. "I prefer it to the purple Kool-Aid. I have a problem with your manufacturing consent by silencing dissent."

"I can't solve your problem. That's not part of my job description." Milo said.

"I have a problem with that." He said.

"The problem is not the problem." Mindbender was apoplectic. "Your problem is not knowing you're the problem. The problem is your attitude about the problem."

"I don't have an attitude problem." Sababa said. "If you have a problem with my attitude, that's not my problem."

"You're enjoying this conversation, Sab." Peter Zaias was smiling.

"This is the type of conversation I do well in." Sababa said. "These Nazis should try to create a better environment for professional patient care instead of threatening to take away our hospital privileges."

"Things without all remedy should be without regard: what's done is done." It was Malcolm's turn. "What's done cannot be undone."

"And nothing is, but what is not." Milo grinned.

"Like a small line of dirt that won't go into the dustpan, Mindbender." Sababa had been saving it. "Si vis pacem, para bellum." *If you wish for peace, prepare for war.*

Peter Zaias adjourned the meeting before the bloodshed began. Milo Mindbender cornered him outside the Board Room.

"You're an emergency doc who has gone into a management position, Milo." Peter said.

228

"You have your own double cross to bear. Sababa sees competing bets from the same person a disgrace to the game. He'll want to beat you."

"What would you do, if you were me, Dr. Zaias?" Milo asked.

"Give him something he values more than honour." Peter said. "And update your résumé."

Far down the hallway, back towards the medical wards, Zaias caught up with Sababa.

"You're not strong enough to withstand this storm."

"I am this storm." Sababa said.

'The cure for anything is salt water: sweat, tears or the sea.'
Isak Dinesen

Sababa's Colombian leather briefcase flew a backwards somersault in its flight path to his computer on the bridge of the Death Star. Its arrival startled the young resident out of her chair and into a posture of defensive indignation. Sababa ignored her in his determination to access his music library, hidden on a secret drive deep inside the hospital computer network. The lyrics of his selection reverberated around the unit, obliterating any remaining serenity in Tranquility Base. *Rage Against the Machine.*

"Sara Reynolds, Doctor Sababa." She said. "I'm your new medical resident."

"Howdy Doody." He pulled the Black Book from its repository. "Are you married or are you happy?"

"No, I'm a doctor." She said.

"So you're not happy." He turned off the music. "No suicidal ideation I hope."

"None." She said. "I was the gold medal winner of my graduating class."

"That's the reason Sababaland issued you a visa, Sara." Sababa said. "Place your right hand on the Black Book of Remedies. I have five rules. Listen and memorize.

Rule number one: When I'm on call, you're on call. No squash games, hockey games, or hot dates when it's our turn at bat. The only exception is a death in the family, and it would need to be yours.

Rule number two: You go first. When your pager goes off, you answer with alacrity and aplomb. The only funeral you can be late for is your own. Sleep when you can, where you can. Which brings me to...

Rule number three: If I'm sleeping, don't wake me unless your patient is dying.

Rule number four: The dying patient better not be dead when I get there. Not only will you have killed someone, but you will have also woken me for no good reason. We clear?"

Sara raised her hand from the Black Book.

"Yes?"

"You said five rules. That was only four."

"Rule number five: When I move, you move. Welcome aboard, Sara. If you're as bright a star as you appear to be, and your CV shows, the hardest part of your job will be trying to be kind to stupid people."

"I've already seen Mr. Harris in Bed #5." She said. "I just need a few more minutes to refine my treatment plan." Sababa smiled a Sababa smile, as Dr. Cliffy Carlton cruised into the unit.

"Have you seen my little midnight special yet?" The ER doc pointed to the man in Bed #5.

"About to." Sababa said. "As soon as my new resident over there finishes her workup." Cliffy let out a long low whistle.

"She has legs that go all the way up to the Yukon." He said. "If I were an enzyme, I'd be DNA helicase, so I could unzip her genes." Cliffy went over to reconnoitre.

"I see you've got the guy with the glass eye and the prosthetic arm." He said. "Welcome to Doctor Sababa's erudite sewing circle."

"I'm not interested." Sara said. What was left of Cliffy limped back to the ER.

"OK, Gold Miss." Sababa said. "Make me proud."

"Seale Harris." She began. "62-year-old saltwater taffy shop owner admitted by Dr. Carlton early this morning for a three-year history of increasing episodes of intermittent prolonged sleepiness and double vision and a low blood sugar refractory to an initial IV bolus of D50W. It's still not normal after several hours of D10W infusion, but he doesn't have any sympathetic symptoms—no tremulousness, palpitations, tachycardia, sweating, hunger, anxiety, or nausea. He's gained a lot of weight. Dr. Oliver Lax saw him in consultation and found his neurological examination normal, including his mini-mental status exam. Physical today is also normal, as were his cerebrospinal fluid examination, brain MRI, and EEG."

"So, what you got?" He asked.

"Whipple's triad." Sara said. "Neuroglycopenic hypersomnia in a setting of documented low blood sugars, and reversibility of symptoms with the administration of glucose."

"You have a name?"

"Insulinoma." She said.

"Four in a million odds." Sababa asked. "Can you prove it?"

"We could do a supervised 72-hour fast with q4hourly reflectance metered capillary blood glucose to see if his insulin levels fail to suppress, increasing the measurement frequency to every hour until he has symptoms or his serum sugars drop to less than 2.7 mmol/L, and then draw bloodwork for glucose, insulin, proinsulin, and C-peptide levels and treat him with IV glucose again."

"Or?"

"Screw it and just get an insulin level, a CT scan, and a surgeon. Rule out the 5% associated with type 1 multiple endocrine neoplasia tumours of the parathyroid glands and the pituitary." She blew on her fingers. Mediocrity knows nothing higher than itself but talent instantly recognizes genius.

"May I pass along my congratulations for your great interdimensional breakthrough?" Sababa said. "I am sure, in the miserable annals of the Earth, you will be duly enshrined. Let's go see him." Mary pulled back the curtain of cubicle 5.

"Mr. Harris, this is Doctor Sababa." Sara said. "He's the specialist I was telling you about."

"Nothing wrong with me, Doc." Seale said. "Nothing that saltwater taffy doesn't take care of."

"We're a specialized hospital here at Harbour City Regional." Sababa shook the man's hand. "We only admit people when they're sick. You're very sick. I like that in a patient. Been eating more and more of your product to stay awake?"

Seale Harris looked terrified.

"You have a benign tumour in your pancreas, Seale." Sababa said. "It appears to be secreting insulin. Too much insulin."

"Can you remove it?" He asked.

"We need to find it first." Sababa said. "But removing it is a cure about ninety per cent of the time, although there is a two per cent chance of your having diabetes after the surgery."

Betty Boop held up a handset.

"Three more for you in the ER, Sab." Sababa looked at Sara.

"Let the games begin." He said.

'While Occam's razor is a useful tool in the physical sciences,
it can be a very dangerous implement in biology.'
Francis Crick, *What Mad Pursuit*

"How are you finding our outlaw god of Internal Medicine,
Sara?" Cliffy Carlton had another chance to speak to the young
resident by referring her next patient.
"He's a cactus fruit." She said. "Spiny on the outside, sweet
heart."
"It's a heart of darkness for those who aren't careful enough."
His grin became a sunbeam. "I'd be more than happy to fill you
in."
"I bet you would." Sara said. "As I told you on the Death Star
Bridge, I'm not interested."
"Your patient is behind Curtain #1." He said. "May the Great
Sababa's wisdom bring success to all your undertakings."
"And to yours."
"And may his radiance light up your life."
"And up yours." She said. Cliffy left her, crestfallen, and Sara
got on with her next assignment.
When Sababa arrived an hour later, she had seen Cliffy's
referral and another from Gung Ho. The portly professor was as
proud as he ever could be.
"Who's on first?" He asked.
"George Anson." Sara began. "49-year old electrician,
unemployed because of knee problems, heavy drinker with a ten-
week history of postural dizziness, dry mouth and eyes, swollen
gums and decaying teeth, halitosis, bone and muscle pain, and a
spontaneous bruising rash and swelling of his legs."
"Exam?" Sababa asked.
"Come see for yourself." She said, pulling back the drapes of bed
number one and making the introduction.
"George, this is my preceptor, Doctor Sababa."
"A pleasure to make your acquaintance, Sir." George said.
"Likewise, George." Sababa was already looking for clinical
signs. There was a faint whiff of ozone.
"His postural low blood pressure didn't respond to fluids." Sara
continued. "He has these peculiar red spots around the hairs on
his chest and abdomen and legs, and this greeny-blue and yellow
bleeding rash on his lower extremities."
"Labwork?" Sababa asked.

232

"Only a mild microcytic anemia." She said.

"You have a name?"

"I'm sure it's a vasculitis." Sara said.

"Uncertainty is an uncomfortable position." Sababa said. "But certainty is an absurd one."

"Voltaire."

"You sure?" Sababa asked. "Squeezing leeches on a patient's skin. What did you make of all his body hairs, the ones with the surrounding petechiae? They're all corkscrewed."

"Genetic." Sara said.

"Acquired." Sababa corrected. "Or the missed observation that some of his old healed skin wounds have reopened, or the unholy rosary of costochondral beading around his breastbone? Did you take a dietary history?"

"I didn't think it was relevant."

"Oh." Sababa turned his attention to their patient. "What do you eat, George?"

"Cheese pizza." He said.

"Anything else?"

"Leftover cheese pizza." Sababa returned to Sara.

"Care to venture an opinion on what condition was first described by Hippocrates, murdered more crusaders than Islam, killed more than two million sailors between the time of Columbus's transatlantic voyage and the rise of steam engines in the mid-19th century, why Vasco da Gama lost 116 of his crew of 170 in 1499, and Magellan lost 208 out of 230 in 1520?" Sababa asked. "What wiped out more English East Indiamen than all their battlefields combined, annihilated 132,108 more men than died in action in Britain's Seven Years' War with France in 1763, lost the French and Spanish fleets the Battle of Trafalgar in 1805, eliminated more gold miners in the California and Yukon gold rushes and ended Jack London's days in the Klondike, murdered urban upper class babies fed pasteurized cow's milk in the 19th century, killed more allied troops than the Turks in Gallipoli in 1915, and plagued prisons, refugee camps, and prisoners of war in the 20th century?"

"Oh, shit." Sara said.

"Close." Sababa said. "Get thee glass eyes, and like a scurvy politician seem to see the things thou dost."

"King Lear." She said.

"George, it appears you have a rare modern case of scurvy." Sababa said. "Most animals and plants can manufacture their own vitamin C, but some mammals have lost the ability, fruit bats and tarsiers and other simians, capybaras and guinea pigs, and a few birds and fish. And us. We lack an enzyme called L-

233

gulonolactone oxidase, GULO for short, required in the last step of vitamin C synthesis. We need vitamin C to make collagen, which is a primary structural protein in our muscle, skin, bones, blood vessels, cartilage, scars, and other connective tissues that comprise 30% of our body protein. Collagen holds our tissues together; the word itself comes from the Greek word for glue."

"I have no glue?" George asked.

"Life is more than USB ports and drink holders and cheese pizzas." He said. "You appear to have come unstuck."

"Can you fix it?" He asked.

"Easy." Sababa said. "Sara, draw an ascorbic acid level for the bean counters, and start George here on a gram of vitamin C for the first 5 days, and then drop it in half forever. You can write up his discharge while I dictate the consult." Sababa pulled *Pink* out of his music library, on a secret drive hidden deep inside the hospital computer network.

> 'Our gums are black, our teeth are falling out
> We've got spots on our backs, so give it up and shout
> We've got scurvy, we need some vitamin C
> We've got scurvy, we need a lemon tree
> We got scurvy, we just chillin' on the sea...
> A pirate ain't worthy 'til he's got some scurvy, Arrgh...
> Pink, *Scurvy*

"Who's on second?" He asked, a few minutes later.

"Zonobia Fasciculata." Sara said. "47-year-old waitress at the Lighthouse Bistro with a 12-year history of type 2 diabetes. Three years ago, she had a rapid weight gain accompanied by a moon face and buffalo hump fat pads, hypertension and high cholesterol, muscle weakness and osteoporosis, memory dysfunction and moodiness, sleep disturbances and depression, and abnormalities of her hair, thin skin with purple streaks and dilation of capillaries and superficial fungus infections, facial acne and armpit skin tags, and acanthosis nigricans and hyperpigmentation."

"You have a name?" Sababa asked.

"Cushing's syndrome." Sara said.

"Half right." He said. "Be more specific."

"Cushing's disease." She corrected.

"Harvey Cushing would be proud." Sababa said. "What's the difference?"

"Cushing's disease is a specific type of Cushing's syndrome caused by a pituitary tumour leading to the excessive production of adrenocorticotropic hormone. ACTH." She said. "While all

234

Cushing's disease gives Cushing's syndrome, not all Cushing's syndrome is from Cushing's disease."

"And we know she also has Harvey's disease exactly how?" Sababa asked.

"The hyperpigmented skin." Sara said. "Melanocyte-Stimulating Hormone is a byproduct of ACTH synthesis from pro-opiomelanocortin."

"Or the high levels of ACTH, β-lipotropin, and γ-lipotropin have weak MSH function, which stimulates the melanocortin 1 receptor."

"Whatever." Sara said.

"There is no ever in 'what,' Sara." Sababa said. "There is only the eternal need to know the answer to every 'what' forever. So then what happened?"

"They did the chemistry and found super high ACTH levels which refused to decrease with dexamethasone suppression testing. An MRI of her pituitary showed a 5x5 mm tumour on the right, consistent with her bilateral inferior petrosal sinus sampling results. They removed it through her nose. Pathology confirmed it. But after her procedure, she still had high cortisol levels and repeat petrosal sampling still showed a pituitary source, so they performed gamma knife radiosurgery."

"So?"

They also did an abdominal MRI for whatever reason." She said. "Sorry, the eternal need to know the answer to every 'what' forever reason. It showed an adrenal adenoma measuring 1 cm in diameter on the left side."

"And then?"

"They didn't think they needed to do anything about it, and they obviously didn't, because she's been fine for three years." She said. "But a month ago, she began to regain weight, her blood sugars went off the charts, and her blood pressures left the flight deck. Her family doc, Dr. James Ruben Andrews, did some blood tests, which found that her ACTH suppressed for the first time since her initial diagnosis. A repeat abdominal MRI showed her left-sided adrenal tumour had grown to 24x18x22 mm with no hyperplasia or atrophy in the surrounding cortex."

"So what you got?" Sababa asked.

"Recurrent endogenous non-ectopic hypercortisolism with a clear shift of ACTH dependency to ACTH independency." Sara said. "But I don't believe it."

"Why not?" Sababa asked.

"What are the odds of two explanations where one should suffice?" She asked. "You know about Occam's razor. The simplest explanation is always the best."

"And you think one is simpler than two?"

"I'm pretty sure it is, yeah." Sara said.

"Why do I have to do this for every whiny resident that comes through here looking for a cookie and a hug?" Sababa asked out loud. "You started with endogenous Cushing syndrome, a rare entity with an incidence of two cases per million per year. Occam's razor is a matter of taste more than of truth, Gold Miss. In Sababaland, Hickam's dictum reigns supreme. 'A patient can have as many diseases as they damn well please.' Let's go see her." Sara muttered under her breath.

"Hickam's dictum. Hmmmmph. More like Sababa's abracadabra."

Behind the second curtain, Zonobia Fasciculata was burning through a book of sudoku puzzles. Sababa and Sara took their time to explain the complexities of her case and the coexistence of functional pituitary and adrenal tumours that had complicated her life. They told her of their deductions and plan to arrange for a surgeon to remove the adrenal adenoma. Zonobia seemed satisfied with their analysis and plan and professionalism.

"Which part of 'no' are you having trouble with?" Sara said. Sababa turned to find Cliffy's smiling face, poking through the curtain.

"He appears to be here on a mission of mercy, not mating, Sara." Sababa said. "Who's on first. What's on second. I don't know's on third."

"One more before you go to your office, Sab." Cliffy said, drawing them out of Zonobia's nine by nine world. John Lykoudis, 51-year-old Chemtrade ammonia supply company owner with a three-year history of chest pain and wheezing between and after meals at night, appetite and weight loss, and nausea and bloody vomiting, unrelated to food and sometimes associated with watery and occasional fatty diarrhea. Our down-island colleagues in Victoria performed several lucrative upper GI endoscopies. In one, they found esophagitis and a large H. pylori-positive bulbar ulcer treated with eradicant triple therapy. They also thought he might have exocrine pancreatic insufficiency and started him on digestive enzyme supplements. He never got better. Abdominal ultrasound and CT showed some small hepatic abnormalities interpreted as angiomyolipomas. MRCP and cholecystectomy for an abnormal HIDA scan were unhelpful. Buddy Benway scoped him again

236

last night and found severe necrotic esophagitis with large ulcers and a scarred narrowing which, after pneumatic dilation, allowed him to discover more ulcers, distal to the duodenal bulb. I sent off some gastric juice, which came back with a pH of 1.8. I tried to call Buddy back, but it's his golf day."

"Golf is nature's way of informing you that you should be dead, Sara." Sababa said. "What do you make of this story?"

"Perplexing." She said. "Although recruiting your passion for Hickam's dictum, I'd say it could still be a combination of gastroesophageal reflux and chronic pancreatitis."

"Light travels faster than sound, Cliffy." Sababa said. "Therefore some people appear bright until they speak. Sara, do you honestly think the severity of this man's condition, his unresponsiveness to conventional therapy, and the low pH level of Mr. Lykoudis's gastric acid could be due to two such mundane conditions?" Sababa pulled up the imaging and laboratory results of his Victoria admission.

"What are you thinking?" Sara asked.

"I'm thinking we're lost in the gastrinoma triangle."

"But see, his gastrin level was normal." She pointed at the screen.

"He was on a proton pump inhibitor." Sababa said.

"Oh." She wasn't so sure now.

"Hah." Sababa said. "Some bright light did a chromogranin A level and forgot to follow it up." It was high, over 1000 mU/ml. He brought up the liver ultrasounds and CT. It showed many contrast-enhanced focal repetitive lesions.

"Those aren't angiomyolipomas." Sababa said. "Let's go see him." The ER doc and the new resident followed him to the bedside.

"Mr. Lykoudis, this is Dr. Reynolds, a post-graduate trainee from UBC." Cliffy said. And this is Doctor Sababa, our on-call specialist in Internal Medicine."

"Is he any good?" The patient asked.

"Sherlock Holmes was autistic by comparison." Cliffy said. Sababa's sensors were in acquisition mode.

"John, you remember that leak that forced the evacuation of the Rec Centre last month and sent three people to hospital?" Sababa asked.

"Yeah." He said. "It was ammonia from my company."

"You know what you get if you spill ammonia?"

"Sure." John said. "Hydrochloric acid. That's what they use to chlorinate the pools."

"Guess what you've got?"

"An ammonia spill?"

"Kinda." Sababa said. "You have a tumour that began in your pancreas. It produces too much gastrin, the hormone that stimulates your stomach to produce hydrochloric acid. In your case, it's become a runaway train with no brakes."

"Began?"

"It appears to have spread to your liver. The condition was first described at Ohio State University in 1955 and named after the two guys that found it. It's called Zollinger-Ellison syndrome."

"Am I going to die?"

"The moment you're born you're done for, John." Sababa said. "But this is definitely treatable. Dr. Reynolds here will admit you to our clinical teaching service." He turned to his protégé.

"OK, Sara." He said. "Repeat fasting serum gastrin and chromogranin, secretin stimulation test, labs to exclude multiple endocrine neoplasia type 1, Octreoscan, 68 Ga-labeled octreotide PET in Vancouver, ultrasound-guided liver biopsy with immunohistochemistry. Start him on TPN and, after they pull his bloodwork, begin high-dose IV PPI therapy and pancreatic enzymes. For what it's worth in terms of the sheer pleasure I will have in seeing the terror in his eyes, consult our itinerant oncologist, Dr. Henry Chibueze, for an opinion on our plan to begin octreotide chemotherapy and receptoral radiotherapy with 1,850 MBq of 90Y-Dotatoc."

"Is that all?" Sara asked.

"Oh, no." Sababa handed her a piece of paper with three names. *Paul Newman... Howard Dell... Hideki Tojo.*

"Page me when you've seen these patients on the fifth floor." He said. "Take care with Sophia. Her first language is Tagalog, and she still hasn't forgiven Phillip II of Spain for his syphilis or Imelda Marcos for her shoe collection. She's the best head nurse on the planet. She can smell fear and incompetence a mile away. If you still have any butterflies in your stomach, you best digest them before the elevator doors open up on her turf."

'Oh,  look around you, all around you,

riding on a copper wave.

Do you like the world around you?
Are you ready to behave?'
Patti Smith Group, *Rock N Roll Nigger*

238

Sara understood our evolutionary imperative of caring more for families and friends than strangers. She reasoned that if we loved all people indiscriminately, it would be impossible to function. If we cared about every suffering person on the planet, life would shut down. Sababa had made a choice between being loved and being feared and decided that fear was better suited to his method. But Sophia had chosen indiscriminate love, the depths of which were fearsome to behold. The elevator doors had opened on the fifth-floor medical ward and the radiant face of the Pinoy Pietà who ruled the fugitive fates of its temporary inhabitants. Sara introduced herself.

"Hello, Sophia. " She said. "I'm Sara Reynolds, Doctor Sababa's new resident."

"He is my payborit." Sophia said. "Did you grud-wait at UBC, like Ductor Dunne?" Sara nodded.

"Ay-bree-buddy has berry sad peelings por him." Sophia said. "But we must rice a-bub trudjety. Welcum to our pama-lee, Suhruh." Sara smiled and handed Sophia her list of three names. *Paul Newman... Howard Dell... Hideki Tojo.*

"Dey are penis dere brick-pus." Sophia said. "Palo me." She led her down the hallway into a four-bed room with three patients. Two hours later she paged Sababa to review her findings. He bounced onto the ward a few minutes later.

"What you got?" He said, finding the room of referrals.

"First is Mr. Paul Newman." Sara began. "56-year-old professional billiards player admitted by Dr. James Ruben Andrews two days ago with a month-long history of headache, nausea and intermittent episodes of vomiting, and a week's worth of thirst and excessive water drinking and urination. Exam shows only tobacco staining of the index and middle fingers of his right hand, and a peripheral visual field defect."

"Labwork?"

"His serum sodium was high on admission." Sara said.

"How high?"

"160 mmol/litre." She said.

"And he wasn't in a coma?"

"Not the sharpest knife in the drawer." She said. "But awake."

"You got a name?"

"Central diabetes insipidus."

"From?" Sara logged into the hallway computer outside the room.

"Brain MRI showed a 1.2 cm dumbbell-shaped sellar mass overriding the posterior pituitary."

"Chest x-ray?"

"Normal."

"I don't believe it." Sababa said. "What's the blood supply to the posterior pituitary, Gold Miss? I'll give you a hint. Posterior pituitary artery. And what's the most common cause of dumbbell-shaped sellar tumours that metastasize via this artery in old smokers?"

"Lung cancer?" She wasn't sure.

"What kinds?"

"I don't know."

"Adenocarcinoma or small cell." Sababa said. "But not squamous. Wait a minute. Here's a CT scan of his chest performed two weeks ago as an outpatient."

"The radiologist reported it as normal." Sababa filled the screen with images and pointed to a small peripheral blur in the right lung."

"Not normal." He said. "My money is on poorly differentiated adeno. Let's go see him." Back inside the room, they pulled the curtain around the professional pool player and spoke softly.

"Paul, it appears you have a small growth in your right lung." Sababa said.

"I've been meaning to cut down on my smoking." He said.

"It may not make much of a difference." Sababa said. "You also have a small abnormality in the back part of a gland in your brain we call the pituitary. It's why you've become so thirsty, and why you pee so much."

"Can you fix it?"

"We can fix the too much peeing part." He said. "Dr. Reynolds will prescribe you a nasal spray called DDAVP which will replace the hormone that helps regulate salt and water balance in your body. She'll also order more hormone tests." Sophia went past the doorway.

"Don't go Jason water, Paul." She said.

"The tumour part is a different question." Sababa continued. "We'll ask two other doctors, Drs. Ed Hyde and Henry Chibueze, our local respirologist and oncologist, to come and see you."

"OK." He said. "We should have a game of pool sometime. Do you gamble, Doctor?"

"Only with peoples' lives." Sababa said. He and Sara left the room to discuss the second case.

"Howard Dell." She began. "23-year-old Harbour Air pilot on disability leave, a patient of Dr. Zaias who's on his day off. Mr. Dell presents with a one-year history of headaches, dizziness, mood swings, memory dysfunction, and abnormal gait, recent appetite loss, skin blisters and dryness, acne, eczema, itchiness, hair loss, mouth ulcers and inflammation of the tongue,

240

impaired wound healing, non-bilious vomiting, and diarrhea, and a two-day history of nosebleeds."

"Exam?" Sababa asked.

"Yellowish skin, early cataracts, mild leg swelling, dermatitis around body openings and the tips of his fingers and toes, and neurological findings of flat emotions, slow and rigid movement and speech, and an unsteady gait."

"Labs?"

"Significant for mild anemia, low bicarb and calcium, high serum chloride, and elevation of liver enzymes, with prolongation of his coagulation times. Those and his nosebleeds responded to the administration of vitamin K."

"Which means what?"

"Liver dysfunction." Sara said. "He also had an MRI of his brain last week." She brought the study images up on the computer screen. Sababa smiled a Sababa smile.

"Ah yes, Grasshopper." He said. "The face of the giant panda. Note the hyperintense basal ganglia and the hypodensities in both lenticular nuclei. You have a name?"

"Not sure." Sara said. "Some kind of hereditary disease affecting his brain and liver? It's a mystery."

"Mystery is the source of all true art and science, Sara." Sababa said. "You're so close, and should have been able to solve this one. Let's go see your Mr. Dell." Back inside the room, they pulled the curtain around the pilot.

"I'm Doctor Sababa, Howard." Sababa said. "Dr. Reynolds has been telling me about your problems."

"Do... do you... do you think you know...what's going on?" He asked.

"Yes." He asked the pilot to extend his arms. They began to flap.

"This is a wing-beating tremor, Sara." He pointed to the man's eyes.

"These are sunflower cataracts. And I know you recognize their outline." Sara flushed with embarrassment.

"Kaiser-Fleisher rings!" She sputtered. "How stupid of me. He has Wilson's disease."

"What's that?" Howard asked.

"It's an inherited condition, usually a mutation of the ATP7B gene on chromosome 13 which codes for a cation transport P-type ATPase enzyme that transports copper into bile and incorporates it into a protein called ceruloplasmin."

"I didn't get any of that." Howard said.

"Your body has trouble getting rid of a certain native metal." Sababa tried again. "The ancient Greeks knew copper as an antiseptic and mixed its glittery flakes with honey as a dressing for wounds. But in your case, the metal has accumulated in your liver until it overwhelmed the proteins that normally bind it, causing oxidative damage through a process known as Fenton chemistry. The free copper precipitates in and damages the liver, kidneys, eyes, and brain. As Dr. Reynolds can tell you, it also caused your zinc deficiency, type 2 renal tubular acidosis, and parathyroid gland failure."

"Will it kill me?" He asked.

"If you were a Bedlington terrier, you would be dead by now." Sababa said. "But we can fix most of this."

"How?"

"First, we need to confirm that this is what you've got." Sababa said. "Dr. Reynolds will order more bloodwork, a urine collection, and a quantitative liver biopsy. We will screen your first-degree relatives for the disease. We'll start you on a low copper diet, supplement your zinc intake, and begin a course of penicillamine or trientine chelation, depending on your initial response, to remove the excess copper from your body."

"What can't you fix?" Howard asked.

"Sometimes the neurologic dysfunction of Wilson's disease doesn't completely resolve with our treatments." Sababa said. "Your Sky King days may have ended. We'll have to see how you respond to our physical and occupational therapies."

"And our continued concern for your best outcome." Sara said. "You know the Rumi poem, Howard?"

"No."

"Through love all that is bitter will be sweet, through love all that is copper will be gold, through love all dregs will become wine, through love all pain will turn to medicine." The pilot put his hands together as if he were praying, and for all Sara and Sababa knew, he may have been.

"Third time's the charm." Sababa said.

"Hideki Tojo." Sara said. "59-year-old sushi chef with a six-month history of nausea, abdominal discomfort, vomiting, and diarrhea, with more recent problems of anemia, and numbness and tingling in his extremities." Dr. Tarmac referred him for B12 deficiency.

"You know what gets on my nerves, Sara?" Sababa asked. "Myelin. And you know what gets on my myelin?" The young resident shook her head.

"Methylmalonic acid." He said. "Why did Tictac ask us to see him?"

"His peripheral blood smear shows anemia with large red blood cells, some with Howell-Jolly bodies, a decreased reticulocyte count, and senile white cells with too many nuclear lobes,

242

suggesting cell growth without division from impaired DNA synthesis."

"You have a name?"

"Megaloblastic anemia."

"Cause?"

"Most likely combined B12 and folate vitamin deficiency. Serum levels of lactic acid dehydrogenase, homocysteine, and methylmalonic acid are up, and B12 is low."

"From?"

"Well, that's the question then, isn't it?" Sara said. He doesn't abuse alcohol or nitrous oxide, doesn't take any vitamin antagonists or antacids or metformin, there's no history of gluten intolerance, abdominal surgery, HIV/AIDS or chronic exposure to toxigenic moulds and mycotoxins in water-damaged buildings, no family history of B12 deficiency, and he's not a vegan. The most likely cause would still be pernicious anemia, but his intrinsic factor and parietal cell antibodies and Helicobacter breath test are negative, and his serum gastrin is normal."

"I would be more reassured if you had started with a classification of B12 deficiency, rather than a checklist." Sababa said.

"OK." She said. "Decreased intake, impaired absorption, and increased requirements. Maybe he has Imerslund-Grasbeck syndrome."

"Except he's doesn't look as if he's from Finland or Scandinavia or the eastern Mediterranean." Sababa said. "You haven't yet told me about his exam."

"Pale conjunctiva, increased heart and breathing rate, smooth red tongue." She said. "And impaired deep touch, pressure and vibration perception, with decreased reflexes."

"So, what you got?" Sababa asked.

"Megaloblastic anemia from B12 deficiency, likely from an unusual cause of impaired absorption." She said.

"What you don't got?"

"Pernicious anemia." She said. "And every other cause I can think of."

"Every healthy body stores up to five years' worth of B12 in the liver." He said. "In the early farming settlements on the North Island of New Zealand, cattle suffered from 'bush sickness' because the volcanic plateau soils lacked the cobalt salts essential for synthesis of the vitamin B12 by their gut bacteria."

"He's cobalt-deficient?" She asked.

"Nope." He said. "Human's don't use cobalt to synthesize..."

"Then why did you bring it up?"

"I'm sorry. Did the middle of my sentence interrupt the beginning of yours?" He said. "It was a digression, a deviation, a departure, an excursus, an incidental remark, an obiter dictum. In the same spirit that you've been missing the all-important context of what you got and what you don't got. He's a sushi chef."

"Meaning what exactly?"

"While you've been travelling the interstellar space of cosmic causes of Hideki Tojo's condition, I've found a month-old upper GI Gastrografin study which shows a faint shadow of the culprit. Look at his duodenum. Which came first, the intestine or the tapeworm?"

"Whah?" Was all she had.

"Sometimes the barium causes detachment and passing of the whole worm, but look at the size of that scolex." Sababa said. "It's half as big as your head."

"It looks like some bizarre, antique tool you'd stumble upon in your grandfather's shed." She said. "With two suction cup-like grooves to grip the poor man's small intestine."

"Or an alien sex toy." Sababa said. "The broad fish tapeworm is the largest known parasite of humans. Its body is made up of thousands of proglottid rectangular segments growing at a centimeter an hour, nine inches a day. These are over thirty feet long and discharge a million eggs per day. The organism can live for twenty years, and there is evidence from South America that they have been infecting humans for over ten thousand. I once had a beef tapeworm, Taenia saginata, in Ethiopia, from eating raw meat my new friends cut off the back of a moving cow, but one of these babies infected my auntie because she tasted her gefilte fish recipe raw. Jewish housewife's disease."

"But isn't there a regulation that requires raw fish to be frozen at −35°C for 15 hours before they can sell it?" She asked.

"It's interpreted as a guideline in the sushi trade." He said. "And cold smoking the salmon doesn't kill these monsters."

"So what kind does Mr. Tojo have? Sara asked.

"It doesn't matter." Sababa said. "Whether it's Diphyllobothrium nihonkaiense from his fresh sockeye sushi, Diphyllobothrium dendriticum from his fresh chinook and Arctic char sashimi, or Diphyllobothrium latum from his trout or Alberta walleye, the treatment is the same."

"What's that?" She asked.

"A single 10 mg tablet of praziquantel." He said. "End of story. I'm surprised that he didn't tell you about seeing thrashing tagliatelle doing a tummy tapeworm tango in his bowel movements. Or maybe you didn't ask." Sara flushed her answer.

244

"This will give me nightmares for a week." She said. "We must miss this all the time."

"Only kings, presidents, editors, and people with tapeworms may use the editorial 'we,' Sara." Sababa said. "Diphyllobothriasis affects twenty million people worldwide, but we don't find them unless we look. Let's go see him."

"Kanazawa no otsu mushi de Tsurumi Kazuhiko no te kara sashimi o tabemashita." Sababa said. *I have eaten sashimi from the hands of Kazuhiko Tsurumi at Otomezushi in Kanazawa.* Hideki jumped up and bowed.

"Nihongo hanasemasu ka?" He asked. *Do you speak Japanese.*

"Sukoshidake." Sababa said. *Only a little.*

"Naze watashi wa byōkidesu ka?" He asked. *Why am I sick.*

"Anata wa sanadamushi o motte imasu." Sababa said. *You have a tapeworm.*

"Ā sōdesu." Said the sushi chef. "Tawagoto, Shārokku." *No shit, Sherlock.*

'Desperately in need Of some stranger's hand In a desperate land...
He's old and his skin is cold
The west is the best... Get here and we'll do the rest.'
The Doors, *The End*

"It's an elemental week, Boss." Her eyes hadn't left the screen of the big G4 computer.

"Justice is for those who deserve it. Mercy is for those who don't." Sababa said. "Mercy, I'd like you to meet our new resident, Sara Reynolds." The medical office assistant looked up from her transcription.

"Are you happy?" She asked. Sara nodded.

"For now." She said.

"Don't let it get behind you." Mercy went back to her typing. Sababa handed Sara the first chart and pointed to the residents' room.

"Come and get me when you're finished." He said. She called her patient and the portly professor called his.

"73-year-old urgent from Dr. Bloom." Mercy said, above her flying fingers.

"Jacob Berzelius?" He watched an old American sailor rise from a chair in the waiting room. Sababa shook his hand and led him into his office. The man gave off the odour of old garlic.

"How can I help?" He asked.

"I'm not doing well, Doc." He said. "I'm losing my hair, my nails are brittle and discoloured, and I salivate all the time. I have muscle and joint pains, and fevers and headaches and dizziness. I'm always tired, my guts gurgle, I vomit for no reason, and I've developed this rash. I had a PSA in Seattle in the spring. It was high."

"So what did you do about it?" Sababa asked.

"All the presented options were unnatural and unacceptable—cutting, burning, poisons—and threatened my sexual potency." Jake said. "So I went on the Internet." It was then he saw the writing on Sababa's coffee cup. *Your Google search does not trump my medical degree.*

"And what did you find?" Sababa asked.

"Selenium." He said. "I bought a bag of sodium selenite powder from a livestock wholesaler. It was cheap."

"And how did you decide the dose?"

"I selected it myself."

"There are three types of medical conditions, Jake." Sababa said. "Too much, too little, and weird. Guess which one you've got."

"Weird?"

"Half marks." Sababa said. "I have your lab results from Dr. Bloom. Your serum potassium and bicarbonate are low. And with your substitution of too much selenium for sulfur in some of your biochemistry, you've inactivated the sulfhydryl enzymes necessary for oxidative reactions in your cellular respiration, which is why your breath smells like a loaf of garlic bread. We don't even have a blood level to help us decide what to do. At this precise moment, selenium poisoning may have made you a sitting duck for a cardiac arrest. I should admit you to hospital."

"Can't, Doc." Jake said. "I don't have medical insurance."

"Our American cousins come to our little corner of paradise all the time, to take advantage of our universal generosity." Sababa said. "And you have a boat."

"It's all I have." Jake said. "It's not an option."

"No, you're right. Let's do it the dumbest way possible because it's easier for you." Sababa wrote a prescription.

"Take these magnesium and potassium supplements." He said. "Throw the selenium away. I'll make a note that you've refused more proper treatment. Go back to Seattle and get your prostate looked after."

"OK." Jake said. "Thanks, Doc. I promise I'll pay you when I get back to the States."

"The only way to know if a man is trustworthy is to trust him."

"Hemingway."

"I'm a big fan." Sababa said. The face of his resident replaced the back of the sailor.

"What you got, Gold Miss?"

"Anthony Stark." She said. "37-year-old welder and owner of Stark Raving Iron Works, referred by Dr. Tarmac for abnormal liver function and knuckle pains."

"Where are you from, Mr. Stark?" Sababa asked.

"I emigrated from Mali ten years ago." He said. "I had trained as a welder in my home country. It was only natural that I carried on that work here."

"What else, Sara?"

"His exam shows a big liver and enlargement of the second and third metacarpal joints on both hands."

"The pain in my hands makes my job difficult now." Anthony said. "That's why I went to see my family doctor."

"Labs?"

"This is where it gets more interesting." Sara said. "Abnormal liver enzymes, elevated blood sugar, hypogonadism, huge hyperdense liver and impaired heart pumping action on ultrasounds, and a raised ferritin."

"You have a name?"

"I would have said hemochromatosis, but there's a catch." She said.

"What catch?" Sababa asked.

"His transferrin saturation index is normal." She continued. "The ferritin could just be an acute phase reactant and everyone has warned me about how much emphasis you place on the transferrin saturation index to diagnose abnormalities of body iron content."

"Everyone?" Sababa asked. "Word gets around. I have extreme views, weakly held. Perhaps it's an irony overload problem." He turned his attention back to the welder.

"Any hobbies, Tony?"

"I make beer at home." He said.

"In what?" Sababa asked.

"Some old ungalvanized drums from work." He said. "Like we used to do back home."

"Hmmm." Sababa said. "How's the beer?"

"Good." He said. Sababa turned back to Sara.

"So do you think he could still have hemachromatosis?" He asked.

"He doesn't fit the Viking hypothesis, does he?" She said. "I can't imagine his ancestors marauding along the coastline of Europe, spreading the genetic fairy dust of iron overload. Besides, his transferrin saturation index..."

"You already said that." Sababa said. "Ever heard of ferroportin? It's the main iron export protein."

"Uh, no."

"Then you wouldn't know about the ferroportin SLC40A1 Q248H aggregate allele mutation in exon 6 that occurs as a polymorphism in people of sub-Saharan African descent." Sababa said. "High ferritin with normal transferrin saturation index. Anthony here has an African iron overload syndrome with involvement of his liver, heart, endocrine organs, and joints, in the form of calcium pyrophosphate deposition in his knuckles. With his homebrew beer making in old steel drums, we used to have another, less politically correct name for his condition."

"What's that?" Asked the welder."

"Bantu siderosis." Sababa said. "But not everyone who drank bush beer got iron overload, and it was only with the elucidation of the specific genetic defects that we came to understand who got it and why."

"Can you fix it?" Tony asked.

"Why is everybody in such an infernal hurry to have his or her disease fixed instead of just appreciated for a while?" Sababa smiled a Sababa smile. "We can fix it, Tony. We'll need a few more investigations to start with. It will mean your giving up homebrew for microbrew beer, and lay off the red meat and bluefin tuna for a while. I'll set up a schedule to remove a pint of blood at longer and longer intervals until your ferritin is normal. Besides, I could use the blood you have on tap for my wife's rose garden. From Timbuktu to here." He looked at Sara. She was not amused.

"Give these requisitions to Mercy and she'll make a return appointment." He said. They went to see the last office patient together. Mercy handed Sara the chart.

"Gary Shadling." She said. The man looked around the waiting room for someone else, in vain. He followed Sara and her mentor into his office. She read the referral note from Dr. Jules Martino. *You'll need another diagnosis.*

"54-year-old bartender at the Dinghy Dock Pub across the harbour on Protection Island." Sara began. You've seen him before."

248

"Indeed, I have." Sababa said. "Four months ago, wasn't it Gary?"

"Four months ago." He agreed.

"History of a kidney stone, with a right nephrectomy eight years ago, if memory serves."

"His GP found high serum calcium and low phosphate, and mild impairment of remaining kidney function." Sara continued. "Your later labwork uncovered a high parathyroid hormone level, and a nuclear scan and neck CT showed a 2.5 × 1.5 cm well-defined parathyroid adenoma posterior to the upper pole of the left lobe of the thyroid."

"Didn't I refer you to Dr. Theodor Billroth for surgery?" Sababa asked. Gary nodded.

"Saw him yesterday, a week after I had this godawful pain in my neck." He said. "Dr. Martino repeated my blood tests and sent me back to you."

"His calcium and magnesium are low and his alkaline phosphatase is high." Sara said. Sababa tapped Gary's right facial nerve and watched him wince in pain. He inflated a pressure cuff on Gary's left arm, producing tetanic spasm. Sababa did an ECG and found a prolonged QT interval.

"There's only one thing that can cause this severe reversal." He said. "Parathyroid apoplexy. He must have spontaneously infarcted the tumour. His low calcium resulted from rapid skeletal recalcification after the sudden fall of the circulating parathyroid hormone level accompanying the hemorrhage into the adenoma, and the inability of the remaining parathyroid glands to secrete adequate hormone. Gary, we'll send you to the emergency room for a repeat CT scan of your neck and some IV calcium and magnesium. Sara and I are heading over there anyway after the clinic and will send you home on calcium and magnesium and vitamin D pills."

"Am I cured?" Gary asked.

"No." Sababa said. "This will probably come back, and Dr. Billroth will still get to remove that parathyroid when it does. And then, I'll get to send him my original letter."

'Is it hot in   here or is it just me?
I've got a knot in my tummy and a tickle in my knees
No you won't hear me cough or sniffle or sneeze
But I think I'm coming down with a rare new disease.'
Lauren Hoffman, *Rare New Disease*

Cheri Sundae greeted Sababa and Sara in the ER.

"Who's the chick, Sab?"

"Sara Reynolds." Sara said. "Doctor Chick to you. I'm with the professor."

"Whoo." Cheri said. "Lah-dee-dah. Happy Doctor Chick2U2. Dr. Capitaine says he gets him first." She pointed to the emergency doc, approaching at a clip.

"How are you, Myles?" Sababa asked.

"Living the dream."

"Dreams can change. If we all stuck with our first dreams, the world would be full of princesses and cowboys. What you got?"

"Verner Morrison." Myles began. "51-year-old BC Ferries captain with five days of flushing, vomiting, and large volume diarrhea."

"Another captain, mon Capitaine?" Sababa asked.

"He saves me a seat at his table on the Queen of Alberni." He said. "Anyway, Verner's diarrhea has worsened from five loose stools daily to ten non-bloody, liquid bowel movements each day. He also has an itchy rash on his inner thighs, now resolved, that started two days before his other symptoms. The man was completely well before this, no previous history of anything."

"Exam?"

"Weak and dehydrated with a rapid heart rate." He said. "That's it."

"Labwork?"

"Elevated hematocrit, white count, liver enzymes, calcium and random glucose, and low serum potassium with a non-anion-gap metabolic acidosis. Fasting and aggressive intravenous fluid resuscitation and potassium replacement and antidiarrheal drugs have failed to improve his loose bowels. Stool studies are pending but I was concerned about contagion and put him in isolation."

"Civilization is the distance man has placed between himself and his excreta." Sababa offered.

"Cholera." Sara said. "I'd say cholera."

"I did a Crystal VC Rapid Diagnostic dipstick test." Myles said. "It was negative for Vibrio cholerae O1 and O139."

"It's not that accurate." Sara said.

"Accurate enough." Sababa intervened. "Context, Sara. He's a BC Ferries captain, for Chrissake. Exhilaration is that feeling you get after a great idea hits you and before you realize what's wrong with it. Does his stool smell like fish and look like rice water, Myles?"

"Nope." The ER physician said. "And his abdominal CT scan showed a solid mass arising from the tail of the pancreas."

"The great tragedy of science—the slaying of a beautiful hypothesis by an ugly fact." Sababa said. "Game changer, Sara. Probable VIPoma. Tumour producing vasoactive intestinal polypeptide."

"That's a one in ten million per year chance of happening." Sara said. "As opposed to him having a separate pancreatic tumour and a two in a thousand chance of having cholera."

"Well, look who's just made the jump from Occam to Hickam without passing through her Royal College exams." Sababa said. "Except that this incidence is for people at risk in endemic countries. Captain Morrison's chance is having cholera is near zero. Stalin once said that a single death is a tragedy; a million deaths is a statistic. Statistics mean nothing to the individual. Not a damn thing. Individual patients are not merely the sum of their probabilities, despite the earnest efforts of VIHA to replace us with the software they claim will make them just that; I'm trying to prevent Verner from becoming one of Stalin's tragedies. His illness is not an exercise in quantum physics, and I don't have the time or the crayons to explain this."

"You don't think probability theory is important?" Sara asked.

"It is a mathematical fact that fifty percent of all doctors graduate in the bottom half of their class." Sababa said. "Of course it is, just not right now. Here's what we're going to do. Serum glucagon, vasoactive intestinal polypeptide level and those of other hormones to rule out Type 1 MEN, and an octreotide scan. Book him for an ultrasound-guided biopsy of the tumour. Get Jules Martino to see him, because he will need surgery when the results are back. Immunize him for pneumococcus, meningococcus and Hemophilus influenzae, because Jules will have to remove his spleen. He may need an octreotide infusion to control his diarrhea. Let's go tell him."

Trace Pangloss was waiting for Sababa and Sara, as they emerged from behind the captains' curtain.

"What?" Sababa asked.

"Got your street medicine hat on tonight, Sab?" He asked.

"I could help you, Trace, but I prefer emergency doctors with newer and more challenging cases right now."

"You're gonna love this one." He said.

"Try me." Sababa raised an eyebrow.

"Rhea Bolger." Trace began. "55-year-old line cook down at Trawlers Fish and Chips. Presents tonight with a Colle's fracture of her right wrist. The on-call orthopod, Piggy Muldoon, came in to fix it because of how bad it was, although he always maintains there's no such thing as an orthopedic emergency. He thought her imaging looked unusual, so he ordered a skeletal x-ray survey, which showed osteosclerosis of the long bones. She's also complaining of several weeks' worth of worsening fatigue and bone pain around the joints of her lower limbs, knees, and ankles. About ten years ago, she began to develop some thickening around her eyelids. Three years after that, she saw your colleague Wayward Woods for a problem of thirst, drinking way too much water, and peeing ten times a day. It even woke her four or five times a night."

"What did Wayward find?" Sababa asked.

"The problem disappeared by itself." Trace said. "So he didn't get to find anything. A year ago she was referred to our own faceless oculist guru, Dr. T.J. Eckleburg, for bulging of both her eyes, after her thyroid tests returned normal. T.J. did a post-orbital biopsy for the thickening he found behind her orbs, but the results were inconclusive. Two months ago she was re-referred to Wayward because of headaches, the loss of full control of her bodily movements, and pituitary hormone abnormalities."

"What kind of pituitary abnormalities?" Sababa asked.

"Low levels of follicle-stimulating hormone, luteinizing hormone, cortisol, insulin-like growth factor, growth hormone, and high prolactin. She was lactating ten years after her menopause."

"Multiple anterior pituitary hormone deficiencies with hypogonadotropic hypogonadism, and growth hormone and secondary adrenal insufficiency. Did Wayward do any imaging?"

"Brain and Pituitary MRI showed symmetrical cerebellar and pontine signal changes, and that her pituitary gland is thinned out and flattened at the floor of the fossa, with loss of the normal posterior lobe hyperintensity."

"Secondary empty sella syndrome." Sababa said.

"That's what Wayward called it, yeah." Trace reported. "Although he thought it was primary."

"It's from something else." Sababa said. "Exam?"

"She has these weird fatty deposits on her eyelids and fatty tumours under her skin."

"Why are they weird?" Sababa asked. "Xantholasmata and xanthomas."

"Her lipid profile is completely normal." Trace said.

"Oh?" Sababa's right eyebrow went up.

"She also has a history of recurrent episodes of fluid accumulation around her heart. Other imaging has shown

252

parenchymal and pleural thickening of her lungs, abnormal soft tissue thickening around her ascending aorta and coronary arteries and left renal artery, and scar tissue behind the posterior lining of her abdominal cavity. And her echo showed a small 2.5 x 1.3 cm mass on the right atrial posterior wall extending superiorly."

"Cheri, who's on call for pathology tonight?" Sababa asked.

"Dr. Leyblanca." She said. "He's already downstairs in the lab working on another case."

"Raise him for me, will ya?"

"On it." She said. "A few seconds later, her left hand gesticulated in the air. "Line two."

"¿What ees it ju want at thees time of night, Cabrón?" Asked the pathologist.

"I want you to pull some slides on a retro-orbital biopsy that T.J. did about a year ago, Juan." There was a feeble grunt of protest on the other end of the conversation. "We'll be right down." Sababa motioned for Sara to follow.

"Come, Watson, come! The game is afoot. Not a word! Into your clothes and come!"

"What are you thinking?" She tried to keep up.

"Perceive that which cannot be seen with the eye. Xantholasma with a normal lipid profile." He said. "Empty sella syndrome from infiltrative hypopituitarism, pleural thickening, pulmonary fibrosis and retroperitoneal lymphadenopathy, recurrent pericardial effusions, osteosclerosis of her long bones— multisystem infiltration by something—heart, brain, bones, skin, lung, and pituitary. The answer is hiding behind her eyeballs, straight ahead." They were in the basement now, where all brilliant troglodyte pathologists lived. Juan Leyblanca was already sitting on the other side of a teaching microscope, making Latin noises of appreciation punctuated in more profane Spanish.

"Hijo de puta!" Escaped his lips as they entered. "I keel that culio."

"Who?" Sababa asked.

"That pendejo of a locum that reported the result of thees biopsee!"

"What's wrong with it?" Sara asked.

"Look." He pointed to the teaching eyepiece. Sara and Sab looked.

"Foamy heesteeocytes, surrounded by scarring." The pathologist said. "The son of a beetch even stained them, and found they were CD68 and CD163 positive, and CD1a and S100 negative.

If he had sent it for electron microscopy, he wouldn't have found any Birbeck granules eether."

"What does that even mean?" Sara was exasperated.

"In 1930, an American pathologist named William Chester came to visit an Austrian pathologist named Jakob Erdheim, in Vienna." Sababa said. "Together they found the first case."

"Of what?" Sara said.

"Of Erdheim–Chester disease." Juan said.

"Rhea Bolger has a diffuse tumour of white blood cells, tissue macrophages called histiocytes." Sababa explained.

"It's rather rare." Leyblanca said. "There are only 500 cases reported in the world medical literature."

"501." Sababa said.

"Soon, Cabrón." The pathologist agreed. "I call ju."

On the way back to the ER, Sara was still unsettled.

"So why did her diabetes insipidus get better all by itself ten years ago, and why is her prolactin level high?" She asked.

"Posterior pituitary lesions rarely cause permanent DI since hypothalamic nuclei can still produce and secrete vasopressin directly into the circulation." He said. "Her prolactin is high because of stretching of her pituitary stalk."

"How do you do that?" Sara asked.

"Do what?"

"Know all this shit." She said.

"How do you get to Carnegie Hall?" He asked. "Practice. Practice. Practice. Think lightly of yourself and deeply of the world. Life is full of obvious things that nobody by any chance ever observes. You will come to learn a great deal if you study the insignificant in depth. Know the smallest things and the biggest things, the shallowest things and the deepest things. It may seem difficult at first, but all things are difficult at first."

"I'm jealous of all the people that haven't met you." She said.

Back in the ER, it took Sababa awhile to explain everything to Rhea Bolger. The middle-aged woman who had spent such a difficult life frying fish and chips and being ill was finally relieved to find out what was wrong with her. Salty trails of tears raced each other down her cheeks.

"Dr. Reynolds here will organize more tests, Rhea." Sababa said. "We'll start you on alpha-2a pegylated interferon, prednisone, and more medications. There are some promising immunomodulator therapies on the horizon. I'll see you in my office for followup. Mercy will call you."

"Mercy?" She asked.

"She's my medical office assistant."

Trace Pangloss was waiting outside Rhea's cubicle.

"I have another referral for you." He said.

"You'll have to go some to beat this last one." Sababa said.

"Neat, eh." He said. "What did she have?"

"Erdheim–Chester disease." Sara volunteered.

"Whatever." Trace said. "Now this next guy, he has something rare."

"Why don't you tell us about it?" Sababa smiled.

"Quinten Massys." He said. "60-year-old owner of The Pirate Chandler, down on the harbour. Arrived in the ER tonight with a long history of headaches and sudden onset of a droopy right eyelid."

"Call Oliver Lax." Sababa said. "He's a neurologist."

"He said to call you."

"OK." Sababa said. "What else you got?"

"Right-sided third nerve palsy on exam." Trace said. "Loose teeth. Bloodwork shows high alkaline phosphatase. Skull X-ray showed both osteolysis and osteosclerosis. Funny looking guy."

"How is he funny?" Sababa pulled up an old Flemish painting on the ER consultants' computer.

"Yeah." Trace said. "Like her."

"The Ugly Duchess." Sababa said. "And the real reason Beethoven was deaf."

"Huh." Trace said.

"Let's go see him." Sababa said. Trace made the introductions.

"Quinten, one of the nerves that supplies your right eye is under some compression force as it enters the fissure above the orbit." He said. "We're convinced that you have a condition called Paget's Disease of Bone, named after the man who discovered it, Sir James Paget. The other name for it is osteitis deformans. It's a disease of osteoclasts, cells responsible for bone remodelling and resorption, and associated with a mutation in a gene we know as SQSTM1, sequestosome-1, which encodes a protein called p62, that regulates osteoclast function. It can sometimes cause arthritis, heart problems, kidney stones, and other neurological problems, but we have excellent therapies that should help prevent these things from happening."

"Can you cure it?" Quinten asked.

"Dr. Reynolds here will organize some further tests as an outpatient—bone scan and urinary hydroxyproline, and give you an infusion of zoledronic acid which you'll have every year. She'll also discuss calcium and vitamin D, diet and exercise, and some other issues before you go home tonight." Sababa said. "Your eye should improve within two months." He handed Sara his pager.

255

"Rule number six." He said. "Everybody goes home. My turn. Make me proud." And was gone.

Sara turned to find Dina, checking off her orders.

"Then there was the time he finished his stint in an Emergency Department in South Africa." She said. "As the story goes, he drove out to a skeet shooting range outside Cape Town, tied his pager onto a clay pigeon, and shouted. *Pull.* An eyewitness saw him blow it to smithereens. The hospital administrator only found out after he left the country." Sara looked down at the pager.

"I know how they both felt about each other."

'I can't get to sleep I think about the implications
Of diving in too deep And possibly the complications
Especially at night I worry over situations.'
Men at Work, *Overkill*

"Doctor Sababa?" Said a disembodied voice. "It's Sara." He looked at his watch. It was after 08:00 a.m. For the first time in a long time, Sababa had slept in.

"Someone admitted last night?" He asked.

"Not exactly." She said. "But I have a commercial fisherman who came in a half hour ago."

"Ernie Hacker is on call today, Sara."

"Dr. Ho said he wanted you to see him."

"You work him up." He said. "I'll be there in half an hour."

Thirty minutes later Sababa's dimpled and dented white Honda Civic swept around the last iconic intersection corner of Dufferin Crescent at Dufferin Crescent on two wheels. A minute later he was flying through the wide automatic sliding frosted glass doors of the Harbour City Regional ER. His Colombian leather briefcase did a barrel roll through to air before coming to rest beside the computer on the consultants' desk. Cheri Sundae pointed to Bed #9.

"Happy Doctor Chick2U2's waiting for you, Sab." He pulled back the curtain to find Sara listening to the chest of a rough lean and leather brown wrinkled alchemy of sun and sea and weather. His eyes were as blue as the ocean, his lips were

256

cracked, and his hands were calloused shovels. He smelled of salt and sweat and tobacco. Then Sababa noticed the painful-looking red sores all over his exposed brown skin. *Bitter days, on the fishing grounds.*

Sara pulled her stethoscope away from her ears.

"This is the specialist I told you about." She said.

"What kept you?" Asked the fisherman.

"I don't ever rise and shine." Sababa said. "Most days I caffeinate and hope for the best. I'm here now. Who is this presumptuous piscator, Sara?"

"Coal Tyee." She continued. "54-year-old salmon fisherman brought in by ambulance this morning because of a fainting episode from severe dehydration. He has a three-month history of facial and upper chest flushing, mouth sores, explosive diarrhea, and abdominal pain, photosensitive rash, hair loss, wheezing, swollen legs, and inflammation of his tongue."

"Not all that wheezes is asthma." Sababa said.

"I feel like a vampire." Coal said. "I have to avoid the sun and I can't sleep at night."

"Not to mention aggressively querulous." Sababa said. "You know the condition that contributed most to the European folklore and vampire legends of the 1700s, Sara, from the corn that Columbus brought back to supplement the continental diet without the secret Native American beneficial knowledge of the necessity for nixtamalization?"

"Say what?" She said.

"I'm talking about Asturian leprosy, the Spring Sickness that afflicted Southerners in Mississippi and Alabama following the corn cycle, and the endemic Northern Italian *pelle agra* 'sour skin' disease, named by Francesco Frapolli of Milan."

"Pellagra?" She asked.

"The one and same." Sababa said. "And it's four D's—dermatitis, diarrhea, dementia, and death."

"Now wait just a goddamn minute here." Coal became aggressively querulous.

"Relax, Dracula." Sababa said. "It takes four or five years, and then only if we don't treat it."

"But how would he get niacin deficiency?" Sara asked. "They put vitamin B3 in everything these days."

"He doesn't have a primary dietary deficiency." Sababa said. "His pellagra is secondary."

"To what?" Coal asked.

"Well, isn't that the question then, Popeye?" Sababa continued. "The big clue here is your flushing. "You have something living in your gut that's using most of the tryptophan you absorb as the source for its serotonin production, which limits the amount available for niacin synthesis."

"Sara...?"

"Nothing to do with me, Coal." Sara said. "Serotonin is a hormone responsible for dilating and constricting the tubes in your body that control luminal flow and smooth muscle activity. We refer to it as a vasoactive substance. It's a monoamine neurotransmitter, an indoleamine molecule that derives from the amino acid tryptophan. Its stimulation of the 14 variants of serotonin receptor has diverse effects on mood, anxiety, sleep, appetite, temperature, eating behaviour, sexual conduct, movement, and gastrointestinal motility. The psychedelic drugs psilocybin, mescaline, some psychedelic mushroom compounds, Ecstacy, and LSD are stimulants of serotonin receptors. The serotonin in insect venoms and plant spines causes pain. Pathogenic amoebae can produce serotonin, and its effect in the human gut is diarrhea. Its widespread presence in many seeds and fruits serves to stimulate the digestive tract into expelling the seeds.

The increased concentration in your body is to blame for the diarrhea from increased intestinal peristaltic transit, wheezing from constriction of your breathing tubes by stimulating their 5-HT2B receptors, and that part of the flushing that isn't from the effects of another powerful vasodilator product called bradykinin. It may also cause scarring of the right side of your heart and the leaky tricuspid and narrow pulmonary valve I can hear when I listen."

"What is doing all that?" Coal asked.

"You have a carcinoid tumour, Coal." Sababa said. "But because it's producing these hormones, we call what you have carcinoid syndrome. Because your liver inactivates serotonin, your tumour is along your gut somewhere and already spread to your liver, or it is only in your bronchi without further dissemination."

"Which one do you think?" Coal asked.

"Most likely the first possibility." Sababa said. "But we'll need to bring you into hospital to find out."

"But my boat." Coal said.

"Will be still at the pier when we let you out." He said. "Sara Tonin here will collect a 24-hour urine for 5-hydroxyindoleacetic acid, order an octreoscan and other imaging, start you on somatostatin analogue monotherapy and nicotinamide. I'll look in on you later."

"Hey, Doc." Coal said.

"What."

258

"Did you know that 3.14159% of fishermen are πrates?" Sababa groaned as he left for the Death Star.

A half hour later, the hospital switchboard operator broke into his train of thought. Lana's overhead broadcast sent along a big chill with the Big Voice. *Code Blue times three... ETA Five minutes... Code Blue. Code Blue. Code Blue... Code Blue. Code Blue. Code Blue...* Sababa had never heard that one before. Nothing got in his path on the way back down the hallways. He arrived to a pandemonium of Brownian motion in uniform. Dina and Michaela and Regina had already assembled innumerable IV poles with bags full of several powerful resuscitation drugs at the ready.

Three ACLS ambulance crews rolled most of their Hopes into the Harbour City Regional Trauma/Resuscitation room. Madelaine Hope had already been disqualified from further participation. Carrie Hope slid under the eyes of Dr. Myles Capitaine and his team of ER nurses and respiratory technicians. Father Darryl fell under the supervision of Dr. Gung Ho and a hybrid group from the ER and ICU. And Dawn Hope might have looked up into the burning eyes of Doctor Sababa and his crack cohort from the Death Star if she would have still been alive.

The EMS technicians who had done all the pumping and bagging since the rescue divers had retrieved the drowning victims, handed off to those chosen to replace their efforts. The nervous silence that preceded the arrival of the Hopes swelled into the sound and fury and bangarang of disassembling crash carts and shouting orders and clangourous clamouring CPR by the three pods of resurrection. The high-pitched whine of ECG flat lines filled the treble spaces. Big Voice filled in the rest. *Code Blue ER... Code Blue ER... Code Blue ER...* But everyone who was a player was already at the game.

Sababa rammed a subclavian central line into the space under Dawn Hope's right clavicle, jammed the end into a hanging bag of warmed saline and began to bark out orders to fill its ports.

"Continue compressions." He yelled. "Epi 1 mg IV."

"Epi 1 mg IV given." Angie called back.

"Bicarb 1 amp IV." Sababa shouted. Angie echoed his every command. After ten minutes of effort, Sababa had given Dawn Hope enough intravenous adrenalin to kill a live horse. Three flat line whines were stuck in the key of B flat. The members of the other two resuscitation pods looked at each other in defeated frustration.

"Call it." Said Dr. Ho. "Time."

259

"10:46 a.m." Mary wrote it down on the resuscitation record. The next admission of failure came two minutes later.

"Call." Said Dr. Capitaine.

"10:48 a.m." Michaela wrote the time on her sheet. Sababa's group looked at him hard.

"Not dead until warm and dead." He said. "What's her core temp?"

"35°C." Angie said.

"Continue compressions." He yelled. "Epi 1 mg IV."

"Epi 1 mg IV given." Angie called back. The high-pitched whine of the monitor gargled a single wide electrical complex of yellow light on a green screen, then another scuttled, and then another.

"Give me a rhythm I can dance to." Sababa muttered. There came a riot of oscillating waves crashing through the flat beachhead along the Styx river underworld, over which Charon had ferried the souls of the dead.

"V-Tach!" Angie shouted. "V-Tach!"

"Yep, that's one." Sababa placed the defibrillator paddles on the gel pads on Dawn's chest. "300 watts/sec."

"300 watts/sec." Angie called.

"Clear." Sababa pushed the buttons with his thumbs. Everything under them jumped a foot into the air. Everyone glared back at the green screen. The yellow returned with a rhythm twice as fast, from the top part of Dawn's heart.

"PSVT!" Angie shouted. "PSVT!"

"Adenosine 100 mg IV." Sababa yelled.

"Adenosine 100 mg IV given." Angie called. Dawn's rhythm snapped to attention.

"Sinus!" Angie shouted. "Sinus!"

"I have a pulse, Sab." It was Mary. "We have mechanical activity."

"Pressure's coming up." From Charmeine. "Now 120/80 mmHg." The nervous silence returned. In the other resuscitation enclaves, Dawn's father and sister had been already declared dead, as should all accidental drownings submerged for more than half an hour.

It's always ourselves we find in the sea.

'Somebody's gonna take the fall There's your quid pro quo
Punish the monkey... And let the organ grinder go.'
Mark Knopfler, *Punish the Monkey*

The casual reader might know that one of the major drawbacks of omniscience was that you have to plan for everything.

Sababa had planned to have an extended family, as he planned the other elements of his future, just as Darryl Hope had built his own pedigree. But they both came through space and time as the philosopher Jagger had observed. *You can't always get what you want.* And ultimately, even though Sababa couldn't figure out why both men ended up in the same place, he realized how much it didn't matter.

True, Darryl had created the perfect family, but a cruel accident took them away. Sababa and Jane ended up never having the family they planned for, but they ended up good with that. Sababa was too busy seizing the day, living in the now forever, to concentrate on having a life outside of his calling. *Carpe diem aeternum.*

In the end, he realized, from his understanding of genetics and the creation and meaning of progeny, that a hen is only an egg's way of making another egg. In the five generations before and after you, there was and would be only 1:32 the amount of you in any relative. So it wouldn't be your eyes that anyone would recognize.

Life wasn't fair. Sababa's cousin, Bill, was a cardiovascular surgeon who woke up on his 63rd birthday, after saving thousands of patients from death and fates worse, with end-stage metastatic squamous cell carcinoma. His only grandson, Max, the apple of his eye, had just celebrated his first birthday.

"What about the *quid pro quo*?" Sababa asked him a week before he died.

"What about it?" Bill asked back and died. Only the dead fish swim with the stream.

Sometimes a shift in perspective makes you see what you've lost. Sababa realized that there was more than one path to the top of the mountain. He understood the difference between the 'dark' and 'light' triads that exemplified the worst and best of humanity. The dark triad brought psychopathy, Machiavellianism, and narcissism; the light triad was about Kantianism (treating people as ends unto themselves, not as mere means to an end), Humanism (valuing the dignity and worth of each individual), and Faith in Humanity (believing in the fundamental goodness of humans). Sababa got beyond love and grief to exist for the good of humanity. He took success like a gentleman and reversals like a man. He treated everyone like they were family. The irony was that, because Sababa had never produced an extended family, he inherited, instead, the ultimate family practice. He became the personification of the generosity of spirit and did nothing of no use. He went on to better things and brighter days. And the reward for good behaviour was always more.

Not everything that counts can be counted, and not everything that can be counted, counts.

A CT scan revealed a 12 x 9 mm cystic nodule in the uncinate process of Seale Harris's pancreas. Sababa was called to the OR to point out the insulinoma to Dr. Martino. Seale never developed diabetes after his surgery and is still sharing saltwater taffy with his customers. Two days after the operation, Dr. Martino called Sababa back to the OR for a second time, to point out Zonobia Fasciculata's left adrenal adenoma. Her blood sugars have stabilized, and she is now back waitressing at the Lighthouse Bistro.

George Anson's serum ascorbic acid level was unmeasurable at <0.12 mg/dL. He responded well to vitamin C and found work again as an electrician. Mambo's pizza now delivers him custom 'Scurvy Pirate' pies topped with tomatoes and broccoli, spinach and sorrel, bell and chili peppers, and watercress and parsley.

The Harbour City Regional clinical oncologist, Dr. Henry Chibueze, developed the predicted terror in his eyes when Sara referred John Lykoudis for an opinion on his Zollinger-Ellison Syndrome. Dr. Martino performed a successful Whipple pancreaticoduodenectomy, that got all the microscopic neuroendocrine tumours and both affected peripancreatic lymph nodes. John is now without symptoms on proton pump inhibitors and pancreatic enzyme supplements. He swims three times a week in the Harbour City public pool, still chlorinated with ammonia from his own supply house.

Paul Newman's thirst and excessive urination responded well to Sara's vasopressin spray, but Ed Hyde's bronchoscopy confirmed Sababa's suspicion of poorly differentiated adenocarcinoma of the lung. Paul lost his last game of billiards a month later.

262

Howard Dell's serum copper levels returned to normal with Sababa's penicillamine chelation therapy, but there were minor residual neurological problems which prevented him from returning to work as a Harbour Air float plane pilot. He spends his time trapping Dungeness crabs that he is quick to point out, have blue blood because the oxygen-delivery hemoglobin in their blood is not based on iron like ours. It's based on copper. *I will make your skies like iron and your earth like copper. Leviticus 26:19*
After a single 10 mg dose of praziquantel, Hideki Tojo gave birth to a 30-foot-long broad tapeworm. All the fish he uses in his sushi restaurant are now frozen at −35°C for 15 hours before he serves them to his clients. Sababa is his favorite customer. *Ā*

s *ō̄desu.*

Ironman Anthony Stark's phlebotomies still perk up Jane Sababa's rose garden. Thanks in part to Sab's influence, Tony has switched to pinot noir and has become something of a Stark Raving connoisseur. He promised to take the stocky savant on a jaunt to Mali, whenever the first wine bar opens in Timbuktu. Sababa took up the offer in the good humour with which it was made.

Four months after Gary Shadling's parathyroid adenoma had its accident, it fired up back into hormone overproduction mode. Sababa sent him back to Dr. Theodor Billroth with a note. *You'll need to fix my original diagnosis.*

Verner Morrison's octreotide scan lit up the tail of his pancreas like a Christmas tree. Both his serum glucagon and vasoactive intestinal polypeptide levels were high, and his ultrasound-guided biopsy confirmed VIPoma. Dr. Martino performed a distal pancreatectomy and splenectomy on the twelfth hospital day. No gross metastatic disease was found intraoperatively. The margins of the pancreas were free of tumour, and the spleen was normal. The patient had an uneventful postoperative course with complete resolution of his diarrhea and normalization of his serum potassium. Follow-up octreotide scan at 15 months demonstrated two new small foci of uptake. CT scanning showed retroperitoneal lymphadenopathy consistent with recurrent disease. At twenty months postresection, the BC Ferries captain declined further workup or intervention.

Quinten Massys's droopy eye returned to normal inside of two months. He sees Doctor Sababa every year before his zoledronic acid infusion, to make sure he has no signs of osteogenic sarcoma, and to say hello. He still owns The Pirate Chandler.

Rhea Bolger's Erdheim–Chester Disease responded well to pegylated IFN alpha-2a and glucocorticoids. She is back working part-time as a line cook at Trawlers Fish and Chips. It appears that she and Jacob Berzelius, once his garlic breath disappeared, sucking on a 'Fisherman's Friend,' have become something of what she refers to as an 'item.' When Jake isn't courting Rhea, he helps Coal Tyee restore his old salmon troller. "Whatever floats your boat." Coal would say. The fisherman's carcinoid tumour and flushing syndrome disappeared with octreotide treatment, and his skin rash and diarrhea and confusion responded well to niacin. And he didn't die.

"Do you know about the Gaelic practice of 'èit'?" Sababa asked him in followup. "Quartz stones are thrown into streams so they sparkle in the summer moonlight. It's supposed to attract the salmon."

"Only if you hit them on the head." He said.

Sometimes virtue is its own punishment. For Sababa, Dawn Hope would always represent the difference between misfortune and calamity. When she fell into the harbour it was a misfortune, but when he brought her back to consciousness, it was a calamity.

Dawn was airlifted from Harbour City to Children's Hospital in Vancouver in critical condition. Awake and struggling, she died there, fresh air gone sad. Doctor Sababa never forgave himself for trying to rescue her from her fate. Sara tried to reassure him, but he was having none of it.

"When people went underwater in movies, I used to hold my breath to see if I could have survived the situation." She said.

"Our motives dictate everything we do, and that is how we should be judged. It was just a dumb mistake."

"I never make dumb mistakes, only clever ones." He said. "As in what usually happens when you poke something big and natural with a stick? It pokes back."

"Any fool can throw a stone into the water that ten wise men cannot recover." She said.

"Sometimes the damage we do to others catches us by surprise." Sababa said. "Sometimes the damage is something we can't even see. Sometimes we can't see why normal isn't normal. And right about now, even though you don't have your basket, oh it's a terrific time for you to skip away."

And Milo Mindbender? Milo continued to plot the downfall of Doctor Sababa. He took great solace in the fact that he would never need to tell the surly specialist to go to Hell because he was building it for him.

8. The Case of the Melting Man

'So come on hitch your wagon
To the living room I'm draggin'
If I can't bring you to my house
I'll bring my house to you.'
Kacey Musgraves, *My House*

It's about habitat. It's always about habitat. The Humpback RV Resort was like an International House of Pancakes, with the customers chained to their booths, swivelling in their chairs.

RVs are the heavy metal Donald trumpets of outdoor concerts— loud and dirty and destructive—a twisted farce of make-believe camping clinging to respectability. They are the inflection point in Maslow's Hierarchy of Living in Nature, halfway between glamping and grizzlies. RVs are doing to wilderness camping what Lonely Planet has done to exotic destinations. Mother Gaia has been profaned, perverted, and commoditized. They call it a lifestyle but there is little recognizable life and no discernable style.

Ever since the Harbour City councillors granted the gated troglodyte colony permission to form a strata corporation, Humpback had devolved into a Star Wars set. From the place where the houses had been on wheels and the cars on bricks, every white-lined parking pad had become an unceasing construction worksite for innumerable concrete foundations, poured into separate times and spaces, of overhangs and pergolas, and sheds and other outbuildings, erected to store the countless crammed cornucopias of Humpback's itinerant inhabitants.

They invested their waning energies into bringing the comforts of home out into the real outside world, with none of them realizing the whole point of going there was to leave them behind. Some dared dream of skyscrapers.

For many, Humpback was the last resort and their RVs antechambers to the next world. This was true for Norbert 'Nozzle' Smart that day, although he didn't see it coming. His brother, Robert, lived in the double-wide next door. They had both tried their luck with Lauren Wasser, the Madrona RV dealership receptionist, but she had rejected him outright for

266

identical reasons, and he knew why. She might sell him a dwelling on wheels, but there was no way in hell she would live in one.

"Go out with you?" She asked, in response to Norbert's bravery. "Why not?"

"I'd sooner put pins in my eyes." She said. "The biggest city you've ever been to is Wal-Mart. Your favorite colour is shiny. Your idea of entertainment involves a flyswatter. You return from the dump with more than you took. When you take your dog for a walk, you both use the same tree.

Look at these tornado magnets." She pointed out into the acre of mutant vehicles in the dealership lot. "Where twisters are born. These things are massive modular millipedes with too many feet. It takes a lot of money to look this cheap, but their value drives off a cliff the minute you pull out of the lot. Every Blue Book appraisal varies as a function of how much gas is still in the tank.

Every off-ramp is a mission to Mars. You get free gravity and radiation protection and oxygen, but everything else costs the moon. All the headaches of home ownership come with no building equity appreciation. Whatever you fork out to keep an RV operational is lost when you sell it for far less than you paid. Every time they break down, the repair process has to navigate through new mechanics and overhaul shops. Not fixing them means being stuck. New RVs are cheap and nasty—materials are light and fragile; construction is poor. To get quality, you need to buy one as old as you are.

Amenities are not designed or fabricated for constant use. When they break, they're expensive to replace. If you squeeze between the wall and the kitchen table, your backside will fracture the table stands and the outdoor range cover. The blinds on the windows and the plastic heat vents in the floor are flimsy. Everything from water systems to fans to seat cushions succumbs to general wear and tear through whatever normal use is, in a fiesta of built-in obsolescence.

Even 'big' RVs feel small and constrained, especially when several people are trying to get things done. Passageways are tight and low and cumbersome. You bang your head on the wooden frames of the pullout, which contains your refrigerator in the poorly engineered heavy massive front drivers-side slide. Your bedroom is over the hitch area of the fifth wheel.

Every space needs to serve many purposes. The dashboard doubles as a religious shrine. Your only table is your kitchen and office and dining room, the only flat space where you can put everything that doesn't have an otherwise obvious home. Coffee and laptops and groceries, and other random items, clutter it up

267

at the same time. Every day that passes when you haven't fried a computer by spilling coffee into it is a celebration, especially if you also own business equipment to make online income. Under the table is a messy swamp of cords, a charging station for the laptops, camera batteries, cell phones, and all other electrical accessories.

The kitchen is a joke, a tiny cooking space with small fragile appliances—no cool toaster ovens, fancy coffee makers, large blenders, juicers, or bread makers. The toy freezer and auto primer-coated fridge restrict having much fresh food on hand. Instead, they're overflowing with nightcrawler chip dip in Cool Whip salad bowls, or peanut noir and nasti spumante wine. And you have to go outside to get it.

The cupboards you see are the cupboards you get. There is no bulk buying. Minimal countertop space requires that cooking is usually one-pot meals, or eating from a can, too much insulin and too little imagination. Dinner parties are an orchestrated ballet of mayonnaise sandwiches beside the can of kitchen table Raid, or they just don't happen. You always have too many dishes and two small sinks to do them in. If you boondock where water is precious, you'll dream of big dishwashers. Your ironing board doubles as a buffet table when you're not cleaning fish on it.

And your expectation for me to sleep six feet from the bathroom where your stepbrother defecates after a dozen Mount Benson lagers is not 'Finding Your Away.' He'll use the toilet brush to scratch his back. There is flea and tick soap in the shower. The toilet paper has page numbers on it. You marvel at how service stations manage to keep their restrooms so clean.

The furniture is crap, smaller than Ikea would make. The Salvation Army refuses it. Rocker recliners are too narrow. The bed is a short queen, four inches stubbier than it should be. The foam inside is of such poor quality and squished down so far, that the underlying springs poke through. And you can't walk into any random furniture store and pick out a heavy replacement. You need to remember not to exceed the weight limit, to avoid overloading your rig.

Storage space is scant and restricted. The closet is two feet wide and you have to share. No room for a winter wardrobe. Clothing ends up all over the trailer. There is no place to put whatever else you own—no basement, no large closets and no garage space for your homestead tools. Over sixty per cent of RVs have the same storage bay locks with the same keys, so kiss your security goodbye.

Home Entertainment is a pipe dream. Forget about pianos or workshops. Portable data costs are prohibitive. You won't have high-speed streaming Netflix or YouTube. Mobile Internet comes in 'buckets' of data for cellular and satellite, and free Wi-Fi is not stable or usable. Hard-mounted satellite dishes are useless in spots with trees and obstacles and infrequent line-of-sight parking. Your working TV will sit on top of your non-working TV.

You have doors but no privacy. Walls are thin, your partner knows all your bathroom habits and, even with stabilizers, nearby neighbours or other people in your rig will recognize and make fun of moments that involve increased physical activity. *If the RV is rockin' don't come knockin.* You will lose your awnings in the wind.

Did I mention fuel? Finding RV-accessible stations is frustrating and fuel costs vary from high to insane. Without deep pockets, you will climb hills at the pace of a snail, pissing off everyone else on the road behind you. Twice a day, you will need to find and hang out in fuel stations to feed your big truck engine, chewing up a gallon of diesel every 10 miles. *More fuel, please.* Again. All these propane cylinders and generator gas cans are always empty. Propane availability and price swing widely. Then comes the job of securing them and making sure everything is safe and not leaking. You will smell like you work in a refinery.

Water tanks need to be monitored and topped up to their proper levels, filled with fresh, emptied of stale. Everything is in buckets and tanks. You'll get tired of sucking on a collapsible water carrier and emptying your trashcans before they get too full. Power sources range from 20A or 30A availability, so you can run the A/C or the microwave but not both, buy all the various adaptors, and manage off-grid power usage when you're dry camping. You'll pay big upfront expenses setting up for extended off-grid periods of time, and you'd better be an electrical engineer.

This level of resource management isn't something you have to deal with in stationary homes connected to a municipal utility. If you suck at managing money in your sticks and bricks life, you will suck at it on the road too."

"But the nomadic RV lifestyle is a healthier lifestyle." Robert insisted.

"Oh?" Lauren was on a downhill roll. "How about the day-night reversal you live in? The interior of your RV is dark, even in the middle of the day, even if you bought extra high-quality lights just to feel alive; and pulling your window shades down at night won't make it ever get dark in the trailer park. Headlights whip around your head all night long, like floodlights finding criminals in an alley. Seasonal Affective Disorder gets real.

Then there's condensation. Mould will destroy your RV and your health if the toxic formaldehyde they used to glue together your particleboard palace doesn't get you first. Perhaps they'll also use it for embalming your dead body, when enough outgasses leak into your mansion, causing asthma or other breathing problems, or cancer because it's a known carcinogen. Your metal home is a bug magnet; the dirt and filth that accumulates is incredible and concentrated in a small space. Don't expect me to sweep it out twice a day.

Every time you flush the throne, your package drops into the belly of the beast and waits for you to do something with it. The crappiest waste management chore is hooking up a poop hose and dumping the tanks, flushing the tanks and hoses, and adding tank chemicals. That job gets old fast. If you're dry camping, you must find local garbage and waste dumpsites.

Sleep is one continuous interruption. If you're double-wide awake in the middle of the night you're out of luck, because there is no space to hang out respectfully while someone else is resting. Did I mention how loud RV roof air conditioners are?

Healthcare sucks enough if you're stationary, but it sucks even more on the road. You will need to buy extended medical insurance when away. Beyond the extra cost, there is a three-hundred-dollar deductible for a doctor visit. In the States, nationwide insurance networks are disappearing and RVers play domicile whack-a-mole to keep on top of it. Managing chronic conditions are challenging. Getting in to see a new primary care physician in every different location is a pain and forget about specialists. It's difficult to keep up on the road unless you always return to your home base. You will suffer through every illness, weighing up if it is serious enough or not to spend the cash, which also affects your future coverage. Prescriptions are a nightmare and finding enough to last a long trip will drive you crazy. You may drive your rig into the third world because the doctors and dentists are cheaper.

RVing is also awkward from a legal standpoint. You'll begin using the words 'health' and 'justice' in the same sentence."

"What if we just take the wheels off and live in Humpback?" Robert asked. "We can do that now."

"What do you own?" Lauren asked back. "Are there rules about reservations and availability, location and pricing, required upfront deposits, amenities offered, and restrictions on age and pets and trailer type? Most camping clubs aren't worth it. You

270

can bet that local RV parking will have the highest nightly rates in the area, as expensive as nearby motels.

Arrival is challenging, depending on how easy the spot is to get into. The tow car and boat and ATV U-turn debacle. Parking your house isn't something stationary life prepares you for. On any tree-lined street, you'll need to break out the chainsaw and amputate protruding tree limbs after running into them and causing damage to your rig.

Watching a poor fool rock around inside his massive, whale-sized mobile mausoleum, neck craned out the window trying to back up into a site, like a boisterous fat man wedging himself into the airline seat next to you, engenders a particular pity.

Spaces are close together, offering no privacy between neighbours, and you never know if you'll end up parked right next to your tranquillity-disturbing pet peeve.

Humpback will be noisy—that metallic shrink crackling of hot vehicles come to rest, hydraulic actuator noises pushing out awnings, levelers, and floor space, the sounds of things being released and pushed apart, generators and power tools, barking dogs whose owner has left them alone for the day, loud music from outdoor stereo systems illuminated with bright outdoor LED lighting or, that new feature on some RVs of an outdoor big screen television in the fuselage side, so people can sit outside their castle and watch television as loud as they want; the boisterous family reunion, CB radio squawk, the non-stop air conditioner on a good open window day, drunken parties, the neighbour who idles his diesel engine or dirt bike for hours on end, screaming kids, lawn maintenance day, or that couple that likes to dine outdoors while listening to polka music.

You expect me to do laundry? First figure out where you will store the dirty clothes. I doubt that even Humpback has well-maintained machines at a reasonable cost, without leftover detergents and fabric softening chemicals from the previous user. Your wardrobe will be fragrant even if I use a non-scented detergent."

"I'll build you a separate shed as a laundry." Robert said.

"Right." Lauren scoffed. "You'd keep your shed more secure than your house. And I'll end up having to share it with all our wonderful new neighbours. Think of the pirate culture you want to become part of. First, these people rape the communities they move into and lock themselves away from. They arrive in town, consume food and other products they don't buy locally, pay no taxes, dump their sewage and trash for free, all the while showing their special disdain for the local economy. Second, they are consumers of junk. After they've unloaded their family car and ATV Roadmasters and motorcycles, and that U-Haul trailer full of souvenirs and other 'toys,' there is always more stationary stuff to covet. The reason that some sleep in the Walmart parking lot is so they can be there for the opening bell. If you want irrefutable proof of Buddha's lesson that possessions are poison to achieving enlightenment, look no further than the RVer, attempting to transcend existence and get 'away' from it all by bringing it along.

Third, most have lost their connection to family except for Facebook and Skype and email, and end up avoiding the new people they meet because that always starts with the same old surface level conversations, requires being in perpetual social mode, and gets old fast. And yet everybody knows and dislikes everybody else. They end up putting more mental time into adapting and less time living, sitting in their folding chairs, feeding Doritos to the geese. It's no wonder that most of responsible society consider them trust fund babies down on their luck, on a permanent parasitic vacation, or on the last hurrah before homelessness. You, Norbert, are just another wannabe Winnebago warrior in a tin can alley. You smell like drama and a headache. Go away."

Norbert 'Nozzle' Smart had no luck with the ladies. He spent most of his time in his trailer beside his brother, Robert, doing who knew what. On the day in question, he waved goodbye to his neighbours on the other side. Muerto Canyon was a true RV lifestyler. His rigmate, Mathias Mamangy, was a missionary from Madagascar, come to rescue the heathens from sin. Muerto pulled their big rig out of its tree-lined space along the lake and rolled down his window to wave.

"Where are you two going?" Nozzle asked.

"New Mexico."

"In the summer?"

"We like it hot." Muerto said. They would live to get their wish.

If you drag a hundred-dollar bill through a trailer park, there's no telling what you'll find. If it stopped at Nozzle's camper any day of the week, you could get a hundred bucks worth of meth. No one knows whether it was the methamphetamine batch or a propane leak or Lauren's rejection, or some combination of all of the above, which set off the explosion in Nozzle's trailer later that night. But it sure looked pretty in the sky.

'Backside melts into a sofa
My world, my TV, and my food
Besides listening to my belly gurgle
Ain't much else to do.'
Faith No More, *RV*

The man who catches a microbe is usually in less danger for his life than a microbe with the bad luck to catch a man. The man was assembled from millions of cells, the microbe only one. But here was no ordinary man, and this was no ordinary microbe.

Roger 'Buttertubs' Marsh was the manager of the Humpback RV Resort. He had been witness to the incendiary nocturnal carnage four weeks earlier. Before that, he had monitored the increase in visitors to Nozzle Smart's trailer from the comfort of his own well-kept conveyance across the convoluted spaces that separated them, within walking distance to the dumpster. He had intended to shut down the illicit activities of both smart alecks, but Robert's skill as a procurer of certain kinds of company had slowed down the planned intervention until only one brother was left.

Within the visible light spectrum, and in the darkness, Buttertubs was extraordinary. He was a big man, double-wide the size of lesser mortals. A fierce defender of his tin can turf, he had fashioned himself into the poster boy for the RV lifestyle, through his dedication to and practice of the seven deadly sins. He could spit without opening his mouth.

Buttertubs was as proud of his luxury RV, as he was wrathful at certain lives outside the Humpback gates. One neighbour, in particular, had railed against and fought the developers he represented, in a useless attempt to thwart progress, with a ridiculous criticism that the Humpback's 'hydrocarbon runoff ran into the lake like the purulence of an open wound.' Buttertubs had become battle-hardened in the mêlée, although he was sometimes envious of others who lived on the other side of the barricades.

He was covetous of and lusted after the wives of some of his more immediate neighbours, and had gained something of a reputation as a cherubic camper Casanova, despite his waning

273

performance, because of the portly results of his unrepentant devotion to the last two deadly impieties. Buttertubs's gluttony and sloth were mythical and had propelled him into the morbid range of obesity. *Thou seest how sloth wastes the sluggish body, as water is corrupted unless it moves.*

His doctors had warned him that his diabetes now required insulin, but Roger was thinking outside his box. Not for Marsh the rigid dictates of hot yoga and ascetic stoicism. Disaster weighed light in the scale against certain pleasure. Instead, Buttertubs drank more of the kombucha he was brewing in his trailer. And more rye whiskey, to fix the kombucha, and what he believed was ailing him. After a new RVer's wife left his trailer that night, Marsh turned on his radio, poured himself a stiff double-wide rye 'n seven, and took two ibuprofen for his bad back.

This is BC Bud, sitting in for your usual Indian country evening host, Silas Seaweed, CNDN Coast Salish radio, 101.3 FM on your Home and Native Band... Silas has come down with a serious case of the shits, but will hopefully be solidly back before too long... Meanwhile, to the guy that stole my antidepressants... I hope you're happy now.

Buttertubs poured a refill and sat back to enjoy the broadcast.

Tonight's program is brought to you by Humpback RV Resort, where you never need a reservation... Find your tribe. Love them hard... You know how you can save a ton of money on your home insurance. Don't buy any... Which way does the road go? Road stay. You go.

The wily mammoth smiled a Buttertubs smile, as BC Bud played a country song that wailed with the bad lyrics of trailer park love. When it finished, the DJ shifted gears and changed course.

Remember. Every white hand you've shaken has touched a penis... Here's an old favourite from Jimmy Buffett...

Buttertubs recognized the words from *Migration*.

Now most of the people who retire in Florida are wrinkled and they lean on a crutch.
And mobile homes are smotherin' my keys; Well, I hate those bastards so much.

The microbe was also exceptional in many ways. Its name was melodious. *Clostridium perfringens*. Buttertubs wouldn't have

274

recognized it if one had stood on his scrotum, which it had done that night. It would have stayed where it was if the wily mammoth hadn't scratched himself to commemorate the pleasure of his earlier activity. The microbe intruded into the man's reminiscence and duplicated. And both of those Clostridium doubled, and they split, and so on, in geometric bliss.

I wish a summer squall would blow them all the way up to fantasy land.
They're ugly and square, they don't belong here. They look a lot better as beer cans.

And they invited their friends, a Rolodex mixture of Gram-positive cocci like Staphylococcus aureus and Streptococcus pyogenes, and enterococci, Gram-negative rods like Escherichia coli and Pseudomonas aeruginosa, and other anaerobes like Bacteroides and the original extraordinary microbe's relatives, Clostridium septicum, and Clostridium sordellii. In their joy, the clones of the exceptional Clostridium began to produce alpha-toxin and theta-toxin, which clumped up Buttertubs's platelets, blocking tiny blood vessels and white blood cell access, destroying red blood cells, suppressing heart function, and creating an ideal oxygen-deficient acidic environment for bacterial proliferation.

Yeah, That's why it's still a mystery to me, Why some people live like they do.
So many nice things hap'nin out there, Never even seen the clues.

The manager developed a severe pain behind where had recently been pleasure. When he scratched again, his finger disappeared into a new surprise space, a crackling cavity flooding a foul discharge, even worse than the hydrocarbon runoff that had for so long drained into the lake under his trailer.

May the medicine be with you, Silas...

Normally idle hands grabbed for the cell phone on the RV table. It fell into the messy cord swamp under it. Buttertubs fumbled for the shape of it and speed-dialled a number. The woman on the other end of the line asked what his emergency was.
"Ambulance." He groaned and gave directions. Minutes later he watched the sign at the gate race by, floodlit behind him.

Thank you for staying with us
Is your antenna down?

275

Are you dragging part of a hose or electric cord?
Did you leave anything or anyone behind, like your tow vehicle or spouse?
Any persons left behind will be used for winter snow removal. No exceptions.

'According to tampon commercials, all women are full of blue windshield washer fluid.'
Will Ferrell

The morning before Buttertubs found the new pathway into his perineum, and a month after Nozzle blew himself into the sky, Sara called Sababa from the ER. She described her patient's predicament as succinctly as she could.

"I'll be right there." Sababa said. She turned to find him beside her.

"What you got?" He asked.

"Lauren Wasser." She said. "29-year-old RV dealership receptionist referred by Dr. Capitaine. She turned to find the emergency physician on the other side.

"How are you, Myles?" Sababa asked.

"Living the dream."

"You're an adult when you've lived long enough for your dreams to become your regrets." He sat on the edge of the consultants' desk.

"She's in shock, Sab." Myles said. "Requiring big league inotropic squeeze just to keep her pressure barely adequate."

"Sara?" Sababa shifted into rapid listening mode.

"Previously healthy." She said. "Penicillin allergy. Developed a sunburn yesterday, even though she hadn't been outside. Came in with a high fever and chills, malaise and muscle aches, nausea, vomiting and diarrhea, and went into shock, with kidney and liver dysfunction, and confusion."

"Exam?" Sababa asked. "Never mind, let's go see her." The three physicians melted into a crease of the curtain around bed 2.

"Her lips and palms and soles are red, Sara." Sababa roused the receptionist from her stupor. "And so are her eyes and oral mucosa."

"Lauren." He shook her. "Lauren!"

"What?" She tilted her head towards the sound.

276

"Have you got a tampon in?" Sababa asked. She nodded her head.

"It needs to come out!" Sababa roared. "Now." His head emerged through the crease.

"Regina, we'll need a vaginal speculum and forceps, a kidney basin, and a nurse in here, please." Together, they set up the stirrups and removed the tampon. Sababa placed it in a sterile bag. He pointed to her vaginal mucosa, also bright red.

"Send it for culture, but we already know what's going on here." He said. "Vanco 1 gram and clinda 300 mg IV now, Regina." The ER nurse went off to mix the antibiotics.

"Cheri Sundae, can you raise the unit for me, please?"

"On it." Cheri said. "Mary on line 1, Sab."

"Little present for you, Mary." He said. "Staphylococcal toxic shock syndrome. Tell your nurses to beware the new high-absorbency tampons, leave no tampon in overnight, and use cotton tampons only, if they can."

"How does that work, Sab?" Myles asked.

"The bacteria produce a TSST-1 superantigen toxin which leeches through the synthetic tampons to activate of as much as 20% of the body's T-cells, causing a cytokine storm which results in multisystem failure."

"Wasn't it supposed to have disappeared with Procter and Gamble's withdrawal of *Rely* tampons from the market in 1980?" Sara asked.

"Tampax." Sababa said. "Stayfree. Be careful out there. It's a type 2 form of necrotizing fasciitis."

"What's the worst kind?" Myles asked.

"Type 1." Sababa said. "You'll know it when you see it."

'Fish, he said, I love you and respect you very much.
But I will kill you dead before this day ends.'
Ernest Hemingway

"While you're here." Myles said.

"While we're here what?" Sababa asked.

"Becky Vulnifica." He said. "48-year-old Seadrift Market fishmonger who got a puncture wound from a vertebral spine of

277

the Fraser River-farmed tilapia fish she was scaling yesterday. Presented with localized pain and redness in her left thumb that we thought was cellulitis. We gave her a gram of ceftriaxone IV and sent her home with some oral antibiotics. Her only other ongoing problem is hemochromatosis, for which she receives regular bloodletting."

"And?" Sababa asked.

"Come see for yourself." Myles made introductions.

"This is Doctor Sababa, Becky." He said. "He's special. And this is Dr. Reynolds. She wants to be." Becky was in obvious pain.

"The redness has progressed up to her armpit and there's lymphangitic streaking." Myles continued. "Her thumb pulp is dusky and cool, with decreased sensation and no capillary refill. Labs show a high white count and lactate and ferritin."

"I don't feel good at all." Becky said.

"Myonecrosis." Sara said.

"What's that?" Becky asked.

"The bacteria are turning your muscles into mush." Sababa said.

"What bacteria?"

"We don't know yet." Sara said.

"Vibrio vulnificus." Sababa corrected.

"What's that?"

"It's a motile, curved Gram-negative rod-shaped bacillus." Sababa said. "It has a protective capsule made of polysaccharides, which prevents it against being eaten by your white cells. It can capture host transferrin-bound iron to grow, so it loves your hemochromatosis. It thrives in summer heat waves and water with low salinity, nature's revenge for our changing the climate of the planet. And it can transfer its DNA between cells."

"Am I going to die?" Becky asked.

"Not if we can help it." Sababa poked his head out of the curtain. "Michaela, can you please bring me 100 mg of IV doxycycline, 500 mg of IV ciprofloxacin, and a gram of IV ceftazidime, in that order." He took his protégée aside. Myles followed.

"Sara, I need you to admit Becky to the Death Star, drain her thumb and send the fluid for stat gram stain and culture, blood cultures with an antibiotic removal device. Get the slasher on call for an opinion about further débridement. Call the freshwater pond aquaculture company where her employer got the Oreochromis niloticus."

"The what?"

"The Nile tilapia." He said. "And tell them we have their worst nightmare. I'll see the referral on the ward. Meet you at my office at one."

"Wow." Myles said. "What a case."

"I'm concerned about what you've cooked up for us today."

"How's that?" He asked.

"Becky has a type 3 necrotizing fasciitis infection." Sababa said. "Lauren has a type 2. Where's the type 1?" Myles laughed.

"Tomorrow." He said. "You've had enough fun for one day."

Dr. Sid Shalimar noticed the three physicians discussing their case and smiled inside. Sid could always create merriment from disaster.

"Hey, Sab." He said. "You're on call today. I've seen a patient who needs admission to the unit. He's back from a trip to China, where he's been eating Horseshoe bats in Yunnan province." Sababa turned to the source of the interruption.

"You have a case of SARS, Sid?"

"Uh... No."

"You have a doppio doppio espresso?"

"No."

"Then go play somewhere else." Sababa said. "We're kinda busy here."

'We got the clap can't be beat
Got it off the back of a toilet seat...'
Infant Sorrow, *The Clap*

Shekina met Doctor Sababa coming off the elevator on the sixth floor combined Orthopedics and Urology surgical service.

"Dr. Muldoon wants you to see one of his patients, Sab." She said. "He's on the phone." Sababa picked up the handset. She handed him the medical record.

"What are the hardest four years of an orthopod's life, Piggy?"

"I'm sure I don't know."

"Second grade." Sababa said. "What you got?"

"Robert Smart." Piggy said. "60-year-old divorced diabetic trailer troglodyte whose right knee I replaced about four years ago. Two weeks back he developed some sweats, malaise, and burning when he peed. A week ago he blew up his right first

279

metacarpophalangeal joint and developed a rash. Came in yesterday with a painful swollen, hot red right knee and a high white count, so I scoped and washed out his prosthesis, did a synovectomy, and started him on some bug juice."

"Where do you hide a hundred-dollar bill from an orthopod, Piggy?"

"Come on, Sab."

"In the patient's chart." Sababa flipped his way through the lab results. "What does he do for a living?"

"Dunno." He said. "Another recreational refugee patient of mine told me he was a pimp."

"Well, that would explain the organism."

"What organism?"

"The one that grew out of the aspirate you got from his knee." Sababa said. "Aerobic, facultative intracellular gram-negative bacteria diplococci. Neisseria gonorrhoea. What antibiotic have you got him on?"

"Ancef."

"Ah yes, the ABCs of Orthopedics: Ancef, Bone, Cefazolin." Sababa said. "What's the difference between an orthopod and a hooker, Pig?"

"Jeezuz."

"A hooker knows more than two antibiotics." Sababa said. "Repeat after me, Pig. Cef-tri-ax-one. Can you say ceftriaxone followed by ciprofloxacin?"

"Would you just go see the guy?"

"Well, since it's an emergency, why not?" Sababa said. "I'll leave a longer note than you wrote. LGFD?" *Looks Good From Door.*

"By the way, Sab." Piggy said. "I didn't tell him you guys were opted out of the government payment plan. He strikes me as a guy that would try to profit from that."

"I'm sure he'll find out soon enough." Sababa said. "Hey, how can you tell the orthopod's car from the other doctors' vehicles in the parking lot?"

"I have no freakin' idea."

"It's the Porsche with the comic book on the seat." Sababa hung up and handed the chart back to Shekina.

"Strong as a mule and twice as bright." He said. "Where is our patient?"

"Room 605." She watched him bounce down the hallway.

"Mr. Smart?" Sababa introduced himself and told the man of how the internal medicine specialists had opted out of their automatic payment plan to pressure the government to negotiate an increase in resources. They would give the patients their billing cards, the patients would remit them, and pass the

280

payment on to the physician. No patient would be otherwise inconvenienced or out-of-pocket. Mr. Smart asked for a specialist that wasn't opted out. Sababa told him there weren't any.

"When was your last sexual encounter?" Sababa asked. Robert denied having any for several years.

"Well, you must be an acrobat to have acquired Trichomonas vaginalis on your urine RT-PCR." He said. "It's the vaginalis part that provides the clue."

"What are you going to do to fix this mess?" Robert asked.

"I'm going to change your antibiotic to something that will kill the infection." He said. "I'll order more x-rays and blood tests, get your sugar out of the clouds, see you every day until it's reasonable to let you out of the hospital, and then make sure you're healed in an office follow-up visit."

"And I will take great pleasure in making sure you don't get paid." Robert said. "I'll keep the money and sue you for more, for defiling the Canada Health Act." We are always the victims of the most selfish among us. They don't even want to be polite.

"You can't be greedy and gonorrheal, Bob." Sababa said. "Pick a struggle."

"It's fruit loop week, Boss."

"Mercy bears richer fruits than justice." Sababa said. Sara had arrived only seconds before.

"First one's yours." He said, handing her a chart. She called a name.

"Jean Molière." A thin middle-aged man got up from his waiting room chair.

"Come see me when you're done." He said, calling his own patient.

"Bruce Darling." A gaunt androgynous woman, or perhaps a man, arose from his seat and followed the stocky savant into his

281

office. A younger creature trailed them, more obviously a female.

"How are you, Bruce?" Sababa asked.

"Brittany." They said.

"How are you, Brittany?" Sababa asked. "Although you are only halfway through your hormones and surgery."

"Not so good, Doctor Sababa." They said. "My sugars are off the chart."

"Remember, I told you that your transformation would play havoc with your type 1 diabetes."

"There's another complication." They said.

"Which is?"

"Lately I've found myself more and more attracted to women." They said. "Do you think I'm becoming a lesbian?"

"Before we embark on any further panel beating, we should pause for a while to decide the proper direction of our metamorphosis." They nodded their heads. Sara's face appeared in the doorway.

"Tell Mercy I'll see you in two months." Sababa watched them leave and turned to his resident.

"Kids these days." He said. "What you got?"

"Jean Molière." She said. "58-year-old Métis carver, a diabetic patient of Dr. Bloom, who presents with an abnormal chest x-ray."

"How so?" He asked. Sara threw the film up on the viewer. Sababa let out a low Sababa whistle.

"Well, lookie here." He said. "Describe what you see, Sara."

"It's weird." She began.

"We do weird." Sababa said. "What's weird?"

"Multiple non-segmental small cavitary nodules involving the lower lobes of both lungs." She said. "Miliary pattern. If this had been present in his upper lobes instead, I would have said that he had TB."

"Poetry and consumption are the most flattering of diseases." Sababa said. "Koch's most original postulate afflicted all your favourite cartoon characters—Tutankhamen, Goethe, Ralph Waldo Emerson, Edgar Allan Poe, Dostoyevsky, Hitler, Balzac, the Brontë sisters, Elizabeth Barrett Browning, Charles Bukowski, Robbie Burns, Albert Camus, Chekhov, Gorky, Dashiell Hammett, Robert A. Heinlein, Kafka, Keats, D. H. Lawrence, Somerset Maugham, Maupassant, Eugene O'Neill, Orwell, Alexander Pope, Rousseau, Ruskin, Sir Walter Scott, Robert Louis Stevenson, Dylan Thomas, Thoreau, Voltaire, Thomas Wolfe, Delacroix, Gauguin, Modigliani, Chopin, Stephen Foster, Paganini, Purcell, Stravinsky, Calvin, Cardinal

Richelieu, Simón Bolívar, Alexis de Tocqueville, James Monroe, Andrew Jackson, Nelson Mandela, Eleanor Roosevelt, Alexander Graham Bell, Sarah Bernhardt, Louis Braille, W. C. Fields, Jay Gould, 'Doc' Holliday, Kant, Vivien Leigh, Mary Todd Lincoln, Dmitri Mendeleev, Florence Nightingale, Spinoza, Ringo Starr, Ho Chi Minh, Edvard Munch, Cat Stevens, and my kabuki cherubic grandmother, Baba Rhea, who blew blue smoke rings as she cheated me during our kalooki card games."

"But it's in the wrong place." Sara insisted. "Isn't it?"

"Red snappers or red herrings?" Sababa said. "TB or not TB? That is the question. I had a nasty examiner give this exact dilemma on my Royal College exam."

"What was your answer?" She asked.

"TB." I said. "And grabbed the fly that had flown between us. I was right. TB prefers the lower lobes in patients with diabetes, although no one knows why. If half the men in the world had TB and the other half had syphilis, what's a girl to do?"

"Dunno." She said.

"Date the ones that cough."

"Four people die of TB every single minute." She said.

"Must make it difficult to sleep at night." Sababa said. "A gift of nature from the Horn of Africa. Let's go give him the happy news."

Sara introduced the carver to her professor.

"Have you ever had TB, Jean?" He asked.

"Not yet." He said.

"Well, that's what we want to talk to you about."

> 'Yeah the candle's burnin' down, now midnight comes around,
> You know the best that we can hope for
> is to be laughin' when we finally hit the ground.'
> The Refreshments, *Sin Nombre*

Drs. Cliffy Carlton and Gung Ho were both waiting for Sababa and Sara behind the wide automatic sliding frosted glass doors of the Harbour City Regional emergency room.

"It's not a propitious sign when there's a welcoming party." Sara said.

"More like an ambush, Sara." Sababa said. "What have you mongrels been up to?"

"Full moon, Sab." Cliffy said. "I would have bet on seeing a werewolf before these two that just came in."

"Let's rule out the lunar god and go from there." Sababa said.

"It's bizarre." Gung agreed.

"We do weird." Sababa said. "We can do bizarre."

"These two drove their RV all the way back from New Mexico, sick as dogs, so they wouldn't have to take advantage of the richly endowed medical care on offer from our American cousins." Cliffy said. "They barely made it."

"It's a beautiful night to save lives. Let's get started." Sababa said. "One at a time, Cliffy. You first."

"OK. Muerto Canyon. 61-year-old RV lifestyler who left with his bible buddy in the next bed a month ago for northern New Mexico. Claims he likes it hot. Got his wish."

"So what happened?" Sababa asked.

"He and buddy settled into a camping spot in Santa Fe County." Cliffy continued. "After a week of spending all their money, Muerto here got a job cleaning the top floor of a barn on the property, unused for ten years following the closure of a chicken farming operation. The equipment that needed removal still contained leftover feed and rodent droppings. Sawdust and manure covered the floor so thick that they couldn't open the inward-swinging upper doors for ventilation. The property owner installed a fan that may have made things even worse. Muerto removed dusty debris for three days. His only protection was nylon work gloves and a dust mask.

About a week ago, Muerto developed what he calls 'the flu'— fevers, chills, drenching night sweats, malaise, muscle aches and pains, headaches, dizziness, and nausea, vomiting, abdominal pain, and some diarrhea, fatigue, and lethargy. Because his rigmate was also sick, and because neither of them had travel medical insurance, they made a run for it and returned to Harbour City. They took turns driving, even though Muerto's friend in the next bed there doesn't have a driver's license."

"Sweet." Sara said.

"Yes, you are." Cliffy said. "Anyway, yesterday, as they crossed the border, Muerto developed a cough and chest discomfort and shortness of breath. And here we all are."

"Exam?" Sababa asked. They entered the cubicle. Muerto's eyes were wide open, but he was barely conscious.

"Fast heart and respiratory rate." Cliffy said. "Fever of 38.3°C, soft blood pressure of 104/69 mmHg. His breathing is laboured,

284

with the use of accessory muscles, difficulty speaking fluent sentences, diminished lung sounds, and diffuse wheezing. No other findings."

"What's this ditzy little #22 gauge IV needle you have in his forearm?" Sababa asked.

"Securing stable IV access is our mission here in the ER, Sab." Cliffy said. "How you define stable is your problem." The portly professor's head disappeared through the curtain the other way.

"Dina, can you bring me a central line tray and intubation kit, please?" He asked. "We're going to have to ventilate Wyatt Earp here. Call respiratory."

"About time." She said. "On it, Sab."

"Funny you should make that decision." Cliffy said. "Turns out Muerto's carbon dioxide levels just zoomed past his oxygenation, he has a respiratory acidosis, and his chest x-ray is unimpressive." Cliffy threw it up on the viewer. Sababa looked at Sara.

"Bilateral diffuse interstitial infiltration and small effusions." She said. "Looks more like acute respiratory distress syndrome than pneumonia or heart failure."

"Bloodwork shows elevated hemoglobin from concentration, a high white count of atypical lymphocytes and immature myeloctyes, and a low platelet count. His kidneys aren't looking so hot."

"Some small creature of the night used his mouth as a latrine and then as its mausoleum. I smell a rat, Cliffy" Sababa said.

"Peromyscus maniculatus."

"Huh?"

"I may not know much, but I know the difference between chicken shit and chicken salad. Deer mice." He said. "You said that Muerto wore a dust mask while he was cleaning out the barn."

"So."

"A dust mask offers no protection against aerosolized rodent urine and feces droplets known to transmit Sin Nombre."

"Sin who?"

"Sin Nombre. Spanish for 'nameless.'" Sababa said. "It's a single-stranded, enveloped, negative-sense RNA virus in the Orthohantaviridae family of the order Bunyavirales. First emerged around two thousand years ago in shrews or moles. Possibly the cause of the Tudors defeating Richard III in 1485 before the Battle of Bosworth Field, over five hundred years before they found his hunchbacked bones under a parking lot. But I digress."

"I'm not getting this." Cliffy said.

"Muerto has hantavirus pulmonary syndrome." Sababa slid an endotracheal into the man's airway, no longer gasping after the sedation he had received. The respiratory technician hooked it up to the ventilator he had brought from the Death Star.

"Sara, make sure the lab collects another 7 ml of clotted blood in a red-topped tube for PCR/immunoglobulin M antibodies to Sin Nombre virus, special delivery to the BC Centre for Disease Control." Sababa said. "He'll need an infectious disease workup for other organisms. Start him on IV doxycycline anyway, and ribavirin. Watch you don't fluid overload him. We'll see this next one together, and then you can finish the orders." He turned to Dr. Ho.

"What about you, Hotshot?" He asked.

"If you liked Muerto, you're gonna love his roommate, Sab." Gung said.

"Try me."

"Mathias Mamangy." He began. "52-year-old missionary from Madagascar of all places, sent here to lead us from the path of sin."

"Credible enough so far." Sababa agreed.

"While Muerto was off cleaning old chicken shit, Mathias was making friends in the RV park." Gung said. "Mostly with a Labrador retriever from the trailer next door."

"What's so special about that?" Sara asked.

"The dog died two weeks ago."

"So?" She asked.

"He was only six months old." Gung said. "A week ago, Mathias developed what he also refers to as 'the flu'—fever and chills, headaches, malaise, muscle cramps, cough, and vomiting, and pain in his groin."

"Exam?"

"Come and see." Sara and Sababa followed him into Mathias's cubicle and waited for introductions.

"May I?" Gung asked the man. Mathias, in obvious severe pain, nodded. Gung folded the sheet that covered him between his legs from both sides, exposing his flanks. Two sets of smooth swollen, ulcerated lymph nodes projected from his groin margins.

"How do you like them apples?" Gung said. Sababa lifted the man's hands. He held out the fingertips.

"Acral gangrene." He said. "Open your mouth, if you can, Mathias." Mathias opened his mouth. Sababa pointed to tiny black dots scattered on the pink inside of his cheeks.

"Lenticulae." He poked his head out through the curtain again. "Dina, can you please bring me 100 mg of IV doxycycline, 500

286

mg of IV ciprofloxacin, and 90 mg of IV gentamicin, in that order."

"Like what you asked Michaela to get for you this morning." She said.

"Different problem." He said. "This guy has bubonic plague."

All activity in the Harbour City Regional emergency department stopped in its tracks. Telephone handsets rose into the atmosphere.

"OK. If you say so." Dina said. "I'm on it."

"If anyone had ever told me that when I signed up for this elective, I'd be looking at a case of bubonic plague, I would have told them they were crazy."

"We do weird." Sababa said. "We do bizarre. Apparently, we do crazy. Madness takes its toll, as long as you have exact change." Sababa pulled a rapid dipstick test strip for Yersinia pestis from his Colombian leather bag and applied it to an aspirate he took from one of Mathias's groin buboes.

"I've been waiting for this opportunity." It was positive. He told Mathias.

"In the good old days you were poor, you got ill, and you died." Sababa said. "I'm afraid I have some good news."

"Why New Mexico?" Gung asked.

"You know the history of plague, Gung." Sababa said. The first recorded pandemic was the Plague of Justinian, named after the ruler of the Byzantine Empire. Its arrival in his capital Constantinople in 542 AD killed 25 million people in and around the Mediterranean and 50 million more over the next two years. The second pandemic, the Black Death in 1347, was even worse. It originated in Mongolian marmots and killed a third of the world's human population. The third pandemic originated in China's Yunnan Province in the mid-19th century and spread to port cities all over the world. When it arrived in San Francisco, President Chester Arthur signed the Chinese Exclusion Act into existence, so your folks might have come before that, Gung. From California, it spread through the southwestern US and took up residence in New Mexico prairie dogs and rock squirrels because the local pinyon and juniper trees supported a diversity of rodents and fleas. Mathias's dog friend was infested with fleas that carry the Yersinia pestis bacillus. He's lucky he didn't get it in his home country."

"Why is that?" Gung asked.

"In Madagascar, even more lethal pneumonic plague is a seasonal speed bump when families dig up the remains of relatives and celebrate reburial in a mortuary carnival ceremony

287

called a *famadihana*. The Turning of the Bones. Antibiotics are imported and unaffordable."

"Why don't they vaccinate the prairie dogs in New Mexico?" Sara asked.

"They're planning on doing just that." Sababa said. "They discovered an endangered black-footed ferret in 1979. Its only sources of food and shelter are prairie dogs and their burrows. When they kill the owner, as a bonus they get to keep the house." Cliffy was back waving another referral.

"Kinda like our local RV park here." He said.

"It turns out that bubonic plague is the biggest threat to ferret survival. The U.S. Fish and Wildlife Service is now using drones to spray peanut butter M&Ms filled with plague vaccine across all the prairie dog colonies they can find. They can cover an acre in less than a minute. The pellets contain a food-grade dye which marks the prairie dogs' whiskers and excreta when they eat the vaccine."

"Maybe they could adopt a similar technique to immunize the tin trailer people against bad taste." Cliffy offered.

"There are still limits to what science can achieve." Sababa offered.

"I have one more case, Sab." Cliffy said.

"Sara, you finish working up and writing orders for our RV duo here, and I'll see this one myself." Sababa said.

"Nursing supervisor on line 1, Sab." Cheri Sundae held up a handset.

"Which one?" Sababa asked.

"'Big Nurse' Ratschet." She said. *The Grand Galactic Governess of Nightingales.*

"I'm sort of busy, Mildred." He said. "It's been a banner day."

"Last time I checked, Sababa, we didn't have a Care Pathway for fucking bubonic plague."

"Two years ago my therapist told me I had problems letting go of the past." He said. "Perhaps it's time for one."

"Get rid of it." Mildred said.

"Much as I'd like to help you out, Mildred, murder violates my parole." He said. "You'll have to find another Care Pathway." Sababa hung up the phone.

"We are here on earth to do good to others. What the others are here for, I have no idea." Sababa turned his attention back to Dr. Carlton. "What you got?"

"Silas Seaweed." Cliffy said. "49-year-old Coast Salish radio host with a two-day history of muscle cramping, vomiting, and profuse diarrhea. He says his stools smell like fish."

"He's First Nation." Sababa said. "Of course his stools smell like fish."

"He also says they look like rice water." Cliffy continued. "I don't remember the Coast Salish as big rice farmers."

"Exam?"

"Profound dehydration." He said. "Cold, clammy blue-grey skin, eyes sunk into his orbits, dry mouth, wrinkled hands and feet, low blood pressure, rapid thready pulse, and Kussmaul respirations."

"He's acidotic?" Sababa asked.

"From stool bicarb losses and lactate from poor perfusion." Cliffy said. "And his potassium is dangerously low. I'm running in Ringer's with extra K^+ as rapidly as I can, and he's soaking it up just as fast."

"Let's go see him." Sababa said. Sara had overheard the conversation.

"Cholera." Sara said. "I'd say cholera."

"Of course." Sababa took another rapid diagnostic dipstick test strip from his Colombian leather bag and dipped it the stool sample in a bedside container. "What's with you and your fascination with cholera?" It was positive for Vibrio cholerae O1. He pushed his head through the curtain.

"Doxycyline 100mg IV now?" Dina asked. Sababa nodded.

"The great tragedy of science—the slaying of a beautiful hypothesis by an ugly fact." Sara said. "Game changer, Sab. The blue death."

"Sometimes, I am wrong." Sababa admitted. "I have a gift for observation, for reading people and situations, but sometimes, I am wrong."

"It doesn't matter what other people think when you're right." Sara said. "You taught me that."

"I've seen this before, in Capetown and in India." Sababa reminisced in his mind.

'In the darkness of the Gaya station, I could just make out the silhouettes of uniformed officials sticking sharp objects into the arms of fellow disgorged passengers, in the line ahead of me. As the queue advanced it became apparent that, while the syringes were occasionally changed, the needles were not. Then, much too soon, it was my turn. A hand grabbed my left arm. My right hand grabbed his.

"What's going on?" I inquired.

"Oh, nothing." He responded.

"Then why the injections?" Says I.

"Only little problem." He offered.

"What little problem? I asked. Because, now I was curious.

"Only little Cholera." He finally admitted.

"I probably already have Cholera". I said. And he let go.'

"But the most immediate question, Cliffy, is 'What's the most important question?'"
"Dunno."
"The most important question is, 'What's the question?'" Sababa said.
"Why does Silas here have cholera?" Sara asked. Sababa nodded.
"And what we do with the most important thing?"
"The most important thing is to keep the most important thing the most important thing." Sara said.
"Where have you been fishing, Silas?" Sababa asked.
"Qualicum Bay." He said.
"And what have you been collecting from the sea?" Silas looked puzzled.
"Salmon." He said.
"And what else?"
"Herring eggs." He said.
"Hearing aids?" Cliffy asked.
"No." Silas corrected. "Herring eggs. We get the roe from the kelp and seaweed."
"You have cholera." Sara said.
"I knew I didn't feel so good." Silas said. "Can it kill you?"
"It killed Tchaikovsky and von Clausewitz." Sababa said.
"I didn't know those guys."
"What did you do with the rest of the herring eggs, Silas?" Sababa asked.
"I sold them to a sushi restaurant in Vancouver."
"Which one?" He asked.
"All of them."
"All the sushi restaurants?"
"No." Silas said. "All the eggs."

'Gangrene, dying one inch at a time
Gangrene, sell your freedom by minutes
Flesh by the pound...'
Utopia, *Gangrene*

Sara called Sababa early the next morning.

"Can you dance with the devil in the pale moonlight?" She asked. "Sorry, Sab, but EMS has just brought in a guy and he's not doing well."

"You know it's a bad day when you wake up and the birds are singing Leonard Cohen." Sababa said. "What's the time?"

"After five." She said. "But this doesn't look like it can wait."

"I'll be there in fifteen." He dressed and brushed his teeth on the way to the dimpled and dented white Honda Civic in his garage. Sara and Dr. Trace Pangloss met him fifteen minutes later, bouncing through the automatic sliding frosted glass doors of the Harbour City Regional emergency room.

"What you got?" He asked.

"Roger 'Buttertubs' Marsh." Trace began. "66-year-old trailer park manager, morbidly obese, uncontrolled diabetic, likes his rye whiskey and escorts, brought in with a sudden fever, vomiting, and a shiny reddish-purple discolouration and painful tense swelling of his groin."

"Where, exactly in his groin?"

"Perineum." Trace said. "Halfway between his scrotum and his anus, and oblivion. One sick bastard." He and Sara watched Sababa wince.

"Who's the slasher on call?" He asked.

"Buddy Benway." Trace said.

"Cheri Sundae, please call Dr. Benway and tell him I've asked for his urgent presence here in the ER." Sababa said. "Tell him to come at once if convenient—if inconvenient come all the same."

"On it." Cheri lifted her handset off its cradle.

"Regina, can you give Mr. Marsh here a gram of imipenem, now, please?"

"On it, Sab." She said.

"Let's go see." Sababa said. Sara made the introductions.

"This is Doctor Sababa." She said. "He knows more homeless people than any of us."

"I recognize you." Buttertubs said. "You're the 'hydrocarbon runoff into the lake' guy. Why haven't you run off into the lake?"

"If they fight you, they're still alive." Sababa said. "I try to avoid arguments, they're always vulgar and often convincing. Mr. Marsh, we need to have another look between your legs." Buttertubs uncovered himself and dropped his knees to the side, just as Buddy Benway entered the cubicle.

"May I?" He asked, as he snapped on a set of gloves, and eased a sterile Magill forceps probe into Buttertubs's wound, now crackling black and angry. The instrument stopped at Buddy's knuckles. Trace's eyes went wide with the rapid change in optics and the smell.

"You seen anybody else with this?" Buttertubs asked.

"Herod the Great." Sababa said.

"The great what?"

"Please excuse us for a moment, Mr. Marsh." Buddy said, drawing the other three physicians outside the curtain and out of earshot. Cheri Sundae handed them the preliminary bloodwork results.

"His LRINEC score is stratospheric." Sababa said.

"What's a LRINEC score?" Sara asked.

"It's an acronym." Sababa said. "Stands for Laboratory Risk Indicator for Necrotizing Fasciitis."

"This is necrotizing fasciitis?" Trace asked.

"Flesh-eating disease by any other name." Sababa said.

"And in Buttertubs's case, and where it is, it's called Fournier gangrene." Buddy added.

"That's horrible." Trace said.

"That it is." Sababa said. "Where there is no imagination there is no horror. Myles said we'd see a type 1 necrotizing fasciitis today. He was too right. We bred these bugs. They're our babies. And they're all grown up now, with tattoos and body piercings and a lot of attitude."

"We need some imaging." Buddy said.

"No time for imaging, Buddy." Sababa said. "No time at all, in fact."

"Cheri, get me the OR please." Buddy said.

"On it." Cheri said.

"I'll go speak to him." Buddy said. "Will you call the unit and arrange a post-op bed?"

"No need." Sababa said. "He won't be coming back."

'Seven deadly sins, seven ways to win,
seven holy paths to hell, and your trip begins'
Iron Maiden, *Moonchild*

We can excuse the casual reader for not knowing whether the Melting Man died of Pride or Lust or Gluttony or Sloth or

Greed or Envy or Wrath, or all or none of the above. Did the Bible not call them lethal for good reason? Or are the Seven Deadly Sins merely a list of victimless crimes, compiled by the righteous to distract our attention from their bloody felonies?

Of these classical vices, Pride is the essence of all sin. Wrath is the healthiest, next only to Lust, which is definitely the pick of the litter. Envy is subtle and impotent and the most insidious, numbed with fear, never-ceasing in its appetite, knowing no gratification but endless self-torment. It is as ugly as a trapped rat, gnawing off its own foot to escape. Anger is the most fun, a feast of licking wounds, smacking lips over grievances long past, tongue-rolling the prospect of bitter confrontations still to come, savouring the last toothsome morsel of both the pain given and the pain given back. But what you swallow is yourself. The skeleton at the feast is you.

The Seven Deadly Sins now have their own websites—move with agility on your mouse pad to the Lust of Tinder, the Greed of LinkedIn, the Sloth of Netflix, the Envy of Facebook, the Gluttony of Yelp, the Wrath of Twitter, and the Pride of Instagram. Pleasure for its own sake. Our evolution has blessed us with a pharmacornucopia of mind-altering recreational substances, in a variety and ubiquitous availability to battle the Mother of all the sins, Monotony.

Both Alfred Nobel and E.I. Du Pont made their fortunes by manufacturing explosives. The first gave us a prize, and the second *Better Living Through Chemistry*, which is now why we live in a cheerful and functional society, so long as the women are on Prozac, the men are on Viagra, and the children are on Ritalin.

For Sababa, Sloth was out of the question. He disdained, was bereft of, and had no tendency toward Pride or Greed or Envy. Lust and Gluttony could only occur on the rare weekend when he wasn't on call. But Wrath he could use at work and inject into his day as a force for good. Sababa knew that, in life, the finest pleasures starburst off the hard work of healing the earth; the best gratifications are delayed. And if we never sin, then Jesus died for nothing.

'There is nothing outside of yourself that can ever enable you to get better, stronger, richer, quicker, or smarter. Everything is within. Everything exists. Seek nothing outside of yourself.'
Miyamoto Musashi

There are two great rules in life: one general and the other particular. The first is that everyone can get what he wants if he only tries. This is the general rule. The particular rule is that every individual is an exception to the general rule.

Lauren Wasser's rash peeled off her two weeks after it began, but she lost both her legs to the life support medication necessary to keep her alive and out of shock. She returned to work as a receptionist for Big Boys Toys and now uses pads instead of tampons during her periods. Becky Vulnifica survived her encounter with the Nile tilapia spine at the cost of some remaining disfigurement of her left arm. She quit her job at the Seadrift market to work as a sales clerk in a local vegan food shop.

Dr. Sid Shalimar never had a patient with SARS but he and Sababa celebrate their birthdays together at the Nori Restaurant with pine mushrooms that the portly professor collects off Mount Benson every fall.

Robert Smart was as good as his word and as evil as his intentions and pocketed Sababa's fee for fixing his leg. He also sued the stocky savant for defiling the Canada Health Act and would have won the ten thousand dollars he was claiming for 'emotional distress' if Sababa hadn't hired a high-priced lawyer to make it all go away. Smart still runs an escort service out of his double-wide in the Humpback RV Resort.

Bruce or Brittany Darling committed suicide before they could decide which team to play for.

Jean Molière is on anti-tubercular triple therapy and is doing well. He has switched to a paleo diet and his blood sugars have normalized off his diabetic medication. Sababa receives occasional carvings of gratitude in his office.

Muerto Canyon and Mathias Mamangy recovered from their respective infections and now spend their time away in Florida. Harbour City Regional now has care pathways for hantavirus and plague. There is still sin in the world.

Silas Seaweed is back hosting the evening programming on CNDN radio. No one in the Vancouver sushi restaurant died of cholera from the tainted herring eggs, although the establishment took a hit on TripAdvisor. The federal Department of Fisheries and Oceans ordered an emergency closure of herring egg harvest in the area. VIHA admitted the outbreak caught them off guard, called the discovery a 'unique situation,' and says it is still 'monitoring the situation very carefully.'

Buttertubs Marsh died in the operating room, with an entire bouquet of IVs in his neck.

And Humpback Resort? It hired a new manager to promote the RV 'lifestyle.' His first task was to come up with a new rallying cry for recruitment and retention. *It's all right letting yourself go, as long as you can get yourself back.*

Closure is an unctuous little word that describes a non-existent condition. Nobody gets over anything.

9. The Case of the Pretty Bird

'Oh, Gabriola What secrets you hide
Left in the ocean, brought in by the tide
Oh Gabriola There's only so much
The green sea can erase
Oh, Gabriola.'
Dean Whitfield, *Three Feet Off Gabriola*

Take me to your island. Back along the fish spine summers, herring schools marooned in long night tides and tangled in the nets below your sleep—surf crashing on the cliffs, seaweed boiling on the teeth of kelp-ringed crags above the misted cove, gulls clawing at the wind in a screeching frenzy, dawn streaming through upper panes of salted glass. Take me to your island.

From across the water, the MV Quinsam pulled into Descanso Bay. *The Bay of Rest.* For many years, there had been a public wharf in the inlet, next to the landing, until the ferry had crashed into it during one bad docking. All that remained were the pilings that had once held it in place.

Diesel engines groaned in their burden. Black water churned the vessel stern towards the expanding jetty. Wet flags flapped in the wind. Sailboats rocked. Behind the Quinsam, Harbour City was the size of his thumb, silent and distant like a toy town.

Binky O'Hare hoisted the backpack and ran his hiking boots up Ferry Hill at a clip, to catch the cars, clanging off the ramp below. He hurried past the assortment of illegal signs and green-nested houses, filled with homework and dishes, dreams and debts, secrets and squabbles, and uninvited guests. Between arrivals and departures, the local boys would blast their bikes down through the open gates and soar off the ramp into Georgia Strait. One crazed unicyclist would play his violin, long hair flying.

At the top of Ferry Hill, at the junction of North and South roads, the old 'T & T' Texaco station used to be the place to find out if the cops had left the island. The owners, Ted and Ted, had the only tow truck, and the police would often consult them after hours to request their services. It was always a risky business because the drivers themselves were in no fit condition to drive. Either Ted would often crawl out from under a vehicle repair bay full of empties to pump gas, smoke dangling from a lower lip. They were 'distracted' at closing time and would often arrive the next morning to find the lights and gas pumps on, and the cash register untouched.

It was here near the post office that Binky O'Hare stuck his right thumb in the air, to catch a ride. An old Ford F-150 slowed and pulled over.

"Where ya goin'?" Asked the backpacker.

"Alder Way." Said the driver.

"Alder way where?"

"Just Alder Way." The old pirate mayor of Harbour City was a property developer and had built the Whalebone Beach Estates on 120 acres along the northeast coast of the island. He named the streets after characters in Melville's Moby Dick.

"Well, I'm going as far as Broadview Turnoff." Binky said. The driver nodded, and the hitchhiker threw his pack in the back of the truck.

"What happened to you?" The man had noticed the sores on his legs and the bandage on his right knee.

"Deer flies." Binky said. The driver nodded and flicked on his radio to a local version of an old Hank Snow tune.

> *I've been to Whalebone, Drumbeg, Sandwell, Orlebar...*
> *Brickyard, Descanso, Spring Beach, Lockinvar*
> *Taylor Bay, Pilot Bay, Silva Bay, Horseshoe Way...*
> *El Verano, Cresta Roca, Berry Point, Daniel Way,*
> *Wild Cherry, Upper Berry, Buttercup, Bluewater...*
> *Red Wood, Pine Wood, Dog Wood, I'm getting good.*
> *I've been everywhere, man. I've been everywhere.*

They passed through what would have been a whistle-stop in any other part of the world, but this was 'downtown' on Gabriola Island. Folklife Village had been a pavilion at Expo '86 in Vancouver. It took two years to barge the twenty truckloads of dismantled posts and beams into Descanso Bay, transport them up Ferry Hill along the narrow winding road to their destination, and reassemble the huge timbers into the grocery store, a real estate office, the fashion boutique, and the Earth Mother Market. Binky had introduced himself to the owner, Mona Pseudos, on his last visit to the island, to meet her resident aromatherapist, Gabriela Sounder. They had shared each other's knowledge with no small enthusiasm. *My dream is to provide natural health through body, mind, and spirit to Gabriolans and island visitors.*

The Ford truck zoomed by Huckleberry Park and what once had been the Firehall Trail.

McConvey, McDonald, McGilvarray, McClay Way...
Ross Way, Coates Marsh, Dragons Lane, Elder Cedar,
Pequod, Quequeg, Spermwhale, Sea Urchin...
Moby Dick, Windecker, Captain Ahab, Seawind
Jolly Brothers, Jolly Close, Barret Road, Wild Rose...
Hoggan Lake, Phase four, Lock bay, Malaspina
I've been everywhere, man. I've been everywhere.

They passed the social and recycling experiment of Tin Can Alley and fields of tansy ragwort, before turning off north onto Barrett Road, at the junction where North Road would have continued on to Colleen and Morleyville. The F-150 rolled downhill towards the northeast.

Old Crow, Wood Fire, Raven Feed, Mad Ronas...
Surf Pub, Skol Pub, Robert's Place for good grub,
Arbutus, Co-op, Credit Union, Gabe Shop...
Giro, Village Foods, Colleens, Wooden Hanger
Drug Store, Wishbone, Gord's Meats, Garden Centre...
Liquor Store, Liquor Store, Liquor Store, Liquor Store
I've been everywhere, man. I've been everywhere.

They pulled over at the Broadview Turnoff. Binky opened his passenger door.

"You headed to Sandwell?" The driver asked.

"Thinkin' about it." Binky was headed to Sandwell.

"You know there's no camping allowed in the provincial park there?"

"I know." He pulled his backpack from the bay of the truck. Binky was going to camp there. He waved as the driver carried on down the road.

Binky knew that that other direction South would take him to the marina at Silva Bay, around the South Road to the

298

dilapidated bench under the old Garry Oak at Gossip Corner, the scenic Joint Point nude sunbathers basking over 'Doc' Nichols' Drumbeg Park on the Gabriola Passage entrance, and the spirits of the flower children that had once camped in Centennial Park on Degnan Road, to pick hallucinogenic psilocybin mushrooms on Eric Bolton's nearby Somerset Farm. Some of the bohemians had bought into the cheap real estate in Hippy Hollow along Coho Drive, half-acre lots offered for 'fifty dollars down and fifty dollars a month.' One free spirit from Ontario held his deposit for a week with a five-dollar bill, until he raised the rest.

Further along were vestiges of Brother XII, a British cult leader from the early 1900s who claimed to be the reincarnation of the Egyptian god Osiris, and had run off with his mistress and the gold of his disciples. He used to dock his boat at The Maples to buy provisions for his faith community. One of his employees, Bill Coates, attempted to build a hydroelectric generator using the water from Hoggan Lake, until BC Hydro beat him at his own game, just as he was getting close to succeeding.

Looking north, Binky had been to Orlebar Point, where an unscrupulous politician had built a luxurious waterfront lot, complete with a desalination plant, with money embezzled from the public purse. The discovery of his crimes sentenced him to house arrest, but the judge had the insight to insist that he serve his punishment at his daughter's home in Harbour City. Beyond were Surf Lodge, the Twin Beaches of Pilot Bay and Taylor Bay in Gabriola Sands Provincial Park, and The Raven Resort, an asylum conference hideaway for wealthy civil servants and corporate gurus endowed with lavish expense accounts. But that was not where Binky O'Hare had made his reservation. Binky had no reservations at all.

The road signs on the route he hiked were misleading. *Bond Street. Fleet Street. The Strand.* Binky walked down a more appropriately named End Road and arrived at Bells Landing.

He walked the wooded trail of ferns and twisted trees to the sea, over steep slippery rock edges and tidepools and the empty long sand beach, collecting jewels wished up on the shore at Lock Bay. The Strait of Georgia glistened. He continued east, past the dunes and shell middens and the prehistoric petroglyph carved into the sandstone, towards the lighthouse. Crabs scuttled, clams hid under their little volcanoes, and starfish and sand dollars did nothing in particular.

Binky would camp here when he was sure that the last visitor had left. He hid his pack in the wooden backdrop to his plan. The sea rolled in over the sandy shoreline on contented waves and came to cool his feet. He retrieved a brochure blowing along the beach. *Visitors should use caution and wear proper footwear. Bring hiking shoes or boots.*

He looked down at an odd number of hiking boots. Including his, there were three. Inside the third, a grisly grey right foot of disarticulated bones—oblivious to the shifting sands and the grips of sun, rain, ice, wind and time, had been cast up like the driftwood that surrounded it, a visitation, yet another illicit incursion. It dropped Binky's knees onto the wet rocks of his salted Salish Sea sanctuary. Take me to your island.

'I'm gonna buy me a parrot, baby,
> And teach him how to call my name.
> Then I won't have to miss you baby
> And I won't have you driving me insane.'
> Eric Clapton, *Sick and Tired*

RRRRrrrrriiinnnngggg RRRRrrrrriiinnnngggg! RRRRrrrrriiinnnngggg!
Gabriela picked up her phone before she realized it was Julius.
RRRRrrrrriiinnnngggg RRRRrrrrriiinnnngggg! RRRRrrrrriiinnnngggg!
"Shut up, you stupid bird." She said. Julius, her Congo African Gray parrot, was ten years old and could live for another sixty. He knew all her buttons.
Good Morning, Binky. Let's do that again. Good Morning, Binky. Let's do that again.
"Shut up, Julius." Gabriela Sounder was late for work, but she knew that Mona wouldn't mind. Gabriela was the aromatherapist at Earth Mother market and, as a consultant, could adjust her own schedule. Mona might not even be at the Folklife Village today. She hadn't been up to her usual wellness level since she lost her appendix in Harbour City Regional a week earlier. Gabriela knew that the appendix was an important part of the holistic whole. She put on the jug for tea.
The sound of boiling water came out of Julius, even before it came out of the kettle.
"Shut up, Julius." She said. It was because of and not despite Julius's intelligence that he possessed the ability to drive her crazy. He had a vocabulary of 300 words, could tell the difference between shades and shapes and knew the names of a

hundred different things. His red eyes followed her every move. The rest of him was the colour of ash, except for his white edging and black beak and nails, and the tinge of carmine in his small short tail. She thought of him as a male, although it was impossible to tell by looking, and she wasn't about to pay for endoscopy or DNA sexing.

Gabriela put a homemade organic gluten-free whole grain muffin in the microwave. Julius made the oven sound before she did. He produced an aria of whistles and hisses, squeaks and shrieks, and clicks and clunks, finishing with an impresario rendition of the doorbell. Tired of Julius expecting her every move, Gabriela switched on the radio.

S'go den... Good Morning First Nations and recent refugees... This is CNDN Coast Salish radio, 101.3 FM on your Home and Native Band. I'm your host, BC Bud...

Gabriela poured herself a cup of herbal tea. From a selection of Nettle & Co. tea, Licorice Lemongrass Mint tea, Love Your Liver tea, Rumble In The Bronchs tea, and Strong Skeleton tea, she chose a bag of the Belly Balm tea and ate her muffin slowly.

To the sweet grass squaw candy Gabriola girl from last night's sweat lodge at Surf Lodge... I had a dream... wait, a vision...

Julius had been a challenge lately. Not that he hadn't always been one. Gabriela had built his cage of fir and medium gauge wire, and filled it with food and water bowls, colourful foraging toys and ladders, a parrot pad and play stand, and hand-shaved natural cedar litter absorbent. It took all her money to buy him a decade ago, and she couldn't afford the expensive South American food pellets, distilled water, and artificial vitamin supplements that should have come with his arrival into her life; nor would she ever consider using chemical Avicare disinfectants, lice and mite sprays, deworming compounds, Cage tidy, or Ozpet litter. Iodine bells were unnatural and cuttlefish bells were cruel. Vaccinations were out of the question. There was no way she would look after an autistic parrot.

During our pow wow under the petroglyphs, you told me you were a vegetarian... For us, it means that you're just a bad hunter...

Gabriela fed Julius apples and carrots and beans and peas and corn and broccoli and spinach from her garden. She bought organic sunflower seeds and peanuts and pine nuts (when she could afford them) from Mona's shop. She tried to clean his cage

301

and bowl every day. In fairness, since Binky had come on the scene, and before their argument, she may not have been as meticulous as she would have liked.

O' Great Spirit help me always to speak the truth quietly, to listen with an open mind when others speak, and to remember the peace that may be found in silence... but the spirits told me you've been talking shit on Facebook...

It wasn't clear when Julius changed. Perhaps it was after his fall. Gabriela had built his new cage taller than the last and made his perches out of local Manzanita wood. She loved its brownish-red and bright orange colours. How was she to know how slippery the smooth bark became when wet? Gabriela had allowed Julius onto the perch above the top of his cage after she clipped his nails and wing-feathers. He was a heavy parrot, and when it happened, he hit the edge of his breastbone and came down hard on his legs. The force drove itself into his shoulders and hips, compressing his chest and pushing the air out of his lungs, and splitting the skin over his breast and under his tail. As he recovered, he began to chew at the feathers there. When Binky arrived on the scene, Julius began to pluck his feathers more furiously, shook his head back and forth like he was looking for somewhere else to go, and became anxious and restless, and aggressive. His vocabulary went sideways. He began to use profanity in creative ways that even Gabriela was unprepared for.

A frog does not drink up the pond in which it lives... When all the trees have been cut down, when all the animals have been hunted, when all the waters are polluted, when all the air is unsafe to breathe, only then will you discover you cannot eat money... I relate to a living universe. You reduce everything to objects...

It was as if the same demons troubled them both. Gabriela developed anorexia and nausea and vomiting and alternating diarrhea and constipation. She had used up her own aromatherapy eye pillows and sleep masks, and raided Mona's shop supply of Eagle Creek and Happy Hippy and Gentle Earth cold-processed soaps, Phillip Adam body care products, Salt Spring Soapworks creams, Synergy Organics natural antibacterial mouth rinses, Dragonfly Dreaming salves, Siglarr Viking naturals, Warm Buddy therapeutic heat wraps, and Salt Spring Naturals thieves' oil and balms, all to no advantage.

Sometimes I go about pitying myself, and all the while I am being carried across the sky by beautiful clouds... The universe is closed. Use the rainbow.

The intermittent abdominal pain that had grown more frequent had become constant and unbearable. After leaving a message on Mona's answering machine, asking her to look after Julius in her absence, Gabriela did the only thing left. She rode her bike down Ferry Hill to wait for deliverance. From across the water, the MV Quinsam pulled into Descanso Bay.

'I've been having a bad bad day,
Come on, won't you put that pad away?'
Joss Whedon, *The Parking Ticket*

It was just one of those things, like Larry Bird's episode of atrial fibrillation after his prostate surgery. Forever grateful for the delivery of 200 watts/sec of electrical energy across his chest while he was still half awake, Larry had returned to work as a Robbins Parking attendant, to hide in wait for a dimpled and dented white Honda Civic, and exact retribution with stiff shocks of his own. It was a Saturday. Sababa was on call, and today was the day.

The portly professor had forgotten his Colombian leather briefcase on his first foray through the automatic wide sliding frosted glass doors of the Harbour City Regional Emergency Department. When he returned to the on-call parking bay, he found a parking ticket under the driver side windshield wiper.

Sababa blew past the security guard in the lobby, on his way to the Administration Office.

"And you all know, security is mortals' chiefest enemy." The sentinel heard only a fading Doppler effect. At the terminal end of a long hallway, Sababa banged on a closed door. Half expecting to find no life behind it, he was half right. In a universe that used chaos as fuel, the man who opened it represented order. Malcolm Canmore was the Chief Hospital Administrator of Harbour City Regional, the CHA, the CEO, the COO, the COG, the CAD, the CON, the CUR, the grand omnipotent stomper of supermen.

"It's Saturday." He said. "I'm not here."

"And I'm on call for Internal Medicine." Sababa handed Malcolm the parking ticket. "Take care of this, or I won't be."

"I'll take care of it." Malcolm took the ticket, in exchange for a death stare.

"I wake up with an erection harder than your job." Sababa said.

"Go back to eating your crayons." He pivoted on tiptoe and was gone.

A few minutes later, his Colombian leather briefcase flew a pirouette and barrel roll in its flight path over Betty Boop and a bank of cardiac monitors, before coming to rest upright beside his computer on the bridge of the Death Star. It missed Sara's head by several inches.

"Why do you do that?" She asked.

"Gravity is a hard habit to shake." He said. "And according to Einstein's General Theory of Relativity, it bends light. What you got?"

"Mona Pseudos." Sara said. "Bed four. 28-year-old owner of Earth Mother market on Gabriola Island. Dr. Martino operated on her perforated appendix three weeks ago. He readmitted her a week ago for abdominal pain and fever. Her white count was on the ceiling. Jules found a small ileocolic abscess on an abdominal CT scan and started her on IV pip/tazo and metronidazole."

"So what's she doing here?" He asked. Sara threw up another image on the cubicle viewbox.

"This was her repeat CT scan two days ago." Sara said. "She had a new huge abscess pocket between the liver bed, transverse colon, and stomach. Dr. Martino took her to the OR the same night, ruptured it with electrocautery, and inserted a closed drain. Her blood pressure was rocky all day yesterday. Hence her appearance here."

"What did the cultures grow?" Sababa asked.

"Nothing." Sara said. "They've been sterile."

"They were incubated at the wrong temperature." He turned to the ward clerk. "Betty Boop, can you raise the micro lab for me, please?"

"On it, Sab." A minute later she held up her handset. "Line three."

"What method did you use to culture Mona Pseudos's abdominal abscess?" He asked.

"Disc diffusion at 37 °C." She said.

"Can you do it again on MacConkey agar at 30 °C?" He asked.

304

"Sure thing." She said and hung up.

"What are you searching for?" Sara asked.

"I'm looking for a bacterium they reported as sensitive to the antibiotics Martino used—a hospital-acquired, glucose nonfermenting, aerobic, gram-negative, mobile, catalase-positive, oxidase-negative, multidrug resistant, biofilm-forming organism capable of producing that big an abscess that fast."

"You have a name?" She asked.

"Stenotrophomonas maltophilia." Sababa said. "Change her bug juice to cotrimoxazole. Call Martino and tell him he's welcome. Let's go see her."

"How do you always know what's going on?" Sara asked.

"A psychic once told me I was psychic." Sababa said. "I didn't see it coming."

'Like the wheel of cheese high in the sky
Well, we're gonna be sinkin' soon.'
Norah Jones, *Sinkin' Soon*

"Cheri Sundae on the line 1, Sab. Two more for you in Emerg." Betty Boop's voice was missing her next cigarette. "One from Dr. Capitaine and one from Dr. Pangloss."

"Tell her we're on our way down." Sababa said.

It was Dr. Capitaine who Sara and Sababa first met behind the automatic sliding frosted glass doors of the ER.

"How are you, Myles?"

"Living the dream."

"Sweet dreams are made of cheese, Who am I to diss a Brie, I Cheddar the world and the Feta cheese, Everyone is looking for Stilton..."

"How did you know?" He asked.

"Know what?" Sababa said.

"The patient I have is a 66-year-old cheesemaker from Saltspring Island." He said. "Gerry Ritz."

"Heuristics." Sababa said. "Bounded rationality."

"Even on a straight road, he's always looking for the shortcut." Sara said.

"OK, Doctor Heuristic, tell me what's wrong with this guy." Myles said.

"Tell us the story first." Sababa said.

305

"The only problem Gerry ever had was hemochromatosis, for which he donated blood every so often on the island. Three weeks after he returned from his holiday in Costa Rica, he developed the flu."

"Meaning what, exactly."

"Fever, chills, vomiting, and diarrhea." Myles continued. "The gastrointestinal stuff went away after three days, replaced by headaches and muscle pains. Yesterday, he began getting confused and fainted for no clear reason. His heart rate went up, his breathing rate went down, and his balance was off. After he had a seizure, his wife called an ambulance, and EMS brought him here two hours ago."

"Exam?"

"He was sick, his blood pressure was high, and his neck was stiff."

"Did you do a CT of his brain?" Sababa asked. Myles threw it up on the nearest viewer.

"Hmmm." Sababa said. "Did you do a lumbar puncture?"

"Results aren't back yet." The ER doc accompanied Sara and Sababa into a cubicle and introduced them to Gerry's wife. The patient himself was elsewhere, hallucinating through a tempest of his own making. His eyes were pointing in different directions. When Sababa picked up his head, the rest of him came along for the ride.

"What kind of cheese does Gerry make on Saltspring, Mrs. Ritz?"

"Goat cheese." She said. "Brie, Camembert, Feta, and Bleu. Gerry doesn't use pasteurized milk. He says it kills the flavour."

"Has he had any other kind of cheese in the last month?" Sababa asked.

"He tried some ricotta salata, a sheep's milk cheese from Italy." She said. "But he thought it would be too much work to make on Saltspring.

"What antibiotics have you got Gerry on?" Sababa asked Myles.

"Gave him a dose of ceftriaxone." Myles said. Sababa stuck his head out of the curtain.

"Regina, can you give the Hallucinator here a gram of ampicillin and 90mg of gentamicin IV please?"

"No problem." She said.

"What do you think this is, Doctor Sababa?" Mrs. Ritz asked.

"Do you remember the outbreak from contaminated Maple Leaf Foods hot dogs, luncheon meats, and deli meats out of Toronto several years ago?" She nodded.

"There were 57 total confirmed cases, resulting in 22 deaths." Sababa said. "The Ontario Agricultural Minister apologized for

306

insensitive remarks. *This is like a death by a thousand cuts. Or should I say cold cuts?* And the lawyers had a field day. Tony Merchant, the Merchant of Menace, filed and won four separate class-action lawsuits in as many provinces claiming damages of $350 million."

"I don't understand." She said.

"Sorry." Sababa backtracked. "I was off with Gerry somewhere. Your husband has meningitis from a bacterium called Listeria monocytogenes. We'll find out for sure when the blood and CSF culture results come back. He may have got it that from the Italian ricotta salata, but there's a lot of work to do here to find out and make everyone safe, regardless of the source."

"Will he recover?" She asked.

"We'll do everything we can to make sure he has the best chance." Sababa said.

Dr. Trace Pangloss poked his face through the curtain.

"You want Doctor Heuristic here?" Myles asked. Trace nodded.

"He's all yours." Sara and Sababa followed Pangloss to another cubicle.

"Bo Geste." Trace began. "72-year-old semi-retired federal civil servant visiting from Ottawa, staying at the Raven Resort on Gabriola. He was making time with another conference delegate's wife in the hot tub every night after dinner. History of chronic obstructive lung disease, still smoking."

"And?"

"Came in last night with a two-day history of fever, chills, muscle aches, headache, fatigue, anorexia, dry cough, chest pain, vomiting and diarrhea, and loss of coordination." Trace said.

"It's peculiar."

"We do peculiar." Sara said.

"His heart rate is slow." Trace said. "Far too slow for what it should be, with his fever."

"Faget sign." Sababa said. "Sphygmothermic dissociation. Seen in infections from bacteria with an intracellular life cycle. Rest of his exam?"

"Bronchial breathing in his lower lungs." Trace said. "Labs show low serum sodium and abnormal kidney and liver function." He put a chest x-ray up on a viewer. Sababa looked to Sara.

"Community-acquired pneumonia with consolidation in the bottom of both lungs." She said.

"The community is always the people who aren't there." Sababa said. "Which community?" Sara shrugged.

"Old-guy-with-established-lung-disease-slow-heart-rate-dry-cough-resort-hot-tub community." Sababa said. "He could have been one of the 2000 attendees of the American Legion convention held at the Bellevue-Stratford Hotel in Philadelphia in 1976, or a guest of Kingsmead Hospital in Stafford, England in 1985, the Westfriese Flora flower exhibition in Bovenkarspel, Holland in 1999, the Murcia Hospital in Spain in 2001, or a victim of the nursing home epidemic here in Canada in 2005." Trace and Sara had the same facial expressions.

Sababa went to the consultants' desk and pulled Bob Dylan from his music library on a secret drive hidden deep inside the hospital computer network.

'Some say it was radiation, some say there was acid on the microphone
Some say a combination that turned their hearts to stone
But whatever it was, it drove them to their knees
Oh, Legionnaire's disease.'
     Bob Dylan, *Legionnaire's Disease*

"Let's go see him." He said.

                                         'Like a
transplant patient
                      Waiting for a donor.
                      Don't let it take the fight outta you.'
                      Ben Harper, *Fight Outta You*

"Dr. Muldoon on line two for you, Sab." Cheri Sundae patched through the call.

"Hey, Piggy, how do you tell an internist, a general surgeon, and an orthopod apart in an elevator?" Sababa asked.

"I don't know, Sab." Piggy said.

"When the door is closing, the internist sticks his hand between the doors to stop it." Sababa said. "The general surgeon sticks his foot in, and the orthopod sticks his head in."

"Funny." Piggy said. "I need you to see a patient here in my clinic."

"As long as it's not an emergency." He turned to his resident.

"Sara, I'll go see Piggy's patient if you pick up Dr. Bloom's referral on Floor 5." He said. "After you finish with Mr. Hot Tub here."

"OK." She said. "I'll page you when I'm done." Sababa made his way down the hallway to Orthopedics outpatients. The cast clinic technician, Michael Eaglefeather slipped a ziplock of smoked salmon into the portly professor's Colombian leather bag. There was communion. Sababa turned to the knuckledragger.

"What you got, Piggy?" He asked.

"Jensen Löwenstein Mott." Said the orthopod. "32-year-old tennis instructor, who works next to your place on the lake." He saw Sababa wince with the reminder.

"Memories are like clam chowder in a cheap restaurant." He said. "It's best not to stir them."

"None-the-less." Piggy said. "We have a problem here."

"Which is?" Sababa asked.

"I operated on this woman's elbow." He said. "And it's not getting better." Sababa looked at Jensen's elbow. It didn't look better.

"What did the cultures show?" He asked.

"Nothing." Piggy said.

"Did you send them for acid-fast bacilli?" Sababa asked.

"Now, why the hell would I do that?" The orthopod inquired.

"Because this looks like an atypical mycobacterium to me." Sababa said. Piggy dragged him aside.

"TB?" He asked. "She has TB in my cast clinic?"

"Relax, Piggy." Sababa said. "She doesn't have Mycobacterium tuberculosis. It's Mycobacterium fortuitum or Mycobacterium chelonae, although we use the same drugs."

"Now how would you know that?" Piggy asked.

"It is my business to know what other people don't know." Sababa said. "Do the acid-fast stains and red snapper mycobacterial cultures on Kirchner or Middlebrook culture media. I'll dictate a consult letter and write up some orders." Sababa's pager buzzed in his pocket.

"What do I tell the tennis instructor?"

"Tell her to keep the grunting and screaming down." He said.

It had been Sara who paged him. Sophia met him as the elevator doors opened on her floor.

"Plis be care-pull, Ductor Sababa." She said. "Mistur Pustulatus is berry inpekchus. I hub him in di-ya-purse, in isolashun room pibe twin-tee. Palo me." They met Sara outside Room 520.

"Bill Koch Pustulatus." Sara began. "56-year-old Seattle businessman off the Sea Princess cruise ship to Alaska that tied up in Harbour City a month ago. Previously healthy, except for the proton pump inhibitor he was taking for some reflux, but he picked up a Norwalk virus on the cruise and started self-medicating with antibiotics, even though they don't work. It was a bad idea."

"How so?" Sababa asked.

"He was taking clindamycin and ciprofloxacin." She said. "And loperamide. His diarrhea got worse. Way worse."

"How worse?"

"They dropped him off the boat here over three weeks ago." She said. "EMS said he smelled like horse manure. His PCR and enzyme-linked immunosorbent assays for Clostridium difficile toxin A and B were all positive. Dr. Bloom's been treating him appropriately, but Bill just blew off the courses of metronidazole, the oral vanco, the cholestyramine, probiotics, you name it. He still has fulminant watery diarrhea and his IV fluid requirements are barely keeping up. He's lost twenty pounds and his serum albumin is in his boots. The only way he's been lucky is that, so far, he hasn't developed pseudomembranous colitis, toxic megacolon, gut perforation, or overwhelming superinfection."

"Deja poo. I've heard this crap before." Sababa said. "He's in deep shit." Sara scowled. "Let's go see him." Sophia ensured everyone washed their hands and gloved and gowned outside the patient's isolation room.

"You can take that away, Sophia." Sababa pointed to the alcohol-based hand cleanser dispenser on the wall. "It doesn't kill the spores." They, unlike the spores, entered single file.

"Bill."

"Doctor Sababa." The patient said. "Sophia told me you might come by."

"I understand your diarrhea isn't getting better." Sababa said.

"Through the eye of a needle, Doc." Bill said. "If I was a rich camel, I'd be in heaven by now."

"You might be mixing your metaphors." Sababa said. "If the camel gets its nose in a tent, then the body will soon follow. Are you eating anything?"

"He eets only ice cream, Ductor Sababa." Sophia said. "Por brick-pus, lunts and deen-ner."

"She's right. Ice cream." He said. "That's all I can get down. That, and my theriac."

"Your theriac?"

"Yeah, my theriac." He said. "You know the physician Galen's ancient Greek universal antidote that heals everything."

"I know about theriac." Sababa said. "But you couldn't have access to all the original ingredients—the 64 roots and stems and barks and leaves and flowers and fruits and seeds and gums and oils and resins and animal parts and products and mineral substances that formed the basis for the ancient Egyptian kyphi recipe, the mithridatium of King Mithridates VI of Pontus, the formulae of Emperor Nero's physician Andromachus and those

310

of the Tang pharmacologist Su Kung and Middle Eastern Tiryaqi, the *Theriaca Andromachi Senioris* Venice treacle of the medieval Worshipful Company of Grocers apothecaries in London, or the concoctions of the Italian Gentile da Foligno, the French Moyse Charas, and the Dutch Amsterdammer Apotheek. You couldn't have sourced and collected and fermented all the constituents, including ground mummy, dried scorpion, viper flesh, opium, Cypriot turpentine, beaver castoreum, myrrh, Dead Sea bitumen, and Canary Island wine, for the several years the recipe requires to make properly."

"Well, no." Bill admitted. "But I make my version from shiitake mushrooms and moonwort, and sea algae and sunflower seeds."

"You do?" Sababa asked.

"I do." He said.

"You don't realize what a perfect shitstorm you've created for yourself, Bill." Sababa said.

"How so?"

"Your ice cream contains trehalose, to lower its freezing point." Sababa said. "All the ingredients of your theriac also contain high concentrations of trehalose."

"What the hell is trehalose?"

"It's a sugar comprised of two molecules of glucose." He said. "Some bacteria, fungi, plants, and invertebrates synthesize it as a source of energy, and to survive freezing and lack of water. It's the major carbohydrate energy storage molecule used by dragonflies and grasshoppers and locusts and butterflies and bees for rapid flight. Both the resurrection plant and New Zealand wetas use it to survive being frozen solid. If you were a Greenland Inuit, you'd have a 15% chance of having a trehalase enzyme deficiency and not being able to break it down. But you're not."

"What's the big deal with this dumb double sugar here?" Bill asked.

"Some strains of Clostridium difficile respond to trehalose." Sababa said. "They grow better and faster and produce more toxins in its presence. You've been feeding them your special theriac and they, in return, have shown their appreciation by trying to kill you faster. We can trace and time the meteoric rise of hospital-acquired C. difficile infections to the introduction of trehalose into the food supply when the cost of its production from corn starch came way down."

"Oh, shit." Bill said.

"Oh, yeah." Sababa agreed. "Not only that, but you may have the more virulent NAP1/027 Quebec strain of the bacterium. Everything here is alive, thanks to the living of everything else."

"Great." He said. "Dr. Bloom says he's run out of treatments."

"Not quite." Sababa said.

"What does that mean?" Bill asked.

"Sara will come back in a few minutes to explain." Sababa said.
"We have to make a phone call to your hometown."

Back at Sophia's nursing station, Sababa handed Sara a piece of paper.

"What's this?" Sara asked.

"Tom Louis's lab number in Seattle."

"What does he do?" She asked.

"Transplants."

"He transplants intestines?

"Nope." Sababa said. "He transplants shit."

"I'm sorry."

"Don't be." He said. "There's no redemption here. Bill requires what we refer to in the trade as a course of fecal bacteriotherapy, the infusion of bacterial flora from the feces of a healthy donor to reverse the bacterial imbalance responsible for the unremitting nature of his infection. You are about to organize a poop transplant transfer transfer."

"Who are the donors?" She asked.

"That is of no great importance." Sababa said. "Many politicos and medical bureaucrats that are chock full of the required material might not be appropriate contributors, given the difficulty of ensuring that they are also not passing on their genetic material."

"Sometimes I wonder if you know the difference between sarcasm and compassion." Sara said.

"Sarcasm and compassion are two of the qualities that make life on earth tolerable." Sababa said. "And passion is 7/10s of compassion."

"That can't be as profound as it sounded." Sara said. "Why don't they make this therapy in a pill form."

"More fun to administer from a Freudian perspective." Sababa said. "They're working on it. Make the call. Then grab a quit bite to eat and meet me at Manzanita at one."

'And if you go chasing rabbits, and you know you're going to fall...'
Jefferson Airplane, *White Rabbit*

"It's all happening at the zoo week, Boss." She played him a recording of a call she had received.

Mercy: Good morning, Doctor's office. May I help you?
Caller: Hello. Is this the colon cleaning clinic?
Mercy: I beg your pardon.
Caller: You know. Do you have a colon cleaner?
Mercy: Well, Doctor Sababa is an internist who does endoscopies and colonoscopies.
Caller: Are those some kind of tests?
Mercy: Yes, but you can't just come in and have one done. You must go to
        your family doctor and be referred.
Caller: Well, I just had my hair cut, and I had some hair sent away and tested
        and it said I should have my colon cleaned. It's getting quite built up in
        there.
Mercy: I'm sorry. You'll have to go to a medical doctor and get a referral.

She passed the mail over her counter.
"The soul closes against hate when dove-eyed Mercy pleads." Sababa examined the bundle.
"Hmmm." He said. "This envelope is strangely hospital privileges-shaped." The wise man always reads a letter backwards. Sababa read the last paragraph and winced. He handed Sara the chart of her first patient. She called his name.
"Binky O'Hare." A young man put down the *Outside* magazine he was reading and followed her into the residents' examining room. Sababa called the name of the second referral.
"Duncan Whippletree." A thin middle-aged man put down a gardening magazine and followed Sababa into his office. He took a moment to read Dr. Tarmac's letter. *47-year-old Native plant nursery owner with a one-month history of fevers, decreased appetite, ten-pound weight loss, weakness, and abdominal pain. Normal bowels. Multijoint arthritis for the previous three years. Please tell me what the hell is going on. TT*
Sababa looked at the man's lab results. He was iron-deficient, his protein was low, and his indices of inflammation were high. Tests for various infections had returned negative.
"What would you like me to do?" He asked.
"Find out what the hell is wrong." Duncan said. "I can't go on like this." The muscles of Duncan's face and eyes performed rapid repetitive movements as he spoke, resulting in the

313

elevation of Sababa's own right eyebrow. After completing his physical exam, Sababa went to get Sara.

"What do you make of this?" He asked.

"I've no idea." She said.

"Oculomasticatory myorhythmia." Sababa said.

"What's that?" Sara and Duncan said together.

"All in good time." Sababa said. "Duncan, are you sure your bowel movements are normal?"

"Well, they smell worse than they used to, and I'm farting all the time."

"His skin is hyperpigmented, he has skin nodules, and his right eye has been to uveitiis.com."

"Huh?" Sara said.

"It's a site for sore eyes." Sababa smiled a Sababa smile. "And he has enlarged lymph nodes all over the place. His low albumin is the likely low oncotic pressure cause of his ankle swelling, and his muscle strength and coordination are off."

The stocky savant pressed the intercom button to his outside world.

"Who's the slasher on call, Mercy?"

"Doctor Doughnut." She said.

"Raise him for me, will you?"

"On it." Mercy said. She patched through the surgeon a few minutes later.

"How's my favourite self-deluded sly connoisseur of his own prodigious powers of creative self-transformation?"

"You forgot 'witty,' Sababa." The surgeon said. "I am not only witty in myself, but the cause that wit is in other men."

"You cannot fashion a wit out of two half-wits, John." Sababa said. "I'm afraid I need your scalpel more than your sagacity this time."

"What for?" He asked.

"Upper gastrointestinal endoscopy and axillary lymph node biopsies." Sababa said.

"What for?" He asked. There was a kind of absolutism about Falstaff's continual search for immediate self-gratification.

"Send a juicy piece of duodenum for Periodic acid-Schiff staining." Sababa instructed. "And an armpit node for PAS and Tropheryma whipplei 16S ribosomal RNA polymerase chain reaction."

"We must get together and quaff some of your fabulous pinot noir." John said. "Together we are more than two half-wits."

"You forgot inebriated, John." Sababa said. "You are not only inebriated in yourself, but the cause that inebriation is in other men."

314

"If sack and sugar be a sin, God help the wicked." The surgeon said. "Toodley-pip."

Sababa replaced his handset and turned his attention back to the nurseryman.

"What?" He said.

"It's a million to one shot." Sababa said. "Unless you're one in a million." The portly professor explained his suspicion and the investigations he needed to perform to confirm or refute it.

"Dr. Falstaff's office will be in touch." He said. "Start taking these medicines after your procedures." Sababa handed him prescriptions for doxycycline and hydroxychloroquine. "You'll be on them for 18 months. Make an appointment with Mercy to see me two weeks after you begin the medication."

"That's it?" Duncan asked.

"I hope so." Sababa shook the man's hand as he left. He took a few moments to recalibrate.

"Dr. Mindbender on line one, Sab." Mercy had derailed his train of thought. There were no survivors. "He's going away on vacation and wants to know if you'll have your new contract and rules and regs signed and turned in by Friday." Sababa picked up line one.

"Nope." He said. "Friday's out. How about never—is never good for you?"

"You have no idea how much I'm looking forward to taking away your privileges."

"I hate it when flies rub their shitty little hands together like they're plotting to ruin my life." Sababa said. "Let me be clear, Milo. I don't exactly hate you but if you were on fire and I had a glass of water, I'd drink it." There came a click, and then another. Sababa looked up to find Sara's face in his office doorway.

"What you got?" He asked.

"Binky O'Hare." She said. "26-year-old seasonal tree planter from Manitoba seen by Dr. James Ruben Andrews six weeks ago for deer fly bites he got while camping in Sandwell Park on Gabriola. He's referred today for a painful lump in his right groin." Sababa's right eyebrow went up.

"Exam?" He asked.

"You need to see this." She said. "He has a suppurating lymph node, like the one from our patient with plague last month. He also has a fever and red eyes." Sababa followed her to the residents' room. Binky O'Hare lay on the examining table, draped and uncomfortable.

"There's nothing going on here." He said. "I'm usually in great shape."

"Every man, wherever he goes, is encompassed by a cloud of comforting convictions which move him like flies on a summer day." Sababa said. "Let's have a look, Binky." He folded the drape to uncover the enlarged lymph node and others.

"Ulceroglandular." Sababa said.

"Ulceroglandular what?" Binky asked.

"Ulceroglandular tularemia." Sababa said.

"TulareWTF?"

"Tularemia." Sababa said. "Fascinating organism, Francisella tularensis, a gram-negative coccobacillus named after Tulare County, California, where it was first discovered in 1911, but it was first recorded as an epidemic in ancient Canaan along the Arwad-Euphrates trading route two thousand years earlier. We sometimes refer to it as muskrat fever or rabbit fever. There are case reports of people getting it from inhaled particles of infected rabbits ground up in lawnmowers on Martha's Vineyard and in Colorado. Only takes ten bacteria to cause infection. It used to kill half the people it infected, which is why it was such a wonderful biological warfare agent. The Soviets used it with success at the Battle of Stalingrad, and the disease is still endemic in Stalin's Georgian hometown of Gori, where I vacationed on Joseph's train last spring. But I digress. The Japanese military used it, and our American cousins turned it into an art form, in their manufacture of the Agent UL Schu S4 strain at Pine Bluff Arsenal, Arkansas, the lethality of which they perfected in their Alaskan 'Red Cloud' testing."

"How did I get it?" He asked.

"Chrysops discalis." Sababa said. "Deer fly bites. You know you're not supposed to be camping in Sandwell, don't you?"

"I broke up with my girlfriend." He said. "I had no other place to go."

"Karma's a bitch. And now you're a cake, left out in the rain." Sababa said. "With tularemia."

"What happens now?" He asked.

"Sara will aspirate your biggest lymph node and send it for isolation on buffered charcoal yeast extract agar. She'll send you to the lab to take blood for serology, and a technique we call 16S rRNA PCR." He turned to Sara. "Make sure you warn the lab about the potential infectivity of our frère rabbit here."

"What about treatment?" Binky asked. Sababa wrote out a prescription for a quinolone antibiotic."

"Everyone wants to go to heaven, but nobody wants to die." He said. "Take every pill—or you'll be back." Mercy intervened.

"Dr. Cliffy Carlton in the ER on line one, Sab." She said. Sababa's contact with the handset was brief.

316

"Sara, there's a patient they've asked us to see in emergency." He said. "Call me when you're done. I'll finish up here and make a brief diversion to this afternoon's x-ray rounds. Dr. Brisk is presenting, and I do so like to enrich his temporal experience on the planet."

'We ate, we drank, and we were merry
And we got typhoid and dysentery.'
Tom Lehrer, *In Old Mexico*

Dr. Sababa didn't get to spend much time at x-ray rounds. His pager went off as Mako Brisk brought up his first set of images on the multi film viewer rotisserie. Sababa stared at the screens on his way out of the dark room.

"Pneumatosis cystoides intestinalis." He said.

"But... but... you just can't..." Brisk's echo followed him down the hallway to Emergency.

"Just give me a chance." Cliffy Carlton was still trying his luck with Sara.

"It's spelled C-h-a-n-c-e-f." She said.

"There's no 'f' in chance." Cliffy observed.

"That's what I've been trying to tell you." She turned to find Sababa, smiling a Sababa smile.

"Wilbur Wright." She didn't break stride. "59-year-old right-handed Gabriola poultry farmer presents tonight with a stroke. Brought in by his next door neighbour, Dave."

"What kind?" Sababa asked.

"Good Samaritan kind."

"I was referring to the stroke."

"Dominant left middle cerebral artery distribution with motor aphasia." Sara said. "He knows what he wants to say, but he can't get it out."

"Cause?" Sababa asked.

"The usual thrombotic or embolic event." She said. "Except for the fever."

"The fever?"

"He has a fever." Sara repeated. "Dave said that he's only just returned from vacation."

"Where?"

"Comoro Islands." She said. "They're in the Indian Ocean."

317

"I know where they are." He said. "What did his brain CT scan show?"

"Well, that's just it." Sara said.

"What's just what?" Sababa asked.

"It should have shown something in Broca's area on the left." She said. "But it showed nothing. No stroke, no abscess, no nothing."

"Rest of his physical exam?"

"Enlarged liver and spleen, and big blanching pink spots on his abdomen."

"Let's go see him." Sababa said.

Wilbur was pleased to see the portly professor, but he couldn't comment either way.

"Tuphos." Sababa said.

"Typhus?"

"No. Tuphos."

"Which is?" Sara asked.

"Apathetic affect from a specific kind of fever."

"What kind?" She asked.

"The kind that killed Pericles and a third of his Athens population, shifting the balance of Greek power to Sparta in 430 BC, the kind that caused 17 million deaths on the Mexican highlands in the mid-1500s, the kind that wiped out the first Jamestown colony in Virginia, the kind that killed two American presidents and annihilated over eighty thousand soldiers in the American Civil War, the kind that killed young Lizzie van Zyl in a British South African concentration camp during the Boer War, and the kind that locked up Mary Mallon in New York for 26 years, because she kept changing her name and causing new outbreaks of dysentery."

"You have a name?" She asked.

"Pythogenic fever." He said. Sara looked puzzled.

"You have another?"

"Gastric fever, enteric fever, abdominal typhus, slow fever, nervous fever." He said. "Take your pick."

"I still don't get it."

"Salmonella enterica serotype typhi." Sababa said. "Typhoid and swans—it all comes from the same place." He focused on Wilbur's consternation.

"You got typhoid fever in the Comoros, Mr. Wright." Sababa said. "It's affected a part of your brain responsible for speech. We will fix it." He handed Sara a piece of paper scrawled with a name. *Gabriela Sounder.*

"I'll write him up, order blood cultures and Widal serology and Typhidot test, and start him on antibiotics and dexamethasone.

You go see this referral from Dr. Martino on Floor 3. He opened her abdomen yesterday and didn't find what he was looking for."
"Why are we seeing her?" Sara asked.
"Because he found nothing at all."

'The camouflaged parrot, he flutters from fear
When something he doesn't know about suddenly appears.'
John Mellencamp, *Farewell Angelina*

Sara introduced herself to Sariel, the head nurse on the third floor general surgical ward. "I love Sababa." She said. "He's like an illegal still, and everything that comes out of him is already moonshine."
"He is definitely the one you want in the boat with you at the end of the world." Sara said. An hour later, after the young resident had paged him to the floor, the stairwell discharged a curly-haired bouncing stout man clutching a Colombian leather briefcase.
"What you got?" He asked.
"Gabriela Sounder." Sara began. "26-year-old aromatherapist from Gabriola Island, admitted yesterday with a two-day history of severe abdominal pain, vomiting, and headache associated with constipation and weight loss over the preceding six months. No history of foreign travel and no risk factors for immunodeficiency. Exam revealed fever, rapid respirations, a bloody nose, and acute surgical abdomen. She had those same rose spots on her trunk as Wilbur did. Heart rate was slow and sodium low. Chest x-ray was unremarkable but her erect abdominal radiograph showed gaseous distension of the small bowel. Dr. Martino did an exploratory laparotomy late last night."
"And?"
"Nada." But she did have another chest x-ray this morning. Sara put a film up on the nursing station viewbox. "New right lower lobe opacification."
"Let's go see her." Sababa noticed Sara's hesitation.
"What?" He asked."You'll see." She said. "People from Gabriola are definitely different."
"It's that snowflake granola vibe—fruit loops, nuts, and assorted flakes." He said. "It's why the island bookstore keeps the

mushroom books behind the cash register because they always get stolen." Sara made the introductions.

"I don't believe in allopathic medicine." Gabriela began.

"And I don't believe in astrology." Sababa said. "I'm a Scorpio and we're skeptical." She pointed to her intravenous.

"I'm concerned about that." She said. "It can't be natural."

"Don't worry, it's a vegan IV. Gluten-free." Sababa offered. "You must hate it when you think you're buying organic vegetables and when you get them home, they're just regular doughnuts."

"I only use carbon-free natural sugar. Look, I know things." Gabriela said. "I'm a sense therapist myself."

"Which senseless therapies are we talking here?" He asked. "Phototherapy, music therapy, healing touch, taste therapy?"

"None of the above." She said. "I'm a licensed aromatherapist. I specialize in the aerial diffusion, direct inhalation, and the topical application of absolutes, aroma lamps and diffusers, carrier oils, essential oils, herbal distillates and hydrosols, infusions, phytoncides, and vaporizers. I'm also a qualified personal health consultant." She handed Sababa her card.

'Creative Health Centre, offering maximum health and performance through wholistic methods using Biokinesiology, Edu-kinesiology, Unique Kinesiology, Jin Shin Do Accupressure, Food Sensitivites, Structural Alignments, Health Analysis, Weight loss Programs, Body Building Programs, Natural Health Seminars.'

"I'm also a consultant for the Centre for Network Care." Gabriela handed him a pamphlet.

'Healing... It's not what you think! Did you know that atoms are electrical energy, and vibrating at a frequency that is individually yours? Research has shown that 99% of people under Network Care who were surveyed wished to continue with care. Available anytime for a remote view and healing which can include a custom homeopathic from the EAV machine, and a look at your energy field to clear any emotional/mental debris and address any past trauma or pain.'

"You may be missing a few skills, Gabriela?" He asked.

"Like what?" She asked.

"Like therapeutic horseback riding and touch, mindfulness and transcendental meditation, the Bates and Feldenkrais methods, Hawaiian and Tantra and Thai massage, crystal and faith and magnetic and pranic healing, Clari-tea and Communi-tea and Immuni-tea and Sereni-tea, acupuncture and colorpuncture and sonopuncture, applied kinesiology and astrology and graphology and herbology and iridology and numerology, Anusara and

320

Ashtanga and Bikkram and Hatha and Hot and Iyengar and Kundalini and Power and Restorative and Siddha and Sivananda and Tantric and Vinyasa yoga, anthroposophical and eclectic and functional and German new and holistic and meridian Chinese and naturopathic and Unani and traditional Chinese and Korean and Japanese and Mongolian and Tibetan medicine, animal-assisted and api- and aqua- and art and attachment and auriculo- and Bach flower and balneo- and biblio- and bioresonance and blood irradiation and body-based manipulative and chelation and Chinese food and chromo- and cinema and coding and colon hydro- and craniosacral and dance and electromagnetic and equine-assisted and flower essence and hydro- and hypno- and light and magnet and manipulative and mega-vitamin and music and herbal and recreational and salt and sound and thalasso- and urine and water cure and natural therapies, acupressure, affirmative prayer, Alexander technique, alternative cancer treatments, autogenic training, autosuggestion, Ayurveda, biodanza Chinese martial arts, Chinese pulse diagnosis, chiropractic, coin rubbing, creative visualization, cupping, dietary supplements, dowsing, ear candling, earthing, electrohomeopathy, Reiki, Qigong, Shiatsu, energy medicine and psychology and therapies, fasting, Feng shui, five elements, Grahamism, Gua sha, hair analysis, havening, herbalism, Hijama, holistic living, homeopathy, home remedies, hypnosis, introspection rundown, isolation tank, isopathy, journaling, Kampo, macrobiotic lifestyle, manual lymphatic drainage, medical intuition, Vipassana, mind–body intervention, autogenic training, autosuggestion, moxibustion, myofascial release, naprapathy, natural health, new thought, neuro-linguistic programming, nutritional healing and supplements, Pilates, psychic surgery, Qi, radionics, rebirthing, reflexology, Rolfing structural integration, self-hypnosis, spiritual mind treatment, structural Integration, support groups, T'ai chi ch'uan, Tibetan eye chart, Trager approach, trigger points, Tui na, visualization, wellness, Zang fu theory, and my personal favourites, vaginal steaming and laser rejuvenation."

"I do homeopathy." She said.

"Of course you do." Sababa said. "In a universe of truth, lies, statistics, and homeopathy, homeopathy is the air guitar of medicine. You do vaccinations?"

"Absolutely not." She said. "Pure poison. They cause autism."

"You remember that time you got polio?" Sababa asked. "No, wait, you don't because your parents got you vaccinated. And I thought therapists were supposed to be nurturing?"

"So what do *you* do?" Gabriela asked. Sara saw Sababa's nose twitch.

"Not much." Sababa said. "Collect a few walls festooned with diplomas, wear bodily fluids that aren't mine, work most weekends and holidays, get screamed at a lot. Oh yeah, and dance with the devil in the pale moonlight. I solve problems you didn't know you had in ways you can't understand. Does your parrot pluck out its feathers?"

"How did you know I have a parrot?" Gabriela asked.

"It is my business to know what other people don't know." He said. "I can smell it."

"Why didn't you tell me?" Sara flushed.

"You didn't ask." She said. "It's an African Gray, from Congo."

"Pretty bird." Sababa said. "With PBFD."

"What's that?" Gabriela asked.

"Psittacine Beak and Feather Disease." Sababa said. "It's a DNA virus, but it can bring secondary bacterial infections, which is what's causing your pneumonia. Birds of a feather."

"I have pneumonia?" Gabriela asked. "But I cleanse regularly."

"The difference between genius and stupidity is that genius has its limits." Sababa said. "You are infected with a chlamydial organism. It's called psittacosis."

"Binky gave me chlamydia?"

"No, your parrot gave you chlamydia psittaci." Sababa said. "I have no idea what Binky gave you."

"So what happens now?" She asked.

"We'll get a Wang's MIF and IgG immunofluorescence confirmation of the diagnosis, a pregnancy test to make sure we can change your antibiotics to something more appropriate, then you'll go home tomorrow with a two-week course of oral therapy, and you'll lose the parrot." He wrote her a prescription. What's this?

"A prescription."

"What for?"

"Tetracycline."

"I don't put chemicals in my body."

"Of course not. I don't blame you. The world is such a complicated place if you have higher reasoning skills." Gabriela pulled out the crystal on her necklace.

"What's that?" Sara asked.

"It's a crystal." She sent it swinging. "If it goes like this, I'll take the pills. If it goes like this, I won't."

"Take the goddamn pills." Sababa and Sara turned to leave the room.

322

"I want reports of my investigations released to my naturopath." Gabriela said.

"No." Sababa said. "And Gabriela?"

"What?"

"Get rid of the parrot."

'Truth is like the sun. You can shut it out for a time, but it ain't goin' away.'

Elvis Presley

The casual reader may realize not only that the fullness of time is precious, but that truth is more precious than time.

Good doctors give medicine, advice, and undivided attention. In return, patients take the undivided attention, while often refusing the medication and the advice. Great doctors also provide the truth. In a time of universal deceit, telling the truth is a revolutionary act. The truth is hard, awkward, rarely pure, and never simple. It might set you free, but the honesty can be hurtful and frightening and impossible to bear.

In return for the truth, patients told lies to their physicians, their spouses, their families and friends, and mostly, themselves. People didn't want the truth.

Everybody lied. The only variable is about what. Deception was a powerful tool for good or evil. It allowed society to function. A lie could travel halfway around the world while the truth was putting on its boots. The most successful marriages are based on falsehoods. *Tell me sweet little lies.* Dying people lie on their deathbeds, wishing they had worked less, been nicer, or sponsored refugees or puppy orphanages. And the truth that was told with bad intent beat all the lies one could invent.

Truth is the torch that gleamed through the fog without dispelling it, onto a path strewn with bodies. The truth isn't where everything ends; it is where a whole new set of questions began. The truth is incontrovertible. Malice might attack it, ignorance might deride it, but in the end, there it is.

Sababa was an incurable anachronism, trying to do good anyway in a world that despised truth-tellers. Every one of his patients would have a moment of truth, and not always what they wanted it to be. But it was what it was, and each would need to bend to its power or live a lie. The Good Doctor's truths were often stranger than fiction because invented narratives had to make sense. His realities lived on the hikes he took with his dog, along the ridges behind the lake where he lived. On the mountain of truth, you never climb in vain.

Truth is a constant. Everything you add to it subtracts from it. The lab tech that incubated Mona Pseudos's blood cultures removed 7 °C of the heat she had added the first time in the second incubation and colonies of Stenotrophomonas maltophilia blossomed like they had won prizes at the Chelsea Flower Show. Sababa sent her home to her Gabriola Earth Mother Market on oral antibiotics three days later.

Gerry Ritz added pasteurization to his cheesemaking skill sets, in exchange for the subtraction of Italian ricotta salata from his potential list of future products. His wife took him home semi-cured.

Bo Geste recovered from his pneumonia, and removed hot tubs and cigarettes and adultery from his bucket list, although he was still a federal civil servant from Ottawa, where truth was forever a negotiable commodity. *But whatever it was, it came out of the trees. Oh, that Legionnaire's disease.*

The tennis instructor who worked next to Sababa's place on the lake, Jensen Löwenstein Mott, got her elbow and her grunt back when her atypical mycobacterium cultures returned positive and the stocky savant's drugs kicked in, but she lost her job when the racquet club owner turned the courts into condos, in another perfect combination of self-indulgent violent action taking place in an atmosphere of otherwise total tranquillity.

When Bill Koch Pustulatus removed the trehalose from his diet and received his poop transplant transfer transfer to and in Tom Louis's lab in Seattle, he became as full of shit as any other Emerald City businessman off an Alaskan cruise.

Dr. Doughnut's subtraction of small amounts of strategic tissue biopsies from Duncan Whippletree's duodenum and lymph nodes confirmed his tropheryma whipplei infection. Sababa's addition of doxycycline and hydroxychloroquine eradicated Duncan's Whipple's disease and all its manifestations, and Falstaff's removal of far too much pinot noir from the grateful portly professor's cellar one night provided him with a reciprocal full-blown epiphany. *In vino veritas.*

Wilbur Wright's Widal serology and Typhidot test confirmed the diagnosis of typhoid fever. True to his word, Sababa fixed his speech loss by adding the proper antibiotic and steroid. In gratitude, Wilbur offered him the carcasses of several chickens from his Gabriola farm. The Good Doctor knew that, although his patient was no longer infected, he could still have been a carrier. Eternally wary of the half-truth, and to avoid getting hold of the wrong half, Sababa declined the generous offer.

Gabriela Sounder made the mistake of trying everything else before taking Sababa's goddamned pills because the most comfortable course was to seek an alternative truth in selfish emotions. Nature never deceives us, we only deceive ourselves, and truth is the daughter of time. Gabriela had to abandon her illusions, in exchange for survival. The truth might set you free, but first, it will piss you off. She gave Julius away to a good home.

Nobody knows what happened to Binky O'Hare. He was last seen camping in Sandwell Provincial Park on Gabriola. Shortly after noon, one Sunday the following May, a local aromatherapist walking along the same beach found a lone hiking boot, with a human foot inside, wedged in a Salish Sea logjam. Take me to your island.

'Yellowed by time and water, like quartz,
Preserved by the rubber and plastic support
And nobody can guess where may lie those left feet
In the deep Strait of Georgia, encased in concrete?'
Dean Whitfield, *Three Feet Off Gabriola*

10. The Case of the Sumatran Mosquito

'Living at risk is jumping off the cliff and
building your wings on the way down.'
Ray Bradbury

The long northern New Hebrides island emerged through the
mist on a calm western shore, a wild wave-battered eastern
coast, and rocky promontories at both ends, where the ghosts
lived. The climate of Pentecost was rainy, the terrain steep and
mountainous, and the in-between a spectacular lush jungle
topography of swollen rivers and crystalline cascades waterfalling
into pristine pools, down to dark little beaches. Treacherous
slippery footpath mud clung to the best efforts to leave it behind.
The landscape was *Lord of the Flies*.

When the Melanesian chiefs, in their prized boar tusk chokers,
were not attacking neighbouring small *kastom* villages with arrows
tipped with the bones of their dead enemies, or settling disputes

in the local currency of long red mats, they could be found as bloodshot and glassy-eyed from all the kava they had imbibed outside their *nakamals* at night, swearing at the sorcery of passing owls.

In the island's southeast corner that morning, a 30-metre high rickety timber tower protruded through the rainforest canopy atop a treeless terrace cut into a fresh cleared rugged hillside. The hundred men and boys under the structure began chanting in Sa, the language of Southern Pentecost. Wearing only penis sheath *nambas*, they broke into dance and stomped the ground. Bare-breasted women in grass skirts issued from the trees and added their native voices to the mêlée, which blended with the primal chanting of older red-eyed men in front of them.

They punctuated their song with throat howlings. Nearby, a line of boys tried to mimic their elders' performance. It was all entertainment for the land divers to encourage their bravery. The day would become festive, with drumming and feasts and grinning celebration. When the elders declared the tower ready, the crowd gathered around, and the chosen ones took their places.

Two of the chosen were Moses, the oldest at 28 years old, and Joshua, his 12-year-old younger brother. Only boys who had been circumcised on their eighth birthday were permitted to join the ritual. They looked up at the wooden tower it would soon be their turn to climb.

Despite its primitive appearance, the *Nagol Adi* was a marvel of intelligent design held together by vines without a single nail or screw. It had taken thirty men seven weeks to build, using brush and wood from the surrounding jungle.

At its core was a lopped tree surrounded by a crisscross of pole scaffolding lashed together and anchored into the earth by vines. The workmen had cut down trees to open a space in the jungle and get building material, cleared a site for the construction of the tower, and removed rocks from and tilled the soil, to soften the ground.

Protruding two metres from the face of the assembly at various elevations were a dozen diving planks, supported by weak struts. The tower was a body, with a head, shoulders, breasts, belly, genitals, and knees. The diving platforms represented penises and the struts below them vaginas. During the jump, the platform supports were designed to snap, causing the platform to hinge downward and absorb some force from falling.

The lowest planks, ten metres from the ground, were for boys performing their first dive; the highest was reserved for the most accomplished—whatever land dive that didn't cripple or kill the bravest contestant would deliver him immeasurable social capital.

"Ranpangran entôô. Yu redi?" Said the red-eyed chief. *Good morning. Are you ready?*

"Redi." Moses and Joshua said in unison.

The men and boys who prepared to fling themselves headlong into space from wooden towers 100 feet high had nothing to break their fall but a slim liana vine tied around each ankle. There were no harnesses, no nets, no helmets, no cushions, and no safety equipment of any kind. God was the on-site Occupational Health & Safety officer. The G forces they took at the lowest point in their dive were the greatest experienced in the non-industrialized world. If either or both of the vines snapped, the solid earth below broke their necks, or their backs, or their legs, or everything, everywhere. *Evri samting evri samwea.*

But the gallant land divers were there for a ritual that tripled as a coming-of-age for young men, a blessing of the earth for the coming yam harvest, and homage to an age-old Pentecost legend.

The origin of *Nanggol* is described in the myth of a woman who was dissatisfied with her husband, Tamalie. Upset by her mate's too vigorous sexual demands, she ran away into the forest. When Tamalie followed her, she climbed to the top of a banyan tree. There, the desperate woman tied a vine around her ankle. Tamalie climbed up after her to make her come down. As he approached the top of the tree, she jumped. Assuming she would die, Tamalie dived after her in anguish and plummeted to his death. His wife survived the fall. Since then, the land diving ceremony has become a show of strength and fertility for men, a defiant confirmation that they cannot be tricked again. At first, the men jumped from trees, but as the ritual evolved, a handcrafted tower was erected instead. The villagers believe that a successful dive can remove the illnesses and physical problems associated with the wet season, and enhance the health and strength of the divers. The goal is to dive from as high as possible and to land as close to the ground as possible. The higher the dive, the higher the yam crops would grow. Men who choose not to dive or back out of diving are not humiliated.

Diving is only permitted in the two months following the wet season to ensure the vines contain the water that lends them elasticity and strength.

While the tower was being constructed, the land divers were prohibited from asking witch doctors to supply them 'love potions.' They lived together in men-only huts and avoided contact with women, to clarify their minds. Women could not

328

approach the tower or Tamalie, who lived in its structure, would seek vengeance, leading to the death of a diver. The men settled any disputes or business affairs or unsettled issues before making a jump, in case they didn't survive. The night before the event, they slept below the tower to ward off evil spirits. Just before dawn, the participants washed and anointed themselves with coconut oil and decorated their bodies. They put on their boar tusks necklaces and traditional penis sheaths. Tradition dictated that there was to be no physical training beforehand.

The precise selection of jumping vines for each individual diver was critical. Although the participants were invited to choose their own lianas (so no one else could be blamed for a fatal accident), a trusted tribe elder supervised the entire process, picking each vine's correct length and girth and moisture content to match each jumper's weight, based on years of trial and error, without benefit of any mechanical calculations. The judgments had to be precise. One ounce too much weight or one inch of dry liana segment could cause the vines to snap, slamming the jumper into the ground. A vine cut too long would cause the diver to hit the ground at a high speed, and a vine cut too short would cause the diver to crash into the tower and destroy it. The vines needed to be supple, elastic, and full of sap to be safe. The ends were shredded, so the fibres could be twisted into a loop for the jumper's ankle.

The ritual began with the least experienced on the lower protrusions and ended with the oldest veterans on the top platforms. Joshua scampered up the tower to the cheers of the shrinking villagers, below. His mother held a piece of cloth from his childhood and planned to throw it away when he completed the feat, a sign that her son had become a man.

Moses called up to his young brother. *Mi hop se trip blong yu i go gud.*

Elders tied one vine to each foot, and Joshua stepped out onto the lowest protruding plank before his debut dive, thirty feet above the crowd, as he had seen his predecessors do every year he could remember. In what could have been his last words, the young boy addressed his village, congregated below. He used a little time to get things off his chest and ensure that he had settled all his issues. He sang a song and made pantomime. The women and men on the ground whooped and danced and clapped their hands, cheering him on. Joshua knew he could change his mind, but that would not happen today.

Minutes passed as the frayed ends of two vines were tied around the boy's ankles. Below, the chanting and dancing intensified. Once the vines were secured, Joshua spread his arms wide and called out for emotional support. The crowd's yelps and whistles reached fever pitch, Joshua crossed his arms over his chest to help prevent injury, and tucked his head in so his shoulders could come in contact with the ground, at the risk of a broken neck or concussion.

He made his leap of faith, trying to put as much distance between himself and the sharp edges of the tower, and reached his terminal velocity of 45 mph. Islanders had tilled the earth below to cushion and soften landings. If all had been correctly estimated, only the top of Joshua's head would brush the ground and fertilize the yam crop.

In the longest fraction of a second in the space-time continuum before impact, the rigid vines around his ankles pulled taut, and Joshua face-planted into the ploughed earth below. *You may talk about your men of Gideon, You may talk about the men of Saul, But there's none like good old Joshua, And the walls come tumbling down...*

The men rushed over and dusted him off, pulled him upright, confirmed he was in one piece, cut the vines off his feet, sent him off into the crowd to celebrate his courage, and prepared the tower for the next diver. Done. Joshua was now a man, although a man with a headache.

As the ceremony progressed, so did the diving heights. The most experienced jumper climbed to the platform at the apex of the tower. Joshua looked up a hundred feet to his older brother, clapping and chanting and signalling to the crowd. Moses curled his toes over the edge of the highest platform, dropped a feather, shut his eyes, crossed his arms over his chest, and pushed off. The sound of breaking wood cracked through the clearing, as the plank gave way. A hundred villagers far below him held their breath and fell silent. He caught the feather on the way down to show his skill.

As Moses approached terminal velocity, he tucked his head in so that his shoulders touched the ground, ensuring fertility for the next season's yam crop. When the vines went taut, the sound of breaking wood cracked through the clearing as the plank gave way, and the muscular man plummeted towards the ground.

Another cadenza of loud and brutal cracking erupted as the vines went taut, but it could have as easily been the cacophonic fracturing of bones. The vines pulled him up so near to the ground that his hair touched and fertilized the soil. Moses had delivered to his people the promised land. The yam harvest would be good this year. A hundred voices roared their approval. No money had changed hands.

A half-century earlier, Mises Kwin of Great Britain had visited Pentecost, to observe the spectacle. The British colonial

330

administration wanted Queen Elizabeth II to have an interesting tour and convinced the Anglican villagers of the Melanesian Mission at Point Cross to perform a land dive. But it was the wrong season, and the vines were dry. One diver had both of his lianas snap, broke his back in the fall, and died later in agony and remorse. He was wearing a good luck charm. The catastrophe made international headlines, horrifying some but inspiring others. In particular, a young New Zealander named AJ Hackett would become the pioneer of a new sport.

At the exact moment that Joshua and Moses made their land dives, halfway around the world, a naked young man, without a penis sheath, perched over a trestle bridge 150 feet above the river near the Harbour City Airport in Cassidy. Mitch Hopper was engaged to be married and was showboating for his fiancé, Melodie, but this had always been on his bucket list, and today was the day. Of the six exciting levels and the dozen styles of bungee he could have selected—classic swan dive Front Flip, Corkscrew, Hover Drop, Prop Plunge, and others, Mitch had gone all out with the Jump Masters choice of the Big Bobowski. It should have cost a grand total of $130 up front and high up, but because Mitch was doing the stunt naked, he got it for half price. He signed the waiver and waved to his fans. *Walk-ins welcome.*

"I'm not jumping to any conclusions here, am I Carlos?" Mitch mused as the new employee of Trébuchet Adventures secured the cords around his ankles. But Carlos didn't know he was using cables that were six years old, and his calculation of the bridegroom's weight and stretched cord length may have been off. Mitch continued to joke with him and Melodie until Carlos indicated that everything was ready. Mitch curled his toes in his boots and made ready to launch himself into the space between him and the rocks and water below.

It was at this point that Carlos should have said 'Don't jump' but he didn't. He said 'No jump,' which for Mitch trying to understand an Argentine accent, sounded like 'Now jump.'

At first, the falling man felt thick air keeping him afloat more than the space-time continuum of Einstein's General Theory of Relativity pushing him down towards the ravine. Mitch forgot to be afraid. He forgot to be anything. He couldn't see why anyone would not do this, over and over again. But then, when the cords went tight, just before they snapped, when the blood in his brain burst through his eyeballs, he couldn't see anything. And, luckily for him, he didn't hear Melodie's screaming when he smashed into the bedrock of the shallow river below.

Moses and Joshua would have called it a *bagarap.*

'There she shook
The holy water from her heavenly eyes,
And clamour moisten'd.'
William Shakespeare, King Lear

Sababa loved to swim across his lake in the summer. Often he would return with an iridescent blue crown of damselflies, a halo of hovercraft head hitchhikers in the heat. Jane waved from the shore, encouraging him to move faster. She had told him earlier that morning.

"You know that Tiki flies in today from Bangkok, so don't take too long for your swim." He had tried to explain the physical laws in play, but his wife was unreceptive to less intuitive forms of logic.

"Don't give me any of your m^2 stuff." Jane looked worried. "My youngest sister has been sick for over a week in Thailand, and she's coming here to recover."

"That might need a dose or two of my m^2 stuff." Sababa's subtle attempt at humour went unappreciated.

Jane drove the twelve miles from the lake to Harbour City airport while, in his passenger seat next to her, Sababa lay back into the streaming sun, listening to the *shah... shah... shah...* of passing fir trees through his open window. They arrived at the low-rise glass and concrete aerodrome on Spitfire Road an hour before Tiki's puddle jumper flight from Vancouver would land so that, in accordance with airline procedures, they could stand around.

Sababa knew that all human life could be found in an airport. In a place with too many faces, he amused himself by scanning for the ones with terminal illness, while Jane paced in front of the plasma screen on the wall of the air-conditioned *Arrivals* lounge. Miles Davis, an ear-budded airport custodian, wet-mopped the nearby restrooms to his Spotify soundtrack. Sababa watched him stop every once in a while and hold a fist to his chest.

Space and time began to fill with the anticipation of those waiting. Some lounged on low chairs; others bounced on their toes. Faint fusion fragrances invaded from the food court.

Sababa bought an espresso doppio doppio from an Ethiopian barista named Isadora Belli, who knew exactly that it was four shots of liquid rocket fuel. The South Sudanese airport screening officer, Charles Donovan, came after him and ordered a spiced *guhwah* special, which Isadora lovingly made. Together they were from the birthplace of the beverage, and both their hearts raced a little faster for the proximity.

Above the sounds of check-in banter and conveyor belts swallowing suitcases, background millennial music whined like the engine noise approaching the tarmac.

There's nothing like an Air Canada Jazz de Havilland Dash 8 to bring you down to earth. Sababa hated Air Canada and, for his passion, they hated him back. Surly stewardesses spoiled all his flights, hungover from the original federal government control of the airline, and its cappuccino communist corporate mantra of service. *We're not happy until you're not happy.*

It was midday, the worst time to arrive. A hole in the rear of the fuselage dispensed travellers returning and arriving from all over the world. Jaroslav Flegr was a local big game trophy-hunting guide who specialized in big cats for big Americans, returning from a cougar shoot in Terrace. David Bruce, manager of the Scotiabank that had been robbed in the early spring, was on his way home from a bucket list East African safari in Tanzania. Sunshine Cruz was a Harbour City downtown social justice warrior returning from a Costa Rican vacation. Justin Beaver was on his way home from hiking the East Beach Trail on Haida Gwaii, the northern BC Pacific islands once known as the Queen Charlottes.

As she followed the other passengers out of the plane, Tiki Lane could barely handle the heat reflecting off the tarmac. The heavy air smelled of salt and pungent kerosene. She was sweating with fever even before she had reached the bottom of the steps, and only the sight of her sister and brother-in-law waving behind the glass of the arrivals lounge held any possibility of relief. She clutched a travel pillow like her first doll. Sababa could see she was not well. Michel Vieuchange, the Air Canada flight attendant last off the plane, appeared worried for her wellbeing, a rare and admirable trait for Sababa to bear witness to.

Tiki and Jane fell into each other with hugs and kisses, in a strange mixture of relief and concern. Sababa knew his most immediate task was to fetch and carry Tiki's backpack, and follow behind the two sisters mind-melding towards his dimpled and dented white Honda Civic, now decorated with a fresh Robbins retribution ticket for his sin of not feeding the parking machinery. He put her pack in the hatchback rear and opened

333

one of the back doors for his sister-in-law. She had been travelling for over forty hours and was shivering so hard her teeth chattered like a typewriter. He drove.

"What happened over there, Tiki?" Jane asked. The cure for anything is salt water: the Salish Sea, sweat, or teardrops, the sacred messengers of unspeakable love and overwhelming grief. Tiki had left a trail of tears halfway around the world, burning down her cheeks into her solitude, the only weapon she had left. The story of how she had fallen from a happy dive shop owner on a paradise island in the Gulf of Thailand, enraptured with her partner boyfriend, to the feverish misfortune in Sababa's back seat, ran through Sumatra, and betrayal, and would take time to understand and put right. Tiki fell asleep with her face still wet. As he drove by the ancient rock carvings of Petroglyph Park, Sababa turned on the radio. Jane turned down the volume.

Leave it to beaver fever and his friends... This is BC Bud, for CNDN Coast Salish radio, 101.3 FM on your Home and Native Band...

In the rearview mirror, Sababa watched his sister-in-law grimace and squirm in a dazed slumber. Rivulets of perspiration ran down her neck.

This is for the newly broken dreamers with that kind of heartache they feel in their bones... who now know that not every sweet root gives birth to sweet grass.

She moaned and cried out and shivered in her suffering. And then she had the seizure.

If you think you are too small to make a difference, try sleeping with a mosquito... The ones in Harbour City are big enough to stand flat-footed and screw a turkey.

'I can see for Myles and Miles
I can see for Miles and Myles
I can see for Myles and Miles and Myles and Miles and Myles...'
The Who, *I Can See For Miles*

Sara Reynolds paged her mentor from the ER early on the morning after Tiki had arrived from Thailand.

"What you got?"

"Referral from Dr. Capitaine, Sab." She said. "Miles Davis, 35-year-old airport custodian with known sickle cell anemia and heterozygous alpha-thalassemia with frequent painful crises. Looks like he had a crisis three days ago and now presents with chest pain."

"I may have seen him at the airport yesterday." Sababa said. "I'll be in shortly."

When she had recovered from her seizure, Tiki had refused Sababa's suggestion that they take her to Harbour City General.

"I just need a good night's sleep and I'll be fine." She insisted. Sababa agreed, on the condition that she went with Jane the following morning to see his own family physician, Dr. James Ruben Andrews. Tiki said she would do that, and Jane said she would take her. Sababa remembered the time when he told Andrews he had chosen him as his GP.

"Why me?" James asked.

"Because of your intelligence." Sababa said.

"My intelligence?" James was stunned. "I have a practice full of sports medicine patients. The last time I looked, there weren't a lot of people who thought of you as a good sport, or me as brilliant."

"You'll give me everything I want because you know better than to argue with me." And so it was.

"How are you, Myles?" Sababa greeted the ER doc that had consulted Sara.

"Living the dream."

"If your dreams don't scare you they're not big enough." He said. "Tell us the rest of the story, Sara."

"Two hip replacements, for avascular necrosis from his sickle cell disease. Because of all his earlier blood transfusions, Mr. Davis had developed iron overload for which he received deferoxamine chelation. Because of chronic pain, he uses cannabis, methadone, NSAIDs, and acetaminophen. A portacath secured venous access. Recently, Miles had severe low calcium from vitamin D deficiency, for which he took cholecalciferol and calcium carbonate. He complains of chest pain behind his breastbone, palpitations and muscle cramps. No shortness of breath. No cough. No fever."

"Exam?"

"Heart rate and blood pressure a little high. Otherwise nothing remarkable."

"Lab?"

"Bloodwork showed anemia with increased bilirubin and lactate dehydrogenase levels and white blood cell count, and decreased calcium, magnesium, and low haptoglobin compatible with smashed red blood cells." Sara threw up a chest x-ray on the nearest viewer.

"Right middle lobe infiltrate."

"Is he getting enough air, Myles?" Sababa grinned a Sababa grin. "Differential diagnosis?"

"Malfunction or infection of the portacath, or pleuritic, thromboembolic, pericardial, myogenic, osteogenic, costochondral or gastrointestinal causes." She said. "But I think it's just acute chest syndrome."

"Second most common cause of sickle cell disease hospitalization." Myles offered. "Set off by lung infection or infarction by bone marrow fat emboli, collapse and spasm of small airways from shallow breathing due to pain, and local shunting leading to further deoxygenation, red cell sickling, and vaso-occlusion. And round and round we go."

"One problem." Sababa pulled up another chest x-ray from a year earlier. "Your right middle lobe abnormality is old, and therefore irrelevant. Where's the ECG?" Sara and Myles looked embarrassed.

"What? No ECG? In a patient with a disease that causes intravascular thrombosis who presents with chest pain. Acute chest syndrome may be the second most common cause of sickle cell hospitalization, but a heart attack is the most common cause of sudden death." He turned his attention to the ER ward clerk.

"Cheri Sundae, please get me a stat ECG and serum troponin on Miles Davis."

"On it."

"At least he's protected against malaria." Sara said.

"Not true, Gold Miss." Sababa said. "He has the disease, not the trait. Miles is more vulnerable to malaria; it's the most common cause of painful crises in malarial countries. Let's go to the bedside." Sara introduced the portly professor.

"They said I'd be seeing God." Miles said.

"God's away on business." Sababa shook his hand. "I'm his locum." The three physicians watched the 12-lead tracing come off the ECG machine.

"It appears you've had a heart attack, Miles." Sababa said.

'I'm a big game hunter
And a sure enough gunner
And I ain't got time for you.'
Buck Owens, *Big Game Hunter*

"Need you here when you're done, Sab." Trace Pangloss had poked his head through the curtain. Sara and the stocky savant met him at the consultants' desk when they had finished rescuing Miles from nowhere.

"Jaroslav Flegr." Trace said. "44-year-old big game trophy hunting guide just returned from a cougar shoot in Terrace. Presents today with headaches, fever, fatigue, muscle aches and pains, and blurred vision."

"Exam?"

"Tender enlarged lymph nodes everywhere." Trace said. "And you've got to see this." He led Sababa and Sara into the patient's cubicle, made introductions, and then handed Sababa an ophthalmoscope. The portly professor looked long and hard into each of Jaroslav's eyes, before handing the instrument to Sara.

"You eat that cougar?" He asked.

"Parts of it." Said the hunting guide. "Mighty tasty."

"Looks like you saved a little bit for later."

"What do you mean?"

"What Dr. Pangloss found in the back of your eyeballs, what my resident is now looking at, is what we call retinochoroiditis, a severe inflammation of the vascular part of your eyes."

"It's like a headlight in the fog." Sara said.

"From what?" Jaroslav asked.

"That cougar you shot." Sababa said. "You ate the tachyzoic merozoites infecting it."

"WTF?"

"The cougar growled the same expletive." Sababa said. "It's a condition called toxoplasmosis, from a protozoan named Toxoplasma gondii. Lab?"

"High white count." Sara said. "Mostly eosinophils.

"What are those?"

"Pink leucocytes." Sababa said. "We see them in worms, wheezes and weird diseases. Revenge of the pink panther."

"So what can you do about this?" Jaroslav asked. "I'm a busy man."

"Some of us wish you were less busy." Sababa said. "I have no problem with hunting for food but consider your activity the ultimate moral perversion. No one should kill an animal just to display its body parts on a wall."

"It's what separates mankind from the other animals, like our opposable thumbs."

"I shudder to think every place your opposable thumb has been." Sababa said. "If there's one thing you can say about mankind, there's nothing kind about man. We're monkeys with too much money and too many guns. Just my opinion, but a well-thought-out, impeccably well-reasoned one."

"You hate me, don't you?" Jaroslav said.

"I don't hate you, although I'm not excited about your existence. Nothing personal, I don't like anybody. I just like you a little less."

"What I do is the ultimate expression of manhood."

"Relative to its size, the barnacle has the largest penis of any animal." Sababa said. "I've never seen one with an AK-47. Everyone who ever loved you was wrong."

"Are you going to fix this, anyway?" He asked.

"Of course." Sababa said. "We fix everybody."

"How are you planning to do that?"

"First, we'll test your blood for the organism with a polymerase chain reaction, a Sabin–Feldman dye test, an indirect hemagglutination assay, an indirect fluorescent antibody assay, a modified direct agglutination test, a latex agglutination test, and an enzyme-linked immunosorbent assay. We're going to test you for HIV, with your consent. Sara, get our own faceless oculist guru, Dr. T.J. Eckleburg, to see Kit Carson here. He'll want to take pictures." Sababa said. "Then we're going to treat you, with a course of endochin-like quinolones if I can get them, or with pyrimethamine and sulfadiazine with corticosteroids, if I can't."

"Anything else I need to know?" Jaroslav asked.

"All you can." Sababa said. "Because toxoplasma can only reproduce in felines, it wants cats to eat its intermediate host, and because cats hunt live prey and do not eat carrion, the parasite must not immediately kill its temporary home. But it should if it could, make it easier for a cat to consume it. With rodents, the density of toxo cysts in the amygdala, a part of the brain linked to anxiety and fear, is double that in other brain structures. Also, the genome of T. gondii contains two lengths of DNA related to mammalian genes involved in regulating dopamine, the molecule associated with reward and pleasure signals in the brain, including in ours. Thus, the protozoan

338

makes suicidal activities, like hanging around places frequented by cats, feel more pleasurable for an infected rodent.

Some people think toxoplasmosis infection can also affect human behaviour—crazy cat-lady syndrome, a higher risk of automobile accidents due to impaired psychomotor performance or enhanced risk-taking personality changes, infected tennis players like Arthur Ashe and Martina Navratilova, and other psychiatric disorders. So there is hope." He saw Myles waving at him from across the ER.

"Now, if you'll excuse me." He said. "Sara, here, will finish your paperwork and arrange for you to see me in my clinic in follow-up." Sababa mouse-clicked his computer and pretended to put another quarter in the jukebox as he left.

'And when the coyotes howl
And the cougar's on the prowl
They ain't lookin' for your customary prey...'
C.W. McCall, *Comin' Back for More*

"Your dance card is already punched for this morning's assembly, Myles." Sababa said.

"You'll want to see this guy, Sab."

"Tell me why."

"Charles Donovan." Myles continued. "38-year-old South Sudanese 'Lost Boys' refugee, working as a screening officer at the airport. You've been there?"

"The airport?" Sababa said. "Yesterday, to pick up my sister-in-law."

"No, the Sudan." Myles said.

"Twenty years ago." Sababa said. "The train broke down in the Sahara for three days, halfway between Khartoum and Wadi Halfa. Biggest Nile rats I've ever seen."

"Must have been horrible." Myles commiserated.

"Best time of my life. Tell me about your Lost Boy here."

"Presented this morning with exertional shortness of breath and coughing blood, fever, weight loss, and fatigue." Myles said. "And a rash that began around his mouth a week ago, and spread to the rest of his face. If I didn't know it wasn't a real thing, I'd have called it mouth measles. Have a look." Myles introduced Charles to the stocky savant.

"When were you last in South Sudan, Charles?" Sababa asked.

"Six months ago." He said. "My mother died."

"I'm sorry." Sababa turned to Myles.

"Rest of his physical?"

"He's a one-man Royal College exam. Enlarged liver and spleen, a mucosal lesion on his tongue, draining sinus of the metatarsal bone of his right big toe. Labwork shows anemia and a predominance of lymphocytes in his white count." Myles threw a chest x-ray up on the cubicle's viewbox.

"At first, I thought he had TB." Myles said. "Bilateral enlarged lymph nodes of his central chest and mediastinum, and thickening of the walls of his large bronchi. But I don't think it is."

"It's not TB." Sababa said. "Cheri Sundae, can you please rescue Ed Hyde from whoever he's currently making enemies with?"

"On it, Sab."

"Regina, can you set us up for a bone marrow biopsy, please? We'll need a consent form." Charles seemed more confident when Sababa explained what he was about to do.

Cheri held up her handset.

"Line 2 for Dr. Hyde."

"Ed, I need you to bronchoscope a patient in the ER. With bronchoalveolar lavage" Sababa said. "Today is good. We'll keep him from food and water until you're done." Sara arrived from working up the cat killer.

"What's the rash from?" She asked.

"PKDL." Sababa said. "Post-kala-azar dermal leishmaniasis."

"Kala-azar?" She asked.

"Black fever in Sanskrit. Assam fever. Dumdum fever. Visceral leishmaniasis." He said.

"It's a fatal disease caused by a protozoan parasite *Leishmania donovani*, transmitted by the female sandfly, *Phlebotomus argentipes*, intermediately hosted by the Nile Grass rat, *Arvicanthis niloticus*. Second-largest parasitic killer in the world after malaria, responsible for 400,000 infections each year worldwide. Misdiagnosis is dangerous. Without proper treatment, the mortality rate for kala-azar is close to 100%. It was the only weapon that Southern Sudanese refugees, moving at foot-speed, could retaliate with against their Upper Nile persecutors during the civil war. Kala-azar arrived with a force comparable to smallpox hitting the American Indians. One village at the centre of the epidemic, Duar, had four survivors out of an original population of a thousand. From the late eighties to the mid-nineties 100,000 succumbed to the sickness in that region alone. Where else in the world could 50% of a population die with no one knowing?"

"But you said the rash comes after the disease." She noted.

"Usually." Sababa said. "Not this time. If you deal in camels, make the doors high."

"Dr. Leyblanca the pathologist on line 3 for you, Sab." He picked up the handset.

"¿Why are ju doing thees bone marrow, Cabrón?" Juan asked. "What are ju lookeeng for?"

"Leishmanial amastigotes." Sababa said. "And organisms cultured in Novy-MacNeal-Nicolle medium."

"JesuCristo!" Juan was excited. "It make the gangleea tweetch! I call ju." *Click.*

Sara did the bone marrow while Sababa supervised.

"So what happens now?" Charles asked.

"We'll draw more bloodwork to look for Leishmania antibodies with a K39 dipstick test, latex agglutination testing and immunochromatography, and administer a leishmanin skin test, courtesy of our Iranian colleagues. Dr. Hyde will get us lavage fluid and sample biopsies from your breathing tubes this afternoon. We'll give you a single intravenous dose of paromomycin and liposomal amphotericin B, and send you home with a 28-day prescription of miltefosine. You'll sleep in your own bed tonight, and I'll see you in a month in my office."

Cheri Sundae was waving her phone at him again.

"Who?" He asked.

"Tictac Tarmac." She said. "Line 2, and T.J. Eckleburg on 3." When Sababa got off the phone, he handed Sara the names he had written down on a piece of paper. *Justin Beaver... Sunshine Cruz...*

"I'll finish up here." He said. "You go see these two new consults on Sophia's floor." He noticed her frown.

"The purpose of today's training is to defeat yesterday's understanding. A thousand days of training to develop, ten thousand days of training to polish. You must examine all this well." Sababa said.

"Miyamoto Musashi?" She asked. Sababa nodded.

"Even in heaven, they don't sing all the time."

'Tony's got a botfly in his forehead
Jenny's got a guinea worm in her shoe
Dave's got leeches, Mike's got flu,
Everybody's got a parasite, I've got you.'
Pain, *Antidote*

"Eksyos me." She said. "Sara. Is statue?" Sophia had found her pulling charts at the Floor 5 nursing station.

"It's me, Sophia."

"Differences hab come bisit as." She smiled. "How berry nice."

"I'm here to see these two patients for Doctor Sababa." Sara handed her the paper.

"Justin Beaver and Sunshine Cruz, anak." Sophia read. "Easttart with Justin." Sophia said. "He has been libbing in diyapurse since plying in prum Queen Charlutt City. He cannot eat pride pooed. We are always changing his bed shits because he is so accident porn."

"Then I'll see Justin first." Sara sailed down the hallway. An hour later Sababa bounced through the stairwell doors in response to her page.

"Ah, my payborit ductor." Sophia said. "Sara is in Room 512 with Meester Beeber." Sababa found his resident, writing in the patient record.

"27-year-old Valhalla Pure Outfitters sales employee, patient of Dr. Tarmac's, just back from Haida Gwaii with a three-day history of sudden onset of fever and malaise, severe nausea and vomiting, abdominal cramps and bloating, foul-smelling floating greasy diarrhea, flatulence with burps that taste like sulfur, and itchy skin, hives, and swelling of his eyes and joints. He had been hiking the East Beach Trail in Naikoon Provincial Park on Graham Island. No pertinent past medical history."

"How was the hike, Justin?" Sababa asked. "I was up there twenty-five years ago when the Golden Spruce was still standing."

"It was great, Doc." Justin said. "Except I can't drink milk anymore, and I can't stop shitting myself."

"Did you filter your water on the hike?"

"Uh, no." Justin admitted.

"Exam, Sara?"

"Not much, Sab." She said. "No fever now, normal blood pressure, fast heart rate. Diffuse abdominal tenderness without peritoneal signs. Labwork shows an elevated white count with a left shift and low CD4+T cell count with negative HIV testing. Flat plate abdominal x-ray normal. His abdominal CT scan got him admitted for what it showed."

"Which was?"

"Extensive bulky mesenteric and retroperitoneal enlarged lymph nodes with inflammatory fat stranding in the mesentery." She took Sababa aside for the next part. "Suspicious for an underlying neoplasm, likely lymphoma."

"What are you two talking about?" Justin demanded.

"Some radiologist wondered about a tumour." Sababa said. "He's wrong."

"How do you know?"

"It is my business to know what other people don't know." He said. "You have acquired a protozoan in your gut from drinking unfiltered water on your hiking trip. It protects its own growth by consuming all the local arginine in the small bowel, the amino acid necessary for your intestine to make nitric acid. Arginine starvation is a cause of programmed cell death."

"So it's killing off my guts?"

"Only the top layer, so it can take advantage of the increased permeability." Sababa added. "The parasite also reduces Bcl-2, a protein that protects against cell death, and increases Bax, a protein that increases it. We call it caspase-dependent apoptosis."

"I call it diabolical." Justin said. "What's the name of this bastard?"

"Giardia lamblia, or duodenalis." Sababa said. "Likely assemblage A or B." Sophia's shining face and starched white cap appeared in the doorway.

"Correk!" She announced. "Are you conpirming dat he has beeber peeper, Ductor Sababa?"

"He has Beaver Fever, Sophia."

"I knew it." She said. "When Justin burps, it smells like da debil."

"It does have a tail, Sophia."

"What now?" Justin asked.

"We sent away some more stool samples for culture and ELISA testing." Sababa said. "And you go home with a five-day prescription of metronidazole. I don't want you in my hospital."

"Great, Doc!" Justin was overjoyed.

"Only one thing, Justin." Sababa said.

"What's that?"

"The antibiotic has a disulfuram effect that will make you ill if you drink any alcohol within two days of its ingestion."

"Oh."

"And Justin?"

"Yeah?"

"You work for Valhalla Pure." Sababa said. "Invest in an expensive MSR water microfilter." Justin nodded in everyone's rear vision.

Sababa and Sara and Sophia walked in on an emancipation event in the next room. A middle-aged woman with a purple Mohawk and a nose ring was holding her lower lip. She was in pain.

"I thought it was a cold sore." The woman said. "What the fuck is it?"

"Allow me to introduce Ms. Sunshine Cruz, Sab." Sara began. "53-year-old social activist returned from vacation in Costa Rica." Sababa extended his hand.

"My o' myiasis." Sababa said. "You have been in Costa Rica I perceive."

"How did you know that?" Sunshine asked.

"It's his business to know what other people don't know." Sara had a program. She knew the players.

"Some circumstantial evidence is strong." Sababa said. "Your T-shirt is emblazoned with the national anthem." *Noble patria, tu hermosa bandera.* "Where exactly were you in Costa Rica?"

"Puerto Viejo de Talamanca." She said. "It's in Limon Province."

"I know it well." Sababa said. "Used to hang out under the Aspirina sign at the Locanda Pura Vida. You look like something or somebody beat you. Did you use a mosquito net when you were there?" One of Sababa's eyebrows went north.

"All life is sacred." She said.

"Right. Look's like you ordered off the menu. Something hijacked your mosquito, Sunshine."

"Get it out!" She shrieked. "I can feel it moving inside me. Get it out!"

"Let me see." Sababa said. Sunshine took her hand away. Her lower lip was red and swollen and encrusted and moving.

"We don't have to get it out." He said.

"You don't?"

"Oh, no." Sababa said. "He's coming out all by himself. Takes about 45 minutes." Her screaming penetrated to adjacent floors.

"Where did it come from?!"

"I could tell you, but you won't sleep." Sababa said.

"What is it?!" She cried.

"Dermatobia hominis." Sababa said. "Bot fly. Also known as warble fly, heel fly and, my personal favorite, gadfly. You're sort of a social gadfly, aren't you, interfering with the status quo of your community by posing novel, upsetting questions directed at authority. Nothing beats the drama of a bullhorn."

"It's a job I'm proud of." She winced with the increasing discomfort of the imminent escape.

344

"And so you should be." Sababa said. "You're in excellent company. Socrates, on trial for his life, pointed out that the gadfly was easy to swat but the cost to society of silencing individuals whose role was 'to sting people and whip them into a fury, all in the service of truth' was, in one of the earliest descriptions of gadfly ethics, quite high. In Greek mythology, an enraged Zeus sent a gadfly to sting Pegasus from under the mortal Bellerophon, attempting to ride to the top of Mount Olympus, believing himself worthy to enter the realm of the gods. Athena spared his life after he fell back to earth, but Bellerophon became blind and wandered the earth until he died, hated by both men and gods. And here we are."

"So, if Justin is da debil, den Sunshine could be da debil's adbocat." Sophia said.

"Or some kind of gainfully employed concern troll." Sababa agreed. "The larva trying to escape out of your lower lip had crawled into the hole made by the proboscis of the mosquito that was carrying thirty botfly eggs under its abdomen. Backward pointing spines make it difficult to remove at the best of times but this guy was pumping you with painkillers and producing antibiotics so you didn't know he was there until he started moving. You could have killed him with iodine or nail polish or petroleum jelly or bacon fat or wax or glue or chewing gum, or even local Costa Rican *matatorsala* tree sap, but you didn't." The next scream pierced everyone's ears.

A lemon yellow peanut with concentric black spotted rings wriggled out of the new crater in Sunshine's lip. It wasn't a peanut.

"You can plant him in soil if you want a perpetual supply of party favours." Sababa said.

"I will get a tee-shoe." Sophia said.

"But that's not why Dr. Rivera admitted you to hospital, was it Sunshine?" Sababa studied the swelling of her left orbit. "Well, the good news is that you don't have a gigantic mutant botfly monster in your eyeball. We've worked the bugs out of that one. The bad news is more interesting. Tell me the rest of the story."

"Nothing much to tell..." Sunshine said.

"I was speaking to Sara."

"Oh."

"Fever, headaches, exertional shortness of breath, decreased energy and appetite, and a blotchy rash most noticeable after a shower and left eye swelling and itchiness. She went to see her GP, Dr. Rivera, yesterday afternoon, who referred her to our own faceless oculist guru, Dr. T.J. Eckleburg, who admitted her to hospital, treated her for an allergic reaction and blepharoconjunctivitis, and consulted us today for what he now presumes is orbital cellulitis."

"Exam?"

"Normal vital signs but left eye is swollen shut, as you can see, with palpable lymph nodes in her neck on the same side... diffuse reddish patches of her skin. Otherwise unremarkable."

"Labwork?"

"Slight anemia. Normal white count with atypical lymphocytes, rest normal."

"Do you know the eponym for Sunshine's swollen eye, Sara?" Sababa asked.

"Is there one?" Sara asked him back.

"Oh, yes." Sababa said. "It's called Romaña's sign, named after Cecilio Félix Romaña, the Argentinian who first described it in 1935."

"What does that mean?" Sunshine asked.

"You didn't use a mosquito net when you were in Puerto Viejo, did you?" Sababa asked.

"No, I didn't." She said. "I stayed in the simple thatched one-room hut of a local woman I met."

"She didn't offer you any insecticide, I suppose."

"She did, but I told her that all life is sacred." Sunshine didn't like the direction of the discourse.

"She didn't mention she sprayed her hut with a protective fungus called *Beauveria bassiana*?

"No, she didn't." Sunshine said.

"She didn't happen to mention the word 'chinche,' did she?" Sababa asked. "They're also called 'vinchucas' in Argentina, Bolivia, Chile and Paraguay, 'barbeiros' in Brazil, 'pitos' in Colombia, and 'chipos' in Venezuela."

"No, I don't think she did. Why?"

"They're a kind of endemic triatomine bug which hide in crevices in the walls and roofs during the day." He said. "They're the principal insect vector, *Rhodnius prolixus*. They're also known as 'kissing bugs.'"

"Vector for what?" She asked. "Why kissing?"

"These sacred bugs of yours emerge at night when everyone is asleep." Sababa said. "They feed on people's faces, hence the kissing reference. After they bite and ingest blood, they defecate on their benefactor, and pass Trypanosoma cruzi trypomastigotes in their feces in or near the bite wound."

"What was that last bit?"

"T. cruzi is the protozoan parasite responsible for Chagas disease, or American trypanosomiasis. Scratching the bite or rubbing your eyes causes the organism to enter the wound and begin invading cells, differentiate, multiply, and pour into the bloodstream. The disease occurs more often in regions where economic exploitation and human habitation have thinned out the sylvatic habitat and its fauna, as in where you were sleeping with your sacred life forms. You have acute Chagas disease."

"What happens now?" She asked.

"That kind of depends on whether you want to remain friends with this part of Mother Nature, or whether you want us to kill it dead." Sababa said. "If you want us to fix this, Sara will order thin and thick blood smears stained with Giemsa, for direct visualization of the parasites, PCR, ELISA, immunoblot, and immunofluorescent antibody tests, call the Costa Ricans and tell them to clean up their act, and send you home with a prescription for benznidazole 150 mg, which you will have to take twice a day for two months. There's still only a 60-85% chance of eradicating the infection if you take every pill prescribed."

"And if I don't?"

"Then you'll enjoy the same natural history as Charles Darwin did. I'll get to see you in less than a year for the chronic manifestations of untreated Chagas disease, parasympathetic nervous system failure, and dilation of your esophagus and colon and heart, and we'll look for a cardiac transplant donor. Karma is everywhere you're going to be."

"OK." She said. "I don't trust my feelings about this bullshit, but I don't think I have a choice." Sababa saluted.

"Other than that, Sunshine, how did you like Costa Rica?"

'He can't fly, but I'm telling you, he can run the pants off a kangaroo.'
John Williamson, *Old Man Emu*

"It's protozoa week, Boss." "The brave love Mercy, and delight to save." Sababa handed Sara the chart of the first patient.

"Ernest Tyzzer?" She watched a middle-aged tanned man in overalls, a flannel checked shirt, and gumboots get up from his chair.

Sababa called the black woman in a *habesha kemis* dress and a *netela* shawl sitting across from him. He recognized her as the barista he bought his espresso doppio doppio from at the airport the previous day.

"Isadora Belli?" She followed him into his office and fainted on the carpet.

"How can I help?" He asked.

"Thank you for seeing me, Doctor. Three weeks ago, my rheumatologist started me on methotrexate and prednisone for rheumatoid arthritis. For the last six days, I've had a fever and abdominal pain, and watery diarrhea, now up to ten bowel movements a day. I've lost so much weight, my clothes no longer fit. I'm dizzy, and scared."

Sababa looked at Isadora. He pulled on the skin of her forearms and watched it slowly return to its original position. Her mucous membranes were dry. Her blood pressure was too low and her pulse too high. She was dehydrated. He examined her abdomen but found no sign of a surgical situation.

Her referring family physician, Dr. James Reuben Andrews, had ordered lab investigations of Isadora's blood and stool. Her white blood cells had turned into lymphocytes and pink eosinophils. *Worms, wheezes, and weird diseases.* The decrease in blood volume and flow had affected her kidney function. She was anemic with large red cells. But the answer to what was causing all this jumped off the stool culture report.

"Cystoisospora belli oocysts and Charcot-Leyden crystals." Sababa said.

"I'm sorry?" Isadora didn't understand.

"You have a coccidian parasite." He said.

"Where did I get it?" She asked.

"It comes from the tropics and subtropical areas of the planet."

"But I haven't been anywhere since I left Ethiopia." She protested.

"Then that's where you got it." Sababa said.

"But that was sixteen years ago."

"The parasite was sleeping." Sababa said. "Your rheumatologist's immunosuppressive drugs woke it up." The barista frowned.

"Can you fix it?"

"Isadora, I need to admit you to hospital for intravenous rehydration and antibiotics." Sababa said. "This can get to be serious if we don't show it the respect it deserves." He picked up his handset.

"Mercy, get me an ambulance, and an ER doc."

"On it, Sab." She said. Minutes later, they watched the paramedics wheel Isadora down the ramp of Manzanita Medical. Sababa turned to find Sara waiting to present her case.

348

"What you got?" He asked, following her into the residents' examining room.

"Ernest Tyzzer." She began. "Referral from Poldy Bloom. 35-year-old emu farmer."

"Emu rancher." Sababa corrected. Ernie nodded.

"Whatever." Sara said. "Presents with a five-day history of intermittent fever with chills, productive cough and breathlessness, and today developed nausea and watery vomiting."

"Exam?"

"He has a low-grade fever and a fast pulse. Right lower lobe noises on listening to his chest. That's it."

"Labwork?"

"High white blood cell count. Chest x-ray revealed right lower zone consolidation." She said. "Sputum staining shows acid-fast structures."

"But not TB."

"Not TB."

"Cryptosporidium parvum oocysts." Sababa said.

"What the hell is that?" Ernie asked.

"Crypto is a disease caused by a genus of protozoa in the phylum Apicomplexa." Sababa said. "It is unusual among eukaryotes because their mitochondria don't contain DNA."

"I didn't get any of that."

"You have a parasite in your gut and your lung." Sara said.

"From what?" Ernie was breathing harder.

"From your emus." Sababa said.

"Impossible." Ernie protested. "I use bleach to clean up after my birds."

"The cysts of Crypto are resistant to chlorine."

"Wait a minute." Said the Emu rancher. "One of my birds, Lucy, escaped for ten days when I forgot to lock the gate to his pen. Flew the coop."

"His pen?"

"Lucy is a male." Ernie said. "I only found out after I named him. He scratched me up real good when I tried to load him into the van last week. He weighs as much as I do."

"Crypto is not uncommon among commercial animal breeders." Sababa said. "Cases have afflicted dealers in leopard geckos, monitor lizards, iguanas and tortoises, and several snake species. We see outbreaks from faulty water filtration plants in British Columbia. In 1996, it infected two thousand people in Cranbrook, and ten thousand in Kelowna a week later."

"What can do about it?" Ernie asked. Sababa wrote a prescription.

"This is nitazoxanide, and loperamide and zinc and oral rehydration therapy." He said. "Take it for three days, and then get me another chest x-ray before coming back to see me in follow-up. Get Mercy to make you an appointment for two weeks on your way out." Ernie got up to leave.

"And Ernie?"

"Yeah."

"If you want to follow this emu bubble thing into the ground, get your waterlines checked, test the droppings, use ammonia and not bleach to disinfect and fumigate your outbuildings, and increase the Vitamin A and K in their diet." He said. "You must give them anti-coccidial drugs on a regular schedule, and still this thing may not fly. Also, it will be hard to get rid of them. The Aussies found this out in 1932. They used Lewis machine guns and unless they hit their tiny heads, the birds were too fast and just carried on eating their crops."

Bureaucrat: One who works by fixed routine, without exercising intelligent judgement.
James MacMillan

After two months as his shadow, Sara could read Sababa's mood swings like an ancient Etruscan Haruspex could read the entrails of a chicken or a sheep. But Sababa was neither a chicken nor a sheep and, after sending Sara to see the two consults waiting in the Emergency Department, he left his office to prove it one more time.

On the eve of the monthly Medical Advisory Committee meeting, that strange, solemn, sacrificial, satanic, shamanic ritual of collision (or collusion, depending on the machinations of the participants) between the medical staff and the health authority bureaucrats, Sababa would get as close to the dark matter of the universe as he ever dared.

The conclave was held in the Boardroom, that same Oracle of Oversight, that identical morgue of ambition, in which Dr. Zaias

350

chaired his Department of Medicine meetings. The only differences were that the light green-yellow padded walls were fuzzier from the static electricity, the white stippled acoustic tile ceiling worked harder to absorb the screams of the defeated, and the Mayline chairs running the length of the long teak conference table held fatter asses, and more of them. The particulate debris lurking under the table became even more agitated.

At the far end of the room, new graffiti marred the melamine whiteboard on an easel:

<u>Mission Statement Generator</u>

<u>Adverbs:</u>
Quickly, proactively, efficiently, assertively, interactively, professionally, authoritatively, conveniently, completely, continually, dramatically, enthusiastically, collaboratively, synergistically, seamlessly, competently, globally...

<u>Verbs:</u>
Maintain, supply, provide access to, disseminate, network, create, engineer, integrate, leverage other's, leverage existing, coordinate, administrate, initiate, facilitate, promote, restore, fashion, revolutionize, build, enhance, simplify, pursue, utilize, foster, customize, negotiate...

<u>Adjectives:</u>
Professional, timely, effective, unique, cost-effective, virtual, scalable, economically sound, value-added, business quality, diverse, high-quality, competitive, excellent, innovation, corporate, high standards in, world-class, error-free, performance-based, multimedia-based, market-driven, cutting edge, high-payoff, low-risk high-yield, long-term, high-impact, prospective, progressive, ethical, enterprise-wide, principle-centered, mission-critical, parallel, interdependent, emerging, seven-habits-conforming, resource-leveling...

<u>Nouns:</u>
Content, paradigms, data, opportunities, information, services, material, technology, benefits, solutions, infrastructure, products, deliverables, catalysts for change, resources, methods of empowerment, sources, leadership skills, meta-services, intellectual capital...

Sara had written it all out correctly. She had left before the committee members began spilling through the Boardroom door and onto the claret pile carpet—medical staff departmental representatives Jules Martino from Surgery, Juan Leyblanca from Pathology, Mako Brisk from Radiology, Trace Pangloss from Emergency, Banjo Paterson from Anesthesia, and Eleazar Sababa from Internal Medicine; and courtiers from the Palace of Administration, and all their urbane appurtenances—Malcolm Canmore, the Chief Hospital Administrator of the silk ties, linen handkerchiefs, silver cuff-links, manicured fingernails, and platinum pens, the new CEO of the new Health Region, and Big Nurse Mildred Ratschet, the Grand Galactic Governess of Nightingales, sporting her string of cultured natural pearls. They would piously collaborate to achieve the magnetic goals that drew their obscene destinies together, always ready and willing to judge and bludgeon the independent outsider—and last but not least, although diminutive, the Chief of Staff and committee chairperson, the most prepotent master of control, Dr. Petronilla de Meath, a Napoleanna bone apart general practitioner, aspirant to and aspirating on gubernatorial greatness. *Something wicked this way comes.*

The harassment haridan picked up a handset from the multifunction business class conference digital phone console and dialled zero.

"Lana, can you announce the beginning of the Medical Advisory Committee meeting?" The hospital switchboard operator's Big Voice broadcast the assembly overhead.

Petronilla called the council to order and requested approval of the previous meeting's minutes. A cacophony of grunts echoed around the room.

"I've tabled the old business." She said. "So we can hear a progress report from William Bligh, the new innovative CEO of the brand new expanded Health Authority. William, please proceed." The innovator rose to the occasion and called for the first slide.

"Thank you for that excellent introduction, Petronilla." He said. "Let me begin by thanking all of you for your patience in the last six months in our reformulation of a new Regional Board, and efforts to refine our Vision and Mission Statements." The first slide was a quote from the new authority's internal newsletter.

CEO Health Matters: The Need for Yet a New Approach
William Bligh, our Chief Executive Officer, has reiterated the need for innovative thinking and process proposals that include a variety of stakeholders and are open to different ideas. We need to encourage other such initiatives to continue to come up with new and innovative ways of responding to challenges in health care.

"A lugubrious concatenation of meaningless clichés skulking in broad daylight." Sababa said. "What happened to Foster Concord's 15-year Action Plan from the last meeting?"

"Last slide, please." There had been only two slides. The second one looked like this:

Central Vancouver Island → Vancouver Island
Health Region   Health Authority
(CVIHR)   (VIHA)

"This demonstrates the evolution of our revolutionary new expanded health region, now encompassing the entire island." William puffed out his chest. "I am proud to have been appointed as its new CEO. We call it VIHA, for Vancouver Island Health Authority."

"Very Iffy Helicopter Access." It was too much for Sababa. "Breathtaking. Like Edward Scissorhands making balloon animals."

"Why is it that you have so little regard for authority, Sababa?" William asked.

"Distrust of authority should be the first civic duty. Bureaucracy is show business for ugly people. A dealer in rubbish sings the praise of rubbish. You have two parts to your brain, Bligh, 'left' and 'right'. On the left side, there's nothing right. On the right side, there's nothing left. Come down off the cross, we can use the wood. Pick one." A gavel came down hard on the sound block.

"That's enough, Doctor Sababa." Petronilla scowled.

"Sorry, your pythoness. I'm allergic to stupidity. I break out in sarcasm." The scowl became a glower.

"The next item of business comes from Mildred Ratschet, the head Team Leader of Nursing Administration. Mildred?" The Grand Galactic Governess of Nightingales handed around a directive.

Memo: Patient Comfort

Until the present heat wave subsides, it is suggested that beds be made up without bedspreads- i.e. with top sheet only. It is hoped that the subsequent decrease in weight and bulk of the bedding would result in increased comfort for patients.

"Patients first." She said.

"We're sitting here for this?" Jules Martino found his surgical self. "It doesn't make sense."

"It's not supposed to make sense." Mildred said. "It's hospital policy. You should read about it sometime." Down came the gavel.

"The next issue is brought to us by Artie Shafer, the new chair of the internal VIHA Research Ethics Committee. Doctor Sababa, you have the most prolific research portfolio so it would serve

353

you well to listen to how our guidelines are going to change. Artie, thanks for coming up to Harbour City. Please proceed."

"Thank you, Petronilla." But for a small mutation in his DNA, Shafer could have been a weasel. "As you all know, clinical investigations have been conducted under the auspices of external research ethics boards which are not suited to our need for more local control. Beginning immediately, all new clinical trial proposals will have to have VIHA Ethics Committee approval. No projects Phase III or below will be allowed. Each review will take approximately six months and will be billed to the principal investigator at our hourly rate." Sababa cleared his throat.

"So, let me see if I understand this." He said. "You have grandfathered my current investigations from your superior internal ethics review process, but I will have to let you make any further research projects become impossible by submitting my proposals to a new and improved local body made up of experts that have never done any clinical trials. Is that correct?"

"That's not fair, but not inaccurate." Artie agreed.

"So, even though I use universally respected state-of-the-art FDA and NIH-vetted institutional review board IRBs to supervise the ethics of multi-centre studies sponsored by the likes of the TIMI boys in Boston, I now have to give all that up for your divine adjudication on the morality of my research?"

"Basically. We need to make sure you know exactly what you're doing."

"If we knew exactly what we were doing, we wouldn't call it research, would we?" Sababa said. "A VIHA ethics committee is an oxymoron. Do you know Barbara Tuchman's three criteria for the definition of political folly?"

"No." Artie admitted.

"One. It must be counterproductive in its own time and not by hindsight, Two. It should be formulated by a group and persist beyond one political lifetime, and Three. A workable alternative course of action must be available. Congratulations. You have destroyed clinical research at Harbour City Regional. How ethical was that?" Petronilla detonated her gavel on the wooden table.

"Last order of business is actually yours, Doctor Sababa." She said. "Something about a protest of blood sugar records removed from patient charts to the medication administration record on the mobile nursing carts? Please proceed with alacrity. We are all busy and need to get home."

"I'm on call, so there's no real hurry." Sababa said. "The removal of the record of blood sugars from the chart poses a

354

danger to patient safety. We will see a lot more low blood sugars and other adverse reactions if this vital information is geographically separated from the central key repository of patient data."

"That decision was made by the Joint Pharmacy and Nursing Administration Task Force." Mildred said.

"Who did they ask?" Sababa inquired.

"The most important stakeholders." She said. "Tell me again what your issue is."

"Do you want the simple but misleading explanation or the one you won't understand?"

"Either is good." Mildred said. "I wasn't planning on listening." Gavel.

"This item is tabled until the next MAC meeting." Petronilla said. "We are adjourned." Sababa rolled his Mayline chair away from the long teak conference table.

"When I die, I want the medical bureaucrats in this room to lower me into my grave, so they can let me down one more time."

It wasn't long before Rage Against the Machine reverberated down the hallways.

'To expose and close the doors on those who try
To strangle and mangle the truth
Cause the circle of hatred continues unless we react
We gotta take the power back!'
Rage Against the Machine, *Take the Power Back*

"And what have you two love birds been up to, while I was attending Black Mass?" Sababa asked. Dr. Cliffy Carlton grinned a toothy grin. Sara rolled her eyes into the back of her head to avert his gaze.

"David Bruce." She said. "49-year-old local bank manager, returned from a 10-day safari in Tanzania, presents with a 3-day history of fevers, sweats, chills, muscle and joint pains, profound malaise and daytime drowsiness, and nighttime insomnia, headache, and an expanding red lesion on his right flank. His only medication at the time was doxycycline for malaria

355

prevention. He recalls being bitten by several aggressive flies during his stay in Tanzania, including while sitting poolside, six days before becoming ill.

"@%#^$ tsetse flies!" Sababa swore a streak so blue it was white. "I know @%#^$ tsetse flies. *Glossina morsitans*. @%#^$ Rwanda. They have @%#^$ tsetse flies the size of eagles. Last time I was down there, one of the game rangers told me to bring along some Dettol in a spray bottle, to prevent @%#^$ tsetse fly bites. They swarmed in through the vents of the Toyota Safari Land Cruiser and pierced us ten at a time. Each bite was like being injected with a large syringe. It took five or six smacks to kill the bastards, and they may as well have drunk the Dettol. We would have preferred drowning in the stuff to avoid getting bitten if it had worked, but the @%#^$ tsetse flies chomped through everything to get at us anyway." Sababa looked up into the concerned expressions on the faces of Sara and Cliffy, and the patient.

"Sorry." He said. "Got carried away. Exam?"

"He has a fever, a swelling below the left lower lip, and a soft, raised, dusky red nodule on his lower right flank." Before Sababa examined the lesion that Sara had described, he ran his fingers down the back of David's neck.

"Feel these." He said. Sara and Cliffy placed their fingers where Sababa had his.

"Lymph nodes." Cliffy said.

"Posterior cervical lymphadenopathy." Sababa remarked. "Winterbottom's sign. The Arab slave traders used it to detect and weed out their ill ill-gotten gains. And your nodule, Sara? It's a site of inoculation by a @%#^$ tsetse fly and called a trypanosomal chancre."

"Hang on." Cliffy protested. "Remember the aphorism of University of Maryland School of Medicine professor Dr. Theodore Woodward." *When you hear hoofbeats, think of horses, not zebras.*

"Except that this guy just came from a place where the zebras outnumber the horses a thousand to one." Sababa said. "In the diagnosis of the disease causation in an individual case, calculations of probability have no meaning. The pertinent question is whether the disease is present or not. Whether it is rare or common does not change the odds. Specific criteria are either fulfilled or not. Labwork?"

"WBC count was normal except for a slight left shift. Thin and thick smears looking for malaria didn't find malaria."

"But they found something, didn't they?" Sababa asked.

"They found trypomastigotes." She said.

356

"What the hell is that?" Bruce demanded.

"A flagellate protozoan called Trypanosoma brucei, in your case the East African *T. brucei rhodesiense*, as opposed to the much more common West African organism, *T. brucei gambiense*, which makes up 98% of cases. Both forms are transmitted to human hosts by bites of infected @%#^$ tsetse flies and both are fatal without treatment." Sababa said. "Although your form is more fatal faster. Seventy million people in twenty countries are at risk, and ☐three hundred thousand are infected each year. Killed over 90% of the cattle and two-thirds of the pastoral Masai of East Africa in 1891."

"So what is it you're telling me I have?" Bruce asked.

"You have HAT." Sababa said.

"HAT?"

"Human African trypanosomiasis." Sababa said. "HAT. Or I'll eat mine. Causes Sleeping Sickness, Brought to you down the Congo River and east by those same Arab slave traders from the sub-Sahara, and now recognized as 'the best game warden in Africa.' Killed more than a quarter million people in a Ugandan epidemic in 1901."

"What does Tsetse mean? Bruce asked. "Why don't the flies get sick themselves?"

"Tsetse means fly." Sababa said. "So a tsetse fly is a 'fly-fly,' just like Lake Nyasa means 'lake-lake.' It's an African explorer thing. On why the @%#^$ tsetse flies don't get affected, they produce vast amounts of hydrogen peroxide that damages the parasite's DNA. But the trypanosomes have a coat made up from variant surface glycoproteins, or VSGs, which can quickly mutate to escape detection by your own immune system. Neither of these animals is nice."

"So what happens now?" Bruce asked.

"I admit you to this hospital." Sababa said. "Sara will arrange for more investigations, including a biopsy of your leg, and a lumbar puncture to collect spinal fluid."

"Why do you need that?"

"It's called Sleeping Sickness, Bruce." Sababa said. "When the parasite crosses the blood-brain barrier, it releases a compound called tryptophol, an aromatic alcohol that induces sleep in humans. We also find tryptophol in Scots pine needles, the unicellular alga *Euglena gracilis*, the marine sponge *Ircinia spiculosa*, as an intermediate catabolite in cucumbers, an autoantibiotic in the fungus Candida albicans, in wine as a secondary product of ethanol fermentation, in the liver as a side-effect of the disulfiram treatment alcoholics take so they won't drink, and as a quorum sensing molecule for the trypanosome parasite itself. We need to know if you're about to enter the second phase of the disease, the period of neurological damage."

"Can you fix this thing?" He asked.

"Sara will give you a test dose of a medication called suramin and then arrange for weekly intravenous infusions of the drug for three weeks." Sababa said. "That should nail it. Do you know why zebras have stripes?" Bruce shook his head.

"They disrupt the light patterns that tsetse flies use to find food and water." Sababa said. "The insects can't decelerate and instead fly over the stripes or bump into them." Bruce turned his attention to Sara.

"Does he always live these kinds of fairy tales?"

"All the time." She said. "He claims that any cases with simple solutions would have been diagnosed by someone else before reaching him. One problem with working for Sababa is you see zebras everywhere."

Sababa had been speaking with Dr. Gung Ho, who replaced Cliffy at the bedside of the patient he had just referred.

"Michel Vieuchange." Gung began. "49-year-old Air Canada flight attendant with a six-week history of blood-streaked sputum, fatigue, fever, chills, and night sweats, and a three-week history of a 22-pound weight loss and five days of diarrhea."

"They nearly didn't let me work my last flight." Michel said.

"Exam confirms fever and diminished breath sounds and audible crackles in his lower right lung." Gung continued. "Lab shows a high white count with a left shift, high alkaline phosphatase, and low albumin and calcium." He threw a chest x-ray up on the bedside viewer.

"As you can see, he has a right pleural effusion, right apical infiltrations and volume loss of the lower lobe of his right lung. I drained some fluid from his pleural space but it, like his sputum gram stain, was sterile. What do you think, Sab?"

"I think you should bring over the portable ultrasound machine." He said. Gung brought the machine. The stocky savant applied some Aquasonic Gel to the head of the probe, applied the device to Michel's abdomen, and adjusted the window. A fuzzy image of his liver flickered on the screen, containing a large, solitary, flask-shaped hypoechoic mass."

"That's not supposed to be there." Sara said.

"Nope." Sababa agreed. "Michel, are you an MSM kind of guy?" The flight attendant nodded. Gung looked puzzled.

"Men who have sex with men." Sara said.

"I remember bringing Jane's friend, Julie, to the Ladakhi hospital lab in far northern India." Sababa mused. "The snow-capped Himalaya were stunning."

"Why did you take her to the lab?" Gung asked.

"We were planning on hiking over the Thorang La pass, but she had developed bloody diarrhea." He continued. "The lab tech mounted a specimen of her stool on their only microscope. He told me there was nothing to see."

"And?" Sara asked.

"It was crawling with amoebas."

"It that what I've got?" Michel said.

"At the least." Sababa offered. "Michel, it only takes the ingestion of one viable cyst to cause infection, a cyst that can survive for a month in soil or up to 45 minutes under a fingernail. Which is where you got yours."

"I did?"

"Transmission usually occurs via what we refer to as the fecal-oral route, but it can also be acquired through anal-oral contact. The four most overrated things in life are champagne, lobster, picnics, and anal sex." Sara and Gung shared a shiver. "Your amoebic cyst hatched into what we call a trophozoite, whose offspring bored through your intestinal wall, ate their way through your bloodstream to reach your liver, and formed an abscess, which perforated your diaphragm, and migrated to your right lung through a hepatobronchial fistula. You have what we call pleuropulmonary amoebiasis."

"Couldn't it be something else?" Michel asked.

"But it's not."

"How do you know?"

"It is my business to know what other people don't know." He said. "Entamoeba histolytica infection is a serious problem. It infects 50 million people worldwide and kills 55,000 of them every year. It caused a thousand infections in an outbreak at the 1933 Chicago World's Fair and killed 98 of them."

"Is there a cure?" Michel asked.

"We treat the infection with an oral tissue-active agent called metronidazole and a luminal cystocidal agent called iodoquinoline." Sababa said. "But I will admit you to hospital."

"What for?"

"For a CT scan of your chest, a consultation with our respirologist, Dr. Ed Hyde, to perform a bronchoscopy, and one to my general surgical expert, Dr. Jules Martino, to make sure we don't have to drain your liver abscess before it ruptures, although that is not likely to happen."

"Isn't there any more natural treatment I could take instead?" Michel asked.

"The Holchu people of the Nicobar Islands in the Bay of Bengal use the bark and seeds of an Indian plant named *Glochidion calocarpum*, to cure amoebiasis, but I don't think I could get a special authority dispensation from Pharmacare. So you're stuck with what works."

"You mentioned that I had an amoebic infection 'at the least.'" Michel said. "What did you mean by that?"

"There is a higher chance of being infected with E. histolytica if one is also infected with HIV. AIDS makes the damage worse."

"I might die?"

"Life is a sexually transmitted disease, Michel." Sababa said. "And the mortality rate is 100 per cent. Sara, please admit Mr. Vieuchange to Sophia's ward on the fifth floor, put in the referral requests I mentioned, and send off stool for direct fecal smear and O&P and antigen and PCR assays and culture in Robinson's and Jones's media. We'll need serum amoebic titres and HIV serology, with Michel's permission. Start him on his bug juice. I have a minor problem to attend to at home, but I will be available by courtesy phone." He handed her his pager and left.

"Is he always that fast?" Michel asked.

"Some people say he was born in a hospital loading zone with the meter running."

'There was once a Hindu sage, who sat down on the banks of the Ganges and thought for seventy years about the millennium. Just as he arrived at the solution and was putting it into verse, a mosquito stung him and he forgot it again at once.'

Don Marquis

Sababa found Jane and her sister at the island in their kitchen on the lake, filling Mason jars with scores of herring from a fisherman friend.

"How are you feeling, Tiki?" He asked.

"A lot better since taking your pills, Sab." She said. "I haven't had any more chills and fevers."

A week earlier, Sababa had asked Juan Leyblanca to look at Tiki's thin and thick blood film slides. The pathologist paged him with the Big Voice the same morning.

"Hey Juan." Sababa began. "How do you tell the difference between an introverted and extroverted pathologist?"

"I have no idea, Cabrón." He said.

"The introvert looks at his shoes while he's talking to you." Sababa said. "The extroverted pathologist looks at your shoes while he's talking to you. What did you find?"

"JesuCristo." Juan said. "¿Where did ju say she went to look at de monkeeys?"

"Orangutans." Sababa said. "She went to look at orangutans. In Bukit Lawang."

"¿Where de hell is dat?"

"Gunung Leuser." He said.

"¿Where de hell ees that?"

"Northern Sumatra." Sababa said. "What did you find?"

"She doesn't have one kind of malaria."

"Huh?"

"She has three kinds." Juan said. "Plasmodium malariae, Plasmodium ovale, and Plasmodium vivax."

"Triple header." Sababa mused. "Thanks, Juan."

"I call ju." The pathologist hung up.

The stocky savant had called in a prescription for chloroquine, and then called Jane to pick it up. Tiki had made rapid improvement from the first pill, although she was initially reluctant to take Sababa's 'chimiculs.'

"Malaria is a monster, Tiki." Sababa told her. "Hippocrates knew about it. It was so pervasive in ancient Rome, they called it Roman fever, and it contributed to the decline of their empire. The term derives from Medieval Italian, 'mala aria.' *Bad air*. Julius Wagner-Jauregg was an Austrian physician who deliberately injected the parasite into patients with tertiary syphilis as malariotherapy, to slow the progression of their disease, the discovery of which brought the Nobel Prize in Medicine in 1927. Other disorders, like sickle-cell anemia and G6PD deficiency, are actually protective against malaria. The history of malaria in war is the history of war itself. During the South Pacific campaigns of World War II, it infected half a million American troops and sixty thousand died. Still kills three-quarters of a million people a year, although there's a new insecticide consisting of a fungus, *Metarhizium pingshaense*, combined with the DNA of a venomous Australian funnel-web spider, which kills 90% of malaria-carrying mosquitos."

"What do people infected with malaria usually die from?" She asked.

"Overwhelming sepsis, ruptured red blood cells, cerebral malaria, blackwater fever causing kidney failure, take your pick." He said. "I hate mosquitoes as much as I hate @%#^$ tsetse flies."

"What if I drink gin and tonic?" She asked.

"Bark of the Peruvian cinchona tree." Sababa said. "Product of the Columbian exchange. More useful to prevent malaria in British India and expand the empire than to treat the disease."

"Have you had many cases in your practice here on the Island?" She asked.

"Every once in a while." He said. "From endemic areas. I remember torturing a poor attending consultant one cold winter with a boatload of infected Vietnamese. That was fun." The sisters finished bottling the fish and sat down for a cup of tea. Sababa enjoyed hearing their laughter again, from the second-floor coziness of his study, overlooking paradise. When the laughter stopped and Jane began calling his name, he knew something was wrong.

Downstairs, he found Tiki shivering again. When that stopped, her face flushed and she began to perspire, and cry. Jane and Sababa piled her into his dimpled and dented white Honda Civic, and roared off down the hill to Harbour City Regional. They waited for Dina to take her into a cubicle, then Dr. Trace Pangloss to see her, then for the phlebotomist to take her blood to the lab, and then for an hour more.

"Doctor Sababa, pick up #2053 for Dr. Juan Leyblanca." The Big Voice had paged Sababa overhead.

"Hey, Juan." Sababa began. "Where do you hide a hundred-dollar bill from a pathologist?"

"I have no idea, Cabrón." He said.

"With his family." Sababa said. "What did you find on the smears?"

"JesuCristo." Juan said. "¿Where did ju say she went to look at de monkeeys?"

"We've done this, Juan." Sababa said. "What did you find—recrudescence, resistance, relapse, or reinfection?"

"None of de above." The pathologist said. "I found de last parasite. She has Plasmodium falciparum as well. That ees some crazeey jungle she found. There ees nothing more dangerous dan a wounded mosqueeto. I call ju."

Sababa thanked him and went back to speak to Tiki Lane.

"What is it?" She asked. "Why didn't the medication work?"

"Congratulations. You seem to have won the Sumatran lottery." He said. "You're infected with all four subspecies of malaria, including the one that originally infected gorillas, falciparum."

"What do we do now? She asked.

"ACT." He said.

"Act?"

"Artemisinin-combination therapy." Sababa said. "Four doses of artesunate followed by two doses of mefloquine.

"And that will kill it?"

"Unless you have something else so new and wonderful that modern medicine doesn't know about yet." Sababa smiled a Sababa smile. "Someday I'll write about the giant rat of Sumatra, a story for which the world is not yet ready. Meanwhile, the most important decision of the day is when to switch from coffee to wine. We have arrived."

'Night and day
Under the hide of me
There's an oh such a hungry
Yearnin' burnin' inside of me'
Cole Porter, *Night and Day*

The casual reader should know that when it is daytime in Harbour City, it is night on the Dark Continent. Beyond the war and poverty and famine and flies, Africa is the origin of our species and our oldest predators. Its plains and savannahs are the evolutionary birthplaces of our cognitive advantage.

But consciousness does not belong to us uniquely. It exists throughout the animal kingdom, a long way down. Even protozoa show signs of learning and consideration. When paramecia are confined to tubes smaller in diameter than their length, they initially need a few minutes to turn but, with practice, become capable of rotating in a few seconds—an observation that shows learning in a single-cell animalcule. Amoebas perceive, identify, choose and ingest a variety of prey not much short of the choices of higher animals; they recognize their own kind and engage in cooperative behaviour, particularly hunting, like lions—observations that show self-awareness.

None of these examples of sentient ability can explain the twisted pack hunting exercise that came through Mercy's intercom one day.

"William Bligh on line 1, Sab." The portly professor took his time picking up the connection.

"The answer is still no." He said. "Where's Milo Mindbender?"

"On holiday for the next month." Said the VIHA CEO. "You know your hospital privileges will end a week from now."

"I read Milo's letter." Sababa said. "What do you want?"

"The Board and I are wondering if you might have some time toward the end of the week for a meeting to discuss this."

"There's nothing to discuss."

"How about Friday afternoon at 4 p.m. in the Boardroom?" Bligh asked.

"It will be a short meeting." Sababa said. "One more thing."

"What's that?"

"The curious incident of worse patient outcomes since you became the health authority CEO."

"As far as I am aware, there have been no worse patient outcomes since I became CEO."

"That's the curious incident."

Men become mortal the night their fathers die. Sababa's father died in a sterile room on the seventh floor of a Toronto hospital, far from the Northwestern Ontario hometown he loved. He had served as its most respected mayor for two decades. As the days passed after his father passed, it forced Sababa to acknowledge that he was alone in a godless, uninhabited, hostile and meaningless universe. Still, he had to laugh.

On his way home, he laughed at seeing Miles Davis back at work as the airport custodian after the successful angioplasty and stent placement he had arranged for him in Victoria. Marijuana had become legal so Miles didn't have to sneak into the airport washroom to relieve his sickle-cell disease discomfort with a spliff. But he have to go outside.

Sababa laughed with Charles Donovan, the 'Lost Boy' South Sudanese airport screening officer as they met by chance in the line at the coffee shop. Charles would order his usual spiced *guhwah* special, and Sababa would comment about the weight he had gained back since his treatment for kala-azar. He laughed with Isadora Belli, the Ethiopian barista, behind the counter at the end of the airport coffee line, now cured of her latent cystoisospora infection, as she handed over his espresso doppio doppio liquid rocket fuel.

Back in his Manzanita Medical office, he laughed with Jaroslav Flegr, the big cat trophy hunting guide, now cleansed of the toxoplasmosis he got by eating cougar meat. He laughed with Justin Beaver, the East Beach Trail hiker who got giardiasis from drinking unfiltered water on Haida Gwaii. When Sababa asked him about the worst part of his ordeal, Justin told him of the unyielding torture of the taste of rotten eggs.

Sababa laughed with social justice warrior Sunshine Cruz, recovered from her botfly and acute Chagas disease. She would never return to Costa Rica and had taken to always sleeping under a mosquito net, even in places with no mosquitoes.

He laughed with Ernest Tyzzer, who, after recovering from his cryptosporidium infection, sold his emus at a loss and entered the potentially lucrative market of cannabis cultivation. Sababa turned down his offer of free samples, in exchange for a single Cuban Montecristo No. 2. He laughed with bank manager David Bruce, who had survived both his East African trypanosomiasis and his suramin treatment, and was planning another safari—to look at polar bears in the Canadian Arctic. His laugh faltered with Michel Vieuchange, the Air Canada flight attendant with amebiasis, whose HIV serology had returned positive.

But he laughed with his sister-in-law Tiki Lane, after the eradication of all four forms of malarial infection, and promised to visit her, as she left Harbour City on the first of her many flights to New Zealand.

On his way home, he laughed at the naked bungee jumper perched over a trestle bridge, 150 feet above the river near the airport.

'When you realize how perfect everything is
you will tilt your head back and laugh at the sky.'
Buddha

11. The Case of the Deadly Tree

'But now I've got the sun
To clear away the clouds

> So why look back
> When there's a stunning, blazing, so amazing
> Now.'
>
> Dixie Chicks, *Now*

No one knows who named that bay on the eastern edge of Vancouver Island, perched along the Salish Sea. A popular and persistent local theory holds that it was Captain George Vancouver in 1792, but his charts show that he never sailed along the west side of the Strait, so that's not right. Some say it was the name of another master and commander who resided in the vicinity but there had been no sea captains living there when it was christened. The most likely explanation is that the appellation had come off the British Admiralty charts of the 1860s, taken from surveys by Royal Navy officer G.H. Richards. But if Richards knew where the designation came from, he did not record the information.

There is another problem with the name. It's also a colloquial term for the buttocks, in North America and, even worse, the vulva, in Britain and most other parts of the English-speaking world. Still, there is no more charming place in Baynes Sound (and some would claim much farther) than Fanny Bay.

A small coastal hamlet of a few hundred human souls and even more Stellar sea lions, the government wharf is decked out with picturesque oyster boats, and the local community hall plays host to aerobics with Suzanne, pickleball, powerhouse fitness, and the Fat Oyster Reading Series. And there's the important clue, for Fanny Bay is world-renowned for its fine oysters.

These are not the *Ostrea lurida* original native Olympia oysters that used to grace the rocky shoreline of the Sound and play a significant cultural and economic role in the emerging city of Victoria.

Four years before their discovery in 1866, the founder of the municipality's Daily British Colonist wrote the newspaper's first editorial, decrying the domination of the local shellfish supply by Native women.

'OYSTER TRADE —Need any be idle when the very squaws are making four and five dollars a day, in bringing in oysters from Victoria Arm, Sooke or Cowichan and peddling them around town? They monopolize the whole trade; not a white nor civilized man enters the field against them. This need not be so – ought not to be so. There is money to be made at it...'

British Colonist, October 21, 1862

367

A few words about the editor—Amor de Cosmos was born William Alexander Smith in Windsor, Nova Scotia on August 20, 1825, but later changed his name in the California gold fields to reflect his 'love of order, beauty, the world, and the universe.' In 1863, he entered politics as a liberal reformer, arguing for the union of Vancouver Island and British Columbia, and the merged colony's entry into Confederation. In the realization of these two goals and his role as the Liberal Member of Parliament for Victoria City and the second Premier of the province, he earned the reputation as British Columbia's Father of Confederation. But Amor de Cosmos had a fierce temper and was prone to public outbursts of tears and fistfights. He had unusual phobias—including fear of electricity. In 1895, they declared him insane.

Enter another colourful Island character, John Hart who with his partner Captain Moses Philips of the liquor smuggling schooner *Explorer*, established the first store in Comox and became the problematic source of alcohol trading to Natives. In November 1865, the settlers described his establishment as 'productive of great evil'. But in 1866, John Hart arrived in Victoria with twenty sacks of oysters, from a recent bountiful discovery in Baynes Sound. The news sparked a frenzy of oyster saloon openings, including Levy's, which boasted a sawdust floor, a parrot and cockatoo for added colour, and world-class cuisine using imported products from around the globe, like turtle meat from Tahiti.

GREAT Big Fellows! THE UNDERSIGNED BEG TO ANNOUNCE to their customers and the public at large that they have now on hand, and will continue to receive a supply of THOSE SPLENDID COMOX OYSTERS! N.B.-- Oyster suppers sent to any part of the city without extra charge. Open at all hours of the day and night. Mind the address—ARCADE SALOON, Government Street, adjoining the New England Bakery. H. E. & J. Levy

British Colonist Newspaper, January 23, 1867

But the gold rush culture brought over-exploitation, habitat alteration, pollution, and near extermination of the only oyster species in British Columbia. The seemingly endless supply from Baynes Sound was in serious decline by 1889.

In 1947, Joseph McLellan, a pioneer in shellfish aquaculture, imported his first batch of oyster seed, inadvertently including Manila clam spawn, from Japan to Fanny Bay. These *Magallana gigas* Miyagi oysters were not as shy or reclusive as their native cousins. The genus Magallana was named for the Portuguese explorer Ferdinand Magellan and its specific epithet gígās was from the Greek for 'giant.' Eating one raw is like French kissing a mermaid. These delicious big, meaty, mineral monsters now account for 98% of the world's cultured oyster production and are farmed in countries all over the world. McLellan's descendants still own and operate the fourth-generation oyster and clam farm in Fanny Bay. Mac's Oysters Ltd. processes more than a third of British Columbia's farmed oysters and clams. Ambrose Bierce defined an oyster as a slimy, gobby shellfish which civilization gives men the hardihood to eat without removing its entrails, but during happy hour at the local pub, they go for a buck a shuck.

Which brings us to the Fanny Bay Inn, a beautiful two-story American Craftsman pothouse still shimmering in its 1938 daguerreotype on a scenic estuary overlooking Baynes Sound. The FBI facade is clad in two-toned blue tinted cedar shingles and double-hung white-framed windows, covered by several clay-tiled low-pitched hipped roofs with deep eaves and exposed rafters and attached to an exterior brick chimney. Tapered river rock columns support the main roof overhanging extension of the front entrance, above which the white sign with black Old English lettering is cantilevered out by silver painted fleur-de-lis wrought scrollwork. *Fanny Bay INN*.

This FBI may be a pothouse but its recent history links it to an entirely different pothouse and another FBI, through a whodunit of global proportions.

After midnight on Nov. 4, 1998, a dump truck backed up onto the government wharf just out of earshot of the Fanny Bay Inn. The five men that got out were met by two more from the *MV Ansare II*, a 60-foot fibreglass fish boat piloted by a 52-year-old captain, Doug Davidson. The men began hauling 480 bales, each twenty-kg bag containing twenty one-kilogram bricks wrapped in Polish-labelled cookie and 'Cappuccino Italiano' foil wrappers, from the boat to the bay of the dump truck. At 2:10 a.m., halfway through their unloading and transfer, a detachment of RCMP swooped in on the operation and seized the ten metric tonnes of Pakistani hashish, so fast that one of smugglers, Rick Farrington of Harbour City, jumped into the freezing waters of Fanny Bay. The first man gets the oyster; the second man gets the shell.

Five hours later, in international waters off the northern tip of Vancouver Island, 540 nautical miles west-northwest of Port Hardy, the US Coast Guard, followed by twenty-five members of the RCMP emergency response team and two dogs on the

Canadian Forces vessel HMCS Huron, boarded a recommissioned scallop dragger, the *MV Blue Dawn*, seized another 2.35 tonnes of hashish, and arrested two more men. Authorities seized a total of twelve tonnes of hash worth an estimated $100 million on board the two ships. They arrested and charged fourteen people. It was the biggest hashish bust in British Columbia history.

The story of the Fanny Bay raid began 16 months earlier, in the spring of 1997, when the RCMP Vancouver drug squad received a tip from their coastal watch program that a suspicious group from B.C. was in Yarmouth, Nova Scotia, pouring money into an aging, 30-metre scallop dragger. The *Blue Dawn*'s massive new fuel tanks and a general overhaul didn't make any financial sense. The tip led to a massive investigation called 'Project EProfit,' involving 150 officers, including manpower from the Vancouver Island detachment and the Greater Vancouver Drug Section of the RCMP, Canada and US Customs, the Canadian Armed Forces, Aurora aircraft stationed at CFB Comox and Greenwood, Nova Scotia, US Customs, the US Coast Guard, the US Drug Enforcement Agency, the Internal Revenue Service, law-enforcement agencies in Europe and the Middle East, and Sri Lanka's Police Narcotic Bureau. The voyage of the retrofitted *Blue Dawn* was doomed from the start.

In December 1997, when the ship arrived in Port Souda, Chania, on the Greek island of Crete, the Hellenistic Coast Guard of Greece notified the Mounties and secretly attached a satellite-tracking device high on the *Blue Dawn*'s main mast.

Investigators followed the mother ship as it left Crete and sailed through the Suez Canal, across the Indian Ocean to Sri Lanka and Phuket, Thailand, where the crew loaded bales of hashish from Pakistan onboard. The floating warehouse was becalmed near Indonesia, before it headed through the Strait of Malacca past Singapore, and crossed the South China Sea and into the North Pacific on its way to the West Coast of Vancouver Island.

On October 26, 1998, a Canadian Armed Forces CP-140 Aurora from 407 Squadron in Comox detected *Blue Dawn*'s tracking device. Five aircraft flew 24 missions, providing continuous surveillance in 300 hours of flying time (and the 415 Squadron at Greenwood, N.S. which flew 100 hours). They noted its meeting with a vessel first dubbed 'Blue Buddy,' and then identified as the *Ansare II*, which a separate RCMP Caravan surveillance plane followed around the northern tip of Vancouver Island, south through Johnstone Strait and into Fanny Bay.

By now, despite an extraordinary ban on overtime for the Mounties imposed at the beginning of October, the dedicated officers continued to work for free for an average of five weeks—between 200 and 250 hours each—of unpaid labour, some away from home and families for over two weeks at a stretch.

After police seized the vessels and their cargoes, they executed search warrants on residences, hotel rooms, vehicles, work places, other vessels, a rented cabin in Bowser, and a leased warehouse in Parksville.

The five men caught unloading the hashish were each sentenced in Harbour City to three years in prison, except for the *Ansare II* captain, Doug Davidson, who got four.

The trial of the nine principal smugglers in Vancouver B.C. provincial court took three years. The case featured 344 exhibits and 103 witnesses. Judge Elizabeth Arnold issued a 256-page ruling. In April 2004, the judge convicted all the conspirators of trafficking in cannabis resin and sentenced them from two to six years in prison. Their two-year appeal was denied. Out on bail, all but one of the convicted smugglers surrendered themselves. The one that didn't was the ringleader who had fled to Mexico after the first trial to escape a five-year incarceration.

Wolfgang Benedict 'Ben' Fitznar had German citizenship—but no Canadian passport—having arrived in Canada from Germany as a child with his parents. He grew up in Maple Bay in Vancouver Island's Cowichan Valley, with one of his co-conspirators, Ken Thomson. Ken thought well of him. *Handy guy and very personable, very talkative. He could charm a snake.*

Fitznar was employed by Ken as a tugboat captain in Bella Coola, before buying the boat he skippered, *Ocean Warrior*, and working it for several respectable years on the B.C. coast. He lived in a Tsawwassen condo. He also had a young 'knock-dead gorgeous' concert pianist wife, Grace Quaglio, and a young son with cerebral palsy, Sebastian Max, who he adored.

Ben left Canada for the tropical state of Yucatan, where his daughter from a previous marriage lived. He enjoyed a public profile in the colonial town of Merida as a real-estate consultant. The world was his oyster. Fitznar was on the management team of Flamingo Lakes Golf & Country Club Resort, as director of the company's Design Centre. They posted his job description next to his photo. *A Canadian national, Ben Fitznar spent 25 years in the marine transportation and hospitality industries in his home country before his entrepreneurial spirit took him to Merida in 2004 to establish a boutique hotel, Villa Merida, in a fine old colonial building.*

Simon Renshaw, the Los Angeles manager of country music's Dixie Chicks, had bought the fine old colonial building.

London's *The Independent* newspaper later named Villa Merida the best boutique hotel in Mexico and one of the top ten such hotels in the world. Fitznar had met Renshaw by fluke, on a beach.

Even as he arrived in Merida, the Mexican government issued a news release on Fitznar's extradition at home in Spanish, even posted a mug-shot photo on its website, in which the smuggler appears to be smiling. Canadian news agencies never picked up on it. Fitznar's name appeared on the Internet, where anyone capable of conducting a Google search could have found him.

Rick Farrington, the Harbour City accomplice who jumped into the freezing waters of Fanny Bay to escape the RCMP back in 1998, was bitter.

"They could have sent Dog the Bounty Hunter down there. Nobody understood it. They worked so hard to prosecute us and put their case together—years and millions of dollars—and short of an airline ticket they could have gone and got him."

Finally, on May 26, 2009, as he was speaking about real-estate development opportunities in the Mayan jungle town of Tulum, the Mexican Federales arrested Ben and extradited him to Canada. The parole board agreed to release him in January 2011, just in time for his deportation to Germany.

If the local expansion of illicit B.C. bud and hashish since Ben's adventure hadn't put an end to such foreign smuggling schemes, the Canadian legalization of cannabis did.

Ben should have read the Globe and Mail review. *Go to Fanny Bay for the oysters, but skip the rest.*

> 'But I'm taking the long way... Taking the long way around'.
> Dixie Chicks, *The Long Way Around*

'Out of damp and gloomy days, out of solitude, out of loveless words directed at us, conclusions grow up in us like fungus: one morning they are there, we know not how, and they gaze upon us, morose and gray. Woe to the thinker who is not the gardener but only the soil of the plants that grow in him.'

Friedrich Nietzsche

South of Fanny Bay, on the old Island Highway further down towards Harbour City, she passed through Bowser, Qualicum Bay, and the Mount Arrowsmith Pipe Band playing at the

Parksville Beach Festival sand castle competition, before turning off into the provincial park.

Rathtrevor Beach was sacred ground for dog walkers in the area. Georgia Strait parked her van among other vehicles she recognized. Rusty was a two-year-old Anatolian shepherd, eager to meet his many dog friends already on the park trails. Georgia had only enough time to hook him on his leash and lock her van doors before Rusty yanked her towards the majestic mature Douglas firs of the old growth rainforest. Together they walked the serenity of a three-kilometre wooded upland park trail and then sat and watched the tide rolling in over the rocks and shells and sand dollars and tidal pools of the wide sun-baked sandy beach. Georgia and Rusty came here every day. There was nothing more peaceful in the world than sitting together in the summer light, saying nothing.

But on this day, Rusty was anxious to return to the vehicle. He kept sniffing and licking Georgia's face and pulling on his lead. Georgia had trouble keeping up on the return leg of the hike. She was more short of breath than normal, and had recently become lethargic and had experienced headaches, sinus congestion, sore muscles, night sweats, and a cough. By the time they made it back to the van, Georgia was feeling dizzy, but she unhooked Rusty into his favourite place, riding shotgun in the passenger seat. Georgia braced herself against the steering wheel to regain her breath and focus and reached over to turn on the radio.

Morning, Palefaces... This is CNDN Coast Salish radio, 101.3 FM on your Home and Native Band. I'm your host, BC Bud... Funny how the Arizona Navaho language they were forbidden to speak was the same one that saved their nation...

Georgia held her head in her hands. It felt like it would explode.

All plants are our brothers and sisters... They talk to us and if we listen, we can hear them... And every animal knows more than you do.

Rusty put a big front paw on Georgia's right shoulder and began to whine.

You might be from Harbour City if you know the provincial flower is mildew... You might be from Parksville if you're newly wed or nearly dead...

The last thing she remembered was Rusty's barking before her world swirled into blackness.

Indians don't knock. It's rude... They honk the horn.

Rusty placed both his front paws on the horn and pushed down.

'Valley of the Fevers
Our time is drawing near
To join the ghost of Cherokees and
Walk the Trail of Tears.'
The Apache Relay, *Valley Of The Fevers*

It would have definitely got him fired if he had ever done it a second time. The day before they extradited Ben Fitznar from Mexico and Georgia Strait collapsed in Rathtrevor Park, Eleazar Sababa had driven his dimpled and dented white Honda through the wide ER doors of Harbour City Regional Hospital. He got out and tossed his keys to the uniformed guard.
"Jerry, call Security." He said. "Some bastard is in my parking space again." Jerry caught the keys and nodded.
"I'll get these back to you, Doc."
She picked him up along his trajectory toward Code Brew.
"I understand you have no regard for Petronilla de Meath." Sara had a head of steam.
"True." Sababa acknowledged.
"That you fight Big Nurse and the other administrators to get what you want."
"Also true."
"And that you hijacked a helicopter from under the feet of the province's first high-profile female Minister of Health."
"Touchdown."
"So they might say that you're a misogynist." Sara was blunt.
"Nah." Sababa said. "I'm a misanthrope, not a misogynist. I hate everybody."
"Good to know." Sara said.
"Although I believe in the existence of satanic witchcraft." He admitted. "What have you got?"
"Referral from Myles." They took the hallway to the ER and to Dr. Capitaine.
"How are you, Myles?" Sababa asked.
"Living the dream." He said. "Wishing for more. Like most people."

374

"If all wishes were gratified, many dreams would be destroyed." When Sababa asked him about the case behind the curtain, Myles pulled it back.

"Charles E. Smith." He began. "66-year-old snowbird. Drives to Arizona every winter to get away from us."

"Oh?" Sababa asked.

"Maricopa County." Charles said. "I have a little dust pad near Vulture City."

"What do you do for fun?"

"I drive over to the greyhound park in Apache Junction to see the races." He said. "The state government plans to shut it down this year."

"Mr. Smith presents with a four-week history of cough, shortness of breath, chest pain, weight loss, fever, and night sweats." Myles continued. "Some walk-in closet doc in Phoenix gave him a prescription for azithromycin. Examination today was remarkable for a temperature of 38.3 °C and decreased breath sounds in the left lower lung field. White blood cell count is high with a normal differential. Chest radiograph and CT showed airspace consolidation and pockets of fluid collection in his left lower lobe." Myles brought up the images on the consultants' computer. "He appears to have a complicated pleural effusion from community-acquired bacterial pneumonia."

"What kind of community might that be, Myles?" Sababa asked. "The man lives on a patch of dirt in the middle of nowhere. His only neighbours are vultures." He turned to Charles.

"You ever had desert rheumatism?"

"Every winter." Charles admitted. "I get fevers and joint pains, and these." The snowbird pulled up the cuffs of his trousers to reveal several red nodules under the skin over the shins. Sababa looked at Myles. Myles didn't look back. Charles winced when Sara pushed on one of his bumps.

"Erythema nodosum." She said.

"Unless you own a scratching cat, Charles, I'd say the likelihood is that you have a coccidioidal empyema."

"Wha?"

"You have what the locals down there call Valley Fever." Sababa said. "From the inhalation of dimorphic saprophytic Coccidioides posadasii arthroconidia. It required rain to get it started. The fungus has formed a closed space infection between your lung and your chest wall."

"Is that good or bad?" Charles asked.

"Not good." Sababa said. "But fixable."

"How?"

"I need to admit you to hospital." Sababa left for a moment to answer his pager, but he was back in a minute. "I need to do a pleural biopsy and place a chest tube to drain what we can, although I suspect you may need a little surgery in Victoria to break down all the pockets of infection. We'll send more bloodwork and the fluid we drain and biopsy material for Grocott's methenamine silver staining, culture, and chemical analysis. You'll get started on daily infusions of liposomal amphotericin B until your transfer but after the surgical procedure in Victoria you may get away with oral azoles or no more antifungal agents at all."

"Life is too damned short." Charles said. "I should have spent more time at the racetrack when I had the chance."

"Even those 'greyhounds in the slips, straining upon the start' are infected with Valley fever." Sababa said. "Coughing more than barking at the mechanical rabbit they were chasing." He handed a piece of paper to Sara, scrawled with two names. *Junmai Daiginjo... Clyde Chestnut Barrow.*

"But wait. There's more." Sababa said. "Welcome back to the sharp end of the rope, Sara. Call me from Floor 5 when you're ready. I'll finish up here."

As he sat down to write out his consultation, Sababa selected The Apache Relay tune from his music library on a secret drive hidden deep inside the hospital computer network.

'To those Joplin Missouri born and raised
Pickin up the pieces blown away
Our hearts are with you...'
Mark Chapman Band, *Where Would You Go?*

"Huppy Ters-day, Sara." Sophia was in her usual ebullient mood. "How is my payborit grud-wait ductor?"

"Fine Sophia." Sara handed her Sababa's paper with the names of his two referrals.

"Mister Daiginjo is berry Japanese." She said. "He doesn't eat any proot or bee gees. Only raw pish wid samurais, por brick-pus, lunts and deen-ner. Mister Barrow is a pat man. His jabetis is prum eating too much cundy and choco-lates. He seems to hab lost his boys obernight. Dey are bote still slipping uk-toowally, but palo me." Sophia knocked before entering Junmai Daiginjo's private room, apologized for waking him and introduced him to Sara before retreating to the nursing station. The young resident spent an hour with him before Sababa caught up with her.

"Still on the first patient?" He asked.

"I'm finished here and was about to see Mr. Barrow." She said.

"Why do we have to go so hastily?"

"Oh, I dunno." Sababa said. "A severed femoral artery empties faster than you can believe—47 fragile organs, 200 miles of delicate blood vessels, 12 million complex chemical reactions to correctly happen every second. Your simple job is to keep it all from bursting, breaking, splitting, spurting or corroding. Every cell in the human body regenerates every seven years, but your patients can't wait that long. You need to work swiftly if your planet is important to you. One patient every four minutes. Time flies. Time waits for no one. Time doesn't heal all wounds. All of us want more time. Time to stand up. Time to grow up. Time to let go. Time. There is too little time."

"Wow." She said.

"In strategy, there are various timing considerations. From the outset, you must know the applicable timing and the inapplicable timing, and from among the large and small things and the fast and slow timings find the relevant timing, first seeing the distance timing and the background timing. This is the main thing in strategy. Whatever the Way, the master of strategy does not appear fast... Of course, slowness is bad. Skillful people never get out of time, are always deliberate, and never appear busy."

"Anything else, Miyamoto Musashi-san?"

"Oh, yeah." Sababa said. "No dog can piss on a moving car. Tell me about Junmai Daiginjo."

"47-year-old artisanal saké maker from Granville Island." She began. "Admitted yesterday by Dr. Tarmac with an intermittent fever and chest burning sensation and persistent cough with scanty expectoration and progressive breathlessness for the last year. Never smoked. No diurnal or seasonal variation of his cough or shortness of breath. No personal or family history of asthma, allergy or dermatitis, or tuberculosis. Spirometry had revealed an obstructive ventilatory defect with partial reversibility to bronchodilator. He was deemed to have difficult-to-treat asthma, according to the four-step Global Initiative for Asthma guidelines, after still unacceptable control with high dose inhaled corticosteroids, long-acting beta2-agonists, montelukast, and oral sustained-release theophylline. He came in last night short of breath."

377

"Exam?"

"Pale." Sara said. "Fast pulse and breathing rate. Barrel-shaped chest with diminished breath sounds and bilateral crackles with occasional wheezing." Sababa unwrapped his Littman Master Cardiology black and brass stethoscope from around his neck.

"Daiginjo-san, anata no mune ni mimi o katamukete mo īdesu ka?" The stocky savant asked to listen to his patient's chest.

"Hai." Junmai consented.

"He speaks English." Sara said.

"I know." Sababa said. "I need the practice."

"Shizuka ni suikonde kudasai." Sababa asked him to breathe in and out while he listened for subtleties.

"Labwork?"

"Elevated white blood cell count." Sara said. "With lots of pink eosinophils. Worms, wheezes and weird diseases, as you would say."

"Not all that wheezes is asthma." Sababa said.

"He also has an elevated serum IgE level." She watched Sababa's right eyebrow ascend into a cloud of black curls. They both left Junmai's room to look at his imaging studies on a hallway monitor.

"Chest x-ray shows collapse of the upper lobe of his right lung." Sara said.

"And tramline shadowing, finger-in-glove opacities and 'toothpaste shadows.'" Sababa added.

"Of course." Sara said. "High-resolution CT scan of his chest reveals a bilateral reticulonodular pattern with patchy consolidation and dilated bronchi." They returned to Junmai's room.

"Daiginjo-san, anata no kokyū wa itsu kaizen sa remasu ka?" Sababa asked Junmai when his breathing got better.

"Watashi ga sake o tsukutte inai toki wa yoku narimasu." *When I'm not making saké.*

Sababa let out a long whistle.

"ABPA." He said.

"Which is?"

"Allergic bronchopulmonary aspergillosis." Sababa said.

"But where would he come in contact with Aspergillis fumigatus?" She asked.

"Not fumigatus." Sababa said. "Aspergillis oryzae."

"Aspergillis oryzae?" Sara looked puzzled. "What's that?"

"Louis Pasteur once said that 'Since the most ancient times, all men, and particularly those who endeavoured in the practice of

378

medicine, have brought closer together two natural phenomena of capital importance: illness or fever and fermentation.'"

"And?"

"And if you knew more about fermentation, you would know that, while the common yeast species known as Saccharomyces cerevisiae can ferment beer and wine, rice for saké does not contain the amylase necessary for converting starch to sugar. It requires parallel fermentation. To hydrolyze the nutrients of the rice and support the growth of the yeast requires the addition of another fungus, as a source of the requisite amylases, glucoamylases, and proteases."

"And that other fungus is..."

"Aspergillus oryzae." Sababa said. "We also see this allergic response in bean paste brewers making miso and shoyu soy sauce. Same fungus."

"Can you prove this?" Junmai asked.

"There are eight major and three minor Rosenberg-Patterson criteria for the diagnosis of ABPA." Sababa said. "You need six to qualify."

"How many do I have?"

"Right now, five." Sababa said. "But we'll get more with intradermal skin testing, looking for specific Aspergillus antibodies in your serum, and with Ed Hyde."

"Who's he?" Junmai asked.

"He's the respirologist who will perform a fiberoptic bronchoscopy and bronchoalveolar lavage to dislodge and culture the mucus plugging up your breathing tubes." Sababa said. "We'll also start you on an oral antifungal agent called itraconazole for four months, and this will allow us to taper off your corticosteroid within six weeks."

"Osoreirimasu." Junmai thanked Sababa with awe. The portly professor bowed in return, not as deep.

"Let's go see our other patient." Sara said. "I have read his chart."

"Tell me about it on the way to his room." Sababa said.

"Clyde Chestnut Barrow." She said. "43-year-old diabetic tourist visiting the island from Joplin, Missouri. Admitted by Dr. Bloom three days ago for a two-week history of progressive headache, nasal obstruction, and black discharge, right-sided hearing impairment, facial numbness, and bulging and blindness of his right eye. No previous rhinosinusitis, dental problems, or local surgeries. Early this morning, he developed left-sided complete facial nerve paralysis in all branches. That's when Dr. Bloom called in the referral."

"Not good." Sababa said.

"I know." Sara pulled up Clyde's CT scans on a hallway monitor.

"Not good." Sababa said.

"I know." She agreed.

"Marked bulging of his right eyeball, thickening of the extraocular muscles, opacification of right maxillary, ethmoid and sphenoid sinuses, bilateral opacification of mastoid air cells and middle ear spaces, and cystic lesions in his neck."

"Let's go see him." Sababa said.

"Good morning, Mr. Barrow." Sara began. "This is Doctor Sababa. He's an excellent magician." Clyde Barrow could only manage a garbled whisper.

"I'm from Missouri, Ma'am." He said. "Home of Budweiser, Kansas City barbecue, and show me. If I was a younger man, I'd be on you like a hobo on a ham sandwich. What's the difference between a good magician and a bad one?"

"A bad magician never gets the good props." Sababa said.

"What's going on with me?" Clyde asked.

"Were you affected by that big tornado two months ago that hit Joplin?" Sababa asked. "The Enhanced Fujita scale 5-rated multiple-vortex monster that killed 158 people, injured 1,150 more, and caused $2.8 billion worth of damage."

"Affected? Hell, I was in the middle of it." Clyde said. "On that Sunday in May, I lost my trailer, most of my neighbours, and any faith I had in FEMA. It was a mile wide. I never used to worry about the tornados back home. Hell, the mortgage on my fifth wheel was so heavy I thought nothing could budge it. Luckily, the insurance paid out enough for me to buy a new one and come up here. Why do you ask?"

"The second principle of magic states' that things which have once been in contact with each other continue to act on each other at a distance after the physical contact has been severed."

"Meaning?"

"There were 18 cases of what you have after the tornado hit." Sababa said. "Some think there was a connection."

"What do I have?" Clyde asked.

"We used to call it mucormycosis." Sababa said. "But we've gussied it up. It's now known as rhino-orbital-cerebral zygomycosis."

"Don't know any more about that than a dead horse knows about Sunday." Clyde said. "But it sounds uglier than three pounds of shit in a two-pound sack."

"Caused by a fungus called Rhizopus oryzae." Sababa said. "If it was Aspergillus instead of Rhizopus, you could have made saké instead of woodpile splinters."

380

"Is it going to kill me?" Clyde asked, with no small interest.

"Not if we work the right magic." Sababa said. "There is a safe spot within every tornado. My job is to find it. Sara here is going right now to page our ENT surgeon, Dr. Theodor Billroth. He will need to perform a biopsy, incise and drain your abscesses, and debride other affected facial anatomy today. We'll start you on an intravenous antifungal agent, amphotericin B, right now. You may need a hyperbaric chamber."

"I don't have any medical coverage." He whispered.

"Doesn't matter." Sababa said. "We'll teach this tornado a thing or two about whirling, just for the pure wine of love and freedom. Don't tell your friends."

"Well, butter my butt and call me a biscuit." Clyde croaked. "Thanks, Doc. I'm happier than a twister in a trailer park."

"That new fifth wheel of yours has four other wheels, doesn't it?" Sababa asked.

"Yep."

"So it shouldn't be too difficult for you to move to a place that isn't smack dab in the middle of tornado alley."

"That's why I'm here, Doc." Clyde said. "Lord willin' and the crick don't rise."

'I've rolled and I've tumbled through the roses and the thorns
And I couldn't see the sign that warned me
I'm heading for the light.'
Traveling Wilburys, *Heading For The Light*

"It's fungus week, Boss."

"Bureaucracy is a fungus that contaminates everything." Sababa said on entering his office. "Hospital administrators are like Old Testament gods—lots of rules and no Mercy. And today is Judgement Day." He handed Sara the first referral chart of the afternoon clinic. She called into the full waiting room.

"Patrick Keeling, please." A well-dressed muscular middle-aged man got up from his chair and followed her into the residents' examining room. Sababa picked up the second folder.

"Too-loud MacLeod?" He said. An elderly man dressed in a semiformal Highland plain cuff charcoal Crail jacket, a grey five-button waistcoat over a turndown collared white shirt, red tie, a tartan kilt, dark green hose, and black sporran and brogues jumped up out of his seat and shook Sababa's hand like he was pumping water.

"Your last name is MacLeod but today you're wearing the honorary tartan of Sherlock Holmes." Sababa observed.

"To see if you would notice." Too-loud said. "You picked up on the lighter blue with the brown edging of the Reichenbach Falls in Switzerland, and the gold strip to show that Holmes was one of London's leading detectives. Thank you for seeing me so quickly."

"You were referred by your GP, Dr. Nicholas Rivera." Sababa said. "But it was the second request from our local respirologist, Dr. Ed Hyde, that got you here faster. How can I help?"

"I have the toxic black mould, Doctor."

"I'm sorry?"

"I am infected with Stachybotrys chartarum, from the mouldy carpet in my flat." Too-loud took a handkerchief from the sleeve of his jacket. "I've complained to my landlord, but he thinks I'm lying or crazy." He coughed several times into the handkerchief and showed Sababa the result of his efforts. It was black.

"Melanoptysis." Sababa said. Black sputum production. Supposed to be rare, but you're the second case I've seen today.

"It's the black mould, isn't it?" Too-loud insisted.

"After a fashion." Sababa poured over his patient's labwork. "What did Dr. Hyde say?"

"He did some lung function tests, CT scan of my chest, and a bronchoscopy." Too-loud scowled. "Said I had delusional infestation. I told him I wanted to see you."

"Why are you dressed like a Highlander?" Sababa asked.

"I play the Great Highland bagpipe in a pipe band." He said.

"How long have you been playing?"

"Since I was a wee bairn." He said. "Although I've cut way back. When I play in the Mount Arrowsmith Pipe Band at the Parksville Beach Festival sand castle competition, we wear the tartan of Cameron of Erracht. I just finished playing a solo at the noontime cannon firing ceremony at the old Hudson's Bay fort here in Harbour City, before coming to your office."

"When did your breathing problems begin?" Sababa asked.

"I used to have a lovely African blackwood instrument, but I finally wore it out about a year ago." He said. "My trouble began when I bought a new set of synthetic Polypenco pipes last spring. They don't need as frequent cleaning."

"Hmmm... Polyoxymethylene." Sababa said. "What happens when you're not playing the bagpipes?"

"Well, that's the strange bit, isn't it?" Too-loud coughed into his handkerchief. "I seem to get better. Took four months off in the fall and my breathing was normal again."

"Your investigations are not unblemished." Sababa said. "Lung function testing showed some mixed obstruction and restriction and a decreased diffusing capacity. Your CT scan showed centrilobular nodules, ground-glass opacities, mild fibrosis, and a few floppy airways in your lower lobes. Your bronchoscopy was unremarkable but Dr. Hyde didn't do a lavage, which in your case would have been a good idea."

"Blaigeard." Too-loud blurted.

"Ed's not a bastard, but he could be of questionable lineage." Sababa said.

"So what have I've got, Doctor Sababa?"

"Saxophone lung."

"I don't play a saxophone."

"The fungus that lives in your bagpipe doesn't care." Sababa said. "You play a woodwind, even though it sounds like you're strangling a goose. It's causing a form of what we refer to as hypersensitivity pneumonitis."

"Does this fungus have a name?" He asked.

"It could be any number or combination of mould species." Sababa said. "Phoma or Rhodoturola or Paecilomyces or Fusarium or Penicillium or Trichosporon or Ulocladium or Cladosporium, or pink yeast, but you are definitely afflicted with one other specific fungus."

"Which is?"

"The clue is the colour of your sputum." Sababa said. Exophiala is a genus of anamorphic fungi in the family Herpotrichiellaceae. There are 28 species, but the culprit here is a dematiaceous mould called Exophiala dermatitidis."

"Can you prove it?" Too-loud asked.

"I'll need you to take your bagpipes down to the hospital lab." Sababa pressed on one of his intercom buttons. "Mercy, can you get me Juan Leyblanca, please."

"On it." She pressed him back a minute later. "Line two."

"Hola amigo mio." Sababa said.

"¿What do ju want, Cabrón?" It was Juan.

"I'm sending you some bagpipes." Sababa said. "I need you to KOH mount and culture them, and the sputum of the man that's bringing them."

"¿What are ju looking for?"

"Exophiala dermatitidis." He said. "And I'll need serum precipitins."

"From the bagpipes?"

"No, Pendejo, from the bagpiper."

"I call ju." There came the sound of Latin laughter. *Click.*

"How often and how do you clean your instrument?" Too-loud squirmed in his chair.

"I brush clean them twice a year." He said.

"So after you take your pipes to Dr. Leyblanca, take them home and clean them every week with isopropyl alcohol. Don't use chlorine bleach or anything else or you'll damage the synthetic material they're made from. A bheil thu a 'tuigsinn?" *Do you understand.*

"Gu tur." Too-loud said. *Absolutely.*

"Tell Mercy to make an appointment for you in three weeks on your way out." Goodtimes shook Sababa's hand like he was pumping water. His departure collected Sara on her way into Sababa's sanctum.

"What do you have for me, Gold Miss?" Sababa asked.

"Patrick Keeling." She said. "44-year-old veterinarian referred by both Dr. James Ruben Andrews and our own faceless oculist guru, Dr. T.J. Eckleburg."

"Excellent." Sababa said. "Not only black sputum day but doubleheader referral day."

"He doesn't have black sputum." Sara said. "He has a painful red left eye."

"Why does T.J. want me to see him?"

"Ten days ago, Dr. Eckleburg did a slit-lamp exam which showed some kind of coarse discrete punctate stuck-on epithelial lesions. The gram stain and Calcofluor White stain showed a unicellular fungus. He started Mr. Keeling on a topical antifungal, 0.3% fluconazole eye drops."

"And?"

"Yesterday, he saw Dr. Eckleburg again." Sara said. "His left eye was even worse. Visual acuity had fallen, conjunctivae were more congested, there was a marked increase in the number of epithelial lesions, and he now has these fungi in the anterior stroma."

"What's the most important question?" Sababa asked.

"Dunno."

"The most important question is 'What's the question?'" He said. "And what is the most important thing?"

"What we do with the most important question?" Sara ventured.

"The most important thing is to keep the most important thing the most important thing." Sababa said. "So I ask again, what's the question?"

"Why is he worse?"

384

"Why is he worse?" Sababa said. "To answer that, you need to know what you got and what you don't got. What you got?"

"A veterinarian with a fungal eye infection?"

"And where did he get that fungal eye infection?"

"Dunno."

"Let's go see." Sababa said. Sara introduced her mentor to the vet.

"This is Doctor Sababa." She said. "When life hands him lemons, he squirts them in peoples eyes." They both watched Patrick Keeling wince.

"How did you get this microsporidia infection, Patrick?" Sababa asked.

"Is that what it's called?" He asked.

"Microsporidiosis." Sababa said. "You have microsporidial keratoconjunctivitis."

"From vaccinating a flock of sheep." He said.

"Did Dr. Eckleburg tell you to stop vaccinating them?" Patrick nodded sheepishly. Sababa turned to Sara.

"What you don't got?" He asked.

"The answer to whether he stopped vaccinating the sheep." Sara said. Sababa turned back to Patrick.

"Did you stop vaccinating the sheep?" Patrick shook his head.

"A sheep in sheep's clothing." Sababa said. "Did you tell Dr. Eckleburg that you stopped vaccinating the sheep?" Patrick nodded.

"Stop vaccinating the sheep." Sababa said. "Continue the antifungals. Mercy will make an appointment for you to follow up with Dr. Eckleburg in two weeks' time."

Sara stared at him after the veterinarian left.

"What?"

"How do you do that?" She asked.

"What?"

"That."

"In science, there is only physics." Sababa said. "Everything else is stamp collecting."

They saw the new referral together. Sara went to fetch the patient and his chart.

"Harry Wheatcroft." She began. "37-year-old Harbour City Regional lab tech referred by Dr. Leyblanca. Wait, he's a pathologist."

"He's a doctor." Sababa said. "He can refer. How are you, Harry?"

"Well, I guess that's why I'm here, Doc."

"I guess it is." Sababa said. "How can we help?" The young man opened his right fist to reveal a bright red index finger.

385

"Ouch." Sara said.

"It's worse than that." Harry rolled up the right sleeve of his shirt.

"Hmmm." Sababa said. "Ascending erythematous nodules and ulcers along the lymphatic vessels. How did you do that, Harry?"

"Got pricked by one of my roses about three weeks ago, Doc."

"How are they looking this year?"

"Fantastic." Harry said.

"You're stealing phlebotomy blood bags to fertilize them with."

"How do you know that?"

"Dr. Leyblanca added Hepatitis C serology to your bloodwork." Sababa said. "It came back positive."

"That means nothing." Harry said.

"Life is the art of drawing sufficient conclusions from insufficient premises." Sababa said. "A growing literature shows that Chronic Hepatitis C infection leads to iron overload. The easiest treatment for iron overload is phlebotomy. You might have got your Hep C a dozen different ways, including needlestick injuries in the lab, but there are no records of your having any such work-related injury, you've been married and monogamous for 20 years, and you have a hobby where you're most likely to poke yourself with thorns. Besides that, Dr. Leyblanca often gives me the leftover phlebotomy bags for Jane's roses, and there have been none available for a while. It's not rocket science, and I used to be a rocket scientist."

"OK, so what's this then?" Harry waved his index finger like an ISIS terrorist.

"That, my dear colleague, is ascending nodular lymphangitis from a dimorphic fungus called Sporothrix schenckii." Sababa said. "Sporotrichosis. Rose-gardeners' disease. It's the main subcutaneous mycosis in Brazil. You're lucky not to have it in your lungs or your brain."

"Is it treatable?" Sababa handed him a prescription.

"Oral potassium iodide." He said. "Make an appointment with Mercy to see me in a few weeks to discuss treatment for your Hepatitis C." He went to shake Harry's hand, but that would not be an option. When Harry had closed Sababa's office door, the portly professor leaned back in his chair.

"Sara, I need you to cover the on-call referrals for a few hours. I have a meeting this afternoon." He said. "I'll be attending as that fungus." *Look like the innocent flower, but be the serpent under it.*

William Bligh, the President and CEO of VIHA, was in a foul
mood. He had driven up all the way from Victoria to chair this
meeting. An army of medical administrators and a conspiracy of
other Suits were already encamped with their local equivalents
in the Harbour City Regional boardroom.

"I thought these Upisland docs had signed onto the new bylaws
and rules and regulations." One mused.

"It's like herding cats." Malcolm said. "But Milo Mindbender
was a son-of-a-bitch, and played Whac-A-Mole until he got
them all."

"All?" Asked yet another Suit.

"All but one." He said. "That's why we're here."

"Who's the outlier?" Asked a third.

"A certain Doctor Sababa." Malcolm said. "He's a bloody
handful. The last MLA had accused him of being a renegade for
telling the media that our funding of his hospital was a 'scam.'"

"Oh, Christ." Said yet a fourth. "We need to squash this one."

"Won't be a problem. It's the little details I love. How to wrap a
piece of smouldering executive fungus in birchbark to carry fire.
These are the things which help a world come alive." Bligh
boomed. "Should be a quick slam dunk."

Dr. Zaias was waiting for Sababa outside the boardroom, pacing
by the time the stocky savant came around the corner.

"Why are you late?" He demanded. "There's a frenzy of sharks
in there."

"Miyamoto Musashi was late for his duel with Sasaki Kojirō,

held on a remote island in the strait separating Honshū and

Kyūshū."

"Who?"

"Miyamoto Musashi was a 17th-century masterless samurai,
philosopher, strategist, and writer considered the Kensei sword-
saint of Japan. He was renowned for his unique double-bladed
fighting and undefeated record in 61 duels. He wrote *The Book of
Five Rings*."

"And the other guy?"

"Sasaki Kojirō, a feudal lord's chief weapons master, renowned as 'The Demon of the Western Provinces.' His favoured wielded weapon during combat was a three-foot blade called the 'laundry-drying pole.' Despite the length and weight of his weapon, Kojirō's strikes were quick and precise. This agility was impressive, but not the source of his lethality. That came from his technique of the *Tsubame Gaeshi* 'Turning Swallow Cut,' which mimicked the motion of a swallow's tail during flight. Striking downward from above, he instantly reversed upward toward the rear, like an eagle climbing after swooping on its prey, the motion could take down a bird in mid-flight, or slice a man in two."

"We don't have time for this, Sab." Dr. Zaias said. "Get to the point."

"On April 13, 1612, according to legend, Musashi arrived unkempt, and over three hours late. His timing was deliberate for three reasons. The first was to unnerve and taunt and goad Kojirō, by showing contempt."

"Congratulations on succeeding in your first goal." Zaias wasn't comfortable with where this was going. "So then what happened?"

"Kojirō shouted insults, but Musashi just smiled. Angered, Kojirō leapt into combat, blinded by rage. The first half of his laundry-drying pole's Turning Swallow Cut manoeuvre came close enough to sever Musashi's traditional samurai *chonmage* haircut but, by then, the second reason that Musashi was late had risen into place. Kojirō was blinded by the sun, ascending into the position that Musashi had waited for."

"You're not going to fiddle with the lights in there?"

"Already programmed." Sababa said. "On the way over to the island, Musashi had used his time to carve a four-foot wooden sword out of one of his boat's spare oars, with his wakizashi. Before Kojirō had finished his swallow cut, this struck Kojirō's skull, smashed his ribs, punctured his lungs, and killed him. The duel had been that short."

"So where's your four-foot wooden sword?" Zaias asked. Sababa tapped his head.

"You have no more time." Zaias looked at his watch. "What is it you intend to do in there?"

"Caedite eos. Novit enim Dominus qui sunt eius." *Kill them. For the Lord knows those that are His own.* He pulled the department head in behind his vortices.

"Wait a minute." Dr. Zaias said. "What was the third reason that your samurai was late?"

"Wait and see." Sababa pushed open the Boardroom door. *When you decide to attack, keep calm and dash in quickly, forestalling the enemy... attack with a feeling of constantly crushing the enemy, from first to last.*

He could smell sulphur.

"Where we are there are daggers in men's smiles." Sababa whispered to Zaias.

He turned on the extra bank of lights that would shine on their faces. *Let your enemies be disarmed by the gentleness of your manner, but at the same time let them feel the steadiness of your resentment.*

At a predetermined time, an announcement from Big Voice resounded from the ceiling.

"Dr. Kevorkian... Dr. Kevorkian... please report to the Board Room." Sababa and Zaias sat across from the Illuminati.

"You had Lana page Kevorkian?" Malcolm asked.

"I thought he should be here." Sababa said.

"Let's begin with introductions." Bligh spread out his arms. "On the other side of the table is the Good Dr. Zaias, Chief of Medicine here at Harbour City, and Doctor Sababa, an Internal Medicine staff consultant, and the subject of today's meeting. On this side of the table are several valued members of our VIHA executive." Bligh swung his arm to his right side. "This is Sanjay Rath, Director, Office of the President & CEO, Ollie Lee Hudson, Vice President Medicine, Quality & Academic Affairs, Mark Savchuk, Vice President Clinical Services Delivery, Robert Garran, Vice President People, Lu You, Vice President Operations and Support, Tim Geithner, Vice President Chief Financial Officer, Legal Services and Risk, Konrad von Finckenstein, Director, Internal Audit Services, Tom Hobbes, Senior Legal Counsel, Vince Bedford, Corporate Director Legal Affairs and Privacy, and Keith Donohue, Corporate Director Care Systems Sustainability." Executive fungus that had formed on a desk exposed to conference. On a boat, this growth would have been a barnacle. The contrast between the friendly greeting and the weapons propped against their shoulders was humorous. There were five more Suits on the other side of him he hadn't mentioned.

"Who are those guys?" Sababa pointed with his elbow.

"Our legal team." Bligh said.

"Send lawyers, guns, and money." Sababa crooned. "You didn't say there would be lawyers."

389

"You didn't ask."

"Excellent. A panel of experts." Sababa said. "Like the bar scene from *Star Wars*. Let me tell you what's wrong with this society. No one drinks from the skulls of their enemies anymore. Where's Milo Mindbender."

"On vacation."

"I'll bet." He said. "Stress leave?"

"I don't think I've ever seen your particular kind of crazy, Doctor Sababa." Bligh continued. "But I do admire your total commitment to it."

"Crazy people don't know they're crazy." Sababa said. "I know I'm crazy so I'm not crazy. Crazy, huh?"

"Doctor Sababa, is it true that you refuse to sign on to VIHA's rules and regulations and also sign a contract with the Health Authority?" It had come from one of the legal Suits. Sababa pointed to a melamine whiteboard on an easel with a tray of desiccated multicoloured felt markers. Whoever had written this message on the whiteboard would have had to have picked the lock to the Board Room.

> Boren's Laws for Bureaucrats
> 1. When in charge, ponder.
> 2. When in trouble, delegate.
> 3. When in doubt, mumble.

Beside the Laws was a familiar equation.

"And what is that?" Asked the Suit.

"Sababa's Equation of Medical-Bureaucratic Inequity." He said. "I can't take your power. I can't educate you. So my only option is to make you accountable."

"You're confusing power with authority."

"No, you are." Sababa said. "Power is the force through which you can oblige others to obey you. Authority is the right to direct and command others. Authority requests power. Power without authority is tyranny. The wisest have the most authority."

"It is not wisdom but authority that makes the rules and regulations." Hobbes said.

"Are you saying that half the bureaucrats in this room are morons?" Sababa asked.

"Take that back."

"OK." Sababa corrected. "Are you saying that half the bureaucrats in this room are not morons?"

"Doctor Sababa!" Malcolm Canmore, the man in the thousand dollar suit, held together with impeccable cuffs and collars, silk ties and linen handkerchiefs, and silver cuff-links in his Cardin shirt, had raised his voice. He drummed his manicured fingers on the table.

"The ultimate authority must always rest with the individual's own reason and critical analysis." Sababa said.

"So now you're the Dalai Lama." Bligh said. "Can you explain to us, in simple language, why you refuse to sign these documents."

"For you, I'll make this as simple as I can." Sababa said. "Your rules and regulations require me to take all the responsibility, and blame, if everything goes sideways, for patient outcomes, with no obligation on your part to provide me with the resources I need to do the job properly. You limit my ability to raise these concerns with facing punishment, and you restrict my ability to dance with the devil in the pale moonlight."

"I didn't get that part." Bligh said.

"No, I'm sure you didn't." Sababa continued. "You can delegate authority, but you cannot delegate responsibility. No authority is higher than reality. And I'm the most real thing in this room."

"Well, here's our solution to this little problem." Bligh sat up in his chair. A sick smile grew and died on his mouth like a fungus. "You have until noon tomorrow to sign a contract with VIHA, or I will terminate your position here at Harbour City Regional. Immediately. This is the conventional wisdom this authority has used to decide the fate of your employment. Do you understand?" If you would know who controls you, see who you may not criticize.

"It's sad to watch authority abused through such Byzantine micromanagement, intimidation, and threats." Sababa said. "Suppose conventional wisdom to be a rainforest. I am a chainsaw. You are squirrels. For most animals, gentlemen, the entire universe is neatly divided into things to (a) mate with, (b) eat, (c) run away from, and (d) rocks. You can't fuck me, you can't swallow me, and it's too late to run. That just leaves rocks."

"What rocks?" Bligh asked.

"I rock." Sababa said. "Together with my colleague, Marquis Shu Ying, I'm on call half of August, while all the other Internal Medicine specialists take their usual holidays. I have seven clinical research projects on the go in this hospital, including two from the TIMI group in Boston, and another two from Paul Armstrong's Vigour Centre in Edmonton. If you rescind my hospital privileges, someone will have to explain, in terms that patients and their families and the medical research establishment and the FDA find acceptable, why I have disappeared from the planet surface, just when things were going so swimmingly. Oh, yes. And you will have to force the other members of my department to return to this shithole as the summer weather climaxes in orgasm. So why don't you and all your confused disciples ride out on the pink ponies you came in on. I have work to do." *In battle, if you make your opponent flinch, you have already won.*

The board room air filled with atomized black spittle.

'It is indeed my opinion now that evil is never 'radical,' that it is only extreme, and that it possess neither depth nor any demonic dimension. It can overgrow and lay waste the whole world precisely because it spreads like fungus on the surface. It is 'thought-defying,' as I said, because thought tries to reach some depth, to go to the roots, and the moment it concerns itself with evil, it is frustrated because there is nothing. That is its 'banality.' Only the good has depth and can be radical.'

Hannah Arendt

'Am I the only one I know
Waging my wars behind my face and above my throat
Shadows will scream that I'm alone...'
Twenty One Pilots, *Migraine*

Sara paged Doctor Sababa out of the showdown at the appointed time.

"How did it go in there?" She asked.

"I appear to be the beneficiary of moral exculpation." Sababa said. "They say the one sure sign of a successful negotiation is when the parties leaving the table both feel like they've been screwed. The goal is a compromise. A situation where everybody wins."

"And?"

"Didn't happen that way." He said. "They also say a man should be judged by his enemies."

"And?"

"Proud of mine."

In the ER, Dr. Cliffy Carlton made for them at a gallop.

"Hello, Baby cheeks." He said. "I've been waiting for you to return."

"Don't call me Baby cheeks." Sara fumed.

"I wasn't talking to you." Cliffy said. Sababa raised an eyebrow.

392

"What you got?" He said.

"Candy Diocese." Cliffy said. "32-year-old naturopath who presents with oral thrush, problem swallowing, vaginal yeast infection and a week-long history of black skin ulcerations. She's convinced she's got something she calls 'candidiasis hypersensitivity.'"

"Ah, yes." Sababa said. "One of the many 'fashionable' cult syndromes, this one was cooked up by the aptly named Drs. C. Orian Truss and William G. Crook. Let's go see." Cliffy made the introductions.

"It's so special to have a sister colleague in attendance."

"I'm not your sister." Sara glowered. "And I'm definitely not your colleague."

"Did you know that our fingerprints are formed by friction from touching the walls of our mother's womb?" She looked at her nails.

"Good to know, Candy." Sababa said. "Now if you would tell us what happened so we can fix this thing."

"Sure." She said. "I don't understand where I went wrong. Two months ago, I mixed up my usual annual kombucha tea starter. Perhaps it was because the new Lapsang Souchong tea I used was incompatible with the previous year's zoogleal mat 'mother.' That's what gave me my candidiasis hypersensitivity."

"You don't have candidiasis hypersensitivity." Sababa said. "You have candidiasis."

"I prefer to think of it as a sensitivity."

"That belief you have in this large pseudoscientific fad." Sababa continued. "I prefer to think of it as a delusion."

"I have thrush in my mouth and cottage cheese in my vagina." Candy pouted. "I should be able to call it whatever I want."

"It's an infection, not an infatuation." Sababa said. "And you also have yeast in the corners of your mouth as angular cheilitis, and it's likely affecting your esophagus."

"And my skin." She said.

"Nope, that's not yeast." Sababa said. "That's something even better."

"Like what?"

"That's cutaneous anthrax." He said. "This last kombucha batch you brewed is a killer."

"But I always thought anthrax was a 100% lethal biological weapon."

"Naw." Sababa said. "This is just skin involvement. Hide-porter's disease. Only 20% mortality, tops."

"My kombucha recipe has cured patients with asthma, cataracts, diabetes, diarrhea, gout, herpes, insomnia and rheumatism,

393

prostate enlargement, impotence, grey hair, wrinkles, hemorrhoids, hypertension, cancer, and immune deficiency." Candy asked. "Are you trying to tell me that my tea mushroom isn't healthy?"

"I'm telling you that your yeast and anthrax infections are from you dabbling in the occult world of fermentation without a roadmap."

"But it's the champagne of life." She said. "A SCOBY 'Symbiotic Culture Of Bacteria and Yeast.'"

"Think of your 'scoby' as the coral reef of the bacteria and yeast world." Sababa said. "A biosorbent binding to contaminants and heavy metals, a dangerous polymicrobial soup that can cause lead poisoning, deadly metabolic acidosis, and severe liver and kidney toxicity. You are not being punished for your kombucha. You are being punished by your kombucha."

"So how would you propose treating my sensitivities?"

"We'll treat your anthrax infection with penicillin, your oropharyngeal thrush with topical nystatin, and your vaginal candidiasis with a onetime dose of fluconazole." Sababa said. "And dump the Kombucha poison."

"Wouldn't I be better off taking bread mould, probiotics, and laser vaginal rejuvenation?"

"Hmmm... A patient with no medical training." Sababa said. "Tell me again how to do my job."

"You have something against conventional wisdom." Candy asked.

"Seems to be a hot topic today." Sababa mused. "The remedy that got you here is an extreme example of unconventional folly because of the great disparity between your implausible, wide-ranging health claims lacking evidentiary support, and its potential risks. The only benefit accrues to those that sell it."

"That's insulting." She said. "And raises questions about your judgment."

"If you want to lecture me about my poor judgment, I can provide you with a list of more relevant examples." He handed her a prescription and indicated for Dina to cut her loose.

"Isn't there anything more natural?" Candy asked.

"Nature is a rotten mess." Sababa said. "If you take your eyes off it for a second, it will kill you. Thorns, insects, fungus, worms, birds, reptiles, wild animals, raging rivers, bottomless ravines, dry deserts, snow, quicksand, tumbleweeds, sap, and mud. Rot, poison, and death. That's Nature. The only reason I ever step outside of my cabin on the lake is that my bravery exceeds my good sense." He went over to the consultants' desk to dictate his report, selecting a tune from his music library, on a secret drive hidden deep inside the hospital computer network.

'Oh my Candida
We could make it together
The further from here girl the better
Where the air is fresh and clean...'
Tony Orlando, *Candida*

Gung Ho pulled back a curtain on the other side of him, to reveal a middle-aged woman with long gray hair, too much black lipstick and eye makeup, and a nose ring. Her choker obscured a neck tattooed with unicursal hexagrams. Circumferential silver bangled her wrists and ringed her fingers. Her nail polish was blood red.

"And?" Sababa asked.

"Need some help with this one, Sab." The portly professor motioned to Sara and indicated he would attend the bedside as soon as he finished his dictation a few minutes later.

"Tell us a story." He said.

"Alberta Hoffman." Everyone nodded at each other. "41-year-old Wiccan priestess..."

"What?"

"Wiccan priestess."

"What?"

"I'm a witch." She said. "Ordained clergy of the Temple of the Green Cauldron."

"Of course you are." Sababa said. "A member in good standing of the local coven of lesbians dancing naked in the forest celebrating the semen stolen from imprisoned hypnotized males, which they then use to inseminate one another using turkey basters to create a legion of demon babies."

"We are also active in community outreach programs." She said.

"Of course you are." Sababa said. "And to what do we owe your materialization in this more secular of asylums?"

"She presents with a 4-day history of worsening limb pain, pallor, and a sensation of coolness aggravated by exertion." Gung said. "Examination reveals high blood pressure and severe upper and lower extremity vasospasm."

"And why is that?" Sababa asked.

"Not sure, Sab." Gung shrugged. "She takes a caffeine-ergotamine tartrate Cafergot preparation for migraine headaches, but she's been on that for eight years."

395

"What else have you taken recently, Alberta?" Sababa asked.

"Nothing." She said. "I don't believe in taking medications unless I have to. Oh, wait. I got this antibiotic for a cough I developed last week." She handed Sababa a small blister pack from her purse.

"Clarithromycin." He said. "A macrolide which can cause inhibition of cytochrome P-450 catabolism of xenobiotics, resulting in elevated serum drug levels and ergot intoxication."

"Ergot?" Alberta had understood none of that.

"Ergot." Sababa said. "It's the active ingredient in your migraine medicine. Potent constrictor of blood vessels. So potent, in fact, that it played a major role in human history."

"How?" She asked.

"We isolated these alkaloids from the *Claviceps purpurea* fungus that infected rye and other cereals, turning the grain into purple ergot bodies. The fungus once caused deadly outbreaks of ergotoxicosis, or ergot poisoning, characterized by medieval epidemics of dry gangrene, and convulsions and other neurological manifestations. People lost fingers and toes and died crazy. It was a fungal party hellscape." He watched the witch's eyes widen.

"They used to call the blight 'cockspur' and the disease it produced 'St. Anthony's fire.' It even affected infants because the alkaloids passed through their mother's milk. They used the infected grain in the ritual killing of certain bog bodies. The earliest reference we have for ergotism appeared in the Annales Xantenses for the year 857. *A great plague of swollen blisters consumed the people by a loathsome rot, so that their limbs were loosened and fell off before death.* And there's a bizarre irony in your particular presentation."

"What would that be?" Alberta asked.

"The convulsive manifestations from ergot-tainted rye may have been the source of accusations of bewitchment that spurred the Salem witch trials." He said. "The crawling sensations in the skin, tingling in the fingers, vertigo, ringing in the ears, headaches, disturbances in sensation, hallucinations, painful muscular contractions, vomiting, and diarrhea, and psychological symptoms of mania, melancholia, psychosis, and delirium, were all manifestations reported in the Salem witchcraft records. There was plenty of rye in the settlement and the climatic conditions that could support its infection. And now you're bewitched."

"Perhaps this fungus became a pipeline into the mind, an entelechy, which we can only image as feminine and can only associate somehow with the environment and the ecosystem."

396

Alberta said. "The Gaian mind is what the goddess is, a network of planetary connective intelligence."

"Enjoy your little heresies." Sababa said. "But it won't save your arms and legs."

"What will?"

"Vasodilators." Sababa said. "And they're on special today. Sara here will admit you for two days of intravenous therapy."

"Is there anyone else I can talk to about this?" Alberta asked. "Do you have a Chief of Staff?"

"We do." Sababa said. "Dr. Petronilla de Meath."

"She's a doctor?"

"Of course."

"Oh? Which kind?"

"Witch."

"Which which?"

"Which what?"

"Which doctor?"

"Right." Sababa said.

'Nature doth thus kindly heal every wound. By the mediation of a thousand little mosses and fungi, the most unsightly objects become radiant of beauty. There seem to be two sides of this world, presented us at different times, as we see things in growth or dissolution, in life or death. And seen with the eye of the poet, as God sees them, all things are alive and beautiful.'

Henry David Thoreau

No matter how complex or affluent, human societies are nothing but subsystems of the biosphere, the Earth's thin veneer of life, and fungi are the interface organisms between life and death. Before heading home to Jane, Sababa had driven up to Witchcraft Lake, to ponder this, and gaze into the twilight. Although it appeared that trees made up the entire forest, he knew the foundation was below ground in the fungi.

The cedars and Douglas fir spoke to each other and shared resources right under his feet, using a mycorrhizal network nicknamed the Wood Wide Web. Some plants used the system to support their offspring, while others hijacked it to sabotage their rivals. Like human societies, Sababa mused.

On his way back down the hill, he pulled an apple out of his Colombian leather briefcase, the one he had lifted from the ER refrigerator earlier in the evening. As he bit into its flesh, his teeth and tongue met a core of bitter soft rot, which stopped him from continuing. He rolled down his driver side window, spit out the mouthful he had taken, and threw the rest of the apple out after it.

The night sky erupted in flaming light and sirens. A kaleidoscope of colour and pandemonium of sound behind his dimpled and dented white Honda pulled him over to the shoulder of Jingle Pot Road. He studied the profile and movement of the officer exiting the police car. The taste of bile replaced the rotten fruit he had bitten into, a few seconds earlier. The flashlight of Veronica Marsden found its mark in the middle of his face.

"Licence and registration." Here was an evil witch. Sababa gave her his documents.

"Do you know why I pulled you over?" Veronica asked.

"Spinal reflex?" Sababa guessed. "The proliferation of luminous fungi in deep caves where the torchless improvident hero needs to see is one of the most obvious intrusions of narrative causality into the physical universe."

"What was it you threw out your window?"

"An apple."

"Now why would you want to do that?"

"Botrytis cinerea." He said. "Anamorph of the discomycete Botryotinia fuckeliana (de Bary) Whetzel, which we place in Sclerotiniaceae of Helotiales."

"What's that?"

"It's a homothallic necrotrophic polyploid saprophyte." She had asked, and would give her a full explanation. "Wine is one of the most complex of all beverages: fruit of the soil, climate, and vintage, digested by a fungus through a process guided by the culture, vision, and skill of an individual winemaker. The fungus is usually a yeast.

But Botryotinia fuckeliana is a fungus that can cause two separate kinds of infections on grapes. The first, noble rot or *pourriture noble* in French or *Edelfäule* in German, occurs when dry conditions follow wet and can create distinctive sweet dessert wines, such as French Sauternes or the Hungarian Aszú of Tokaji or Romanian Grasă de Cotnari. The fungus removes water from the grapes, leaving behind a higher percent of solids, in the form of sugars, fruit acids and minerals. This results in a more intense, concentrated product. The wine is often said to

398

have an aroma of honeysuckle and a bitter finish on the palate. Last year, I visited Chateau d'Yquem, the only Premier Cru Supérieur in Sauternes, to taste *en primeur*."

"And?"

"The second kind of Botryotinia fuckeliana infection is Botrytis cinerea, derived from the Latin for 'grapes like ashes,' referring to the colour of the grey mould that causes bunch rot when wet conditions follow wet. They can destroy the entire crop of a vineyard just before harvest after the farmer has invested an entire season's work. It can cause a rare form of hypersensitivity pneumonitis called 'winegrower's lung.'"

"What does that have to do with the apple you threw out your window?"

"The apple was rotten with Botrytis cinerea." Sababa said. "It has also infected my pinot noir and chardonnay vines this year, despite the Trichoderma harzianum fungus I sprayed them with, to kill the first fungus. All this must have left a bad taste in my mouth."

"There are only two things you can throw out the window of a moving car, legally." Veronica wrote him out an expensive ticket. "Water. And feathers. Everything else you get in trouble for." She passed the citation through the window and tipped the brim of her hat.

"Why, thank you, Officer." Sababa said. "Always a pleasure." He called to her again as she opened the driver side door to her Ford Interceptor cruiser.

"You know the German botanist who they named Botryotinia fuckeliana for?" He asked.

"No idea." She frowned. He shouted it back to her as he drove away.

"Karl... Wilhelm... Gottlieb... Leopold... Fuck..."

The last thing Veronica Marsden saw was a hand thrown out Sababa's driver-side window, one prominent finger raised into the night sky.

'Watching in slow motion
As you turn around and say
Take my breath away.'
Berlin, *Take My Breath Away*

"Bruce Chatwin." Sara met Sababa on the bridge of the Death Star the next morning. "39-year-old Harbour City Star Reporter admitted late last night by Dr. Pangloss. Two weeks before his presentation, his GP evaluated him for a 'mono-like' illness characterized by night sweats, diarrhea, loss of appetite, transient rash, and a documented 20-lb weight loss. Two days ago, he spiked a fever, associated with non-productive cough, and progressive shortness of breath. In the ER, he developed acute chest pain and respiratory embarrassment. Trace found he had blown his right lung, put in a chest tube, and called me in to work him up post-intubation and transferred him here for mechanical ventilation."

"Charmeine?"

"Close enough." Said the patient's critical care nurse.

"Exam?" Sababa asked.

"Febrile, fast heart rate with soft blood pressure." Sara continued. "Enlarged lymph nodes everywhere. Decreased breath sounds and crackles at both lung bases."

"Lab?"

"Significant for anemia, sky-high lactic dehydrogenase level, elevated liver enzymes, and prerenal azotemia. Initial arterial blood gas analysis showed a high pH of 7.506, low PaCO2 of 27 mm Hg, low PaO2 of 63 mm Hg, and oxygen saturation of 90% with a huge alveolar-arterial gradient of 53 mm Hg. Low CD4/CD8 cell count ratio. As you have likely already surmised, his ELISA and Western blot analysis came back positive for HIV." Sara brought up a series of chest x-rays on the mechanical viewer.

"Well, lookee here." Sababa said. "Quelle surprise. Bilateral, patchy, interstitial infiltrates. Do we have a sexual history?"

"Trace recorded that Mr. Chatwin appears to like both girls and boys, a lot." Sara said. "From his own account, he wasn't particularly fussy about protection or heartbeats or number of limbs."

"It is unseemly to provide more information than is necessary to make a diagnosis, Sara." Sababa said. "When the AIDS epidemic started to hit America, we called it '4H Disease' after the people at most risk—Haitians, Hemophiliacs, Heroin Users, and Homosexuals. The gay community had an in-joke: 'What's the worst thing about catching AIDS? Having to convince your parents you're Haitian...'"

"So what have you got?"

"Probable primary HIV infection with Pneumocystis jiroveci pneumonia." She said. "I started him on IV ceftriaxone,

400

azithromycin, trimethoprim/sulfamethoxazole, and corticosteroids."

"This week I appear to be collecting spores, moulds, and fungus." Sababa said. "No HAART antiretrovirals?"

"Not until we kill his fungal infection." Sara said. "We need to delay that to cut the risk of immune reconstitution syndrome while treating his acute opportunistic infection."

"Trick question." Sababa said. "Solid pass. You know, I think I looked after one of the first HIV index cases in my internship. Haitian guy. Worked on him tirelessly 24/7 and couldn't find a damn thing. The ICU attending kept busting me for not finding out what was killing him, but he didn't know either. I only found out about AIDS when I worked in Africa, in my five-year hitchhiking trip around the world."

"Someone told me you admitted an injured black puppy to a whites-only pediatric ward in South Africa." Sara said. "That true?"

"Let's organize an HIV RNA level and genotype." Sababa said. "Get Ed Hyde to bronch and lavage him for toluidine blue, periodic-acid Schiff and silver stain, and direct fluorescence antibodies to P. jiroveci. Tell Juan Leyblanca we're looking for crushed ping-pong balls." He left the bedside to answer a page.

"We have another new one in the next cubicle, Sab." Sara shouted after him. He was back in less than a minute.

"Jane wants me to stop at the store to pick up some victuals when I finish today." He said. "We're having you for dinner tonight. That'll obviate the need for me to run over something on the way home."

"Your wife is too kind." Sara said. "She asked me over without telling you, for some peculiar reason."

"The same reason glue doesn't stick to the inside of the bottle." Sababa said. "What you got?"

"Georgia Strait." Sara began. "After midnight special, courtesy of Dr. Pangloss again. 53-year-old widow from Parksville admitted for pneumonia and meningitis. Several month-history of productive cough, chest pains, sinusitis, headaches, dizziness, muscle aches and pains, night sweats and weight loss. Didn't seek medical attention. Yesterday, after she had finished walking her puppy in a local park, she collapsed in her van. Her dog alerted attention by leaning on the horn."

"Man's best friend." Sababa said. "Which park?"

"Rathtrevor." Sara said. "She walks her dog there most days. Why?"

"Truth grows in my mind like a fungus, and though I try to sleep it out, there is no resisting the epiphanies."

"Sometimes I don't get you." She said.

"A hero ain't nothin' but a sandwich." Sababa shrugged. "Carry on."

"Initial exam performed by Dr. Pangloss showed lethargy and confusion, fever, rapid heart and breathing rate, stiff neck, light sensitivity, abnormal breath sounds, and skin lesions. Trace intubated and ventilated her for respiratory failure, did a lumbar puncture, and then called me."

"And what did you do?" Sababa asked.

"Started her on intravenous antifungal therapy." Sara said. "Amphotericin B and flucytosine."

"Now why would you do that?"

"Because her serum and CSF cryptococcal antigen test returned positive." Sara said. "She has cryptococcal neoformans meningitis and pneumonia."

"She has cryptococcal meningitis and pneumonia." Sababa corrected. "Who said anything about neoformans?"

"What other kinds are there?"

"Does she have any risk factors for the acquisition of invasive neoformans disease?" Sababa asked. "HIV, decompensated liver cirrhosis, inherent cell-mediated immunity dysfunction or suppressive regimens without calcineurin inhibitors, autoimmune diseases?"

"Not that there's any history or evidence for." Sara said. "So what other kinds of cryptococcus can do this in an otherwise immunocompetent patient?"

"I've been waiting for this one for a while." Sababa said. "There's a tropical fungus called Cryptococcus gattii, most prevalent in Papua New Guinea and Northern Australia but also reported in India and Brazil."

"Why would it appear on Vancouver Island?" Sara asked.

"Climate change, Gold Miss." Sababa said. "Climate change."

"But where would Georgia Strait have caught it?"

"It lives in Rathtrevor Park." He said.

"But where?"

"In the second deadliest tree on the planet." Sababa said. "The poisonous shade of our own Douglas fir."

"What's the deadliest?" Sara asked.

"The manchineel tree of the coastal beaches and brackish mangrove swamps of the Caribbean, Florida, Bahamas, Mexico, Central America, and northern South America." He said. "Manzanilla de la muerte." *Little apple of death.* Every part of the beach apple contains strong toxins, some unidentified. The fruit is fatal if eaten. Its milky white sap contains phorbol and other skin irritants. Standing beneath the tree during rain causes

402

severe skin blistering. *A single drop of rain or dew that falls from the tree upon your skin will immediately raise a blister.* The sap can damage the paint on cars. Burning the tree will cause eye injuries if the smoke reaches the eyes. The Caribs would poison the water supply of their enemies with the leaves. Spanish explorer Ponce de León died from an arrow dipped in manchineel sap."

"Dr. Leyblanca on line 3, Sab." Betty Boop held up her handset.

"Saprophyte Central." He answered.

"¿Hey Cabrón, what are ju growing up there?"

"Tropical fungus."

"We need to wait a week, but the KOH stains of sputum and cerebrospinal fluid look like cryptococcus also."

"Probably gattii, serotype B, subtype VGIIa." Sababa said.

"Well, knock it off." Juan said. "Ju are killing my micro budget. I call ju." *Click.*

"What now?" Sara asked.

"Now we blow a little smoke through the fir trees and the Parksville Chamber of Commerce." Sababa said. "Betty Boop, can you please connect me with the VIHA Medical Health Officer and the BC Centre for Disease Control?"

"On it, Sab."

"Sometimes, I'm just a fun guy." He said. "Fun gi, get it?"

"It's scary." Sara said.

'So soon as prudence has begun to grow up in the brain, like a dismal fungus, it finds its first expression in a paralysis of generous acts.'
Robert Louis Stevenson

The casual reader would love to have dined at the Sababa homestead that evening.

"This is delicious, Jane." Sara dug her spoon into the broth for more. "Thank you for inviting me."

"I'm glad you're enjoying it, Sara." Jane said. "Eleazar made it." Sara looked up into Sababa's grin.

"You promised me there wouldn't be any roadkill." She said.

"There isn't." He said. "The duck is from Jane's Muscovy pen, and the chicken is from the Benedictine sisters next door."

"You have a name?"

"Longevity Soup." Sababa was between slurps. "It's Tibetan."

"It's wonderful." Sara said. "Exotic, even. Does it have any special ingredients?"

"One." Sababa passed her the pepper. यार्सागुम्बा, Yartsa gunbu, or Dōng Chóng Xià Căo, in Mandarin."

"Which is?"

"Its literal translation means 'winter worm, summer grass.'" He said. "In Linnaeus's binomial nomenclature, its Latin name is Ophiocordyceps sinensis."

"Sounds like an Asian organism." Sababa fetched a photo of a caterpillar, with a long dark brown horn emerging from its head. It could have been a unicorn if the unicorn had no legs and a tusk longer than its mummified corpse. Sara choked back the urge to vomit.

"It's a fungus?" She asked.

"It germinates in the living ghost moth larva underground, which it kills and then emerges from the soil as an upright fruiting body." He said. "The other misnomer for it is 'vegetable caterpillar.' It was the most important source of cash income in rural Tibet, but the fungus is nearly extinct now because of climate change."

"Where did you get it?"

"I have a Tibetan friend who sells them at the Third Month Fair in Dali Prefecture in Yunnan Province. I can't afford them, but he sends me a few every year."

"In the mail?"

"He can't afford FedEx." Sababa said. "It's funny. The Chinese refer to this caterpillar in English language texts as 'āwheto,' from the similar Māori fungus which infects Kiwi Forest Ghost Moth larvae, Ophiocordyceps robertsii."

"A rare delicacy in New Zealand in the old days." Jane added.

"The fruiting bodies do contain high concentrations of arsenic and other heavy metals." Jane said. "So you can't consume too much. I won't give you another bowl of soup, but it's also in the main course I made."

"What's that one called?" Sara asked.

"Failing Energy Chicken." Sababa said. "I thought it was an appropriate dish."

"How valuable is this Tibetan fungus?" Sara asked.

"About $30,000 a kilogram." Sababa said. "They're like blood diamonds. Inter-village conflict over access to its grassland habitat has resulted in the murder of several people. They killed seven farmers in our old stomping ground of Manang in June

404

2009 after they went to forage for it. In 2011, a court in Nepal convicted nineteen villagers over the murder of other farmers during a fight over it. The fungus played a role in the Nepalese Civil War when Maoists and government forces fought for control over the lucrative export trade during the summer harvest season. I was there with Gung Ho and Tictac Tarmac and Cliffy Carlton."

"Doing what, exactly?"

"I planned our trek to Rara Lake in the western part of Nepal." He said. "No one told me there was a war going on."

"Isn't there another kind of fungus that affects the behaviour of wasps and ants?" Sara asked.

"It's called adaptive parasite manipulation." Sababa said. "Ophiocordyceps unilateralis is a tropical fungus that infects Camponotus leonardi ants that live in tropical rainforest trees. Once infected, spore-possessed zombie ants will climb down from their normal habitat and chomp down with a lock-jaw 'death grip' into specific north sided veins on the underside of leaves 25 centimetres above the ground in an environment of 95 per cent humidity and temperatures between 20 and 30 degrees Celsius. The fungus then kills the ant and sprouts a fruiting body from the back of its head, which then releases spores onto a new infectious killing field. Ophiocordyceps sphecocephala can cause similar behavioural changes in median wasps. There are thousands of cordyceps fungi, each having evolved to prey on a specific victim. The Massospora fungus drugs cicadas with psilocybin—the potent hallucinogen found in magic mushrooms, and cathinone, the active amphetamine in the khat plant, incessantly chewed by its addicts in the Horn of Africa. The fungus causes their butts to fall off, triggering the dispersal of thousands of spores, and turning the cicadas into 'salt-shakers of death.'"

"Thankfully, there is no human equivalent for any of these monsters." Sara said.

"Oh?" Sababa smiled. "Ophiocordyceps bureaucraticus. Physicians only cross to the dark side when their brains are infected with a mandarin functionary fungus that turns them into rigid zombies. I've seen the red tape growing out of their heads. They're the fungus among us, controlled to become the last of us."

"And?"

"The administrators tried to bury us in paper and protocol." He said. "They didn't realize we were seeds."

You think you want the blue skies, the open road, but you want the tunnel, you want to know how the story ends. Sometimes there is light at the end of the tunnel. Sometimes there is more tunnel. And sometimes there is cold coalface dirt, where the fungus lives.

Tunnels have become crowded and cosmopolitan, and travel through them no guarantee of survival. Consider the case of Charles E. Smith, the elderly snowbird who flew the metal tube tunnels every winter to Arizona. Charles underwent a left posterolateral thoracotomy with decortication and drainage of the complicated pleural effusion and received antifungal medication for several months until, on his way back to Vulture City from the last greyhound race in Apache Junction, a drunk driver from Phoenix ran him over.

Consider also the rush hour French traffic tunnel, where an English princess was killed with her Egyptian boyfriend by a Belgian drunk on Scotch whiskey driving a German car with a Dutch engine, followed by Italian paparazzi, on Japanese motorcycles, despite final treatment with Brazilian medicines by an American doctor.

It was a carpal tunnel and not allergic bronchopulmonary aspergillosis that forced Junmai Daiginjo from saké making to saké marketing. He still sends Sababa a bottle of his best every year during the sakura cherry blossom season. The wind tunnel that blew *Rhizopus oryzae* fungus into the diabetic face of tourist Clyde Chestnut Barrow made him the last victim of the infamous Joplin, Missouri tornado. Despite antifungals and a radical debridement of all involved sinuses, orbital exenteration, incision and drainage of parapharyngeal abscess, and myringotomy and aspiration of middle ear effusion, he succumbed to Sababa's diagnosis of rhino-orbital-cerebral zygomycosis. They that sow the wind shall reap the whirlwind.

It was a tunnel of silence that helped cure Too-loud MacLeod of his Saxophone Lung, even though he played the bagpipes. His sputum fungal culture grew Exophiala dermatitidis. Sababa's six months of daily itraconazole, a prolonged period of abstinence, and a strict isopropyl alcohol cleaning regimen for his pipes had him back puffing out his chest and reproducing expert strangled goose noises in time for the following year's Parksville Beach Festival sand castle competition.

Tunnel vision is caused by an optic fungus that multiplies when the brain is less energetic than the ego. If the ego is large enough, there is no light at the end. Fortunately, veterinarian Patrick Keeling swallowed his pride, halted his sheep vaccination program, and bought a pair of safety glasses for the next time. His corneal edema resolved in three weeks, and his visual acuity returned to normal.

From the tunnels of blood that provided Harry Wheatcroft with his rose fertilizer, did he also get his chronic hepatitis C infection. Sababa fixed his sporotrichosis with potassium iodide and then his hepatitis with antiviral therapy. Harry, in his gratitude, supplies Sababa with ongoing laboratory-sourced nourriture for Jane's own rose garden.

Sometimes the light at the end is in the next tunnel over. Candy Diocese agreed to Sababa treating her anthrax with penicillin but refused treatment for her cutaneous and mucosal candidiasis, holding fast to her delusion of hypersensitivity syndrome. She is still self-prescribing naturopathic nostrums and making fresh batches of kombucha from the previous year's 'mother'. Here is a hall without exit, a tunnel without end.

Alberta Hoffman, the Temple of the Green Cauldron Wiccan priestess, came through Sababa's vasodilator tunnel of hope, and recovered from the Pablo Neruda St. Anthony's 'fire that dances and climbs up the invisible stairs and awakens the blood in the tunnel of sleeplessness.' *You must take care to light the matches one at a time.*

Sometimes that light at the end of the tunnel is a train. Sometimes the light is at the other end of the tunnel. Bruce Chatwin wrote an article for the Harbour City Star, thanking Sababa for treating his Pneumocystis pneumonia and later, an ode to his Burkitt's lymphoma, from which he would die. Poetry is the tunnel at the end of the light. What we call the beginning is often the end. And to make an end is to make a beginning. The end is where we start from.

The night is a tunnel, a hole into tomorrow. After a series of antifungal therapies, Georgia Strait is back walking Rusty, although she now drives to Sababa's lake, just to be safe.

Ben Fitznar's escape tunnel into the Yucatan terminated in a German courtroom dead-end. Sababa finally told Dr. Zaias the third reason that Miyamoto Musashi had been late for his duel

with Sasaki Kojirō, on that remote island in the strait separating

Honshū and Kyūshū. Musashi had used the time tunnel of his

arrival to match the turning tide, which carried him away to safety.

The bureaucratic tunnel rats of VIHA solved their Sababa problem by asking the portly professor if he had read the new rules and regulations.

"I've read them." He said. "But I won't sign on to them. I've worked at Harbour City Regional for two decades and never needed them."

"Would you agree to sign something to state that you've read them?" Bligh asked.

"What good would that do?"

"It might help us save face."

"Yours is looking like a bag of smashed crabs right about now." Sababa said. "There would be no obligation for me to follow any of these guidelines?"

"None." Bligh said. The important thing in strategy is to suppress the enemy's useful actions but allow his useless actions.

Sababa signed the paper already typed up in Victoria earlier that day and was gone with the outgoing tide. But there is always more tunnel. *The big print giveth and the small print taketh away.*

Milo Mindbender, at the end of Sababa's terror tunnel, had been strong enough to kill but not resourceful enough to survive. VIHA had a rule that anyone under investigation by the College of Physicians and Surgeons of British Columbia was automatically ineligible to work for the Health Authority. The pulse is your friend. The College is not your friend. Sababa had complained to the College about Milo, and VIHA had fired Milo into the cold coalface dirt, where the fungus lives.

Oh, and Dr. Reynolds, Sababa's resident? Sara would soon spin wildly, in a tunnel of love.

12. The Case of the Double Double Whammy

'Hot weather opens the skull of a city, exposing its white brain, and its heart of nerves, which sizzle like the wires inside a lightbulb. And there exudes a sour extra-human smell that makes the very stone seem flesh-alive, webbed and pulsing.'

Truman Capote, *Summer Crossing*

High summer had opened the skull of Harbour City, and removed the entrance gates from the chain-link fence that had encircled the eight-acre land reserve on Port Drive. The mayor said their removal was to allow more rapid access to any required emergency medical response, but the squatters inside the enclosure didn't feel any safer without them.

The homeless encampment hadn't started on the south downtown Port Way waterfront property that ran beside the Gabriola ferry across the wrong side of the railway tracks. It began in late spring on the lawn of the City Hall, as a protest organized by the Society of Living Illicit Drug Users because, apparently, the dead ones couldn't make it. An eviction notice provoked the Alliance Against Displacement, a local group of social justice warriors, into breaking the locked barriers of the empty industrial lot, through which poured dozens of vagrants, some from tent cities on the Lower Mainland, and establishing a colony of campers which would swell to a population of three hundred protesters before the story ended. The new name they chose for the lot on which they had claimed their new living spaces was authentic enough. *Discontent City*.

They planted flags and signs.

409

Homelessness is not a crime... Homes Not Hate...
Fight4Homes.Fight4Justice... #SquatTheEmpties... Tent Cities Unite...
The War on the Poor Must End Now...
ThePeopleUnitedWillNeverBeDefeated... Discontent City against Racism...
There were some who would become patients of Doctor Sababa
in the coming weeks—Ned Sparks, John Ormond, Al
Ginsberg—but these were early heady days.

The sweltering seasonal heat would show little mercy, fading the
tents pitched on black tarmac and scorching their inhabitants,
cracking the spirit of those encamped on more earthen areas
baked hard as a concrete biscuit, in wrinkled dereliction and
defeat. Sweat trickled into eyes and down shirtless backs until it
didn't, and then heat stroke drew torpor and buzzing flies.

But if the settlers were on fire with an insurgent zealotry for
solving the collective social injustice issues of homelessness and
poverty and affordable housing, they were equally back-
illuminated with their individual developmental failings to solve
problems of personal mental health and drug addiction, the
catalysts most responsible for the coming wave of criminal
activity and tragedy that would befall their community.

Those opposed to the establishment of such a homeless petting
zoo in the middle of the city warned of being buried in 'needles,
condoms and garbage,' and having to deal with a 'vortex of
disruption' that would result in countless health, safety, fire and
legal issues and crime in the surrounding area. Individuals and
agencies whose funding depended on the perpetuation of
poverty and its patrons shouted them down.

But the predicted criminal activity came to pass. The RCMP
and BC Ambulance and Harbour City Fire Rescue personnel
responded to unending disturbances and drug overdoses.
Firefighters attended the camp 98 times, for reasons that
included four calls for help, 14 burning complaints, 13 fires, one
for hazardous materials and 66 medical aids, responses for
opioid overdoses, some of which were fatal, despite the
ubiquitous availability of intranasal naloxone harm reduction
kits, and the mutually agreed injunction of Rule #1- *No one does
drugs alone.* There must have been some money to pay for all the
irony. How could these indigent occupants afford pets and nose
rings and other transdermal metal and subdermal ink and
cigarettes and drugs and bottled water, and mobile phones and
Facebook pages? How could you collect welfare without an
address? Many of the people living at Discontent City weren't
even homeless. The police took no direct action.

Open flames inside tents for cooking and warmth were a
constant concern. A woman suffered burns when she lit a pipe

and caught her bedding on fire, smoking her tent and belongings instead.

The drugs and the need for drugs spawned an internal economy to procure them based on what you had to sell. Property theft and extensive shoplifting from downtown merchants could make you money. If you couldn't sell purloined products, then you only had one other thing you could sell. Depending on your infatuation with progressive liberalism, this activity fell into the category of prostitutes or sex workers. Underage prostitutes became 'street-engaged youth sex workers' who were also taking intravenous drugs. Political correctness collided with visceral excess. The police took no direct action.

This drew out the crazies from the other end of the political spectrum. The Soldiers of Odin and a group called Action Against Discontent City were more disturbed than usual by reports of 'child sex trafficking' and were on their way to fix it. This immediately produced a backlash of hypersensitive verbiage from the alternative lifestyle advocacy brigade.

'Harbour City itself legislates and normalizes anti-homeless hatred, which the general public and hate groups like the Soldiers of Odin then pick up and run with, inciting moral panic over child welfare in order to justify anti-homeless violence, in order to justify a displacement that would only send hundreds of people into isolated survival, putting them at greater risk of violence. The Soldiers of Odin's call-out has nothing to do with youth welfare or the safety of people engaged in sex work, and everything to do with misogyny and hatred of homeless people. We denounce attempts to market violence against vulnerable communities as concern for street-engaged youth. A group of grown men posturing as protectors of women's bodies, whether adult or minors, sex-working or not, is a deeply paternalistic, misogynistic trope that furthers violence against women and children. The figure of the macho man who uses violence to unilaterally intervene in exploitation, imagined or real, is just the other side of a patriarchal coin that portrays women and children as victims who are passively in need of rescue by self-interested men. Whereas the Soldiers of Odin gesture superficially at youth vulnerability in service of their racist and misogynist agenda, Discontent City stands for the self-determination of all oppressed peoples, including women and youth alongside homeless people, Indigenous people, and sex workers.'

Then came the violence. A Discontent City resident began throwing rocks at the media. An 18-year-old camper inflicted a 'life-threatening stab wound' into a 27-year-old squatter, and another stabbing incident occurred a few weeks later. And then, along with the anarchy, came bombs.

411

No one knows the reason these campers for social justice felt they needed to store fireworks inside their shelters. In one tent, a man sustained severe burns to his legs and feet.

But there was also another man living under nylon, recognized for his fascination for building pipe bombs with fireworks components, and then exploding them on Discontent City's railroad tracks. He crossed the last line with a homemade shrapnel device of commercial fireworks components inside a needle sharps container, positioned against the chain-link fence opposite the shopping centre. The police took direct action.

The anarchy radiated out at the speed of sound. Activists seized an empty school in Harbour City's north end and tried to make it their home. There was a propane explosion at a satellite outpost on the Millstone River. Flames shot higher than nearby tents. Four explosions at the Anita Place tent city in Maple Ridge ignited a tall tree.

It cost Harbour City a half-million dollars to host Discontent City, not including policing costs or legal fees, undisclosed because of solicitor-client privilege, allowed under the province's privacy act.

Enter Dr. Spud Hasselbeck, VIHA's Medical Health Officer for Central Vancouver Island. Spud wasn't aware of a single social justice contradiction he didn't adore—youth unemployment, child poverty, harm reduction—he loved them all as one.

In a fireworks display of Medicine Nobel explosive prize-seeking exuberance, he had ordered the city to provide Discontent City occupants with municipal water, portable toilets, and hand-sanitizing stations. The city spent five grand on a water pipeline and vastly more on litter pickup and security.

Spud could have made it much easier. Spud could have done his job. Spud could have issued an evacuation order, flesh-alive, webbed and pulsing.

'Now it could be said that Starbucks gets more flavour from their bean
And a single can of Red Bull will provide you more caffeine
But there's more to drinking Timmy's than the coffee that they brew
For Canadians it's just the patriotic thing to do.'
Brad and Robert Nelson, *Timmy's Anthem*

Around the corner from Manzanita Medical and down from the law offices of Miles, Frum, and Romeda, a kilometre northwest

of the winter of our discontent made glorious summer, the doors
to the busiest downtown coffee shop in Harbour City were also
always open.

A notice hung on the elevated brick and cement and glass
shopfront behind the red umbrellas and awnings—coffee • donuts
• espresso • latte • bagels • sandwiches • smoothies.

And above that, and all the compass points of the building, four
red signs glowed in the founder's own handwriting font. *Tim
Hortons... Always Fresh.* (Or in satire: *Because Canadians have nothing
better to do.*)

Except that the name didn't have an apostrophe, to comply with
Quebec's draconian language sign laws, and it wasn't fresh at all.
Oh, it had been once, but the doughnuts which they used to
make at night to be ready for the morning rush, were now
parbaked—partly cooked and then frozen and delivered to every
restaurant in Canada from Brantford, Ontario. Muffins were
flash-frozen, pre-made and pre-wrapped.

Tim Hortons is quintessentially Canadian. Its cups are the most
recognizable litter in the land. Canadians eat more doughnuts
and have more doughnut outlets per capita than any other
country.

Pierre Berton, that most iconic of Canadian authors, wrote of its
prominence in the nation's life. *The story of Tim Hortons is the
essential Canadian story. It is a story of success and tragedy, of big dreams
and small towns, of old-fashioned values and tough-fisted business, of hard
work and of hockey.*

Tim Hortons was the cathedral of the Double Double, a coffee
with two sugars and two creams, the Maple Chill, a maple
milkshake topped with regular whipped cream and sprinkled
with maple flakes, and the Honey Dip doughnut, in every small
town and rural patch of habitation from sea to shining sea to
shining sea. A marketing campaign, *Roll Up the Rim to Win*,
handed out so many prizes and was so popular that someone
invented a mechanical 'rimroller' device for rolling up the paper
cup rim. They had even sold the doughnut holes, calling them
'Timbits,' filling all the other holes in our precious heritage with
millions of priceless chocolate coconut cream-filled Dutchie
glazed crullers. A beacon of refuge for the road-weary traveller,
a home away from home for the lumpenproletariat, Canada was
the Timbit Nation.

Except it isn't Canadian anymore. It's Brazilian. And before Rio
de Janeiro-based 3G Capital bought it, Timmies was owned by
Wendy's International and then Burger King. There are 4,613
restaurants all over the world, including seven on Canadian

413

Forces stations (and Kandahar, Afghanistan) and five on US military bases, bringing in over $3 billion a year.

Before dawn on this most fragrant of summer mornings, he parked his dimpled and dented white Honda astride two white lines in the empty lot. Under the ceiling halogen lights, so bright as to sear the retinas out of both your eyes, and a visor and a hairnet, he found unpretentious Jan behind the counter, dressed in the saddest shade of brown.

"Hey, Doc." She said. "Picking up some Timbits for the ICU nurses?" Johnny Reid played behind her on the radio.

When I'm runnin' on empty... and it's cold and dark... with wings on my wheels... and a hunger in my heart... That's when I know... I need a little taste of home.

Sababa, involved in several of his own TIMI clinical trials, nodded, and Jan began filling a box with sugary spheres of many colours. He wasn't a regular patron of the place, preferring the doppio doppio of Code Brew or Jane's espresso at home.

He went to Starbucks even less often, and only when he wanted to see what the world would have been like if Hitler had won the war. There was something about the fresh-faced Aryan efficiency of the baristas that sent a shiver up his spine. To compensate, when they asked him his name, he would say 'Penis' with a short 'e', and they'd get him to spell it and then when his doppio doppio was ready, he'd get them to say it.

But he didn't have any such apprehensions in Tim Hortons. The odours made sure of that.

The coffee smelled like burnt aluminum watered down with warm skunk urine. The coffee trays smelled like human shit because that's what they were made from, integrated solid bio-waste. All the food reeked of dead chicken on a sponge wrapped in with wet cardboard, seasoned with battery acid and mustard gas. The washrooms smelled like the food.

Good Morning Harbour City... This is CNDN Coast Salish radio, 101.3 FM on your Home and Native Band. I'm your host, BC Bud... On this day in 1876, Custer died for your sins... A big shoutout to our Western Inuit brother Orpingalik, down from Tuktoyaktuk for medical treatment...

Jan was finishing Sababa's order when the stocky savant noticed the local Coast Salish community nurse seated at a table with a quiet older Mongoloid man with dark sallow skin, and a flattened wide face and nose with almond-shaped eyes. His small body was thick and robust, his arms foreshortened, adapted for limiting heat loss. He was drinking tea.

"Doctor Sababa." She pointed with her lips. "Good to see you."

"Good to see you too, Stanzy." He had great respect for this home care nurse, who looked after the sickest patients in her community, ensuring that they all had referrals to see the portly professor. Sababa remembered his initiation into a traditional smudging ceremony, when he held a cedar branch, as she fanned him with sage smoke and ritual cleansing.

"Who's your companion?" He asked.

"His name is Orpingalik." She said. "He's an Inuit hunter from the high arctic. I'll bring him to your office this afternoon. Dr. Tarmac has put in a referral."

"Kina una?" Orpingalik asked *Who is this.*

"Una Doctor Sababa." Stanzy said. *This is Doctor Sababa.*

"Where in the world did you learn to speak Sallirmiutun, Stanzy?" Sababa asked.

"I spent two years in Inuvialuit after my training." She said.

"The Place of the Real People." He added. Stanzy raised her eyebrows.

"Qanuq itpit, Orpingalik?" Sababa asked. *How are you.* His almond eyes opened wide.

"Nakuuyunga, Doctor." He answered. "Ilvitmi?" *I am fine. How about you.*

"Nakuuyunga, Orpingalik."

"Where did you learn your Sallirmiutun, Doctor Sababa?" She asked.

"It's a hobby I wish I had more time for." He said. Orpingalik let loose with a barrage of cacophonic consonants.

"He wants to know who this Tim Horton is." She said.

"Was." Sababa said. "Tim Horton was a bruising blue-liner in the last glory days of the Toronto Maple Leafs hockey team, onboard for their four Stanley Cup victories. He played for 22 years and migrated from the New York Rangers, Pittsburgh Penguins and finally, the Buffalo Sabres." There was a flurry of more quiet consonants.

"He wants to know what a sabre is." Stanzy said. Sababa drew a picture on a napkin and explained how the Syrians used to quench their Damascene blades by shoving them into the bodies of slaves. Orpingalik lit up like the Aurora Borealis at the imagery.

"By the time the Leafs traded him to the Sabres, Horton wasn't even interested in playing anymore. He was thinking retirement, but Punch Imlach, the team's General Manager, sweetened the deal of a one-year contract by adding one heck of a car. Tim went down to Gateway Lincoln Mercury in Thornhill, Ontario where he drove away in a $17,000 signing bonus—a coach white 1972 De Tomaso Pantera Lusso, with a black front bumper and Goodyear Arriva tires.

But Tim Horton was 44 years old by now, playing against younger, faster NHL players not even born in his rookie year. He was taking speed to stay competitive.

He played his last game at the Maple Leaf Gardens in Toronto on February 21, 1974. The day before the game, Horton had taken a puck to the jaw during a practice in Buffalo. He had made an appointment to see a doctor for some x-rays next morning. Despite the swollen bruising of his face, he took a handful of painkillers and insisted on playing. With his family and many friends in the crowd at the Gardens, he skated for two periods before the intense pain forced him into leaving the game shortly into the third period. The Leafs won, 4-2. They selected Tim as the third star.

The veteran defenceman drank eight vodka and sodas in less than an hour, double double double double. He took a handful of Dexamyl 'purple hearts', a mixture of dextro-amphetamine and a barbiturate, amobarbitol, and an unknown amount of Dexedrine, another amphetamine. It was the perfect cocktail for disaster—vodka for recklessness, speed for speed, barbiturates for obliviousness, and a soupçon of narcotic painkillers, driving off at 175 kilometres an hour down the Queen Elizabeth Way.

When his white Pantera roared into St. Catharines around 4:30 a.m., Ontario Provincial Police constable Mike Gula was waiting for him. He gave pursuit in his cruiser, lights on, but couldn't catch him. *I was doing over 100 mph, but I lost sight. I never even got close.*

A few minutes later, the Pantera's tires sank into the soft shoulder with two of them coming off their rims and slicing the treads. *Roll up the rim to win.*

Tim Horton's signing bonus careened out of control. The left front tie rod snapped and at one point the right rear wheel assembly broke loose and was shorn off from the control arm mounting. The impact ripped apart and destroyed the upper ball joint. The car hit a lamppost at speed and hurtled into the concrete wall on the west side of the highway, shattering the steering rack. It barrel-rolled several times before coming to a rest upside down on its roof, in a westbound lane facing north.

The Pantera's passenger compartment was intact. They found Tim's body on the grass of the median, ejected from the car 200 feet away. He was wearing a brown checked topcoat, a yellow sports coat, a yellow shirt, brown boots, and brown pants. The physics had broken his neck and crushed his skull. Police found a 40-ounce bottle of Smirnoff Vodka with its top broken off, orange and green pills, a package of Old Port Cigars, six eight-track stereo cassettes, and two cheques from the Buffalo Sabres totalling $1,792.

Who was Tim Horton? He was one of this country's most famous drunk drivers. The irony is that his name now adorns the hundreds of doughnut shops where so many late-night drivers come for coffee to help stay awake." It was quintessentially Canadian. Another patron had pushed in front of Sababa while he had been telling his story.

The tragedy of life is not death but what we let die inside of us while we live... Sing your death song and die like a hero going home.

"His first name was actually Miles." The man said. "That's my last name." Sababa recognized the name, the man, and the smell of expensive single malt on his breath.

Leon 'Shady' Miles was a local lawyer, from the offices of Miles, Frum, and Romeda. While Sababa was heading off to work, Shady was attempting to recover from a night of revelry, before trying to do the same.

Leon was a true professional—a medical malpractice lawyer, Queen's Counsel, loyal Rotarian, a warrior with his mind, his pen, and his computer. He was rich, rapacious, progress without a conscience, paving everything in his path. He was in the 1%, consuming 25% of the earth's natural resources. His truth was not Truth, but a consistent expediency. He paid a lot in taxes and did some charity work, most of which was tax-deductible. One thing was for certain. Leon 'Shady' Miles had impeccable taste in the booze.

"You know you get more sugary glaze or chocolate or sprinkles if you buy the doughnuts and not the holes." He garbled.

"Actually, that might be correct if the volumes were equal, but they're not." Sababa said.

"Nonsense." Shady slurred. "It's a simple ratio of surface area to volume, comparing a torus to a sphere."

"You can't discount the isoperimetric inequality in your assessment." Sababa said. "Compare $(R^2 - r^2) \pi^2/(\pi r^2)(2\pi R)$ of the toroidal doughnut to the $4\pi r^2/4/3\pi r^3$ of the spherical Timbit and you'll see your error." But Shady didn't realize his error, nor the Tim Hortons team member with Hepatitis A who had served him a month earlier at a different location, nor that he would return in the same condition later that night and crash his black Audi A3 into the brick and cement and glass storefront,

417

but not quite as terminally as Tim Horton had crashed. Shady grabbed his order and pushed Sababa out of the way as he left.

By now there were five people waiting behind the portly professor in the early morning queue. There were Arthur Looss and Charlotte Manson and Priscilla Plantagenet and Robert Picton and Sababa's colleague and fellow department member, Dr. Wayward Woods, who was always late, convinced that the only reason for time was so that everything didn't happen all at once. When Sababa left, Wayward would order a Double Double on the double.

"See you later, Doctor Sababa." Stanzy called after him.

And remember this lesson from our Hopi brothers... The one who tells the stories rules the world.

Sababa felt a chill of terror run through his marrow halfway up Comox Road, on his way to the hospital. He knew the kaleidoscopic pandemonium that Veronica Marsden always seemed to save for his special enjoyment. She took her time getting to his driver side window. Red lights revolved in the leaves.

"Do you know why I pulled you over?" She asked.

"You knew I had doughnuts." He said, one eyebrow raised.

'Another face erased From this tidal pool
Found one day Then swept away...'
Cowboy Junkies, *The Summer Of Discontent*

Larry Bird had been smoking an Export, waiting near the Harbour City Regional Specialist parking bay for the dimpled and dented white Honda to arrive. Ever since this driver had shocked his chest while he was still awake, and he could resume his job as a Robbins Parking attendant, this windshield had become a bulls-eye for frequent parking violation tickets, whether there had been any criminal intent or act committed. Sababa emerged from the Honda's interior, balancing his Colombian leather briefcase with two boxes of Timbits. Bird stubbed out his cigarette and began to write out his form of retribution.

"I'm on call today." Sababa protested. "Get away from that car, or I'll drink your blood." Larry backed off, to light another coffin nail.

"Export, eh?" Sababa smiled.

As he dropped off one box of doughnut holes in the ER, Dr. Myles Capitaine indicated he wanted a word.

"How are you, Myles?" Sababa asked.

"Living the dream."

"Who looks outside, dreams." Sababa said. "Who looks inside, awakes."

"I need to tell you about a patient that Sara and I just admitted to the Death Star." Myles said. "Discontent City squatter. Came in last night with a broken hip from a fall on the railroad tracks. Piggy Muldoon operated on him in the wee hours, and then called me because he wasn't doing so well. Said he had some kind of bowel obstruction."

"Did you tell him you weren't the right guy to call?" Sababa asked.

"He told me there was no such thing as an orthopedic emergency."

"And?"

"He said this was an emergency, and I was an emergency doctor, and yadda yadda." Myles said. "I called Sara. He's in the unit."

"OK, I'll deal with it." Sababa said. "You know what's eleven inches long and hard in the hands of an orthopedic surgeon?"

"No."

"An ECG." Sababa waved with the arm that wasn't carrying his other box of Timbits and Colombian leather briefcase. Sara met him at the door of the Death Star.

"What you got?" He asked. She handed him a chart with two brief early morning consultation notes. Piggy Muldoon had written the first: 'Ortho H&P: BBMF.' *Orthopedics History and Physical. Bone Broke, Me Fix.* Sara had supplied the second: 'FOOSBA.' *Found on Ortho service, barely alive.*

"Ned Sparks." She began "43-year-old homeless gold prospector camped out in Discontent City."

"And?"

"Piggy fixed his hip in the early hours." She continued. "About 5 a.m. Mr. Sparks developed sudden nausea, vomiting, abdominal swelling, and pain. Examination showed gaseous distension with sluggish bowel sounds." Sababa could see how bloated Ned's abdomen was from the bridge of the Death Star. It looked like he was about to explode.

"On rectal, I found ballooning without fecal impaction." She said. "No evidence of infection or electrolyte abnormality or excessive narcotic administration." Sara put up an x-ray on the viewer.

"Plain films of his belly showed massive colonic dilatation involving the entire colon with a cecal diameter of 11 cm, and without any air-fluid level." She said. "I put down a nasogastric tube, but it did nothing."

"So he's not mechanically obstructed from any surgical reason." Sababa observed.

"It appears not."

"What you got you got. What you don't got you don't got." He said. "So you have a name?"

"Acute megacolon?" Sara wasn't confident.

"$T = Pr/2t$." He said. "Where T is wall tension, p is pressure, r is radius, and t is wall thickness. You may have heard of it. It's called Laplace's law. Since the wall tension is proportionate to the radius, a dilated intestinal segment has a greater wall tension than one that is not; if the dilatation and tension are severe enough, obstructed blood flow and gut ischemic necrosis will result. Mortality rate is 30%."

"Do YOU have a name?" She asked.

"Idiopathic acute colonic pseudo-obstruction." Sababa said. "Otherwise known as Ogilvie's syndrome." He turned to Ned's nurse.

"Mary, please draw up a milligram of atropine to have by the bedside in case we need it for wheezing or too slow a heart rate. Then give Mr. Sparks 2 mg of IV neostigmine over five minutes." Mary went to the drug cupboard to get the medications.

Five minutes after the first five minutes, Ned's colon decompressed and his abdomen deflated to its normal size.

"And that's how you do the hoochie coochie." Sababa blew on his fingers. Betty Boop had five of hers in the air.

"Dr. Pangloss on line 1, Sab." She said. The portly professor picked up the call.

"We'll be down." He said, and hung up, motioning for Sara to follow him.

Trace was waiting for them in the ER.

"John Ormond, a 51-year-old homeless man, squatting in Discontent City." He said.

"We appear to be having too much of those with too little." Trace made the introductions.

"This is Dr. Reynolds." He said. "She's a resident in Internal Medicine. And this is her preceptor, Doctor Sababa." Trace said. "He doesn't enjoy dealing with patients."

"Isn't treating patients why he became a doctor?" John asked.

"No, treating illness is why he became a doctor." Sababa said. "Treating patients makes him miserable." He asked Trace to tell them the story.

"Mr. Ormond came in early this morning with astronomical blood pressure, accompanied by severe headache, generalized weakness, and bilateral back pain. He's lost ten pounds in eight months, but he hasn't been eating regular meals."

"Exam?"

"Blood pressure was 220/180 mm Hg." Trace said. "We're having some difficulty getting it down. I also found bilateral lumbar tenderness and a painless mass on deep palpation in the left renal lodge, mobile with respiration."

"Labwork and imaging?"

"Bloodwork showed a normochromic macrocytic anemia and an elevated C-reactive protein. Thrombotic disorder screen negative. Doppler ultrasound found a narrowing of the right renal artery. CT angio showed a total thrombosis as the cause, with the presence of a half-centimetre hypodense circumferential sleeve surrounding the aorta next to it. Renal scan confirmed the non-functionality of that kidney."

"So he has severe renovascular hypertension from a clotted off right kidney artery." Sababa said. "What's the question?"

"Why did it clot off?" Sara ventured.

"Someday all this will be yours, Gold Miss." He spread his arms. "And the answer?"

"Could be embolic, inflammatory, could be fibromuscular dysplasia." Trace said.

"You're blowing smoke, Trace." Sababa said. "Leonard's Law of Physical Findings—it's obvious, or it's not there. Look at that CT angio. What is that 'sleeve?' Roll up the rim."

"Retroperitoneal fibrosis." Sara said. "RPF. Also known as chronic periaortitis."

"Head of the class." Sababa rocked from side to side. "And the most likely cause?"

"Could be medication-induced, like from methysergide or hydralazine, or infection, or radiation or malignancy."

"What?" John blurted.

"More smoke." Sababa said. "What is the most common cause of RPF?"

"Dunno." Said Sara and Trace and John, together.

"Correct!" Sababa said. "We don't know. It's called idiopathic for just that reason, although there is some suggestion that, at least in half the cases we see, there is some association with an excess of IgG4-secreting plasma cells. Some circumstantial evidence is strong, like when you find a trout in the milk."

"Should we get a biopsy?" Trace asked.

"What?" John re-blurted.

"Only necessary in specific unusual cases." Sababa said.

"Can you fix it?" John asked. "I have to get back to my tent."

"Millions long for immortality who do not know what to do with themselves on a rainy afternoon." Sababa said.

"Well, can you?"

"Maybe not today, maybe not tomorrow, but soon and for the rest of your life." He handed Sara a piece of paper. There were two names. *Emma Nem... Al Ginsberg.*

"Call me." He bounced and bounded down the long hallway back to the Death Star.

    'While   velocipedes   among
the weeds will scare you
    And the menopause with hungry jaws ensnares you...'
              Don McLean, *On the Amazon*

"Where's Sophia?" Sara inquired of the pant-suited woman giving orders at the Floor 5 nursing station. Her scarf was Valentino Garavani silk. She clutched her hundred-dollar clipboard like she was walking through a dark alley.

"Who's Sophia?" She asked.

"She's the Head Nurse of this medical ward."

"Not anymore." Pantsuit said. "I'm the new Team Leader and Care Coordinator."

"I'm Sara Reynolds, Doctor Sababa's Internal Medicine resident."

"Ah, yes." Pantsuit's pupils constricted. "We've all heard of the great Sababa. There won't be any more special indulgences for his esoteric behavior."

"His patients do tend to have esoteric conditions." Sara said. "Sometimes that calls for an esoteric approach."

"Not on this unit." Pantsuit made a clicking noise with her tongue. "Not now."

"Do you have a name?" Sara asked.

"Samara." Pantsuit said. "Samara Morgan. Professor Morgan. VIHA designated me an influential educator."

422

"I need to see these two patients." Sara handed her the piece of paper. "They're referred in consultation."

"We don't call our customers patients anymore." Samara said. "We speak of them as clients. You can look up their rooms on the chart rack." Sara found the records and began to scan the first one.

"We are trying to encourage visiting physicians to find a place other than the nursing station to write their reports." Samara pointed to a distant room. Sara thought of how much she would enjoy Sababa's interaction with the new Team Leader. She had to wait for an hour.

A large blur came off the elevator like a clay pigeon on a skeet shooting range. His Colombian leather briefcase barrel rolled over the nursing station and landed next to a pant-suited woman with a fancy scarf and clipboard. There may have been an element of surprise.

"Doctor Sababa, I presume." She struggled to catch her breath.

"Presumptuous." Sababa said. "But correct. Where's Sara?"

"She's down the hall in the space I've reserved for visiting physicians." One eyebrow headed for the ceiling. Sara had listened for Sababa's arrival, and made her way back to the nursing station, slow enough to not interfere with the natural history of what was about to happen.

"Who are you?" Sababa asked. "Where's Sophia?" The answers Samara provided were not to his satisfaction.

"You can tell a lot about someone's personality from what they're like." He said. "And I can tell right off that you're no angel of mercy. I miss Sophia's healing touch already. Don't even think about making my job more complicated than it already is."

"Curly hair, curly thoughts." Samara said. "From now on, you tie your own shoelaces. I'm sure you already hate me. I know I don't like you."

"I don't hate you." He said. "I don't care enough about you to hate you. If you ride off on that broom you came in on, Sara and I can get on with our little lifesaving lemonade business." Samara stormed off down the stairwell to see the Grand Galactic Governess of Nightingales.

"You were rude." Sara reeled in the receding haze of Samara's departure.

"It seldom pays to be rude." Sababa said. "It never pays to be half rude."

"She's not your enemy." She said. "Sometimes you overplay your righteous indignation."

"Even though the snake is small, it is wise to hit it with a big stick." Sababa said. "Let's go see your clients."

They entered a four-bed room, and Sara introduced her mentor to the woman on the right-hand side beside the window.

"Contestant Number One." Sababa turned to Sara. "What you got?"

"Emma Nem." She said. "52-year-old Dragonfly herbalist admitted by Dr. Bloom for a two-week history of fatigue and nausea and muscle aches and right upper abdominal pain, and a three-day history of dark urine and clay-coloured stools. She denies any alcohol use, and her family history is negative for liver or autoimmune disease.

Exam shows tenderness in the right upper quadrant and jaundice with no signs of chronic liver disease. All her liver function tests are way up—bilirubin, alkaline phosphatase, alanine transaminase, and aspartate transaminase. Acetaminophen level, urine drug screen, viral hepatitis panel, ceruloplasmin protein electrophoresis, and genetic testing for hemochromatosis were negative. But she has an elevated anti-nuclear antibody and anti-smooth muscle antibody."

"You got a name?"

"Autoimmune hepatitis." Sara was confident.

"From what?" Sababa asked.

"Dunno." She said. "It's associated with other conditions like celiac disease, vasculitis, and autoimmune thyroiditis, but she doesn't have any evidence for those. I'd just call it idiopathic. I learned that one from you."

"You haven't mentioned her medication history." Sababa said.

"I don't take synthetic medications." Emma said.

"I'm sure you don't." Sababa said. "But I'll bet you dip into the herbs. I smell body odour and furniture polish. What are you taking for menopause?"

"Something natural for what is a natural part of life."

"Death is a natural part of life, but we try not to roll over for it too much." Sababa said. "What are you taking?"

"Black cohosh extract." Emma admitted. "I started a month ago."

"Actaea racemosa, a flowering plant of the family Ranunculaceae." He said. "Also called black bugbane, black snakeroot, and fairy candle. Contains triterpene glycosides and some other phenolic constituents."

"It's natural." She said.

"So are strychnine and cyanide and arsenic and uranium235." Sababa said.

424

"I know more about menopause than you do."

"People who think they know everything are especially annoying to those of us who do."

"What do you propose to do?" Emma squirmed cross-legged on her bed.

"We need to find out for sure and treat this thing." Sababa said.

"I won't allow for any physical or chemical assault." She shook an ISIS-like index finger in the air.

"What would you like me to do?" Sababa asked. "In fact, this is an ideal situation for my special blend of psychology and extreme violence." "One, you need a liver biopsy, which I will do later this morning. Two, you need to stop the black cohosh, which you will do today. Three, we'll start you on a steroid called budesonide and an immunosuppressant, azathiaprine, which we'll do after your biopsy."

"And if I refuse?" Emma asked.

"Well then, right in the middle of the woodland you prefer to live in, will come the smiling mortician." Sababa said. "Or you might be lucky and get a liver transplant." Emma's eye movement scanned for a way out and then focused on her hands.

"Sara will be back to get a signed consent for the biopsy." Sababa said. "See you later." The two physicians left for another four-bed room, further down the hallway. In a mirror image bed of the first client, Sara introduced Sababa to her second consultation.

"Al Ginsberg." She began. "42-year-old poet and Discontent City dweller, admitted yesterday by Dr. James Ruben Andrews." When Sababa shook his hand, he howled.

"Suffering is what was born, ignorance made me forlorn, tearful truths I cannot scorn."

"Yeah, my wife tells me I squeeze too hard." Sababa said. "Sorry about that. Carry on, Sara."

"Chief complaint of progressive headaches and an increasing painful swelling over his anterior chest wall over the last two months." She said. "History of untreated chronic hepatitis B and C."

"Why haven't you sought medical attention before now, Al?" Sababa asked.

"I've been busy trying to find affordable housing for the homeless." He said. Sababa looked at Sara.

"Exam was remarkable for an 8 cm × 6 cm mass over the sternum, immobile and firm, with no local rise of temperature." She continued. "The overlying skin was tense, with dilated veins over the mass. The rest of his physical was unremarkable."

"Maybe it was a metaphysical." Al added. "Is the pain in my chest all in my head... or is the pain in my head all in my chest." Sababa smiled a Sababa smile.

"Lab?"

"Elevated liver function tests." She said. "And then there's the small matter of his serum alpha-fetoprotein result."

"Which was?"

"34,300 ng/dL." Both of Sababa's eyebrows flew into the sky after it.

"Did you listen for sounds over his liver?"

"It doesn't have a mouth." Sara said. Sababa unwrapped his Littman Master Cardiology black and brass stethoscope from around his neck, placed first the bell and then the diaphragm of his instrument over Al's liver, concentrated for a full minute, and then showed her where to listen. Sara also took a full minute before removing her own stethoscope from her ears.

"He has an abdominal venous hum indicative of portal hypertension, also called Cruveilhier–Baumgarten syndrome." Sababa said. "He has a hepatic arterial bruit from either increased arterial flow, partial obstruction to arterial flow, or arteriovenous shunting. And he has a hepatic friction rub from local inflammation. That he has all three means that he had cirrhosis and now has a hepatoma."

"What's that?" Al asked.

"Hepatocellular carcinoma." Sababa said. "Primary liver cancer."

"I see the poem ending with an open door." Ginsberg said.

"It may not lead to somewhere you want to go, Al." Sababa took his hand again, gently this time.

"Hey Father Death, I'm flying home, Hey poor man, you're all alone, Hey old daddy, I know where I'm going."

"Statutum est hominibus semel mori." Sababa said. *All men are destined to die once.*

Outside Al's window, a seagull passed alone, wings spread silent over roofs.

'The worms crawl in and the worms crawl out
The ones that crawl in are lean and thin
The ones that crawl out are fat and stout...'
The Pogues, *Worms*

"It's worm week, Boss." Even while typing, Mercy had heard Sababa jouncing through the antique stained glass door of Manzanita Medical. His resident was already probing through the referrals.

"It is Mercy, not justice or courage or even heroism, that alone can defeat evil." He said, to Sara's continued consternation at his bizarre references to his office assistant. She had also been combing through the patient medical history forms, more for amusement than erudition:

> Main Problem: tyerd
> Past Medical History: Foar concutions... Wisdom teeth out
> Medications: pant lock... nightrow... pro sack... assburn
> Sexual Problems: depends on female
> Drug Allergies: Pennicillin Reaction- Fatal
> Marifine makes me hilusinate

"Busy clinic today, Gold Miss." Sababa handed her the first chart. "Best get started." She called into the full waiting room.

"Arthur Looss, please." A middle-aged man with sunburned skin and yellow eyes rose from a corner chair and followed Sara into the residents' room. Sababa called the next contestant.

"Charlotte Manson?" A young potbellied woman stood up and accompanied the portly professor into his office. Her eyes were spectacular—almond-shaped with double eyelids, and irises so dark brown, they were black.

"How can I help?" Sababa began.

"Ductor Sababa, I yam Sophia's cousin." Charlotte said. "She suggested I be reppered to you."

"Where is Sophia?" Sababa asked. "What happened to her?"

"Pull it ticks." Charlotte said. "De nurse dat replaced her has union sceneyority. She put a bluck mark on Sophia's name. Aybree-buddy is berry sad but she has decided to return to the Pilippines. In lipe, dere are wieners and losers."

"That is unfortunate news, Charlotte." Sababa said. "If there is anything I can do, tell her to let me know. She was the best head nurse Harbour City Regional ever had."

"I know dat, Ductor." Charlotte said. "I will tell her."

"And you?" Sababa said. "It appears that Dr. Buddy Benway did a colonoscopy and found a prize polyp."

"It was a sur-prize polyp, Ductor."

"It also surprised Dr. Juan Leyblanca, the pathologist, judging by the Spanish profanity in the margins of the report he sent me."

427

"Dere are many people with snail peber in da Pilippines." She said.

"Eight hundred thousand to be exact."

"Most in my home island of Mindanao."

"Over 200 million people worldwide." Sababa said. He took a more complete history, performed an examination, and reviewed Charlotte's labwork and imaging.

"You appear to only have the hepatointestinal form of the disease, Charlotte." He said. "But we'll have to do some more tests to make sure.

"Thank you, Ductor."

"Dr. Leyblanca found Schistosoma Japonica blood fluke flatworms and their eggs in your polyp. The ancient Egyptians considered the blood in the urine it caused in young boys to be a male version of menstruation. We also call this condition bilharzia after the German physician who first discovered the worms in 1851, Theodor Bilharz."

"Can you treat it, Ductor?" Charlotte asked. Sababa handed her several requisitions and wrote a prescription for a single tablet. *Praziquantel.*

"One pill?"

"One pill, Charlotte." Sababa said. "Please tell Mercy to book another appointment in four weeks time, and give my best to Sophia."

"Thank you, Ductor Sababa."

"My pleasure."

As Charlotte left, he found Sara hovering on the other side of his door.

"What you got?" He asked.

"Whoa." She said.

"You have woe?"

"No, I have whoa." Sara said. "W-h-o-a. Whoa."

"Tell me about whoa." He said.

"Arthur Looss." Sara began. "48-year-old Namibian tanzanite and diamond merchant referred by Drs. Poldy Bloom and Jules Martino. He's been in hospital twice already. The first time was a month ago for a ten-day story of upper abdominal pain aggravated by food intake. Dr. Martino scoped him and found only a preponderance of eosinophils on his gastric biopsy. He made a slight improvement. Jules discharged him home on omeprazole and a course of oral steroid, budesonide, with a provisional diagnosis of eosinophilic gastroenteritis."

"And then?"

"Dr. Martino readmitted him two weeks ago for persistent epigastric pain, now radiating through to his back, and one

428

episode of vomiting. He had lost ten pounds in the previous three weeks. This time he had a high count of eosinophils in his blood. His amylase and lipase enzymes were high. Mako Brisk reported his CT scan and ultrasound of his abdomen and pelvis as normal, but there were technical issues. The surgeon thought he had acute pancreatitis from his steroid therapy and discontinued the budesonide. He managed Mr. Looss with intravenous fluid and discharged him two days ago."

"Stools for ova and parasites?"

"Done repeatedly and all reported negative." Sara said. "Jules booked him for an ERCP as an outpatient.

"And now?"

"And now he's yellow."

"Let's go see him." They walked down to the residents' room, where Sara introduced the portly professor.

"She says you're a rocket scientist." Arthur said.

"Former life." Sababa said. "Mercifully, laughter intervened."

"I'm sick, aren't I?" He asked.

"Yes." Sababa said. "Does it hurt?"

"A little."

"We'll take it." Sababa said. "It's the painless jaundice that will kill you." Mercy cut in on the conversation.

"Dr. Leyblanca on line two, Boss." Sababa picked up the handset.

"Give me a rhythm I can dance to." He said.

"Hola, Cabrón." Juan said. "Ju weel never guess what I found on one of Martino's duodenal biopsies. Hees name ees Arthur Looss. He is with ju now."

"Strongyloides fuelleborni fuelleborni." Sababa said.

"¿How do ju know thees sheet?"

"It is my business to know what other people don't know." He said.

"¿How did ju know eet was thees subspecies of worm?"

"Arthur is from Namibia."

"I call ju." Sababa heard the click of a busy Latino pathologist hanging up on him.

"It's refreshing when the cause of biliary obstruction is a worm." Sababa turned to Sara. "The clue was the eosinophilia. In the conundrum of worms, wheezes and weird diseases, sometimes it's just worms."

"Is it rare?"

"About a hundred million people in the world have strongyloidiasis." Sababa said. "You're not alone."

"Can you kill these things?" Arthur asked.

"Oh yeah." He pressed his intercom button.

"Mercy, cancel Mr. Looss's ERCP and let Martino's office know."

"Done, Boss." She said. Sababa wrote out more lab and imaging requisitions, and a prescription for two pills of Ivermectin. He handed them to Arthur.

"Only two pills?"

"Only two pills." Sababa said. "The medication doesn't kill the Strongyloides larvae, only the adult worms. Take them two weeks apart. Tell Mercy I'll see you in a month."

"Thank you, Doctor Sababa." Arthur said. "Much appreciated."
He turned to leave.

"Oh, and Arthur?"

"Yes, Doctor."

"Life is hard. Then you die. Then they throw dirt in your face. Then the worms eat you. Let's make sure it continues to happen in that order."

"Yes, Doctor."

Sababa and Sara accompanied Arthur to see Mercy and to recharge with two more patients. The portly professor recognized Stanzy and Orpingalik from their early morning encounter in Tim Hortons and asked Sara to do the consultation. He called the last referral.

"Priscilla Plantagenet, please." He said. A middle-aged woman followed him into his office. Sababa noticed she was protecting the left side of her chest with her right arm."

"How can I be of service, Priscilla?"

"Doctor Falstaff wants to operate on my left breast." She said.
"For?"

"Well, that's just it." Her arm position was defensive. "He said he doesn't know. I asked to see you." Sababa read the referral and pushed his intercom button.

"Mercy, see if you can raise John Falstaff for me." He said.
"Please and thank you."

"On it, Boss."

"I've had this painful mass in my left breast for eight months now." Priscilla said. "Dr. Falstaff says it's not cancer, but he doesn't want to operate until he knows what it is."

"Sometimes you don't know what something is until you operate." Sababa said. "Although I try to make that as unnecessary as possible. What do you do?" He motioned for her to get changed so he could examine her.

"I'm a professional dog groomer at Pawcific Coast." She said. "Been doing it for thirty years." Sababa found a mobile mass on Priscilla's anterior chest wall, peripheral in the left breast. The nipple, areola, and overlying skin were normal. There were no

430

palpable lymph nodes in either armpit. He poured over the imaging studies on his desktop.

Mammography had shown a dense mass in the same place at 9 o'clock, with a regular, sharply defined lobulated contour in the left breast, with no calcifications. Ultrasound showed a semi-solid mass with a 'water lily' internal detached membrane and circumferential loculations divided with septations, resembling fractal offspring. Intracystic spaces contained a homogenous 'sandy' echogenic material in the lesion centre, creating a 'wheel-spoke' pattern, like the rose window of Notre Dame.

Doppler showed no internal vascularity. Her MRI was a rosette from outer space.

"Doctor Doughnut on line one, Boss." The quality of Mercy was not strained.

"Hey John, what do you call two surgeons reading an EKG?" He asked.

"I'm sure I have no idea."

"I'm sure you don't either." Sababa said. "A double-blinded study." He heard good-humoured chortling on the other end of his handset. "I'm seeing Priscilla Plantagenet. She tells me you want to operate on her breast lesion."

"Beauty of general surgery, Sab." John said. "See badness surrounded by goodness. Cut out the badness and all's right with the world. It's you and your blade, one on one, *mano a mano*. Whoever said winning wasn't everything never held a scalpel."

"Be that as it may, you'll have to be careful with this one."

"And why is that, my precious pinot provider?"

"Never bring a knife to a gunfight." Sababa said. "This time you'll have a 3.8% chance of inducing anaphylactic shock."

"Why is that?"

"Because she has a hydatid cyst." He said. "And if you rupture it, you may not find its soul with your scalpel."

"Anything you can do to make me look good?"

"I'll start her on albendazole and give her some H_1 and H_2 blockers before you operate." Sababa could see the fear forming on Priscilla's face. "You remember to give her a milligram of dexamethasone before you pick up your 'healing steel,' to upregulate her Treg cell IL-10 and TGF-β1 levels, and inhibit her helper T cell 2 cytokines. Gotta go." He put down the receiver.

"What is it?" Priscilla asked. "What have I got?"

"One or more of those thousands of dogs you groomed over the years has given you a tapeworm called Echinococcus granulosus sensu lato. It has formed a cyst in your left breast. This kind of

431

thing has been happening for a long time. There are references to such cysts in ritually slaughtered animals as far back as the Babylonian Talmud."

"So dogs gave us these tapeworms?"

"Originally in evolution, we gave the worms to the dogs, and different tapeworms to pigs and cattle." He said. "I had such a worm once. Got it in Ethiopia at a feast where we ate raw beef. Explorer David Bruce used to watch the locals bring a live cow into their tents and slice off pieces of what they wanted to eat. It was prime rib prime tapeworm real estate. The answer to William Burroughs's famous question about which came first, the intestine or the tapeworm, is the intestine. All happened a few months after a Xhosa mother slapped her infant on his back and the foot-long Ascaris lumbricoides he coughed up did a loop-de-loop onto my clinic desk in Cape Town. Serves me right for not believing her."

"What now?"

"Dr. Falstaff will book your surgery, and I'll get you to go for this bloodwork, and take this medication. Tell Mercy to book a return appointment a week after your procedure." After Priscilla had thanked the Good Doctor and left to see Mercy, Sababa meandered down the hall to the residents' room. He knocked and then entered.

"Qanuq itpit, Orpingalik?" Sababa asked. *How are you.*

"Nakuuyunga, Doctor." He answered. "Ilvitmi?" *I am fine. How about you.*

"Nakuuyunga." Sababa said. "Sara?"

"Mr. Orpingalik is a 41-year-old Western Canadian Arctic Siglit hunter referred by Dr. Tarmac." She began. "Two-year history of progressive shortness of breath, fatigue, muscle aches and pains, and ankle swelling. He also remembers having transient eye puffiness, gastroenteritis, fever, and blood in his eyes. He had an echocardiogram yesterday that shows a weak contracting left and right ventricle with other signs of heart failure. Mr. Orpingalik is quite distressed about this because it means his hunting days are over." Sara and Sababa went over the physical exam again, together, and looked at the other investigations that Tarmac had ordered. Sababa posed more questions.

"Sumik anguniariagaqsivit?" *What do you hunt.*

"Aiviq anguniariagaqsiyuami." *I hunt walrus.*

"Hmmm." Sababa mused.

"Hmmm?" Sara asked.

"Eosinophilia, elevated muscle enzymes, dilated cardiomyopathy." Sababa said. "He has trichinosis."

"From what?" Sara asked. "He lives in the high Arctic. There's no Trichinella spiralis or pigs up there."

"No, but there is Trichinella nativa, which has a high resistance to freezing, and there are walruses. The eggs hatch inside the females as mature larvae." Orpingalik let loose a string of clicking and clacking.

"I've told him what it is, Doctor Sababa." Stanzy said. "But he wants to know what it is we should we do."

"Tell him we need to send him to Victoria for a biopsy of his heart muscle." Sababa said. "We'll also do trichinella bentonite flocculation titres, but they are only positive in 70% of cases. I'll make the referral and he should be down there in two or three days. Then we'll start him on a worm-killing medicine and he should get better."

Stanzy explained all this to the Inuit hunter. Sababa retrieved a tune from the office computer network as Orpingalik flashed him a grin of two upper tooth pegs, white as bone.

'I am the egg man
They are the egg men
I am the walrus
Goo goo g'joob.'
The Beatles, *I Am the Walrus*

'My   head's

exploding

My mouth is dry
I can't help it if I've forgotten how to cry...'
Tuxedomoon, *No Tears*

Dr. Gung Ho was gung-ho to speak to Sababa and Sara when they arrived in the Harbour City Regional ER after their afternoon clinic.

"Talk to me." Sababa said.

"Jan Mikulicz-Radecki." Gung began. "55-year-old Tim Hortons counter attendant. She says she knows you."

"She does." Sababa said. "Why is Jan here?"

"She had an abdominal ultrasound today which showed an incidental pericardial effusion."

"Why did she have the ultrasound?" Sara asked. Sababa beamed.

"Two-week history of right upper abdominal discomfort, loss of appetite cough, fever, shortness of breath, and sharp chest pain worse with deep breathing." Gung said. "In the previous four months she has lost 15 pounds, her eyes and mouth had been dry, and she was 'itchy.'"

"Exam?" Sara asked. Sababa smiled.

"She was small-framed, thin, and alert. Her pulse and breathing rate were borderline fast. Oral mucous membranes were dry and crusted, the tongue was red and smooth, and there were ulcers in the mucosa of her right cheek. Jugular veins were distended, and breath sounds were decreased on the left, with dullness to percussion and decreased tactile fremitus. Deep palpation in the right upper quadrant produced pain."

"Lab?" Sara had hit her stride as a fledgling consultant.

"High white count with left shift, and elevated sedimentation rate and direct bilirubin and gamma-glutamyl transferase and alkaline phosphatase. Antinuclear antibody returned with a titre of 1:640 in a homogenous pattern. She has a polyclonal hyperglobulinemia. Chest X-ray showed mild heart enlargement and a left pleural effusion."

"Hmmm." Sara mused. "There are three important features of this case: 1) she is a 55-year-old woman, 2) she has Sicca syndrome, and 3) she has elevated cholestatic liver tests. As Doctor Sababa never tires of explaining, Internal Medicine is an artful science that follows Confucian rules. Most things occur in threes. Although there are three clinical possibilities, there is one that makes the most sense.

Approximately 15% of patients with Sjögren's will have liver disease, and that disease is usually primary biliary cholangitis. We need two more tests, an antimitochondrial antibody, and a needle core liver biopsy, to confirm the diagnosis."

"What are you saying I have, Dr. Reynolds?" Jan asked.

"Not for certain." Sara said. "But primary biliary cholangitis is a disease of unknown cause, characterized by the inflammation and destruction of small intrahepatic bile ducts."

"Is there any effective treatment?"

"Treatment, yes." Sara said. "Effective, not so much. We'll give you ursodeoxycholic acid to stabilize the hepatocellular membrane, reduce cholestasis, and improve your liver function tests, and indirectly reduce the itchiness. We'll give you cholestyramine to bind bile acids and help eliminate the itch directly. We'll monitor, and replace as needed, your poor lipid-dependent absorption of Vitamins A, D, E, and K. We'll watch for osteoporosis and enlarged esophageal veins. We must discuss the use of methotrexate, and we may someday have to talk about the only intervention with a 5-year survival of about 70%, liver transplantation. We'll follow your serum bilirubin level to decide on the timing."

"So you know what has caused this?" Jan asked.

"No, we don't." Sara said. "Several reports suggest that an environmental Gram-negative alphabacterium, Novosphingobium aromaticivorans, causes a cross-reaction between the proteins of the bacterium and the mitochondrial proteins of the liver cells. But we don't know."

"We will work to ensure you get the best care we can provide, as long as we need to provide it." Sababa said. *Your friend along the way.*

Dr. Cliffy Carlton had been waiting on the sidelines of this conversation and took the first opportunity to corral the consultant duo before they went to other parts of the hospital, to see other referrals.

"Need your opinion on this one, Sab." Cliffy said.

"What you got?" Sara asked.

"One Robert Picton." He began. "57-year-old pig farmer with a five-day history of nausea, fatigue, and jaundice associated with elevated liver enzymes." Sababa and Sara could see into the patient's cubicle. Robert Picton was as yellow as hot buttered corn on the cob.

"Why didn't he come in five days ago?" Sababa said. "You would have."

"Said he was taking care of an outbreak on his farm." Cliffy made introductions.

"They call me Pork Chop Rob." Picton said.

"I'll bet." Sababa said. "What's in the syringe?"

"What syringe?"

"The 5 cc syringe profiled in the stretch of your blue jeans pocket."

"Oh, that syringe." Pork Chop pulled it out of his pocket. Inside was a blue liquid. "Windshield washer fluid."

"You got a tiny windshield washer?" Sababa asked. Pork Chop grinned with as many teeth as he could muster.

"What kind of outbreak did you have on your farm?" Sara asked.

"The guy from the Food Inspection Agency came back over a week ago and told me my hogs had Hepatitis E, or HEV." Picton replied. "Said there weren't no treatment, but I had to pay more attention to regular cleaning and disinfection of the pens, and to clean out the pig shit more often." Sababa left the gathering, heading to the consultants' desk computer.

"Where are you going?" Cliffy asked.

"Need to hack a database." Sababa said. "Sara, please continue with the history and examine Mr. Pork Chop while I do this." After a quarter of an hour, he returned to the bedside in time to hear Sara's findings.

"Nothing more?" He asked.

"Nothing." She said. Sababa noted what other items Pork Chop Rob had emptied onto his bedside table. There was a pair of night-vision goggles, a set of faux fur-lined handcuffs, and a small 7.5 ml bottle of liquid with a label. *Canthcur.*

"It's for my warts." He said. "So what's wrong with me?"

"Don't know yet." Sababa said. "Still working on it. Why did you come in tonight of all nights?"

"Not sure." Pork Chop squirmed on the stretcher. "This bullshit doesn't get any better. Do you think I have the same virus as my pigs?"

"There's a high probabilty." Sababa said. "Hepatitis E is in the genus Orthohepevirus, reassigned into the Hepeviridae family. It's a small nonenveloped positive-sense particle with a genome of about 7200 bases, a polyadenylated icosahedral single-stranded RNA molecule that contains three discontinuous, overlapping open reading frames along with 5' and 3' cis-acting elements, which play important roles in its replication and transcription."

"I didn't get a goddamned word of that." Pork Chop said.

"Here's an interesting part." Sababa continued. "A few hundred years ago, this virus diverged into two clades—an anthropotropic form which evolved into genotypes 1 and 2 and an enzootic form—which evolved into genotypes 3 and 4. The first two only infect humans; the second two infect pigs and humans, and a bunch of other hosts."

"I'm still not getting this." Picton frowned.

"Here's the most interesting part." Sababa was building something special. "I hacked the Food Inspection Agency database, hardly a difficult task."

"And?" Sara asked.

"Robert's hogs should be infected with genotype 3 if this was a North American-acquired porcine zoonotic infection."

"And?" Cliffy asked.

"They're not." Sababa said. "They're infected with genotype 1, unheard of, as it's usually only found in human outbreaks, usually in Asia."

"What does that even mean?" Picton demanded.

"It means that, while you may have contracted HEV from your pigs, your pigs got their infection from a human." The redness

436

drained from Picton's face. He looked like a lemon with pineapple sauce.

"I should go." He said.

"Yes, you should." Sababa said. "We've drawn your blood, and can add the extra testing with another requisition. If you'd like me to follow up to discuss treatment, call my clinic and ask for Mercy."

"Ask for Mercy?"

"Ask for Mercy." Pork Chop gathered up his things and bolted for the door. Sababa turned to Sara.

"You find any warts?"

"No." She said. "What was in the small bottle?"

"Cantharidin." Sababa said. "It's an odorless terpenoid secreted by male blister beetles and given to the female as a copulatory gift during mating. Afterwards, the female covers her eggs with it as a defence against predators. They use it for warts, but in darker places, it has another name."

"What?" Cliffy asked.

"Spanish fly." Sababa said.

"I'd be happy to mix you a cocktail, my little pork chop." Cliffy said to Sara. She vaporized him with a glare.

"So what is a guy doing with Spanish fly, handcuffs and a syringe full of windshield washer fluid?" She asked.

"Nothing noble." Sababa said. "More alarming, why are his pigs infected with a genotype of Hepatitis E that normally only infects humans?"

"What are you going to do about it?" Sara asked.

"I'll give the RCMP a call." He said. "There is one officer at the local detachment who likes to pull me over because she's lonely. I'll ask for someone else."

'I jumped across for you
Oh what a thing to do
Cause you were all yellow.'
Coldplay, *Yellow*

Early next morning, Sababa picked up his doppio doppio espresso from Code Brew and his pace to catch up with Dr. Marquis Shu Ying. He had great affection for his colleague, whose simple erudite genius was at least as remarkable as his own darker variety. There were fond memories of meeting him in other hallways in other Augusts when all the other internists were on their holidays, and comparing the lengths of their inpatient lists, often as long as they were tall. There were other stories that had hardened into legend, of Shu Ying's razor-sharp humour, and his usual response on the other end of the phone, when called to attend an emergency. *Heh, heh, heh...* And then he would be there before anyone worried about whether he was coming.

One late night in the ICU, Charmeine had called him about her patient. After relating her concern, she listened for a response. Hearing nothing for a minute, she reacted with indignation.

"The asshole has fallen asleep." She announced to the other nurses.

"*Heh, heh, heh...*" Shu Ying said. "The asshole is thinking."

On another occasion, patients in the reverse isolation room of the Death Star were developing hospital-acquired pneumonia from a rare organism. The infection control brigade was having puppies trying to figure out why. When Marquis took a magnifying glass to examine the tracheostomy of the latest victim, he found a profusion of tiny drain flies around the stoma, and later determined that they had built the fancy new room exactly over the hospital sewer.

Sababa remembered when some of his department members had gone to a local pub after work. Shu Ying ordered a hundred prawns. The waitress asked him how many plates and forks she should bring to the table.

"One of each." He said. When Marquis had finished those hundred prawns, he ordered a hundred more. Sababa lined up on Shu Ying's trajectory and slid up alongside him.

"How's the yin-yang duality today, Shu?" He asked.

"Strong." Shu said.

"This patient you will see in the unit." Shu continued. "The one Sara admitted early this morning."

"What about him?"

"An inch of time is an inch of gold, but you can't buy that inch of time with an inch of gold." Shu said. "According to the Five Elements, his element is wood, his emotional activity anger, his environmental factor wind, his sound calling sound, his time of day 11 p.m. to 3 a.m., his subjugation spleen, his yin organ liver, and his taste..."

"You're not helping me here, Shu." Sababa protested. "Is?" Marquis smiled.

"Sour."

"He sounds like a lawyer." Sababa said.

438

"He is." Shu veered off towards the Electrodiagnostic lab. Sababa continued down the corridor, past an anguished assembly of four people in the waiting room, and through the hiss of the frosted automatic door. *ICU—Tranquility Base.*

"Nice of you to drop by." Sara had been up all night and was looking somewhat worse for the ordeal.

"I was coming in anyway." Sababa smiled a Sababa smile. It wasn't contagious. "What kept you up?"

"He did." Sara's head nodded towards the patient in Cubicle 9.

"And who might he be?" Sababa asked.

"He might be Albert Schweitzer, but he's not." Sara fumed.

"And?"

"Leon 'Shady' Miles." She began. "65-year-old lawyer, a senior partner at Miles, Frum, and Romeda. Brought in early this morning after driving his Audi A3 into the Tim Hortons brick storefront."

"Injuries?"

"Not from the accident." She said. "But his hobby is about to finish him." Sababa looked at the large number of CADD pumps surrounding the counsellor, each one contributing to finite finality in the predictive equations for the end of life and the beginning of lawsuits, those machines you enter as a pig and come out as a sausage.

"What hobby?" Sababa asked.

"Dipsomania." Sara said. "Nothing but the finest brands."

"Ah, yes, alcohol, the cause of, and solution to, all life's problems." He said. "First the man takes a drink. Then the drink takes a drink. Then the drink takes the man. Absinthe makes the heart grow fonder."

"He's an alcoholic lawyer, Sab."

"Abraham Lincoln was an alcoholic lawyer."

"This guy was no Abraham Lincoln, Senator." She said.

"Was?"

"Come have a look." She and Sababa entered his cubicle. Mary was suctioning Shady's endotracheal tube. It made a noise like dishwater going down the drain.

"Leon here is a patient of 'Big Easy' Hacker." She said. "Ernie's been following his borderline liver for a year."

Sababa remembered his first shift on call at Harbour City Regional. Hacker had signed off to him just before a gruelling three-day holiday weekend with a few words of reassurance. *If you're still alive on Tuesday, you can stay.*

He looked at Shady's sallow skin and the thousand other clinical signs of alcoholic liver disease he could appreciate at a glance. Leon's abdomen was draining amber ascites the same colour as

439

his favourite double double single malt. His organs were floating and his mind was swimming in a sea of ammonia, like the rainstorm from a Jovian cloud. Shu Ying knew Jupiter as mùxīng, the 'wood star,' and would have known Leon as a block of wood, a closed mind, a closed book. The room smelled of sweet musty mice and fragrant fish. Shady's eyes were wild and confused with terror, his hands shook and his arms flapped in Mary's restraints. Sababa didn't like lawyers. They hired out their words and anger and posed a perennial threat to his ability to function as an effective medical consultant. They all treated their laws as if they were infallible and divinely inspired, but justice was an eternally elusive commodity in their artificial space-time discontinuum. Barristers and solicitors and judges considered Sababa's courtroom testimony 'like nailing Jell-O to a wall.' Mother Nature made the laws under which the portly professor operated and she tolerated no mistakes. Sababa knew that there was no law except the law that there was no law. Leon's eyes were grey; if they had ever been any other colour it had leached away with his humanity.

"So what tipped him over?" Sababa asked.

"This." Sara showed him Shady's Hepatitis A test. It was positive. "Probably got the virus from a counter server at Tim Hortons who left Harbour City about a month ago. And now he has this." Sababa saw the rest of the lab results. Leon was also in kidney failure.

"The good news is, he's running out of organs to fail." He said. "You're not usually allowed over three dead ones before the shovels come out of the shed. Why is he in renal failure?"

"Ernie saw him in the ER yesterday afternoon and drained off several litres of ascitic fluid from his belly."

"Several litres too much?" Sababa asked.

"He hooked his drainage up to wall suction and left for a while." Sara said.

"That's how he does stress tests." Sababa winced.

"He didn't give him any intravenous albumin or other fluid."

"That'll do it." He said. "So, you have a name?"

"Type 1 hepatorenal syndrome." She said. "I've been up all night trying to expand his intravascular volume with albumin, and given him midodrine and octreotide to reduce the doses of the three vasopressor medications I'm using to keep his blood pressure from tanking. He's on continuous veno-venous hemodialysis. And you saw the dearly beloved in the waiting room."

"Who's there?" Sababa asked.

440

"His son and daughter, and his law partners Frum and Romeda."

"Where's his wife?"

"She went home earlier on." Sara said. "She says she's available by phone if we need her."

"And what would we need her for?" Sababa asked.

"To tell her when he dies, I guess." Sara rubbed her temples. "I'm not sure which side she's pulling for."

"And the others?"

"It's been a nightmare." Sara said. "The two law partners keep asking legal questions. The son has been threatening to fire me all night long. And the daughter visiting from California has been on her phone to various consultant physician friends in Los Angeles, to collect whatever orders she wants to issue next."

"I'll go speak to them."

"Thanks, Sab." Sara leaned back and exhaled. "I would appreciate that." The portly professor left the unit to meet the anguished assembly.

"I'm Doctor Sababa." He began. "Dr. Reynold's preceptor."

"Where have you been?" The daughter asked. "Why haven't you been here?" Sababa told them about physician qualifications and delegated responsibilities and teaching and learning, but no one showed any interest.

"I have it on good authority from a relative on staff at Ronald Reagan UCLA Medical Center that my father's MELD score is only 36 points, which gives him a 3-month mortality of only 52.6%." The daughter said. "We should send him for a TIPS procedure and then a liver transplant, to a centre where they know what they're doing, as soon as possible."

"We use the Model for End-Stage Liver Disease mortality scoring you've mentioned to stratify stable patients already on liver transplant waiting lists." Sababa said. "Your father has a condition called hepatorenal syndrome. He's in shock. He's in grade 4 hepatic coma. We have another prognostic scoring system called Apache II. He will die whether or not we ship him anywhere."

"So why not send him?"

"Because, number one, I wouldn't be able to find anyone who would take him." Sababa said. "And number two, even if I could, I'm trying to tell you that, if I try to send him anywhere, it will not be a tranquil transfer, and he will not have a peaceful end." He watched four cell phones come out of separate spaces.

"I'm going back into the unit to check on what's happening." He said. "I'll be back with any news." No one was listening to anything but dial tones.

"Doctors are the same as lawyers." Frum said. "The only difference is that lawyers merely rob you, whereas doctors rob you and kill you too."

"Chekhov was a physician, Mr. Frum." Sababa said. "He meant that in jest." No one thought it was funny.

Back inside the unit, Sababa followed Shady's ECG monitor tracing into the dirt.

"Flatline!" Mary shouted. Sara looked at Sababa who made the hockey referee interference sign. The pressure inside the Death Star deflated. Sababa went out to speak to Shady's family and colleagues.

"I'm sorry." He said. "But Leon is gone."

"Gone?!" Screamed the daughter. "Gone?! I didn't hear you call a Code Blue."

"No, you didn't." Sababa said. "It wouldn't have made any difference." The cell phones reemerged from their hiding places.

"You say you're sorry like it's some kind of weapon or an excuse." Said the son.

"No, I am sorry." Sababa said. "And I'm using it correctly. Every time I walk into this room to tell someone that a person they love has died, I know they were fine before they met me. I know they're here so I can give them the worst news of their life. I am responsible for when someone goes from loving wife to grieving widow, or orphan, or alone in a cruel world. We both get to remember and change each other for the rest of our lives. So I take that seriously. I recognize the importance of my role. I respect that your pain is the biggest thing in this room. When I said I'm sorry, I meant it. 'I'm sorry' is perfect. 'I'm sorry' is redemption."

He called Reverend Gory to comfort the son and daughter, and counsel the counsellors. He called Shady's spouse at home to give her the news.

"Nothing in his life became him like leaving it." She said.

His emotional activity is anger, his time of day 11 p.m. to 3 a.m., his yin organ liver, and his taste..."

"Is?"

"Sour."

A half hour later, Dr. Hacker strode into the ICU, asking after Leon 'Shady' Miles. Sara told him what had happened.

"He was all right when I left him yesterday." Ernie remarked, before heading out to make his tee time at the Cottonwood golf course. Cottonwoods are the trees that dropped large branches on unsuspecting Conestoga wagons in the middle of the night. The pioneers used to call them 'widow makers.'

'Neither fire nor wind, birth nor death can erase our good deeds.'
Buddha

The casual reader is likely less ambivalent about death than 'Shady' Miles was about his own Double Double Whammy. For Leon, after a meaningless life of easy evil and exploitation and mediocrity, a meaningful death would have been hard, if not impossible. Guilt was its painful companion. The opposite of life was not death, it was indifference, and because of Leon's assumption that the story was only about him, his death was truly the end of him. No one is dead until the ripples they had caused in the world die away. You die twice, the first time when your heart stops and the second when somebody says your name for the last time. For Shady, they both occurred in the next instant.

For Sababa, the goal wasn't to live forever. The goal was to create something that would. He lived hoping to become a treasured memory, or an anonymous benefactor, doing good anyway.

The meaning of life is that it stops. The ancient Egyptians believed that upon death they would have to answer two questions to decide whether they could continue their journey in the afterlife: (1) Did you bring joy? (2) Did you find joy? Although Sababa knew that the answer to both questions would be yes, he wasn't sure about what he would do in Paradise, if the geography were to present itself. They might not allow him his obsessions. He would ask for a library. If Jane and Shiva couldn't with him, he wanted nothing to do with the place. If they could, he would go into that good night and through eternity holding infinity in the palm of his hand.

And when he shall die, take him and cut him out in little stars, and he will make the face of heaven so fine that all the world will be in love with night and pay no worship to the garish sun.

'To every man upon this earth
Death cometh soon or late.

And how can man die better
Than facing fearful odds,
For the ashes of his fathers,
And the temples of his gods?'
Thomas B. Macaulay

Death is a delightful hiding place for a weary man. For some, it is a beautiful doom. But if you cheat death today, you still die a little anyway. And no one is getting out of here alive.

Ned Parks got his colon back. By the time he had recovered enough from his broken hip and its complications, Harbour City had demolished Discontent City. Backhoes, city workers and police had moved in to disassemble and clean up what was left. But the provincial government had purchased nearby land and built 170 units of 'modular housing,' at a cost of $3.6 million. The Minister of Municipal Affairs and Housing said it was a good start.

"We have this wonderful opportunity to be successful in changing lives." She said.

As a recipient of one of the new units, Ned had front row seats for the ribbon cutting. His response to the Harbour City Star reporter who interviewed him sitting in his furnished new digs was illuminating.

"What do you expect me to eat?" Ned asked. He that is discontented in one place will seldom be content in another.

All Harbour City's mayors had been pirates or lawyers, or both. The current burgermeister's solution to the perceived shortage of affordable housing was to promote the construction of a stack of condos overlooking Sababa's homestead on the lake, right next door.

John Ormond not only lost his tent and belongings in the demolition, but he also misplaced a kidney, removed by endoscopic nephrectomy in Victoria, performed to normalize his blood pressure. He is now living in a van down by the river.

Emma Nem's liver biopsy showed findings consistent with autoimmune hepatitis. Two days after starting treatment with prednisone and azathioprine, her elevated liver enzymes began to normalize, and she was able to come off the medication six months later. She traded her black cohosh menopausal mixture for a more natural history of hot flashes and bone loss and night sweats and vaginal dryness and painful sex and reduced libido and insomnia and anxiety and poor memory and concentration. She now takes St. John's wort for the depression.

Shakespeare had posed the question. *What is more miserable than discontent?* Al Ginsberg, who had seen the best minds of his generation destroyed by madness, vanished into nowhere Zen during the demolition of his former colony.

Sababa cured Namibian diamond merchant Arthur Looss of his strongyloidiasis with two pills; he cured Charlotte Manson of her schistosomiasis with one.

Orpingalik's cardiac biopsy in Victoria showed an infestation of Trichinella nativa. He called them glowworms because they had lit the way to Sababa. He took the Good Doctor's mebendazole until the pumping action of his heart normalized. Orpingalik is back on his trapline and walrus hunting expeditions in the western high arctic. Stanzy and the local Coast Salish sent him home with an Outwell Jimbu Camping Stove, a shipment of gas cartridges, and a box of Timbits.

Dr. John Falstaff removed Priscilla Plantagenet's left breast dog tapeworm collection. The surgical specimen showed characteristic daughter cysts of hydatid disease. After finishing Sababa's course of albendazole, she resigned her position as a dog groomer for Pawcific Coast and opened Harbour City's first cat café.

Jan Mikulicz-Radeck's liver biopsy and antimitochondrial antibody results confirmed Sara's diagnosis of primary biliary cirrhosis. Her minor salivary gland biopsy showed Sjögren's Syndrome. Her itch is gone, her mucosal membranes are more comfortable, and she has returned as a counter attendant at Tim Hortons.

The RCMP arrested Robert Picton for feeding his victims to his pigs. He is receiving off-label ribavirin therapy in prison, released and provided under the BC Pharmacare and Correctional Service of Canada compassionate care program. The ironic difference between hyphenated and non-hyphenated; Inflammable means flammable. What a country.

Leonard 'Shady' Miles is still dead. His surviving partners are still Frum and Romeda.

Dr. Sara Reynolds broke her news to Sababa as delicately as she could. Harbour City Regional's plastic surgeon, Dr. Christian 'Pretty Boy' Troy, had asked her to marry him. She was now planning on specializing in dermatology.

"Is that one or two things?" Sababa had asked.

"Three." Sara said. "I'm pregnant. Christian and I plan on opening a high-end cosmetic surgery clinic on the island after the baby is born." The portly professor bit his tongue and uttered all the usual platitudes one offers in these circumstances. Later that night, he told Jane of his disappointment.

"This is a happy event." She chided him for his insensitivity. "Think of their love and good fortune in a positive way."

445

"Her departure will raise the IQ of both departments." He conceded.

Epilogue

'Look to the seasons when choosing your cures.'
Hippocrates

So, how was Harbour City? Aren't you glad you stopped? You appear to have survived the ordeal and, as importantly, gained new skills of observation and analysis.

One of the questions you might have is why are there only two seasons in Sababa's Casebook, when everyone knows there are more—like the Humours of Empedocles, the Diatessaron's

447

honeyed treacle and voices, Sababa's Levels of Medical Intervention, his doppio doppio espresso, Loeb's Laws, the diagnostic methods of physical examination, Shu Ying's possible elemental relationships, the massive fluted columns on the façade of The Great National Land Building, Sophia's prides of the Philippines, the most common OB-GYN surgical procedures, the hardest years of an orthopod's life, the D's of pellagra, the number of people who die of TB every minute, the number of subspecies of malaria or Tim Horton's Stanley Cup victories, the most overrated things in life, and the number of chambers in a human heart—Even Antonio Vivaldi knew there are four. Se questa non piace, non voglio più scrivere. *If you don't like this, I'll stop writing.*

As spectacular as spring and fall are in Sababaland, in autumn and winter you can feel the bone structure of the landscape. The fires burn and the kettles sing, and earth sinks to rest until next spring. Falling leaves hide the path so quietly.

Sababa's creator has a Faustian pact with the devil that, if he is allowed to live that long, he would write a sequel to The Casebook.

Wait for it.

Characters

Family
Eleazar Sababa
Jane Sababa
Shiva

Administrators
Malcolm Canmore- Site Administrator, Harbour City Regional Hospital
Foster Concord- Chief Executive Officer, CVIHR
William Bligh- Chief Executive Officer, VIHA
Dr Milo Minderbinder- Executive Vice President and Chief Medical Officer, VIHA

Dr Petronilla de Meath- Chief of Staff, Harbour City Regional Hospital
Corky Mcfail- Minister of Health

Moa
Mercy

Paging Operator
Lana

Internal Medicine
Dr Peter Zaias
Dr Eleazar Sababa
Dr Marquis Shu Ying
Dr Ernie 'The Big Easy' Hacker
Dr Dasco Boet
Dr Wayward Woods
Dr Edward Hyde (Respirology)
Dr Sidney Shalimar
Dr Commodus Sitsofsky (Dermatology)
Dr Henry Chibueze (Oncology)
Dr Oliver Lax (Neurology)
Dr. Gerry Genial (EP Cardiologist, Victoria)
Dr. Ricardo Wineburger (Interventional Cardiologist, Victoria)
Dr. Manfred Mann (Echocardiologist, Victoria)

Surgery
Dr Theodor Billroth (ENT)
Dr Buddy Benway (General)
Dr John Falstaff (General)
Dr Jules Martino (General)
Dr Olaf Octagon (OB/GYN)
Dr TJ Eckleburg (Ophthalmology)
Dr Piggy Muldoon (Orthopedics)
Dr Christian 'Pretty Boy' Troy (Plastics)
Dr Harry 'Doc' Martin (Urology)

Anasthesiology
Dr Banjo Paterson

Pathology
Dr Juan Leyblanca

Psychiatry

Dr Robert La Capuche

Radiology
Dr Alan Statham
Dr Mako Brisk

GPs
Dr Tictac Tarmac
Dr Poldy Bloom
Dr Petronilla de Meath
Dr James Ruben Andrews
Dr Nicholas Rivera

ER Physicians
Dr Myles Capitaine
Dr Trace Pangloss
Dr Cliffy Carlton
Dr Gung Ho

Ward Clerks
ICU- Betty Boop
ER- Cheri Sundae

Nursing
Grand Galactic Governess of Nightingales (Big Nurse)- Mildred Ratschet
Director of Medical Nursing- Edith Mortley
Director of Surgical Nursing- Daisy Daws
ER- Dina, Michaela, Regina
ICU- Mary, Charmeine, Angie
Floor 1- Serafina
Floor 3- Sariel
Floor 5- Sophia, Samara Morgan
Floor 6- Shekina
VIU Nursing professor- Amber
Coast Salish Community Nurse- Stanzy

Internal Medicine Residents
Dr Jamie Dunne
Dr Sara Reynolds

Biomedical Engineer
Murray 'Leatherman' MacGyver

Medical Advisory Committee
Dr Petronilla de Meath
Malcolm Canmore
Dr Jules Martino
Dr Eleazar Sababa
Dr Juan Leyblanca
Dr Trace Pangloss
Dr Mako Brisk
Dr Banjo Paterson

RCMP
Veronica Marsden

Patients
1. The Case of the Ultimate Artery
Sam Kee- City Councillor
Man Singh- Blueberry Farmer
Murasaki Shikibu- Pianist
Julius Noh- Stamp Dealer
Paul Hewson- Catholic Priest
Yuri Heilongjiang- Amur River Prisoner
Edie Sitwell- Dental Hygienist
Rod Duterte- Drywaller
Linda Blare- Health Food Shop Owner
Randy McCoy- Cattle Rancher
Britney Pratt- Methamphetamine Addict

2. The Case of the Broken Heart
Linley Valley- Realtor
Meisie 'Stretch' van der Merwe- Travel Agent
Fred Hundertwasser- Guest House Owner
Mingtao Wang- Chinese Restaurant Owner
Victoria Huckell- Scotiabank Teller
Cathy Bates- Jewelry Store Employee
Pinky Floyd- Busker
William Paxton- Theatre Manager
Hank Gathers- Hotel Maintenance Man
Pfeffer Bach Reiter- Second Hand Bookstore Owner

3. The Case of the Cornelian Dilemma
Rick Erscurve- Fisheries Biologist
Sam McGee- Bed and Breakfast Owner
Stephen Dedalus- Parks Supervisor
Aurora Leigh- Salon Hairdresser
Jerome Conn- Canada Fisheries Salmon Officer

452

Louisa Musgrove- School Teacher
Brad Eggleston- BC Conservation Officer
Sherry Rogers- Single Mother
Dr. Jeremy Bentham- Family Physician

4. The Case of the Parthian Shot

Harewood Mines- Geotechnical Engineer
Elizabeth Barnes- Housewife
Mallory Weiss- Paving Contractor
Bernadine Soulier- Golf Widow
Martha Lillard- Pub Waitress
Henri Mygold- Canadian Tire Auto Parts Specialist
Herb Hancock- Fireman First Responder
Hillary Flinston- MLA
Amato Lusitano- Coast Guard Officer

5. The Case of the Syncopated Rhythm

Jasmine Place- Dance Teacher
Brian Hugh Warner- Singer
Alexander Asteras- Greek Tourist
Larry Bird- Parking Attendant
Barry Keliher- Government Liquor Store Worker
Daisy Miller- Pregnant Canada Post Letter Carrier
Torsades de Pointes- Chef
Mathew Damon- Casino Croupier
Rich Cheney- Steakhouse Manager
Cara Cicatriz- Cosmetician

6. The Case of the Lush Vegetation

Gulch Galloway- Dairy Farmer
Walt Gropius- Architect
Toni Brachstone- Laughter Yoga Teacher
Michael Verigin- Doukhobor Meats and Delicatessen Owner
Edmond Nocard- Horse Trail Ride Guide
Ed Derrick- Wildlife Recovery Centre Volunteer
Duck Jones- Qualicum Trading Post Employee
Les Hart- Country Market Produce Worker

7. The Case of the Flushed Fisherman

Coal Tyee- Fisherman
Seale Harris- Salt Water Taffy Shop Owner
Dawn Hope- Alberta Student
George Anson- Unemployed Electrician
Zonobia Fasciculata- Bistro Waitress
John Lykoudis- Chemical Supply Owner

Paul Newman- Pool Shark
Howard Dell- Pilot
Hideki Tojo- Sushi Chef
Jacob Berzelius- American Yachtie
Anthony Stark- Welder
Gary Shadling- Bartender
Verner Morrison- BC Ferries Captain
Rhea Bolger- Fish and Chips Line Cook
Quinten Massys- Chandler

8. The Case of the Melting Man
Roger 'Buttertubs' Marsh- Trailer Park Manager
Lauren Wasser- RV Dealership Receptionist
Becky Vulnifica- Fishmonger
Robert Smart- Scam Artist/Pimp
Jean Molière- Metis Carver
Bruce Darling- Transsexual
Muerto Canyon- RV Lifestyler
Mathias Mamangy- Malagasy Missionary
Silas Seaweed- Native Fisherman

9. The Case of the Pretty Bird
Mona Pseudos- Natural Products Shop Owner
Gerry Ritz- Saltspring Island Cheesemaker
Bo Geste- Retired Federal Civil Servant
Jensen Löwenstein Mott- Tennis Instructor
Gabriela Sounder- Aromatherapist
Bill Koch Pustulatus- Seattle Businessman
Duncan Whippletree- Nursery Owner
Binky O'Hare- Tree Planter
Wilbur Wright- Poultry Farmer

10. The Case of the Sumatran Mosquito
Miles Davis- Airport Custodian
Jaroslav Flegr- Big Game Trophy Hunting Guide
Charles Donovan- Airport Screening Officer
Justin Beaver- Haida Gwaii Hiker
Sunshine Cruz- Social Justice Warrior
Ernest Tyzzer- Emu Farmer
Isadora Belli- Barista
David Bruce- Bank Manager
Michel Vieuchange- Air Canada Flight Attendant
Tiki Lane- Jane Sababa's Sister

11. The Case of the Deadly Tree

454

Georgia Strait- Dogwalker
Bruce Chatwin- Harbour City Star Reporter
Charles E. Smith- Snowbird
Junmai Daiginjo- Saké Maker
Clyde Chestnut Barrow- Tourist from Missouri
Too-Loud MacLeod- Bagpiper
Patrick Keeling- Veterinarian
Harry Wheatcroft- Lab Tech
Candy Diocese- Naturopath
Alberta Hoffman- Wiccan Priestess

12. The Case of the Double Double Whammy
Leon 'Shady' Miles- Lawyer
Ned Sparks- Gold Prospector
John Ormond- Discontent City Squatter
Emma Nem- Herbalist
Al Ginsberg- Poet
Arthur Looss- Namibian Diamond Merchant
Charlotte Manson- Filippino Nanny
Orpingalik- Inuit Hunter
Priscilla Plantagenet- Dog Groomer
Jan Mikulicz-Radecki- Tim Hortons Attendant
Robert Picton- Pig Farmer

The Analects of Doctor Sababa

A. The Science

1. Sababa's Existential Slap:
What's the question?

2. Sababa's Three Rules of Medical Analysis:
1. What you got you got
2. What you don't got, you don't got

3. Context is everything

3. Sababa's Three States of Natural Imbalance:
1. Too much
2. Too little
3. Weird

4. Sababa's Four Levels of Medical Intervention:
1. Etiologic- causal
2. Symptomatic- anywhere
3. Geographic - ICU
4. Existential - DNR

5. Loeb's Laws
1. If what you're doing is working, keep doing it.
2. If what you're doing is not working, stop doing it.
3. If you don't know what you're doing, do nothing.
4. Never make the treatment worse than the disease.
    Robert F. Loeb, 1895-1973- Loeb's Laws

6. Leonard's Law of Physical Findings
It's obvious or it's not there.

7. Sutton's Law
Perform first the diagnostic test expected to be most useful ('Because that's where the money is.'—Willie Sutton was a bank robber. This was his response when they asked him why he robbed banks.)

8. Occam's Razor
The simplest explanation is always the best."

9. Hickam's Dictum
A patient can have as many diseases as they damn well please

10. Three laws of Thermodynamics
1. You can't win.
2. You can't break even;
3. You can't get out of the game.

11. Sababa's Aphorisms:
The Internist exists to solve the 5% of medical problems that other intelligence, artificial or otherwise, overlooks.

456

The T6 somatotome is the final common pathway to all chest pain.
Serum sodium is not about sodium; it's about water.
The retina is a window into the world of disease.
Not all that wheezes is asthma.
Alternative Medicine is an alternative universe.
The pulse is your friend. The College is not your friend.
When in doubt add sugar; when in more doubt add thiamine.
Your most important detector is the First Cranial Nerve.
Phlebotomies are good for your rose garden.
Never choose a subspecialty career path based on a single 3 a.m. orgasm.
If they fight you, they're still alive.
Round numbers are always false.
You either (1) don't know (2) don't care or (3) don't know you don't care
They're not dead until they're warm and dead
Liver AST:ALT>1.6 = alcohol
Risk of Lawyer Death = $\dfrac{\text{Number of CADD pumps}}{\text{Number of organ systems}}$

12. Sababa's Research Jargon Interpreter

It has long been known: I didn't look up the original reference
A definite trend is evident: the data is practically meaningless
While it has not been possible to provide definite answers to the questions: An unsuccessful experiment, but I still hope to get it published
Three of the samples were chosen for a detailed study: The other results didn't make any sense
Typical results are shown: This is the prettiest graph
These results will appear in a subsequent report: I might get around to this sometime, if published/funded
A careful analysis of obtained data: Three pages of notes were obliterated when I knocked over a glass of beer
After additional study by my colleagues: They didn't understand it either
Thanks are due to Joe Blotz for assistance with the experiment and to Cindy Adams for valuable discussions: Mr. Blotz did the work and Ms. Blotz explained to me what it meant
A highly signifigant area for exploratory study: a totally useless topic selected by my committee
In my experience: Once
In case after case: Twice
In a series of cases: Three times
It is believed that: I think

It is generally believed that: A couple of others think so too

Correct within an order of magnitude: wrong

According to statistical analysis: Rumour has it

It is clear that much additional work will be required before a complete understanding of this phenomenon occurs: I don't understand

A statistically-oriented projection of the significance of these findings: A wild guess

It is hoped that this study will stimulate further investigations in this field: I quit

13. Sababa's Medical Glossary

Appy: a person's appendix or a patient with appendicitis

Baby Catcher: an obstetrician

Babygram: x-ray of an entire infant

Bagging: manually helping a patient breathe using a squeeze bag attached to a mask that covers the face

Banana: a person with jaundice (yellowing of the skin and eyes)

Beemer: A patient with a high body mass index (BMI), obese.

Blood Suckers/Leeches: those who take blood samples, such as laboratory technicians

Body: big bag of unknowable goo

Bounceback: a patient who returns to the emergency department with the same complaints shortly after being released; readmission

Bury the Hatchet: accidentally leaving a surgical instrument inside a patient

Cath Jockey: Invasive cardiologist

CBC: complete blood count; an all-purpose blood test used to diagnose different illnesses and conditions

Circling the drain (CTD), PBAB (pine box at bedside): A patient who can't be saved and death is imminent.

Clinic unit: 200 pounds—'three clinic units' means the patient weighs 600 pounds

Code Brown: a patient who has lost control of his or her bowels

Code Yellow: a patient who has lost control of his or her bladder

Crook-U: similar to the ICU or PICU, but referring to a prison ward in the hospital

Departure Lounge: geriatric ward

Discharged to God or discharged to heaven: Patient has died.

Donorcyle: motorcycle, whose riders often become donors

DNR: do not resuscitate; a written request made by terminally ill or elderly patients who do not want extraordinary efforts made if they go into cardiac arrest, a coma, etc.

Doc in a Box: a small health-care center, usually with high staff turnover

Dusting and Cleaning: dilation and curettage

dyscopia: difficulty coping at home; often used by internists to imply that the patient requires admission to hospital despite having no obvious acute illness

FLK: funny-looking kid

fluffy: fat

Foley: a catheter used to drain the bladder of urine

FOOBA (Found on orthopedics barely alive): A patient who has had a joint operation, but has developed heart failure or another critical internal condition not recognized by the orthopedic surgeon.

food snorkel: feeding tube

Forehead sweat: When your gut says your patient is going to circle the drain but you got no objective data yet. see Sniff test.

Frequent flyer, cockroach: A person who turns up repeatedly at the emergency department with a variety of ailments.

Freud Squad: the psychiatry department

full code: full cardiac resuscitation according to Advanced Cardiac Life Support (ACLS) guidelines

Gas Passer: an anesthesiologist

GI Rounds: a clinicians meal or snack, typically consumed in the hospital cafeteria

Goat Rodeo: an emergency where nothing goes right

GSW: gunshot wound

Hanging crepe: Preparing family that patient is dying and cannot be saved.

Headshrinker: psychiatrist

The Hole: used by surgeons to describe the appearance of the operative field in an obese patient undergoing abdominal surgery, when fat has to be moved to the sides to view abdominal structures

Horrendoma: Refers to a horrendous medical condition; patient or situation fraught with many complications and often associated with a bad outcome

House Red: blood

Knife and Gun Club: an emergency room in a rough neighbourhood

Knuckle Dragger: orthopedic surgeon

M & Ms: mortality and morbidity conferences where doctors and other health-care professionals discuss mistakes and patient deaths

Milwaukee goiter: protruding abdominal fat

MRI: a big fancy machine that prints money

MVA: motor vehicle accident

O Sign: an unconscious patient whose mouth is open

Parentectomy: removing one or more parents from the examination room or hospital bedside

Pediatron: pediatrician

Pharmacologically-enhance: strongly medicated or 'stoned' personality

Plumber, Stream Team: urologist

Q Sign: an unconscious patient whose mouth is open and tongue is hanging out

Rear Admiral: proctologist

selfie: a person with a self-induced injury or illness

Shotgunning: ordering a wide variety of tests in the hope that one will show what's wrong with a patient

Sieve: resident physician who seems to admit every patient encountered

Slasher: surgeon

Slow Code, Hollywood code, Light Blue Code: slow-motion or half-hearted attempt to resuscitate a patient in cardiac arrest

Soft Admission: a patient a Sieve would admit but a Wall would not

Sniff test: When you walk into a room and something smells bad, but you can't immediately put your finger on it.

Stat: from the Latin statinum, meaning immediately

Status dramaticus: A patient who loudly and dramatically magnifies symptoms to get quicker medical attention.

Swallower: A term used for certain psychiatric patients.

Tox Screen: testing the blood for the level and type of drugs in a patient's system

Train Wreck: a case in which one complication follows another

Turf: a term meaning to refer a patient to another specialty service

UBI: unexplained beer injury; a patient who appears in the ER with an injury sustained while intoxicated that he or she can't explain

Unclear Medicine: nuclear medicine

Virgin Abdomen: a patient who has never had abdominal surgery

Vitamin C: the antibiotic ceftriaxone

Walker: ironic term for elderly patient with dementia and a poor quality of life, often bedridden

Wall: the opposite of a Sieve, a Wall is one who is skillful at preventing soft admissions to the hospital

Yellow submarine: An obese patient with jaundice caused by cirrhosis of the liver.

Zebra: a very unusual disease

14. Laws of the House of God

1. GOMERS don't die. (GOMER = Get Out of My Emergency Room)
2. GOMERS go to ground.
3. At a cardiac arrest, the first procedure is to take your own pulse.
4. The patient is the one with the disease.
5. Placement comes first.
6. There is no body cavity that cannot be reached with a #14G needle and a good strong arm.
7. Age + BUN = Lasix dose.
8. They can always hurt you more.
9. The only good admission is a dead admission.
10. If you don't take a temperature, you can't find a fever.
11. Show me a BMS (Best Medical Student, a student at The Best Medical School) who only triples my work and I will kiss his feet.
12. If the radiology resident and the medical student both see a lesion on the chest x-ray, there can be no lesion there.
13. The delivery of good medical care is to do as much nothing as possible.
14. Connection comes first.
15. Learn empathy.
16. Speak up.
17. Learn your trade, in the world.
    Samuel Shem, *The House of God*, 1978

15. Sababa's Rules for Residents

1. When I'm on call, you're on call.
2. You go first.
3. If I'm sleeping, don't wake me unless your patient is dying.
4. The dying patient better not be dead when I get there. Not only will you have killed someone, you will have woken me for no good reason.
5. When I move, you move.
6. Everybody goes home.

16. Sababa's Empiric Guidelines for ICU Patient Management

1. Intubate and attach the trachea to an MA-2 respirator. Adjust the machine so that the pH = 7.40, PCO2 = 40, and PO2 = 100. Do not permit any deviation from these numbers.

2. Insert a large bore triple lumen catheter into the neck. Its precise location will determine whether it will be used for infusing IV fluids, or NG feeds or for measuring blood gases.

3. Insert an arterial line, through which blood can be drained continuously for lab tests. If the mean arterial pressure is less than 70, infuse albumin, dopamine, dobutamine and levophed; calculate the appropriate dose (in micrograms per kil per minute), and then run them in wide open. A litre of premixed solution can be kept at the bedside and forced in using a pressure bag. There is no need to waste time thinking about what kind of shock is present, as this mixture will correct all of them.

4. Insert a rectal tube. This keeps the sheets clean, the laundry happy, and makes rectal exam impossible.

5. Insert an NG tube, and infuse Mylanta. The resultant diarrhea will prevent clogging of the rectal tube.

6. Insert a foley catheter. Keep the urine output at 40+/- 2 ml/hr. If less than 40, give a bolus of Lasix (the dose can be calculated as: creatinine squared X number of hours since you last slept. Use the hearing aid provided by the maufacturer. If urine output is greater than 40, tighten the clamp on the Foley.

7. Insert CVP and Swan-Ganz catheters. Keep the CVP at 10 and the wedge pressure at 16. While this may be difficult, it is your most important job in the ICU. All else pales in comparison. If a pressure is low, give a bolus of fluid (this can be premixed with Lasix just in case). Is it is high, remove blood through the appropriate port. Ignore any physical findings that don't fit with the wedge pressures on the chart.

8. Start all patients on Ranitidine, Mylanta, heparin, tobramycin, clindamycin, cefotaxime, INH and Solu Medrol. Culture every orifice daily, but continue this drug regiment regardless of the results. If the patient begins to look uncomfortable, add amphotericin B.

9. Consult nephrology, hematology, cardiology, neurology, and infectious disease as soon as the patient arrives in the unit, Let them derive lists of differential diagnoses. Follow any suggestions that agree with the data derived from the Swan-Ganz catheter.

10. Don't waste valuable time doing a physical exam (if God had intended for us to do physical exams he would have never given us Swan-Ganz catheters). If you try to examine the patient, you will only get tangled up in the lines and tubes or trip over a wire, Also, the nurses will be busy putting on eye patches, TED stockings, mittens and bunny boots. You will only get in the way.

11. Write in the patient's chart continuously. This created the illusion that you are busy, and keeps you from finding more problems with the patient, which would only complicate matters.

12. Always keep in mind that your patient may be dead. This is easily overlooked. The respirator makes it look like he is breathing, the pacemaker keeps his heart beating, an arterial pressure reading of zero is probably a clogged line, and pulses are never palpable because of edema and hematomas. Don't be fooled. If in doubt, ask.

B. The Snowflakes

1. Sababa's Homeopathy: The Evolution of Medicine
I have chest pain...
2000 BC - Here, eat this root.
1000 AD - That root is heathen. Here, say this prayer.
1850 AD - That prayer is superstition. Here, drink this potion.
1940 AD - That potion is snake oil. Here, swallow this pill.
1985 AD - That pill is ineffective. Here, take this antibiotic.
2000 AD - That antibiotic is artificial. Here, eat this root.

2. Sababa's Homeopathy: The Logical Fallacy Laws
1. The Law of the Similars
2. Hering's Law (Direction of Cure)
3. The Single Remedy Law
4. The Law of Minimum Dose
Homeopathy is mostly water. Plants crave water. Ergo, plants crave homeopathy.

C. The Suits

1. Sababa's Equation of Medical-Bureaucratic Inequity:

$$x = \frac{Power}{(Knowledge + Accountability)}$$

$$where\ x_{ideal} = 1;$$
$$x_{bureaucrat} = Infinity;$$
$$x_{physician} = 0$$

2. The Fatal Law of Gravity
When you are down, everything falls down on you.

3. Ellard's Laws

1. Those who want to learn will learn.
2. Those who don't want to learn will lead enterprises.
3. Those incapable of either learning or leading will regulate scholarship and enterprise to death.

4. Boren's Laws for Bureaucrats
1. When in charge, ponder.
2. When in trouble, delegate.
3. When in doubt, mumble.

5. The Law of Inverse Relevance
The less you intend doing about something the more you have to keep talking about it.

6. Sababa's Mission Statement Generator
17 Adverbs: quickly, proactively, efficiently, assertively, interactively, professionally, authoritatively, conveniently, completely, continually, dramatically, enthusiastically, collaboratively, synergistically, seamlessly, competently, globally
26 verbs:
maintain, supply, provide acces to, disseminate, network, create, engineer, integrate, leverage other's, leverage existing, coordinate, administrate, initiate, facilitate, promote, restore, fashion, revolutionize, build, enhance, simplify, pursue, utilize, foster, customize, negotiate
39 adjectives:
professional, timely, effective, unique, cost effective, virtual, scalable, economically sound, inexpaanisce, value-added, business quality, diverse, high-quality, competitive, excellent, innovation, corporate, high standards in, world-class, error-free, performance based, multimedia based, market-driven, cutting edge, high-payoff, low-risk high-yield, long-term, high-impact, prospective, progressive, ethical, enterprise-wide, principle-centered, mission-critical, parallel, interdependent, emerging, seven-habits-conforming, resource-leveling
20 Nouns:
content, paradigms, data, opportunities, information, services, material, technology, benefits, solutions, infrastructure, products, deliverables, catalysts for change, resources, methods of empowerment, sources, leadership skills, meta-services, intellectual capital

7. Kohlberg's Stages of Moral Development
A. Premoral of Preconventional Stages
Stage 1. Punishment and Obedience

Stage 2. Instrumental Exchange
   B. Conventional Morality
Stage 3. Interpersonal Conformity
Stage 4. Law and Order
Stage 5. Prior Rights and Social Contract
Stage 6. Universal Ethical Principles

8. The Creation

In the Beginning was the plan
And then came the assumptions
And the Assumptions were without form
And the plan was completely without substance
And the Darkness was upon the faces of the workers
And they spake unto their Group Heads, saying:
'It is a crock of shit, and it stinketh.'
And the Group Heads went unto their Section Heads, and
Sayeth:
'It is a pail of dung, and none may abode the odour thereof'
And the Section Heads went unto their Managers and sayeth
unto them:
'It is a container of Excrement, and it is very strong,
such that none here may abide by it'
And the Manager went unto their Director, and sayeth unto
him:
'It is a vessel of fertilizer, and none may abide its strength'
And the Directors went unto their Director-General, and sayeth:
'It contains that which aids plant growth, and it is very strong.'
And the Director-General went unto the Assistant Deputy
Minister,
and sayeth unto him:
'It promoteth growth, and it is very powerful'
And the ADM went unto the Deputy Minister, and sayeth unto
him:
'This powerful new plan will actively promote the growth and
efficiency of the Department, and this area in particular'
And the Deputy Minister looked upon the plan,
And saw that it was good
And the Plan became Policy.
Amen

9. Voltaire's Lexicon:

Accountability: not us
Action Plan: schedule of meetings
Agenda: what is never hidden

Barrier: protection against conception of universality
Bias: characteristic of anything we don't agree with
Care Provider: person sued when things go wrong
Chair: where the Chairperson's mind is resting
Chairperson: neutered Chairman
Collaboration: this is how you will do the labour
Community-Based: Home alone
Confidential: don't let the press get this
Consultant: American expert
Consumer: the person with consumption
Deputy Minister: Big shot technocrat with tenure
Disease: effect of Kryptonite
Doctor: Bad guy
Document: war against the forests
Downsizing: you're fired
Empowerment: piss off and do it yourself
Envelope: funding container with a sealed top and a hole in the bottom
Environment: everything we are screwing up
Executive Summary: limit of our attention span
Expedite: make several copies of a document or push down the handle
Expert: Technocrat from another province
Facilitate: empower the front line
Fee for Service: the root of all evil
Front Line: where the effect of firing is absorbed
Fundamental: bottom line of this insanity
Gatekeeper: the fellow you meet after crossing the River Styx
Gender: Technocrat's substitute for sex
Government: Where children of unmarried parents work
Holistic: referring to the middle part of the Health Care doughnut
Illness: Bad stuff; costs money; not the business of the Ministry of Health
Impact: How we break things that work
Leading Edge: Closest to the precipice
Mandate: means to an end which justifies the means; single exception to gender policy
Matrix Management: mother of all muddles
Meetings: technique to keep ideas form being translated into action by spending hours collecting minutes
Minister of Health- Count of Phlebotomy
Ministry Data: bovine ordure arranged on tables
Ministry of Health:
Ministry Plan: Ultimate oxymoron

466

Mortality: One less bell to answer

MPP: Many perks and pensions

Multidisciplinary: Collaboration of Care Providers

NDP: Numbingly Draconian Palatines or Nearly Dead Philosophy

New Paradigms: Ideas from the 1970s

Outplacement: You're fired and we're escorting you out of this place

Overheads: Where we never hide the agenda (never circulate before a meeting)

Paradigm Shift: All we've got is loose change or 'we're going through the change'

Personalize: what technocrats never do—always remove the person the public will accept will stomp out disease so we don't have to pay for curing it

Policy: current favored positions

Politics: a career that does not require credentials

Position Paper: Kama sutra of policy

Preferred Future Survey: dreaming in technicolour

Preliminary Report: it was out idea if it works

Priorize: Confirmation of a faulty education; means to put something or someone into a priory. technocrat means list all the things we aren't going to pay for but prioritize ain't a verb

Program Management: passing out copies of our overheads

Rationalization: turning subtraction into addition

Reform: Curriculum of Health Care Reform School

Repatriation: sending refugees back where they came from

Restructuring: Perestroika

Retreat: technocrat's way of moving forward.

Role Statement: outline of how to respond to the punches

Senior Consultant: Junior technocrat; little shot

Service: what you can't get any of around here

Sex: probably neutered

Specialist: Worse guy

Subspecialist: Lex Luthor

Stakeholders: people who will be out for the count

Strategic Planning: reading the writing on the wall while you have you back to it

Task Force: Lots of meetings

Technology: the machines that go 'ping'

TQM: total quandry management

Transfer Payments: the money that's been transferred to technocrat pensions

Treasury Board: the root of all money

Trial Balloon: inflatable structure which rises rapidly if contents are hot or excessively vapid
Universality: Mythologic concept linking champagne taste to bee budget; a 'sacred trust'
VIHA: Very Iffy Helicopter Access
Wellness: Great stuff; costs small change
    (with thanks to Philip Hall UofM)

'Their standard procedure when faced by outside questioning is to avoid answering and instead to discourage, even to frighten off the questioner by implying that he is uninformed, inaccurate, superficial, and, invariably, overexcited, If the questioner has some hierarchical power, the experts may feel obliged to answer with greater care. For example, he may release a minimum amount of information in heavy dialect and accompany it with apologies for the complexity, thus suggesting that the questioner is not competent to understand anything more. And if the questioner must be answered but need not be respected—a journalist, for example, or a politician—the expert may release a flood of incomprehensible data, thus drowning out debate while pretending to be cooperative. And even if someone does manage to penetrate the confusion of material, he will be obliged to argue against the expert in a context of such complexity that the public, to whom he is supposed to communicating understanding, will quickly lose interest. In other words, by drawing the persistent outsider into his box, the expert will have rendered him powerless.'

                    Saul, JR *Voltaire's Bastards*

10. Sababa's Military Terminology

Big Voice: On military bases, loudspeakers broadcast urgent messages. When incoming rocket or mortar fire is detected by radar systems, the Big Voice automatically broadcasts a siren and instructions to take cover. The Big Voice will also warn of scheduled explosions, usually to destroy captured weapons.
Bird: Helicopter. 'Chopper' is rarely used, except in movies, where it is always used. A chopper is a kind of motorcycle, not an aircraft.
Black (on ammo, fuel, water, etc.): Almost out.
CHU: (pronounced choo) Containerized Housing Unit. These small, climate-controlled trailers usually sleep between two and eight soldiers or doctors and is the primary unit of housing on larger bases. A CHU Farm is a large number of CHUs together. CHUs are unarmored and very vulnerable to rocket attacks.

COP: Combat Outpost. A small base, usually housing between 40 and 150 soldiers, often in a particularly hostile area. Life at a COP is often austere and demanding, with every soldier responsible for both guard duty and patrolling.

DFAC: (pronounced dee-fack) Dining Facility, aka Chow Hall. Where soldiers eat. At larger bases the meals are served by contracted employees, often from Bangladesh or India. These employees are called TCNs, or Third-Country Nationals.

Dustoff: Medical evacuation by helicopter. For example, 'dustoff inbound' means that a medevac helicopter is on the way.

Embed: A reporter who is accommodated by the military command to observe operations firsthand. Security, food, shelter and transportation are provided by the military for the embed.

FOB: Forward Operating Base. Bigger than a COP, smaller than a superbase. A FOB can be austere and dangerous, but is more commonly provisioned with hot, varied meals, hot water for showers and laundry, as well as recreational facilities.

Fobbit: Combination of FOB and Hobbit. Derogatory term for soldiers who do not patrol outside the FOB.

Geardo: (rhymes with weirdo) A soldier who spends an inordinate amount of their personal money to buy fancy military gear, such as weapon lights, GPS watches, custom rucksacks, etc. Generally refers to a soldier with little tactical need for such equipment. See: Fobbit.

Green Bean: A civilian-run coffee shop common on larger bases in Iraq and Afghanistan, often the locus of the base social scene, such as it is.

Green Zone: In Iraq, the heavily fortified area of central Baghdad where most government facilities are located. In southern Afghanistan, refers to the lush, densely vegetated areas following rivers that Taliban fighters defend vigorously. As opposed to the Brown Zone, which refers to the more barren mountains.

Groundhog Day: From the Bill Murray movie, the phrase is used to describe deployments where every day proceeds the same way, no matter how the individual tries to change it.

Gun: A mortar tube or artillery piece. Never used to refer to a rifle or pistol. Military-issued pistols are usually called 9-mils.

IED: Improvised Explosive Device. The signature weapon of the insurgencies in Iraq and Afghanistan, IEDs are low-cost bombs that can be modified to exploit specific vulnerabilities of an enemy. They range in size from a soda can to a tractor-trailer and are initiated by anything from a pressure sensor to a suicidal attacker.

IDF: Indirect Fire, or simply Indirect. Mortars, rockets and artillery. Term generally used to describe enemy action.

Inside/Outside The Wire: Describes whether you are on or off a base.

Joe: Soldier. Replacement term for GI.

Kinetic: Violent. Example: The Pech Valley is one of the most kinetic areas in Afghanistan.

Mark: The Mk-19 40mm grenade launcher.

Meat Eater: Usually refers to Special Forces soldiers whose mission focuses on violence, as opposed to those whose mission focuses on stability and training.

Medevac: Medical evacuation of wounded personnel by helicopter.

MRE: Meal, Ready to Eat. Vacuum-sealed meals eaten by soldiers when no DFAC or local alternative exists. Shelf life is approximately seven years.

OPTEMPO: Operational Tempo, high or low. Describes the pace at which a soldier works, whether that work is combat patrols, making PowerPoint slides or training.

Oxygen Thief: A useless soldier, or one who loves to hear himself or herself talk.

Pink Mist: Produced by certain gunshot wounds.

Plant Eater: See: Fobbit.

POG: (pronounced pogue) Person Other Than Grunt. Derogatory term for a soldier lacking combat experience. See: Fobbit.

POO: Point Of Origin. The site from which a rocket or mortar was launched at U.S. forces. Most easily calculated by tracking the projectile's trajectory with radar. Example: 'We're going out POO hunting.'

Powerpoint Ranger: A soldier who is tasked primarily with building PowerPoint presentations for commanders' briefings.

Rack Out: Go to sleep.

Rumint: A combination of rumor and intelligence. Gossip, scuttlebutt.

Secret Squirrel: Highly classified, top secret. Secrecy confers tremendous status upon soldiers—the most classified missions are often the most prestigious in soldiers' eyes.

Self-Licking Ice Cream Cone: A military doctrine or political process that appears to exist in order to justify its own existence, often producing irrelevant indicators of its own success. For example, continually releasing figures on the amount of Taliban weapons seized, as if there were a finite supply of such weapons. While seizing the weapons, soldiers raid Afghan villages, enraging the residents and legitimizing the Taliban's cause.

470

Speedball: A body bag filled with supplies, usually ammunition and bottled water, dropped from a plane or helicopter to resupply soldiers far afield or in dire need.

Squirter: A person, assumed to be an enemy, running away from a military attack.

Superbase: Kandahar Airfield and Bagram Airfield in Afghanistan. They are built around supporting the regional military commands, and are logistical hubs for forces in the area. Soldiers stationed at these bases have access to the most comfortable living quarters, the most variety in food, shopping and socializing. For example, Kandahar Airfield has a weekly 'Salsa Night' dance party near the TGI Friday's.

Tango Mike: Thanks Much.

Terp: An interpreter, usually a local Afghan or Iraqi hired by the military to translate for military personnel when they are communicating with a local. This abbreviation is considered somewhat rude.

TIC: (pronounced tick) Troops In Contact. Usually means a firefight, but can refer to an IED or suicide attack.

Whiskey Tango Foxtrot: What The F#@&, Over.

Songs and Poems

Sababa's Playlist (from a secret drive hidden deep inside the hospital computer network):

1. The Case of the Ultimate Artery
Dean Whitfield, *Three Feet Off Gabriola*
Bonny Tyler, *Total Eclipse of the Heart*
Rise Against, *Help Is On The Way*

Max Avelyevich Kyuss, *Amur Waves*
Joe Hedges, *Mitral Valve Prolapse*
David Adkins, *Blood Feud*
Waylon Jennings, *Luckenbach, Texas*
Old Crow Medicine Show, *Methamphetamine*
Faker, *This Heart Attack*
The Decembrists, *This Why We Fight*
JAMA, Jan 31 1942, *The Limerick of Syphilis*

2. The Case of the Broken Heart
Kenny Chesney, *Boston*
German Folk Song, *Schnitzelbank*
Led Zeppelin, *Heartbreaker*
Blue Oyster Cult, *Don't Fear the Reaper*
Peter Cornelius, *Horst Wessel Lied*
Bee Gees, *How Can You Mend a Broken Heart*
Robert Frost, *The Bear*

3. The Case of the Cornelian Dilemma
Mariah Carey, *Heartbreaker*
Woody Guthrie, *Worried Man Blues*
Huey 'Piano' Smith, *High Blood Pressure*
Bruce Springstein, *Blinded by the Light*
Terry Gilkyson, *The Bare Necessities*
Billy Lee Cyrus, *Achy Breaky Heart*

4. The Case of the Parthian Shot
Steve Earle, *Lungs*
Sade, *Smooth Operator*
Three Days Grace, *Pain*
Rage Against the Machine, *Killing in the Name*
The Police, *Every Breath You Take*
Rolling Stones, *Gimme Shelter*
Genesis, *Land of Confusion*
Radiohead, *My Iron Lung*
Samuel Butler, *An Heroical Epistle of Hudibras to His Lady*

5. The Case of the Syncopated Rhythm
The Cascades, *Rhythm of the Rain*
Michael Jackson, *Beat It*
Richard O'Brien, *Time Warp*
ABBA, *Dancing Queen*
Backstreet Boys, *Quit Playing Games With My Heart*
Mötley Crüe, *Kickstart My Heart*
Kiss, *Shock Me*
Johnny Cash, *Get Rhythm*
Debarge, *The Rhythm of the Night*
Linkin Park, *In the End*

6. The Case of the Lush Vegetation
Arrowsmith, *Livin' on the Edge*
John Gorka, *Winter Cows*
Toni Braxton, *Un-Break My Heart*
Simon & Garfunkel, *The Sound of Silence*
Wizard of Oz, *If I Only Had a Brain*
Joe Cocker, *Unchain my heart*
Rod Stewart, *You're In My Heart*
U2, *I Still Haven't Found What I'm Looking For*
Mötley Crüe, *Dr. Feelgood*
Rush, *Closer To The Heart*
Led Zeppelin, *Stairway To Heaven*

7. The Case of the Flushed Fisherman
Ken Hamm, *Fishing Grounds*
Fleetwood Mac, *Storms*
Pink, *Scurvy*
Patti Smith Group, *Rock N Roll Nigger*
The Doors, *The End*
Lauren Hoffman, *Rare New Disease*
Men at Work, *Overkill*
Mark Knopfler, *Punish the Monkey*
Rolling Stones, *You Can't Always Get What You Want*
E. E. Cummings, *maggie and milly and molly and may*

8. The Case of the Melting Man
Kacey Musgraves, *My House*
Faith No More, *RV*
Jimmy Buffet, *Migration*
Infant Sorrow, *The Clap*
ZZ Top, *Consumption*
The Refreshments, *Sin Nombre*
Utopia, *Gangrene*
Iron Maiden, *Moonchild*

9. The Case of the Pretty Bird
Dean Whitfield, *Three Feet Off Gabriola*
Hank Snow, *I've Been Everywhere*
Eric Clapton, *Sick and Tired*
Joss Whedon, *The Parking Ticket*
Norah Jones, *Sinkin' Soon*
Eurythmics, *Sweet Dreams (Are Made Of This)*
Bob Dylan, *Legionnaire's Disease*
Ben Harper and The Innocent Criminals, *Fight Outta You*
Jefferson Airplane, *White Rabbit*
Tom Lehrer, *In Old Mexico*
John Mellencamp, *Farewell Angelina*

10. The Case of the Sumatran Mosquito

Jay Roberts, *Joshua Fit The Battle Of Jericho*
The Who, *I Can See For Miles*
Buck Owens, *Big Game Hunter*
C.W. McCall, *Comin' Back for More*
Pain, *Antidote*
John Williamson, *Old Man Emu*
Rage Against the Machine, *Take the Power Back*
Cole Porter, *Night and Day*

11. The Case of the Deadly Tree

Dixie Chicks, *Now*
Dixie Chicks, *The Long Way Around*
The Apache Relay, *Valley Of The Fevers*
Mark Chapman Band, *Where Would You Go (If You Couldn't Go Home)?*
Traveling Wilburys, *Heading For The Light*
Tony Orlando, *Candida*
Berlin, *Take My Breath Away*

12. The Case of the Double Double Whammy

Brad and Robert Nelson, *Timmy's Anthem*
Johnny Reid, *A Little Taste Of Home*
Cowboy Junkies, *The Summer Of Discontent*
Don McLean, *On the Amazon*
The Pogues, *Worms*
The Beatles, *I Am the Walrus*
Tuxedomoon, *No Tears*
Coldplay, *Yellow*
Thomas Babington Macaulay, *The Lays of Ancient Rome*

Other Works by Lawrence Winkler

www.ingramcontent.com/pod-product-compliance
Lightning Source LLC
Chambersburg PA
CBHW030911050726
47498CB00003BA/681